Gables
Against the Sky

Gables Against the Sky

A Novel

ANITA STANSFIELD

Covenant Communications, Inc.

Covenant®

Cover inset photo, © *Lost Images,* Al Thelin
    Taken at The Armstrong Mansion Bed & Breakfast, Salt Lake City
Cover background photo, ® 1999 PhotoDisc, Inc.

Published by Covenant Communications, Inc.
American Fork, Utah

Printed in the United States of America
First Printing: March 2000

07 06 05 04 03 02 01 00   10 9 8 7 6 5 4 3 2 1

ISBN 1-57734-607-6

To Alyssa Dawn
For bringing the light of heaven into our home

THE GABLE FACES EAST
Jess Davies
Alexandra Byrnehouse

GABLES AGAINST THE SKY
Emma Byrnehouse-Davies
Michael Hamilton
Tyson Byrnehouse-Davies
Lacey Byrnehouse-Davies

THE THREE GIFTS OF CHRISTMAS
Richard Byrnehouse-Davies
Jesse Michael Hamilton II
LeNay Parkins

THE FIRST LOVE TRILOGY
J. Michael Hamilton III
Emily Ladd Hall

HOME FOR CHRISTMAS
Allison Hall

BYRNEHOUSE-DAVIES & HAMILTON

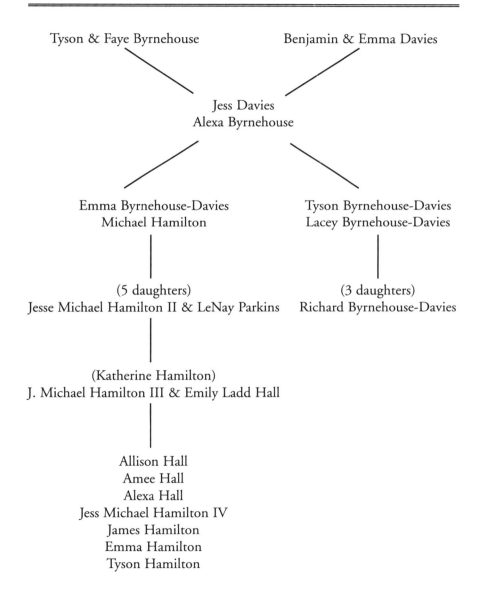

Tyson & Faye Byrnehouse   Benjamin & Emma Davies

Jess Davies
Alexa Byrnehouse

Emma Byrnehouse-Davies   Tyson Byrnehouse-Davies
Michael Hamilton   Lacey Byrnehouse-Davies

(5 daughters)   (3 daughters)
Jesse Michael Hamilton II & LeNay Parkins   Richard Byrnehouse-Davies

(Katherine Hamilton)
J. Michael Hamilton III & Emily Ladd Hall

Allison Hall
Amee Hall
Alexa Hall
Jess Michael Hamilton IV
James Hamilton
Emma Hamilton
Tyson Hamilton

PROLOGUE

South Queensland, Australia—1897

"Michael? Michael, are you all right?" He could hear Miss Sarina's voice, although it sounded distant and hollow. And he was having difficulty focusing on her face. The usual noises of the schoolroom seemed far away and hazy.

"I'm fine!" Michael snarled, unwilling to admit that he was far from it. In the two years he'd been here at the Byrnehouse-Davies Home for Boys, he'd never once allowed anyone to believe that he was anything but independent. He'd survived completely on his own for nearly four years before he'd been brought here at the age of eleven. And he'd do it again if he had to. A part of him couldn't deny that he was grateful to know his next meal didn't have to be stolen or fought for, and he would be protected from those who might threaten his safety and well-being. Still, a much bigger part of him was terrified of letting anyone get close enough to see the truth. Therefore, Michael had worked very hard at keeping up the toughness he had learned on the streets—and surviving there had been far better than what he'd left behind at the age of seven. But now, for the first time since he'd run away from the hell that most people called home, Michael was *not* in control. He felt as if he was drowning in some overpowering whirlpool that catapulted him from blinding heat to freezing cold and back again.

"Michael?" Miss Sarina's voice was gentle, and he couldn't help being grateful to know that he would be cared for. Whatever was plaguing him, he knew he wouldn't have had the slightest chance of surviving it if he had still been living on the streets. He felt a gentle hand on his face and heard her exclaim, "Good heavens! He's burning up with fever. Get the other boys out of here, and tell Ben to come quickly and help me get him to bed."

"Yes, ma'am," a distant voice responded, and Michael's next conscious realization was finding himself in his own bed, while his surroundings blurred around him. That hot and cold feeling continued to consume him, but now it was accompanied by an intense pain that crept into every minuscule part of his body. It seemed that even his fingernails hurt. He'd survived many beatings on the streets, and he'd learned to hold his own. But he couldn't recall ever hurting like this.

Michael struggled to maintain some semblance of control while he drifted in and out of consciousness, with bits of conversation floating about his ears and spinning into his dreams. *Send for the doctor . . . Hope it isn't catching . . . Don't think I've ever seen a boy this ill . . . Must inform Mrs. Davies as soon as she returns . . . A pity if he didn't survive.* Michael clung to that last thought, almost hoping he wouldn't. He couldn't recall life ever giving him anything really worth cherishing. In fact, he'd always found his desperate fight to survive somehow ironic—even pathetic. Against his will, the horrors of his past filtered into his delirium, as if they had found him weak and vulnerable and were determined to plague him, given the opportunity. He became a small child again, curled up on a dirty blanket at the bottom of a closet, praying he wouldn't be found. The pain suddenly became familiar as he was lured into memories he had ached to be free of. He felt terrified all over again—terrified of the very people who should have nurtured him, loved him, cared for him. The pain inflicted by his father became real, and Michael heard himself cry out. He was vaguely aware that he was dreaming, but unable to bring himself back to the present and away from the fear.

"Don't let him find me," he muttered. "Please, God, don't let him find me!"

"I won't," a gentle voice murmured, accompanied by a pleasant touch. He couldn't quite place the voice, but it was familiar in a way that eased the fear, and he drifted into an oblivion that was almost peaceful.

Alexa Davies wiped another stray tear on her sleeve and wrung the rag out into the basin of cool water for what seemed the thousandth time. She laid the wet cloth across Michael's forehead and fought to keep from sobbing aloud. Since the day Michael Hamilton had come here nearly two years ago, she had felt drawn to him as to no other boy in their care. And yet, he'd always been the most difficult.

Alexa had returned home from a lengthy shopping trip in town to the news that Michael had suddenly come down with a raging fever. The doctor had come and gone, declaring there was nothing to be done but try to keep his temperature down and wait it out. She had immediately taken over caring for him, perhaps hoping this could be the opportunity she'd longed for to somehow get past the impenetrable walls that Michael had kept so firmly in place around himself. At the age of thirteen, he was more tough, more manipulative, more obnoxious, and more wise than most of the adults she knew. He had countered her every attempt to break into his hardened heart and help him accept the love and protection they were trying so hard to give him.

Not unaccustomed to caring for ill boys, Alexa rolled up her sleeves and set to work, attempting to keep him cool and bring his fever down. Since he was lost in delirium and apparently unaware of her presence, he didn't oppose her effort as he might have if he'd been coherent. She efficiently unbuttoned his shirt in order to put a cool compress over his chest, but what she saw there made her freeze. The horrifying remnants of Michael's past glared blatantly up at her from a variety of ghastly scars.

Alexa completely lost track of time as she wept over the reasons for Michael's hardened heart. She understood now why he was the way he was, even if she didn't know how to cope with it.

"Are you all right?" Jess Davies asked, startling her to the realization that her husband had entered the room.

Without saying a word, Alexa clung to him and cried. When she finally calmed down, he looked into her eyes, silently demanding an explanation. "I'm so grateful for you," she said, and he responded with a baffled chuckle. "If you hadn't been so determined to create this place where we could take these children in, what would have become of them? Oh, Jess, I love you."

"I love you, too, Alexa. Now, why don't you tell me what's brought this on?"

Alexa moved to Michael's side and carefully pulled down the sheet to reveal his scarred chest.

"Merciful heaven!" Jess gasped. "How do you suppose that happened?"

"They're far too . . . *orderly* . . . to be any kind of accident. And there are far too many of them to be the result of his life on the streets. You don't get those kinds of scars from fist fights."

"Who do you suppose . . . ," Jess began, but he didn't seem to want to finish.

"We can't be sure, but we could wager a fair guess."

"Yes, I suppose we could," Jess snarled with a voice that shook from compassion as much as anger.

"How is Lacey doing?" Alexa asked, drawing her attention briefly away from her patient. Her only real worry in spending so much time with Michael was a deep concern for the little girl who had come to live in their home recently. She'd come to them when she'd been found on the streets, dressed as a boy. No one had claimed her, so they had made the decision to raise her along with their twins, who were about the same age. Jess and Alexa had repeatedly tried to get Lacey to open up about the circumstances that had brought her here, but she refused to say anything. Alexa had finally concluded that they just needed to love and nurture her and hope for the best. She was well behaved for a seven-year-old, and the twins had taken her into their little circle without any apparent difficulty.

When Jess didn't seem to hear her, Alexa repeated the question. "How is Lacey doing, love?"

"Oh, she seems to be fine," he said, startled away from his obvious concern for Michael. "As long as she's with Emma, she seems perfectly content. The two of them have really taken to each other."

"That's good, then," Alexa said, turning her attention back to Michael as he moaned and shifted in his bed.

In spite of Jess's concern for Alexa, he allowed her to stay continually with Michael. They agreed to keep their discovery to themselves in order to protect the confidentiality of a very sensitive issue. Alexa left Michael's bedside only when Jess himself took over long enough for her to see to her own needs. But she was never away for long. After days of sitting with his hand in hers, she had tallied up a number of clues from the rantings of his delirium.

Alexa's relief was beyond description when the fever finally broke and it looked as if Michael would make it through. She made certain he was wearing a shirt before he became fully aware of his surroundings, as she didn't want him to feel that his privacy had been violated. She was sure to be at his side when he opened his eyes and showed the first sign of coherence in nearly a week.

"Hello," she said with a smile.

"I've been sick," he said with a raspy voice.

"Yes, you have. You've been very sick. But you're going to be fine."

He attempted to sit up, muttering angrily, "I need to—"

"Hold on there," Alexa said, putting firm hands on his shoulders. But it didn't take much effort to make him lie back down when the weakness obviously overtook him. "The world has gotten by just fine for more than a week. It will do fine until you get your strength back."

Michael looked bewildered, afraid, and comforted all at once. Then he turned his face away from her and went to sleep. He woke up a while later, declaring he was hungry. Alexa ordered a tray from the kitchen and sat with Michael while he ravenously downed every bit of it . "Careful," she said. "You mustn't overdo."

Michael just scowled at her and ignored her warning. Alexa smiled, actually grateful to see him coming back to his usual self—gruff and obnoxious as it might be.

Alexa was moving the tray from the bed when a young boy burst into Michael's room without knocking and said breathlessly, "Mrs. Davies! You gotta come quick. There's a commotion in the stable. Hurry! Hurry!"

Alexa noticed Michael looking alarmed. She gently put a hand over his arm and smiled. "I'm certain it's nothing. You rest. I won't be long."

Alexa didn't know what she'd expected to find as she came through the wide stable doorway, but she stopped abruptly, coming upon a scene that made everything inside of her freeze. A man she had never

seen before actually had a gun pressed to Emma's head, and his arm
was firmly around Lacey as well. Emma's eyes were wide with fear, but
the horror in Lacey's expression was chilling. The child was frozen
with a terror that made her as white as the ribbon in her hair.

Jess was already there, and he glanced in Alexa's direction at the
same time as the villain in question. She quickly surmised that Jess's
fear matched her own. And if she had any doubt as to whether or not
this man was serious, her eyes were drawn briefly to one of the stable
hands who was lying on the ground, unmoving, bleeding profusely
from a bullet wound in his side. Meeting the eyes of this man who had
the audacity to kill and was threatening to kill again, Alexa's breath
escaped her. Never in her life had she seen such blatant evil. Peering
between his dark, unruly hair and unkempt beard were eyes that
burned with malevolence and depravity.

Alexa felt herself come back to life as the reality descended. Her
heart pounded fiercely, and her breathing became sharp. A scream
threatened to erupt from her throat, but Jess's voice broke the air,
keeping her silent. "You might as well put the gun down and leave
now. You won't get what you came for." She thought he sounded
awfully confident, given the situation.

"I *will* get my son," he retorted in a voice that was deep and grav-
elly, "or I will shoot a hole in this pretty little head."

Lacey whimpered at the same moment Alexa gasped. A quick
glance at the child made Alexa wonder if she would actually faint. The
terror in her eyes was beyond description. Then it seemed that Lacey's
fear crept into Alexa, and the reality began to sink in. *This fiend was
attempting to take back one of the boys in their care. He had shot a man
who could be dead for all they knew, and he was using Emma and Lacey
as a means to get what he wanted.* Alexa slapped a hand over her mouth
before she made everything worse by expressing her deepest fear.

"Get him!" the man shouted, startling Alexa and making Lacey
scream. Emma's face just tightened in determination. "Now!"

Alexa closed her eyes and prayed until Jess finally said, "Over my
dead body."

She opened her eyes and gasped, not liking the implication at all.
The man laughed very much like a villain in a melodrama. He smiled
cruelly and muttered, "That could be arranged." He moved the gun

away from Emma and pointed it toward Jess. A shot rang out, and Alexa screamed. It took her a moment to realize that Jess was still standing, and Emma scrambled into her father's arms as the man holding her and Lacey fell to the ground. He groaned once, then became still. Two of the hired hands hurried to the side of the wounded man and determined that he was still alive. One of them quickly mounted a horse to go for the doctor. Alexa forced herself to breathe, then she turned to meet Jess's eyes just as he tossed a revolver to the ground.

"Where did you get that?" she demanded, wishing she'd known that he had it. He wasn't known to carry a gun.

"I just came in from trying to find that dingo that's been in with the sheep."

Alexa took a deep breath. "It would seem we're being looked out for," she said, noting that she was starting to shake. Jess knelt down to make certain Emma was all right. Through her sudden surge of tears she nodded to indicate that she was fine. Alexa forced away her own fear of what might have been and rushed to Lacey's side. The child was staring in horror at the lifeless form lying on the ground.

"It's all right now, love," Alexa said gently, scooping Lacey into her arms. "No one is ever going to hurt you, or Emma. I promise."

Lacey didn't cry the way Emma did. She just clung to Alexa, her entire body trembling. Jess gave orders to the hands to make certain everything was under control, then he scooped both the little girls into his arms and carried them toward the house. Alexa hurried to catch up with her husband. She sensed the anger and fear hovering in his eyes, and knew his feelings were much the same as hers. He'd just killed a man, for heaven's sake, and one of his employees was barely clinging to life. She couldn't imagine how he must be feeling.

"Are you all right?" she asked, attempting to keep up with his stride as he carried the girls into the house and up the back stairs as though they weighed nothing at all. She noted how Lacey clung to Jess's shoulder as if she never intended to let go.

"I'm still alive, aren't I," he growled.

Alexa opened the door to Lacey's room, and Jess put both the girls on the big bed. He sat between them and held them close. "Everything's all right now. I promise," he murmured in a comforting voice that belied the anger in his eyes.

Alexa sat down near the window and watched the girls closely as they gradually relaxed. She wanted to discuss what had just happened with Jess, but she didn't want to upset the girls. Emma didn't appear to be any more ruffled than she might have been if she'd fallen off a horse or skinned her knee. But the terror in Lacey's eyes hadn't gone away. Alexa wished there was a way to calm the child's fears. But it seemed likely that if Lacey hadn't been willing to talk about what had happened prior to coming here, she would be reluctant to talk about this. All Alexa could do was hope and pray that the child would grow out of her fears. She truly believed that with enough love and nurturing, and with God's help, such a thing was possible.

When the girls were finally asleep that night, Alexa ventured to ask Jess exactly what had happened. He told her how the girls had ridden out with him to check the sheep. They had just returned and were seeing to the horses when this man appeared out of nowhere, demanding that his son be returned to him. Only then did it occur to Alexa that they had nearly twenty boys in their care at present. Over half of them could possibly have a wretched father who might be wanting to get a son back for any number of deplorable reasons.

"Who?" she asked simply, knowing that he was well aware what she meant.

Jess's eyes became angry and sad all at once. Even before he said it, Alexa knew from his expression what the answer was. Through a brief moment the events of the last few weeks paraded through her mind: the way Lacey had come into their family, and the discovery of Michael's secret. All of it suddenly culminated inside of her with a sharp sense of poignancy, irony, and a deep gratitude for the work they were doing here.

"Michael Hamilton," he said in little more than a whisper.

Alexa just looked toward the window and sighed.

One
THE THIRD TWIN

1908

Michael Hamilton pressed his hand lovingly over the neck of Emma's gelding as he deftly put the bridle in place. Knowing that Emma would appear any minute to go riding, he wanted to be certain her favorite mount was saddled and ready to go. Tightening the strap beneath the horse's belly, his heart quickened just to imagine how Emma looked when she rode around the gallops, as if she'd been born to it. He became so caught up in his fantasies that he was startled to hear her voice.

"Good morning, Mr. Hamilton," she said with a kind smile that quickened his heart further. But his deepest hopes were dashed, as always, when she seemed to look right through him. He was no different to her from any of the other hands who worked the stables and tracks. But a tiny flicker of anticipation within made him believe this time might be different; perhaps today she would see something beyond the usual trivialities that passed between them, mostly in silence. He watched her face closely as her hand slipped into his and she gently placed a booted foot on his thigh in a well-practiced manner so that he could lift her easily into the saddle. She glanced down and smiled as she muttered the usual, "Thank you." But as always, she looked right through him.

Michael briefly felt a temptation to be angry at her indifference, but he reminded himself that he'd never done or said anything to make her take notice of him. She would be eighteen soon. Perhaps now was the time to finally make a step toward winning Emma's heart. But how? Just the thought of exposing his true feelings was utterly terrifying. He'd never opened his heart to anyone, especially not a woman. And how could he possibly explain that she was the biggest reason he had stayed here to work these past six years, since he'd graduated from the boys' home? Well, he didn't have to spill it all in one conversation. He just had to give her the opportunity to get to know him better. It was as simple as that. All he had to do was open his mouth.

As Emma situated the reins in her delicate hands, Michael cleared his throat carefully, attempting to come up with any trivial thing he could say to strike up a conversation. He was startled by a boisterous, "Hold on there, Emma! I need to talk to you."

Michael turned to see her brother, Tyson, enter the stable. Emma's face lit up, as it always did when he was around. The two of them were practically inseparable. Just finding Emma without him or Lacey was nearly impossible. Emma jumped down from the gelding to talk with her brother while he saddled his own horse. Michael discreetly moved away to curry one of the other horses, trying to convince himself that having such feelings for Emma Byrnehouse-Davies was tantamount to insanity.

❦   ❦   ❦

Lacey hovered a moment in the stable doorway, not surprised to find Tyson and Emma, their heads bent together, giggling like children. Or more accurately, Tyson was bent over in order to meet Emma eye to eye. In spite of being twins, Tyson had surpassed Emma's height at the age of thirteen, and now he stood a head taller.

"Talking about me?" Lacey teased with a light slap of her riding crop to Tyson's arm.

"What else would we talk about?" Emma answered lightly while Tyson rubbed his wound and made a martyrish noise. "You know our motto . . ."

"If you're not here, we're going to talk about you," they all said at once, Tyson's voice raised to mimic an old woman.

"Well," Lacey giggled, "you could be making plans for your birthday. I just realized this morning that you'll be eighteen in less than a week, and I haven't a clue what to get for either of you."

"I don't need anything," Tyson and Emma said at nearly the same time, then they shared a gaze of mock disgust.

"Besides," Tyson added, "it's as much your birthday as it is ours."

Lacey gave a noncommittal shrug and urged her favorite gelding out of a stall in order to saddle him. She'd never been comfortable with sharing the twins' birthday. But since the day their father, Jess Davies, had taken her from the streets and brought her home to his family, it had been decided that since her birthday was unknown, and she was about Emma's size, Lacey could simply have the same birthday. Tyson and Emma had never seemed to mind. They'd never made much of the day anyway, but Lacey had always felt as if she was taking something from them. Still, she couldn't once recall even a hint of anything less than complete acceptance through all their years together.

Lacey was continually in awe of all she had been given as a result of being discovered huddled on a city street when she was less than seven—or so they had guessed. Jess had come to collect her from the constable's office. Of course, Jess had believed she was a boy, and so did everyone else. Her parents were dead. That was all they knew.

Despite much protest from Lacey, Jess had carted her home to his Queensland estate with the intention of adding her to the population of his self-founded Byrnehouse-Davies Home for Boys. But turning her over to his wife and Miss Sarina for a good cleaning, the discovery was soon made and a family conference had followed.

Lacey well remembered sitting timidly on the sofa in a drawing room unlike anything she had ever seen. Everything surrounding her was fine and elegant, though the room was comfortable, with a homey feel. Its lack of fragility was proven by the way Tyson repeatedly somersaulted from the overstuffed chair onto the floor, while Emma played quietly with pieces to a wooden puzzle spread out around her. Lacey just sat, wearing a dress borrowed from Emma's closet, and black shoes that were so shiny she could almost see her reflection in them.

Lacey recalled wanting to cry when Jess and Alexandra Davies came into the room and sat on either side of her, calling the children to attention. Jess calmly announced that they couldn't take the child back because there was nowhere for her to go, and she couldn't stay in the boys' dormitories for obvious reasons. It was little Emma who stepped forward and took the newcomer's hand. "She can be our sister, Papa," Emma announced. "Since Mama can't have any more babies, she can be our sister."

Lacey would never forget the tears in Alexa Davies' eyes, and the gentle way Jess had asked the twins, "What should we call her? She can't seem to remember whether or not she has a name."

"Lacey," Tyson had piped up. "I read it in a book, and I was saving it for my most special foal. But it was born a boy. I want to name her Lacey."

Alexa nodded, Jess smiled, and Lacey Byrnehouse-Davies became her name. Like the others, she shortened it to Davies for the sake of convenience, but on anything written, Jess had made it clear their name was Byrnehouse-Davies.

Since that day, Lacey had been raised side by side with Emma and Tyson. Their common gender made it easier to be close to Emma in all things, but she shared no less of a bond with Tyson. Every day of their lives they had ridden and raced, traveled and talked, schemed and lived life to its fullest. The Byrnehouse-Davies fortune surrounding them was far more than acres of land, dozens of race horses, and the power to purchase nearly anything money could buy. The wealth that surrounded Lacey was the incomparable love, abounding far more than the constant evidence of money. Over the years, Lacey had witnessed many discoveries of homeless or mistreated boys, and she had watched the majority of them respond and grow from the love and discipline given here. She had gone with her adopted family to the outback and watched them give away wagon-loads of necessary food and commodities to the natives. And she had felt their unquestioning acceptance of her. An ordinary urchin had been lovingly transformed into a young woman who wanted for nothing.

Lacey loved her family, she loved life, and more recently she had realized that in a very different way, she was falling in love with Tyson. She'd had trouble with her feelings at first, certain it was nothing more than a childish infatuation resulting mostly from her dependence on him. He'd always been more like a brother to her. But the brother she'd grown up with had become a man worthy of admiring. To watch him now as he teased Emma, Lacey was moved. His long legs were clad in high riding boots and narrow breeches, and a white shirt bloused over his broadening shoulders, while his capable hands bridled a horse as effortlessly as breathing. Tyson was a unique combination of his mother's aristocratic blood and his father's rugged appeal. His subtly red-tinted brown hair waved off his forehead and hung in loose curls over the back of his neck. His mostly hazel eyes changed colors with his moods. His manner radiated soft-spoken strength.

Lacey was gradually coming to accept her new awareness of Tyson as something real and undeniable, and a week shy of their eighteenth birthday, her greatest fear was the thought of living out her life with anyone other than Tyson Byrnehouse-Davies. But she had no reason to believe that such a thing had ever even crossed Tyson's mind.

"Hey, are you listening to me?" The subject of her thoughts interrupted them.

"I'm sorry." She focused her eyes on him. "Did you say something to me?"

"I said hurry up, or we'll leave you."

"I'm ready," she announced, throwing herself into her custom-made racing saddle.

"I'll race you ladies to the border," Tyson announced with a sly grin.

"You're on." Emma met the challenge and the three galloped across the yard, jumping fences with room to spare.

Jess Davies had been in the business of breeding and racing horses long before he'd opened a boys' home. So naturally, racing had been almost a daily ritual since the children had been old enough to control a horse at high speeds. But one of the girls usually won, since Tyson had become too tall to carry off being a jockey. Occasionally, however, they conspired to let him win, only so they could tease him about it the rest of the day.

For the next mile and a half, Lacey saw only brief glimpses of the scenery that blurred past her as she left the others in the dust. She reared the gelding back and laughed as she raced toward the appointed finish line: the border. It had once been the dividing line between Davies land and Byrnehouse land. But now it was the line that merged the two enormous pieces of property together. Lacey dismounted and turned to find Tyson alone, staring down at her from atop his stallion.

"Where's Emma?" she asked in concern as he lifted a long leg over the horse's mane and slid a short distance to touch his boots to the ground. "She's returned to the stable, I would assume," he answered with a quick upward twitch of his lips.

"But I thought that—"

"I bribed her," he interrupted with a conspiratorial grin.

Lacey's heart began to pound. She couldn't recall him ever seeking out her company exclusively. "But . . . why?" she asked, feeling suddenly timid.

"I wanted to be alone with you," he stated as if it was the most natural thing in the world. He tethered the horses to a leafless tree, then leaned a sturdy shoulder against it. Lacey watched him, wondering what to say. Her feelings for him seemed to blossom tenfold with no one else around.

"I need to talk to you, Lacey," he said. "I was going to wait until we were eighteen, but I don't want to. This is close enough."

Again Lacey was surprised. It had always been Emma whom Tyson confided in. The twins were practically of one mind.

"I'm flattered," she admitted, hoping it didn't sound too forward.

"Lacey . . ." He seemed a trifle nervous, and she wondered why. It was so out of character for him. "I'll be eighteen soon, and . . ." He hesitated, and his countenance changed. His eyes seemed to catch fire with a familiar zeal.

"Oh, no," she groaned and turned her back to him. All joy was dashed when it became evident what he wanted to talk about.

"What do you mean by that?" he insisted.

"If you came to tell me your glorious stories about the world and how you're going to discover every inch of it on your own, I don't want to hear it."

"It's not just talk any longer, Lacey," he announced. "I'm leaving next month."

Lacey turned toward him, gaping, her heart pounding. He had always shown signs of discontent, and she often sensed an unexplainable resentment in him that was usually well hidden. But she had never dreamed that anyone in their right mind would want to leave this place. "But why?" She nearly choked the words out.

"Don't you understand?" he asked with a vehemence she had never seen. She found her shoulders clasped in his hands, her toes barely touching the ground. "I have to!" His eyes took on a deep green hue as they blazed with dreams of glory. "Every day of my life, all I ever see is misery. Miserable urchins brought off the streets, starving and abused. Natives being neglected and mistreated. This island is a prison, Lacey. It always has been. There's got to be a place on earth where such misery doesn't run rampant."

"How dare you speak of misery?" she snapped. "You've never wanted for anything, Tyson Davies. What could you possibly know of misery?"

"It's been there at every turn, as long as I can remember. My parents seem to thrive on it."

"Your parents thrive on *easing* it. There is a lot less misery in this world, thanks to them. You're a fool, Tyson, if you think there is any such place where misery doesn't exist—and don't forget that you are looking at one of those miserable urchins."

"That's just it." He smiled brightly. "I want to take you away from here, Lacey." He took a deep breath. "I want you to come with me."

Lacey had to remind herself to start breathing again. "But why?" she asked again.

"We could see the world together, Lacey. We wouldn't have to stay here and watch the suffering any longer."

Lacey tried to concentrate on one thing at a time in an effort to sort out the overwhelming reality of what he'd just said. "But . . . I love it here. We have a good life, Tyson. There is everything we could ever want, and—"

"I want more," he muttered, pulling her closer. For a moment, the world stood still. Their eyes met with electricity, sparking blue to green.

"Tyson," Lacey finally found the voice to say, "why are you holding me this way?"

Tyson looked down at his hands and seemed surprised. For a moment, Lacey thought he was going to let go of her and break the spell. His hands left her shoulders and she gasped, certain she would collapse. But his arms broke her fall, and she found herself so close to him that no breath of wind could have whistled between them.

"Tyson," was all she managed to say. He smelled of leather and earth and horses—all the smells she related to security. All she had come to feel for him began to hammer in her chest.

"Lacey," he replied in the same tone, "I can't keep this distance between us any longer. Haven't you seen it? Haven't you felt it?" His eyes blazed with the same glory as when he'd spoken of leaving; his voice rang with the same vehemence. "I won't let anyone try to tell me that you're my sister and I'm not allowed to feel this way. I've felt it every minute of every day since I have known what it feels like to be a man."

Lacey could only hold her breath and wait for him to catch his. She recalled how young he had been when his shoulders had broadened and the shadow of a beard had appeared on his face. Had he felt such things for so long? She couldn't believe it. This was like some kind of a dream.

"Have you felt it, Lacey?" he repeated, searching her eyes.

"Yes," she murmured, and he smiled.

"Lacey," he whispered hoarsely, and she recognized a passion for life that his father possessed. "I want you to come with me. I want us to share it, all of it."

"Why . . . ," she stammered, wondering how to contain the joy of knowing she was not alone in her feelings, and at the same time attempt to ignore his plea to leave. "Why haven't you said any of this before?"

"Do you realize," he laughed softly, lifting a hand to touch her hair while his other arm only tightened around her, "how difficult it is to be alone with you? Besides," he seemed to be searching her eyes, "until we're eighteen, our parents will regard us as children. They have made that quite clear. A child can't march home one day and announce that he's marrying his adopted sister."

Lacey felt the blood rush from her face, resting in her throat with a pulsebeat that was deafening. A thousand thoughts tumbled through her mind, the utmost being a gratitude that fate had offered so much to one who had been destined to an orphaned life in the pit of the city. But all she could think to say was, "I'm not."

"You're not what?" He sounded panicked.

"I'm not your adopted sister. It was never legal. Father and Mother are my guardians. That is all."

Tyson's eyes lit up freshly while she felt them crossing a bridge that would change their lives forever.

"Tyson?" she questioned carefully. "Are you trying to ask me to marry you?"

Tyson only smiled, then the world fell away as his lips came over hers with all the vehemence he was capable of.

"Tyson," she gasped, lifting her head to take a breath. His lips moved to her throat. "We're so young," she protested. "What do we know of marriage and—"

"We'll figure it out." He overpowered her lips again and she thought she'd die from the wonder and bliss of the moment. Her hands went into his hair, while she wondered how long she had ached to just touch it.

"You didn't answer me," he whispered against her face.

"You didn't make the question clear," she argued softly.

Tyson drew back to look into her eyes. "Will you marry me?"

Lacey could only smile and nod her head. Tyson lifted her off the ground to spin her around and they laughed together with perfect happiness.

❦　❦　❦

Emma sailed over the first fence and reined her horse to a halt, smiling to herself as Tyson and Lacey disappeared in the distance. Tyson turned back briefly with a casual salute. Emma didn't know what Tyson was up to, but she had noticed long ago the way he observed Lacey. Of course, Lacey watched Tyson, too. But Emma wasn't certain if they ever watched each other at the same time. Lost in her speculations, Emma trotted back toward the stables, actually glad to have some time to herself. She loved Tyson and Lacey dearly, and could not comprehend life without either of them. But still, there were times when solitude was appreciated. If something evolved between Tyson and Lacey, Emma could likely become an outsider in a circle she had always been a part of. She felt a subtle ache in that possibility, but she reminded herself that it was inevitable. They were growing up.

Emma was beginning to remove the saddle when a deep, firm voice startled her. "I thought you left with the others."

Emma turned to see Michael Hamilton, a wayward boy turned stable hand. "Ah," she smiled politely and returned her attention to the saddle, "they wanted to be alone."

Michael chuckled casually, though she sensed an unusual tenseness about him. "Is romance in the air?"

"One never knows," Emma replied nonchalantly.

"Come now." His voice filled with pleasant mischief. "Those two have been gawking at each other for months."

Emma turned in surprise but said nothing. She didn't know whether to feel disconcerted or somehow consoled to realize she wasn't the only one who had observed the changes between Tyson and Lacey.

Michael continued in a tone that bordered on compassion. "Sort of leaves you out in the cold, doesn't it."

The comment suddenly touched something in Emma that she didn't want to look at too closely. She tried briefly to perceive Michael's motives, but all she could gain from his expression was genuine concern.

"You're a very observant man, Mr. Hamilton." She returned to her chore, not accustomed to having Michael make conversation. He had always kept to himself.

Michael Hamilton had a reputation that preceded him. Of all the difficult boys who had filtered in and out of their lives, whether orphans staying here into adulthood, or children fostered from miserable situations, Michael Hamilton was at the head of his class. He'd been harsh and obnoxious as a youth, always picking fights with the other boys and defying the adults who governed him. As a result, he was generally disliked. His maturity of twenty-four years had mellowed him into a quiet, sinister-looking man who went about his business, seeming to appreciate Jess Davies allowing him to stay on and work. Either Michael had nowhere to go, or he had some aversion to the world beyond Byrnehouse-Davies. Emma suspected it was a little of both.

In the six years he had been employed here, since his graduation from the boys' home, Michael had been working in this stable, willing to assist Emma nearly every time she'd come here. But only today had he chosen to speak beyond their usual and necessary exchange.

A long moment of silence forced Emma to turn and affirm his presence. He stood unmoving, dressed as always in black from neck to toe, in well-worn but highly polished riding boots, narrow breeches, and a loosely fitting muslin shirt, hanging open slightly below his throat to reveal a hint of hair as dark as the neatly mussed hair on his head. His brows were thick and dark, often furrowed close together, turning his brown eyes into narrow, cynical slits. He wore a thick mustache that looked so at home on his face, one might think he'd been born with it. But Emma recalled the teenager who had had little choice but to show the jagged scar above his upper lip that looked as if someone had purposely carved a piece out of his face.

"Did you need something?" she asked, not disturbed by his hovering presence, but perhaps baffled by it. She knew that Lacey was afraid of Michael, but Emma had observed her mother handle Michael in a way that made his reputation seem insignificant. If her mother didn't fear him, then Emma didn't see any reason to, either.

"Let me help you with that," he said with a ring of gentleness as he urged her aside and lifted the saddle off the horse to put it away. "Such delicate beauty should not work so hard." The tender words and silky voice belied all she knew of him.

"Michael," she laughed softly, "you flatter me."

"No." He smiled, and Emma believed it was the first time she'd seen him do it. A row of straight, white teeth overbit slightly to mostly conceal a few barely crooked ones beneath it. She decided then that he was actually handsome—in a roguish kind of way, much like the heroes of the romance novels she was always reading. Until now, his appeal had always been hidden behind his mask of severity.

Emma smiled back and began to curry the horse. Again Michael came beside her and took the brush, elusively touching her hand for a lingering moment as he did.

"Is there a reason you're being so kind to me?" she asked, leaning against the stall to watch him.

"Bribery," he said with no expression. He was serious.

"To what end?" she inquired, wondering whether to feel leery or intrigued.

"Perhaps to soften you up a little before I ask you to go riding with me."

Emma couldn't find words to respond. Had he just admitted to having some romantic interest in her? Was he attracted to her? The realization left her decidedly nervous, though she wasn't certain why. Perhaps she *was* afraid of him. Or perhaps she'd simply been caught off guard.

"If you don't want to," he responded to her silence by brushing the horse more vigorously and avoiding her eyes altogether, "all you have to do is say so."

She didn't want to hurt him, but something formless made her hesitant to accept. "Michael, it's not that I don't want to. It's just that—"

"Don't worry about it," he interrupted tersely. His entire countenance changed, reverting to the hard reticence that was more characteristic of him.

Emma could neither leave nor speak. She watched him in silence, hating the regret that consumed her, despite wondering if her emotions were genuine or if she was being manipulated into feeling them. She recalled the many times her mother had cautioned her not to let a man goad her into doing something she didn't feel right about. Still, she felt regret. She nearly considered accepting his offer, finding a certain intrigue in it. But before she could contemplate an appropriate response, Michael paused in his work to look at her with a cruel finality that made his gentle conversation of moments ago seem imagined. Emma opened her mouth to speak, but no sound came out. She felt certain that nothing she could say now would make any difference.

"Good-bye, Miss Davies." He dismissed her with a hard arrogance that made her momentarily forget that *he* was the servant.

"Thank you for your help," she stated, unable to avoid the terseness his manner provoked.

"Any time," he said tonelessly.

"Perhaps I'll see you tomorrow," she added, certain a good night's sleep would help her see this in a clearer perspective.

Michael's eyes narrowed further before he turned back to curry the horse as if she wasn't there. Emma turned and walked away, wondering why she felt changed by the encounter. She had always been fascinated by human behavior, and her mother's guidance in such things had left deep impressions. But she'd never felt so affected by an exchange of conversation, which she suspected had barely scratched the surface of something she didn't understand. That, combined with the realization that Tyson and Lacey were likely beginning a relationship she could have no part in, left Emma certain that Michael Hamilton had been right. She was left out in the cold.

❦   ❦   ❦

Lacey found herself on the ground, giggling like a child as Tyson collapsed from dizziness and they landed together in a heap. She felt her every nerve became taut with awareness. The world spun around her, but in the center was Tyson, making perfect her already blissful life.

"We'll get married soon, Lacey," she heard him whisper against her ear, "and we'll honeymoon our lives away. I'll take you to Europe, the Americas. And we'll go to the—"

"But . . ." The word sounded like a boulder crashing into a still pond. "I . . . don't want to leave here."

Tyson sat up. "You just said you would marry me," he protested, barely calm.

Lacey reminded herself of one of the many things Alexa Davies had taught her and Emma as they'd matured into women: never let a man goad you into doing something you don't feel right about. Alexa's words gave Lacey strength now, even though the goading man was Alexa's only son.

"I *do* want to marry you, Tyson," she insisted. "But I don't want to leave. Everything I love is here."

Tyson came abruptly to his feet. "I won't be," he retorted, his eyes revealing that often-concealed streak of rebellion.

"Tyson," she soothed, standing beside him to touch his face, "it's all right. We'll work it out. We can't plan our lives in an hour." Instinctively she reached up to kiss him, holding his stubbled chin steady with her fingers. She had just been offered the love she'd been dreaming to have, and she was going to fight to keep it. Tyson's lips went from cold and hard to warm and fervent in less time than it took Lacey to thread her fingers through his hair.

"Oh, Tyson," she drew back to take a breath, "I can't believe this is happening."

"But you love me," he stated with confidence. "You *do* love me."

"How did you know?"

"I've been watching you." He grinned like a child with a secret. "I could feel it. I could see it in your eyes."

Lacey put her face timidly to his shoulder and he pulled her close as she said softly, "I suppose I was too shy to look into your eyes, or I might have realized you felt this way, too."

Again Tyson kissed her, and Lacey felt an unspoken promise of many secrets yet to be shared.

"Lacey, my dear Lacey. If anything could make me stay, you could." He smiled. "Now I understand why my parents are kissing every time I turn around."

Lacey giggled and nuzzled against his throat.

"I suppose we should get back," he sighed, "before Emma comes after us."

"Does she know?" Lacey asked while Tyson helped her mount the gelding.

"Why I bribed her, you mean?" he said, and she nodded. "I didn't tell her, but it's unlikely that she wouldn't figure it out. You know how she can practically read my mind."

"Will you tell your parents?" she asked while they rode side by side at a slow pace.

"Do you want me to?"

"Let's wait." She smiled, and he nodded in agreement. "Let me get used to all of this first."

While their conversation settled into a typical exchange of trivialities, the stables of home came into view too soon. Tyson drew back the reins to stop for a moment, and Lacey did the same. Their eyes met with fresh intensity, and Lacey nearly wilted from the emotion he betrayed in his expression.

"Meet me tonight," he said, "in the gabled attic . . . at eleven."

Lacey nodded and moved her mount forward, fearing she would give in to the urge to kiss him otherwise. They returned quietly to the stable, knowing immediately that Emma had returned, since her gelding was being attended to by one of the hands. Being the only one there, he came from the stall to take their mounts.

"Thank you, Hamilton," Tyson said, handing over Lacey's reins, but seeing to his own personally.

Lacey quietly observed Tyson, admiring the way he never took advantage of the servants, which was something their parents had admonished strongly. At Byrnehouse-Davies, the servants worked *with* the family, not for them. But Lacey wished that Michael Hamilton was not here with them. Not only did she want to be alone with Tyson, but Michael simply made her uneasy. She could never explain it. She only knew that she was never comfortable in his presence.

Lacey was relieved when Michael inquired, "Will there be anything else?"

"No, thank you, Michael," Tyson said.

Michael looked briefly at Tyson, then Lacey, as if he sensed the changes they were experiencing. Lacey felt herself shudder, then she sighed audibly when he turned and walked out toward the carriage house.

Tyson apparently noticed her reaction. Once they were alone, he asked, "What's the matter with you?"

"I don't know why Father was so willing to let him stay on. I wish he'd left a long time ago."

"What? Hamilton?" Tyson laughed. "He's harmless."

"I'm not so sure," Lacey muttered.

Tyson finished caring for the horse and put his arms around her, saying with mock gallantry, "I'll protect you from the beast."

She laughed. "I'm counting on it."

Tyson put his hands into his pockets as they walked into the house. Lacey thought how natural it felt to be with him. Yet everything was different. The house seemed different. The normal daily routine felt different. The meals with the family, her time alone in her room. Everything was different. Tyson Davies was in love with her.

Keeping their secret was more difficult than Lacey had imagined. She wanted to shout the news from the rooftop. And when Tyson reached beneath the supper table to squeeze her hand, it wasn't easy keeping a straight face. Jess and Alexa seemed oblivious to the electricity in the air, but Lacey had little doubt that Emma had figured it out. Once when Lacey caught Tyson's eyes and held them for a long, spark-filled moment, she heard Emma clearing her throat ridiculously loud. They turned to find her grinning conspiratorially, while their parents seemed to think it was just another private joke among the three of them. No words were exchanged, but Lacey felt certain Emma knew everything. Watching her through the remainder of the meal, Lacey realized that her sister looked distracted. She wondered if Tyson's attention to her had left Emma disoriented. She didn't know how it couldn't. They were twins, for heaven's sake.

Lacey's suspicion was confirmed during the usual bedtime ritual of brushing through each other's hair.

"It's true, isn't it," Emma said, smiling slyly into the mirror. Lacey glanced innocently back at her while she brushed Emma's wavy brown hair with long, even strokes. She'd always envied Emma's hair, which had just enough natural wave to make it do what she wanted it to. To Lacey's consternation, her own dark brown hair didn't have even a hint of curl. She thought of how Emma's hair betrayed subtle red highlights in the sun, which was one feature she shared identically with her brother. Their hair was exactly the same color—and texture, she thought, recalling that she'd touched Tyson's hair earlier today.

"What is, darling?" Lacey replied nonchalantly.

"You're playing a pointless game, sister," Emma's smile deepened, "if you think you can keep it from me. It's easy to see the meaning behind those longing gazes Tyson is giving you." Lacey stopped brushing, but her expression remained steady as she met Emma's eyes in the mirror. "Oh, he does well at keeping it subtle," Emma continued. "I don't think Mother and Father have a clue. But you should know that Tyson can't keep anything from me." Emma's tone deepened with the intensity in her eyes. "I can almost feel how he loves you."

Lacey turned away, not certain how to react to such sudden changes in their comfortable triangle. She felt as she often had—that she was infringing upon something she should not have been a part of.

"Lacey," Emma rose and turned to face her, "what is it? Did I say something I shouldn't have?"

"No," she insisted. "It's only that . . . I . . . well, he's such a part of you that . . ."

"He is my brother." Emma laughed softly, taking Lacey's hand into hers. "It has always been accepted that one day we would have to give each other up for the sake of love. What better woman to give him up to than you?"

Lacey knew Emma was being honest with her. They had never been otherwise. But she sensed a subtle uneasiness between them. It wasn't that the changes were wrong. They were simply difficult.

Lacey couldn't think of anything to say that wouldn't make the strain more evident. Emma urged her to the chair and took her turn brushing through Lacey's straight, dark hair that fell to the middle of her back. The difference in their hair was a fair representation of their other differences. Emma was confident and adventurous, while Lacey was timid and needed security. Alexa, in the psychological analogies that she used in dealing with wayward boys, had speculated that these differences were likely a result of the contrast in the girls' first seven years of life. Emma's childhood had been secure and peaceful. Lacey's still gave her nightmares.

Beyond that, they could not have been more the same if they had been natural-born sisters. There was less than an inch difference in their height, Lacey being taller at five foot five inches. Their clothes were interchangeable, except for shoes. Emma's feet were a size larger. The girls' similarities had been enhanced through their lifestyle. They practically lived in breeches as a result of always riding and assisting in the training of racing stock. They had grown up seeing their mother rarely wear skirts, and it suited them fine. It was rare that they did anything more with their hair than simply tying it back to keep it out of the way. Seclusion on an Australian station made fashion and social convention hardly relevant. Their lives were full enough without it.

Emma and Lacey's contrasts and similarities had kept them comfortably close through their years of growing up, and their mutual sensitivity to the need for time both together and apart had helped strengthen their closeness. And Alexa had always been a big part of their lives. She was open and honest, with the wisdom of a mother when necessary and the enjoyment of a good friend when appropriate. Sharing time as a family was also important, and the five of them often spent hours together at various activities. Jess and Alexa were always open with them about the happenings at the boys' home, over which they kept close supervision. Alexa believed it was an important endeavor that the children should be involved in, and Jess hoped that one day they would grow up to take a more active part in it.

When Lacey contemplated the close relationship she had with Emma, she hoped that Tyson would not come between them. The prospect seemed unlikely as soon as she thought it. But then, she wondered if one day another man might do the same. What kind of man would Emma love when the time was right? Perhaps someone like Tyson. *Tyson.* Lacey felt warmed just to think of him.

"What are you thinking?" Emma finally asked when Lacey smiled timidly with distant eyes.

Embarrassment momentarily flushed Lacey's cheeks. She didn't want her thoughts read so easily. Emma's eyes widened as if to repeat the question, and it became evident that attempting to keep any of this a secret from her was futile.

"He asked me to meet him in the gabled attic."

Emma was obviously surprised. "Of course you will."

"I did promise," Lacey said. "Not that it will be any great sacrifice." This brought out a mutual giggle that dispelled the tension. Emma continued to brush Lacey's hair while her speculations over Tyson and Lacey somehow took her mind to Michael Hamilton. After an unusual length of silence, she was surprised to hear Lacey ask pointedly, "What are *you* thinking?"

Emma hesitated, certain Lacey could never understand the subtle regret she couldn't seem to ignore. Emma's indifference to Michael had never matched Lacey's obvious distaste of him, which became evident whenever he happened to cross their paths. There was little point in trying to explain it, so she simply smiled and insisted, "Nothing, really. What time are you meeting Tyson?"

"Eleven."

"It's getting close to that now." Emma glanced toward the mantle clock. "We must have visited longer than we thought after supper."

Lacey felt warm to recall how different their usual evening in the drawing room had seemed. They had done all the same things: toying with the piano, chatting, and even singing a little. But everything was different. Everything had changed.

Lacey noted the clock hands hovering together over the eleven, and her heart quickened. Abruptly she came to her feet, grabbed her wrapper from the foot of the bed, and tied it around her.

"Lacey," Emma stopped her at the door, "be careful." She paused. "You know what I mean."

Lacey fought the urge to feel embarrassed as she nodded and hurried into the hall.

Emma sighed, suddenly feeling the first real hint of loneliness she had ever known. It was difficult for a twin to feel lonely. Tyson had always been there, and if he wasn't, Lacey had been. Never once had she felt any jealousy or resentment toward Lacey. What Lacey shared with Tyson had come close to what Emma shared with him as brother and sister. But Emma had always known that she and Tyson shared something no one could ever understand or take away. Still, it was evident that Tyson and Lacey were crossing bridges that Emma could never share. Tyson was a man now, and he was in love. It was a good match, Emma told herself with genuine warmth, in spite of their being so young. She hoped that everything worked out between them.

Fluffing the pillows on her bed, Emma leaned back and took up a novel from the bedside table to lose herself in a common pastime. Her mind soon became lost in the ridiculous tale of a roguish hero carting some dazzling young woman through outlandish adventures, eventually to meet with a happily ever after. These books were all the same. That's why Emma loved them. But tonight, not even fictional escape could erase her growing regret. Inwardly she cursed Michael Hamilton and read more fervently. He was nothing more than a grown-up bully, manipulating her with his cruel eyes and hard stares to believe she had wronged him. She was justified in turning down his offer. Wasn't she? Carefully she rationalized the guilt away and read until her eyes burned.

❦ ❦ ❦

The gabled attic was set high in the front of the boys' home, adjacent to the family residence. The room was large with sloped ceilings, a polished, clean-swept floor of wood slats, and three large gables with window seats, facing east. There were no furnishings beyond a pile of blankets kept in a corner in case they were needed. The room had not been built this way accidentally, but rather the entire home had been built around the concept of this room. Its purpose was very defined.

When a boy's misbehavior called for time alone, he was sent to the gabled attic to contemplate the results of his bad choices. And often group discussions were held here to help the children work through their problems and feelings. But the room had escaped the reputation for punishment. In truth, it had become an experience most boys treasured, to be allowed time alone in the gabled attic. Gradually it had become a reward rather than a punishment, and the room was said to hold good luck. It took only one evening seated in a gable, looking toward the sky of Australia, to feel its magic.

Lacey had often escaped to the attic room for her own peace, when she knew it would not be in use, and often Emma had come with her. She could recall only a handful of times when Tyson had joined them. But tonight it would be just the two of them.

Lacey figured it was just past eleven when she pushed open the door to find moonbeams shining through the southernmost gable. Instinctively she moved to stand in the light, and had barely absorbed it when the door squeaked softly and she turned to find Tyson leaning against it. She held her breath as he locked the door and moved stealthily toward her, the leather of his boots creaking.

"Today has been so wonderful," she said as he stood beside her and took her hand, gazing toward the three-quarter moon. "I almost feared it had been a dream."

"Dreams are for sleepers," he murmured, then turned toward her. They seemed to share an unspoken need to further explore the feelings that had sparked to life between them earlier. Tyson reached out a hand to touch her face, and she felt his words brush her skin. "Do you know how long I have wanted to be with you this way?"

"Tell me."

"Forever, it seems."

He kissed her then, and Lacey could feel a firm strength in him that made her long to be held and coddled. But a thread of sense forced her to realize the situation was precarious. Emma's words of caution came back to her.

"We must be careful, Tyson," she whispered.

He sighed. "I suppose we must."

"Come," she lightened her tone, "sit with me." She led him to the window seat, and they gazed together toward the sky. At the risk of shattering the mood, she added, "I don't want you to leave here, Tyson."

He circled her shoulders with his arm. "I'll make no promises," he said with a hint of dilemma seeping into his voice. "But right now, I could not leave you."

Lacey felt enough relief to push all of her fear away.

"I'll just have to talk you into going with me," he added lightly.

Lacey said nothing more, but deep inside she knew she couldn't go. Her heart was settled here. And there was something indescribably frightening about the world beyond this place, and the parents who had so lovingly nurtured her.

They talked far into the night, parting with a vow to continue their secret and meet again. For Lacey, life could be no better.

🍃 🍃 🍃

Long after Emma put down her book and tried to sleep, she was still haunted by the image of Michael Hamilton and that intense finality in his eyes. But a finality to what?

Attempting to analyze the situation in light of his personality—or what she knew of it—Emma realized that his overture toward her had likely been very difficult for him. And she had brushed it off so easily. Could it be possible that she had truly hurt the tough Michael Hamilton?

By morning, with very little sleep behind her, Emma had resolved herself to find Michael and accept his offer. What could it hurt? It was only a little ride with one of the stable hands. In essence, she'd done it many times with others who worked here. She had just never been formally approached before.

Emma skipped breakfast and went to the stable. But Michael wasn't there. She checked the tracks, the carriage house, everywhere he might be. Then she finally asked the stable master. "Murphy, do you know where I can find Michael Hamilton?"

Emma expected to hear that he'd gone into town or taken one of the racers out for a run. But she felt something die a little inside her when the answer was, "He left last night. Quit his job and was packed and gone before you could blink. Can you imagine that? Been here since he was eleven, then gone in less than an hour."

"Did he say where he was going?" she asked dryly.

"Didn't say a word to anybody. He just left."

Emma thanked him and hurried from the stable, where she leaned against the outside wall and tried to catch her breath. She couldn't rid herself of the feeling that something significant had just passed from her life—perhaps forever. She didn't understand why or how, and she could never begin to explain these feelings. But they were so vivid she could almost touch them.

She pondered briefly over the timing of his departure. The coincidence couldn't help but make her think she had something to do with it. Had he actually felt something for her? If so, how long had he felt it? How long had his attention to her been brushed carelessly aside while she'd been oblivious and perhaps insensitive?

"Emma!" Tyson's voice startled her, and she turned to see his expression filled with concern. "What on earth is wrong?" he asked, obviously sensing her distress.

"It's nothing." She attempted a smile, but he gave her a dubious glare. "Really, Tyson," she insisted. "I'm fine." But she gladly let him put his arms around her. There was no place so comforting as her brother's embrace.

"You're certain?" he asked, looking into her eyes. She hesitated, then nodded firmly. Tyson gave her a sly grin that was typical of him. "Does it have anything to do with me and Lacey?" he asked, his voice turning more severe.

"No," she answered with conviction. "I mean . . . well, it's going to take some getting used to, but . . ." She smiled up at him. "It feels so right, doesn't it?"

"It does to me," he said ardently.

"If I can't keep you from venturing out into the world, perhaps she can, eh?"

"I don't know," he said reluctantly, his expression faltering. "Maybe."

Murphy walked out of the stable, heading toward the tracks. He paused and spoke to Emma. "If he's not here, is there something I can help you with?"

"No, thank you, Murphy. I just wanted to ask him something. It's not important."

Murphy nodded and walked away. Tyson turned curious eyes to his sister. "Who?" he asked.

Emma had no choice but to answer. Still, she did her best to make her voice sound indifferent. "Oh, just Michael Hamilton."

Tyson narrowed his eyes, and it became one of those moments when Emma knew it was futile to keep anything from her brother. "Is that why you're distressed?" He chuckled dubiously. "Because Michael Hamilton left?"

"How did you know he left?" she insisted, wishing her tone hadn't betrayed her lack of indifference.

"Father told me last night," he answered. "He collected his wages and left. He had apparently been having Father save most of it for him, right from the start. It was a fair amount of money. What difference does it make to you? What haven't you been telling me?"

Emma had no desire to try to explain something that she didn't understand herself. Tyson was obviously sharing secrets with Lacey that he would never share with her. In that moment she cleared both points by saying, "I don't have to tell you everything, Tyson. I've got my own life to live, just as you do."

Emma moved away, but Tyson caught her arm. For a long moment their eyes met, and they shared a realization that becoming adults would, at least in some ways, compromise the closeness they had always known. And it hurt.

"Are you going to be all right?" he finally asked.

"I'll be fine," she insisted and walked away, silently cursing Michael Hamilton for having the nerve to manipulate her into feeling this ridiculous, unexplainable apprehension.

Two
NO PROMISES

The day prior to the twins' birthday, Emma decided that being with Tyson and Lacey was becoming unbearable. Everything they did was the same as before. They raced, they worked on the tracks, they shared their meals. They went through the trivial normalcy of every-day life just as they always had. But the tension between them was as tight as a bowstring. Emma decided that if they didn't get all of this out in the open soon, she was going to do it for them. She wanted life to be the way it had been before they had started sneaking around with these secrets. She missed them.

As a result of the changes, and certain regrets that Emma tried not to think about, she spent the majority of her time reading. She found an opportunity to go into town with Murphy when he went for sup-plies, and she bought every romance novel she could find that she hadn't already read. With a healthy stack of them on her bedside table, she read herself into exhaustion at night, then slept past breakfast and read instead of riding with her lovesick siblings. But the more Emma read, the more lonely she felt. Every romantic scene became Tyson and Lacey in her mind. And every roguish hero, no matter the physical description in the text, was vividly Michael Hamilton. The adventure in the books belonged to him, and in her mind he was out there some-where living it—while she sat in her bed with a sitting room between her and her sister that might as well have been a mile wide. Every evening she heard Lacey leave at bedtime, often not returning until the middle of the night. She could only hope they were minding the morals they'd been taught. In the meantime, Jess and Alexa didn't seem too concerned with the late hours all of their children were sleeping these days, as long as they managed to get their assigned work done. Everything apparently seemed normal enough to them, or they would have mentioned it by now.

On this night before their birthday, Emma heard Lacey sneak out of her room as usual. She glanced at the clock. Sure enough. Five to eleven.

Emma sighed, sank down into her bed with her latest paperback escapade, and tried to become lost in it.

❦   ❦   ❦

Lacey hurried down the hall and turned her key, identical to one each family member possessed, into the lock on the door between the residence and the boys' home. She locked it behind her and hurried on, wanting only to be with Tyson.

Through the days they had done well in keeping their secret, though it was beginning to get tiresome and Lacey longed to have it in the open. But tomorrow Tyson would celebrate his adulthood, and he'd expressed a desire to surprise his parents with their intentions at the appropriate moment. Then they could finally get on with their lives.

Each night, as they shared deep conversations of the future and past, it was becoming increasingly difficult not to express all they felt for each other. It seemed they were suited perfectly for each other—except for one issue, and that was merely avoided. But deep inside, Lacey believed that eventually he would come to see her reasoning, and his love for her would be enough to make him content to stay and put aside his desire to travel.

Lacey entered the attic to find it chilled from a heavy rainstorm that had set in unexpectedly after supper. She huddled in a window seat, pulling her wrapper tightly around her, waiting anxiously for Tyson to appear. She heard him come in and lock the door, then she listened through the darkness as he spread a blanket on the floor and wrapped another around her shoulders.

"Is that better?" he asked, pressing a kiss to the side of her neck.

"Much better, thank you." She touched his face, and he eased her to sit beside him on the floor.

"It's warmer here," he said and lay on his back, crossing his booted ankles and clasping his hands behind his head. For a long while Lacey sat beside him, trying to think of something to say. They usually couldn't find enough time to say all they wanted to, but for some reason, conversation felt difficult to come by at the moment. But being with him was comfortable, and she relaxed and wrapped her arms around her knees, relishing the feel of just being near him and listening to the rain beat on the roof so close above them.

Lacey was beginning to wonder if he'd fallen asleep when he said, "Come here."

Lacey hesitated. To this point they had just sat together and talked, and sometimes they'd kissed each other. She knew the rules of propriety they'd been taught, and she knew that this was risky.

"Oh, come on." He laughed, turning to pull her down beside him where he eased her head to his shoulder and relaxed with his arms around her. Lacey tried to relax too, but his nearness distracted her. The rain could only be entertaining for so long, and she went nearly crazy from the silence between them. Frantically she searched for something to say. But she didn't come up with anything before Tyson turned abruptly, whispering in a husky voice, "I can't bear this any longer, Lacey. I love you so much, I . . . ." His words faded into a throaty growl that made her giggle.

"Let's get married soon, Tyson," she said, feeling her resolve to keep the rules beginning to waver. How long could they be expected to carry this burden?

"We'll tell them tomorrow," he said with conviction.

Lacey felt relieved by his promise. She knew their parents would not be so liberal with them if they had any clue of how their feelings had changed.

He kissed her again with more ardor than before. But it only took a moment for Lacey to realize that she was not enjoying this. It was wrong and she knew it. Panic exploded in her mind, and she was suddenly very afraid. Afraid of their immaturity, their differences—however few—and their lack of commitment. She had been taught very clearly about such things, and she knew Tyson had been taught the same. She tried to ease away, but he seemed oblivious to her discomfort. Finally she had no choice but to sit up and move back. "No, Tyson. I can't," she said firmly.

Tyson hit his fist on the floor and groaned in frustration. She reached out to touch his hand. "I'm sorry, Tyson. But it's . . . too soon. We must—"

"Yes, I know." Anger crept into his voice. "We must be careful. I've asked you to marry me. What more do you want?"

"I want what I was taught to demand. More than asking. More than promises."

Lacey felt his anger deepen, even though she could barely see him in the darkness. He came abruptly to his feet, and without another word, he left her alone with the chill and the rain.

At first Lacey cried. The rejection was almost unbearable. When she realized that crying wasn't going to help any, she returned to her room and listened to the rain from her bed, feeling confused and alone. She wanted to talk to her mother, but Alexa was only a foster mother to her. And she knew she must wait until Tyson took the first step of revealing their circumstances. Jess and Alexa were *his* parents, and she would not step over those boundaries in this situation. She had already stepped over too many of them through her growing years.

Lacey nearly went to Emma's room to tell her of the problem, but the same reasons kept her pinned to her bed. Emma was like the other half of Tyson, and for the first time in her life, Lacey felt unable to reveal her thoughts to her closest—and only—friend.

With little sleep behind her, Lacey went straight to the stables early, needing the invigoration of a brisk ride. She had barely approached the gelding's stall when Tyson's voice startled her. "I'm truly sorry, Lacey," he said with total sincerity. "I've been here for hours. I figured you would show up eventually."

He smiled, and everything was all right. Relief flooded through her. "I understand, Tyson. Really I do." She looked away timidly. "I want you too, but . . ."

"Yes, I know." He lifted her chin to look at her, and the meaning in his gaze brought memories back to flush her cheeks. "I'll tell them at supper," he stated. "Then we can get married."

Lacey nodded in firm agreement. Tyson turned and walked away as one of the stable hands appeared in the opposite doorway.

"Tyson," she called after him, "happy birthday."

He smiled and winked. "You, too."

The hours until supper seemed endless to Lacey. In order to pass the time, she even asked Emma to tell her the plot of the novel she was reading. But she came to the usual conclusion. "They're all the same, Emma. I don't know why you read those things."

"I've got to do something besides watch you and Tyson ogle at each other."

Lacey laughed. "I suppose you're right. I doubt this is easy for you."

"I'll get even one day." Emma laughed. "At least, I hope so."

"I'm certain you will," Lacey agreed. "Some lucky man is out there looking for you right now."

"There aren't a lot of men to choose from around here," Emma said, feeling sad for some reason. Diverting the topic, she asked, "So, how are things with you and Tyson?"

"He's going to tell your parents today at supper." Emma made an exaggerated noise to indicate that she was impressed. Lacey giggled and added, "I guess we'll decide a date from there."

"A date?" Emma couldn't help being surprised.

"For the wedding. I thought Tyson would have told—"

"Wedding?" Emma didn't want to admit her true feelings. She knew Tyson better than anyone, and she couldn't find any evidence to see that he was ready to get married. "I knew you were getting closer. And I knew it was becoming . . . well, romantic, but . . . *a wedding?*"

"He asked me a week ago," Lacey said with apology in her voice. "Of course I said yes."

"But you're both so young still, and Tyson is so . . ."

"What?" Lacey insisted.

"Restless."

Lacey looked downhearted, and Emma checked herself. She had to learn to think before she spoke. She should have learned that from her experience with Michael Hamilton. "I'm sorry, Lacey. I must remember that this is not my relationship. If you and Tyson are ready to be married, you have my blessing. I know you will be very happy together. I'll miss you."

"But we'll live here, of course," Lacey insisted.

"If Tyson has his way," Emma tried to say lightly, even though she knew it had a great deal of truth, "you won't live here all of the time. That boy's got wanderlust." Again Emma felt she had to partly retract her statement. "I'm certain he loves you enough to do what's best for you, Lacey."

Lacey smiled weakly, trying to ignore her nagging doubts. She loved Tyson and he loved her; of that she was certain. The rest would surely come together.

They were both relieved to put an end to the conversation by going down to supper. Tyson smiled knowingly at Lacey as they were seated, then he winked at Emma. They all took notice of the sealed envelopes set over their plates, with each of their names scribed in their father's eloquent hand.

"Aren't you going to open them?" Jess Davies asked, barely seated. He grinned at his wife, who returned an emotional smile. This day was significant for them, as well. An important season of their lives was behind them. Their children were grown.

"You go first," Tyson said to Lacey.

"No, Emma should go first."

"I think you should all do it at the same time," Alexa suggested, and the three of them almost reluctantly picked up the envelopes. They glanced back and forth at each other to assure themselves that they were all equally ignorant. As they unanimously removed the contents, their breath caught in unison. They stared at Jess in disbelief while he gave a quiet speech.

"I told you a long time ago that when you were eighteen, we would consider all of you adults. I will continue to provide the basic needs of life for you, and your mother and I both hope that you'll be under our roof as you raise families of your own. Alexa and I have discussed this thoroughly, and we decided there was no need for us to die before you received your inheritance. So, there it is. I would suggest you invest it and use it wisely, and it will last you a lifetime. And please, don't bet it on any horse races."

This brought a tense chuckle from the recipients. Tyson finally spoke with a tight, incredulous voice. "A hundred thousand pounds?"

"Each," Jess stated.

"But . . . ," Tyson began.

"Oh, I'm sure there will be more when I die," Jess quipped. "We won't miss that too much. Your grandfather," he pointed to Tyson, "your namesake, Tyson Byrnehouse, was a very wealthy man. We can thank him for the life we live."

"Not only him," Alexa added affectionately, gesturing toward her husband. "Your father worked very hard to get and keep all that he has. Remember that as you decide how to use what is in your hands."

"Thank you," Tyson and Emma said at nearly the same time, which lightened the mood a little further.

"I don't think I can accept this." Lacey set the bank note carefully onto the table and folded her hands in her lap. All eyes turned to her, baffled and astonished.

"I will not allow you to do otherwise," Jess insisted. Lacey looked up at him with tears in her eyes. "You are as much our child as Tyson and Emma. Sometimes I think we should have adopted you officially from the start, and—"

"Personally," Tyson interrupted, "I'm glad you didn't."

Alexa glanced inquisitively toward her son, as if to question him on that. But the first course was brought in by Mrs. Brady, who announced proudly that she had prepared the best of everything for the big day.

Just into the second course, Tyson flashed Lacey a knowing smile, and her heart began to pound.

"Father, Mother," he began carefully, "now that we're eighteen, I've been thinking that it's time to get on with something I've felt strongly about for a long time, and—"

"Yes," Jess smiled, "you're a man now, and I've been thinking myself that it's high time you started taking over."

Lacey felt immediate tension descend over the room as Tyson's eyes flashed with vivid rebellion. And she was frightened.

Alexa apparently sensed it as she spoke gently to her husband. "Jess, I believe you interrupted Tyson. He was about to say something."

"So I did. Forgive me," he apologized sincerely. "Go on, son."

Lacey waited tensely for Tyson to complete his announcement, but a silent moment later she realized he wasn't going to.

"What do you mean by 'take over'?" Tyson demanded, his voice deep with anger and frustration. Lacey had witnessed many episodes such as this, but life had always gone on, and their parents had generally credited it to the adage of *boys will be boys*. But tonight, Lacey felt her future resting in the midst of it. And the rebel who occasionally surfaced in Tyson was someone who frightened her. Perhaps she didn't know him as well as she thought she did. Or maybe love was blinding her discernment. The fear deepened as she realized that Tyson was no longer dependent on his parents. She looked warily at the envelope sitting next to his plate.

"Well?" Tyson demanded of his father.

"I would think it's obvious," Jess concluded, apparently baffled by Tyson's anger.

"I thought I had made it clear that I have no desire to take over," Tyson insisted. "I have other plans."

"I thought you would have grown out of such plans by now," Jess said, his calm demeanor beginning to crumble.

Lacey felt helpless. She met Emma's eyes and recalled their earlier conversation. It was true that Emma knew Tyson in a way that Lacey never could. She looked to Tyson, then to Jess, the tightening anger evident in their faces. To a degree she could understand both points of view, but neither of them was doing very well at expressing himself. She was relieved when Alexa said gently, "Must we argue? This is a special occasion, and—"

"Yes," Tyson interrupted with sarcasm, "this is the night when I'm expected to take the reins. Pun intended." He threw his napkin to the table. "Well, I don't want to spend my life betting on races and collecting lost boys. And sheep? I hate sheep! I won't do it."

"Tyson," Emma pleaded softly, "calm down. We can talk about this."

Lacey could feel the pain in their parents and Emma that closely matched her own as Tyson's expression only hardened further. "I'm leaving tomorrow," he announced coldly, and Lacey felt her heart drop to the floor.

"Tyson," Alexa muttered with a quiver in her voice, "you can't just leave here and—"

"Watch me." He stood so abruptly that his chair spun and tipped.

"But Tyson." Lacey came to her feet in protest. He glanced at her briefly, as if he'd just now remembered where this conversation had begun.

For a moment, Lacey felt a glimmer of hope. The moment passed quickly as he added, "Any of you are welcome to come with me." His voice rang with finality as he left the room.

Emma noticed that he took the money with him. All she could think was how long a man could live on a hundred thousand pounds. She looked to Lacey and wanted to cry on her behalf, if for no other reason.

Lacey glanced around quickly at the regret and fear showing in the grim faces of her family. Instinctively she offered, "I'll talk to him. Perhaps I'm not so involved."

The words echoed in her ears with irony as she fled from the room, realizing she was far more involved than she dared admit. Her heart was breaking, and her desperation mounted as she flew up the stairs. She found him standing in the fading light of the gable windows, his hands plunged deeply into his pockets, his head bowed.

"Tyson," she whispered, closing the door behind her. His head shot up, his eyes ablaze with rebellion and challenge.

"Are you coming with me?" he asked.

"No, I'm not," she replied, and his face hardened further. "Why don't you stay, and we'll work it out?"

"In other words, all of you will work me out to your specifications."

"Tyson, your father tries hard to do the right thing. You must not judge him so harshly."

"You just don't understand, do you," he retorted.

"I understand that you want to travel. All right," she conceded, realizing she would have to give in to a degree if she was to have him. "I'll go with you, but not tomorrow." His eyes widened. "Let's get married—soon. And we'll take some time to travel before we—"

"Come back here and live out our lives," he said, the hardness returning to his eyes.

"I love it here, Tyson. I don't understand why you can't see the value of all that we have here. All I see here is love and goodness. All you see here is misery."

"That's right."

"Tyson," she decided to try guilt, "you'll break our hearts if you leave. We all love you."

"What about *my* heart?"

"Stop being so selfish, and try to think beyond the moment."

"I've been thinking beyond for years. Now it's time to *do* something about it."

"You're angry. You need to calm down and think rationally before you make such decisions."

"Yes, I'm angry. I just don't understand why . . ."

Intuitively Lacey rushed to him, silencing him with a kiss. Desperation seeped into it. He'd once said that if anything could make him stay, she could. She believed he had two passions, and one of them was her. In that moment she made the decision to relinquish herself to him, praying he would put her above his desire to leave. In spite of knowing how wrong it was to take such a step under the circumstances, deep inside she believed he couldn't possibly leave her with such a bond between them.

She turned in his arms to face him, wanting him to see the tears in her eyes. "I need you, Tyson." She could only hope he would sense the deeper implication. She needed him to be here tomorrow, next month, always.

❦   ❦   ❦

Tyson quietly walked Lacey to the door of her room, pausing there to hold her and kiss her. He followed her into her room where they sat in silence, sharing an occasional kiss that filled Lacey with peace. She knew in her heart he could never leave her now. They were both startled when a knock came at the sitting room door.

"Who is it?" she called, not wanting their time together interrupted by the realities of life.

"It's me, silly," Emma called back, wondering who else would come through the sitting room—especially this late at night.

"Just a minute," she said, and shared one more long kiss with Tyson. Then she whispered, "Just act innocent. We were only talking, right?"

"Right," he chuckled.

She impulsively decided to leave the room dark, hoping it might keep Emma from sensing the guilt that she knew wouldn't be easy to hide. Tyson moved to a chair by the window and sat casually, situating himself to look as if he'd been sprawled there for hours.

Lacey opened the door and Emma moved into the room, ignoring the sensation of something being different in order to get to her point. "Did you talk to him?"

"I still am," Lacey replied.

"Hello, Emma." Tyson's voice came out of the darkness.

"I was wondering where you'd run off to," Emma said.

"I've been with Lacey."

"So I see." Emma wished the room was light so she could see his face. She sensed something different about him but couldn't quite grasp it. No one else seemed inclined to light a lamp, so she resigned herself to have her say in the dark. "You left your mother crying." Her tone was firm but not harsh.

"I'm sorry about that," Tyson admitted. Lacey sat on the edge of the bed to listen, feeling the magic of the past hours shattering around her.

"Don't tell me, Tyson," Emma said. "Tell her. She's your mother as much as she is mine."

"You were born six minutes earlier," Tyson quipped, but his attempt to lighten the mood was lost.

"Tyson," Emma said carefully, "you cannot hurt those you love for your selfish purposes, and not pay for it in the end."

"Why doesn't anyone ever mention how *I* get hurt?" He stood and turned to show his silhouette against the window. To look at him now, Lacey could hardly imagine the gentleness he had shown toward her only minutes ago.

"I understand your need, Tyson. But there is a way to fulfill it without causing so much hurt."

"I'm not sure you do understand it," Tyson said almost sadly.

"If you believe that," Emma's voice betrayed some of the hurt she'd referred to, "then there is no point discussing this at all."

"There," he said tersely, "we agree on something." He turned and pointed a finger at Emma. "If you want to solve the problem, then talk to your father. He needs to figure out that I am not going to follow in his footsteps."

"I don't think that concerns him nearly so much as his fear of your leaving. If you would sit down and discuss your feelings with him rationally, instead of arguing about it, I'm certain the two of you could come to an agreeable position."

"I wonder," Tyson said cynically.

"You're acting like a child, Tyson. You may look twenty-five, but you act like a twelve-year-old," Emma replied with the same cynicism. "When you're ready to communicate like an adult, come and see me." She moved to the door, adding tersely to Lacey, "I don't think your talking did much good."

Tears burned into Lacey's eyes, and she was grateful for the darkness that hid them from Tyson. She had failed. She had given him everything she had, and it wasn't enough. The humiliation was too much to bear.

In one last, desperate attempt, she moved close to him and touched his face. "Tyson, we must be together. You're a part of me now."

"Lacey," he said with passion, wrapping her in his arms, "I want you to come with me. It would mean so much more if you were there. Please, Lacey."

"Marry me first, Tyson. Just wait a couple of weeks and—"

"I don't know if I can. Let's leave tomorrow. We'll elope, and—"

"I don't want to elope. Mother and Emma would be so hurt if we—"

"And I'll be hurt if you don't come with me."

"Wait, and I will," she said, certain they could come to a compromise.

"I can't wait. I've got to get out of here."

Lacey pulled away from his arms. "I never would have believed it, but you are a selfish man, Tyson Davies. Or perhaps you're just trying to be a man so quickly that your concern for others isn't keeping up. You were not raised to be this way."

"I am what I am, Lacey. Not what I was raised to be. You have to love me as I am or not at all."

"And you have to do the same. But if that's the case, then maybe it's better this way." She heard her voice crack.

"What are you saying?" He sounded panicked enough to give her one last glimmer of hope.

"There is a part of you I don't understand, Tyson. And neither does Emma, or anyone else. I can't love that part of you. I can't love something in a man that would make him turn his back on so much because he's so full of youthful rage that he can't compromise to any degree."

"Admit it, Lacey." He turned the anger back as if he'd not heard anything she'd said. "You don't want to come with me. A month away from here, and you'd be lost."

"You're right, Tyson. But I said I would go anyway."

"I'm not going to drag you around the world while you're longing to be here."

"Then it would appear that we have come to cross purposes."

Lacey tried to keep the tears silent, but the reality of what she'd just said caught in her throat and forced a sob into the open air.

"Lacey." He touched her face and kissed her brow. "I love you. Maybe you're right. Maybe we can come to a compromise. I don't want to be without you."

Lacey sighed and nearly collapsed against him. His words were enough to give her something beyond despair.

"Perhaps we should sleep on it." He lifted her chin to kiss her. Lacey savored it carefully, as if it might be their last. "And remember, Lacey, whatever happens, I love you. I will always love you." His words made Lacey realize that his conciliatory remarks about staying had only been momentary consolations to patronize and soothe her.

Tyson moved toward the sitting room door, and Lacey felt suddenly panicked. "Please," she said, "don't leave without . . . please tell me you'll stay until we can . . . at least talk and . . ."

The reality of his words were like a dagger in her heart. "Right now, I can give you no promises."

He disappeared in the dark, and Lacey could do nothing but collapse on the bed and cry.

❦ ❦ ❦

Emma found it impossible to sleep with the muffled sounds of arguing voices filtering through the sitting room. She hadn't realized they had stopped until she heard her own door opening and footsteps that could only be Tyson's.

"Emma," he whispered, kneeling beside the bed. She reached out and took his hand in the darkness.

"You seem different," she whispered, unable to pinpoint it, but sensing a strong change in him.

"I'm a man now, Emma," he said after a long pause.

Emma said nothing more, but she knew something had happened to change him that had nothing to do with coming of age.

"I beg you to understand why I have to do this, Emma." His voice trembled with urgency.

"You're leaving, then," she stated, feeling as if a part of her blood was literally being drained away.

"I don't know for certain, but I . . ."

He hesitated and she said with finality, "You're leaving." He made no response. "And what about Lacey?"

"She'll get over it."

"None of us will get over it, Tyson. You're a fool if you think you can just walk away and not affect us."

"I love you, Emma." He ignored her wisdom. "You must remember it." He left the room, and Emma felt silent tears trickle into her hair, which slightly distorted the sound of Lacey quietly sobbing in the other room.

❦ ❦ ❦

Emma came awake suddenly in the morning light, tuning her ears to the rumble of contentious voices floating up the stairs. In a flurry she threw on her wrapper and headed through the sitting room to wake Lacey, but she was already on her way to the door. Neither of them dared speak as they flew down the stairs in their bare feet like a couple of avenging angels, lifting their nightgowns to avoid tripping, their unfastened wrappers flying behind them.

Their abrupt arrival at the bottom step silenced the angry exchange taking place in the entry hall. For a moment they were stunned. Tyson stood with his hand on the doorknob, a long coat hanging over his lean frame, hat in hand, bag at his feet. Alexa was crying on Jess's shoulder. Jess stood firmly, anger keeping the hurt in check.

Emma finally spoke up. "You were going to leave without even saying good-bye?"

"I did that last night," he said flatly.

"Is that what it was?" Emma retorted as Lacey's trembling hand took hold of her arm.

"You must forgive me for not meeting your expectations," Tyson said, his sarcasm piercing her deeply.

"I don't believe it." Lacey stepped forward, wondering why all they had shared meant so little to him.

"I believe it," Emma said bitterly.

Lacey couldn't begin to find words to express the hurt she felt from his callousness, the anger at his irresponsibility and selfishness, and the regret over her foolishness in believing that her sacrifice would make a difference. The humiliation threatened to strangle her. How could she have been so stupid?

"And that's it," she stated, echoing Emma's bitterness.

"There's no point in trying to stop him, Lacey." Jess spoke in a voice more acrid than she'd ever heard. "His mind is made up."

"Perhaps it is." Lacey brushed past the others to face Tyson directly. "But I've got a few thoughts I'd like him to take along."

For a moment she looked at him deeply, wondering who this man really was. Tears nearly surfaced, but she choked them back and urged the anger forward. "One day, Tyson Byrnehouse-Davies, you're going to stop in the midst of your great quest and wonder what you're doing. You're not going to find the glorious place you're dreaming of, because it doesn't exist. What you're looking for is right here!" She hit his chest, none too softly. "You're a fool, Tyson, but until you find that out for yourself, I will give you exactly what you gave me: no promises." He lifted his chin abruptly, as if she had struck him. "And when the loneliness starts to seep in, I want you to think about what you left behind, and I want you to ache the way I'm going to ache, the way we're all going to ache. You don't deserve the way you are loved. You don't deserve the life you've been blessed with. Try to make some sense of that. And have a wonderful time."

"Are you finished?" he asked coldly.

"No." Her voice softened with her eyes. "I . . . I . . . hope you come home . . . before it's too late."

"Too late for what?" he asked.

"You figure it out," she concluded fiercely.

"Are you coming home?" Emma asked, her voice strained with emotion. She felt as if half of her flesh and blood was being torn away. And for what?

"Eventually . . . perhaps." With that, Tyson put on his flat-brimmed hat and picked up the lightly packed bag.

"Good-bye," was all he said before he threw open the door and strode out without looking back. Emma moved to her father's other shoulder to cry with her mother. Jess's lip quivered as he looked toward the ceiling and squeezed his eyes shut.

Lacey still felt too angry to cry. Matching his vehemence, she went after him, calling his name from the porch. He turned back with obvious reluctance and she ran toward him, stopping only inches away.

"There's something I want to give you before you go," she said softly. "Take it with you and remember it when you feel alone." His eyes softened and she wanted to kiss him. She knew that's what he was expecting. But with all the strength she could muster, she drew her hand back and slapped him. His head reeled to the side, and Lacey turned to walk back into the house before he recovered. She paused on the porch and turned back briefly. Their eyes met across the distance. He turned and walked briskly toward the stable.

Three
CONSEQUENCES

The sting in Lacey's hand rushed to every nerve in her body, settling into her heart with an ache that she knew would never dissipate. An oppression filled the house in lieu of Tyson's presence. Laughter was hard to find, and tears were quick to surface. Everything had changed. Lacey felt the intensity of his absence as she continued to harbor her secret from the family, ashamed and distraught over all that had transpired between her and Tyson. And still, she had failed to keep him here.

The regret over her transgression began to consume her like a dark cloud that infiltrated every part of her heart and soul. She felt cheap and dirty, and too ashamed to admit it to anyone—not even Emma. At times it felt as if the darkness would completely devour her, and she often believed that she deserved such a fate.

Weeks passing didn't ease the pain for any of them, but perhaps they learned to keep it from affecting their daily lives. Lacey knew what she felt could be no worse than what Emma or their parents were going through—as far as missing Tyson was concerned, at least. It was the consequences of her actions that now separated her from the family in a way that nothing else ever could. It all became very clear to her on a morning much like every other morning since he'd left—except for the dull, throbbing realization that the signs and symptoms were no coincidence. She was pregnant.

Lacey couldn't begin to know how to react. The darkness that had hovered with her since that fateful night now became full-blown. She could almost literally hear some evil voice whispering taunts in her ear. The only thing she found herself capable of was sobbing helplessly into her pillow. A part of her hoped that Emma would not hear her, while another part longed for her sister's strength. If she had to face this alone, she felt certain the darkness would completely and irrevocably devour her.

"Lacey." Emma was holding her before she realized she wasn't alone. Like an immediate answer to her faithless prayers, Lacey held to her sister as if to a lifeline.

"Lacey, what is it?" Emma insisted. She knew Tyson's absence had been somehow more difficult for Lacey, although they had avoided discussing the reasons. But the emotion Emma saw now was far too anguished to be any kind of reaction to the simple fact of Tyson's absence.

Lacey couldn't find the words to tell Emma. But she had to. There was no keeping her secret now. She couldn't possibly hide the nausea and weight gain for long when her daily activities involved wearing breeches and riding horses.

"Lacey," Emma urged. "Something is terribly wrong. You must tell me what it is."

Lacey saw no point in prolonging this any further. "Oh, Emma, I don't know how to say this. I . . . well . . . Tyson and I . . ." She wiped helplessly at her tears while Emma looked on with expectancy and compassion. "He . . . I mean . . . I . . . I . . ."

"Come on, Lacey. It can't be as bad as all that."

Lacey took a deep breath. "I'm pregnant, Emma."

Emma gave no reaction at all. She felt as if time had just frozen around her while she tried to put the elements together. Tyson. Her brother. Her twin brother. And Lacey. Her friend, as good as her sister. Emma had imagined Tyson kissing Lacey, even kissing her passionately. She knew they had become close, but she could not imagine what might have possibly possessed them to allow such a thing to happen under the circumstances. Alexa had often told them how passion could make anyone, man or woman, lose all reason. But they had always been taught the importance of maintaining control outside of marriage.

Emma wanted to ask a hundred questions. How had it happened? Where? Why? But she knew it was none of her business. She wanted to scold Lacey for being foolish enough to let it happen. But Emma knew better than to judge something that she knew absolutely nothing about. Emma had never even been kissed. She'd never come across anyone worth kissing. And here Lacey was *pregnant!* And Tyson was as gone as any man could be. She wanted to scream at her and demand to know how she could have been so stupid. But looking into Lacey's eyes, it was evident that she was punishing herself plenty. She didn't need Emma to add to the burden.

"Emma!" Lacey finally shrieked, certain she would far prefer outward anger over this blank, stunned silence. "Say something! Anything!"

"We've got to tell Mother and Father," she stated calmly, putting her speculations on hold long enough to think rationally. Lacey was in no position to do so. "I know you must be terrified, but we'll work it out. You know you're not alone."

"Dear, sweet Emma." Lacey threw her arms around her sister's neck. She had expected to be scolded and ridiculed—and she knew well that she deserved it. But Emma was offering nothing but perfect love. She wondered how she could be so blessed. "What would I ever do without you?"

"There is no reason to wonder. I will always be here."

"But Emma." Lacey pulled back. "How can I tell them? They've been through so much with having him leave. This will only make everything worse."

"You've got to just tell them, Lacey. They're the only parents you've got. And you certainly can't hide it."

"Perhaps I should go away for a time, or—"

"I won't hear of it," Emma insisted. "And neither will they." She patted Lacey's hand with genuine reassurance. "Now get yourself dressed. We'll tell them now."

"I've got to have something to eat first," Lacey insisted.

"Fine, we'll tell them after breakfast. Hurry along."

The meal passed in quiet tension, but with Tyson's absence, nothing seemed too out of the ordinary. Jess rose to excuse himself, but Emma stopped him.

"Before you start your work, Lacey and I need to discuss something with you." She looked to her mother. "Both of you. It is important."

"All right," Jess stated, passing a glance of curiosity toward his wife. "I'll be in my office. I'll see you as soon as you're finished."

Emma nodded gratefully while Lacey turned pale.

"Are you feeling all right?" Alexa asked her.

"Oh, well enough." Lacey gave a phony smile. "I'm sure I'm fine."

Alexa looked doubtful, but she rose to follow her husband from the room.

"I don't want to hurt them," Lacey whispered across the table.

"Well, I think that's unavoidable. But you'll hurt them more by not confiding in them. They are quite used to dealing with problems."

"Yes," Lacey agreed, "but I doubt that any of their wayward boys ever got pregnant."

They shared a brief chuckle. "No, but some of them were likely the cause of such things."

"That's true," Lacey had to admit. But it didn't make her feel any better. "Emma," she spoke shyly as they moved down the hall, "I don't want to tell them it's Tyson's baby."

Emma stopped to stare at her in disbelief. "You think they won't find out?"

"Then let them find out later, when his leaving is not so prominent." She gave a hopeful smile. "Perhaps Tyson will be back before it's born."

"Perhaps," Emma moved on and Lacey followed, "but don't count on it."

"Will you, Emma? Will you please not tell them?"

"I suppose I'll leave that up to you. But they'll find out. I would bet on it." Emma appeased Lacey's concern by adding, "But they won't find out from me."

"Thank you, Emma. You're a dear, as always."

They paused before the office door, and Lacey drew a deep breath to swallow the lump in her throat. "I'm not sure I've ever done anything so difficult in my entire life," she admitted.

"It'll be all right. I'll stay with you," Emma reassured her, then turned the knob before their courage was lost.

They entered to find Jess behind the desk at his paperwork, while Alexa stood behind him, rubbing his shoulders. Lacey thought briefly of how much she loved and admired them. They were good people, and the love they shared was evident in the way they gave it to others at every turn.

"We need to talk to you," Emma announced.

"No," Lacey put a silencing hand on Emma's arm. She knew Emma would gladly buffer it for her, but she had to do this herself. "This problem has nothing to do with Emma. She's here to keep me from running away."

Emma gave Lacey an encouraging glance as the curiosity intensified on their parents' faces. Lacey took a deep breath. "I hope you won't be too disappointed with me," she began. "I've made a foolish mistake that will not easily be rectified."

"What is it, love?" Alexa encouraged when the silence grew long.

Lacey glanced to Emma, who nodded firmly. She decided to just get it over with. "I'm pregnant."

The room became so still that the clock on the mantle sounded like a time bomb. Lacey bit her lip to stop its quivering. The hurt was apparent in their faces, but they appeared too shocked to respond. The regret Lacey had felt since Tyson had left suddenly magnified a hundredfold. "I'm sorry to hurt you this way," she murmured. "You've given me so much, and this is how I repay it." She attempted to choke back the tears. "I wish I could just go away and—"

Alexa was at her side in a flash. "You'll do no such thing. I'll not lose any more children." Lacey found her face against Alexa's motherly shoulder, where she cried and gratefully absorbed the much-needed comfort. But her regret deepened when she realized that Alexa was crying, too.

"I'm so sorry," Lacey said when she had calmed down somewhat. "I'm so sorry to disappoint you this way."

"Well, we are disappointed," Alexa said with a sniffle, glancing toward Jess, who said nothing. His face was hard, and the displeasure in his eyes was harsh. "But that doesn't mean we don't love you."

Lacey began to cry again, knowing that their quiet disappointment was the most painful thing of all. *How could she have been so stupid?*

"I'm so sorry," she said again when the tears finally ran dry, if only for the moment. "I don't think I've cried so much since . . ."

"Since when, love?" Alexa pressed when she hesitated.

"Since my parents were killed. I barely remember it."

"At least we can say your life has been good since then." Alexa gently wiped at Lacey's tears with a delicate handkerchief. "And we'll just have to do all we can to help you through this."

Jess apparently took this as his signal to step in. "Who is the father?" he asked, anger tinging his voice.

Lacey quickly covered her fear and found a suitable answer. "It doesn't matter. He won't marry me."

"It matters to me," Jess stated, the anger becoming more evident. "If someone has taken advantage of you, I want to know about it."

"It was my fault it happened," Lacey argued. "Please . . . I don't want any trouble caused over this. I . . ."

"Well, it's too late for that," Jess shouted.

"Jess," Alexa insisted. "She will suffer enough consequences without having you yell at her. Your temper will solve nothing."

"Lacey," Jess said gently, though his anger was still obvious. "I have seen too much pain in my life as a result of children being born where they were not intended." A sharp glance passed between Jess and Alexa. A similar look was exchanged by Emma and Lacey as they realized there was something significant that they were unaware of.

Lacey remained silent and Jess came to his feet, setting his palms on the desk to look directly at her. "Listen to me, girl. It takes two people to create a child. That child belongs to someone else every bit as much as it belongs to you. We cannot approach this effectively until we have all the facts. Now, again I ask, who is the father of the baby?"

"I don't want to tell you," Lacey cried.

"Lacey." Jess sighed with an obvious attempt to keep his temper under control, and Alexa squeezed her hand reassuringly. "We love you. You have been a great blessing to us." Fresh tears filled her eyes. She'd never heard him say it that way before. Lacey looked to Alexa, who nodded to confirm it. "We want to help you," Jess continued, "but you're not doing anyone any good by protecting the other guilty party. If we can talk to the young man and—"

"You can't!" she shot back, realizing she was slowly being cornered. She felt certain he would not let up until he got the answer.

"Why not?"

"He's gone."

"Gone where?" Jess demanded.

"I don't know," she whimpered.

"Is it one of my employees?" His voice continued to gain volume.

"No!" Hers did as well.

Lacey looked to Alexa with pleading in her eyes. Jess Davies could be a difficult man to talk to. Alexa gave her a look of reassurance, then her eyes narrowed, as if she could sense what Lacey was trying to convey. Something apparently clicked in Alexa's mind as she breathlessly murmured, "Oh, no."

Realizing that Alexa had perceived the truth, Lacey pressed a hand over her mouth in a feeble effort to hold back the sobs racking her chest.

"What?" Jess insisted.

"Oh, no," Alexa repeated. "Lacey, you're not trying to tell us that . . ."

"What?" Jess shouted.

"You've got to say it, Lacey," Alexa insisted gently. "I won't believe it until you say it."

Lacey looked to Emma, who nodded firmly with encouragement. She drew back her shoulders and took a deep breath to gain some control of her emotion. But the words came weakly. "It's Tyson."

"What about Tyson?" Jess asked without stopping to think, then he gasped deeply as he apparently realized that his question had been answered.

"It's Tyson," Lacey nearly shouted, glad to have it out. The guilt and shame had been borne secretly for too long. "Tyson is the father of the baby."

Jess sat down, while Alexa and Lacey nearly collapsed against each other. This seemed a good time to finally take a chair, and the three women were seated, all holding hands.

"I don't believe it," Jess said. "I had no idea that . . ."

"That Tyson and I loved each other?" Lacey provided, gaining a degree of courage now that the worst was out.

"And was it love?" Jess asked cynically.

"Did you credit me with less?" Lacey asked.

"No, Lacey," his voice softened, "I'm sorry. I only meant that . . . perhaps I might credit Tyson with less."

"Perhaps Tyson suffers from inheriting his father's passion," Alexa interjected while Lacey felt herself being regarded as Tyson's lover.

Jess's eyes widened, as if he was surprised that his wife would say such a thing in front of the children.

"They're grown up now, Jess," she said. "And we have a very grown-up problem on our hands."

"Yes," he agreed, "I suppose we do." All was quiet for a thoughtful moment, except for Lacey's sniffling.

"Emma," Jess said, "I know that you and Lacey are very close, but I think we'd best talk to her alone."

"I understand, Papa." She looked to Lacey with an expression of support and left the room, closing the door behind her. "Oh, Tyson," Emma whispered. "I understand now what had changed you. Come back," she pleaded into the empty hallway. "You must come back."

"Have you been feeling ill?" Alexa asked Lacey with a comforting squeeze of her hand. Lacey nodded, but didn't feel much like elaborating at the moment.

"I still can't believe it." Jess chuckled in disbelief and pushed a hand through his hair.

"I'm so sorry," Lacey attempted to console him. "I don't know what to say."

Jess leaned back and sighed. "Maybe you'd better tell us what happened."

"Jess," Alexa scolded, "I should think it's obvious."

"I don't mean that," he retorted. "I mean . . . ," he turned gentle eyes to Lacey and her heart filled with fresh respect for this man who was a father to her, ". . . how the two of you came to cross the line . . . from friendship into . . . something more."

Lacey blew her nose and swallowed. "Tyson and I have always been close, but we were always together with Emma. It had always been the three of us. Many times I felt like I was intruding upon something that should not have been mine." She paused a moment and looked at her hands while Jess and Alexa seemed to absorb this revelation.

Lacey proceeded to tell them briefly of her feelings for Tyson, and the way he had sought her out. When she related how they had been spending late hours alone in the gabled attic, Jess pushed a hand over his brow and sighed.

"But I kept it under control," Lacey said, "until . . ." She bit her lip for composure, but her voice cracked when she said it. "Until the night before he left." The sobbing returned as she finished. "I thought he would stay if I let him have his way."

Jess came to his feet and reached for the closest object on his desk, which happened to be a glass of water. His groan of frustration was overshadowed by the glass shattering against the wall. Silence encompassed the room following the crash. Jess stood before the window, hands behind his back, until Lacey came behind him, speaking softly. "I love Tyson very much, Papa." He turned to look at her. "In many ways, he is a great deal like you."

"Perhaps he is." Jess put a fatherly arm around her. "I love him too, Lacey. I suppose that's why it hurts so much."

No family conference was held to decide how to handle the situation, mostly because there were no options. Lacey gave birth to a son, who came breech after twenty-eight hours of harrowing labor. There had still been no word from Tyson.

The event was a combination of joy and pain for the family. Alexa cried when she held the baby, declaring that he looked so much like his father. Then she turned to Jess and added with warmth, "It looks as if Tyson has left us something to remember him by." This made Lacey glow with a degree of pride that eased the heartache—if only a little.

"What will you name him?" Jess asked distantly.

"Richard Tyson Byrnehouse-Davies," Lacey declared proudly.

"It is convenient," Emma sat on the edge of the bed near Lacey, "that he can still bear his father's name, in spite of the circumstances."

"Yes, convenient," Jess echoed with a touch of sarcasm.

"It's a fine name," Alexa concluded, still gazing at the baby. "But why Richard?"

"I saw it on a grave by the old house," Lacey answered absently, but she didn't miss the sharp glance that passed between Jess and Alexa.

"Is it significant?" she asked.

Alexa said nothing, so Jess apparently figured it was up to him. "Richard was a dear friend of mine, and . . . your mother's first husband."

"Oh, I'm sorry," Lacey murmured in surprise, noting from Emma's expression that she too had been ignorant. "I had no idea. Perhaps you would prefer that—"

"Oh, no," Alexa smiled, "the name is perfect."

"If he was your husband," Lacey pressed, dying of curiosity, "then the baby's grave—"

"Yes," Jess answered, then abruptly changed the subject. "Let me hold him, Grandmama. It's my turn."

Alexa handed the sleeping infant over reluctantly. Jess smiled and cooed a little, then said with conviction, "I didn't think I'd ever say it, little guy, but we're sure glad you came."

Everyone had to agree, especially Lacey. In spite of the circumstances and the heartache, she would not trade her life for this beautiful child who was so much a part of the man she loved. If only the man she loved was here to ease this emptiness inside of her. This baby needed a father.

Lacey was up and about quickly in spite of her ordeal. A suitable nanny was hired, a Miss Leeds whom the family adored. The vibrant, gray-haired spinster was left alone with her charge for the first time so that Lacey could share dinner with the family.

"It feels good to be somewhere besides the bedroom," Lacey said with enthusiasm. The seven weeks she had been confined to bed prior to the birth had been unbearable.

"It's good to have you looking so healthy," Alexa commented. "We've missed you, or at least we've missed having you to visit with somewhere besides the bedroom."

A lull in the trivial conversation brought Alexa's attention to her husband's glum countenance. "Is something troubling you?" she asked gently.

Jess looked up from his meal in surprise. "I was just thinking about something I heard in town today," he admitted.

"Is it worth sharing?" Alexa asked.

"I had intended to tell you . . . eventually."

"What is it?" Alexa's tone turned wary.

"You know how I often visit with the constable. He enjoys keeping me posted."

"Oh, no." Alexa leaned back. "Which one of them is in trouble now?"

It was common for Jess and Alexa to keep track of the boys who had come through their lives, and Alexa knew there was only one reason why her husband would mention the constable.

"Michael Hamilton," Jess answered quietly. Emma's head shot up from the attention she was giving her steak. Her heart hammered involuntarily, but she credited that to her vivid imagination in having put Michael's face into the books she read. "He was arrested last week," Jess added.

Alexa said nothing, but her troubled expression was not lost on Emma. Sadly she said to her husband, "I had always held such high hopes for him."

"We can't succeed with them all," Jess consoled. "That's a fact of the work we do. And he was a difficult one to reach."

Emma put down her fork, suddenly not hungry. She'd hardly thought of him for months, mostly because she hadn't been reading as much while she'd stayed close to Lacey through her pregnancy. "What was the charge?" she heard herself asking, not certain she wanted to know.

Jess seemed surprised by her interest. Alexa didn't appear to be. "I believe he said disturbing the peace and disorderly conduct; something to do with a woman." Emma squeezed her eyes shut. "He was sentenced to three years."

"He should never have left here," Alexa said wistfully.

"I fear that was my fault," Emma spoke up, unable to bear the regret of that day any longer.

"Now, how can that be?" Lacey finally showed some interest in the conversation.

"He asked me to go riding with him," Emma admitted, catching her mother's empathetic eye. She could swear that Alexa knew something she didn't. "I declined, and he left that very night."

"I'd say it's a good thing you did," Lacey insisted. "Personally, I think behind bars is a good place for him. I wouldn't trust him to curry my horse."

"Actually," Emma said more to herself, "he did a rather good job of it."

"You mustn't let it bother you, Emma," Alexa said with wisdom in her voice. "Michael is a free agent, acting for himself. If you did what you felt was best at the time, you cannot be responsible for his reaction."

Emma tried to smile. Her mother's words were consoling, but she still felt bad about it. She didn't know whether it would remedy or worsen the regret, but she went upstairs and opened an unread novel. Sure enough, Michael's image quickly filled her mind. Emma shook her head in disbelief. What a dull life she must lead to be fantasizing adventure with a street-tough criminal she had barely exchanged words with.

Emma set the book aside. She needed to find a *real* man!

Analyzing the situation further, Emma realized she knew of no man worth having, or even spending time with. She was familiar with all of the stable hands and racing employees. None of them even came close. At one time she had fancied traveling jockeys, but the good ones were arrogant and the others were eccentric. Some were both. And they were all short.

Emma had to face it. Living this kind of life would not bring around any *real* men. What she needed was adventure. If she had gone with Tyson . . . The thought was immediately squelched. If she had left then, or if she left now, she would break her parents' hearts. And Lacey needed her.

Emma sighed and picked the book up off the bedside table. The image in her mind became very clear.

❦ ❦ ❦

Lacey hoped and prayed that Tyson would return before his son changed too much. But Richard crawled, cut teeth, walked and talked. Still no Tyson, or any word from him.

Gradually Lacey lost more and more of her vitality and spirit. In spite of the love she had for her son, it seemed that one bad choice had sent her into a continual downward spiral. She became more absorbed and preoccupied with Tyson's absence the longer he was gone. His name was not mentioned without bitter, cynical remarks from Lacey. Her parents and Emma had continually attempted to distract her, talk it through with her, and help her work out her feelings. They talked about forgiveness, and the need to be at peace with herself as well as with Tyson. But they gradually just came to avoid the subject altogether. Lacey was oblivious to the depth of her own bitterness, and in her view, no one but Tyson could change it. They only hoped he would come back before it was too late, when even he wouldn't be able to change it.

A week past Richard's third birthday, a letter finally came. Emma answered the door when it was delivered. She stood for some time in the entry hall just staring at the envelope, trying to determine what it might be. It was addressed simply Byrnehouse-Davies, followed by the location of the home. And in the upper corner was scribed nothing more than TBD.

"Lacey!" Emma shrieked when she realized what she was holding. She tore up the stairs, holding the tattered envelope high above her head as if it was a beacon.

"What is it?" Lacey met her at the top of the stairs. "Is Richard all right? Is he—"

"He's fine. He's with Mother in the garden. Look, Lacey." She waved it in front of her face frantically, then she shouted when Lacey didn't seem impressed. "I think it's from Tyson."

Lacey felt something come alive inside of her that had been dormant for more than three and a half years. She tore the envelope from Emma's hands to examine it, then they sat together on the top stair, squeezing each other's trembling hands. "You open it," Lacey said to Emma.

"I couldn't possibly," Emma argued. "With all I have felt since he left, I fear what I might read. You open it."

"What do you mean by all *you've* felt?" Lacey demanded, temporarily ignoring the letter.

"I can't explain," Emma shrugged. "It seems I've always sensed his emotions to some degree. But I always had him close by. Since he left, I think of him and I feel . . . well, at first it was a sense of freedom. No," she corrected, "a bitter freedom. But it has gradually turned into something resembling . . . grief."

"Why didn't you say anything before?" Lacey demanded.

"It sounds so silly. It's probably nothing. Open the letter. I can't bear it."

Lacey took a deep breath and pressed a finger beneath the seal. She pulled out a single page, and a small photograph fell to her lap. Emma picked up the photo and wrinkled her nose. "It looks like a grave, but I can't read what it says. Hurry. Read the letter."

Lacey cleared her throat carefully and began.

"Dear family, I hope you don't find me a hypocrite if I say that I miss you—all of you. Today I stood where my great-grandfather was buried. Enclosed is a photo I had taken of his grave. I know you can't read it, but it says: Paul Jesse Davies, Dear Husband, suffocated in coal mine. He was thirty-one when he died. Did you know, Father, that you were named after him?

Europe is beautiful, and so different from home. The Americas, too, are something to see, with country so diversified, there is no beginning to explain. I spent some time in the Orient as well, but I think I prefer Europe.

Mother, I love you. Father, I'm sorry. Emma, is everything all right? Sometimes I feel anxiety on your behalf. And Lacey, are you married yet?"

Lacey threw the letter down and shouted at it. "How can I get married? Your son comes with the bargain." She stepped on the paper, then stomped on it and hissed through her teeth. Emma calmly pulled her back onto the stair and picked up the letter, straightened it, and continued to read.

"I might get back to Australia one of these days, but I'd like to see more of Europe first. I hope you'll want to see me if I stop by. I love you all. Tyson."

"How kind of him," Lacey spat. "To do us the honor of his presence if he *happens* to get to Australia. And of course, he didn't have the decency to leave a return address, but then he doesn't stay in one place long enough to have one. Ooh, I'd like to give him a piece of my mind. I hope he does stop by. I'll—"

"But, Lacey," Emma interrupted with a hand on her arm, "he's all right."

Lacey buried her face in her hands. "I know," she cried.

"And there was a tone of regret to the letter, don't you think?"

Emma's question went unanswered. She laid her head on Lacey's shoulder and shed silent tears.

"What's all the noise?" Jess called from the foot of the stairs.

Lacey ignored him. Emma held up the letter.

"He's not dead, is he?" Jess asked tonelessly.

"No, of course not," Emma answered, and Jess came up the stairs to take the page and read it himself. Emma watched him blink several times and press a thumb and forefinger over his eyes to rub them. He swallowed hard and said, "I think I'll go show this to your mother."

Emma put her arm around Lacey, feeling a vivid spectrum of the effect Tyson's absence had had on their lives. In that moment, she believed a day would come when he would catch that same spectrum. It would not be an easy thing for any of them. But most especially for Tyson.

Four
HIS RETURN

Another six months passed with no word from Tyson, and Lacey began to give up what little hope she had left. Deep within, she had always dreamed of the day he would come home, learn of the existence of his son, and marry her. But real life had taught Lacey that such dreams were nonsense.

With sheer determination, she settled herself into the reality that this would be all for her. She focused her entire life on her son, certain he would be her only child, her only source of love beyond Emma and her parents. No man worth having would want a woman with an illegitimate child. Even Emma, unattached and attractive, had found no man worth any effort. The consequences of Lacey's choice became more obvious and difficult as time passed. She loved Richard, yes. But having him under such circumstances was a crime, and she was being punished for it daily. Lacey was at least grateful that her parents were willing to let her stay, and their love and enjoyment of Richard made up for a great deal.

"What are you so glum about?" Emma inquired one evening, plopping onto the sofa in the sitting room they shared.

"I was just telling myself that I must face the fact that Tyson will not come back, and if he does, he will not want me."

"You've told me that before. Why so glum now?"

"I suppose I've told myself I should believe it, but now I've got to *make* myself believe it."

"Personally," Emma consoled with all honesty, "I believe he will come back, and he will want you."

"I can't count on that."

"And so you're resigning yourself to life as it is."

"What more is there?"

"Some adventure, I would hope." Emma's eyes beamed with some of the same anticipation Lacey had seen in Tyson. And she didn't like it.

"You and your talk of adventure," Lacey grumbled. "You read too many of those stupid books. I'd rather stay home, personally. What I saw of the streets as a child was enough adventure to last me a lifetime."

"I suppose you're right. But for me, I still dream of adventure." She giggled. "Dreaming may be all I'll ever get."

"You look tired," Emma observed when Lacey didn't respond to her humor. "Is Richard still keeping you awake?"

"Yes," she sighed. "Since that last bout with earaches, he's never gotten back into good sleeping habits. I'll be glad when Miss Leeds returns from Sydney. At least she takes turns with me."

"Why don't you sleep in my room tonight, and I'll get up with him. You'll feel better after a good night's sleep."

"No, that's all right, really," Lacey insisted. "Mother always hears him. If he fusses for long, she comes to my rescue."

"I know, but you need an uninterrupted night of sleep. Go on now, get into my bed. I'll see to Richard."

Lacey did as she was ordered, grateful and relieved—but knowing still that no amount of sleep could erase the pain Tyson Byrnehouse-Davies had etched into her heart.

❧ ❧ ❧

Lacey had barely fallen into a fitful sleep when terror woke her, making her heart pound. Rough hands forced a silk scarf into her mouth, while others bound her hands in front of her. In the darkness she could see little but shadows, and all efforts to scream or struggle were thwarted. In all her wildest imaginings, Lacey couldn't fathom who would do this to her, or why.

Another scarf came around her eyes while her captors silently worked together with deft efficiency. Tears leaked into the scarf and sobs wretched in her throat as she was hoisted out the window and let down a ladder on the large shoulder of a man the likes of which she had never smelled. Her fear deepened as she was lifted onto a horse and held tightly by the rider. Her home, her child, and all she loved disappeared behind the blackness of being abducted.

After a ride of nearly twenty minutes, Lacey was relieved to feel the animal beneath her slowing, then coming to stand where voices filtered to her ears.

"We got 'er, boss," a gruff voice announced behind her.

"Good," replied a deep, sinister sounding man. The voice alone sent shivers of fear through Lacey. She struggled to no avail while that voice added, "Uncover her eyes."

Lacey felt the heat of a torch near her face as the scarf was removed. The light was blinding, and she could see nothing beyond it. But she could smell the leather of a gloved hand that pulled back her head as the voice shrieked in anger near her face, "You stupid, idiotic fools! You've got the wrong girl!"

Lacey's heart pounded freshly. Whoever this was, he was after Emma. But why? Who would have believed that spending a night in Emma's bed would result in such a horrid misunderstanding? She wondered what to expect now. As if to directly answer her silent question, the conversation around her continued.

"Cover her eyes again and put her over there," the leader ordered. "You've got to go back and get the other one."

"But we went in th' room you told us to, boss."

"I don't care! You've got the wrong girl, and we're not leaving here until I get the other one."

"What about this one?" a squeaky voice asked while her eyes were covered and she was forced to sit on the ground in itchy meadow grass.

"We'll have to take her, too," the leader stated, calculating and cold. His words filled Lacey with dread. This was all so awful!

"Do you think we can get twice as much ransom for two of 'em?"

"Don't count on it," the leader insisted. "Now get back there and hurry up, or we'll never reach the first point before morning. And change the note," he added loudly, "so they'll know we have them both." Horses galloped away, and Lacey heard him add quietly, "I hope the stupid fools can write."

Kidnapping for ransom. Lacey couldn't believe it! Of course they wanted Emma. She was the blood daughter of one of the wealthiest men in Australia. Oh, Emma! If it's adventure she wanted, she was about to get it. But what about Richard? Would they hurt him? Likely not, if they wanted ransom. But what would happen when Emma wasn't there to hear him? At least his grandparents were there, but . . . Oh! Lacey just wanted to die! She had thought nothing could be worse than Tyson's abandonment. But this was definitely worse!

❦ ❦ ❦

Emma woke to find herself being blindfolded, bound, and gagged. She was efficiently hoisted down a ladder, a wild fear enveloping her as she soon learned that any struggling was pointless.

"We got yer sister," a gruff voice proclaimed as she was hoisted onto a horse. "Now we want you, too."

Emma could do nothing but absorb the fear as she was taken into the dark night, for herself as well as for Lacey. She was finally set on her feet, but her arms were held firmly behind her and she remained blindfolded and gagged. If this was adventure, she could do without it!

"We got th' right one this time, boss," the gruff voice announced proudly.

"Uncover her eyes," a sinister voice commanded, and Emma felt a deep shiver sputter to every part of her. She felt the scarf being untied and prepared herself, wanting to show as much defiance as she could muster. Whoever was doing this had a lot of nerve! But she wasn't about to allow them to think she was intimidated.

"Michael!" she gasped, but it came through the scarf as a mumbled astonishment.

"Hello, Emma," he said as if he'd asked if she wanted butter on her bread.

Knowing she couldn't speak, Emma did her best to convey a hundred questions with her eyes. For a moment she was actually glad to see him. Then she surveyed her surroundings, and the fear returned.

On either side of the black-clad Michael Hamilton stood two cruel-looking thugs, holding torches that illuminated Michael's imposing stance. His hair was longer, waved with loose curls that hung down the back of his neck, and he wore a neatly trimmed beard. Lines around his eyes were beginning to betray the life he'd led. The cold indifference in his eyes betrayed nothing. Another man held the reins of several horses, while still another held Lacey, blindfolded and gagged. Beyond that, Emma could see little but darkness in spite of the full moon that somehow gave Michael the appearance of not quite being real. Despite his reputation, she never would have believed him capable of such madness. Whatever he wanted, this was not seemly, to say the very least.

"Would you like to go riding?" he asked soberly, then one corner of his mouth turned barely upward. "Just a little joke," he added, apparently insulted by her lack of response. Still, Emma did nothing. After a moment's contemplation, he continued, "I can see by your eyes that you want to speak quite badly. I would be willing to allow that, only because we are far enough away from your home that any effort to scream would be futile. In that light, you'd do well to spare the attempt. I do so detest screaming." He gave that crooked smile again, and she wanted to ask if the comment was another joke.

"Remove it," he ordered, and Emma fought her temper. She was not going to give him the pleasure of watching her throw a fit.

"Hello, Michael," she mimicked in the tone of his own greeting. He folded his arms across his chest. Lacey struggled and moaned. "Let her go," Emma demanded. "This has nothing to do with her."

"It does now."

"And how is that?"

"I can't let her go running back to your mother and let the cat out of the bag, now can I? Besides, how would you know what this is about?"

"Forgive me for attempting to read your mind, Mr. Hamilton. Just what *is* this about? An explanation would be in order, don't you think?"

"It's about money," Michael announced with a slight bow from the waist.

"Ransom?" She laughed. "Why didn't you just stay and keep your job?"

"Stable hands don't make a hundred thousand pounds for so little effort."

"My father won't pay it," she insisted, once she'd recovered from the shock she refused to betray.

"He will if he wants his daughters back, shall we say, unscathed?"

Again Lacey struggled. "Let her go." Emma tried to match his cruel voice.

"Uncover her eyes," Michael ordered, "but keep her mouth covered. I'm in no mood for any more female prattle."

The thug holding Lacey pulled the scarf from around her head none too gently. Emma met Lacey's eyes and saw terror there. Emma gave their captor a spiteful glare and complimented him with sarcasm. "Nice guys. Cell-mates?"

Michael was a difficult man to read, but Emma knew he was surprised that she knew where he'd been. "Actually, no." He shifted his weight to the other booted leg. "*They* were much worse. Enough idle talk." He waved his hand through the air impatiently. "We've got miles to go before sunrise. Mount up, boys."

Lacey struggled, and tears showed in her eyes. Emma caught the pleading and acted on it. "Let her go back," she said more humbly. "She has a child who needs her. I'll go with you."

Michael shifted his eyes back and forth between the two women. "No," he said. Lacey would have screamed if not for the gag. "Tie her to the saddle horn," he added, and Lacey was hoisted onto a sturdy mare. Her bound hands were secured as ordered, and she had no choice but to stay in the saddle or suffer great injury.

"I trust that with your skill you can handle the gentle creature," Michael spoke to Lacey as if she bored him terribly.

"What about the other one, boss? We only got one horse."

"That's because you were only supposed to get one girl, you twit!"

"Should we put 'em together?" another thug asked.

Please, yes, Emma prayed silently.

"Mercy, no." Michael was insulted at the very idea. "The last thing I need is the two of them conniving together. Distance between them is mandatory for now." He mounted his horse, which Emma noticed was black—of course.

"Where's she gonna ride?" inquired the smelly semblance of a human being holding Emma.

"With me, of course," Michael stated, hardening his gaze on Emma. This made her struggle as her fear deepened—although she couldn't be certain of what exactly she was afraid of. Less than gently, Emma was lifted into what little room was left in Michael's saddle. She felt sandwiched between the saddle horn and his body. "Bind her," Michael said quietly, and his bidding was seen to immediately. Emma tried to lean into her hands and away from the hard chest behind her, which was far from comfortable. Just as she noticed with Lacey, her nightgown pulled up in order to straddle the horse, leaving her lower legs exposed. Emma had done a lot of riding in her lifetime, but never in bare feet and a nightgown.

Michael took the reins into a black-gloved hand. When the thugs were all mounted, two of them came on either side of Lacey to guide her. The torches were doused, and seven horses galloped into the darkness. When Emma's eyes finally adjusted, she could see ahead for some distance by the light of the moon. She knew they were going west, and that could mean only one thing. The outback.

In the silence as miles passed behind them, Emma's heart turned sad. What of her parents? And Richard? Of course they would hear Richard when he awoke, and they would care for him. But what would result from this madness?

Michael set the pace for the group with a steady gallop. They were in a hurry. Emma had to admit she was impressed with his skill as a rider, and also the horse's ability to carry two for so long with little deviation in its stride.

"You might as well relax," Michael said at last. "We've got a long way to go."

Emma said nothing, and she didn't move. Abruptly Michael pushed a brash arm around her waist, practically slamming her back against him. It became immediately evident that there was no moving away from him, but once she got used to it, she had to admit that this wasn't so hard on her back. And after a while, she found herself relaxing from exhaustion.

She felt her head jolt up and realized she'd been asleep. Still they rode at a steady pace as the rosy hues of dawn were beginning to appear around them.

"Did you have a nice nap?" Michael asked in mock concern.

Emma kicked her heel against his booted shin. She knew it wouldn't hurt him, but it expressed what she felt.

"Ouch," he said tonelessly.

"It was just a little joke." She mirrored his toneless voice.

"The lady speaks," he fairly hissed. "The spoiled little rich girl honors me with her voice."

"I'd honor you with a good slap if I had a hand to do it."

"Yes," he tightened his arm in a threatening gesture, "I bet you would. But only if I give you the chance." She felt his nose burrow into the hair hanging behind her ear. "There are other chances I'd rather take," he whispered in a perfect balance of cruelty and seduction, making his intentions very clear.

Emma squirmed in protest, but it only made her acutely aware of how helpless she was. The sun rose higher in the sky, and what had been miserable became worse. She distracted herself by contemplating the plot of the novel she had been reading, until the reality struck her. The coinciding circumstances were unbelievable. She was being kidnapped by Michael Hamilton! She couldn't suppress a throaty giggle, and Michael's head bent forward curiously.

"Is something amusing you, Miss Davies?"

"Nothing of any interest to you, Mr. Hamilton," she said tersely.

A moment later she felt his beard rumpling her hair, while he whispered like a gallant suitor sitting in the parlor, "Your hair smells good, although I've never seen it quite so . . . free."

His unusual attention seemed worthy of posing a question. "Why are you doing this, Michael?"

"I told you. I need the money."

"Is that the only reason?"

"Money, money, money." He said it like a bored banker, and Emma decided he enjoyed doing imitations.

"And that's it?" she persisted.

"That's it," he echoed conclusively while he tightened his arm around her waist. The gesture stated very clearly what his words had denied. His motives were more than money alone. But what exactly? Vengeance for a thoughtless spurning? Or perhaps some perverse attempt to retaliate for something he hadn't liked about her family? Or the boys' home?

His arrogant behavior could be frightening, but perhaps Emma had read too many of those books. Despite being disgusted by his actions, she couldn't help feeling a degree of intrigue. Her mother's voice came to mind, cautioning her against being manipulated. She tried to tell herself that Michael Hamilton was likely nothing more than a cold-hearted beast with heinous plans for her. But no matter how she tried, Emma couldn't feel completely afraid. If Lacey were safe at home, Emma decided, she could likely handle this adventure.

❦ ❦ ❦

Alexa came awake to a familiar young voice calling for his mama. Richard called several times then started to cry, and Alexa rolled over reluctantly.

"I'll get him," Jess muttered sleepily. "It's about my turn."

"No, that's all right." Alexa kissed his brow. "I want to talk to Lacey anyway. This might be a good time." She rose and put on a wrapper. "Go back to sleep, love."

Jess pressed his head back into the pillow and sighed just as the night was shattered by an urgent scream.

"Jess!" Alexa's voice sent him flying through the door and down the hall. "Jess!" she screamed again as he bounded into Lacey's room.

"Is Richard—"

"He's fine," Alexa cried, clutching the child, who was crying at his grandmother's display of fear.

Jess quickly absorbed the empty bed, the open window, the paper in Alexa's hand. A hundred possibilities flooded his mind, but none of them made sense.

"Is Emma—" he began to ask.

"Her room looks the same. She's gone."

"What does it say?" Jess snatched the paper from her.

"I don't know," she cried softly, attempting to soothe Richard. "It's dark."

Jess lit the lamp and held the note beneath it while Alexa moved close beside him. Together their eyes scanned the eloquently scribed words that made the heartache of losing Tyson seem trivial.

*I've got your daughter*s. (The "s" was scribbled in a different hand.) *I assure you she will be fine, as long as you play the game right. Just relax and enjoy the peace and quiet. I'll send word with further instructions in a few days. Oh, and don't be harassing my courier. He doesn't know anything. You might want to be gathering the money and getting the mules packed. It could save time. See you soon.*

Alexa drew in a loud gasp that wouldn't let go until she began feeling lightheaded. Jess muttered in angry disbelief, "I don't believe it! Ransom? Kidnapped for ransom? Who on earth would—"

"Jess," Alexa whispered unsteadily, "we mustn't upset Richard further."

Jess looked to the child's inquisitive, tear-filled eyes and wanted to cry himself. It wasn't bad enough to never know his father; now the boy's mother had been kidnapped.

Alexa quietly took him to the nursery to settle him back to sleep. Jess went to the window to investigate more closely, trying to ignore the sick dread in the pit of his stomach that he knew Alexa must be feeling as well. He found scuff marks on the sill, traces of dirt, and looking down to the ground, he could see a long ladder lying across the lawn.

Cursing under his breath, he went to Emma's room, finding similar circumstances. By the condition of the beds, it was apparent they'd been dragged from their sleep with a great deal of struggle. The thought of his beautiful daughters in the hands of who knew what kind of men made his stomach roil in heated knots.

"He's asleep," Alexa said behind him, startling him from his blank stare at the note in his hand.

"Just relax," he quoted in angry sarcasm and crushed the paper into his fist.

"Jess," Alexa cried and moved into his arms, where he cradled her as much for his own comfort as hers. "What are we going to do?"

"All we can do is wait. They could be hours away by now. I'm certain any search would be futile."

"You don't think they'll be . . ." She looked up at him, not daring to say it aloud.

"If it's ransom they want," he said with a calm logic that defied all he felt, "they wouldn't dare harm them."

"I pray you're right." She put her head back to his shoulder. "Oh, if only Tyson were here. If only—"

"He's not, Alexa. There's no point in wishing it."

"Oh," she sobbed freshly, "my poor darlings. They must be so frightened."

"Come back to bed, Alexa," Jess urged. "There is nothing we can do right now. If we're going to worry, we might as well do it lying down."

"We must stay close to Richard." She wiped at her face helplessly. "We can lie down in here."

They climbed into the bed and held hands, staring helplessly at the ceiling until the room filled with daylight. Nothing meant more to them than their children, and nothing was more unbearable than their absence, and the fear they felt in not knowing where they were.

🌢 🌢 🌢

Emma nearly collapsed with relief when Michael announced, "We'll stop up here and sleep a few hours."

They rode near an outcropping of rock where two of Michael's thugs dismounted and disappeared, returning with crates of supplies, then going back for more. Looking closer, Emma realized there were two more men and several mules waiting here.

Michael swung down from his horse and looked up at Emma, seeming terribly amused.

"My, but aren't we well prepared," she said, stretching her back while she kept her eyes pinned on him.

"If you're going to play a game," he said like a cautious gambler, "you've got to play it right."

"And how long have you been formulating this delightful little game?"

"Long enough, my sweet."

"I am not your sweet."

"Nor would I want you to be."

"And what do you want me to be, Mr. Hamilton?" She lifted her chin defiantly.

"Right now," a dark brow went up in severe mischief, "you are a game-piece. Nothing more."

"Where do you want this stuff, boss?" a voice called, and Michael looked irritated by the interruption.

"Set the tents up there, where the sun won't hit them so much. Figure the rest out yourself." He turned back to Emma, pleased and expectant.

"My father will not be amused by your little game."

"The amusement is for me alone. Everyone else is just a pawn."

"And disrupting lives is nothing to you?"

"Nothing."

Emma felt a rush of fear from his coldness. What little good she had sensed in him four years ago was obviously buried deeply beneath his warped cruelty. She reminded herself to take care and not let her adventurous fantasies become confused with the man Michael Hamilton really was.

"Must I sit here all day?" she asked to distract herself from the intimidation in his eyes.

He began untying her from the saddle horn. "Do you think you can walk after so much time in the saddle?"

"I am quite accustomed to being in a saddle, Mr. Hamilton."

"So you are." He took hold of her waist and set her on her feet.

After only a moment she announced, "The sand is hot."

"So I must carry you after all." He pulled her up into his arms as if she weighed nothing. "How tedious."

Emma was set down in the shade of the overhanging rock, where Michael hovered near her with his back turned, observing the activity taking place.

"What about Lacey?" Emma attempted to sound demanding.

Michael looked over at the other girl, sitting on her horse in the sun, forgotten and looking distraught. Emma was thirsty, hungry, achingly tired, and her bladder was full. Lacey was likely worse off, not having another rider to lean against all this way.

"Oh, yes. Poor Lacey." Michael was obviously bored.

Emma wanted to cry on Lacey's behalf as Michael sauntered away and took Lacey down from the horse, carrying her over to set her beside Emma.

"Hold on." Emma stopped Michael as he turned to move away. "Your game-pieces deserve some common decency."

Michael lifted his brows, his eyes daring her to make demands on him.

"You can make the whole affair just as miserable as possible for us, and we'll make life miserable for you in return. If you must play this game, so be it. But we will not be treated like animals."

"And what is it that you desire, my lady?" Sarcasm was comfortable for him, Emma decided.

"First of all, there is no good reason why Lacey and I shouldn't be freed from these ropes. You've got us now, so you might as well untie us while you're at it. There is nowhere we could run without ending up dead eventually."

"That's true." He lifted a finger. "But why should I?"

"Because we need some privacy," she insisted.

"Privacy?" He sounded baffled.

"You figure it out."

After a moment's contemplation, Michael quietly knelt before Lacey and removed the scarf from her mouth, pausing to study her expression.

"You fiend!" Lacey spat when her voice was freed.

Michael laughed and patted her face like he might a puppy. Lacey recoiled from his touch. She absolutely loathed the man.

"How dare you drag us away from our home, forcing me to leave my baby and—"

"Lacey," Emma said firmly, knowing her protests would do little but feed his ego. And though she intended to keep him on his toes, she didn't want to anger him.

Michael gave Emma a glance of appreciation that might have warmed her had there not been so much coldness at its source. He forcefully untied Lacey's hands, pointed a silent threatening finger at her, then he leaned over Emma to do the same, watching her eyes closely as he did. Emma stopped to wonder why his treatment of her was so different from that of Lacey. Either of them would bring ransom. But then, Lacey hadn't rejected him carelessly four years ago.

"Now," he said while the women rubbed their wrists, "you can go right over there." He pointed to some brush the opposite direction of where the men were working. "Mind your manners and sing."

"Sing?" Emma wrinkled her nose.

"Sing whatever you want, my sweet. But if I can't see you, I want to hear you. You stop singing, and I will come and hold your hand. Do I make myself clear?"

"Quite," she snapped and took Lacey's hand. They rushed away while she sang a childish tune, just as obnoxiously as she could manage. There was so much she wanted to say to Lacey, but she couldn't talk and sing at the same time. Lacey looked too afraid to speak. They were relieved and back in no time. The hot sand on their bare feet urged them along.

"How was that?" Emma asked as they dutifully sat on the ground again in the shade.

"Let's just say I'm glad my fortune doesn't depend on your vocal abilities."

They were dismayed when he produced a pair of handcuffs, and without a word, cuffed Lacey's ankle to Emma's. He leaned back, apparently rather proud of himself.

"That should keep you from going too far."

"As if we could, dressed like this," Emma spat.

"Go ahead and give me misery, Emma." He took hold of her chin firmly. "Misery with such beauty could be very pleasurable."

Emma jerked her face out of his reach, then she growled under her breath when he walked away to supervise the men who were setting up camp.

"Are you all right?" Emma asked, putting a comforting arm around Lacey.

"I suppose," Lacey admitted. "What about you?"

"I'm fine."

Lacey wanted to cry, but she feared bringing attention to herself and choked it back. "I'm just so worried about Richard and—"

"Richard is just fine," Emma assured her. "He wouldn't have cried long before Mother heard him. She always does. They'll take good care of him."

"They must be so worried," Lacey whimpered.

"Yes, well . . . there's nothing we can do about that."

"What are we going to do, Emma?"

"There is nothing we can do except behave ourselves. You let me do the talking, and we'll just have to take it on the best we can."

"I never did like him," Lacey sneered, glaring toward Michael, who happened to glance their way at the moment. "I should have known he'd be capable of such treachery."

Michael smiled as it became apparent he was being discussed, then he turned his attention back to the men.

"The fiend," Lacey hissed. "I wouldn't be surprised if he . . . Oh, Emma." She gasped. "What if he tries to . . ." Lacey couldn't bring herself to say it.

Emma bit her lip. She couldn't quite imagine Michael doing such a thing. But what did she know of men? To console Lacey she said lightly, "He's not after that. It's money he wants." Emma chose not to relate the implications of his behavior as they had ridden together.

"Do you think Father will pay him?"

"Of course he will. He'd do anything for us. You know that."

"Yes, I know. If only Tyson—"

They were interrupted by Michael's return. Emma gratefully took the canteen he offered and handed it to Lacey to drink first. She took her fill then handed it back to Emma, who eased her thirst and returned it to Michael. "Thank you," she said sincerely.

"I might be a wretch, but I'll not treat you any worse than my horses."

"How comforting," Lacey muttered with sarcasm, but Emma garnered a degree of peace from his statement, recalling Michael's careful attention to the horses he'd cared for in their stables. She knew he respected horses, and under the circumstances, she could be satisfied with such respect.

Michael took a swallow from the canteen before he turned and walked away.

"Do you suppose he's going to starve us?" Lacey grumbled.

"Not if he treats us like his horses," Emma stated, and she had no sooner said it than he returned with an ample meal of jerked meat, cheese, bread, and canned peaches.

"Thank you," Emma said again, willing to be gracious when it was warranted. She couldn't deny that he was in control, and she was not going to let his kindnesses go unappreciated.

Michael nodded. "We'll have a hot meal before we set out. Enjoy." He left them eating too busily to talk, and returned just as they were polishing off the last, to offer the canteen again.

"You're an excellent cook, Mr. Hamilton," Emma quipped while

Lacey drank, then glared at Emma in disgust for attempting humor under the circumstances.

"You can thank Corky for that. But let's hope he comes up with something a little more delectable next time."

Emma drank and returned the canteen to Michael. He set it aside and knelt to unlock the cuffs and remove them. He motioned for the women to follow him, and they quickly gathered their dishes. Michael led them to the smaller of the two tents and pulled aside a flap for them to enter. Emma wanted to squeal with excitement, but she managed a straight face and was glad to see that Lacey was not affected.

"Don't let it be said that Michael Hamilton treats his hostages poorly," he announced presumptuously. Emma's eyes went to the boots and clothing laid out, then she looked to Michael in question. "You always kept a spare pair of boots in the stables, did you not? Ian had the good fortune of grabbing both pairs, not certain which was yours. I assume, then, that the other is yours." He nodded toward Lacey. "The clothes I purchased." He bowed slightly and took on the tone of a fussy tailor. "Charming yet practical, for the lady with an adventurous spirit." His demeanor returned to cruel kidnapper. "I'll be sleeping in here with you. I'll be back in five minutes." He lifted a finger of warning. "And don't try anything stupid, or you will be miserable, I can assure you."

With that he left. Emma and Lacey proceeded to examine what he'd provided. There was a hairbrush, hair ribbons, a riding cap, and a wide-brimmed hat. It seemed he'd wanted to give options, which left plenty for both women, and they were grateful. There was a pair of riding breeches, a little large but usable; a split skirt; and four different white shirts—men's shirts in a small size, which was what they were quite used to wearing much of the time. Finding clothes for women that suited their lifestyle was not easy unless they were custom made. They also found several pairs of stockings, a jacket, and a long riding coat.

"What are you more comfortable with?" Emma asked Lacey, already knowing she would choose the skirt and the cap, which was fine with Emma, since she preferred the breeches. And the low, flat-brimmed hat had a look that appealed to Emma. If she was going to have to brave the outback, she could at least do it looking reasonably good.

"Why are you getting dressed?" Emma asked. "We're going to sleep."

"I feel safer fully clothed." Lacey hurriedly pulled on the skirt and tucked in the big shirt, its looseness disguising the lack of suitable underclothing.

"I suppose that's true," Emma admitted and quickly changed. "It was thoughtful of him," she added while Lacey brushed through her hair and tied it back, pausing to give Emma a glare of disgust.

"You've gone mad. It's the least he could do, the brute."

Finding her statement humorous for some reason, Emma played it a little further, if only for the sake of distraction. "Actually, I think he's rather handsome."

Lacey's glare deepened. "And so is the devil." She shook the hairbrush at Emma.

"Or so they say," Emma added, taking the brush. "Personally, I've never seen him."

"I have." Lacey looked up with purpose as Michael returned to find them sitting on two of the bedrolls, completely dressed minus boots, Emma brushing through her hair.

"Don't we look fine," he quipped. "Riding in nighties and sleeping in clothes. Aren't we a strange lot."

"One does what one has to," Emma growled.

"And you'd do well to remember that applies for me, as well."

Lacey made a noise of disgust that turned Michael's amused eyes toward her. He seemed to relish her attitude toward him.

With no warning, Michael pulled a dagger from inside his boot. The women gasped, and he eyed them carefully while they held their breath. Then with purpose he knelt in front of Emma, gently moving the tip of the blade over the side of her face. "It would be a pity to mar such beauty," he said as if he meant it. Emma hardly dared move. She couldn't imagine him doing something so heinous as drawing blood, but what did she know? His other hand moved into her hair, fingering and tugging until he separated a small lock, withdrew the dagger from her face, and cut the piece of hair with one swift movement. Emma gasped and met his eyes in question.

"We don't want your father to have any doubt that I've got you, now do we," he stated coldly. Then he took hold of Lacey's hair and did the same. He stuffed the hair into his pocket and turned away, sticking the knife in the ground near the door of the tent.

"Get some sleep," he barked, "while you can. We've got a long way to go yet. I trust you are comfortable."

"For the moment," Emma retorted.

Michael grunted and settled onto a bedroll right in front of the door. He checked a pistol to make certain it was loaded, then tucked it beneath his pillow before he turned his back to them and settled into a comfortable position.

"I hope you don't snore," Emma said.

"Shut up and go to sleep. And take care," he added. "I can have six loaded barrels staring down your noses in thirty seconds flat."

"I suppose that's threat enough to sleep on," Emma said to Lacey, and they gratefully sunk into an exhausted slumber.

❦   ❦   ❦

Tyson arrived on Australia's eastern shore, homesick, humiliated, and scared to death. He wanted to go home so badly that it ached through him night and day. But he'd been a fool. Such an all-fired, blasted fool. And facing the people he'd hurt would not be easy.

With a combination of emotions, he headed home in a roundabout way, justifying to himself that he wanted to see his own country, too. But he had seen it all before, and his memories of this place had become nearly sacred. He pretended to enjoy the sights, but he could always hear voices in his head. His father shouting, his mother crying, Emma pleading—and most prominently, Lacey. Sweet, beautiful Lacey. She had given him no promises and a healthy slap to remember her by.

He had traveled the world and seen it all, while Lacey's words continually haunted him. It first happened when he came upon slums in New York City, and Lacey whispered in his ear, *There's no place on earth where misery doesn't run rampant.* And then when he'd found a tribe of American Indians, cold and starving because their buffalo had been slaughtered and they were living on barren reservations, Lacey's voice told him, *Your parents thrive on easing misery.* Each country he thought would be better, but it wasn't. He found beauty, yes. But he also found the misery. He found homeless children in every city, poor and needy people, crime and depravity. And always Lacey whispered, *What do you know of misery?*

Tyson turned to high society. He had the money and enough refinement to fit in, but he couldn't stomach the way they were living in such vulgar excessiveness while misery abounded all around them. He'd seen attractive women, and women who would have eased his loneliness at the drop of a hat. And more than once he was tempted. But Lacey would always slap his face and remind him of what he'd done to her the night before he'd left. His lack of commitment to her evoked sick knots in his stomach. He had turned his back on her and left after she had given him everything. How could he betray her further by seeking affection elsewhere? The women of the world only proved one thing: none of them were Lacey. The misery of the world proved another: he'd been wrong and he wanted to go home. But the prodigal son was not an easy thing to be. What does a man say to the people he loves after four years of absence and neglect?

Tyson nearly made up his mind to explore the outback a little, since it had been a long time. But a sensation came over him that put everything into perspective. He had been riding west, lost in thought, when he looked down and realized that he had turned around and was riding east. He didn't know why he'd turned, so he guided the horse west again. And this time he was paying attention when, for no apparent reason, he turned the reins and found himself facing east.

"Why?" he asked aloud, and then it hit him. It was like those moments when he thought he felt Emma's emotions. But all he could feel now was fear—cold, black fear. The following morning, Tyson found himself staring at the gabled attic of the boys' home. From the distance it stood silhouetted against the sky like a beacon, beckoning him to gallop the final distance. Moments later he was on his own front porch, drawing courage to open the door.

Coming quietly into the entry hall, Tyson set down his bag and removed his hat, tossing it onto a nearby chair. He stood for a moment just to absorb his surroundings. Home. He sighed, recalling the story of his father having rebuilt this house to replace the one Jess's father had built, after it had burned to the ground. That's what home was, he thought. The privilege of living in a place crafted by the sweat

and tears of those who shared his own blood. Home was where someone cared about more than a handsome face or a wad of money.
"Home," he whispered aloud. He felt an eerie silence answer him,
bringing back the sensation of fear that had turned him around. He
wondered where the girls were, and his parents. His disoriented feelings deepened when he caught an unusual voice—a child's voice—
coming from the drawing room.

Spurred on by curiosity and a desperate need to touch someone
that shared his flesh and blood, Tyson pushed away his fears and quietly opened the drawing room door. His eyes went first to the small
boy stacking wooden blocks on the floor. As if he sensed that he was
being watched, the child looked up with curious eyes. For a long
moment they stared at each other, as if trying to accept the other's
unfamiliar presence in surroundings so familiar.

Jess and Alexa didn't hear the door as they attempted to busy
themselves with trivial pastimes, wishing it would ease the heartache
of their children's absence and the tension of waiting. The silence was
broken by Richard's curiosity. "Who are you?"

Tyson was about to ask the same. But his eyes went quickly to his
parents as they turned their astonished faces toward him. He had
pondered over this moment hundreds of times, and the best he'd ever
come up with for a greeting just didn't seem right now that he was
here. The well-rehearsed words, *I'm back,* stopped in his throat.
Instead, his voice cracked as he said, "I'm home."

"Tyson!" his mother breathed more than spoke, and rushed into
his arms. The feel of her brought tears to his eyes. He squeezed her so
tightly that he feared she would break. But she looked up at him, wel-
coming tears streaking her face. She touched his face, his hair. She
laughed, and Tyson laughed with her. "You're safe. You're home. How
I prayed you would come!"

As if she sensed Jess behind her, Alexa stepped back, and Tyson
met his father eye to eye in a moment he'd dreaded for years. It was
his fear of this encounter that had kept him away much longer than
he'd wanted to be. He knew he'd lost his father's respect, and earning
it back would not be easy.

The only comfort in the tense silence was a reassuring squeeze of
his mother's hand. The words that bridged four years and three

months of separation hit Tyson between the eyes. But he knew he deserved it.

"Did you run out of money?" Jess asked tersely.

"Jess . . ." Alexa began to scold him, but Tyson put a gentle hand over her arm to stop her.

"It's all right, Mother." Tyson took a deep breath. If nothing else, he felt some assurance from the evidence of his own maturity. He had no desire to snap at his father or make an issue out of his comment. He simply told him the truth. "I ran out of what I took with me over a year ago. I could have got more without coming here. That's not why I came home."

Tyson expected Jess to ask why he *had* come home, or perhaps lecture him about the hurt he'd inflicted. But as if Tyson's reaction was proof enough that he'd grown up, Jess only extended his hand. "Welcome home, son."

Tyson took it firmly and saw his father's face mirror his own emotion as their grip tightened. Before their hands parted, Jess put his other hand to Tyson's shoulder. Tyson squeezed his eyes shut in a silent prayer of gratitude as he embraced his father.

"Come and sit down," Jess invited quietly. Tyson tried to make himself comfortable while his eyes scanned the room, absorbing the memories. And the peace. He felt his mother's hand press into his as his eyes focused again on the child that had been briefly forgotten amidst the reunion. Those curious eyes were still intently fixed on Tyson.

"Who are you?" Tyson returned the child's question, recognizing toys scattered about that had once been his own.

"Richard," he answered proudly.

"Richard what?" Tyson persisted, missing the sharp glance between Jess and Alexa as they silently agreed that it was not up to them to tell Tyson about his son. Lacey could tell him when she came back.

"Just Richard," he answered. His grandparents sighed in unison, grateful he hadn't yet been taught his surname. "What's your name?" Richard asked.

"Tyson Byrnehouse-Davies, and I'm proud of it." A smile toward his father added meaning to his announcement.

That seemed to satisfy Richard's curiosity for the moment, and he returned to his playing. But Tyson had to ask, "Did I miss something?" He pointed casually to the child.

The irony in the statement made Alexa unable to answer. She was grateful when Jess said coolly, "Just another boy abandoned by his father."

Tyson nodded his understanding. "A little young to blend in with the others, eh?"

"Something like that," Jess stated nonchalantly.

"He was very young when he came to us," Alexa added. "He needed special care."

"And his mother?" Tyson asked with a concern that deepened the evidence of his maturity.

"She's gone," Richard provided, as if it was obvious.

"Got into some trouble," Jess added, and Alexa marveled at the deepening of their deception.

"Grandpapa," Richard said. His timing made Jess sigh with exasperation. "Will you fix my horse?"

"Grandpapa?" Tyson chuckled.

Jess lifted an embarrassed brow. "It just seemed to fit." He gave a look toward Alexa that he was grateful she understood. It was a silent confession at not being a good liar.

"I don't think it's fixable," Jess said gently after a close examination. Richard sighed and left it with Jess, returning to some other toy horses that had four good legs.

An uncomfortable silence made Tyson ask in a tone of light expectancy that brought tears to Alexa's eyes, "So, where's Emma? Lacey? They didn't run off and get married or anything, did they?"

There was enough hesitance that Tyson looked quickly to his parents' faces and caught a severity that eerily combined with the silence of the house. The feelings that had shortened his journey home meshed with recalling his mother's initial greeting. He took a deep breath and asked, "Why were you praying I would come?" She didn't answer. He moved to the edge of his seat. "Where are they?" he demanded. She put a hand to her mouth and started to cry. Tyson pulled her to his shoulder and turned insistent eyes to his father, whispering with a fear that cracked his voice, "Where are they?"

"If we knew . . ." He didn't finish.

"What do you mean by that?" Tyson shouted, coming to his feet.

"They're gone," Jess said. "They were—"

"Gone?" Tyson repeated breathily, interrupting Jess's attempt to explain. For months he had been imagining a reunion with his sister and sweetheart. He'd imagined them terse, joyous, forgiving, indifferent—even married. But he'd never imagined them *gone*. "What's happened?" he demanded.

Jess pulled the only clue out of his pocket and handed the note to his son, figuring it would explain better than the rambling of emotional parents.

Tyson first noticed the worn look of the piece of paper, as if it had been read hundreds of times. He began to read and had to find a chair. Finally he looked up, shocked and dumbstruck.

Jess answered the silence. "All we can do is wait. But when that next message comes, we could use you."

Tyson nodded firmly, suppressing the urge to scream and throw something. He wanted to say that they couldn't possibly just *wait*. But he felt certain such feelings had already been voiced. And it was apparent that when he'd entered the room they had been trying to occupy themselves. Tyson recalled again the sensation that had brought him home now. Had he sensed Emma's fear as she'd been dragged away from home? The thought made his voice return. "How did it happen?" he asked.

Jess glanced toward Richard, making certain that he wasn't paying attention. They had been vague in explaining where his mother and Aunt Emma had gone. In a low whisper he answered, "Just taken from their beds in the middle of the night."

Tyson hit a fist against his thigh and looked again at the note. "It looks as if they only intended to take one. Which one, I wonder? And what made them change their minds?"

"Only time will answer such things, Tyson," his mother said so sadly that he knew he had to change the subject.

In a frantic search for distraction, Tyson turned his gaze to Richard. "What are you doing there, boy?"

"The horses are eating," Richard announced.

Alexa put an unnoticed hand to her heart when Tyson moved to sit on the floor beside Richard, saying in a tone that sparked the child's attention, "Are they racing horses?"

Richard nodded proudly. "Like Grandpapa's horses."

"Then they have to eat just the right things," Tyson said. "And we'll have to make certain they're trained properly right from the start. Do you know where we can find one of the best horse trainers in the country?" Richard shook his head, obviously fascinated by this grown-up conversation being directed at him. Tyson pointed proudly to his mother and whispered loudly, "She's sitting right there. Why don't you go ask her if she will train your horses to race, then maybe we could make a bet."

"What's a bet?"

"If my horse wins, I get to take you for a ride on a real horse. And if your horse wins, you get to go for a ride on a real horse."

"Yeah." Richard grinned in a way that made Alexa wonder why Tyson couldn't see himself in the child's face. "Let's make a bet."

Alexa made Richard believe that she trained his horses, and Tyson lost three races. Tyson promised to fulfill his bet after lunch, and Miss Leeds came to get the boy for his story time.

"How can we just wait?" Tyson shouted, coming to his feet. No one answered.

"Tell us about your travels," Alexa finally said in a poor attempt to sound cheerful.

"There's nothing to tell," he said firmly and sat beside her. He figured now was as good a time as any to make a point clear. He added with strength, "It's good to be home."

The silence became unbearable again. Neither Jess nor Alexa could think of anything to tell him that didn't have to do with Richard.

"Does anyone care if I take a walk?" Tyson stood up again. "I'd like to have a look around."

"Make yourself at home." Alexa's eyes warmed to his.

"If I still have a room, I'd like to unpack."

"It's just how you left it," Alexa told him. "Perhaps more orderly."

Tyson smiled and bent to kiss his mother. How good it was to know she had been wanting all this time for him to come home. He looked to his father and felt moved to repeat, "It's good to be home." He moved to the door and paused. "If I find the nursery, do you think Miss Leeds would mind if I joined their story time?"

"You'll have to ask her." Jess managed a smile. "But she's fairly agreeable."

Tyson left the room, and Alexa reached for her husband's hand. "Why do I feel like it never happened?"

"What do you mean?"

"He's gone one minute, here the next. He sits down like he's just come in from a long ride. It's as if he's never been gone. He looks older, but he's still the same."

"Not completely." Jess tapped his fingers on his thigh. "In a certain way, I believe he's changed very much."

"He's grown up," Alexa agreed.

"Yes, but I also believe he has a long road yet to travel before he rebuilds all the bridges he burned when he left."

Alexa absorbed the reality of his statement, her brow furrowed in concern.

"And you thought it would get easier when they turned eighteen," Jess said almost lightly. "That was the day the real trouble began, my dear."

"I'm afraid you're right. And I have a feeling there is a great deal of trouble ahead."

Jess nodded and squeezed her hand. "That's what you get for being so beautiful."

Alexa was warmed by the compliment. "What has that got to do with—"

Jess leaned closer and touched her nose with his. "If you weren't so beautiful, I wouldn't have fallen in love with you. And if I hadn't fallen in love with you, we wouldn't have always been—"

"I get the idea," Alexa said and pressed her fingers over his lips.

Five
AT THE MERCY OF
MICHAEL HAMILTON

Lacey woke with a start and sighed heavily as she absorbed her sur-roundings. They were a poor disappointment in contrast to the dream she'd just emerged from, where Tyson had returned to find her gone, and, like a knight in shining armor, had ridden across the outback to rescue her, killing Michael Hamilton on the spot. She contemplated the dream in an attempt to ignore the sounds of the other tent com-ing down while the men joked crudely and loaded the pack mules. The thought of Tyson rescuing her was something worth pondering, but it was futile and she knew it. So she pushed the idea away, remind-ing herself that she'd been listening to Emma relate too many plots of those books she read.

Facing reality with a practiced bitterness, Lacey made up her mind to not think about Tyson, or Richard, or anything else. She opened her eyes and saw Michael Hamilton standing above her, hands on his hips. She'd think about him, she decided. He sneered at her and she sneered back. It would give her a great deal of strength through this ordeal to contemplate how much she hated Michael Hamilton.

"Pleasant dreams?" He bent forward slightly and gave her a mock-ing grin.

"Actually, yes," she snapped. "I dreamt you were dead."

Michael gave a disgruntled noise and nudged Emma in the ribs with the toe of his boot. "Wake up, Emma." She groaned. "Emma, my sweet." He spoke to her as if she were his spouse of twenty years. "I've thought it over, and you were absolutely right. Are you listening to me, dear?" She groaned again and attempted to focus on him hovering above her. "As I was saying, you were right and I admit it. The next time you give me advice, I will heed it implicitly."

"What are you prattling about?" Emma said with irritation. She didn't feel nearly rested enough to face what was awaiting her.

"I was talking about your sister," he said, as if she were inane not to know. "She's very funny, you know. She's having dreams about me dying, and she's enjoying it."

"Are you making sense, or am I still asleep?" Emma attempted to sit up.

Lacey observed the conversation in gaping disbelief.

"You aren't listening to me, dear." He leaned onto one leg and tipped up the toe of his other boot, digging the heel into the ground. "I said I should have taken your advice."

"About what?" Emma yawned.

"I told you already. Are you daft, woman? I was referring to your sister."

"What about her?" Emma glanced at Lacey, wondering if she had missed something, but it was apparent they were both equally ignorant.

Michael sighed in exasperation, turned his back to them, and threw his hands in the air. Then he turned to face them again and immediately regained his stance. "You were right!" he nearly shouted, enunciating each word. "We should have left her home!"

"Brilliant!" Lacey said with bitter sarcasm. "It's not too late to take me back, you know."

"Oh," he grinned, "but it is. Besides, the game has just begun." His voice returned so quickly to his cruel monotone that Lacey had to blink twice to make certain it was the same man. "Now hurry up and get moving. We've got miles to ride before sundown, and it's already past noon."

"Where are you taking us?" Lacey asked fearfully.

"China," he answered, and she gasped. He turned to Emma and added, "Just a little joke."

"Amusing," she muttered, coming to her feet and stretching.

"Did you want to eat breakfast first, or would you rather sing?" He might as well have asked them if they would prefer white wine or red with their meal.

Emma glanced at Lacey and they said together, "We'll sing."

They were given a good breakfast, which should have been lunch, while their tent and bedrolls were packed away. Their belongings were put into saddlebags provided for each of them, and they were allowed to sing their way through private matters once more before they were hauled onto horses and tied just as the night before.

"Hold it!" Michael shouted before they had gone three steps, and the entire group came to an abrupt halt. "Bring her over here." He nodded toward Lacey, and one of the guards ushered her horse within Michael's reach. He shifted the reins to one hand while both women held their breath. Abruptly Michael removed Emma's hat and handed it to Lacey's guard, then he took Lacey's hat from her head and put it on Emma's.

"There!" he announced, taking the wide-brimmed hat from the baffled guard and patting it onto Lacey's head. "Now I can possibly bear this journey without a hat brim in my throat. Is everybody happy?" No one answered. "Then move out!" he shouted, and they did.

"You know, my sweet," Michael said, "your being so . . . shall we say . . . not so tall, does make this much easier."

"Then it's too bad I'm not taller," she said to be obnoxious. "And don't call me your sweet."

"Oh no, you're just right." He put that menacing arm around her waist. "My sweet."

Emma sighed in exasperation and chose not to argue. The man had to be mad.

"Which is convenient," he continued.

"What is?" she asked when silence made her realize he wouldn't continue until she asked.

"To be so . . . well, not so tall, and to be in the business of racing horses."

"I suppose."

He briefly tightened his grip. "The perfect woman jockey."

"I haven't raced since I was sixteen."

"Yes, I know. You prefer to train and observe."

"How is it that you know so much about me?" she asked, slightly unnerved.

"You once told me I was an observant man," he said, his voice lowering dangerously. "I'm just living up to my reputation."

Emma thought of the full spectrum of his reputation, and her uneasiness increased. She was glad when he said nothing more.

They moved at a slower pace due to the mules joining their team. And from the way they were loaded, Emma realized this would not soon be over. From the treks she had taken with her father to associate with the natives, she guessed by the supplies that they were expecting to be gone two to three weeks. She groaned audibly at the thought and attempted to shift to a more comfortable position in what little room she was allowed in the saddle.

"Is something troubling you, my sweet?" Michael asked while the horse lumbered along beneath them.

"I'm certain you've gained weight since we last shared this wondrous experience."

"Perhaps it's you who has put it on." He patted her leg none too softly. "Although I should compliment you on your choice of clothing. I must confess, there is nothing like a woman in breeches."

They went several miles in silence. It was growing dusky before Michael announced they could stop for the night. He ordered the men to work before quietly untying the girls to send them singing. When they had finished their necessities, Emma put a hand to Lacey's arm and gestured for her to be still and follow her. They moved quietly toward the camp, but stopped behind a huge rock. Lacey whispered frantically, "What are you doing? We'll never get away from him by—"

"I'm not trying to get—" She stopped as Michael ran past them, nearly sliding to a halt in the sand. He turned frantically to look in every direction until he saw them. His eyes narrowed angrily, but Emma only laughed, and Lacey realized it had been nothing more than a practical joke. At times she felt as if this was nothing more than a game between Michael and Emma, and she was nothing but an unwanted pawn.

"I thought I told you to sing!" he said through clenched teeth.

Emma continued to laugh until Lacey hit her, not liking the growing disdain in Michael's eyes.

"It would seem we had your nerves riled there for a minute, Mr. Hamilton." Emma fought for a straight face.

Lacey let out a gasping scream as Michael stepped forward and took hold of Emma's arm, twisting it until she had no choice but to kneel on the ground in front of him. He looked down at her as if he'd like to tear her to pieces. Lacey took a step back, but Michael's eyes shot to her, full of fire. He lifted his free hand to point a menacing finger at her. "You stay put, Miss Davies." His tone made Lacey cringe. "Don't move. Don't talk. And breathe quietly. Or your sister may not emerge from this conversation quite the same."

Lacey bit into the back of her hand as Michael's eyes returned to Emma. She couldn't move, but she did her best to show all of the heated defiance she could muster in her expression.

"Am I hurting you, my sweet?" he asked with mock gallantry, smiling with a phoniness that added malevolence to the intensity of his eyes. Emma couldn't deny that she was afraid, but she wasn't about to show it.

"No," she answered quite honestly. Despite his firm grip, she felt no pain as long as she didn't move.

"Good." His lips spread further over his teeth. "I wouldn't want you to be distracted while I tell you how foolish it is to amuse yourselves at the expense of the man who is presently holding your lives in the palm of his hand."

Michael gently put his hand into Emma's hair, then he tugged at it abruptly, forcing her head back as he bent from the waist to look her in the eye. He was so close she could feel his angry breath. Her heart pounded into her throat. He moved his mouth to her ear, and she felt his beard brushing her face as he whispered, "Perhaps I could send home a little souvenir for your father, my sweet. It would give me a great deal of pleasure to poison the great Byrnehouse-Davies household with some . . . bad blood."

Emma felt the fantasies of paperback novels and roguish heroes come shattering down around her. The vengeance in his voice rang strong and true. She felt certain his need for money was real, and perhaps his hateful desires were as well. But she now knew his strongest motive. Vengeance. For what she wasn't certain, but the fear in her now was real. She felt moisture building in her eyes, but she doubted her tears would do anything but urge him on. She would not make this enjoyable for him by revealing her true emotion. With angry defiance, she drew a deep breath and whispered in return, "It would be the best thing that could possibly happen to a child of yours."

Michael's eyes shot to hers and Emma gave him a quick, triumphant smile that she had learned from him. He let go of her hair and hauled her to her feet, retaining his grip on her arm. It was obvious she had silenced him by the way he continued to stare at her with those cruel, imposing eyes. But his mouth remained shut in a rigid line. Emma took the opportunity to add in a voice still soft enough to avoid Lacey's ears, "The curse would come back to you, Michael. You would forever wonder about that child, and you would ache to know it. You would always wonder what kind of masterpiece I had created with your bad blood. I would refine it and mold it, guide it and nurture it, while you could only spend the rest of your life remembering what it was like to touch, for only a moment, the one thing that could have saved you."

As soon as the words escaped her, Emma stopped to wonder where they'd come from. Her mother had spoken of times when she had said something so right that she had believed she'd been speaking on instinct. Or perhaps some kind of inspiration. Emma could find no other explanation for words she hardly understood herself; words that made Michael Hamilton let go of her and recoil as if she had prophesied his certain destruction.

"Go on." He waved a hand toward the harsh land surrounding them. "Run. Get yourself killed. It would be good riddance."

"We would," Emma announced, sauntering past him toward the camp, "but we're hungry." Lacey followed and passed Emma, wanting distance between her and Michael. Emma turned back briefly to add, "And I will admit that you're right about one thing. Our lives are in your hands. We can't survive out here without you."

"You'd do well to remember it," he sneered, a deeper anger still hovering in his eyes. "And remember also, my sweet, that perhaps you credit me with too much emotion." He gave a sideways nod, a subtle pronouncement of triumph, of getting the last word. "I could care less what you do with my blood."

Emma suppressed the shudder threatening to seize her and walked toward camp, feeling Michael Hamilton's eyes piercing through the back of her as he followed.

They sat on the ground near a fire where a man in his fifties, the one Michael called Corky, was busily creating some culinary delight that actually smelled good. Michael sat near Emma, leaning on one elbow and stretching his legs out. Corky began babbling about his expertise in the art of cooking, but it didn't dispel the tension hovering between Michael and Emma. Lacey seemed oblivious to it, as if she didn't want to know what they'd said to each other a few minutes ago. But Emma felt Michael's eyes on her; they were manipulating brown eyes. She felt certain he was making good on his threat, if only in his imagination.

As the men gradually finished their work, they came one by one to circle the fire as Corky completed the meal and began dishing it out. He served Michael first, who casually handed his plate to Emma, scolding Corky tersely. "Ladies first, you imbecile."

Emma nodded her thanks to Corky and ignored Michael. She waited to begin until Lacey had hers. Eating was an easy way to ignore the brash group of men surrounding them. But some things could not be ignored, and the girls winced visibly as the conversation turned crude and the language more foul. She was gratefully surprised when Michael said in a firm voice that caught the men's attention, "Mind your mouths, boys. You're in the presence of ladies."

All eyes turned humbly back to their meal, except for one pair that showed courageous defiance. "You got a problem with that, Bud?" Michael asked.

"Maybe I do." Bud's gruff voice made it clear this was one of the men who had dragged the women from their rooms.

Michael had a dagger out of his boot, his plate on the ground, and was standing over Bud so quickly that it was all a blur until the blade was pressed against Bud's cheek. A taut hush fell over the group, broken only by Michael's voice. "Perhaps taking a slice out of your tongue would help you deal with it."

It was Corky who piped up with a confident willingness to adhere to their leader's specifications. "I'd say if the boss wants clean language, you'd do well to mind it."

"Thank you, Corky," Michael said and backed up to where he'd been sitting. He didn't take his eyes off Bud for even a second as he was seated and stuck the dagger into the ground in front of him for quick retrieval. He picked up his plate and continued to eat as if nothing out of the ordinary had transpired.

When they were finished eating, Emma handed their plates to Corky, who took them eagerly. "Thank you, Corky," she said, finding him the only one in the group worth speaking to. "It was delicious."

"Glad ya liked it, ma'am." He nodded, then smiled at Lacey, who ignored him.

Emma came to her feet, and Lacey followed. "Where do you ladies think you're going?" Michael asked without looking up.

"To bed," Emma retorted. "We're tired."

"You'll go to bed when I go to bed," he stated. Lacey took Emma's arm and nodded toward the dagger. They sat back down. Less than a minute later, Michael came to his feet and put the dagger into his boot. He hauled Emma up by her arm, and Lacey followed willingly. Once inside the tent with a lantern, he muttered, "Say your prayers, girls. I'll be right back."

He returned to find them settled into their bedrolls for some much-needed sleep. Emma heard him removing his boots, checking his pistol, then the lantern was doused. She knew it was a stupid, foolish thing to do, but she couldn't bite back the urge to say, "Back so soon, Mr. Hamilton? We didn't hear you singing."

She held her breath, wondering if he would hit her... or worse. He only grunted and went to sleep.

The girls woke feeling rested from a good night's sleep, and glad to see that Michael was in a tolerable, quiet mood. Emma was relieved to have survived the night with her virtue. When she stopped to think of the reality of his threats, she felt a fear that made her heart pound—and a mild intrigue that reminded her she had read too many novels.

Breakfast and loading up passed without incident, and they were again moving toward some unknown destination. Its only significance to Emma and Lacey was the distance from their home.

A bright spot came when Michael allowed them to ride without their hands tied. If nothing else, Emma thought, yesterday's drama had perhaps convinced him that they were aware of the foolishness in attempting to escape.

A pattern was established that carried them through four more days. Or was it five? Emma lost track. They ate and rode, slept and sang, while Michael remained quiet and aloof but constantly present, keeping watch over them like a hovering vulture.

Lacey became despondent as her thoughts were obviously with her son, and she was longing to be home. Emma might have been prone to feel depressed by the entire production, but she chose to distract herself by observing their captor. She had always been fascinated with people— what made them think and behave the way they did. And Michael Hamilton was very complex indeed. When her mind became bored or discouraged, she thought of all she knew of Michael, his background, his behavior, and she tried to mix it with the man before her—the same man she had spent so much time in the saddle with that she was beginning to believe she couldn't ride without him. There was a hollow between his neck and shoulder that was custom tailored to the back of her head.

While his presence surrounded and supported her, Emma pondered his mind. To look at his obvious traits, it might have made simple sense. He was cruel, a twenty-eight-year-old bully with nothing better to do than inflict his bitterness on others. But Emma had seen hints of something that made her believe there was more to Michael than that. There was evidence on several counts that cold cruelty was not his only characteristic.

Comparing him to the men they rode with was a good place to start. He didn't blend in with the crowd. They were crude and crass; he was refined and eloquent in his own villainous way. He smelled of leather and horses, and the sweat and dust of their journey—not the rank odor of personal neglect that hung about the others. His defense at their first meal around the campfire was some evidence of respect to their gender, and perhaps their background, despite his actions that subtly defied that concept.

Beyond that, Emma recalled her first out-of-the-ordinary encounter with Michael Hamilton more than four years earlier. She remembered his gentle attention to her gelding, his insightful words concerning her being alone, his genuine smile as he complimented her beauty. More recently, he had displayed a satirical humor that Emma found enjoyable. She had come to miss it in the stead of his quiet malevolence. She thought of his procuring clothes for her, which was not necessarily a kind act, but a necessary element of the game. It was rather what he had provided that intrigued Emma. He seemed to know her so well, when he had not even seen her for years.

Emma pondered again his motives for this escapade. Vengeance stood out stronger than greed or lust. And she was gradually focusing in on the belief that his vengeance was aimed more at her than her family. Had she hurt him so badly by her thoughtless rejection? If that was the case, perhaps his mind had warped this into much more than she could ever comprehend. Perhaps he had awful things in store for her out of some perverse obsession. His lack of physical attention so far was a relief, but it didn't necessarily make her believe it wouldn't happen. She knew he was capable of carrying out his threats, and she knew she had to be on guard. In that respect, she was grateful that his interest was in her and not Lacey. With her sensitive nature and precarious childhood, Emma felt certain that Lacey would never recover from such a thing. Emma had to admit that she was likely displaying her own ignorance when she told herself she could get over it without too much trauma. But she mentally tried to prepare herself for the possibility, hoping that if nothing else, figuring him out to some degree would give her a few cards to play in this game.

In observing the apparent cruelty in Michael, Emma wondered why it came so naturally for him. But she was more intrigued by the way her one attempt at counterattack had sent him into days of intense severity, with no hint of the subtle humor he had displayed prior to that time. She wondered over the true source of Michael's desire for vengeance. The reality that he had been living at Byrnehouse-Davies even before Lacey could be unnerving if she contemplated it too deeply. Had he watched her when she was a child and formulated plans for years? She realized that she knew nothing of him prior to his residence at the boys' home. And this made her wonder what kind of childhood he'd had, and how it had molded the man he was now.

Such questions concerned Emma, but they also intrigued her in a way she couldn't quite pinpoint. She couldn't help wondering what it might be about herself that would make a man go to so much trouble. If this kidnapping venture was truly for more than money or sport, then his avid attention to her, while indifferently disregarding Lacey, made the game very complicated. The whole thing left Emma wary. The bottom line was evident: she was at the mercy of Michael Hamilton, whatever kind of man he proved to be.

Emma couldn't describe the relief that she knew Lacey shared when they apparently reached their destination. Now they could stop riding continually, and also stop putting distance between themselves and all they loved. Camp was set up in a more permanent manner near a typical cluster of overhanging rock, which was also the entrance to a deep cave where more supplies had been left—supplies that could mean an even longer stay than Emma had feared.

❦   ❦   ❦

Tyson pushed open the door to the nursery and announced to Miss Leeds, "Here he is!"

"Riding again, Master Richard?" The woman spoke to him as if he was lord of the manor.

"Yes, and Tyson says tomorrow we can go on a picnic. Mrs. Brady said she would pack us a lunch, with little cakes and everything!"

"How delightful." Miss Leeds grinned and winked at Tyson.

"You be good now, and take your nap." Tyson tousled Richard's hair. "I'll see you later on."

Richard happily stayed with the nanny while Tyson went down to the dining room to eat with his parents. Meals had become the most difficult time of day for him, and he suspected for his parents as well. The absence of Emma and Lacey was felt keenly and seemed to be intensified by the empty chairs and lack of conversation. In contrast, Tyson found his time with Richard to be the easiest. The child was purely delightful—as were his imaginary friends who had accompanied them on various excursions. Tyson didn't recall ever making up friends as a child. But then, he'd always had Emma. Richard was likely a lonely child in need of such imaginary companions, although Tyson found a desire to eventually replace them with their own budding and very real friendship. There was something about Richard, perhaps because he was a fatherless child, that eased the misery of the past four years. He was one hundred percent boy, and Tyson found an uncanny rapport with the child as he rode with him, played with him, and took him for long walks, during which they communicated somewhere between their different levels of intellect. Richard was bright and witty for a three-and-a-half-year-old. Tyson was fun-loving and boyish for a man of twenty-two.

Tyson found himself spending more and more time with Richard. The enjoyment of his company made time fly and reality less prominent. He had a desire to inquire more about the boy's background, but there was too much on his father's mind right now. When everything was back to normal, Tyson was determined to find out more.

"How is Richard this morning?" Alexa asked as Tyson was seated.

"Charming as ever." Tyson managed a smile. He wanted to ask if there had been any word yet, but he knew they'd have said something if there had been. A week with no message was beginning to make them fear the worst.

Halfway through the meal, the miserable quiet was broken by heavy footsteps running up the hall. As they came closer, a familiar voice shouted, "I got it! I got it!"

They were all on their feet when Murphy bounded through the dining room door, holding an envelope in a tight grip. "I got it!" he repeated breathlessly.

"How?" Jess insisted, taking it from him to read the familiar script on the outside that simply said *Mr. Davies.*

"A rider galloped in, handed it to one of the lads near the track, and told him to give it to Mr. Davies immediately. He was gone in a flash. The boy brought it to me right off."

Jess looked to Tyson and Alexa, then he drew a deep breath and broke the seal.

"What does it say?" Murphy asked impatiently.

"Hush up and give me a minute," Jess insisted, opening the letter carefully, as if his daughters' lives were literally folded inside. Something fell to the floor and Tyson bent to pick it up, feeling his heavy heart turn heavier.

"What is it?" Alexa demanded.

Tyson rose and held out his hand as he fingered the long locks of hair, one reddish brown, the other dark. Anxious glances replaced the need for words. They all knew beyond any doubt that whoever this was had both Emma and Lacey. Tyson curled the hair into his fist and pressed it against his lips.

"Read it aloud, please." Alexa nibbled tensely on her knuckles.

Jess cleared his throat and tried to ignore the knots in his stomach as he read.

"My dear Mr. Davies, Your daughters are very beautiful. It would be a shame if something happened to them, but beauty has a price, and I feel quite certain a hundred thousand pounds could insure their safety."

Alexa gasped. "I don't believe it."

"I've got more than eighty thousand," Tyson announced readily, willing to give anything to have them back.

"It's all right, son," Jess said calmly. "The money isn't a problem." He continued to read.

"By the time you receive this message, we will have arrived at our destination, and we will be anxiously waiting for you to join us here. It's a quaint little place, somewhere in the middle of Australia. I only said that to make you appreciate that I didn't take them to China."

"The man is full of laughs," Tyson interrupted angrily. "I'd like to—"

"Hush!" Alexa ordered, and Jess read on.

"You should be able to find us easily enough, as we are waiting near a place you people call Crazy Rock."

Jess looked up at Alexa as they both perceived this was someone who knew them well. "You don't think that one of our boys . . ." Alexa couldn't finish.

"I don't know who else would know about Crazy Rock." Jess showed fresh anger in his eyes.

"Finish the stupid thing," Tyson insisted.

"I will have two men waiting each morning at ten o'clock until you arrive, near a solitary gum ghost two miles southeast of Crazy Rock. Don't come any closer to our camp than that, and bring the money with you. Then, and only then, will your daughters be returned to you. And please, let's not do anything foolish, or they will certainly regret it. See you soon."

Jess continued to stare at the letter, saying calmly, "Murphy, get Ben and tell him to meet me in my office immediately." Murphy left quickly. "Ben knows the outback like his own bedroom," Jess added.

"Isn't Crazy Rock a five-day journey from here?" Tyson asked.

"At least," Jess said soberly.

"Then we'd better get the preparations underway." Alexa managed a steady voice. "I want my daughters back as quickly as possible."

"Come along." Jess put his arm around Alexa, and they hurried to the office with Tyson close behind.

Ben arrived to find maps of the outback spread over the desk. "You needed me?" he asked coolly.

"We need your blood," Tyson stated quite truthfully. Ben was half aborigine, and during his childhood had spent half of each year in the outback with his mother's parents. He'd spent the other half of his life at Byrnehouse-Davies with his mother, Sarina, who had been a maid here long before Alexa's initial arrival. Sarina was now head mistress of the boys' home, and Ben was head administrator. He was quietly tough and expertly intelligent. But beyond that, there was a bond the family shared with Ben that few were aware of. He was actually the source of inspiration for the Byrnehouse-Davies Home for Boys. He had been born illegitimate, and would have been left to a life of poverty if Jess Davies had not taken his mother in and helped her raise the child. Jess loved Ben, and had made good on his vow that if money ever came into his hands he would help boys like Ben. But the bond between them went even deeper. The man who had fathered Ben and abandoned Sarina was the late Chad Byrnehouse. And that made Tyson and Ben cousins by blood. But it was the other half of Ben's blood they needed now—his aborigine blood.

"I'm assuming you got the message?" Ben asked, only to have it handed to him. He read it quickly and looked up at Jess soberly. "There are very few boys who would know of that place, and they would all be men now."

"Didn't you take several treks there?" Alexa asked.

"No," Ben said in his usual matter-of-fact way. "I only took one group there. The purpose of getting the boys to appreciate the harshness of nature proved to be accomplished much more easily with fewer days' journey. Crazy Rock was an experiment that wasn't necessarily successful."

Jess leaned forward intently as he realized that this could be narrowed down, and they might have some idea of who they were dealing with. "Do you remember who?" he asked.

"No, but I've got records." He pointed. "They're in that drawer with the general files."

"Get it," Jess directed.

Ben went to the drawer and turned a key in the lock, speaking as he thumbed through the files. "It's a six- to seven-day journey with mules, which we must have to take enough supplies to survive it. Fortunately, this is not the hottest season of the year. But then, I'm certain this great kidnapper had that in mind. He didn't likely have a desire to roast any more than the rest of us." He pulled out the file and looked through it as he continued. "Crazy Rock is a nice place, considering. Of course, you've all been there."

"I remember." Tyson's eyes lit up. "That was the trek we took the winter after we got Lacey and . . ."

"That's it," Jess added when Tyson faltered at the mention of her name.

"I remember very little about it," Tyson added. "Didn't it have a pool or—"

"That's right," Ben answered. "An exquisite artesian spring, carefully hidden in the rocks. There are also a number of deep caves in the area. If you had to have a kidnapping, I'd say he picked a good spot."

"Go ahead," Jess attempted a light tone, "compliment the beast."

Ben shrugged his shoulders and held out a sheet of paper. Jess took it and read frantically.

"Who was there?" Alexa insisted. She prided herself on keeping track of these boys into adulthood.

"Bobby Downs."

"Married. Lives in Sydney."

"Gar Krebbs," Jess continued.

"Married. Moved from Melbourne to Adelaide last year. He sent me a letter at Christmas. He has three children."

"Tom Black."

"He died in an accident nearly three years ago."

"Guy Winston."

Alexa hesitated. "I don't know. He never kept in touch."

"That's a possibility." Jess drew his attention from the page in his hand. "Do you remember much about him?" Jess asked Ben.

Ben tilted his head thoughtfully. "Quiet, self-confident. Never caused any trouble. Seems like he wasn't too fond of the outback, but he handled it well enough."

"Alexa?" Jess posed the same question to her.

"He doesn't stand out strongly one way or another."

"Sometimes the quiet ones are the most difficult to understand," Jess added thoughtfully.

"Is there anyone else?" Tyson asked.

"Yes," Ben answered. "I always took five boys. You only read four."

Jess scanned the page to find his place. Alexa saw his eyes widen as he perceived something significant. "What?" she insisted.

Jess looked up and said the name as an obvious answer to the ultimate question. "Michael Hamilton."

"Oh, no." Alexa's voice became heavy. "Why would he do such a thing?"

"I don't believe it," Tyson added tersely. "I always thought he was a little brash, but I wouldn't have thought him capable of something like this."

"Wasn't he in prison not so long ago?" Ben gave an important fact.

"I'm afraid so," Jess answered, perceiving the downhearted expression in his wife's eyes. "But we won't know for certain until we get there, so there's no point speculating over it any further now. There is always the possibility that whoever is doing this simply heard about Crazy Rock from one of these sources. The important thing now is to get there."

Ben found the appropriate map and traced the journey with his finger.

"All right," Jess concluded as they stared down helplessly at the appointed spot, all too many miles away. "Ben, I want you to supervise getting the supplies loaded and the animals ready. I know you won't forget anything. Get Murphy and Jimmy to help you. Tyson, you ride into town and get the money from the bank. I'll send a letter with you so Mr. Kline won't give you any hassle. We're leaving at dawn."

Ben and Tyson left to see to their orders. Alexa moved into Jess's arms. "It's him, Jess. I can feel it."

"I know, but I don't understand it."

Alexa picked up the letter and shook her head. "It's his voice, his style."

"But why?" Jess curled his hand into a fist. "After all we've done for him, why would he turn around and do this? I just don't understand."

"I would venture to say that his reasons are very complex, which makes me believe it may not be as bad as it appears to be."

Jess turned to look at his wife carefully. "You know something I don't."

Alexa hesitated. "We both know things about Michael Hamilton that no one else knows," she stated.

"Yes, but there's something else." He stepped toward her abruptly. "What makes you think it's not as bad as it appears?"

"Call it instinct," she replied noncommitally.

"I will call it a lot more than that, Alexa." He took her shoulders into his hands. "You have an insight that I will never understand. I know how you feel about Michael, and before I go out there and face him with my daughters' lives in the balance, I want to know everything you know. Everything!"

"I know very little, Jess. But I have suspected for many years that . . ."

"What?" he demanded when she hesitated.

"It has something to do with Emma."

"You don't think that . . ." He couldn't find the words.

"Yes, I do. I believe he felt something for her. I believe that's the biggest reason he stayed on to work. And I believe that's why he left when he did. She told me herself that he left here the same day she refused his offer to take her riding."

"I remember." Jess sat down thoughtfully.

"It's impossible at this point to know what traits have taken dominance in Michael's mind. We both know he's had things to deal with that . . . well, you know what I mean."

"Yes, I know." Jess's answer was heavy with sadness.

"I know I shouldn't do it, and I would never admit this to anyone else, but . . . it's difficult to look at the boys we've had here and not pick our favorites. If I am completely honest, Jess, Michael Hamilton has meant more to me than any other beyond my own children."

"Yes," Jess nodded, "I know. The one who gave us the most trouble had to be the one you loved the most."

"Perhaps because he needed a mother's love more than any other."

"Perhaps." Then Jess brought them back to reality. "And now he's got my daughters, demanding a ransom of a hundred thousand pounds, implying threats against their safety."

"Maybe he needs the money," she observed, attempting to defend him.

"What he needs is a good, swift kick in the rear."

"Perhaps that, too." Alexa leaned toward her husband. "Jess, as I said, it is impossible to know where his mind is. Maybe he has become a victim of his circumstances and let them overtake him. If that's the case, I say get the girls out of there at all costs. All I ask is that you keep an open mind. Try to read between the lines in what you see happening. Maybe we can help him."

"And maybe we can't."

"I do feel some relief," Alexa admitted.

"How is that?"

"If it was Lacey alone out there, I'd be scared to death for her. But he's got Emma." She smiled and Jess caught the implication, chuckling dubiously.

"Yes," Jess rubbed his chin thoughtfully, "the man will get a run for his money, if nothing else."

"Michael's a tough kid," Alexa added, "but I really don't believe he'd hurt either one of them. Oh, he'd likely threaten and put on a pretty fair act. But there is something inside of him that will respect those girls the way he respected me."

"Only because you demanded it."

"But I think he learned from it. Let's just hope he hasn't changed too much."

"Yes," Jess agreed, "let's hope."

❦   ❦   ❦

Just before dawn, Tyson peeked into the nursery to gaze for a moment at the sleeping Richard. He smiled to recall the boy's excitement when he promised they would share a picnic when he returned. It was a pleasant contrast to the tears the boy had shed when Tyson had announced that he had to leave for a couple of weeks. But this parting was different for Tyson. This time he said firmly, "I'll be back, Richard. I promise."

The sky was barely showing hints of light when Jess, Tyson, and Ben set out with a loaded mule team and extra horses. Alexa stood on the side veranda, watching them ride away, blowing kisses and wiping tears. In that moment she could only long to have her family reunited. She felt certain that she would be truly happy when they were all safe and sound at home again.

❦   ❦   ❦

"Now what?" Emma insisted when Michael entered the tent to find the girls lounging while they nibbled jerky and cheese.

"We wait," he announced, settling into a comfortable position close to Emma. Too close.

"For what?" she asked.

"Your father should have gotten our second message by now, giving him instructions. I suspect he'll be here in less than a week, give or take a little." No comment followed from any of them. Michael's eyes focused on Emma, and she felt his motives shifting now that the journey was behind them.

Emma turned her attention back to the food until she saw Lacey's eyes widen, and she realized that Michael was idly toying with her hair where it hung over her shoulder. Though his rekindled interest in her was somewhat unnerving, Emma could find no reason to protest. He wasn't hurting anything, so she simply said, "I can't imagine your fascination with it, Mr. Hamilton." He met her eyes in questioning surprise. "I'm certain it has half of Australia caked in it by now." She sighed. "I swear I'd give anything for some scented shampoo and enough water to wash my hair. Wouldn't you, Lacey?"

If Lacey wasn't surprised by Emma allowing his attention, she was certainly surprised by her attempt at casual conversation in his presence. Lacey could hardly tolerate his presence to any degree. But this certainly wasn't the first time she and Emma had disagreed on something, and Emma seemed to know how to handle him, so Lacey just sat back and said nothing.

"Lacey?" Emma added. "Did you hear me?"

"Yes, I heard."

"Wouldn't you give anything to—"

"Almost anything," Lacey answered tersely, setting her eyes on Michael. Her gaze obviously didn't go unnoticed as he lifted one brow into a cruel arch, then purposely turned to watch his hand toying in Emma's hair.

It was some time later when Michael came to his feet, picked up a saddlebag, and headed out, pausing to say sternly, "You ladies stay put. I'll be back shortly."

"You really shouldn't let him do things like that," Lacey scolded when they were alone.

"He wasn't doing any harm. If I tolerate such harmless gestures, he's less likely to make bigger demands."

"I'd be more prone to say that if you give him an inch, he'll take a mile."

"I have to do the best I can, Lacey. I'm having trouble understanding why he behaves the way he does. But making him angry is not going to help either of us."

"You never did tell me what he said to you after you got him so angry."

"You never asked."

"We've hardly been alone," Lacey added, then she waited for Emma to answer. When it became apparent she wasn't going to, Lacey persisted. "Well, what did he say?"

Emma looked at her sister carefully. "You don't want to know. Trust me." The memory of Michael's threat came back to her clearly. Sharing Lacey's caution just now, she realized that Michael Hamilton's game was likely only beginning. Emma closed her eyes and prayed silently that she might emerge from this escapade unscathed. She thought of the trauma Lacey had suffered through the years as a result of her one stolen night with Tyson. And they had loved each other! What kind of long-range consequences would Emma endure if Michael Hamilton had his way with her? The thought made her nauseous. She squeezed her eyes together more tightly and prayed harder. She prayed not only for herself and Lacey, but that there might be something good in Michael that could be reached. She prayed that she would come to understand him, if only to help her deal with him. And she prayed that if there was anything redeemable in Michael at all, she would be able to reach it—if only to save herself.

With the long journey behind them, boredom compelled Emma and Lacey to lie down and take a nap. Emma woke to the feel of late afternoon. She first noticed Lacey still sleeping, then she turned to find Michael staring at her. The difference in him was immediately apparent.

"You're clean!" she exclaimed, whispering to avoid waking Lacey.

"But still despicable," he answered, as if to convince her. He took a sip of coffee from a tin cup wrapped in his hands. Emma watched him closely, thinking that it smelled good, but she didn't want to make any demands on him. As if he'd read her mind, Michael held the cup out toward her. Emma hesitated a moment, then she reached up a hand to take it. Michael was slow to let go, resulting in a lingering touch of their fingers against the warm tin. He finally relinquished his hold, but his eyes never left her as she took a long, careful sip, savoring the smell as something that reminded her of home. She held it up for him to take back, but he nodded slightly, which she interpreted as permission to drink more. She took another long swallow, then she gave it back, and he repeated the same lingering touch as the cup traded hands. Michael held her eyes to his with an unspoken magnetism as he immediately took a long sip, then brushed the back of his hand against his mustache to pull away the droplets of moisture clinging there.

Emma was surprised to feel her stomach flutter and her heart pound a little faster. She took a deep breath in an effort to dispel the feeling, but it only brought to her senses the clean, masculine smell of him that reminded her of that first night they had shared in the saddle. Her thoughts wandered as he drank again, and she scolded herself for bringing to mind the image of a roguish hero in a romance novel.

Emma felt his gaze deepen, as if he sensed what she was feeling. His piercing brown eyes scrutinized her, leaving her self-conscious as she tried to imagine how she must look after a week in the outback. Timidly she lowered her head to look away, but his finger touched her chin, lifting her face back to his gaze, silently challenging her to look at him.

"Emma." He drew her name out in a husky whisper, as if he meant to imply a hundred other words that she couldn't begin to grasp. For a moment Emma became lost in the depths of his eyes, searching for the motives she had often pondered. She saw his expression change, his eyes soften, and for a moment, she nearly expected him to apologize or confess something humbly. But he shook his head slightly and the coldness returned, though not so harshly as before.

"I have something for you," he said in a toneless whisper. He set down his cup and reached for the saddlebag he had taken with him earlier. Emma watched him throw open the flap and rummage inside while she drew a deep breath and pondered the feelings she had just experienced. It was as if a part of him held some magic over her that she was powerless to dispel.

"Here." He tossed a small bottle onto the blanket beside her leg. Emma reached down to pick it up and smiled. Lavender shampoo. "You said you would give anything," he added in such a harsh tone that Emma had to look up to see if it was the same man. "We'll discuss payment later."

"Then I don't want it," she insisted.

"It's too late." He picked up his cup and came to his feet. "Use it or don't. The payment will be what I decide. I've got some water heating for you outside. You can clean up and wash some clothes if you like." He glanced toward Lacey. "You'd better wake your sister or she won't sleep tonight."

Temporarily ignoring his demand for "payment," Emma looked again at the bottle in her hand. She couldn't help wondering and impulsively asked, "How did you know?"

"Know what?" He paused with the tent flap in his hand.

"Lavender. It's my favorite."

"Oh, that was easy." He smiled mischievously, almost endearingly. "I just went to this little shop and smelled them all until I found the one that smelled like you."

He left Emma wondering what Michael Hamilton suffered from. Was it insanity? Or something else that controlled his mind? Infatuation? Had he taken such notice of her that after four years he would recall how she smelled?

With no conclusive answer, Emma woke Lacey with the exciting announcement. "Look what I've got."

"Shampoo?" Lacey nearly squealed. "But is there any water?"

"There's some heating outside. Come on. Michael says we can clean up and wash some clothes."

They hurried outside to find Corky working on supper near the fire where Michael was testing the temperature of a kettle of water with his finger. The rest of the men were occupied with a rowdy game of cards near the other tent, far enough away to avoid being annoying. Michael caught Emma's eye. He bowed gallantly and motioned toward the water as if he were a valet. He sat on the ground and leaned against a smooth rock, making himself comfortable with a book. *So he reads,* Emma thought, wanting to get close enough to see what it was. But there were better things on her mind at the moment.

"There are towels in that box over there." Michael pointed, then returned to his reading, mumbling under his breath, "Nobody else uses them."

Lacey sat on another smooth rock, and Emma poured warm water over her hair. The shampoo was strong with fragrance and rich with lather. As Emma lathered and scrubbed, Lacey sighed gratefully and gave a genuine smile for the first time since this ordeal had begun. The suds soaked into the back of her shirt and trickled from the ends of her hair onto the ground.

"Can you smell this?" Emma asked. "It's fabulous."

"It reminds me of the soap Papa bought us last Christmas," Lacey replied brightly. "Here, give me some." She held up her hands, and Emma pulled suds from her hair to put some there. Lacey laughed and wiped the suds over her arms and throat. Emma pulled more suds from Lacey's hair and did the same.

"Should I rinse it now?" Emma asked.

"Oh no," Lacey insisted, "let it soak. I'll wash you first."

With her head and arms covered with suds, Lacey traded places with Emma and proceeded to wash her hair in the same manner. Emma pulled off her boots and stockings and rubbed her feet in the lather. Lacey laughed and did the same once Emma's hair was sufficiently scrubbed. Moments later, they were spreading suds over their clothes and giggling like children.

"Do you think they'll get clean while we're wearing them?" Lacey laughed.

"It couldn't hurt." Emma started rubbing suds over Lacey's back. She'd almost forgotten that they weren't alone until she happened to glance up and catch Michael's eye. His book was set aside as he watched with amused interest. His smile was almost pleasant, and Emma chose to smile in return. His smile deepened, and Emma felt warmed by it.

It was late before they made it to their beds, all spare clothing cleaned and left to dry, hair rinsed and brushed smooth, and bodies washed as much as possible with water they had taken into the tent to use in privacy.

Emma lay staring into the darkness while Lacey's breathing indicated an even sleep. She could hear the men talking and laughing in the distance, but she wondered where Michael was. Only then did she stop to consider how very separate he kept himself from his hired thugs, as if they held no interest for him outside of the work they could do. Emma could understand such bias, and she was grateful herself for the separation. She could stay near Michael and the others could keep their smelly, crude distance. Despite traveling together, she and Lacey had not been allowed close enough to them to even know most of their names. And that suited her fine.

Emma felt tired, but sleep eluded her in the face of what were becoming habitual thoughts. She pondered the many faces of Michael Hamilton she had seen, even today. And she found herself aching to know the real man. Or did she *really* want such a thing? Perhaps the truth of him was the part she didn't want to know. But what was it about him that intrigued her? And what about him had sent her heart pounding and her stomach fluttering earlier today? Was it possible that she'd become attracted to the man? A repeat performance of sensations filled her, as if to verify the answer. Looking back, she had to admit that not once had she felt repulsed by his presence. She had been disgusted by his behavior, yes. But villain or not, Michael Hamilton was an attractive man. How clearly she could imagine his long legs encased in narrow breeches, tucked into classic riding boots. His shirts were always black, and always elusively clinging to a hard chest and arms that she knew to be muscular by the easy way he could hoist her on or off a horse, or carry her as if she weighed no more than his saddlebags. She liked the way he looked in the flat-brimmed hat he often wore in the sun, tilted at a precarious angle to hide one eye just so. His stride was long, his stance wide, his hands large and capable. And his eyes—those vivid brown eyes, capable of implying more emotion than words ever could.

Yes, Emma had to admit it. As she realized how long she'd been lying here thinking about nothing but the way Michael Hamilton looked, she was attracted. Perhaps that made her as wicked as he, but denying it would only make her a hypocrite.

WAITING

Emma's thoughts stopped, along with her breathing, as Michael entered the dark tent. She could see his shadow hovering above her, and only then did she recall his repeated mention of "payment" for his gift. Like the devil coming to collect for indulged sins, Michael took a step toward her, whispering hoarsely, "Are you asleep?"

Emma felt her heart pound, though she had to wonder if it was from fear or from the thoughts that had been preoccupying her for the last hour. She was tempted to pretend she was asleep, but saw little point. He would likely do as he wished, whether that meant waking her or not. Before she could answer, he proved this with a gentle booted toe to her ribs. "Emma, are you asleep?"

"Lacey is, but . . . I can't seem to relax."

"Good." He knelt down beside her, and she recoiled. All thoughts of attraction and intrigue fled like mice scurrying from a huge, menacing, very hungry cat. Attractive or not, could she bear what he might do to her with motives far from love?

"How much do you think a bottle of shampoo is worth?" he asked like a proprietor.

She couldn't resist saying, "Only half as much as it was worth when you gave it to me."

"Why is that?"

"We used half the bottle."

"As I noticed." He chuckled.

"You found it rather amusing, then?" she asked, hoping this encounter would remain in clever conversation.

"I found myself thinking about you." His voice lowered and fear seized her. "I like to think about you, Emma." He touched her face with the back of his hand. "You didn't know that, did you."

"I do now," she replied, wishing her voice hadn't trembled.

Abruptly Michael sat close beside her.

"Michael," she breathed with difficulty.

"What?" he finally said, so close to her face that it startled her.

"What are you going to do to me?" she asked.

"I thought we could discuss that souvenir for your father."

"I thought we were discussing payment for the shampoo."

"Perhaps we could accomplish both with the same task." Panic set in and Emma squirmed in a futile effort to push him away.

"Michael, no!" she insisted, but he clamped a hand over her mouth.

Lacey woke up with her heart pounding and listened for what might have caused it. A brief silence was followed by a muffled moan, and she panicked. It happened again, and she whispered frantically, "Emma, are you all right?"

"Blast!" She heard Michael's voice through the darkness and her fear increased. Drawing great courage, Lacey felt for the lamp, struck a match, and lit it. What she saw made her go cold with a fear that seemed to tease at something long buried inside of her; something she didn't want to look at and chose to push away. She concentrated instead on the moment, wondering what kind of fiend they'd been imprisoned by. It didn't take much imagination for Lacey to guess what Michael's intentions were. His hand over her mouth and the fear in Emma's eyes were all too evident. Once the situation was absorbed, Lacey found the iced fury of Michael's eyes cutting into her. But for the moment, she didn't care.

"You fiend!" she spat, and Emma admired her courage. She knew it wasn't easy for Lacey to be so bold with those who intimidated her. But she was doing it for Emma's sake. "How dare you think you can—"

"Do you mind, Lacey?" he interrupted with calm irritation. "We were just discussing payment for certain . . . niceties."

"I will not stand by and allow you to—"

Her words were cut short as Michael's hand left Emma's mouth and reached beside her head to pick up a pistol that Emma hadn't even known was there. He cocked it carefully and pressed it to Emma's temple. Lacey gasped and her face turned red from anger, then white from fear. Emma's breath turned sharp with fearful gasps. While she truly believed he would never do something so barbaric, the possibility was terrifying. The incident stirred a childhood memory that in itself had little effect on Emma. But she wondered if Lacey had made the same connection.

"Lacey," Michael said calmly, "douse the light and go back to sleep, or I shall blow a hole into your sister's pretty little head. Do I need to expound on that?"

Lacey hesitated. "Do it, Lacey," Emma insisted, her voice trembling in conjunction with the fear pounding in her chest. Lacey immediately doused the flame.

Emma let out a slow breath of relief when he removed the gun and set it back on the ground beside her. He was still for a moment, and she wondered what he would do now. Would he have the nerve to persist with his threats, knowing that Lacey was wide awake? Abruptly he let out a heavy sigh and muttered angrily, "Go to sleep, Emma." There was something subtle in his voice that made her wonder if he was actually glad to have an excuse to back down.

Michael settled his head next to hers, and she felt him relax. She eased a safe distance away and he didn't protest. Emma attempted to relax, hardly daring to breathe too deeply. Her mind raced through the encounter over and over. She couldn't deny the fear she'd felt. But neither could she deny the instinct surging through her that Michael Hamilton was little more than an overgrown bully. Perhaps it was the memory of his tenderness toward her in the stable years ago that made it difficult to believe he would really hurt her. Or maybe it was more. Still, she couldn't be completely comfortable, knowing there were complexities in Michael's head that she could never understand.

Emma was finally able to relax when she heard his breathing fall into a steady rhythm. When she knew he was sleeping, she whispered carefully, "Lacey, are you asleep?"

"You must be joking," she replied quietly.

"It's all right, Lacey. He didn't hurt me."

"But what about next time?" Lacey asked.

"I don't know, but . . . We'll talk tomorrow."

She heard Lacey moan in angry frustration and added, "It's all right, Lacey. Go to sleep."

"Eventually," was all she said before Emma finally drifted off. She awoke to sunlight and found Michael sleeping soundly. The reality caused Emma to pause and watch him in a whole new light. In sleep, all cruelty and menace was absent from his face, and something innocent shone through that was almost startling. That sensation of attraction overwhelmed her, and the man who had held a gun to her head in the night seemed nonexistent. Emma felt an entirely different type of emotion fill her as she pondered the reasons why Michael would behave so cruelly. To see him now, she could almost imagine the hurt, lost little boy who had come reluctantly into her parents' care. She wondered what kind of horrors he might have encountered prior to that time, and her heart went out to him. She recalled her mother's frequent adage in dealing with difficult people—most specifically the boys she had counseled and nurtured. "Unconditional love is vital," she would say, "but no more vital than firm boundaries. If you allow someone to treat you badly, then the love can't get through."

Emma marveled at the love her mother had given those who had passed through their lives, and for the first time in her life, Emma felt a desire to emulate that love. Was it possible for her to reach beyond Michael's cruel exterior and find something good in him? Only if she didn't allow him to bully her, she concluded from her mother's advice. Of course, he was physically stronger than she was, and she didn't know which characteristics were most prominent in his mind. Still, she couldn't help feeling drawn to him now.

Once she had confirmed that her sister was asleep, Emma tentatively reached out a hand to touch Michael's face, noting the masculine texture enhanced by sun and wind. In his sleep, Michael moved closer to her hand and she retracted it briefly, fearing he would awaken. Was it her touch that made him dream? She softened her touch as her motivation shifted to an offering of comfort. He groaned again, and Emma felt almost afraid on his behalf. She was wondering if she should wake him when Michael came awake with a breathy, fearful gasp. He lifted his head to look down at her, his eyes wide with unconcealed terror. The brief fear was washed away by a vivid relief as he saw her there and Emma could hear him attempting to steady his breath.

"Are you all right?" she felt compelled to ask. He nodded quickly. "You were dreaming," she whispered gently.

"Yes, I know," he admitted, rolling abruptly onto his back, his eyes distant, still betraying a hint of fear.

Emma wanted so badly to ask what frightened the tough Michael Hamilton. But the question was pointless. She knew he wouldn't answer any such inquiry. She opted instead to ask, "Do you want to tell me about it?"

He turned to look at her in surprise, and for a long moment they silently attempted to absorb the other's thoughts.

"Why do you care what I was dreaming?" he asked with cynicism.

"Why did you buy me lavender shampoo?" she retorted, almost certain that both questions had similar answers. If Emma could admit that she was intrigued with Michael Hamilton, then it was apparent by his actions that he was at least the same with her.

Michael turned his eyes back toward the roof of the tent. He said nothing.

"You don't have to tell me, but it might make you feel better," she urged.

"I doubt it."

"Try."

"Fine. I was dreaming about my father. I've had the same dream for nearly twenty years. There. I don't feel any better."

Emma leaned onto one elbow to look down at him. "But you didn't tell me about the dream."

Michael looked at her deeply, and a sudden chill rushed over her as she saw a hint of something raw and vulnerable and scared. With more sincerity than she had ever heard from him, he said deeply, "Trust me, Emma. You don't want to know."

Emma held his eyes for a moment and saw evidence of what she had suspected. There was something deeply troubled in him; something that caused behavior worthy of her fear. But she also realized that there was something inside of him that he feared as well. The man was afraid of himself. Emma recalled her father briefly mentioning something about a time in his life when he had feared himself. She would give a great deal to discuss this with her father now—and her mother, as well. She knew Alexa had a great deal of insight concerning Michael, and her wisdom would have been very useful at the moment.

But Emma was on her own, fighting to defend herself and her sister from this unpredictable man with dual natures of black and white, and a good deal of gray in between.

Michael came to his feet, looked down at Emma with contemplative eyes, then stooped to pick up his pistol from the ground. "I'll get you some breakfast," he announced, and left her alone. Emma sighed, wondering where all of this would take them in the days left before her father's arrival. It seemed like forever.

The reality of the long days ahead came in the afternoon, as Emma and Lacey found themselves intolerably bored. At home they would have gone riding, or played with Richard, or any number of other pastimes. Emma decided she'd give anything to have a romance novel to read. On second thought, to have *anything* to read. They might have been able to ease the boredom with some good conversation, but Michael was rarely far away. And more often he was in the tent with them, sprawled over his bedroll, reading that book. That book! Michael had a book, which he had been totally absorbed in over the past several hours.

Curiosity and desperation spurred Emma on without thought. She eased closer to Michael to examine the book more closely. His eyes shifted to her quickly, but he ignored her and returned to his reading.

"*Rogue of the Plains?*" She read the title aloud, grabbing the book from his hands. "I've read that one."

"Then kindly let me do the same." He tersely took it back. "You lost my place," he growled, thumbing through the pages in blatant irritation.

"What are you reading that stuff for?" she questioned, while Lacey looked on in practiced disbelief.

Michael quipped like a bookseller, "It has all the adventure and romance we readers hunger for." His voice returned to normal. "Don't ask stupid questions. Now leave me alone and let me read!"

"Do you have any more?" she asked far too humbly. Lacey rolled her eyes, foreseeing this obvious setup.

Michael looked cautiously over the top of the book, his eyes over-flowing with mischief. "I might."

"I'd give anything to have a book to read," Emma said impulsively, then slapped a hand over her mouth as the words came back to her.

Michael raised an eyebrow and Emma retorted, "You know that's simply a figure of speech."

Michael casually opened a box that had been present since their arrival, and he pulled out another half dozen novels.

"You brute!" Emma scolded. "You've been holding out on me!"

"Do you enjoy reading?" he asked with such obvious innocence in his eyes that Emma knew he was teasing her. If he had observed her enough to know that she preferred lavender, he had surely seen the way she often carried a novel wherever she had gone during her teen years.

"Quite," was all she said.

"I trust you can find enough there to entertain yourself for a few days."

"Thank you." Emma gave him a mocking smile, and Michael returned it.

"Lacey?" He held a book out toward her as Emma chose one that seemed intriguing. Lacey hesitated and he added, "I realize it's not your favorite pastime, but seeing that Tyson is not with us . . ."

He left the sentence unfinished as Lacey's eyes filled with fury at having a sore nerve too closely touched. She grabbed the book from him, turned her back and commenced reading, knowing she would go insane otherwise.

As Emma became involved in the story, the habitual image of Michael Hamilton came into her mind. With an eerie reality, she lifted her eyes from the pages to observe him stretched out on his chest, his knees bent upward so that his booted ankles were crossed in the air. As a recently familiar tremor of intrigue filtered through her, the reality dawned in her mind. There was only one reason these books were here. He had known she loved them. It was just like the shampoo. And she would wager a great deal that his biggest motive in reading the book in his hands was simply to draw her attention to the fact that he had them.

Not wanting Lacey to overhear and misconstrue her bizarre interest in Michael, Emma scooted toward him and imitated his position right beside him.

"Michael," she whispered. He grunted softly but continued to read. "Why are you reading a romance novel?"

"I told you already. Why are we whispering?" Emma glanced toward Lacey, who was reading, oblivious to their conversation. He nodded slightly and returned his attention to his book.

"No, you told me why readers in general read them," she retorted. "I want to know why *you* read them."

Michael turned his head to look at her eye to eye, almost touching his nose to hers. His lips spread over his teeth with no evidence of a smile. "I'm looking for ideas of how to torment you. The villains in these books are great inspiration."

"Some of them end up being the hero in the end." She played along.

"But not the kind of hero for you, Emma," he said too seriously. "In real life, rogues with bad reputations and bad blood do not end up happily ever after with spoiled little rich girls."

There was something cutting in his statement that, for no good reason, brought a burning of moisture into Emma's eyes. After all he'd said and done to her, she wondered why she would be prone to tears when he told her she was spoiled. Or perhaps it was the disillusionment of romantic stories in contrast to real life that prompted her emotion. Whatever it was, Emma was caught off guard, and unable to hide the tears before Michael saw them.

"What?" he quipped with malice, and she turned abruptly away. He caught her chin and forced her to look at him. A tear trickled over her cheek. "Did I hurt your feelings? How brash of me!"

"Shut up and read!" she said loudly enough to draw Lacey's attention. Emma turned and sat up, putting her face into her hand until the emotion was under control. They all went back to their books and remained there, except for mealtimes, until it was too dark to read.

When they were finished with the evening meal, Lacey and Emma returned to the tent to go to bed. Emma wondered where Michael was, but gave it little thought as they pulled off their boots in the darkness and found their beds. Emma's question was answered when a familiar hand clamped over her mouth. Her heart pounded as she realized he was beginning to make her afraid of the dark.

"Don't do anything," he whispered in her ear, his words barely audible, "to indicate that I'm here, or you will regret it, I promise you." He hesitated a moment, and she absorbed his threat. "All right?" he added. She nodded firmly, and he removed his hand to allow her to breathe.

Emma tried to relax, but her every nerve was rigid with awareness and fear. She hoped that Lacey would fall quickly to sleep. But as if to directly contradict the thought, her sister's voice came out of the darkness. "Emma, have you thought much about Tyson lately?"

In all honesty, her mind had been quite preoccupied with Michael. "Not much, why?"

She felt Michael's bearded lips come against the side of her neck, and she had to use great self-discipline to keep from reacting audibly. His hand pressed down her arm with a touch that was gentle, almost fragile.

"I was just wondering," Lacey answered as if nothing was out of the ordinary, "if you had sensed what he was feeling."

Michael became still for a moment, as if he had paused to ponder Lacey's meaning.

Lacey went on and so did Michael, moving his fingers tentatively up and down her arm as if it was terribly fascinating. "The last time we talked about it," she said, "you told me you could sense . . . how did you put it?"

"Grief," Emma answered. Michael paused again, then he leaned onto his elbow to reach further down her arm, seeming fascinated by her fingers before his hand moved back up with gentle purpose to her shoulder.

"Has it changed?" Lacey asked with longing.

Emma wasn't certain she wanted Michael to be a part of this conversation, but she could see no way to avoid it. She had to be truthful with Lacey, or she would sense that something was amiss.

"I don't know," Emma answered. "I haven't thought about him much, and—"

"Think about him now," Lacey nearly pleaded, "and tell me what you feel."

"It's not as easy as all that," Emma justified. "It's not like I can just look into a crystal ball and see his feelings."

"I know, but you can sense them."

"Not necessarily at my own will. Sometimes it just . . . happens."

"Try," Lacey pleaded. "Just think of him, and try. I miss him so desperately."

"I'll try," Emma conceded, knowing it would at least temporarily end the conversation. But it was difficult to gear her thoughts to Tyson while Michael's lips were toying freely with her ear. She squeezed her eyes closed and tried to think of Tyson, attempting to shut out the reality of Michael's touch and how it affected her. *Tyson!* She told herself to think of Tyson.

"Tyson," she said aloud in an effort to focus on him. Michael paused at the sound, and for a full minute he did nothing. "Tyson," she repeated in a whisper, trying to envision what he looked like. Michael relaxed beside her, as if he was allowing her undistracted time to achieve her purpose. Something about the act warmed her.

Gradually a clear image of Tyson came to mind. She could see him sitting on the steps of the porch, his elbows on his knees, a day's growth on his face, a sly smile sparkling in his eyes. The picture became vivid, and she felt a longing for him that she hadn't had the capacity to feel since she had been dragged from her bed by Michael's hired thugs. With purpose she concentrated on him, wanting to feel his thoughts. She couldn't recall ever doing this consciously before. It had always just come accidentally. When the feeling struck her, Emma gasped. She was both surprised that it had come at all, and shocked by what she felt.

"What?" Lacey insisted. "Is it Tyson?"

"I think so," she whispered. "Just a minute. Just a minute." Emma squeezed her eyes shut. Michael withdrew further, as if to allow her more space for thought. The gesture seemed to show respect for her relationship with her brother.

"Tyson," she said with longing, catching the spectrum of what he felt with enough verity to know that it couldn't be anything else.

"Tell me," Lacey insisted.

"It's anger," she reported quietly. "The longing and grief are still there. But the dominant feeling is anger. No," she corrected, "angry fear. But the fear is not for himself."

Lacey sat up. "Perhaps he is coming for us," she said with a gleeful hope.

"Perhaps," Emma said noncommittally, "but don't count on it."

"Do you feel anything else?" Lacey asked expectantly.

"No." Emma's voice turned downhearted as a combination of realities consumed her. "Perhaps we should get some sleep." Michael apparently liked this suggestion as he resumed his game.

"Emma?" Lacey asked cautiously. "Aren't you afraid Michael will . . . well. . . you know."

Emma felt a devious chuckle come softly into her ear, but she took the opportunity to display some open trust toward Michael, whether he deserved it or not. "No," she said, and Michael froze. "I don't believe he really wants to hurt me, and I don't think he will."

"I hope you're right," Lacey remarked with doubt in her voice. "Good night, Emma."

"Good night."

"Good night," Michael whispered in her ear, adding with malevolence, "You don't know me very well, do you."

Emma thought further on trust, recalling her mother's observation that displaying trust could often bring miraculous results. Alexa had told her that often the boys in the home had never been trusted, and they lived up to that reputation. But when they were given trust, they usually acted on it.

With a combination of defiance and longing, Emma turned to face Michael. She found his ear with her lips and whispered carefully, "Perhaps it's the other way around."

Michael sighed and rolled onto his back. Emma pushed her trust one step further and laid a relaxed head on his shoulder. When it became apparent that his advances were temporarily put to rest, Emma lifted her head long enough to whisper, "What's the matter?"

He gave no response, and Emma fell asleep before he made any attempt to move. She awoke the following morning to find him gone. She picked up her book and began to read until Michael came in with some breakfast. Without a word exchanged, he sat to begin another novel, having finished *Rogue of the Plains* the previous evening. It was shortly after their noon meal that he abruptly came to his feet and held out a hand toward Emma.

"Where are we going?" she asked without taking it.

"For a walk," he insisted, the cruelty glaring in his eyes.

Emma hesitated. He grabbed her arm and forced her to her feet.

Lacey gasped and gave Emma a pleading look that Michael answered with a firm, "You stay put and keep quiet."

"Rafe!" Michael called when he had Emma outside. "Guard that girl, and don't let her out of your sight."

"You're hurting me," Emma protested at the firm grip he held her with as he dragged her along.

"How dreadful for you," he stated in boredom without relinquishing his hold in the slightest. He forced her to climb up smooth rocks that seemed vaguely familiar to her, and she wondered if she might have come to this place as a child. With the treks her family had made to the outback, she decided it was likely.

They moved up and around, coming to the top of the cave that was presently storing supplies. Michael stopped near a steeply rising rock wall that shielded the sun this time of day. He pushed Emma's back up against the rock and placed his hands on either side of her head, moving his feet out behind him until the two of them were equal in height.

"What do you want?" she hissed.

"I want to be away from observing eyes—and ears. It's about time we got on with the best part of the game. I call it . . . ," he drew his lips back to enunciate, "payment of debts."

"And what exactly would that be?" Emma managed to keep a steady voice.

"Don't play stupid, Emma." He chuckled from his throat. "Surely you know what I want." His voice turned almost warm. "Actually," he added, "I'm tired of playing games with you, Emma."

Emma turned away, but he jerked her chin back to face him. When it had been made clear that she was not to move, Michael rubbed his thumb over her cheek, commencing in a detailed exploration of her face with hot, calloused fingers. Emma held her breath, feeling neither afraid nor angry. But perhaps puzzled. His repeated advances in the past had never proven to cross the borders he'd threatened, and she prayed this encounter would end as favorably. She watched Michael closely, fascinated to observe him now, when his prior advances had taken place in the dark. She was more convinced each day that the truth behind Michael's motives significantly involved his feelings for her, however misguided.

After minutes of play with her face, Michael pushed his hand behind her neck, lifting her throat to his lips. Emma gasped and found her hands at his shoulders, resisting futilely. Her heart began to pound. Emma tried to feel her instincts, waiting for the fear and disgust to come forward and provoke her to fight him off. But they didn't come. She felt her palms turn sweaty and heard pulsebeats in her ears. But what she felt deep within had nothing to do with fear. She couldn't will herself to fight, or even to respond. So she did nothing. Michael looked at her face, seeming to question her willingness to allow this, and Emma realized that he wanted her to protest. He wanted her to fight. Was that part of his game? If so, she would not allow him to win.

"I thought you would find me repulsive." He affirmed her suspicions in a roundabout way.

"And why should I?"

"I'm everything you would never want to have holding you."

"Are you trying to tell me that you are as devilish as you are devilishly handsome?" Emma had to fight for a straight face, seeing how she'd thrown him off guard.

"You flatter me, Miss Davies."

"No," she nearly whispered, compelled to press her confrontation as she began to see that she was more in control here than she had realized, "one of us is honest."

"I am many deplorable things, Emma, but I am not a liar."

"And how would you know?" She gained confidence as she felt herself beginning to figure him out, if only a little. "You're so dishonest with yourself that you wouldn't know truth if it spat in your face."

For a moment, Michael showed no emotion. He was completely unreadable. Only the silence indicated that her statement had bitten him.

"Let's get on with it, shall we?" he asked, as if his physical supremacy was his only defense. He pulled her closer, reminding her formidably that what control she had gained was no match for his strength. His eyes pierced hers, arrogantly implying that he had every right to hold her this way.

"You won't get away with it," she said, wondering once again if he would actually have the nerve to make good his threats. "Damaged goods don't bring a high price."

"And how would your father know?" Michael's face was so close she could feel the heat from his eyes.

"I would tell him."

"Not before I have the money, you won't." Emma felt the dismay in her eyes, and he chuckled. "Nice try, Emma, but I'm still in control here."

"Is that what this is about? Control?"

"Quite."

"Don't get too cocky, Mr. Hamilton. You might find yourself out-done yet."

"By a couple of cackling hens, I suppose." He laughed and brought a finger to her lips, touching them in meek exploration. His gentle manner contradicted his cruel attitude. He moved his face toward hers, and Emma turned her head quickly.

"What's the matter?" He chuckled, then his voice lowered rough-ly. "Do I frighten you?"

"No," she lied. "I . . . I just don't want you to kiss me."

"Why not?" He seemed to find her bluntness amusing.

"Because I . . ." She turned to look at him, almost wanting to admit that she feared her own emotions. . . emotions that seemed to weaken her resolve to stand up against his threats. But she opted to tell him a different truth. "I've never been kissed before," she admitted, and his eyes widened in genuine surprise. "I have no desire for my first kiss to be forced and manipulated. If you must do it, try to gather some decency and bear that in mind."

Michael's eyes actually softened. But Emma wondered if he was acting the gentle suitor now, just as she had seen him act many other parts in the past several days.

"How do you want it to be, Emma?" he whispered, elusively brushing the back of his hand over her face. "Do you lie awake at night and dream of being kissed? Is that why you read those books, Emma? Can you see yourself being carried across the plains by a rogue on a black stallion?" He urged her face closer. Emma felt her shoulders rise and fall with each breath she took. He took hold of her chin to prevent her from moving. "And when he takes you in his arms, despite all your fears, is there something in you that longs for his kiss?" His voice lowered further, his face came closer. "How do you want it to be?" he repeated. "Timid? Passionate?" He pressed his mouth to her cheek. "Or both?"

Emma's lips parted with a longing that she knew couldn't be concealed. Michael drew back only slightly. She saw him close his eyes and she did the same, holding her breath as his lips timidly met hers. He drew back again. Their eyes opened and met. He touched her lips again while he watched her. Emma closed her eyes to avoid reality.

When she felt certain she could bear no more without making a complete fool of herself, Michael pulled away, his eyes seeming to question her response. Emma felt a defensiveness rise in her, not willing to admit what she felt for him, when the majority of his actions made him so undeserving of her affection.

"Now we're even," she said even more spitefully than she'd intended. "I have given you my first kiss. My debts are paid."

The hurt that came into Michael's eyes was so brief that Emma might have believed she'd imagined it, except that it was so vivid and undeniable. As his now-cold eyes searched her expression, Emma contemplated his reaction briefly. Her denial of response to his kiss had hurt him. In that instant, a very big piece of the puzzle fell into place. She had taken his motives through many stages, but none of them had felt quite right. She had seen his purposes evolve from greed to desire to vengeance. And perhaps there were degrees of all those things involved. But what Emma saw now was startling. Michael Hamilton was after love. In disbelief she tried to absorb it. He kissed her again as if it might bring back the response he had felt initially. Emma fought to hold back, and sure enough, when he pulled away, he was disappointed. And though the hurt was guarded, she saw it unmistakably. But what did he expect after the way he'd treated her? It wasn't like he'd been courting and wooing her all these days.

Impulsively she said, "If it's love you're looking for, Michael, you won't get it for nothing."

"I can steal love," he retorted, urging her closer as if to prove it.

"What you may choose to steal will never bring you love. Only when you give love will it come back to you."

He seemed to contemplate the theory, but his eyes turned cold and harsh. His defenses went up like a brick wall. With a purpose that left Emma downhearted, Michael repeated, as if it was his only defense, "I can steal love." Then he silenced her with a kiss.

❦   ❦   ❦

As soon as Lacey was left alone, she felt a cold fear on Emma's behalf. But the fear quickly shifted to herself when the smelly impersonation of a human being entered the tent, his eyes blazing with mischief. He licked his lips in a way that made Lacey want to throw up, and it took only a moment to be certain that his motives were not to guard her as he'd been ordered.

"I been wonderin' when I'd have a chance to get my hands on one o' you pretty little things," he mumbled, looming toward her. Lacey came carefully to her feet and backed away, well aware of the knife in his hand. Trying to be courageous, she reasoned logically that Emma couldn't be far. Silently she prayed they would return soon as she took one bold chance and ran for the door. Rafe grabbed her around the waist, and she screamed with everything she could muster, praying Emma was not too far away to hear. As Rafe attempted to cover her mouth with a filthy hand, Lacey squirmed out of his reach and bolted away. She felt his hand come around her ankle, tripping her so that she fell halfway out of the tent, struggling to get free. She screamed again and became aware of the other men moving closer. But she'd wager they would be more willing to cheer than assist her. As she attempted to wrench her ankle from the firm grip holding it, Lacey felt Rafe's other hand take hold of her leg—the hand that held the knife. She felt the accidental slicing of her lower leg, and looked down to see Rafe let go as blood spilled over his hands.

Lacey's fear shifted again as she became lightheaded from the sudden loss of blood, and she could only hope her sister returned before she passed out.

❦   ❦   ❦

Michael's forced kiss was interrupted by a high-pitched, feminine scream that could only be Lacey. Michael ran like a madman, seeming to know that Emma would follow to come to the aid of her sister.

Emma could only see Michael's back as his stride far outdid hers, leaving her frantically running, aching to get to Lacey.

"What are you doing?" she heard Michael shriek, but it was directed at Rafe, not Lacey.

"She tried to run," the big oaf defended, wiping the blood on his breeches. "I had to stop her!"

Lacey cried out in her own defense. "He tried to have his way with me." She sobbed with an edge of pain, and Emma brushed past Michael in search of the source of blood.

"No," Emma cried, going to her knees beside Lacey, gaping in disbelief at the deep slash running vertically up her lower leg. Blood gushed onto the ground while Lacey turned steadily more pale from the shock.

"Do you see what your game has done now?" Emma screamed at Michael, but he obviously wasn't listening. He moved ominously toward Rafe, who backed away reluctantly, fear showing in his eyes.

Emma quickly found her long-unused nightgown, which she started tearing apart, pausing to urge Lacey to remain calm. While Emma worked to put pressure on the wound, she kept half an eye on Michael, wondering how he would handle this.

"You fool!" Michael shouted. "You stupid fool. I didn't tell you to play with her. I told you to guard her. Now look what you've done." He quoted Emma, "Damaged goods don't bring a high price! You stupid, idiotic fool!"

He stopped talking, and Emma turned her full attention to Lacey until she heard Rafe give a guttural moan. She snapped her head back to find him doubled over in pain. A moment later Michael sent a fist into Rafe's jaw, not once, but twice, three times, four, until Emma started to wince on Rafe's behalf. Rafe was a hand taller than Michael and weighed at least fifty pounds more. But he appeared helpless against Michael's quick agility and well-rehearsed fist. Rafe began to fall, but Michael took hold of his shirt to hold him steady while he hit him a few more times, ending with a knee in the stomach and a boot in the backside for good measure. Rafe fell to the ground with an anguished groan. Michael turned and walked away as if he'd just fed his horse or closed a gate.

"Why did you do that?" Emma insisted as he approached her. "It won't do any good now."

"The others won't want to bother either one of you, now will they.

Besides, any man who would try to force himself upon a helpless woman deserves more than what I just gave him."

Emma wanted to ask if that was another of his jokes. But he was so intently serious that she wondered if he was mad. Outright hypocrisy was one of the symptoms. Or perhaps he was implying that Lacey was helpless, and Emma was not.

"How bad is it?" He knelt beside Emma and removed the compress she held against the wound. "Blast!" he muttered under his breath and pressed it back. He looked at Lacey's paling face, then he met Emma's eyes with intensity. Emma felt a warming between them as she read sincere apology there, though he would likely not admit to it verbally. In view of what he had just done to Rafe, who was beginning to drag himself off the ground, Emma began to see Michael more as a protector than a persecutor.

"What do you have in the way of medical supplies?" Emma asked.

"I fear that's something I overlooked." His voice turned regretful, almost humble. That rare sincerity was evident. He wasn't acting.

"Well, surely there is a bottle of alcohol somewhere around here that we can clean it with." She glanced toward the other tent to indicate the rough bunch they were living with.

"I told them no drinking, and they knew I meant it."

"You mean there's nothing?" Emma squeaked.

Michael hesitated, then shook his head. Emma closed her eyes and swallowed hard. "And I'm certain that Rafe kept his knife as impeccably clean as he keeps himself," she snapped with sarcasm. "He probably uses it to pick his teeth and clean his fingernails, if such a notion ever crossed his mind."

Michael said nothing, but she felt his eyes on her, the apology deepening. "We'll just have to do the best we can," he said. "I'll get some water, and we'll try to clean it."

Michael returned moments later and lifted Lacey onto her makeshift bed. Four hands worked as two, gently flushing the wound and bandaging it tightly.

"Perhaps we should stitch it," Emma said as an afterthought.

"We have nothing to stitch it with," he replied soberly. Emma gave a sigh of disgust. "Well," he justified, "I was not coming out here to mend my breeches."

"Next time you plan such an escapade, perhaps you should consult a woman."

"I'll be sure to drop by and solicit your opinion." The anger in his voice began to rise.

"Oh, stop it," she demanded, too concerned for Lacey to have the strength to banter.

"I'm so sorry, Emma. You must believe me." Emma looked up in search of sincerity and was surprised to find it. "We'll do everything we can." He said it as if she had already been pronounced dead. If infection set in before her father got there, she likely could be.

"So am I." Emma shot her eyes back to Lacey, dismissing Michael's presence. But he stayed, quietly observing her gentle care of her sister.

Time flew and stood still until he asked in a low voice, "Are you hungry?"

"No, but Lacey should eat something."

"I'll get it." He stood and walked out.

Emma put a comforting hand on Lacey's brow. "Is the pain any less?"

"Let's just say I'm getting used to it. I thought he'd never leave."

"He's concerned."

"If he was concerned, we wouldn't be here."

"He beat Rafe into the ground."

Lacey looked surprised but said nothing. Michael returned with plenty of food for both Lacey and Emma. Lacey ate heartily with her leg propped onto a folded blanket. But Emma felt little appetite while she contemplated why, after all that had happened, she was defending Michael Hamilton to her sister.

That night while Lacey slept soundly, Emma lay in the darkness, listening as Michael came in and groaned out of his boots. All became silent, but she felt his presence fill the confined space of the tent as his eyes absorbed her through the darkness. She couldn't see his face any more than he could see hers, but still, she felt his presence. Something formless drew her to him, and the reality of that was disturbing. Was she so naive, so thirsty for adventure, so wanton, that she would find herself warming to such a villain?

He moved, and she was not surprised to find his touch on her shoulder. She turned toward him and he whispered against her face, "Your sister is asleep. Don't scream or I'll have to cut out your tongue."

"One of your jokes?" she whispered back. "Amusing, I must say." Her sarcasm was intense.

"I don't think it's very amusing." His tone was so fierce that she could easily fathom him being the worst of men. But at the same time, she found it difficult to take him seriously when he said such things. "I dare say it would make a terrible mess."

Impulsively Emma reached beside her head and found Michael's pistol in the usual place where he left it while he played this game. She heard him catch his breath as she pressed the barrel to his throat. Emma knew she could never pull the trigger. But the bluff was worth indulging in, if only to see his reaction. He didn't move or speak. Emma cocked it.

"Go ahead, Emma," he said, sounding more sad than anything, "put me out of my misery. I've never had the guts to do it myself. But before you get trigger happy, I want you to consider one thing. If I'm gone, you'd be at the mercy of far worse."

"That's true," she said, knowing he was absolutely right, especially after what had happened to Lacey today. "Besides, it would make a terrible mess."

Carefully she retracted the gun and reset the hammer efficiently, making it clear that she knew how to use a gun. She set it aside, admitting quietly, "I couldn't have done it anyway."

"I know," he replied with arrogance.

"What are you going to do to me?" she asked, realizing she hardly cared.

"Anything that might humiliate you and make you plead for mercy. Anything to put the spoiled little rich girl in her place."

"Is that what this is all about?" she asked.

"I've told you before, and I hate to repeat myself. I need the money."

"And something more that you're not admitting to."

"I don't have to admit anything to you, my sweet. Right now you are mine, and I intend to take advantage of it before your gallant father arrives. Perhaps your brother will come as well, and we could have a party."

"My brother is long gone."

Michael lifted his head from his attention to her ear, expressing surprise through the darkness.

"He left home four years ago. I thought you had figured that out by now."

"Forgive me. I didn't. Fine. No parties."

Emma felt compelled to add, "He left the same week you did."

Michael ignored her. Instead he turned her to face him, pressing his mouth over hers. Emma consciously tried to detach her mind from what he was capable of making her feel, certain that being cold would achieve more for her than putting up a fight. She kept expecting him to get serious, but he seemed content to kiss her, almost timidly, without becoming too bold or presumptuous.

"Emma," he murmured, and she realized his menacing side was completely absent. The Michael with her now was sensitive and loving in spite of himself, and she found it impossible not to respond.

She pressed her arms around him and returned his kiss. "Oh, Michael."

She gasped, then held her breath as Michael bolted to his feet as if he'd been struck by lightning. Emma lay feeling empty from the sudden distance between them. She could hear his heated breath that matched her own, while she gazed at his tense form silhouetted in the darkness. With no further exchange, he tore out of the tent like fire was at his heels. He didn't return until he brought breakfast, which he left without a word spoken; there was only a coldness in his eyes that made Emma wonder over her own motives.

Pushing her confusion away, Emma stayed near Lacey, seeing to her needs as much as possible. The bleeding had stopped, but the wound didn't look good at all. Emma was worried—with good reason.

Seven
THE STORM

Two days passed while Lacey remained mostly bedridden, and Michael remained aloof. He kept a vigilant eye on them, but all bantering between him and Emma ceased. Emma sensed signs of disgruntlement rising in the camp outside. She felt this was partially due to Michael's treatment of Rafe, and enhanced by his sour mood, which had worsened considerably since Emma's last encounter with him. Had her brief response to his affection struck him so deeply? She speculated over it until her head ached, then she had to ask herself why she even cared.

Emma's thoughts were interrupted by Michael's loud voice outside. The commotion brought Lacey to a sitting position. They looked at each other anxiously, but there was so much shouting they could hardly discern more than a word here and there. Eventually they recognized Corky's voice, as if he represented the rest of them in coming against Michael's leadership. Words filtered through: disrespect, money, lives, coward, going soft, stupid fool. Then all of it stopped cold as a gun cocked and Michael stated clearly, "Get on your knees and take off the hat."

"No," Emma said aloud, attempting to stand. But Lacey mustered all her strength to hold Emma back.

"You mustn't get involved. He'll kill you, too."

"No," Emma repeated, feeling far more unsettled than Lacey could ever understand.

Two shots rang out, then a hush followed until Michael's cold voice said, "Get him out of here!"

Another day's silence left Emma continually sickened by the reality that Michael had killed a man in cold blood. Had his cruelty pressed him to kill before? Had he forced himself on other women and succeeded? The confusion tore at Emma and she ached to be away from here, away from him. But far worse was the reality of Lacey's leg becoming infected, and she was helpless to do anything about it.

Emma was distracted by another commotion outside and hurried out before Lacey could stop her. She could see Michael arguing with Rafe while the others hovered around curiously. Emma was about to move closer so she could hear better when Rafe pulled a gun and pointed it at Michael. At the moment, all she could think of were Michael's own words: *If I'm gone, you'd be at the mercy of far worse.*

Panic rushed to her heart and she began to run, but she'd barely taken three steps when a shot rang out, then another. Emma screamed, and all eyes turned to her as Michael fell to his knees and rolled forward.

"How could you?" she screamed at Rafe, kneeling beside Michael and turning him over. The men all stood silently observing as she pulled his head into her lap. Michael coughed and gasped, clutching helplessly at his chest.

"Oh, Michael." She felt his eyes focus weakly on her. She was unashamed of the tears she shed on his behalf, and her feelings for him hit her between the eyes as she faced the reality of losing him. "Michael, you mustn't die. Please don't die."

He reached a trembling hand toward her face and she guided it there, holding it against her tear-dampened cheek. "Kiss me, Emma," he said weakly. Emma bent down and put her mouth over his, doing her best to give him a taste of all the passion she felt, hoping it would give him the will to hang on. She felt his hand move around her neck, holding her to him with a strength that began to seep into his response. But it was only when he started to chuckle that she jerked her head back and realized there was no blood. She looked at Michael in fury as his laughing eyes met hers, and for the first time ever, she saw him laugh. He laughed so hard that moisture glistened in the corners of his eyes. Emma growled at him and stood up, leaving his head to fall to the ground with a thud. But still he laughed. "It would seem I had your nerves riled there for a minute, Miss Davies," he managed to say. Emma growled again, and he pointed a finger at her. "Now we're even."

He jumped to his feet, and the men all took a startled step backward. "You're all a bunch of fools," he laughed. "There isn't a real bullet within miles of here. I loaded everything with blanks before we left." Michael seemed to find it terribly amusing, but Emma sensed that the men didn't share his sentiment, and it made her nervous.

"Go mind your business," he ordered. "This'll be over in a couple of days."

The men dispersed slowly, pausing to look inside their revolvers to assure themselves that what Michael had said was true. The cartridges were all blanks.

Michael turned to Emma, still chuckling. She walked away without a word.

Emma's attention was quickly diverted from Michael's little joke when she returned to the tent to find Lacey growing warm with fever. "Please, God, no!" she prayed aloud, and turned to find Michael looking down at her.

"What is it?" he insisted.

"She's got a fever," Emma answered gravely.

"Blast!" he muttered under his breath.

"How long before my father is supposed to be here?" she inquired, barely calm.

"We were almost expecting him today," Michael answered. "It's likely he'll be here tomorrow, but if they had any trouble, it could be longer."

"Get me some water and clean towels," Emma ordered, and he did it without hesitation.

For the first time since Emma had responded to Michael's passionate kisses, he stayed in the tent, sitting close to her, offering quiet support as she attempted to keep her sister's fever down. He said nothing, but once while she was bent over Lacey, pressing a cool towel to her face, Michael pulled a stray lock of hair away from the sweat that held it to Emma's skin. She tried to ignore the gesture, but she couldn't ignore the intensity in his eyes as he watched her. Even without looking at him, she could feel it.

❦   ❦   ❦

Michael Hamilton watched Emma's tender attention to her sister and felt a familiar ache. He knew the games were coming to an end. And something desperate erupted inside of him. Time was running out, and he felt emptier than he ever had in his life, while something base in him believed that he should feel deeply gratified over the misery he'd brought into *her* life. There were so many things he wanted to say, but one thought stood out prominently, and it pushed its way to his lips before he could find the will to hold it back.

"I didn't think you would even notice when I left," he said. She turned to him in question and he clarified, "When I left Byrnehouse-Davies."

"I noticed." She looked away.

He broke the following silence with a breathy, "Why?"

"You want to know why?" He nodded slightly and she went on. "All right, I'll tell you why. I had reconsidered, Michael. I hardly slept that night. I decided that I had been thoughtless and presumptuous. I went out to find you first thing the next morning, to apologize, to accept your offer." She looked deeply into his eyes. "But you were gone."

"Maybe I should have stayed," he admitted, unwilling to look at the full gamut of stupidity that had evolved from that choice.

"Yes," she spoke angrily, "maybe you should have. But you didn't. You were a fool, Michael. You turned and ran without giving me half a chance to look past your reputation. But nothing has changed, has it. You're still a fool if you think all of this is going to work. It's falling down around you, and I'm not even sure what it is you're after. I'm not sure that *you* know what you're after."

"I need the money," he defended, as if it were a new concept.

"Yes, I know." Emma tersely put an end to the conversation and turned her attention back to Lacey. She wondered if the things he'd just said had anything to do with what they might both be feeling. But then, her father would be here soon and all of this would be over. For Lacey's sake, she was grateful. But for her own, she felt a desperate, uncanny yearning for more time. More time to learn the truth from him, to find the real Michael Hamilton, the one she was coming to care for in a way that was evidenced by her reaction when she thought she might lose him forever.

Following a tense silence, Emma decided that if they were attempting to clear the air in preparation for the end of all this, she might as well have it out.

"Why did you do it?" she asked. He looked puzzled. "Why did you kill him?"

Michael's eyes widened in surprise, but he said nothing.

"Did you think I couldn't tell what was going on out there?"

Silence hung like a threatening storm, more tensely than it ever had before. Michael had to stop and try to comprehend what was happening here. True, it surprised him that his ridiculous attempt to maintain discipline in this chaotic camp had been misinterpreted as murder. Hadn't she just heard him say there were no real bullets in camp? Did she think that meant his gun was excluded? But more than that, Michael couldn't deny that Emma was disappointed in him. But why? He wanted so badly to know that he nearly asked her. But this charade was almost over, and what she believed him to be was vital until that money came into his hands.

Emma watched him expectantly, waiting for an answer to her question. But he didn't have one to give. This wasn't turning out at all like he'd planned or expected. She was right when she said it was falling down around him. The devil be cursed, everything that should have felt better by now only felt worse. He had wanted her to hurt, to beg and plead. But she had done nothing but match him at every turn, making him stop to wonder what he was even doing here. And what *was* he doing here? Of course, it was the money. But all else he'd been attempting to prove was coming back to him in a way he simply wasn't prepared for. And when he thought of the way she had reacted to his kiss, he nearly wanted to die.

Michael watched her now and saw pain in her eyes. But it was not for herself. It was concern for her sister that grieved her, and he found compassion within himself—something he was quite unaccustomed to. And now there was more pain. Something new. Emma was grieving for him.

At this moment, Michael could no more admit the truth to her than he could give her the moon. So he just stood up and walked away, longing for this to be over . . . and wishing it would never end.

Emma was left baffled and somehow hurt. But she turned her attention to Lacey with a prayer on her behalf, and Michael's too.

The night was long and harrowed as Lacey slipped in and out of fever. Emma stayed with her continually, and Michael stayed with Emma, bringing her fresh water when needed for Lacey, and hot coffee for Emma.

When morning came, Lacey didn't seem any worse. Michael brought in breakfast for Emma, wishing she would ask who had cooked it. He wanted to tell her he hadn't murdered the cook, but he didn't know how to say it without sounding like a fool.

When they had eaten, Michael took the dishes and left her alone. Emma lay beside Lacey and drifted into another short bout of sleep, praying that all of this would end soon, for Lacey's sake.

❦   ❦   ❦

Tyson found it ironic that he had cut short his explorations of the outback so he could go home and begin a trek into the outback. He had seen this land before. But just as with the rest of this country that he had seen since his return, it was different. This was not the way he had remembered it. This was a land rich and raw, with unspeakable beauty, and elements to be respected. This was the greatest land on earth. Australia. Home.

When Tyson wasn't contemplating the land, his mind was focused on his destination. With a combination of anger and fear, he rode steadily onward, his father and Ben always near. But for the most part, they quietly allowed him time to ponder what faced him ahead. Each mile made his longing for Lacey and Emma grow deeper, along with his regret at leaving them. He realized that beyond his concern for their safety, his greatest fear was the prospect of not spending the rest of his life with Lacey. There was nothing to indicate she had found someone else in the time he'd been gone, but he wondered if she would want him. He couldn't blame her if she didn't, but that wouldn't make it any easier.

When his thoughts turned to whoever was behind this ridiculous escapade, Tyson felt his anger deepen. He'd like to have his hands around the man's throat and squeeze the life right out of him for doing this to the women he loved. But for now, all he could do was keep riding and bide his time, longing, praying, hoping that everything would come together.

Tyson lost track of the days, and it was a relief when Ben finally pointed west and announced, "Crazy Rock is about five miles that way. There is a good place to camp among those rocks up ahead. There's enough of a cave to shelter us from the elements, and a bore nearby for water."

"Good," Jess said firmly, "we'll set up camp and meet them tomorrow at ten."

Nerves were tight through the evening, but exhaustion made them all sleep well. When morning came and breakfast was finished, Tyson was so filled with raw emotion that he felt sure he'd explode. There was joy in the prospect of being reunited with Emma and Lacey, the fear of Lacey's rejection, and concern for their safe return. And then there was enough anger directed toward the man responsible for this to make Tyson want to kill him.

When it was nearing time to head out, Tyson couldn't believe it when his father declared sternly, "You wait here and keep an eye on that." He pointed to the saddlebags containing the money. "We'll see you in a while."

"Whoa!" Tyson protested. "Wait a minute. I'm not going to sit here and wonder what's going on out there while you—"

"Son," Jess calmly mounted his horse, "you are as strung out as a cocked crossbow. I am not taking you out there and having you put one or both of my daughters' lives in jeopardy because you're so all-fired full of vengeance. Watch the money and sit tight."

"I thought you were supposed to take it with you," Tyson argued.

"I am. But if he wants it and I've got it, that leaves me in control to some degree. Besides, I'm not giving up anything until I see Emma and Lacey and talk to them. When I know they're all right, I'll give him the money. Not before."

Jess and Ben rode away, leaving Tyson to curse unnoticed into the open air. He paced until his feet ached, but still his nerves were raw. What could he do but wait?

❧ ❧ ❧

"What time is it, Ben?" Jess asked as they approached their destination.

"Getting close to ten, I'd guess," he answered after a squinting appraisal of the sun as it moved into darkening clouds that they hadn't noticed until now.

Jess checked his watch and replaced it, smiling at Ben. "Right, as always."

The solitary gum ghost mentioned in the letter appeared in the distance, and Jess and Ben perked their instincts keenly. The two men sitting on horseback near the tree showed alertness as they approached and slowed down.

"You Davies?" one called.

"I am," Jess called back, slowing and then stopping close enough to get a good look. Bile rose in his throat as he surveyed the lowlife scum before him. He couldn't fathom his daughters at their mercy.

"You got the money?" the bigger one asked.

"It's close by, but I want to see my daughters first."

"I'll get Hamilton," the other said to his mate. Jess and Ben exchanged a sharp glance at the mention of the name. It confirmed their suspicions, and Jess reminded himself to heed Alexa's advice to keep an open mind—a task that he knew wasn't going to be easy.

One rider turned and rode the other direction at a swift gallop, while the more despicable of the two sat dumbly on his horse, picking his rotting teeth. Jess looked up at the gathering clouds and sighed. All they could do was wait.

❦   ❦   ❦

Emma was awakened by the Michael he was comfortable being. "Your father is here," he said, speaking like a confident gambler. "Dean just rode in. Rafe is waiting with the esteemed Mr. Davies, who is claiming he will not give over the money until he knows you're safe. Put your boots on. Let's go."

"But Lacey is—"

"Coming as well." Michael scooped her up carefully and followed Emma outside to the waiting horses. He handed Lacey up to Dean, one of the gentler thugs, Emma observed. "Be careful with her,"

Michael said sternly. Dean nodded and situated her carefully across his broad lap. Lacey woke up looking disoriented, and Emma reached up to squeeze her hand.

"It's all right, darling. Papa is here. We're riding out to meet him."

"She'll be all right," Dean said to Emma with a genuine note of kindness.

"Get over here," Michael demanded. "We haven't got all day." He lifted Emma into the saddle, tied her hands to the horn, and mounted behind her. It seemed so long since she had been next to him this way, yet it felt so familiar—except for the evidence of a pistol between them, tucked into his belt.

They headed out at a steady gallop, Dean following more slowly for the sake of Lacey's comfort. Emma saw the solitary tree come into view, and the silhouettes of three riders. She recognized the first as Rafe, much to her dismay. But gradually the others came into focus, and her heart pounded with joy and relief to recognize her father and Ben. Michael tightened his grip around her waist, and her joy melted into confusion. A part of her wanted to take hold of Michael and plead to stay with him, to have just a little more time to perhaps break through the walls between them. But the rest of her ached to be home and safe from the danger as much as from the wrestling she felt within.

They slowed, then halted. Michael nodded toward Rafe, who backed away to hover several yards behind, near Dean as he approached with Lacey. Michael stopped directly in front of Jess and Ben. Emma smiled warmly at her father, wanting to convey a thousand thoughts. His expression remained steady, but she caught the affection in his eyes before they moved down to survey her bound wrists and Michael's possessive hold on her.

"Michael Hamilton," Jess said to begin the formalities. Emma was surprised that her father seemed to have expected this turn of events. "I would never have thought you capable of such a thing."

"Come now, Mr. Davies. Think back. You know what kind of boy I was."

"That's just my point," Jess said almost smugly. Michael didn't have a clue what he was talking about.

"Are you all right, Emma?" Jess added carefully.

"I'm fine," she responded eagerly. "Michael has treated us very well."

Michael was surprised, knowing she could have truthfully spouted off a long list of awful things he'd done.

"But Lacey is hurt," she added. "It's her leg."

"What happened?" Jess asked with urgency.

"A little accident," Michael stated. "But unfortunately, we had nothing to treat it with. She's not doing well." Michael paused and shifted his tone from concern to malice. "Where's the money?"

"It's nearby. But I've got a mind not to give it to you."

"We can play by your rules, Mr. Davies, but I don't think you'll like the way the game ends."

"Give it up, Hamilton," Jess retorted.

"Give up the money, and I will."

There was a brief battle of silent wills until Michael announced, "You can take Lacey. We have nothing to help her with, and I don't want to deal with it anymore. You can come back for Emma in three days—with the money. Play it right, or you won't get her back at all."

Michael pulled the gun out for emphasis, and Emma saw her father's jaw tighten just before Michael turned the horse and rode away, pausing a moment to shout at Rafe and Dean, "Give her to them and hurry back. Don't let them follow you."

Thunder cracked overhead to remind them that the sky had turned black during the course of their exchange. Ben glanced upward warily, while Jess kept his eyes fixed on the approaching rider. Their horses came side by side, and Jess's heart fell to see Lacey's pallor. She was gently handed over, the rough-looking Dean defying his nature to help Jess situate Lacey carefully. "I hope she'll be all right," he added.

Jess nodded and Dean rode away at a gallop, Rafe joining him as he passed.

"Is there any shelter between here and camp?" Jess asked Ben as the sky rumbled again.

"No."

"Then we'd better hurry."

"Papa?" Lacey muttered, opening her eyes with effort.

"It's me, darling." He smiled warmly. "I've got you now. Everything's going to be all right."

Lacey smiled and closed her eyes. Jess nodded to Ben, and they rode out as quickly as they could manage with their ailing passenger. Heavy drops began to fall, and Jess called out in disgust, "It rains once every ten years in this country, and it had to be now."

Ben shrugged his shoulders and rode on.

❦   ❦   ❦

Emma didn't even have time for a glance back, but she sensed her father's disheartenment. Her heart ached, but she was relieved that Lacey was in his hands. She knew he would have come prepared with medical supplies. And now, if nothing else, she could confront Michael without distractions. Confront him about what exactly, she wasn't certain. She only knew she had to do something. Now that she was relieved of the responsibility of Lacey, it all became clear in her mind. Her feelings resembled those of the night she had regretted accepting his offer to take her riding, but a thousand times stronger. Now Michael was here, and she was going to make up for it. Her heart demanded it. Whatever became of this, she would not be separated from him again and be reduced to wondering what might have been.

Emma was thoroughly absorbed in her thoughts until a loud crack of thunder drew her attention to a sky so black with clouds that it threatened to upheave everything in sight. Emma gasped, which muffled the mumbled cursing uttered behind her ear.

"Oh that's just what we need." Michael turned the horse about quickly, searching for someplace, anyplace to wait out the downpour that he knew was only moments off. Seeing what might be a narrow overhang of rock, he heeled the stallion into a brisk gallop. Thunder broke again, and the heavens opened with a rare offering to bathe the desert. Michael pushed the horse for all it would give while Emma bowed her head against the rain, feeling a fear that could only come from being at the mercy of the elements. Menacing sheets of rain soaked them to the skin in moments. But the weather was only a catalyst for bringing to the surface everything else she felt. She was afraid for Lacey, missing her parents, longing for Tyson, and aching for Michael.

Emma felt more alone than she ever had in her life as Michael edged the stallion beneath the rock. It was barely wide enough to shield them, but it was sufficient and they were grateful. Michael slid down, untied Emma's hands, and quickly tethered the horse to keep it from bolting. Then he turned to help Emma, but she was already out of the saddle, huddled on the ground, pressing her back as close to the rock as she could. Michael sat next to her, mostly because there was nowhere else that was remotely dry, except for the area the horse was hoarding.

"It probably hasn't rained here for years," Michael commented like a newspaper reporter. "One wonders how long it will last."

Emma found his attempt at humor irritating when she was so consumed with unventable emotion. It suddenly became too much to bear, and she put a hand over her mouth in a feeble effort to stop the sob catching in her throat.

"Oh, please," he drawled with disgust. "You're not going to cry, are you? It's just a little rain."

"Shut up!" she screamed at him, deciding it was about time he received some of the wrath he had so painstakingly earned. "You're the stupid fool who got me into this mess. If it weren't for you, I'd be home with my family and my sister, sleeping in a warm, dry bed. But no! Here I am, out in the middle of nowhere, with you," she hissed. "You," she repeated huskily, turning on him like a rabid cat, transferring all her hurt and confusion into cold, blatant anger. "You . . . you brute. You cold, black-hearted, unfeeling, sinister, wicked fiend!"

"You flatter me." He arched an eyebrow and lifted a crooked smile. To Emma, it was the straw that broke the camel's back. All this time she had struggled to keep her dignity, if only to keep his ego in check. And now that she couldn't hold it any longer, Michael was lapping it up like a starved puppy, arrogance and pride filling his brown eyes with amusement. At the risk of drenching herself further, Emma moved away enough to get some good momentum behind the hand that slapped him. It stung her hand so badly that fresh tears burned into her eyes. But Michael hardly flinched, as if taking such pain had been well rehearsed. With no hesitation she slapped his other cheek with her other hand, doing her best to make it hurt more. Still, he hardly moved. But the humor fled from his expression, leaving only that cruel *I dare you to cross me* glare.

Emma groaned in frustration. He was enjoying her misery, and she wanted to see some misery from him. "You're not even human." She grabbed his shirt collar into her fists and shook him, wondering where her resolve had gone to tenderly confront his feelings. He still showed no reaction, and she started hitting his chest with her fists. "What kind of awful thing happened to you to make you so horrible?" she shouted.

With little effort, Michael took her wrists into a firm, powerful grip. "I think that's about enough," he stated calmly, but Emma fought with everything left in her to continue her fruitless retaliations. Michael shook her abruptly, forcing her to realize who was in control. When physical release was no longer possible, Emma succumbed to a throaty sob that ushered her tears back tenfold. She tried to break free, if only to hide her emotion, but Michael maintained his grip, holding her, watching her, as expressionless as the rock protecting them from the storm.

Emma hung her head forward and found it had nowhere to go but against Michael's chest. Once more she tried to hit him, but ended up with her face buried in the rain-soaked shirt that was plastered to his skin. Her fists futilely pushed him away, then suddenly she took hold of him in blatant desperation. The cause of her pain became the buffer, and she cried helplessly while he just held her.

Michael gave in to the urge to put his arms around her, wondering what he was doing here. Emma was right. She should have been home, and he should have gone to China or someplace equally distant. Every name she had called him was pure truth, and the sting in his face reaffirmed it. So why was she holding to him as if letting go would leave her to drown?

Michael willed himself to release his grip, wondering if she would do the same, but he only felt the wet fabric tighten around him as she drew more of it into her fists, her knuckles turning white from exertion. He felt helpless and confused, and it wasn't easy for him to put his arms around her again, more tightly, in a feeble attempt to offer the comfort she was seeking. The part of him that longed to give it was too lost in the rest of him, the man responsible for her pain. Her obvious vulnerability made him wish she were dependent upon anyone but him at this moment. He was not the kind of man who should be holding her this way. He had been certain, when all of this began, that he hated Emma Byrnehouse-Davies. He had wanted to make her hurt the way he had hurt. She was hurting, yes. But it was at his expense—again. And the thought made him angry. Forcing logic to the surface, Michael took hold of the back of her hair to force her to look at him.

"It's not working, you know." His voice was sheer malevolence. "Tears will not soften my motives. You're not going back until I have that money."

"To the devil with you and your money, Michael Hamilton! The two of you deserve each other."

He lifted an amused brow. Her anger was much easier to handle than her tears. "I couldn't agree more."

Emma watched him closely, hating herself for wanting him to kiss her. When he did she gasped from shock, and a fear more tangible than anything she had known before. Michael did have power over her; a power more intense than any cruelty could match. And he wasn't even aware of it. As far as she could see, Michael didn't have a clue about what was happening between them. He was so absorbed with his greed, or whatever else might be motivating him, that he couldn't even see beyond it. Emma willed herself not to respond, but the power was too great. Her strength left her and she succumbed, wondering if he would bolt and run like he had before when her true feelings had slipped through.

For a long moment, it was as if their minds became detached from their hearts, and their kiss became deep and mutual. Emma felt herself drowning. Her fingers threaded and tugged through his hair, thick and wet and dark. Michael's kiss deepened with some kind of desperation. Emma instinctively eased closer as his embrace tightened.

Michael groaned suddenly and jerked his lips free as if they'd been burned. His eyes turned fierce, and he took her shoulders into a firm grip. "Stop it!" he demanded. "Do you hear me? I said stop it! What warped notion possesses you to behave that way? Are you wanton, girl? Or just daft? Don't you know what kind of man I am? Don't you know why you're here? I hate you, Emma. You . . . you spoiled little snob. I hate you!"

Emma watched him rant much the way she had ranted not so many minutes ago. She listened with no expression, and she gave no resistance to his spiteful lips as they fell against her throat, nearly devouring her with kisses, while he said it over and over, "I hate you, Emma. Can't you see how I hate you?"

Emma said nothing, her only conscious thought being the memory of one of her mother's lessons in human behavior; words that echoed over and over in time to his helpless ranting. *Love and hate are very close in the heart.*

Michael's lips met hers again in direct contradiction to his words, and the truth fell over Emma like the warmth of the sun penetrating the storm surrounding them. Maybe he did want ransom; he had said it enough to make her believe he meant it. But money, along with his other motives, all fell into place now as his passion betrayed him. It was Emma that Michael Hamilton wanted. He claimed it was hate, and he had intimidated her, held power over her, cruelly threatened her enough to almost make her believe it. But in that moment, Emma recalled his little kindnesses, his endearing traits that had seeped through, and she would have bet her life that the line between love and hate in Michael's heart was very thin.

He took her face into his hands as the scale tipped to the light side of his heart, kissing her, drinking her in like the desert drank the rain. Then the scale tipped into blackness and he nearly threw her from his grasp, coming to his feet, his back to her, fists clenched, standing boldly in the deluge of rain as if it might wash away the confusion. In one snapping movement he turned toward her, eyes imposing, finger lifted in threat, shouting through the rain pouring over him.

"Don't do that again! You're just trying to distract me, you little wench. And I'm not going to fall for it. I would have thought a woman of your birth had more to her than that."

"You don't have a clue what I have or haven't got inside of me," she shouted back. "You don't even know your own mind. How could you possibly know mine? You're nothing but a fool, Michael Hamilton. A coward and a fool."

Emma had meant to strike a nerve, but she wasn't prepared to have him leap toward her, lunging like an animal out for the kill. With thoughtless purpose, he lifted a hand to strike her. Emma cried out and recoiled, pressing her eyes shut in preparation for the blow. Instantly her mind went through her response. If he actually had the nerve to strike her, she doubted that she could ever get past his base nature to make anything good out of what she felt. She wouldn't tolerate it, plain and simple. But the blow never came. She looked up to see his hand curl into a fist, then he willfully dropped it to his side. Her eyes plumbed his, questioning him silently. He moved beside her beneath the rock and sat down, wiping the rain from his face. "I may be cruel, but I'm not a barbarian. I will not allow the blood in my veins to rule me."

Emma didn't have a clue what he meant. She was only relieved that he had not stooped so low as to really hurt her. Still, his rejection of her feelings—and his own—was hurt enough. In that moment, as they silently watched the desert bathe, Emma felt near despair. It was apparent that the walls surrounding Michael's heart, Michael's true emotions, were not within her power to break down. It would take something more humbling than a woman's scorn to beat pride unbeatable.

Through the noise of the pounding rain, Emma became conscious of a clicking sound. It was so rhythmic that it reminded her of a clock ticking off seconds. She turned to Michael and found him flicking his thumbnail repeatedly over the edge of his tooth. His eyes blazed in conjunction with the nervous gesture, and Emma felt a fresh pounding in her chest. It was as if she had just lit the fuse to a time bomb buried deep within him, and it was now threatening to explode. Emma couldn't recall ever being more afraid in her entire life.

❦ ❦ ❦

Tyson stood at the mouth of the cave, watching the rain in disbelief. He ached to know what was going on, and hoped it would all be over soon. In the midst of the beating rain, he was startled to see Ben come around the rock. "I'm glad you've got that fire going," he announced, hurriedly spreading blankets out next to it.

"What happened?" Tyson demanded, only to see Jess come around the corner with a soaked, limp woman in his arms. He couldn't tell if it was Emma or Lacey. Either way, he wanted to die.

"What's wrong with her?" he persisted, noting she was unconscious. "What happened?"

"She's been hurt, and I assume it's infected," Jess reported, easing Lacey carefully down to the blankets and pausing to wipe the water from her face. "The storm didn't help. She lost consciousness about a mile back." Tyson's heart raced just to see her. She had changed. Or maybe it was the dripping hair and pale skin that made her look different. This was not how he'd imagined seeing her again.

"Where's Emma?" Tyson questioned.

"Get more blankets, Ben," Jess ordered. "Tyson, help me get her out of these wet clothes before she freezes to death. With the fever she had when they handed her over, I wonder if she's strong enough to survive the chill."

Tyson hesitated only a moment before he knelt to assist his father. "What happened?" he repeated. "Where's Emma?"

"Emma's fine." Jess's tone made it clear he was in no mood to talk. "Right now, Lacey isn't. Build up that fire," he said to Ben. "But don't overdo it. Then get some food heated, and make some coffee— lots of hot coffee. Then find those medical supplies and have them ready. When she warms up, we're going to have to work fast to save that leg."

Tyson felt a lump growing in his throat. He tried to imagine Lacey losing her leg—or her life. The thought was unbearable. If only he'd been here. If only . . .

Jess moaned in frustration, momentarily interrupting Tyson's thoughts of regret. It seemed nothing more could be done for the moment, and Tyson just stared at her, shocked and afraid.

Jess looked up at Tyson and shouted, "Take off your shirt and boots and get in there with her!"

"What?" Tyson shrieked.

"You heard me, boy. It's a fact that the fastest way to warm a human body is with another human body. Just do it."

"But . . ."

"Don't stammer! Just do it!" Jess shouted. Tyson couldn't recall *ever* seeing him this angry. "It certainly won't be the first time."

A moment of shock, reflected in their eyes, passed between them. Jess remembered Alexa making him promise to let Lacey tell Tyson about Richard, while Tyson was obviously wondering how on earth his father knew what had happened between him and Lacey. Jess took care of both problems when he said quickly, "Yes, she told us. She felt so awful after you left that she nearly fell apart."

Tyson still found it difficult to move. This new picture of events during his absence was not easy to take. He supposed that he deserved the guilt and humility he was feeling, but he had to believe it was only just the beginning.

"Hurry up, boy, before she freezes to death. She's not strong enough to stay that cold for long. And you're the only one not wet. Now get in there and wrap yourself around her."

Tyson hurried to remove his shirt and pull off his boots. "I didn't mean to hurt her," Tyson attempted to justify.

Jess looked nothing short of astonished as Tyson slipped between the blankets and eased close to Lacey. Her coldness made him ache with regret.

"Why don't you say it," Tyson said without looking at his father.

"Say what?"

"Ever since I came back, you've been wanting to say something to me. I can feel it. I wish you'd just get it over with."

"All right, I will." Tyson looked up at his father over the top of Lacey's head. With a stern finger pointed at him, Jess spoke in a low, angry voice. "It wasn't easy on any of us when you left to conquer the world. But after you were gone I got to thinking, and I could see why you had to do it. I could also see that I was partly to blame for your anger. Your absence itself was perhaps excusable. But I will never understand what possessed you to think you could make love to that girl, then simply turn your back on her and leave."

Tyson squeezed his eyes shut in an effort to block out the pain and humiliation. But Jess's continued speech demanded that he open them and face up.

"I'm only going to say this once, and then I'm going to try to let it rest. So listen well, Tyson, and think about it long and hard. When you turned fifteen, I sat you down and we had a good, long talk. Do you remember it? Speak up, boy."

"I remember."

"Not very well, I'm afraid, because I said then what I'm going to say now: The power to create life is a sacred responsibility, and any man who is a man does not exercise that power then turn his back and run. That power should only be used when deep love, mutual respect, and *commitment* abide between two people."

Tyson groaned from the anguish of regret. His father might as well have beat him with a riding crop. The welts went deep, and he deserved every one of them. "I'm so sorry," was all he could think to say.

"Don't tell me you're sorry. Tell her." He pointed to Lacey's still form, wrapped in Tyson's arms. "If she lives long enough to listen."

Tyson groaned again, and Jess headed out of the cave to the outcropping of rocks where their supplies were kept. "I think I'll see if Ben needs some help."

Once alone, Tyson's little remaining composure faded quickly, and no force on earth could keep him from crying. He pulled Lacey closer, pressing his lips to the top of her head, sobbing like a child. "Forgive me," he begged of her silent form. At first the tears were painful to the core, racking pain from the deepest part of him in heaving sobs. But as the tears went on and on, they became silent and cleansing. He was grateful for his father's words that had cleared the air. He was glad to have it out in the open, although it seemed ironic to be holding her this way while he was seeking inner penitence. But all he felt for her now had nothing to do with the lust he had allowed to rule him before. Now, he could only pray that she would live.

"Live," he whispered against her face, over and over. "You must live. I have so much to make up for." He could feel her body turning warmer, but only when she began to shiver did she move at all.

"Father!" he called, quickly wiping his face dry with the edge of the blanket.

"What is it?" Jess rushed in, fear burning in his eyes.

"She's shaking. What's wrong?"

"I think that's good," he said.

"You think?"

"I read a lot," Jess argued. "I'm no doctor."

"Well, I'm sure glad you're here." Tyson gave him an affectionate smile.

"I'm glad you're here, too," Jess replied, and Tyson felt some peace. Somehow he believed everything would be all right.

❦ ❦ ❦

The rain slowed to a trickle and finally ceased as Michael hoisted Emma into the saddle. The clouds separated and disappeared as quickly as they had come while the horse's hooves plodded through the muddy earth. Emma's mind replayed what had just transpired between her and Michael. She had witnessed passion to match his anger, and a display of emotions so incongruent that she could only believe the confusion was making him crazy. She could almost feel his every nerve ticking in conjunction with the bomb in his head. The prospect of three more days in his company, without Lacey's chaperoning presence, suddenly turned what little resolve she had left into a fuel that fed her smoldering fear.

With more instinct than thought, Emma pushed her elbows back into his ribs, jerked the reins from his hands and threw them free. She reached behind her to pull his head forward in an effort to throw him off balance enough to get him out of the saddle. It might have worked if Michael hadn't taken hold of her on his way down, and Emma tumbled with him into the mud. She almost got free in the confusion, but as she stood to run, he grabbed her ankle and wrestled her to the ground, straddling her on his knees, pinning her wrists into the mud. He laughed, and Emma felt angry. Before now, escape would have been futile. But now she knew her father was within a few miles.

"It was a worthy effort, I'll grant you that." Michael chuckled and lifted an eyebrow. Oh, how she hated it when he lifted that brow! "But I think escape is not in the rules. I haven't suffered through putting up with you this long so you can foil my game now."

With that he stood and heaved her over his shoulder, keeping a strong grip despite her fists beating against his back and her screaming protests. Somehow he managed to get in the saddle and lay Emma, stomach down, over his lap.

"All right," she shouted, "I yield. I will not ride like this."

"You will if I say you will," he retorted matter-of-factly and urged the horse into a steady, jolting trot.

"You're impossible!" she shrieked.

"Yes, I know," he muttered proudly. "It's my best trait."

Emma could have sworn he was purposely going in circles to drag out her time in this ridiculous and uncomfortable position. The hot sun returned so quickly that their clothes were almost dry by the time camp came into view.

Emma sensed trouble immediately. She couldn't see anything beyond the ground and the horse's legs, but she felt Michael go tense, and he seemed suddenly oblivious to her as he let her slide to her feet. He dismounted without taking his eyes off the men, as if he was accounting for the presence of each one.

"Go into the cave," he said warily, barely moving his lips, "and don't come out."

"What is it? Do you think I—"

"Just do it," he demanded, easing her behind him to keep himself between the men and her destination. Emma's fears fell into perspective as Michael suddenly became her protector.

Emma sat tensely amid the cold walls, wondering frantically what was happening. Would they kill Michael for real this time, leaving her at their despicable mercy? One of the men came in, and Emma felt afraid until she realized he was just bringing things in and setting them down—things that had been in her tent.

"What's going on?" she asked, and he looked up. She recognized him at once. "Corky? I thought you were dead!"

"Dead?" He laughed. "Nah, Mike Hamilton wouldn't shoot a wallaby. We was just funnin', him an' me. Though the rest o' those oafs didn't take it that way. They got no sense o' humor. Mike just likes t' be showy, that's all."

Emma's heart leapt for joy as her instincts concerning Michael suddenly made so much sense. But the fear quickly returned to blanket her excitement. "What's going on, Corky?"

"We're leavin'."

"Who is?"

"All of us. 'Cept Hamilton, o' course. I suppose he'll look after you. The tents an' stuff belong t' Dean, so I guess you'll be stayin' in here."

"But why?" Emma persisted, taking advantage of this opportunity to be alone with Corky and his willingness to talk.

"Well, he paid us some advance. Good pay it was, I'll admit. But most of 'em ain't bankin' on gettin' the rest without trouble. We're gettin' out while the trouble's not s' close. That's all." Corky gave a reasonable smile, and Emma almost liked him. He *was* a good cook. "I'd better be gettin' th' rest o' yer things, ma'am."

Emma moved to the entrance of the cave and watched everything being packed up and moved out while Michael stood, holding his horse's reins, his face completely unreadable. He turned to look around as if to confirm that everything was gone. The stream of mules and horses eventually disappeared. Michael tethered his horse and removed its saddle. Emma watched him, wondering if this could possibly be the humbling element he needed to face her with the truth. It couldn't hurt to try, she told herself, drawing fresh courage. The circumstances weren't likely to get any worse.

Michael entered the cave and threw the saddle on the ground. Emma looked to him in silent question.

"They called me a coward and a fool," he reported, brushing past her. "They must have heard you shouting at me earlier."

"For miles? Through the rain?" she asked, keeping her tone light.

Michael turned and regarded her for a long moment. "You were yelling rather loudly."

Emma gathered her courage. He'd proven time and time again that he was not capable of hurting her physically. "Are you afraid?" she asked.

"If I were, would that make me a coward?" he retorted.

"It takes a brave man to stay when he's afraid."

Michael fought to study her face in the dim light. She had a way of putting him in his place with her simple wisdom. There was so much he wanted to say to her, and so little time to say it.

"I guess it's just you and me now," he said, not liking the humble way it sounded. "I suppose you could run away if you wanted to badly enough."

"If I did," she challenged, "would you run after me?"

"I need the—"

"Yes, I know," she interjected, "you need the money." She smiled. "Well, I'll give you a run for your money, Mr. Hamilton."

After Emma's failed attempt to escape earlier, watching her run out of the cave seemed ridiculous to him. And he wondered what she was trying to prove.

Emma turned back to be certain he was following her. She purposely left the horse for his use.

Michael mounted bareback and took out after her, reminding himself with each gallop of what he was supposed to be doing here. By the time he caught up with her he felt in control of himself again, and determined to carry this through. Without dismounting, Michael reached down and caught an arm about her waist, hoisting her up in front of him.

Emma feigned protest, if only to rebuild his confidence. He quickly sat her in front of him in spite of her struggling, and turned the stallion back toward the cave. Emma could feel him maneuvering the horse with his thighs as much as the reins, and couldn't help but admire his skill. Of course, he had been taught to ride at Byrnehouse-Davies as a boy, but he obviously had a natural gift.

Michael kept an arm around her while he tethered the horse, then he hoisted her over his shoulder and took her into the cave. Under much protest he tied her hands behind her back, then left her to call him awful names while he attempted to put their belongings in order, completely oblivious to the humor in Emma's eyes.

❦ ❦ ❦

Lacey became vaguely aware of her surroundings as her body began to warm. She couldn't recall for certain how she'd gotten where she was, but she could hear her father's voice in a distant kind of way, and it gave her comfort. Seeking warmth, she instinctively nuzzled closer to an enveloping heat. Gradually it became more distinct, and Lacey knew she was dreaming. It was Tyson's warmth she felt, Tyson's voice she heard, whispering over and over, "It's all right, Lacey. I love you. I'm so sorry. You must forgive me. I love you." She felt his lips on her brow, her cheeks, her eyelids. With purpose she concentrated on the dream, squeezing her eyes shut, not wanting to awaken while she obliviously murmured his name.

Hearing his name voiced over and over, Tyson glanced to his father with hopeful eyes.

"I think she'll be all right," Jess said gently. "As soon as she stops shaking, let's get some warm clothes on her, and Ben can have a look at that leg." Tyson nodded and eased her closer.

As Lacey gained warmth, her breath became more steady and her body still. Tyson eased carefully away to get dressed, feeling a subtle fear at the prospect of facing her when she regained consciousness fully. He helped Jess pull an oversized shirt over her head, but he remained behind her when Lacey looked up at their father with recognition.

"Hello, darling," Jess smiled. "I think you're going to be all right. Ben and I are going to have a look at that leg. It won't be pleasant, but we'll get it healing."

Lacey nodded, and Jess touched her face affectionately. Tyson hovered at a distance while Jess held Lacey, and Ben carefully lanced the festering wound. Lacey cried out in anguish, and Tyson bit into his hand. He felt so helpless, and his self-imposed distance from her seemed momentarily impossible to cross. Lacey cried out again as the wound was cleaned with disinfectant, then Ben put some aboriginal concoction on it before it was bandaged with clean linen.

"I think it will be fine," Ben announced quietly. "It cleaned pretty easy, and the redness hasn't spread."

There was a unified sigh of relief, especially from Lacey. Tyson was drawing the courage to approach her when she drifted into an exhausted slumber, and he could only watch her. He felt like a fool, such an utter fool. And his deepest hope was that Lacey would forgive him and allow him to make it right. He wondered about Emma, and again wanted to have his hands around the throat of the fiend who was responsible for all of this. Seeing Lacey suffer only deepened his anger.

A prominent question came to mind, and he realized the details had been forgotten in the heat of the drama. He turned to his father, who was frying salt pork over the fire. "You didn't tell me what happened out there, and who is behind all of this."

Jess continued to stir the meat, and he spoke without changing his expression. "It was Hamilton."

Tyson turned his eyes back to Lacey, swearing loudly.

"Watch your language," Jess said without looking at him.

"You said Emma was all right," Tyson added. "I assume you saw her."

"Yes, we did."

"Do I have to force every word out of you?" Tyson shouted in a whisper. "What happened, for crying out loud?"

"We met two rough-looking men at the appointed spot. One stayed with us while the other rode out to get Hamilton. It was quite some time before they returned."

"Long enough to ride to Crazy Rock and back," Ben inserted.

"That's likely."

"And?" Tyson persisted.

"The rider came back, holding Lacey, but he kept his distance. It was Michael Hamilton who approached me. He had Emma in the saddle with him."

Tyson began to mutter more profanity, but Jess gave him a hard stare and he finished, "The brute!" His voice raised. "Why didn't she just jump off, or take the reins, or—"

"Well," Jess said so calmly that Tyson wanted to shake him, "he had a gun, for one thing, and—"

"A gun?"

"Are you going to let me tell this story or not?" Tyson sighed, and Jess continued. "Yes, he had a gun, and Emma's hands were tied to the saddle horn." Tyson stiffened but said nothing. "But she told me she was fine, and to be perfectly honest, she didn't look at all distressed, except concerning Lacey."

"And what was their explanation for that?"

"Michael said it was an accident. I believe him."

"Why would you believe that—"

"Because he wants ransom," Jess retorted, beginning to get irritated over the entire thing. "And I don't believe he would deliberately allow one of them to be hurt. I just don't think it's in him."

"So now what?" Tyson asked quietly.

"Well, Hamilton was upset because we didn't bring the money out as specified. I really thought he'd be a little more open-minded than that."

"So he still has Emma. Shouldn't we—"

"He said we can come back for her in three days."

"Three days?"

"Be glad he didn't say a week. You might as well face it, Tyson. He's the one in control here, and we're just going to have to live with it. You're going to have to learn to look on the bright side a little.

Lacey is going to be fine. Emma is obviously all right. In a few days we'll all go home and catch up on some sleep." Jess felt compelled to add, even though he didn't want to, "And perhaps all of this is not nearly so bad as it seems."

"What do you mean by that?" Tyson insisted.

"Ask your mother when you get home," Jess added, already regretting that he'd brought it up when he didn't know how to explain it. "She's the one who said it." Jess paused thoughtfully. "I suppose she still hopes to find something good in Michael."

"I'd say it's hopeless," Tyson uttered.

"Perhaps." Jess moved the pan off the fire and began to dish up the pork and some fried potatoes. "But we obviously don't know the whole story. And I promised your mother I would keep an open mind. You should do the same."

Tyson only grunted. Ben smiled to observe them. They ate their meal without conversation, then bedded down around the fire with Lacey between Jess and Tyson so they could be aware of her needs if any arose. Just before Tyson drifted to sleep, he reached over and took Lacey's hand, holding it as if it were a lifeline.

Eight
TRUTH

Michael paced nervously until Emma thought she'd scream. And far worse, he was almost continually clicking that thumbnail off his teeth.

"Is something vexing you?" she asked tersely.

"I can't imagine whatever gave you that impression." He was serious.

"I don't know why you insist on leaving me tied up this way." She attempted gentle reasoning. "It's very uncomfortable."

"You tried to run away." He pointed a stern finger at her, but at least he'd stopped pacing and clicking off the seconds of that time bomb.

"You can't blame me for trying," she said, mostly to make conversation.

"I can't possibly let you go until I get the money."

"But it's not really the money, is it," she pressed cautiously.

"What are you implying?" He sounded astonished, as if it had never come up before. "If you think for one minute that I am anything more or less than a ruthless, black-hearted man, you are quite mistaken. I will stop at nothing to get what I want, Emma."

Emma forced herself not to smile. She knew he was lying—to himself as well as her. "And what exactly do you want?" she persisted. She had begun to believe she had him figured out, and if she didn't press for the truth now, she might never get the chance. "It's just you and me, Michael. You don't have to impress anyone, because I already know what you really want."

"And what might that be?" He squatted in front of her and gave a phony smile.

"You want me," she said with conviction. Michael's eyes narrowed, then they shifted tensely to look her up and down. "Maybe I do," he finally said, so low she could barely hear him. Emma could see the ticking of the time bomb in his eyes. At this point, it alone made her fear him. He must have sensed this as his expression turned confident. "You're afraid of me, Emma."

"Not nearly so much as you'd like me to be."

"You truly test my patience, Emma my sweet."

"And you truly test mine," she retorted.

He didn't respond for several moments, but Emma could almost audibly hear the ticking in his head.

"And what if I said that I do want you?" His tone treaded carefully.

"I'd say it's about time you told me the truth."

Michael stopped to analyze where he stood. Emma was right. She was always so blasted right! It was just the two of them now; no one to impress but her, no one to interfere or interrupt. And here she sat, claiming to know his motivations, implying that she knew him better than he knew himself. His impulse was to be cruel and angry, and convince her that she was wrong. But his feelings were in that vein less and less. Something deep inside, something achingly cloaked with fear, longed to give her the truth she was demanding. But he'd never told anyone the whole truth before.

Silence ruled while Emma watched a span of inner debate showing in the narrow slits of his eyes. A confident lifting of his chin indicated which side of him had won—at least for the moment.

"And what if I told you more truths?" His voice held that familiar sinister ring as he leaned onto one knee, bringing his face cautiously close to hers. "I'll tell you everything, Emma, if that's what you want."

"I want the truth," Emma demanded, feeling hopeful and afraid at the same time. "No more hiding. No more acting."

"Are you certain?" he asked, and one brow rose deviously. "Perhaps the truth would make you more afraid."

"I would venture to guess that no one is afraid of your truths except you."

"My, my." He chuckled tensely, wondering how she always managed to strike so close to the core of him. But he did well in covering it. "Aren't we bold!"

"One has to be, under such . . . circumstances."

"I would venture to guess that your boldness hides your true fear of me."

Emma laughed, not caring if it angered him. "You can venture to guess anything you like," she growled, "but until you face the truth, everything you've sacrificed to get me here will be worth nothing. You'll get the money. I'll go free. And then what will you do? Kidnap another innocent woman and pretend it's me, while you—"

"I think you're pressing the issue a bit." His anger turned genuine as she struck a nerve she couldn't possibly understand. He gripped the back of her neck with a firm hand, forcing her to look into his eyes. "I say truth for truth, Miss Davies. No more taunting."

"I'm not certain you know the difference."

Michael felt himself seething. What gave Emma Byrnehouse-Davies the right to probe into his soul and pick apart all that was tucked away there in deep, painful caverns? Still, there was something about her demand for truth that enticed him toward the light she represented. And if it was truth she wanted, he had to admit there was a part of him that wanted to tell her. But even the thought of facing it verbally nearly tore him to pieces inside. The fear overruled. The cruelty surfaced.

"Well," his eyes turned to fire, "see if you derive any truth from this."

With no warning, Emma became suffocated by something that resembled a kiss. She knew he was trying to make her feel used and humiliated, but all she felt now was anger.

"Stop it!" she insisted when he pulled back to catch his breath, but he drew her against him and pressed his mouth over hers again with a complete absence of the warmth and affection that she had felt creep through in the past. "Stop it," she repeated, trying to squirm away.

"You see," he said against her ear, "you are afraid of me."

"No, I am not!" she insisted. "I'm disgusted."

Michael contemplated that but persisted nonetheless, while her protests only seemed to prove his point.

With a prayer in her heart, Emma searched quickly for another avenue, feeling that if she didn't get through to him now, she never would. She was surprised to be suddenly overcome with tears as she growled at him, "Truth for truth, you say." She reached deep inside herself for the words that would prove that she *did* know him better than he knew himself; words that would cut him to the quick. "The truth, Michael Hamilton, is that what you really want is love. But you can't steal it, Michael. You have to earn it."

Michael drew back to look into her eyes, and her voice deepened in an effort to drive home a point she sensed he was absorbing. "What do you know of love, Michael?" She sniffled and wished she could wipe her nose on her sleeve, but her arms were still tied behind her. The tears flowed freely as she went on. "Did you ever let anyone break past your walls of bitterness and cruelty enough to touch your will to love?"

Michael came to his feet so quickly that Emma thought the walls surrounding them would crumble. He stood like a wild beast that might be sizing up its prey, contemplating whether to strike or run. Emma quickly sought for words that would discourage him from doing either. "You once loved an eighteen-year-old girl," she cried, putting her assumptions boldly into the open. His shoulders went back. His stance stiffened. "But how can you judge love by her inexperienced reaction, which you obviously interpreted as blatant rejection?"

Again she felt his mind ticking. But was it digesting information, or threatening to explode? Still, what frightened Emma most was tied into the words she'd just voiced, which forced her to face some truths of her own. Now, four years later, she finally understood what she had subconsciously felt when Michael left.

Watching him closely, she sensed something yielding, however slight. And she softened her voice to match the fragileness appearing in his eyes. "You're not nearly so cruel as you are trying to prove, Michael. And I am not nearly so confident as I might seem to be. Even spoiled little rich girls have pain."

"What would you know of pain, Emma?" he asked in a toneless voice that defied the spinning wheels behind his eyes.

"What would you know of love, Michael?" she retorted gently. He lifted his chin again, not in confidence, but as if he was expecting a blow that might knock him over. "Perhaps sharing some truths could benefit us both."

Michael was at a complete loss for words, but the tension had to be broken or he would scream. In a word, he *was* afraid. All of this was treading too close to something that he both longed for and feared.

Emma held her breath as he knelt before her and leaned forward. For a moment she feared that she had misjudged him and there was true reason to fear. But her breath escaped with relief when he reached around her to untie the cords about her wrists.

Michael rocked back on his heels and studied her a long, defining moment. The game was over, he told himself. And Emma had won. He could do nothing now but give her the truth. But a part of him wondered if this was what he'd truly been hoping for all along. He couldn't deny that he'd imagined such a moment as this, but the biggest part of him had never believed it would happen. He'd convinced himself that she was a spoiled brat, and he was base and unredeemable. But she had proven him wrong—perhaps in both respects. She was demanding the truth from him. And she had earned it.

Pushing his fear to a place where it couldn't be felt, Michael drew all the courage he could muster as he ventured to cross a bridge he'd never crossed with anyone—not anyone. He doubted it would take any more courage than this to walk onto a battlefield, toward a volley of cannon fire.

Emma watched his eyes and saw them go through many phases of thought and emotion. He returned her gaze so vividly that she felt as if he was attempting to convey some silent message or meaning. She held his gaze with the same intensity, hoping to grasp whatever he might convey to her. He rose to his feet and took a few steps back, still riveting his focus on her. She sucked in her breath as he untucked his shirt and began to unbutton it. She glanced away, feeling suddenly timid, while she searched for the words to ask his intentions. But all she could come up with was simply, "What are you doing, Michael?"

Her voice seemed to shatter the mood that had hovered around them as she'd sensed they were on the verge of crossing a significant bridge.

"Look at me, Emma," he said, and the vague hint of a quiver in his voice restored that mood instantly. She slowly moved her eyes toward him as he added, "I want you to know why I am the way I am. If nothing else, I want you to go home with some kind of understanding, and perhaps you won't remember me so . . ." His voice trembled more intently and he stopped abruptly. He unbuttoned the cuffs of his shirt, hesitated a moment, then let it fall over his shoulders to the ground. While she resisted the urge to turn timidly away, Emma tried to discern what purpose he might have had for doing such a thing. But it only took a quick glance for the answer to slap her in the face with a reality she couldn't even fathom. It was beyond her power to hold back an astonished gasp. Michael stood as he had before, his stance wide and strong, his chin high, his shoulders back. But glistening over his chest and ribs were a number of horrid scars, the likes of which she had never conceived possible. She felt her eyes widen in horrified disbelief, and she could see Michael's chest rising with each labored breath, making it evident that facing her this way was taking great courage.

"Yes," he responded to her expression, "they are ghastly. And, so you don't have to embarrass yourself by asking, they are my father's attempt to teach me about pain." He turned and held up his arms in a gesture of surrender to display countless deep welts across his back. "That man had better uses for a belt than to hold up his breeches," he stated coldly, as if the experience had left no scars beneath the skin at all. He turned to face her again, pointing carelessly to random scars. "This was how he used a hot fire poker, and this was a broken whiskey bottle. I nearly died from that one. But my parents wanted me to live. They frightened me into stealing for them while they lay around and indulged in their bad habits. If I didn't steal enough to support those habits, they inflicted pain."

Michael drew a deep breath. Emma saw his fists clench. "Do you know, Emma, what my clearest memory of my mother is? My mother, the woman who gave birth to me? I was seven. I called my father a monster after he had given me the usual beating. He pulled a knife on me, but for the first time in my life, I fought back. In the struggle, he accidentally sliced my upper lip. He didn't like that. He'd made it clear that he wanted the scars hidden. He didn't want anybody to know."

Michael stopped to swallow the bile rising in his throat, and the words nearly choked their way out. "My mother laughed. She *laughed,* Emma." His eyes narrowed, then closed, then opened again. "She said, 'That'll teach the little brat to mind his manners.' Then she threw me a dirty rag and told me not to bleed on the floor."

Michael looked down and swallowed hard. "One day soon after that, I realized that I could steal for myself and avoid the pain. I never went back. Your father came for me after I was found sleeping in a gutter after some thugs beat me to a pulp when I was eleven. I'd been on the streets for nearly four years, stealing and fighting to survive, sleeping anywhere I could find where I thought I might wake up still alive."

Emma didn't know she was crying until a tear fell against her hand. What could she possibly say? The truth was evident in his eyes. She had suspected that his anger and cruelty were a cover for pain. But she never would have believed this!

"Yes," he said, "that is pure truth. Perhaps the only real truth I know. You asked what I know of love, and the truth is that it was never a part of my world. I believe your mother tried to teach me love, but it was something that frightened me at the time, and I rejected it. Perhaps it still frightens me."

"Do you believe that any amount of love could ever ease such pain?" Emma's voice betrayed the compassion she felt.

His eyes narrowed, not with cruelty, but sincerity. "If anyone but you were to tell me that, I would not believe it."

"Why me?" she asked, in awe that he would share something so obviously difficult with her.

"Partly because you are so much like your mother. She is the only human being who ever really cared about me, in spite of my efforts to keep anyone from caring. My entire life, pain has burned inside of me, Emma. And in so little time, you seem to have somehow doused a lifetime of fire."

"Can it be doused so easily?" she asked.

"I don't know," he admitted. "Perhaps it's still smoldering. Perhaps there is still more to fear. Sometimes I feel like it will explode and kill me from the inside out." He deepened his gaze on her. "I don't want you to be caught by the flying pieces."

A taut hush fell between them and Michael went to his knees, as if his confessions had exhausted him. When his eyes lifted again to meet Emma's, they were full of regret. He chuckled with irony. "I'm a pretty bad guy, eh? Kidnap a woman and threaten her with life, limb, and virtue. Then pour my heart out to bleed all over the ground." He held out his arms in a resigning gesture. "Trample on it if you must. I wouldn't blame you, and I might not even feel it. Pain is my best subject."

"Enough of pain," she whispered.

"Ah, yes." He smiled with little humor. "I've fulfilled my part of the bargain: truths of pain. Now it's your turn, Miss Davies." Michael's expression turned more severe than his greatest attempt at cruelty had ever shown as he threw Emma's question back at her. "What do *you* know of love?"

Emma didn't know what she could possibly say to even attempt dispelling such pain. Would words mean anything to him now? Not words alone, she answered herself with confidence. In that moment her instincts meshed with her feelings, which until now had made so little sense. It was easy to reach out her hand, but he only stared at it like a wild animal, afraid of human contact.

"It's all right," she whispered, like she might have to a skittish colt. "Take my hand." It was a long moment before he reached out and pulled her dainty fingers into his, calloused and hard. His touch was timid, nothing like the man who had abducted her and threatened her with her virtue. This was the real Michael Hamilton. Emma gave a gentle squeeze and his grip instantly tightened, as if she had become a lifeline. His hold on her became almost painful, but Emma welcomed it, sensing the trust it betrayed.

Treading carefully, Emma came to her knees before him, setting a gentle hand to his face. A combination of surprise and caution filled his eyes. Emma held her breath and ignored her pounding heart as she leaned forward and pressed her lips to his. She watched his wary eyes, then closed her own to avoid the distraction. He gave little response, but she persisted, softening her lips to his with little more than instinct to guide her. She felt him relax, then pushed a hand into his mussed hair as his kiss deepened. With his response, a warmth filtered through Emma from the inside out. Combined with the pounding of her heart, she knew beyond any doubt that her affection was genuine. She loved him. She loved him, heart and soul.

Michael tried to discern where her motives were coming from. He wouldn't have been surprised to have her respond to the truth with repulsion and disgust. At the very best, he had hoped for compassion and tenderness, not unlike he'd found in her mother. But this? What kind of woman would be confronted with what he'd just revealed to her, then respond with a kiss unlike anything he'd ever known in his life? It was as if she could draw his pain into her and somehow buffer it, and at the same time feed him with perfect affection and acceptance. Was this the answer to his question? Was this somehow what she knew of love? The thought was too incredulous to even consider. But he didn't have to understand it to know how it warmed him.

Their kiss seemed to last forever, an eternity of questions answered, pains faced, and hopes fulfilled. When Emma finally eased back, her villain, her rogue, the scoundrel who always wore black, had tears glistening in his eyes. His grip on her hand tightened further, as if to maintain a bond between them.

"Is something wrong?" she asked.

He blinked, and the tears spilled over his face. "After all I have done to you," his voice cracked, "all I have admitted to," he sighed and drew a sustaining breath, "you would give such perfect affection to me?"

Emma wrapped everything into a neat little package when she said, "No amount of hate or pain can stand with truth in the face of genuine love and forgiveness."

Michael drew back to absorb her words, as if a splash of cold water had struck his face. And then it happened. Something in the deepest part of him began to tremble, like a volcano threatening to erupt. It was as if his conscience had just received the message that he had bared his soul, and it was now reminding him that there was a price to be paid. A lifetime of pain and fear that had been carefully tucked away, bit by bit, was suddenly overflowing, bubbling through him, demanding to be felt and acknowledged before they would leave him in peace.

Emma felt Michael's grip tighten even further, and she held to him with equal force. She watched his eyes and saw something frightened and vulnerable pass through them. He unconsciously lifted his free hand to his mouth and expertly clicked his thumbnail off the edge of his tooth with the perfect rhythm of a ticking clock. She could almost feel his mind spinning. Pulsebeats pounded in her ears. The ticking ceased. For a long moment, Emma wondered if the bomb would explode or diffuse. Michael bowed his head forward. *It's diffused*, she told herself just before an anguished groan emerged from the depths of him. He let go of her so suddenly that it left her startled. His arms went over his head as if he could fight off some kind of unbearable pain. Emma bit into her lip to keep from crying out as she took hold of his shoulders in a firm grip, fearing she would lose him if she let go. His groan deepened until he gasped for breath and threw his head back in an agonizing wail.

Emma could only cry and watch as twenty-eight years of pain exploded before her eyes. In helpless frustration, she called to him as if he were miles away and drowning, "Hold me, Michael. I'm here. Hold me." She felt some relief when he pulled her against him where she could absorb a degree of his pain, rather than just observing help-lessly. She kept expecting him to gain control and bring this torment to an end, but it went on and on. He groaned and cried, sobbed and muttered incoherent phrases. He held to her as if for life itself. And only when the cave had turned dark and cold did he settle enough to simply cry into her lap, like a lost child, finally come home.

Emma lay back on the ground, holding him to her in the dark-ness, crying silent tears to match his own. Deep into the night, Michael finally slept. But Emma could not. She fingered the scars across his back, wondering why such misery existed in the world. Then she thought of her parents and felt a deepening of gratitude for the life they lived, the misery they eased, and the heritage they had given her through their example. She knew now that their love for Michael at a tender age had softened him for what he had faced today. Seeds planted many years ago had helped him cross bridges that many pained souls could never attempt.

For what seemed hours, Emma contemplated and analyzed what had transpired. She was grateful, not only for her mother's insights on human behavior, but also for Alexa's willingness to share her knowledge with her children as they had grown and matured.

Understanding what had happened to Michael gave her confidence that she could handle what might still lie ahead.

Realizing she was cold, Emma eased away, knowing Michael must be more so without his shirt. Tenderly she covered him with a blanket and rolled another gently beneath his head. He was so completely exhausted that he hardly moved a muscle. Finally she lay next to him and slept at last.

❦   ❦   ❦

Far past breakfast, Lacey still slept. Ben declared she had no signs of fever, and the sleep was likely giving her much-needed revitalization. Camp was in order, and there seemed little to do except wait—and watch Lacey. Ben whittled. Jess read a book. And Tyson watched Lacey. He leaned on one elbow and idly tossed pebbles. He sat up and scratched lines in the bottom of his boots with a stick. He shifted and explored nervous gestures until Jess and Ben glared at him. They were all relieved when Lacey began to stir.

Lacey felt physically better even before she realized she was awake. Her leg didn't hurt so much, and her body felt normal instead of weak with fever. She was lying on her back when she opened her eyes to see the rock of the cave opening above her. Quickly her memory filled in the pieces and she turned, searching for her father. Their eyes met in a warm exchange. She looked to Ben, and he nodded in his typical way. There was no describing the peace she felt to know that she was in their care.

Recalling her vivid dreams, Lacey unconsciously glanced around further, if only to reassure herself that Tyson was as absent as he had always been. Her breath caught in her throat when she saw him. Her stomach tightened. As her memories of drifting in and out of consciousness began to take shape, she had to admit that it hadn't been a dream.

The silence became excruciating as their eyes met with a once-familiar electricity. There was so much Tyson wanted to say, but the only words that came to his lips were simply, "Hello, Lacey."

His voice seemed to bring her to life, and she sat up abruptly. Tyson leaned forward, expecting a much-longed-for embrace. But instead his face met with a slap to outdo the one she'd sent him away with.

Lacey waited for a reaction, and felt gratified as he turned slowly back to face her, the hurt evident in his eyes. "Oh, fine," he said with sarcasm. "It's the last thing you do before I leave, and the first thing when you see me again. Couldn't you come up with something original?" Lacey immediately slapped him equally hard with the other hand, sending his face the opposite direction.

Jess and Ben started to laugh, and Tyson growled, "What's so funny?"

"Looks like she's feeling better," Ben chortled.

"I'd have to say you deserved that," Jess added.

Tyson turned humble eyes back to Lacey, attempting to put across a point as he said firmly, "Yes, I think I did."

"You'd better believe it," Lacey snarled, peering beneath the blanket covering her. "Could I get some breeches, perhaps? I'm starving. And I'm not going to hide under this blanket all day."

"Your mother sent some things," Jess announced, coming to his feet. "I'll get them. Tyson, heat her some breakfast."

Tyson did as he was told as Ben went out, mumbling something about the mules being better company. Jess produced a saddlebag and tossed it next to her. "I think everything you'll need is in there. If not, say so. It's just a suggestion, but why don't you wear that skirt you had on? It would make it easier to treat that leg."

"That would be fine." She gave her father a warm smile that made Tyson envious. Jess brought her the now-dry skirt, then left to join Ben and the mules.

"Do you need some help with that?" Tyson asked as she struggled to pull the skirt on and remain covered.

"I'm just fine," she spat. "I've managed fine without you for more than four years, so turn around and mind your business."

Tyson turned his back and dumped her breakfast from the pan to the plate. Lacey struggled with the skirt until she bumped her tender leg and couldn't help releasing a startled gasp. Tyson turned without thinking, and she glared at him. He sighed and looked away until she was ready to eat.

"Thank you," she said tersely as he handed her the plate. Lacey used great willpower to avoid his gaze. The reality of his presence clashed with everything she had come to feel inside. She caught his eyes briefly as he sat across from her, his expectant expression making it clear that he was going to say something. Lacey ignored him and began to eat.

"Mother said you missed me," he ventured.

Lacey's eyes shot up. Did he know about Richard? "What else did Mother tell you?" she asked with her mouth full.

"That's about it." His tone was dry. Lacey sighed with relief. She didn't want him to know about Richard; not yet, at least. "Although she did say you would be glad to see me." She continued to eat as if he'd said nothing. "It would seem that even Mother is wrong occasionally."

Lacey paused and looked up at him. In truth, she was so glad to see him that she could hardly bear it. She had longed for this moment since the day he'd left. But there was too much deeply carved pain for her to simply set it all aside and throw herself at him in joyous reunion. It was going to take time to heal the wounds he had caused. But she relinquished her anger enough to truthfully admit, "I am happy to see you, Tyson."

"Oh?" He chuckled humorlessly. "Was that the message I was supposed to get from the right hand, or the left?"

"At least I know you're alive," she said and took another bite. Tyson shook his head in disbelief. This was not the reunion he'd expected. But then, as his father had said, it was likely what he deserved.

"Lacey," he said gently, figuring now was as good a time as any, "I have something to say to you. I can only ask that you listen."

"I'm listening," she said distantly, then she pointed. "Is that coffee hot?"

Tyson poured her a cup and handed it to her, hating the indifference in her expression. It was only her painful greeting that let him know she cared at all.

"Lacey, I'm sorry."

"You're sorry?" She laughed.

"I was a fool, Lacey. Everything you said before I left was true."

Lacey paused a moment to absorb it. At least he'd come back humble, but that didn't come close to rectifying the circumstances. "You're right, Tyson. You were a very big fool, and you're an even bigger one now if you think you can just come back after all this time, say you're sorry, and forget it ever happened. You have no idea what I went through in your absence." She pointed a fork at him. "Don't you even begin to think you know the suffering you left behind."

"Why don't you tell me?" he asked softly.

"Why don't you figure it out!" she retorted.

Tyson squeezed his eyes shut a moment and drew a sustaining breath. "Lacey, we can never resolve this if we can't talk about it maturely."

"Don't you dare talk to me about maturity!"

"Lacey, I was eighteen."

"So was I! I didn't run out on you! And you were certainly man enough to . . ." She stopped when his eyes went wide. She knew he'd perceived the implication as he glanced elsewhere abruptly.

Lacey began to eat again while Tyson searched for words. She was setting her empty plate aside before he said, "I was relieved to hear that you hadn't married."

"What are you implying?" she asked pointedly, inwardly hoping he still cared enough to marry her. It was the only thing she wanted. All this time, she had longed for nothing more than to have Tyson return and marry her—not because they had a son, but because he loved her. That was it. She wanted to know beyond a doubt that he was marrying her for love, not out of obligation. The best way to do that was to keep him ignorant of Richard's existence until she was certain that Tyson still loved her. Only then could she truly forgive him.

"I'm not implying anything," he insisted. "I simply said that I was relieved."

"Used women have a difficult time finding suitable husbands." Lacey saw the hurt in his eyes, but she didn't regret saying it. That was how she felt, and he needed to hear it.

"I did not use you." An edge crept into his voice.

"And what would you call it?" she demanded.

Tyson couldn't answer her. Any claim to love would only deepen his hypocrisy.

Jess eased the tension by returning with Ben, who knelt next to Lacey. "Let's have a look at that leg," he said kindly while untying the bandages.

"Did you get enough to eat?" Jess asked.

"Yes, thank you," she said gratefully.

"And how are you feeling?"

"Quite good, actually," she admitted. "I'm so relieved to be away from that . . . ," she shuddered visibly, "that beast." She looked around frantically as she finally became distracted from Tyson's return enough to perceive a reality. "Where's Emma? Good heavens! He's still got Emma, hasn't he!" She looked to Jess, who nodded just enough to answer her question. "Papa, no!" She would have jumped off the blanket if Ben hadn't been holding her leg down. "You can't leave her alone with him. He'll . . . he'll . . ." Tears welled into her eyes, and she bit her lip.

Jess and Tyson exchanged an anxious glance. Tyson relied on his father to handle this calmly. He was seething so much from the thought that he wanted to scream.

"He'll what, dear?" Jess asked carefully.

"He'll have his way with her," she stated. Tyson came to his feet, not knowing how to react any other way. "He was always threatening her, but she . . ."

"She what?" Tyson insisted when she hesitated.

"She remained so calm. I don't know how she did it. Most of the time she acted as if everything was under perfect control. There were times when she almost seemed to enjoy herself. But the man is crazy, I tell you. He'd be joking one minute and have a knife at her throat the next."

Jess fought his instincts and tried to keep Alexa's words in mind, asking calmly, "Did he hurt her?"

"Not to my knowledge," Lacey had to admit. "But I suspect there were times when I was asleep that he . . . well, I'm not sure."

Tyson asked in a barely calm voice, "Wouldn't she have told you if something had happened?"

"I don't know. She seemed . . . different. I had to wonder if he was threatening or manipulating her to keep quiet."

"Lacey," Ben brought up an important point, "how did he behave toward you?"

"For the most part, he ignored me. He came right out and said they should have left me home. I wish they would have."

"Then why did he take you to begin with?" Tyson asked.

"I was sleeping in Emma's bed that night so she could . . ." She stopped, realizing she was about to mention Richard. She finished by saying, "It's a long story. But they got me by mistake, then they went back for Emma."

Ben gave a nod toward Jess that seemed to echo Alexa's speculations. "That doesn't make sense," Tyson said.

"It does if Michael Hamilton has motives beyond money," Ben replied.

"Like what?" Tyson and Lacey said at nearly the same time.

"Like Emma," Ben answered. Tyson and Lacey looked surprised. Jess obviously wasn't. "Why else would he behave the way he has?"

"I'd say that speculating over this is pointless," Jess concluded. "When we have Emma back, we will get the truth."

"But you can't leave her there." Lacey took hold of his arm with pleading urgency.

"I'm afraid we have no choice," Jess said gravely. "There is no way we can get her back without jeopardizing her safety until the day after tomorrow. If something was going to happen, it would have by now. There is no point in risking her life. Michael's not the only one out there, and I didn't like the looks of them."

Tyson groaned in frustration and pushed a hand through his hair. "How did that happen?" He pointed to Lacey's leg as Ben returned his effort to removing the bandage. "Was it an accident, like they said?"

"I suppose you could say that," Lacey said, feeling knots gather inside of her to think of it.

Jess saw her turn toward him, as if seeking support, and he could tell the ordeal had been very trying. Her sensitive nature would not handle such things as well as Emma's natural confidence.

"Michael took Emma away for a while," she began, which made Tyson even more tense, "and while they were gone, one of those awful . . . men . . . tried to . . ." Her lip quivered.

"He didn't succeed, did he?" Tyson demanded.

"No," she said firmly. "Michael and Emma came back when I screamed, but when I was trying to get away, the man grabbed me with a knife in his hand and . . . well, I suppose it could be justified as an accident."

"An accidental attempted rape," Tyson grumbled, and Lacey started to cry again.

Jess hit him in the shoulder for his lack of sensitivity, then he asked what he considered an important question—if he was supposed to be keeping an open mind. He was beginning to be extremely irritated with Alexa for making him promise to do that. "Lacey, what did Michael do after it happened?"

"I didn't see it, but Emma said that he . . . he beat the guy up pretty badly."

Jess actually smiled. "I don't think Emma's in too much danger," he concluded. "How's the leg, Ben?"

"Does it hurt much?" Ben asked, removing the last of the many layers of bandaging.

"Not nearly so much as it did yesterday."

Ben smiled as he uncovered it, saying with a cheerful tone, "I don't think we could expect any better than that."

They all leaned over to look. The reddish swelling was completely gone, and there was no sign of fluid in the wound.

"It's going to heal just fine," Ben announced, then Lacey groaned as he cleaned it with disinfectant.

"That's wonderful," Jess sighed. "It will make it easier for you to start home." Only Ben seemed to know what he was talking about.

"We can't go without Emma," Lacey protested.

"Ben and I will get Emma. I'm sending you home with Tyson." Their eyes met quickly, and Lacey knew she couldn't protest without looking foolish. But she couldn't decide whether to feel relieved or petrified at the prospect of a week's journey with only Tyson's company.

"I want you to start within the hour," Jess added, "so get ready." He gave a subtle grin. "And with any luck, you'll work out your differences before we get back."

"Yeah," Ben chuckled, "out of earshot."

Tyson and Lacey remained silently embarrassed as Ben dressed the wound, pointing out to Tyson exactly what he was doing as it became evident that Tyson was going to be solely in charge of Lacey's well-being for the next several days. Tyson knew it wasn't going to be easy, but maybe it was what they needed. He wouldn't be surprised if that was the biggest reason his father was doing this.

Ben finished up and left them alone. "Find my boots, please," Lacey ordered. "I need some fresh air."

"You can't walk on that!" Tyson insisted.

"I can certainly try. Will you please find my boots?"

Tyson found them while Lacey dug through her bag for stockings and eased them on, going carefully over the bandage. She tugged one boot on easily, but Tyson saw her grimace as the other moved into place.

"You all right?" he asked.

"I'm fine. Help me up."

Tyson helped her to a standing position, wanting so badly to just take her in his arms and hold her until he died. But all he could do now was help her hobble unsteadily out of the cave into the sunlight. Frustrated and concerned, Tyson finally lifted her into his arms, saying with sarcasm, "All right, here's your fresh air. Now what?"

"I need some privacy," she said with quiet intensity, relieved when he didn't act embarrassed. He simply carried her to some brush, set her down carefully, and moved several paces away with his back turned.

The remainder of their preparations to leave passed in miserable silence. When they were ready to set out after receiving careful instructions, Jess lifted Lacey onto a horse and helped her get situated, laying her lower leg over a folded blanket in front of the saddle to keep it elevated.

"It's a good thing you learned some side saddle." He smiled up at her. "Are you comfortable?"

"I'm fine." She bent to kiss him. "Thank you, Papa. And please, get Emma back safely."

"I will," he promised. "And you, don't be too hard on Tyson." Lacey looked down, then she looked at Tyson, who was quietly talking to Ben.

"I'm not sure how to be."

"Just try to remember where it all began, Lacey. It seems overwhelming now, but time will work it out."

"He doesn't know about Richard?" she asked to verify her suspicions.

"Let's just say that he doesn't know who Richard belongs to." Jess smiled slyly.

"You mean he . . ."

"He was rather taken with the boy." Jess squeezed her hand. "Just let it take its course, Lacey. And work toward forgiving him. You will have no peace until you do." She smiled timidly and he added, "Be careful. We'll be just a few days behind you."

Jess moved to Tyson as he mounted his horse. "You take good care of her, now," he cautioned with a smile.

"I will," Tyson said with conviction, his eyes moving to Lacey.

"Get going," Jess said, standing back as the animals moved forward.

"How you doing?" Tyson asked quietly, riding next to Lacey.

"Better than the journey out," she admitted, then her eyes became distant. "If only I could stop thinking about Emma. I hate to imagine what awful thing is happening to her right now."

"Then don't think about it." Tyson reached a hand over to squeeze hers, and he felt some relief when she didn't pull away. "Emma will be fine."

Lacey could only hope he was right as she focused her mind toward going home. Home, with Tyson at her side.

Nine
STARTING OVER

Michael opened his eyes and felt completely disoriented, as if he'd been transported to another time and place since he'd last seen daylight. His eyes burned with an unfamiliar dryness as he attempted to focus on his surroundings. For a moment, the sensation in his head was like those times when he couldn't remember anything between the first drink and the hangover. The last time he'd felt that way, he'd ended up in prison. The fear of such a thing ever happening again made him sit up abruptly. The familiarity of the cave took hold, but the realization that he was without his shirt brought the memories flooding over him. He'd hardly been without his shirt since the day he left home as a child, except when he bathed in total privacy. And now here he sat, exposed and vulnerable.

Sunlight stingily filtered through the cave entrance, illuminating a path across the ground that his eyes followed, coming to rest on the motivation behind all he'd done since he was eighteen. Emma. She was the biggest reason he'd stayed at Byrnehouse-Davies to work, rather than going into the world as most of the others did. And she was the reason he'd left. The reality of his feelings for Emma had provoked the drunken fit that had landed him in front of a judge. And thoughts of longing, combined with vengeance, had driven his carefully laid plan, now laid waste. She had given him what he'd never expected. He'd been certain she would be haughty, full of arrogance, fighting him tooth and nail at every turn—and he would have relished it. It would have convinced him, along with everything else in his life, that he was worthless, cruel, and black-hearted. And that she was nothing more than a spoiled brat.

But Emma had thrown him way off course. He'd felt the self-confidence and discernment of her mother right off. And Alexa Davies was a woman he respected. But Emma had something more than even the great Mrs. Davies; something courageous and unexplainably right that had thwarted his plans at every turn. And now . . .

Michael put his face into his hands and groaned. He wasn't even sure what had happened to him last night, but he knew it had changed him. Recalling the events that had exhausted him to the core, Michael felt awed, embarrassed, confused, afraid, and wonderful all at once. But in the center was an unfamiliar peace where only pain had existed before. He felt as if the long-buried demons that had hovered mercilessly inside of him for as long as he could remember had suddenly been set free.

Michael felt inexplicably afraid as Emma stretched herself awake and turned warm eyes upon him. He couldn't begin to know what to expect after what she'd witnessed last night. But she leaned forward to kiss him as if it was the most natural thing in the world. His fear evaporated, but he still felt embarrassed when she gently asked, "Are you all right, Michael?"

"I think I'll make it." He tried to keep his voice light, but she didn't smile. "I'm a pretty tough guy. I've got the scars to prove it."

"You don't have to be tough for me," she whispered, brushing a hand over his bearded face. "Unless you want to, of course."

"I think I'm tired of pretending to be something I'm not."

Emma smiled. "And I think I'm hungry." Her stomach growled to echo her announcement, reminding them both that they'd not eaten since yesterday's breakfast.

Michael was relieved by the distraction. He came to his feet and offered her a hand. Emma stood and turned to survey the situation. "I'll find a lantern," he offered, noting that it was too dim in the cave to accomplish much of anything without some light.

Emma picked up Michael's shirt and briefly inhaled its subtle masculine fragrance before she tossed it playfully toward him. She watched him put it on, and their eyes met with newfound interest. Was he as in awe of what they had shared as she was?

Relieved to have the scars concealed, Michael said, "I'll build a fire. You find the food."

A short while later, Emma sat on the ground with her feet tucked beneath her, holding a plate of heated beans, hot biscuits cooked on a stick, and canned peaches. Michael sat before her, his long legs nearly encircling her.

"I could only find one cup." He offered it to her and she took a careful sip of the rich coffee. She gave it back, and he did the same without taking his eyes from her. While Emma had her plate in one hand and her loaded fork in the other, Michael put a peach slice into her mouth, but most of it stuck out since it was too big.

"I'm going to drop it," she managed to say with a chuckle. Michael laughed, then impulsively took the other half of the peach with his mouth, kissing her as he bit into it. Then he kissed her again. She looked at him in a way that made him remember all the other times he had kissed her. Recalling his insensitivity and brashness made him turn away, embarrassed and wondering how to deal with these changes.

They finished eating in silence, then cleaned the dishes together with water heated over the fire. When everything was in some semblance of order, Emma excused herself to go out and find some privacy. She returned to find Michael standing beside the cave entrance, studying the landscape as if he'd never seen it before. He wore his hat and a long coat that she'd seen on him only once before during this excursion. The coat was pushed behind his arms, and his hands were deep in the pockets of his breeches.

"Going somewhere?" she quipped.

"Crazy perhaps," he said too soberly.

"Do you want to talk about it?" Emma urged one hand out of his pocket and held it.

Michael brought her hand to his lips with a gallant kiss that made her tingle. "I can't think of what to say."

"What are you feeling, Michael?" she asked.

He looked at her and chuckled, not certain he liked dealing with his emotions in such a straightforward manner. "Overwhelmed."

"That's why you should talk about it."

"Is that what your mother taught you?" he asked, clearly hearing Alexa Davies coming through in Emma's simple wisdom.

"Emphatically," Emma said.

With a desperate need to understand what was happening to him, Michael told himself he had come too far with Emma to have any good come of holding back. She couldn't possibly see or hear anything from him now that could shock her. And their time together was brief. Instinctively he believed that she could help him heal and start over, provided he wasn't stupid enough to waste away this precious time together. Too soon, it would be over and she would be going back to the world he'd torn her away from.

With that in mind, he banished his self-consciousness and decided that he would face all of this now or never. He sighed deeply. "I feel out of sorts with myself," he admitted. "The man I am accustomed to being does not fit any more with what I feel inside. I don't know how to face anything. I'm nearly afraid to speak, for fear I will betray something unfitting."

"Perhaps I could be your interpreter until you learn the language."

He gave her a warming smile that lit up his eyes. "Why, Emma? I don't understand why you have given so much to me."

"I haven't given you so very much." She laughed it off, certain her real reasons were not something he was prepared to hear just yet.

"You've given me a lot more than I ever deserved," he said, and felt unexpected moisture on his cheeks. Hurriedly he wiped the tears away and laughed from embarrassment. "I haven't cried since I was seven, when my father held my arm against a hot stove because I cried when he beat me with a belt." Emma put a compassionate hand to his face, touching his tears with acceptance. Michael turned his arm over and pulled up his sleeve in search of the evidence.

"It's this one." He lightly pointed to a burn welt, then pulled the sleeve back over it. Fresh tears spilled, and he hurried to wipe them away. "I haven't cried for more than twenty years, and now I can't seem to stop." He felt embarrassed, but he doubted it made much difference after what Emma had witnessed last night. "I'm sorry," he said. "I feel as if I've fallen off some great pedestal that I'd placed myself on. Somehow I feel like less of a man."

"No, Michael. Today you are on a higher plane than you have ever been. Today you are more of a man than some men ever dream of being."

"Where do you find such wisdom?" He touched her face with awe.

"Mother always told me I have a gift of discernment."

"I should like to tell your mother how your gift has saved me."

Silence brought to mind something Michael felt he had to say, and he figured now was as good a time as any. "Emma, I have been thinking and . . . well, you asked me why I left Byrnehouse-Davies four years ago." He cleared his throat tensely. "I'm not sure I can tell you why exactly, but I want to say that I was wrong to leave. Perhaps if I had not been so hasty . . . but I never dreamed you would change your mind." He sighed and bit his lower lip. This confession and apology business was not comfortable for him. "I can see now that I had underestimated you, Emma. And I can also see that I have brought much of my misery upon myself."

"You are not to blame for the pain inflicted on you as a child, Michael. But good can only come from it if you learn to rise above it."

"And that would make me more of a man?" he asked with a dubious chuckle. Emma nodded firmly, completely serious.

Michael paused to try and grasp the full spectrum of what was happening here. He looked to Emma, and panic gripped him. She would be gone from his life so soon, and he was powerless to change it. With his desperation growing stronger, he drew courage to get to a point that he knew he had to face.

"Emma," he said deeply, "through the days we have been together, I have seen your . . . discernment, as you call it. You understand me, though I will never understand how. Emma, I trust you. I trust your wisdom. You must tell me. Tell me, Emma, what happened to me last night." His voice unconsciously lowered to a hushed whisper, as if he was discussing a dark secret that he didn't want the land and sky to overhear.

"Let's walk." Emma took his hand and moved in the direction he had taken her once before. She had thought all of this through last night while he'd slept, and she felt certain that she understood what had happened. But explaining it to him would not be easy. Michael had likely never thought past his own surface emotions. His entire background, his way of thinking, his manner of living was different from hers. Talking to him of such things would not be like discussing it with a member of her family, all of whom had grown together with an awareness of the human mind and how it related to the pained children they were trying to help, as well as to their own personal issues.

They walked together in peaceable silence, climbing the rocks to return to the place where he had once behaved so obnoxiously with her. "I'm not certain I like the memories here," he said when she stopped.

"There will be memories everywhere you turn. You can't hide from them. Besides," she smiled, "I think I like the memories here." She glanced around. "Here is where I was first kissed."

Michael lifted a skeptical brow before he looked down to ward off his embarrassment once again. His behavior with her had been appalling, and he knew it. Attempting to stick to his original purpose, he pressed gently, "Tell me what happened, Emma."

"As far as I could see, Michael, your willingness to face the truth, combined with your trust in me, triggered the release of all you have feared and hated."

"What do you mean by . . . release?" His eyes filled with a puzzled concern.

"My mother once explained it like this. Most people have things happen in their lives, to varying degrees, that are painful or difficult to deal with. If they are not dealt with and felt, they are bottled up inside . . . stored away, so to speak. It's like everything you have ever felt that hurt you was pushed into a corked bottle. Last night, you were given an offering of genuine love in the same moment that you were humble enough to be willing to accept it. Combined with your trust in telling me about your pain . . . well, the cork blew off, Michael. It hit you right between the eyes."

Michael leaned against the rock wall and sighed. She could see him trying to piece it all together, and she allowed him the time to do it. Several minutes later he stood straight, holding up a hand as his brow furrowed with deep concentration. "Wait a minute. Wait a minute." He looked at her hard. "An offering of what?" Emma hesitated, trying to recall how she'd said it. "I could have sworn you said an offering of genuine love."

"I don't think I stuttered." He seemed so surprised, when to Emma it felt so natural.

Michael attempted to fit that in with everything else he was trying to grasp, and decided that she had to be speaking of her love for mankind—the type of love her mother gave to lost boys. Anything else was too preposterous to even be considered.

"Do you understand it now?" she asked gently.

"I think so," he answered, feeling like a boy in the schoolroom, discussing a scientific concept. He had to stop and remember that they were discussing his heart and soul. And on the same topic, he recalled again that his time left with Emma was very brief. She had somehow ushered him across a bridge into a world he was unfamiliar with, and the thought of facing it without her was terrifying.

"Then what's the matter?" she asked, startling him from his thoughts.

Attempting to give a truthful answer that wouldn't sound foolish, Michael stated, "I was just thinking how different it feels . . . between us. I know somehow that you were a very big part of what has happened, and I . . ." He stopped, realizing he was sounding foolish after all.

"I think I know what you mean." She took his hand. "I feel as if you and I have shared a complete emotional unity." Michael's eyes narrowed in question. He didn't understand, and she didn't know how to explain it. Tyson or Lacey would have understood, but they knew how her mind worked. Michael would have to get used to her ways, just as she would his.

"It's like . . ." She looked at him closely. "Well . . . like . . ." She blurted it out. "Like making love is a complete physical union, what passed between you and me was a complete emotional union that few people share unless . . ." Oblivious to Michael's widening eyes, she went on to add, "My mother often told me that one without the other can leave a person feeling empty and discontent—in marriage, that is. It takes a careful balance for true happiness to evolve between two people."

Emma turned to Michael and saw the understanding in his eyes. Then she watched it fade into a warm desire that made her realize what she'd just said. "Oh, my!" She turned away, feeling herself turn warm. "I was simply repeating how Mother explained it. I didn't mean to imply that we . . . I mean . . . oh, help." She got so flustered that she started to walk away as the warmth in her face deepened to a hot blush.

Michael took the error at face value and grabbed her arm to stop her. "It's all right, Emma. I understand." She still looked embarrassed, but Michael misinterpreted it. "Emma, you must believe me when I say that I never had any intention of really having my way with you. For all my indiscretions, I would not have wanted to hurt you that way. I was just trying to be . . . well, you know."

"No," Emma took the opportunity to get to the bottom of all this, "I'm not sure I do know. You've told me a great deal, Michael. But you haven't told me why you're really here; why you've treated me the way you have."

Michael put his hands behind his back and looked at the ground. He didn't know where to begin. How could he possibly explain away and justify all he had done? He decided to begin at the beginning. "I suppose it all goes down to that day in the stables."

"The day you left."

"I can see now that I had misjudged you, that I was too hasty, but at the time . . ."

"All you felt was rejection."

"That's right," he said.

"And you wanted vengeance."

"I wanted to see you hurt the way I had hurt."

"I was hurt when you left, Michael, although I'm not certain I fully comprehended why at the time."

"I understand now why you turned me down," he said.

"Why?"

"You were afraid of me. You had reason to be, I suppose. I wasn't such a nice person."

"But you wouldn't have hurt me any more then than you would now."

"You didn't know that. I suppose I wanted to prove to you that I was someone worthy of fearing."

"Did it work?"

"You tell me, Emma. Are you afraid of me?"

"At times my fear was very real," she admitted.

"And yet you never screamed and fought like I expected you might."

"I didn't think it would do me any good."

"And now?" he asked. "Are you afraid of me now?"

"Why should I fear you now?"

"I might take you here and now and ravage your virtue."

"But you wouldn't, would you." It wasn't a question.

"No," he answered without hesitation.

"You still haven't told me the real reason we're here, Michael."

His reluctance to answer brought their conversation to a temporary standstill. They were both aware of the high-strung emotions hovering beneath the surface, but all they had come through and all they had to face in the little time left to them seemed presently overwhelming and insurmountable.

Emma felt a drop of rain and looked skyward to find it gray with clouds, though not nearly as oppressive as the day before.

"Oh, not again," Michael said with a comfortable sarcasm, although he welcomed the distraction. The drops came faster, but neither of them felt compelled to move the several steps back to the overhanging rock. Michael handed Emma his hat. She smiled at his humorous gallantry and put it on, giving him a mockingly wanton glance as she lowered her voice. "How do I look?"

"As beautiful as ever," he said, as if he'd asked her to pass the bread.

It gradually became evident that they were in for a good rain, and Michael urged her back to the rock wall where they leaned side by side, silently watching the storm. Memories of yesterday's storm filtered over them. Emma removed his hat and toyed idly with it, liking the feel of the rich, black felt.

"How long do you think it will rain?" he asked as if they were standing on a street corner, total strangers huddling beneath a shop awning.

"If we're lucky, all day."

Michael smiled at her, relieved to see some of the normalcy returning between them. Taking notice of a visible shiver that went through her, he asked gently, "Are you cold?"

"Not especially," she replied.

"Then why are you shaking?"

"I don't know," she answered honestly. "Maybe I *am* cold."

"Here." He began to remove his coat.

"Oh no," she insisted, "I'm all right. I just . . ." She stopped when he threw it around her shoulders and she eased her arms into it. Michael rolled up the sleeves so that her hands showed beneath them, but the coat was so long on her that it actually brushed the ground. He took the hat and put it back on her head, surveying her with a delighted chuckle, then he realized she was still shaking.

"Still cold?" he questioned. Emma shook her head firmly. "Afraid?" he asked quite seriously.

"No," she said with strength, then she chose to return to her unanswered question. "Why, Michael? Tell me why we're here like this."

Michael looked out to the pouring rain, then he looked at her. "You're still shaking," he commented lightly. But as Emma looked into his eyes, she understood why. It was his nearness, his newness of spirit, his innocence of his own goodness; it was the reality of how much she loved him. Michael put an arm around her and pulled her close to him in a gallant offering of warmth, but her trembling only increased.

"Why?" she whispered, and set a quivering hand against his chest as she looked up into his eyes.

"I assume you want me to be completely honest," he stated with reluctance when it became evident he couldn't avoid this. It wasn't that he was afraid to admit it, but rather the hopelessness of such an admission that made him hesitate.

Emma nodded. The question in her eyes deepened.

"There is no reason not to tell you." He looked toward the rain. "I'm certain it's already become evident. I can make no more a fool of myself than I already have."

Michael turned his eyes to bore deeply into hers. The severity in them suddenly stilled her shivering. For a moment there was no sound, no movement. Only the continuing rain.

"Emma," he spoke her name as if for the first time. His voice turned low and husky, and the emphasis on her name was passionate. He put a hand to her face and brushed back a stray lock of hair. Emma closed her eyes momentarily and leaned her face into his hand. "My sweet Emma." His voice lowered further and she opened her eyes. "I have loved you for so long, I don't remember when I started loving you."

Emma felt her chest rise and fall as her breath became labored. Her vision of him blurred as her eyes filled with mist. She felt him moving closer as the warmth of his breath caressed her face. She closed her eyes and the tears spilled as his lips timidly touched hers, moved away, then touched again. Emma felt his arm come around her, his fingers threading into her hair, his hand pressing against the back of her head, tilting it back to accommodate his height. The hat fell to the ground unnoticed. His lips softened. She eased closer and accepted a kiss unlike anything she had ever dreamed existed. All the misguided emotions settled around them in that moment as everything became perfectly clear.

Emma pulled her head back, gasping for air as if her head had exploded through the surface of glassy waters. She willed her lips back to his with a kiss that made the last one seem mild in comparison. Then all became still.

Emma found the will to open her eyes. Michael's face hovered close to hers, expectantly watching her. She kissed him and touched his cheek. He buried his face in her rain-dampened hair, muttering like a helpless child, "This can't be happening to me."

Emma pushed a hand into his dark hair and looked into his eyes. The longing she saw there compelled her to ask, "What is it, Michael? What are you thinking?"

"Oh, Emma," he murmured, "I want so badly to just take you in my arms and . . ." He stopped abruptly, realizing that he was treading toward boundaries that were simply off limits for him.

"What?" she asked. "What do you want?"

Michael took her shoulders into his hands to put distance between them. He forced logic into his mind, fearing he would hurt her even further if he didn't. "What I want is irrelevant, Emma. It's simply not possible."

"How do you know if you don't try? Just tell me what you want, Michael. You're not going to embarrass me."

"No," he chuckled and looked away, "I don't think that's possible."

He turned back to face her, and Emma searched for the answer in his expression that he seemed unwilling to verbalize. The desire in his

eyes was so evident that she turned warm and looked away. She
searched her mind for the words to tell him that they wanted the same
thing, without giving him the wrong impression.

"Apparently you were wrong," Michael said.

"About what?" she asked, still not looking at him.

"You said I couldn't embarrass you. But you're blushing, Emma.
And I didn't even say anything."

"You didn't have to," she said.

"Forget about it, Emma. It's impossible."

"No," she said, facing him again, "not impossible. Nothing is
impossible."

"Your innocence warms me, Emma." He brushed the back of his
hand over her face. "I never dreamed you would put such faith in me."

"I never dreamed you would give me such adoration, such devotion. I would never have believed that any man would go to so much
trouble for me."

"My devotion to you has been very misguided, Emma. I fear your
faith is not warranted."

Emma shook her head to disagree. "I want you, Michael," she said
quickly. Before she had the chance to clarify herself he went on, and
she was afraid he'd gotten the wrong idea.

"I'm flattered, Emma," he chuckled, "and it goes without saying
that the feeling is mutual." He lowered his voice intently, and a sadness filled his eyes that made Emma nervous. "But you are a lady,
Emma. You should be loved with a wedding ring on your finger."

"I would expect nothing less," she said, grateful for the chance to
clarify her stand on such things. He hung his head as if the conversation should be finished, but she added firmly, "Then you must put a
ring on my finger, Michael."

Michael's head shot up. He couldn't believe what he was hearing.
This kidnapping venture was not supposed to end in marriage pro-
posals! It was true that he wanted her in his life. But the reality of the
circumstances made the very thought preposterous. It was likely the
most difficult thing he had ever done, to say to Emma Davies, "I
cannot."

Emma felt certain the rain had distorted her hearing. "I'm sorry. I
don't think I heard you correctly."

"Emma," he said, his tone apologetic, "you have been very kind to me, and don't think I'm not appreciative of that, but I—"

"Kind to you?" She couldn't believe her ears. "Michael, has your memory failed you so quickly? Do you realize what you and I have been through together?"

"Yes, Emma." He took her hand. "Your discernment has helped me immeasurably, and I am forever indebted to you, but—"

"Michael! Haven't you been listening to me?"

"Why should I, when you won't let me finish a sentence?"

"I won't listen to anything that begins with the word *but*. Michael, what happened last night didn't happen because I was *kind* to you. I have not put up with you, argued with you, and forced you to face up to the truth for the sake of my own entertainment. It happened because there is something significant between us that is stronger and more binding than I believe either of us can comprehend. It happened because in spite of all that's transpired, we trust each other implicitly. I'm certain you heard me say it, because you repeated it back to me. But I'm going to say it again so you don't misunderstand me. What triggered the changes in you was an offering of genuine love. *My* love, Michael." Michael only stared at her, completely unreadable, so she shouted at him, "I love you, Michael. Do you hear me? I love you!"

Michael wanted to tell her that he didn't believe it. But to see all she had done, he could think of no other explanation. It was so wonderfully incredible, but it still didn't change the reality.

"Emma," he touched her face as if to memorize it forever, "I will never forget you. I . . ."

Emma backed away as if she'd been struck. "You'll never forget me?" She put a hand to her heart and tried to catch her breath. This was not how it worked out in those romance novels. "Michael, did I not just hear you say that you love me, that you have loved me for years?" He didn't answer. "Well?"

"Yes."

"When you asked me to go riding with you so many years ago, did you really believe it would just end there? Can you tell me that you didn't have intentions of pursuing it further?"

"That was one of the bitter realities I had to face when I left there. You and I simply could never be."

"Haven't you felt what happens between us? Don't you understand what's going on here? Why do you think I'm standing here pouring my heart all over the place? Michael, I—"

"Yes, Emma, I feel it." He stepped forward and took her shoulders. "I feel it so strongly that it consumes me, it obsesses me. But look at me, Emma. Take the passion out of your eyes and look at me. Stop and consider who I am, what I am. Look at what I've done to you, to your family. What you are implying here is impossible."

"Nothing is impossible, Michael."

"You've read too many of those stupid books."

"Perhaps you haven't read enough of them."

"I only read one," he admitted. "But it was enough to know that real life isn't like that. You and I are from different worlds, Emma."

"We grew up in the same place. You lived at my home for thirteen years of your life. Don't try to tell me our worlds cannot mesh and—"

"We grew up on different sides of the same door, Emma. And what I lived through before I came there is something you could not fathom in your worst nightmares. You are a lady, Emma. For six years *I was your servant.*" He enunciated each syllable with bitter emphasis.

"This is not the old world, Michael. We are living in a golden age, in a country full of freedom and opportunity. We are not ruled by social conventions. This is Australia. Our forefathers came here to be free of such nonsense."

Michael chuckled humorlessly. "Yours might have, but mine . . ." He chuckled again. "My forefathers, Emma, were the epitome of everything Australia was originally intended to be. My forefathers were the unwanted garbage of Europe, dumped here to be gotten rid of. I am the result of generations of lowlife breeding. My blood *is* bad. I was quite serious when I said that it would do nothing but poison your line."

"No, Michael, you are strong and good, and capable of overcoming your past. Your blood would strengthen my line. You and I both know what happens when horses are interbred too much. Eventually they become too soft or too uncontrollable. It takes a delicate mixture to produce good, solid stock. My line could use some good, strong blood."

"Your father is no soft man, Emma."

"No, but Tyson?"

"Tyson can hold his own."

"Not like you can. Don't get me wrong, Tyson is as much of a man as any woman could ever want. But his life was too easy, like mine. He's refined and gentle. I wouldn't want him any other way, but I hope his children marry into some strength, or the softness will become too dominant."

Again Michael became unreadable. "Do you understand what I'm saying?" she asked.

Michael sighed and looked away. He sounded genuinely irritated as he murmured, "Must you always be so blasted right?"

Emma smiled, but her expression quickly faltered again as he turned hard eyes toward her, saying intently, "But that still doesn't change the reality that your family will not want anything to do with me after what I've done." Emma said nothing, and he gave that dry chuckle. "No, I didn't think you'd have a comeback for that one. As I see it, if you and I were to marry, we would have two choices. We could go back to Byrnehouse-Davies and live, or we could go somewhere else and live. The first problem with either choice is that I have nothing. Let me repeat that: nothing! Wherever we choose to live, I would have to work to support you. And I can assure you, it would not be the way you are accustomed to being supported. I have no skill, no background except a prison record."

"You're wrong, Michael."

"Of course," he said with sarcasm.

"For one thing, as long as you work hard, the manner in which you support me means nothing." She didn't bother to tell him that she had a hundred thousand pounds put away. "Not only that," she said, "but you have a very worthy skill. Your knowledge and natural ability with horses are impressive. You received training at Byrnehouse-Davies, Michael. I don't need to tell you what kind of reputation goes behind that name when it comes to horses."

Michael shook his head, not liking the irony under the circumstances. "Oh, well, fine," his sarcasm deepened, "maybe you know of a place I could get a job with horses."

"Actually, I do."

Michael turned cynical. "Of course. Good morning, Mr. Davies. I would like to marry your daughter, and could you give me a job as well?" He shook his head soberly. "I don't think so, Emma." He chuckled ironically. "I would be lucky if he didn't shoot me on the spot." He leaned back against the rock wall and put his foot up behind him.

"Oh, I see now." Emma's voice turned angry. "I can see what all of this boils down to. You're afraid. You're afraid to take on the commitment, to fight for what you want. You're not even willing to try, because you simply are not committed, Michael."

"Let me tell you something." He took a step forward and grabbed her arm. "Commitment is watching a child grow into a woman, being constantly absorbed with a fascination that gradually grows into something more each time you see her from a distance, and when she comes close enough to see the features of her face, it renews life and builds hope. Commitment is being there every single time she sets foot in the stirrup, helping her at every turn while she looks right through you. But even that didn't dispel the commitment. Commitment, however misguided, is years of obsessive planning and carrying through with a quest to find her, obtain her, believing that vengeance is the motive, when in truth it was all a mad search to have those feelings returned, to know that I wasn't alone. To just have a part of you, Emma. Don't stand there and try to tell me that I . . ." Michael stopped when he realized she was smiling. She was amused. He considered what he had just said, then took a step back. "You did that on purpose."

"Yes, I did," she said proudly. "I think we have established the fact that you *are* committed. Now I want to establish one more. You are a fighter, Michael."

"I *was* a fighter," he corrected. "I'm not sure what I am anymore."

"You are still there." She pressed a hand over his chest and looked up at him with intensity. "There are simply some things that must be redirected. You can't solve these problems with a fist fight. But you can fight just the same to prove yourself, to prove what you've become, to achieve what you want. I can't tell you how my family will react to all of this, but I can remind you that my parents are good people who have dedicated their lives to forgiving and accepting the victims of misery in this world. All I can ask is that you try. If it doesn't work out, we'll go somewhere else and make a fresh start."

"I couldn't take you away from your family, Emma. I'm not sure I could make up for the sacrifice."

"I think you underestimate yourself. But I believe they will eventually come to see you the way I see you."

"And how is that?"

"You're a good man with a good heart, Michael. And you deserve a chance to prove it."

"Emma," he touched her hair in adoration, "you silence me every time. But I'm not certain I can live up to the faith you are putting in me."

"I put faith in your commitment, Michael; in your love for me, your ability to fight. Fight, Michael." She lowered her voice in challenge. "Fight for me, Michael. Fight to have me. I love you more than life, Michael Hamilton. I know that now. Don't sentence me to life without you. You must fight."

"Emma." He pulled her to him and held her fiercely. "Oh, Emma." His embrace tightened and she pressed her hands to his back, her face to his chest, feeling the desperation of her entire future hanging in the balance.

Michael's mind skimmed briefly through everything she had said, all that had happened, everything he felt. It all came down to one undeniable conclusion. "I can't believe this is happening to me," he muttered.

Emma looked up with hopeful eyes. "You mean . . ."

"After what you just said to me, I could never walk away from you and live with myself. There have been too many times in my life when I have taken the cowardly way out. But I won't do it now. Not for you, Emma."

Her face brightened. "Then you . . ."

"Yes, Emma. I will fight for you." His voice lowered intently. "I would die for you."

Emma's eyes filled with tears of perfect gratitude. Michael chuckled and asked, "Why are you crying?"

Emma laughed. "Look who won't let who finish sentences."

Michael grinned and wiped away a tear as it spilled over her face. "Well, let me finish the whole conversation with this." He dropped to one knee and took her hands firmly into his. "Will you marry me,

Emma?" She opened her mouth to answer, but he went on. "Will you
fight by my side to have a life together? Will you accept me in spite of
me? Will you forgive me of everything I have done to you? Will you
bear my name, my children? Will you . . ." He chuckled softly. "How
did you put it: nurture them and refine them?" He returned to his
impassioned tone. "Will you do the same for me? Will you guide me
into your world and teach me how to live there, teach me how to
become what I want to become? Emma, my sweet Emma. Will you
marry me?"

Emma squeezed his hands as tightly as she had strength, attempting to convey what her tears and the conviction of her voice could not.
"Yes, Michael. Yes. Yes! A hundred times yes. It would be an honor to
be your wife."

Michael remained on one knee as he pushed his arms around her,
holding her to him, trying to comprehend the reality and intensity of
what he had just done. Emma laughed, and he looked up. "It would
seem I'll be taking home a souvenir for my father after all."

Michael groaned and pressed his face against her in an attempt to
hide his shame. She laughed again, and he had to admit it was funny. It
scared him to death, but it *was* funny. Emma pushed her hands into his
hair, lifting his face to look at her. "It's not going to be easy, Michael."

"No, it's not. It will be as difficult for you as it will for me."

"But we can do it!" She pressed her hand to his cheek and he
turned into it, kissing her palm. "We'll fight together, Michael, and we
will win."

He looked up at her again, and all his fears briefly fled behind the
joy. Nothing had ever felt so good, so right, so wonderful in all his life.
And it was only made better by the reality that Emma felt it, too. His
happiness suddenly became too much to contain, and Michael stood
abruptly, lifting Emma with him. He laughed deeply as he turned circles in the lessening rain, while Emma held out her arms as if she
could fly.

"Did you hear that, world?" she shouted to the sky. "I'm going to
be Emma Hamilton."

Michael laughed and spun her again, slowing as he allowed her to
slide down to a point where she was at eye level with him, her feet
dangling above the ground.

Emma looked into his eyes and pressed her hands over his shoulders, marveling at his strength, his ability to hold her suspended as if it were nothing to him. She followed her urge to say, "I love you, Michael."

"Yes, I know." A corner of his mouth twitched upward.

"I don't want you to forget."

"I won't, as long as you keep telling me."

"Forever," she whispered.

"Emma," his tone deepened, making it evident he needed to say something important, "I have nothing to offer you."

"I know. You already told me that."

"I mean *nothing*, Emma. My life has just started over, and I might as well be a newborn babe. I have nothing but what you see here." His voice softened. "But all I have is yours." He chuckled and shook his head.

"What's funny?"

"I can't even believe I'm saying this. How does a man like me happen to be saying such things to Emma Byrnehouse-Davies? Do you realize what that name has meant to me? I have always been in awe of everything associated with Byrnehouse-Davies. And here I am . . ."

"And you're doing just fine." Emma smiled. Michael looked doubtful, and she searched for a way to give him some encouragement. She kept expecting him to put her down, but he seemed content to hold her against him. "Did you know that when my parents came together, neither of them had anything? She had been disowned by her family, and he was betting everything he owned on a horse race that would either save him or leave him destitute."

"You're joking." Michael gave a wide smile. It was strangely comforting, in a way, to imagine Jess Byrnehouse-Davies destitute. "So what happened? As if I didn't know."

"Mother told me that the day Tyson and I were born, their solicitor came with news that they had inherited all of Byrnehouse, and my grandfather, Tyson Byrnehouse, was one of the wealthiest men in Australia. And of course, by then, Father's estate was secure as well."

"Because he won the race?" Michael asked, intrigued.

"Of course," she smiled. "My mother was the jockey."

Michael laughed, then followed his urge to kiss her. He kissed her again, and a recently familiar spark came to life inside of him.

"Emma." He attempted to distract himself.

"Yes?" She seemed to prefer kissing over talking at the moment, so he let her slide to the ground and put some distance between them.

"We're getting wet," he said. "It's still raining."

She looked up as if she'd just noticed. "Not much. It's nearly stopped." She chuckled. "Maybe it will wash yesterday's mud out of my hair." Her eyes turned humorously vicious. "You remember that, don't you. You wrestled me to the ground—in the mud—you fiend."

Michael laughed. "You tried to throw me off my horse." His eyes turned mockingly cruel. "You feisty little wench."

"Well, at least you got mud in your hair, too. That makes us even." Her eyes lit up. "You didn't let them get away with my shampoo, did you? I paid a high price for that."

"An argument broke out over it. Rafe especially gets pretty excited about lavender, but I put a stop to it. I told them if they wanted your shampoo, they would have to kill me first."

"And of course they wouldn't dare cross you." She went along.

"They handed it over without hesitation; trembling in their boots, they were."

Emma smiled. "I'm glad to see that you haven't lost your sense of humor."

"What sense of humor?" he asked with perfect innocence. She glared at him dubiously, and he finally chuckled.

"Do we have enough water to wash my hair?" she asked like a child after candy.

"I can get you all the water you want," he lifted his brows quickly, "for a price."

"All right. I will marry you if you will wash my hair."

"Oh, no," he shook his finger at her, "you're not going to bribe and blackmail me like that. But I am willing to bargain." He lowered his voice. "I will marry *you* if *you* will wash *my* hair."

"Done!" she said like an auctioneer finalizing a bid.

"Could we play in the suds?" Now *he* was the child after candy, though his enthusiasm was ridiculous, even in that light.

"If you wish." She took his hand and headed back toward the cave.

"You did make it look like such fun."

"Wait!" She stopped walking abruptly.

"What?" he asked in panic.

"You forgot your hat."

"No," he held up a finger, "it's *your* hat. I just told you that all I have is yours." She hurried to pick it up and he added, "It looks better on you."

Emma grinned, and Michael watched her intently as she brushed off the hat and put it on. He had to be the luckiest man in the world. He was going to marry a woman who lived in breeches—Emma Byrnehouse-Davies, no less. It had to be a miracle.

❦   ❦   ❦

While Tyson rode close beside Lacey, he pondered happier times between them when they had talked endlessly. And now, he couldn't think of any avenue for conversation that he hadn't already attempted. Every question he asked her came to a dead end with her brief, terse responses. The only thing she would talk about at all was her ordeal at the mercy of Michael Hamilton, and her concern for Emma. But since there was nothing to be done about that for the moment, he tried to steer around it rather than discussing something that only seemed to feed her anger. And so he settled for silence, saying nothing at all beyond necessary exchange.

By the time Tyson was setting up camp that evening, he felt as if he would scream from frustration. He'd been aching for years to be with Lacey, and now he felt as if there were still hundreds of miles between them. Of course, that was his fault, and he knew it. But he simply didn't know how to bridge the chasm he had created from his mistakes of the past. He just had to do it, he told himself over and over.

"Lacey," he finally said once they'd finished eating their evening meal, "there's something I need to say."

"I'm listening," she said, but she seemed guarded and distant.

"Then could you at least look at me?" he asked. She turned toward him reluctantly, as if his very presence only annoyed her. "Thank you," he said, forcing a civil tone. Reminding himself of his purpose, he cleared his throat louder than he'd intended and spoke firmly. "I want to say that . . . I was wrong. What I did was wrong, and—"

"What exactly are you referring to?" she asked tonelessly, as if the conversation bored her terribly.

Tyson swallowed hard and persisted. "I'm talking about the way I left, and . . . what I did to you before. I was young and stupid, and there are no words to express my regret. I know that words alone mean little, but . . . I intend to spend the rest of my life proving to you that I . . ." Tyson felt his voice catch and attempted to gain control of his emotion before he went on. He thought he had it mastered, but his next attempt was even more cracked. "I . . . I . . ." He stopped again, but felt some hope as Lacey's eyes softened on him. He looked at her deeply, and emotion overtook him. Impulsively he gave up his efforts to maintain control, and decided that she needed to see the evidence of his sincerity.

"I'm so sorry, Lacey," he cried. "I intend to spend the rest of my life proving to you that I . . . I love you, Lacey. And I pray that one day you will be able to forgive me . . . and that you'll be willing to take me back."

Lacey felt as if she were in a trance, watching from a distance as Tyson poured out his heart, tears streaming down his face. She had dreamt of this moment so many times that it was difficult for her to believe it was real. A part of her just wanted to throw herself in his arms and put the past completely behind them. But something bigger and stronger protested. What if she opened herself to him again, only to have him take off on another exploration of the world? What if he was just saying what he felt he had to in order to make peace for the moment? Of course, his apology deserved acknowledgment, but she couldn't bring herself to just throw away the past as if it had never happened. They had a son, for heaven's sake—a son that he knew nothing about. Had it ever occurred to him to even ask if something had resulted from their night together?

Lacey looked away and cleared her throat, attempting to keep her mind on the moment. She was still trying to find the right words to express the combination of joy and fear she felt when he said timidly, "Don't you have anything to say?"

Lacey turned back to face him and instinctively reached out to wipe away his tears. Her love for him briefly overruled all else as she whispered, "I love you, too, Tyson." He squeezed his eyes shut and gave a breathy laugh of relief that stopped abruptly when she added, "But you can't expect me to just let it go with a snap of your fingers. It's going to take time to get back to where we were before."

Tyson swallowed and coughed to suppress another onslaught of emotion. "I understand," he said. He wanted to have her forgive him and get on with their lives. But he'd left her waiting four years, and he couldn't expect it to be undone instantly. Still, he had to ask. "But . . . can we work toward it together?" He reached out a hand toward her, feeling as if he'd exposed himself to a man-eating crocodile.

Lacey looked at Tyson's hand and decided a measure of compromise was in order. She took his hand and squeezed it gently, bringing a subtle smile to his face.

Tyson acted on impulse alone as he let go of her hand and pushed his arms around her, holding her close. "I missed you so desperately, Lacey," he murmured close to her ear.

"I missed you, too," she replied, but the way she returned his embrace seemed withdrawn and cautious.

He reminded himself that it would take time as he eased back, saying gently, "It's late. We should get some sleep."

Lacey nodded and eased away. And Tyson resigned himself to a long, hard road ahead. But at least he had taken the first, most difficult steps. He only prayed that it wouldn't be too long before she found it in her heart to forgive him. He needed her as much as he loved her. And he loved her more than life.

Ten
MENDING BRIDGES

After rooting around in the cave for several minutes, Emma finally found the shampoo and towels. "So, where's the water?" she asked.

"Come along." Michael took her hand, and they walked from the cave in the opposite direction from where they had gone before.

"Michael," she said after they had walked several minutes, "you didn't bring anything with you to take the water back in, or . . ." They came around a cluster of huge stones that concealed a small pool, glistening in the high sun that was finally breaking past the clouds. "I've been here before," she said as the childhood memory took hold.

"I suppose that's likely." Michael squatted down by the edge of the water and urged Emma's hand to the pool's surface.

"It's warm." She smiled. "You've been holding out on me again."

Michael only kissed her. "Sit down, and I'll make your hair smell good." He rolled up his sleeves, and with the cup they had shared coffee in for breakfast, he lifted water into her hair until it dripped over the ground and onto his breeches. With a gentility that seemed to defy him, Michael lathered Emma's hair, toying, massaging, and scrubbing. Emma tilted her head back with a pleasurable moan.

"I bet they never had a scene like this is those silly books you read," he said.

Emma tipped her head back further to look at him, and he kissed her nose. "Do you find it romantic?" she asked.

"I do," he said with a little laugh, "perhaps because it's so thoroughly innocent. I suppose I can admit now that watching your sister wash your hair nearly drove me mad. I have been fantasizing about doing just this ever since."

Emma felt a warm gratification from his confession. Not only was he telling her his innermost thoughts, but it made her realize they had something in common.

"I suppose I fantasize in a way as I read," she admitted. "There must have been a part of me that always wanted such things in my life."

"Such things?" he asked as he coiled her hair on top of her head and kissed the back of her neck.

Emma did her best to sound dramatic. "Like having a handsome rogue kidnap me, carry me across the outback, and blackmail me into letting him wash my hair."

"Oh, you did not," he insisted.

"Well, not that exactly, but . . ."

"Yes?"

"The heroes were always you."

Michael took hold of her head and turned her to face him. "Yes," she admitted gingerly, "since the day you left, I could not read one of those silly books without seeing you."

"I should be flattered."

"Yes, you should. Are you?"

"Amazed would be more accurate."

"And tell me, Michael, what else have you fantasized about?"

"More things than I could have a chance to show you in a lifetime."

"We could try." She put a hand on his booted lower leg, noting the feel of the well-worn leather. Michael pushed his hands down over her arms, leaving a trail of lather over her shirt. Emma lay her head back against his shoulder and reached up behind her to put a hand into his hair.

"Now it's your turn." She imitated the way he often lifted his brows in mischief.

Michael eased away and knelt to lower his head into the pool, then he flipped it back and wiped the water from his eyes. He sat to face her and bent his head forward, mumbling with mock irritation, "Just what I need—to smell like lavender. If my hired thugs could see me now."

The thought made Emma laugh as she massaged the lather through his dark hair. Michael moaned pleasurably and lifted his head to look at her. Impulsively she worked the lather into his beard, sniggering as she watched him.

"What's so funny?" he sneered.

"You look like Father Christmas."

"There's no relation, I can assure you." A moment later he added, "I think that's enough. I believe I prefer that you smell this way."

"Fine." Emma wiped her hands over the front of his shirt, only to have Michael retaliate by pulling off one of her boots, then her stocking. He reached up to pull a handful of lather from her hair and began massaging her foot. Emma decided that she liked it until a corner of his mouth twitched upward and he started to tickle her.

"Oh, Michael, no! Don't do that!" She laughed with no control, wiggling and writhing, attempting to get free. He sneered wickedly as if he was operating some ancient torture device, and he didn't stop tickling until she was lying back on the ground, laughing helplessly and out of breath.

"Oh, look what you've done," he said like a mother disgusted by her soiled child. "I just washed your hair, and you have to go lying around in the dirt."

"It was your fault!" she protested, scrambling to her knees to tug on his boot until it came free. Michael leaned back on his elbows and watched her smugly until both his feet were bare. She pulled lather from her own hair and started to play with his feet while she watched his eyes. She got no reaction from him beyond an arrogant, "I'm not ticklish."

Emma grinned, recalling a particular spot where Tyson was ticklish. It was a worth a try. With careful purpose she moved her hands up his lower leg, barely touching him behind the knee.

"Ah!" He sat upright as if he'd been struck. "Emma?" He laughed. She did it again. "That's not fair!"

"Fair is relative, Mr. Hamilton."

He laughed, and she went back to gently massaging the lather on his feet.

"Did I ever tell you how I love the way you call me that?" She looked up in question and he clarified, "I mean, nobody ever called me that. It was always just Michael, or just Hamilton. You are the only person who has ever called me Mis-ter Hamilton."

"I shall have to do it more often, Mis-ter Hamilton."

"I wish you'd do that more often, as well." He nodded toward his feet. "I can't say I ever fantasized about it, but I think I'll start."

Emma smiled, then she looked down as her fingers became aware of something unusual. Impulsively she pushed the lather aside with her palm. It only took her a split second to realize what it was. There were cigarette burns on his foot. Startled, she looked up at him in question. As he realized her discovery, he retracted his foot and looked away tersely.

"Michael," she said, but he didn't look at her. She took his foot back with gentle insistence and continued to massage it. "Look at me!" Slowly he did. "No shame, Michael. You have to accept it. The scars are there. They will not go away. But they are not there because of anything you are, or anything you did. Your father had a problem. Not you."

Michael squeezed his eyes shut, wishing he could even begin to express what those words meant to him. For years he had tried to believe that it had nothing to do with him, but hearing her voice it that way dispelled more pain than she could ever realize.

"Thank you, Emma," was all he said, but she smiled, seeming to know how he felt. "Give me your foot," he said to change the subject, and she lifted the one that was still booted. He quickly bared it and cleaned it as he had the other, tickling for just a few seconds before she gave him a hefty kick with her free leg. Michael responded by dramatically rolling over and falling into the pool. Emma laughed as he stuck his head completely under and came up lather-free. He stood in the water that came half-way up his thighs, and reached out a hand. His smile turned subtly mischievous.

Emma put her hands behind her back. "Did you really think I would fall for that? You're perfectly capable of getting out of there on your own."

"It was worth a try," he said, then he bolted toward her, grabbing her around the waist before she even got to her feet. With ease he threw her gently into the water, just enough to rinse her off, then he helped her to her feet. Emma pushed her hair back off her face and wiped her eyes dry.

Their laughter stopped as she looked up at him. She could feel the changes between them in his gaze; changes that had come so quickly, and yet she could see they'd been evolving for years.

Michael wanted more than anything to just take her in his arms. But memories of all he'd threatened in the past made it difficult to fathom the trust in her eyes. And he had to wonder if he could trust himself with Emma Davies' virtue. It would take time to prove to her—and to him—that his affection was genuine, that he respected her and wanted the best for her. The expectancy in her eyes was evident, but he only kissed her quickly and took her hand to lead her out of the pool. At all costs, he would not allow anything more than that to happen until he put that ring on her finger and made her his wife.

"Put your boots on, woman," he ordered. "I've got a fantasy for you to fulfill."

"And what might that be?" she asked as she sat on the ground to pull on her boots and stockings.

"I want to watch you ride," he said, and Emma was surprised. "I'll saddle the stallion. It's been so long since I've just . . . ," he hesitated and she looked up, "just watched you."

"I'd love to," she admitted, longing to feel a saddle beneath her with a sense of freedom. They walked back to the cave to leave what little was left of the shampoo, and to retrieve the saddle. Emma watched Michael as he gently placed it on the fine stallion. She felt a vague sensation stir her memory as she realized how many times she had watched him do this without even thinking about it. When the saddle was in place, he turned and held out a hand, saying with natural gallantry, "Your mount, my lady."

The memory became more vivid as Emma slipped her hand into his in a way that made her realize they had shared this exchange hundreds of times before. As she lifted her foot toward the stirrup, Michael bent one knee to place his thigh beneath it as a stepping stone the perfect height for her to put her foot, enabling her to step gracefully into the saddle rather than having to practically jump in as she usually did on her own. The process felt so thoroughly natural that

Emma had to pause once she was seated and look down at him as if she was seeing him for the first time.

Michael caught the implication in her eyes and felt the years of hope becoming fulfilled in that moment. He knew she was perfectly capable of getting in and out of the saddle without assistance. And when he'd been employed at Byrnehouse-Davies, no one had ever even suggested that he be there to assist the ladies into their saddles. But he had done it. He'd done it for the sole purpose of being able to touch her at least once a day. And each time it happened, she had politely thanked him and disregarded him. He remembered lying awake at night, imagining and hoping that one time she would stop and look down at him, just as she was now, and somehow realize the feelings behind his gestures.

Emma felt a subtle ache rise in her as she comprehended his noble love that had gone so utterly unnoticed. She played it through again in her mind, and found herself deeply moved by the practiced way he had bent that knee below the stirrup more times than she could count. They had touched so often, and she had never stopped to see him, never comprehended that the hand helping her into the saddle would be the hand she would hold when she married.

There was so much she wanted to say, but fearing she would become overly emotionally, she summed it up with simply saying, "I love you, Mr. Hamilton."

Michael smiled. His ultimate fantasy had just come true. He gently slapped the animal's rump and Emma galloped away. As he watched her go, he realized what a display of trust it was to set her free on his only means of transportation out of this desolate place. Emma urged the animal into a cantor, moving in broad circles from where Michael stood, feet wide apart, arms across his chest, watching her with a sense of adoration.

To Michael, there were two things in this world that he considered pure beauty. The first was Emma, and the other, horses. He had developed an acute appreciation for equine in the thirteen years he'd spent in Byrnehouse-Davies stables, first as part of his daily routine as a resident of the boys' home, then as an employee. And Emma had been in the saddle practically from infancy. Her mother had been a trainer before she'd become a mother, and Emma not only had the best possible background, she had the inborn gift of a oneness with her mount. Some of his fondest memories were of simply watching Emma ride.

When the animal was warmed up, Emma pulled her legs up into a racing position, improvising with the saddle the best she could. She whispered in the animal's ear and patted him in a way that made Michael envious. The stallion, though not a trained racer, took off at her command and bolted across the outback, dust flying behind, until all he could see was dust. For a long moment, Michael felt afraid. Had she been lying to him? Was this her way of weaseling an escape? It didn't make sense with all he'd felt, but he still felt relieved to see her returning. He had given her trust, and she had proven herself worthy of it. If she didn't leave him now, he knew she never would.

Emma pranced over to Michael, slid forward in the saddle, and held out her arm. "Ride with me, Michael. Hold me like the night you abducted me."

"Why?" he laughed, mounting behind her.

"Even then, I couldn't deny wanting to be close to you. You felt so strong . . . and you smelled good."

"Not as good as I smell now," he quipped. "Lavender's my best fragrance." He pushed an arm around her waist, heeling the stallion to a hearty gallop while Emma leaned back against him, relishing the hot wind in her face and the way it seemed to press her closer to him.

An hour later they returned to the cave. Emma watched as Michael attended to his horse with water, feed, and affection. She realized that horses had likely received his pent-up affection for many years.

Somewhere in the late afternoon, they shared a meal that greatly resembled their breakfast. But they added variety by feeding each other and talking of trivialities. When they had finished eating, he stood up abruptly.

"Where are you going?" she asked.

"I have to shave," he stated, "before it gets too dark to see."

"But you have a beard."

Michael turned to look at her as if she was daft, so she followed him curiously outside where he leaned a small mirror against a rock and pulled a straight blade from its sheath.

"You aren't going to shave it off, are you?" she asked like a child.

"I'm not going to shave any more than I have every other day since we've been out here."

Emma looked puzzled until he soaped up only his cheeks and expertly shaved down to the point where his beard began in a neatly trimmed frame of his jaw-line.

"Oh, I see." Her expression filled with enlightenment. She'd seen men with all kinds of beards, but she'd never stopped to think what made them look different. Emma had watched Tyson shave before, but she'd never found it so intriguing.

"You do look handsome," she said.

"You're daft, woman." He wiped off the blade and sheathed it. The entire process had only taken a couple of minutes. "Hand me that stuff." He pointed to a bottle on the rock behind her, which he took and poured a small amount into his hand, slapping it on his face.

"Ooh." She stepped closer and touched his face. "So, that's why you always smell so good." The scent was vague but distinctly masculine, distinctly Michael. "And I am not daft."

"Look at me." He pointed into the mirror and comically examined his profile.

"I always do."

"My nose is too big."

"Good, strong nose."

"And I have this little crease between my eyebrows."

"That's from trying to look so cruel all the time. But I like it."

"You really think I'm handsome, eh?"

"The most handsome man in the world."

Michael stuffed the mirror into his saddlebag along with the shaving items. "You're daft, woman."

Emma laughed, realizing then that he was a man who cared about his appearance, without being the least bit vain. He was clean, but rugged, the result being a carefully mussed look that suited his nature. The fact that he was oblivious to what Emma found attractive only added to his appeal.

Emma cleaned the dishes and put things in order while Michael built up the fire in the mouth of the cave, more for protection than warmth. He replenished their store of firewood and stacked it neatly while he pondered the events of this day, marveling that he could be so lucky. The sun went down, and by the light of the fire Michael prepared two bedrolls, side by side. Recalling that they'd slept on the ground the night before, he became freshly amazed at all that had happened since then.

When Emma was finished, she sat down on her bedroll and hugged her knees to her chest, watching Michael as he sat down to pull off his boots. Then his eyes became distant, and she wondered where his thoughts might be. In considering all the changes they'd experienced together, was he as overwhelmed and in awe as she? It seemed so perfectly natural to be with him this way, and to want to be near him always. She found her mind wandering. Butterflies swarmed inside her as she pondered how it felt to be in Michael's arms, consumed by his kiss. And when he turned to look at her, as if he'd just been snapped out of a daze, she had little doubt that his thoughts were similar. The desire in his eyes was evident. And while it warmed her with sweet anticipation, she knew they had to discuss the situation. She would not leave such an important issue to chance.

"Michael," she said, "we . . . have to talk."

His brow furrowed in concern. "Okay. I'm listening."

"It's about . . . well . . ." She looked away, wondering how to approach this without embarrassing herself. It had come up before, but not like this. She cleared her throat, more loudly than she'd intended, then forced herself to spit the words out. "You know, Michael, what we shared last night was no small thing, and . . . we've become very close in a very short time. I'm certain it's natural for us to want to be even closer; to be . . . intimate, and . . ." Emma sensed his surprise without even looking at him. She hesitated, wondering how to make it clear that her desires were real and strong, but she couldn't, under any circumstances, be intimate with him before they were married. His emotions were raw and vulnerable, and in light of his childhood experiences, she could understand how his perceptions of right and wrong might be distorted. She didn't want him to feel rejected or hurt by her determination to remain chaste; she simply wanted him to understand that their relationship would be better and stronger if they waited. She just didn't know how to make that clear without hurting him.

Emma drew her courage and hurried on, sensing his impatience. "Of course, we're engaged to be married now, and I know our commitment runs deep. I want more than anything to—"

"Emma," Michael interrupted, taking her hand. He couldn't be certain what exactly she was trying to tell him, but her nervousness was evident. He hoped that making his intentions clear might put the issue to rest. "If you're trying to offer yourself to me, I'm very flattered, however . . ." Emma opened her mouth to clarify herself before he got the wrong impression, but he quickly went on. "I hope you can understand, Emma, why it is so important for me to wait until we are married for anything more to happen between us in that respect."

Emma drew in a sharp breath, then she let it out slowly with a little laugh of relief. "You see," he said, looking down in a way that made his nervousness apparent, "most of my life I have considered myself a bad person. Your mother worked very hard to teach me that I had a great deal of good in me, and I had to believe that of myself in order to overcome my past. But I never believed it; not consciously, at least." He laughed softly, but still he wouldn't look at her. "I wonder now if some of her teachings penetrated my thick skull, even against my will." He looked briefly into her eyes. "I can't think of any other reason that you might find something redeemable in me."

Emma touched his face, and for a long moment their eyes met in the firelight with a thousand emotions passing between them. Then he noticed her tears and wondered if he had hurt her feelings somehow. Feeling the need to finish his thought, he fought the distraction and turned away.

"Emma, I want you more than I've ever wanted anything in my life. But you must understand how important it is to me that we wait until we're married; to do it properly. Perhaps this is a way I can prove to you—and to myself—that I *am* a good person; that I can be disciplined; that I can put my respect for you above my desires."

He chuckled tensely, wishing he had even a clue what she was thinking. "I know it must sound so hypocritical," he murmured, still not looking at her. "After the way I've treated you, making horrible threats and being so obnoxious, you must find such a declaration ridiculous, but—"

"No, Michael." Emma touched his face, forcing him to look at her. "I find your declaration sweet and stirring. No woman has ever felt more loved and respected than I do at this moment." He looked confused and she hurried to add, "You *are* a good person, Michael. That's why I love you." She laughed softly. "And that's what I was trying to say, Michael. I know this is a difficult transition in your life, and I can understand how the closeness we've shared could help you through. But I wanted you to understand that I couldn't let our relationship go any further in that respect until we're married. And I didn't want you to feel hurt or rejected. I want you to know how very much I love you."

Emma pushed her arms around him and held him tightly, finding immeasurable comfort in the way he returned her embrace with fervor. She could feel his love surging through her, and when she looked into his eyes, the feeling only deepened.

"Okay," he said like a storekeeper bartering over the price of sugar, "you've talked me into remaining chaste until marriage, but don't think I'm going to stop holding you like this."

"I wouldn't want you to." She smiled and kissed him.

Their kiss turned passionate, then he drew back only enough to say, "And I won't stop kissing you this way."

"I should hope not," she said and urged him to kiss her again, looking forward to the day when she would be his wife.

❦ ❦ ❦

Tyson sat up in the dark, suddenly overcome with a sensation that was not so much disturbing as it was puzzling.

"Emma," he said aloud, wondering why a sudden wave of passion would bring her to mind. Or perhaps it had been the other way around. Lying here next to Lacey, attempting to go to sleep, he could explain his feelings because of her nearness. But the connection to Emma made no sense.

"Did you say something?" she muttered sleepily. "Is everything all right?"

"Everything's fine," he soothed. "I was just thinking about Emma."

"You feel something?" she asked, sitting up next to him. "Do you think she's hurt? What do you feel? Fear? Anger? Tell me, Tyson."

Tyson chuckled, unable to explain it and not wanting to admit it.

"I'm not certain that what I'm feeling has anything to do with Emma."

"But you said you were thinking about her, and . . ."

"I know, but . . ."

"What is it?" she pressed when he hesitated.

"What I felt, Lacey, was passion. Pure and simple."

Lacey grunted and lay back down. "Go to sleep, Tyson. I think you're confused."

"I'm glad we agree on something," he muttered with subtle cynicism and lay down again. But as his mind returned to Emma, he felt it again. The ache for her filled him like it never had. He missed her in a way that only the same flesh and blood could. He wanted to talk to her about all he'd felt on her behalf during their separation, and he wanted to ask if she had felt the same for him. And he was dying to know why, at this moment, Emma was feeling passion.

The following day, Tyson felt some hope in regard to his relationship with Lacey. As they worked together to break camp, she spoke with him comfortably. It nearly felt as if he'd never been gone. Their relationship felt very much like the brother and sister they had once been. Of course, he longed for more. But it was a step in the right direction.

As they rode slowly side by side, the long spells of silence were broken by brief bits of casual conversation. Their topics never went beyond trivialities that had occurred in the past four years and the weather, but at least she wasn't ignoring him.

Lacey enjoyed the opportunity to be with Tyson in a way that felt comfortable from their years of growing up. But she had to stop herself more than once from saying something about Richard. She simply wasn't ready to tell him yet—not until she knew that his commitment was for her, not out of obligation. Still, she felt hope. They were together again, and it was evident he loved her. And for now, hope was the best bridge she could ask for.

❧ ❧ ❧

Emma woke with the late-morning sun shining into the mouth of the cave. Michael slept beside her, as content as the child he'd never been allowed to be. For a long while she was content to just watch him, pondering all they had shared and their lifetime together still ahead. She recalled the faceted conversation they'd shared far into the night; deep, invigorating discussions that she'd never had with anyone beyond her immediate family. Michael proved more and more that he was intelligent and profound.

Suddenly missing him, Emma gave in to her urge to kiss him awake. He stretched before his eyes came open, squinting to adjust to the light, then they sparkled as they focused on Emma.

They spent the day in quiet conversation, avoiding the fact that reality would soon have to be faced. Late in the afternoon, they shared the usual meal of canned peaches, beans, and biscuits. Emma sensed Michael becoming distant with thought, but he said nothing until he'd finished eating.

"Emma," Michael soberly set his plate aside when it was empty, "I fear your father will not have me after what I've done. I can't blame him, but it frightens me."

"I can handle my father," Emma assured him.

"I believe you can. You can certainly handle me, but . . . Emma, I'm the one responsible for all of this. And I've got to be the one to make it right. I've been thinking about it, and I've decided that I've got to take you back before he has a chance to come looking for you."

"You're not taking me back tonight?" she asked in a panic, wanting as much time as possible alone with him. She sensed a need to strengthen the bonds between them before they were assaulted by the waiting consequences.

"No, not tonight," he said, unable to deny feeling relieved by her insistence on staying together as long as possible. He needed the strength she gave him, but he also knew he had to face the inevitable. "But . . . ," he added, "we must leave first thing in the morning, before he sets out to meet us."

Emma nodded firmly, praying in her heart that the fight ahead for Michael would not do him in.

Michael took her hand and kissed it, determined to spend their little remaining time together to its fullest. He could face the consequences tomorrow.

While they cleaned the dishes together, Michael's mind went again to his foreboding meeting with Jess Davies. He decided it was his commitment to Emma that mattered, and they would find a way to be happy together no matter the circumstances. But he knew Emma would be happier at Byrnehouse-Davies, and her parents' support would make a great difference in their lives. Admittedly, Michael could think of no better place to live out his life than her home, the only place on earth that had ever been home to him. To look at the situation ideally, he could hope that Jess would tolerate him enough to give him back his job in the stables. He wouldn't make much money, but they could be happy there. Yes, it all depended on his reconciliation with Jess Davies. If that worked out, he believed the rest would eventually fall into place.

The sun was going down when Emma suggested they go riding. Michael smiled and bent to pick up the saddle, but Emma stopped him, feeling the urge to ride bareback. Michael lifted Emma onto the bridled stallion then mounted behind her. Together they galloped and cantered, while no words were necessary to express all they were feeling. There was something peaceful and stirring as the newness of their love combined with the raw earth and the endless sky surrounding them. The setting sun forced them to stop and watch as the sky lit up in flamboyant hues of pink and orange.

"It's so beautiful," Michael whispered behind Emma's ear, feeling as if he'd never really seen the sun go down in his entire life. He wondered if his efforts to hold the world at bay had taken so much out of him that he hadn't had time for sunsets.

Together they returned to the cave, where Michael built up the fire before they crawled into their bedrolls and slept. Emma could hardly remember what it was like to sleep in anything but her clothes, which was likely best under the circumstances.

Emma woke the following morning feeling disoriented. She groped for Michael's watch and squinted to read the time, then she panicked.

"Michael!" She shook his shoulder and stood up, searching frantically for her boots.

"What? What is it?" he murmured groggily.

"If we don't hurry, my father will be on the doorstep, so to speak."

"Oh, that would be great," he said with practiced sarcasm. "Just great. Where is my other boot?" he asked, then their eyes met and everything froze for a long moment.

"Emma," he said, touching her face. There was so much he wanted to say, but the urgency of the situation shocked him back to the present. Their time alone was over for now. The consequences had to be faced.

"Here," she said, handing him his missing boot.

"Thanks," he said, pulling it on. "You'd do well to brush your hair, I think. I don't want you looking too scandalous, or your father might hang me from the nearest gum ghost. He might anyway."

"I won't let him," she said firmly, tugging the brush through her hair.

"Give me that," Michael said when she was finished. While she was tying her hair back he muttered with disgust, "I still smell like lavender."

Emma only smiled and led the way out of the cave, leaving everything as it was. Michael saddled the horse, then helped Emma mount. She took his hand and paused to say, "Whatever happens, remember that I love you, and everything will be all right."

He nodded, wanting to believe her. He was barely seated in the saddle behind her when he broke into a gallop, heading the direction where he knew they were camped.

Michael had thought all of this through very carefully the previous night while Emma had slept beside him. And he felt certain he knew the best way to handle it. He had intended to discuss it with Emma, but their sleeping late had left no time to talk. He felt a degree of relief to pass the appointed gum ghost and not find anybody waiting there. But as they rode on, the reality of what he was about to face made his heart hammer wildly.

"Emma," he felt a need to explain this much, "however all of this may appear, I want you to trust me and go along."

"Whatever are you talking about?" she asked, feeling her nerves turn raw with a fear on his behalf, combined with a little of her own. Much of their future was hinged on this moment, and he was asking her to go along with him as if they were playing a game. But there was no time for questions.

"Michael, I want you to remember the man you are now, not the one you were before. You have a right to happiness."

He pushed an arm around her waist and held her tightly. "Tell me you love me, Emma."

"I love you."

"Say it again."

"I love you. I love you more than life. And what about you?"

"I love you, Emma."

"Say it again."

"I love you, and I will fight for you."

The words settled into a knot in his chest as a small group of horses and mules came into view, tethered together in the shade created by a rock formation that blocked the morning sun. Michael slowed down to approach just as Jess Davies came around the rocks, carrying a saddle, with saddlebags over his shoulder.

"I'd say that was cutting the time a little close," Michael muttered in her ear as Jess caught sight of them from the corner of his eye and stopped. Michael dismounted and dropped the reins of the well-trained stallion. He turned to help Emma down, appreciating her one final whisper, "I love you, Michael."

Emma met her father's eyes as he set down the saddle. She wanted to embrace him, but she hesitated and looked at Michael, feeling somehow torn. "Go on," he urged. "Don't make him think I'm holding you back."

Emma attempted to assure him with her eyes, then she turned and ran the short distance to her father's arms. Jess dropped the saddlebags into the dirt and pulled her against him, muttering quietly, "Oh, thank you, God." He drew back to look at her. "Are you all right?"

"I'm fine, really," she said with enthusiasm.

Michael felt almost sick inside as he observed the reunion. They were so happy to see each other, and he had been the cause of their separation. Jess Davies had obviously been very worried, and he'd been through a great deal of trouble. Michael swallowed the lump in his throat and drew back his shoulders as Jess's eyes fell on him. Michael took it as his signal to move in, and he walked steadily toward them, stopping an arm's length away.

Emma felt the tension in the air immediately as these two men faced each other with a duel of fire in their eyes. She held her breath, waiting for one of them to speak, praying they would each say the right things. When she couldn't bear it any longer, she began, "Papa, I . . ."

Michael put an arm up to stop her. "I think I need to handle this myself."

Emma stood beside him, watching his face as he watched her father's.

"Where are your hired thugs?" Jess asked, bitterness edging his voice.

"They abandoned me," he stated flatly.

Jess gave no hint of reaction in his expression. "I've got the money," he stated, nodding toward the saddlebags on the ground.

Michael took a deep breath. "I don't want your money, Mr. Davies. I'm certain I should not expect to get paid for all of the difficulty I've inflicted upon your family."

Emma sensed the surprise in her father. She looked up at Michael, admiration shining through the tears in her eyes. As if he sensed her gaze, he turned to look at her, his eyes sparkling with the peace that was still so fresh in him. He took her hand, kissed it in a gesture of respect, then he put it into her father's. He gazed long and hard at Emma, as if he was trying to convey something, and she wondered if this was what she was supposed to go along with.

"Again, I apologize for my indiscretions," he said gently. "Goodbye, Emma. Mr. Davies." He nodded at her father, then turned on his heel and walked away.

Emma couldn't believe it. "Are you all right?" Jess asked, noting her distressed expression. Emma nodded absently, then muttered quickly, "Just a minute." And she ran after Michael.

"Michael, wait," she called. He stopped near his horse and turned slowly. Emma searched his eyes, relieved to see the amusement. But she was still puzzled by his behavior. "What are you doing?" she asked quietly, hoping to avoid her father's ears.

"It's all right, Emma," he assured her, wanting to kiss her so badly that he ached. "I had to turn away and let you come after me. Now he'll know I'm not coercing or manipulating you into any of this."

Emma sighed and took both his hands into hers, wondering what their silhouette might bring to her father's mind. As if he'd read her thoughts, Michael turned to look at Jess. His stance looked as if he was ready to lunge and kill.

"Do you still want to go through with this?" she asked, mostly for the sake of allowing him to reassure himself.

"Of course I do." He looked at her deeply. "When I told you I was committed, I meant it. I will do whatever I have to."

"I love you, Michael," she said with strength.

"Yes, I know." He smiled. "Just keep saying it." Michael hesitated only a moment before pulling her into his arms, holding her as close as humanly possible. Out of the corner of his eye, he felt Jess Davies coming toward them, tense and alert. "I think your father is coming to shoot me between the eyes," Michael said too seriously.

"Nonsense," Emma quipped. "He doesn't have a gun."

"At the moment."

Emma turned to face her father, easing Michael protectively behind her. "I want to take Michael home with us," she stated, figuring that was already obvious.

Jess looked closely at Michael, then at Emma. For the first time since this had begun, he was grateful for Alexa's advice. At this moment, he definitely needed an open mind. "Why?" was all he said.

"It's the only home he's ever known," Emma replied.

"You're not getting to the point, woman," Michael inserted.

"And what point is that?" Jess asked, not certain he wanted to know.

"I am a misguided, love-starved child, as you once called me. And until a few days ago, little had changed since you called me that. The entire truth, Mr. Davies, is that I put on this ridiculous charade and caused all of this pathetic trouble out of a misguided, childish intention of proving to Emma that I love her."

Jess was stunned. He really wished Alexa was here. She'd probably be laughing by now, all smug and proud of herself for having figured all of this out right from the start. But at the moment, Jess was simply stunned. "You're trying to tell me," he said, "that you stole my daughters from their beds in the middle of the night, dragged them across the outback, left us sick with worry, and sent us on this wild goose chase, because you . . ."

"I love her," Michael finished for him, almost proud of his list of accomplishments.

Jess really wanted to feel angry. In fact, he tried very hard to feel angry. But all he could do was shake his head and heave a deep sigh. He absorbed it a long moment, then wrapped all of his questions up into one word, "Emma?"

"It's true, Papa. He's been good to me. I love Michael. I trust him completely, and I want him to come home with us."

"You want him to move in with us—is that what you're trying to tell me?"

"I suppose that's it," Emma said timidly, squeezing Michael's hand tightly.

"Michael?" A whole new set of questions was put forward.

"I'm not going to pretend I am anything I'm not. I'm sick to death of pretending. I have absolutely nothing to my name, nothing to offer Emma but my love and respect. I suppose I'm not much better off than when you collected me from the constable's office after he found me in the gutter."

Jess shook his head and chuckled in disbelief. "You smell a little better."

Michael sighed, hoping he didn't mean the lavender. While Jess Davies seemed to be taking this positively, Michael figured he should get to the real point. "I want to marry Emma, sir. I can't expect you to forgive me, or even like me. I only ask that you tolerate me, for Emma's sake." Jess looked up with an acceptance seeping into his eyes that urged Michael to add, "And perhaps you could give me back my job. I can't come back without a way to earn my keep."

With Alexa's insight and an open mind, Jess could find absolutely no reason not to accept this. Begrudgingly he had to admit that if Michael was attempting to prove himself, he was doing it rather well. He had no reason to believe that he wasn't completely humble and sincere, and his attitude seemed healthy. But the clincher was Emma. Of all his children, Emma had always shown insight and wisdom that had often left Alexa in awe. She was a mature, level-headed woman, in spite of those stupid books she read. And Jess had to admit that if Emma felt that way about Michael, there was no reason not to trust her judgment.

With no hesitation, Jess stretched out his hand. Michael looked at it in disbelief, then he warily reached out to take it, shaking it firmly, dumbstruck by Jess's acceptance. It should have been harder than this.

As if to answer what Michael couldn't ask, Jess said with conviction, "If I didn't forgive you, Michael, I would be a hypocrite in the face of my own life's work." Jess smiled and touched his daughter's chin. "Now, why don't you go and get your things." He looked directly at Michael as he added, "Let's go home."

"We'll be ready in no time," Emma announced, throwing herself into her father's arms. "I love you, Papa. Thank you for everything, for both of us."

Jess laughed. "Hurry up now." Emma mounted the horse with Michael's assistance. He bent to retrieve the reins as Jess called, "Just a minute, Michael." Michael looked toward Emma warily but handed her the reins and walked back to where Jess was standing. He stopped when Jess threw a pair of saddlebags at his feet.

"What is this?" Michael asked cautiously.

"A hundred thousand pounds."

Michael looked at the bag as if it might bite him. He set narrowed eyes on Jess Davies, certain this must be a test. "I told you I didn't want the money, and I meant it."

"Michael," Jess pointed a finger, "I would have given that and much more for my daughter's safe return. There is no way on heaven or earth to put a financial figure on someone you love. Her happiness is worth much more than that to me, and it seems you have given her that." Jess waved his hand through the air. "It's only money, and you need it more than I do." Michael still said nothing. "Take it as an advance on your new occupation."

"Occupation?" Michael laughed. "The only occupation I've ever had is thief and liar."

"I would assume that's set aside from now on, or we wouldn't be standing here like this."

"You assume right."

"Take it, Michael, or it will just rot in the sun."

"But why?" Michael asked, thinking he'd prefer to let it rot. "I had hoped for tolerance. But you not only forgive me, you give me everything I could ever hope for and more. Why?"

"I've seen a lot of misery, Michael, but you've been honest with me, so I'm going to be honest with you. You always had a place in my heart."

"I would have thought I was more a pain in the—"

"That too," Jess interrupted with a chuckle. "But you must understand that people are often a product of their upbringing, and some things are more difficult to undo than others."

"But you knew nothing about me," Michael insisted.

"Oh, you worked very hard at keeping it hidden, and you did well at being the tough kid, keeping everyone at a distance. But I bet you never stopped to think what might have happened when you had that fever at the age of thirteen, did you? My sweet wife sat by your bed for days, crying over those carefully hidden scars. She always believed in you, even when I didn't. She always seemed to understand. I think she loved you more than any other boy that passed through our lives, per-haps because you needed it most."

Michael was struck as dumb as if his tongue had been cut out, but Jess didn't seem to want any response. "Take the money, Michael. Consider it a wedding gift." Jess laughed. "It'll be worth it. When I walk through the door with humble you, my wife will forgive me for all the years I've snored in her ear." Michael managed a chuckle. "Hurry up now. Let's go home."

"I won't let you down," Michael stated with fervor, but he didn't pick up the money.

"I know." Jess bent to retrieve the saddlebags and slapped them into Michael's arms before he turned toward an impatient looking Emma, waiting just out of earshot.

"What did he say?" she insisted as Michael approached her.

"I'll tell you later." He handed the bags to Emma and mounted behind her.

"What's this?"

"A wedding present."

Emma opened the flap to investigate while they rode. "Michael!" She laughed. "I don't believe it!"

"I don't either, and I'm not sure I like it. But I know what he's doing."

"And what's that?"

"He's trying to make me so humble and grateful that I wouldn't dare back down."

"And is it working?"

"Yes, blast him, he's just like you—always so intolerably right."

Emma laughed, and Michael urged the horse to a gallop.

❧   ❧   ❧

"Maybe it's none of my business," Ben said and startled Jess. "But . . . well . . . am I mistaken, or did Michael Hamilton just ride off with the girl *and* the ransom?"

"It would appear that way," Jess said nonchalantly. Then he laughed. "Actually, I think he gave the ransom to the girl."

"Kidnapping is not necessarily a common thing around here," Ben quipped, "but I don't believe that's generally the way it's supposed to work out."

"Quit jabbering and get those mules packed," Jess chortled. "We're going home."

❦ ❦ ❦

Little was said between Michael and Emma as they gathered their few personal belongings and blankets, leaving the canned food, utensils, and firewood for anyone in need who might come across this shelter.

"I guess that's all," Michael said, looking around one last time, then he looked toward Emma and laughed. "I just don't believe it."

"Maybe this will help." Emma pushed her arms around him and reached up to kiss him, knowing they might not have this opportunity again for a long time. Eagerly she expressed every emotion they had shared since his pain had fallen into her hands. Michael dropped the saddlebags into the dirt and pulled her closer, relishing the tangible evidence that love and truth had come into his life.

"Do you believe it now?" she asked, breathing the words onto his lips.

"Not quite," he said like a wine taster attempting to grasp the flavor fully. "Let's give it another try."

He kissed her again until he nearly devoured her. Then he forced himself back with a sigh of self-discipline. "Let's go home and get married," he said. Emma smiled and he picked up the saddlebags, motioning her outside. "After you, my lady."

Michael secured everything to the saddle, and they rode back to find Jess and Ben loading up the last of the supplies onto the mules' backs. "I think that's all," Ben called to Jess, then he turned to acknowledge Michael as he dismounted. "How are you, Michael?" he asked, seeming amused if anything.

"Fine, and you?" Michael replied as if they were at a social gathering.

"I'm great," Ben said as Michael turned to help Emma down, holding to her waist longer than necessary.

"Where is Lacey?" Emma asked fearfully as it became evident they were preparing to leave, and she hadn't shown herself yet.

Michael felt sick with dread. He could just imagine that they had buried her by now.

"She went home with Tyson," Jess answered casually.

"Tyson?" The word practically burst out of Emma. Michael smiled, recalling her deep affection for her brother. Their closeness was something he'd always envied, but now he felt the peace of knowing he held a part of Emma's heart that no brother could ever share.

"When did Tyson come back?" Emma demanded. "Did he look different? Was he all right? Did he—"

"One question at a time, girl," her father laughed. "He came back the day after you left. His timing's impeccable, eh?" He grinned. "He looks older, but he's still the same Tyson. A little more humble, perhaps." Jess and Emma shared a knowing smile. "I'm sure you'll have plenty of time to catch up with him when we get back."

"Is Lacey all right?" Michael asked, fearing what the answer might be.

Jess looked at him severely, but without malice. "She nearly didn't make it through that first night. When the rain hit, she became unconscious. But she was doing beautifully when I sent her off. I'm certain she'll be fine."

"I'm sorry about that," Michael had to say. "I really never intended for anyone to get hurt, and I—"

"I know." Jess put up a hand to stop him. "Enough said. We can just be grateful it turned out all right."

Ben mounted his horse as if to announce that they were ready to go.

"Emma," Jess said, "you can ride Vertigo there." Michael and Emma exchanged a quick, unnoticed glance of disappointment, but they both knew it was highly illogical to ride together such a long distance when there were plenty of horses available.

They rode through the day in peaceable silence. They ate in the saddle, jerked meat and biscuits that Ben had cooked earlier that morning, and drank from canteens. Michael drank from his and passed it to Emma, saying for her ears only, "Drink up, honey. It's the closest thing you'll get to a kiss for a while."

Emma took it from him, recalling all the times they had shared cups and canteens, and she wondered if that's what he had been thinking.

When Jess and Ben were ahead of them, Michael reached over and took her hand, holding it with casual familiarity as they rode. When he was certain they wouldn't be noticed, he leaned over and kissed her. She sniggered like a schoolgirl.

"Don't fall off," Jess called without turning, and Emma blushed prettily. Michael sighed.

As the sun lowered in the sky, Jess suggested, "Michael and Ben, why don't you ride up ahead and make sure our intended stopping place is in order."

Ben acted immediately on the standard procedure, and Michael followed without hesitation. Jess held back until Emma was riding beside him. "How you doing?" he asked casually.

"I'm wonderful," she said brightly.

"It's mild to say that I'm curious about what happened out there that brought you and Michael to this end." Emma looked down timidly. "You don't have to tell me if—"

"There's no reason not to," she said directly to him in the same open manner that had always been evident within their family. "But it's kind of difficult to explain. There were times when he had me downright scared to death, but there was something that kept shining through; something about him that didn't make sense." She shrugged her shoulders. "I just kept at him until I got him to admit to the truth."

Jess chuckled. "Boy, that must have been something to see."

Emma's eyes blurred with mist as she recalled it. Her expression didn't go unnoticed. "If you had seen what I have seen, you would know, as I know, that he is a man among men."

"That privilege is for you alone, Emma. And next to me, he is the luckiest man alive."

Emma smiled. "What about Tyson?"

"Tyson will be lucky if he survives the week in one piece. He's traveling home with Lacey's scorn."

Emma laughed, then she took her father's hand and said, "Thank you again, Papa, for your acceptance. This is not easy for him."

"I know, and I would be a fool not to accept him." He squeezed her hand in return. "Believe it or not, girl, I can understand a great degree of what Michael is feeling."

Emma's eyes widened curiously, but Michael and Ben approached, denying her the opportunity to inquire further.

"Looks all right," Ben announced.

"Good, we'll be having a hot supper within the hour."

Michael leaned toward Emma and whispered, "I hope it's not beans and peaches."

❦   ❦   ❦

For Jess, the journey home was a mending of bridges with Michael, as the journey out had been with Tyson. The attitude of humility and penitence from both of them became more evident in the time they shared. Tyson and Michael were finally growing up— just as Jess had once been forced to do, long after he had considered himself a man.

They rode long and slept hard, while Michael tried to be content with an occasional sly squeeze of Emma's hand, a stolen kiss behind backs, and gazes with deep meaning. But every moment of it, Michael felt grateful for the love they shared that made all of this possible. He often wondered what Jess Davies was thinking of the entire situation, which was a mild concern in view of what was facing him when he arrived *home*. If Lacey was arriving only a few days earlier, the name Michael Hamilton would likely not have a good ring when he walked in to announce that he would be joining the family.

As the days wore on, the mood became more comfortable. One evening while they were gathered around a campfire to eat before bedding down for the night, Jess took some significant steps in mending those bridges.

"You know, Michael," he began, leaning on one elbow and stretching his legs out, "I've been thinking lately about a time in my life when I was perhaps more like you than you might realize."

Michael chuckled dubiously, expecting some patronizing story about how he'd told a lie or stolen some candy. But Michael checked himself against jumping to conclusions when Jess's eyes turned deep. "When I first met Alexa, she was like a balm to my life. Everything that I did wrong, she made right." He spoke as if he was among friends, rather than a parent to children. "I wanted to love her, to give her what she needed from me, but I was so full of fear and pain that I found myself pushing her away, then hating myself for doing it. But I just couldn't bring myself to face the problem."

With empathy Michael said, "You must have worked it out—obviously." He still found it difficult to believe that Jess Davies could have caused the suffering he had.

"Oh, eventually," Jess chuckled, then he turned serious eyes to Emma, and she perceived some kind of warning, as if what he intended to say might be a shock to her. "But not right away."

"What happened?" Emma persisted, realizing she'd not heard any of this before.

"He became ornery and nasty as an old Scrooge," Ben laughed, nudging Jess's boot with a cooking stick. "I remember it well."

"Mind your business, boy," Jess said in mock anger. "You were just a kid. What did you know?"

"I know you were ornery and nasty as—"

Jess kicked him teasingly and he laughed, but the mood changed abruptly when Jess looked at Michael hard, as if to drive home a point. "She married another man; my closest friend, in fact." Michael couldn't believe it. The Jess and Alexa Davies he knew were confident, self-assured people who loved each other and had no purpose in life but to give to others.

"You mean," Emma gasped, "that Mama married Richard after she had met you?"

"Quite," Jess answered. "I became so angry, so belligerent. I started drinking too much and . . . well, finally I just left. It took a lot of humility and soul-searching to come to the conclusion that I had driven them to it."

"What happened to Richard?" Emma asked quietly, recalling the grave by the old house.

"Your uncle killed him. Shot him square in the chest."

"You mean . . . murder?" Emma gasped again.

"That's what I mean," Jess said. "He admitted to it before he died, but . . ." His gaze hardened again on Michael. "It was supposed to have been me. He thought it was me when he pulled the trigger."

A profound hush fell over them as Jess's statement was perceived. He went on in a quiet voice, speaking to Michael, "Now, I don't doubt the internal struggle you're presently having is difficult. But while you're facing up to it, I want you to wonder how it might feel to be given back the woman you love because her husband was killed in your stead. I caused her a great deal of pain and misery, but she loves me, Michael. And she loves you, too." Jess smiled. "I just want you to know that."

"Thank you," Michael said, so stunned that he couldn't think of anything else to say. He just hoped Jess knew that he meant it.

"Thanks for the bedtime story, Uncle Jess." Ben slapped his shoulder lightly. "I think I'll get some sleep."

The others agreed and settled into their bedrolls around the fire, except Michael, who stayed as he was, gazing into the dying embers. Ben began to snore, and when Emma made no protest, Michael knew she was sleeping as well. Some time later, Jess leaned up onto one elbow to meet Michael's surprised gaze in the firelight.

"Can't sleep?" Jess asked.

"I suppose you could say I've got a lot to think about."

He found himself watching Emma, then felt embarrassed when Jess caught him at it and grinned. His embarrassment deepened when Jess asked, "Did you sleep with her?"

Michael's eyes widened in surprise, then they narrowed as he felt cornered. He thought quickly of all he and Emma had shared, and reminded himself that he had nothing to regret. He was grateful to be able to answer with confidence, "No." Jess lifted an eyebrow as if to question Michael again, and he clarified carefully, "Emma and I have become very close. She has ushered me through hell and back. But nothing inappropriate has passed between us—and it won't. I told her I would marry her first, and I meant it."

Jess's smile was barely noticeable, but it warmed Michael through. "Well, that's good," Jess said. "Because I don't want any more illegitimate children on my hands."

Michael thought he meant some of the boys he'd grown up with, but he sensed something more personal and asked, "Any more?"

"You'd do well to have the family gossip before we get home," Jess answered easily. "My dear son Tyson got Lacey pregnant and left the country."

"You're joking." Michael couldn't help laughing.

"No," Jess laughed too. "But I think everything will be all right now. She didn't seem very happy with him when they left, but they'll work it out. I believe they've got what it takes."

This story added one more layer of strength to Michael's concerns. Even Tyson Davies had his faults and had caused others grief. Not that any other man's deed excused Michael, but it gave him the hope of empathy from others.

"I want to thank you, Mr. Davies," Michael uttered with strength, "for all you're giving me."

"Call me Jess." He chuckled. "And don't get *too* humble on me, Michael. I've got work for you that's going to take a tough man. In truth, you might just be the answer to my prayers—if you're willing, of course."

Michael had been a lot of things to many people, but he'd never been the answer to anyone's prayers. "How can all the trouble I've put you through have anything to do with prayers?"

"Sometimes the best things come out of difficult circumstances."

"That's true," Michael had to admit.

"You see, Michael, Ben has been telling me for quite some time that he has a desire to leave us and go back to his people. I can understand that; he wants to help them, and I know he can. But that leaves me without an administrator for my boys."

Michael didn't dare speak for fear that it would break the spell and he'd realize he was only dreaming.

The silence urged Jess to clarify what he was asking, so there wouldn't be any room for doubt. He'd always had the belief that giving a wayward boy some responsibility he was capable of handling could do wonders. He figured the theory applied now. "They need someone who is as tough as they are, but good enough to see through their barriers. They need someone who is willing to search until the little bit of good can be found, and they need help nurturing it. That would be one aspect of your responsibilities. The physical means to carry that out would come in as you oversee the boys' activities, most specifically supervising them with their horses. They need to learn to work, and to focus their attention on something within their control. Those horses have taught many a hurting boy how to love."

"Yes, I know." Michael managed to keep his voice from cracking.

"That's why I think you're the man for the job."

"And you really think I could do it?"

"Do it? You could excel at it. If it's what you want, of course. If you would prefer something else, I can arrange any number of—"

"No," Michael interrupted, and Jess grinned subtly. "I think I would like to at least give it a try."

"Good, you can start as soon as you get settled in. Ben will be glad to know that I've replaced him. He's been getting antsy."

With that, Jess turned over and went to sleep. But Michael lay awake for quite some time, just contemplating the goodness of his life.

Eleven
COMING HOME

"It looks really good," Tyson said as he performed the daily ritual of bandaging Lacey's lower leg. "You'll be good as new in no time."

"In a manner of speaking," Lacey said scornfully, visibly shuddering to recall the intensity of her ordeal in the outback. She prayed that Emma was all right, and longed for them all to be reunited again.

Tyson watched Lacey's eyes grow distant and felt certain her thoughts were with the drama of the last couple of weeks. "I wish I would have been there," he said gently.

"What?" she asked, startled from her thoughts.

"I wish I would have been there . . . to keep him from hurting you."

"Well, you weren't," she said with a bitter edge. Of course, it was ridiculous to think that his being around would have saved her from being kidnapped. But there were far too many other things he had missed, and his presence seemed to have a way of reminding her of those things, rather than offering much comfort.

Tyson chose not to comment, and turned instead to clean up the mess made from their supper. When everything was ready to bed down for the night, he found Lacey sitting on her bedroll, brushing out her hair. He watched her for a few minutes, then impulsively took the brush from her hand and began to do it for her.

Lacey wanted to protest, but she couldn't deny the way her heart fluttered each time he made some little effort to let her know he cared.

If only she could get past the hurt and just enjoy being with him! But there were moments when it took hold of her so strongly that it squelched all affection and desire. Still, there were other moments, like now, when all she could think was how she loved him; how she'd missed him.

Cautiously Lacey turned to look at him, and he stopped brushing. Their eyes met in the firelight, and Lacey wanted more than anything to just have him kiss her. Her heart began to pound when she realized that he intended to do just that. As their lips met meekly, Lacey thought she would melt from the memories it stirred. By their own will, her arms moved up over his shoulders, where she held to him with everything she had. Their kiss became warm and sweet, so new and yet so familiar, and Lacey wanted it to go on and on.

Tyson thought he might die from the relief he felt in the evidence of Lacey's affection. The road to healing everything between them might be long, but he knew beyond any doubt now that she still loved him. And that made the future bright.

"I love you, Lacey," he murmured and kissed her again. "I love you so much. I want more than anything to just put the past away and pretend it never happened. Can we just start over and wipe away the last four years?"

Lacey looked into his eyes and saw a startling resemblance to her son. The reality hit her like a cold splash of water. And it made her angry. Quickly she put distance between them, snapping firmly, "How dare you whisk back into my life and assume you can just wipe away what I've been through in your absence. You have no idea what you're talking about."

The astonishment on his face reminded her that he was completely ignorant of what he'd left behind. But then, he'd never bothered to ask.

Tyson sighed and took a deep breath. "You're right," he said gently, attempting to keep this from turning into an argument. "I have no idea what I'm talking about. So, why don't you tell me."

Lacey looked at him long and hard before she finally said, "I'm tired. It'll have to wait."

"We'll be arriving home tomorrow," he stated as she settled huffily into her bedroll.

"Good," she said, while at the same time she felt a nervous twitter at the thought of being forced to tell him he had a son. She couldn't put it off forever, even though a part of her wanted to.

Lacey hardly slept that night as images crowded through her mind. Her love for Tyson became mixed up with intense feelings of confusion and anger. And her concern for Emma led her mind directly to her intense hatred for Michael Hamilton, a man who somehow represented everything she feared in the deepest caverns of her mind. And her love for her son struck chords of irony in realizing that his birth was a mistake. How could the joy Richard had brought into their lives be the result of something so painful as his father's abandonment and the sin they had committed? All of it swirled together endlessly until her head ached clear down her back. She finally drifted off from sheer exhaustion, knowing she was poorly prepared for the final leg of their journey.

Tyson was immensely grateful to know they'd be home by afternoon when Lacey woke up with a grim silence that hovered through the day. Her cold attitude made him wonder where her affection for him had gone in the hours since they'd shared that kiss in the firelight.

Lacey restrained herself from squealing with delight when the gables of the boys' home came into view. She'd never been so grateful to see them, and never so glad to be home. Alexa greeted them excitedly and insisted on a detailed report. Lacey was surprised to hear Tyson immediately inquire over Richard's whereabouts, and she was relieved to hear that he'd gone for a long walk with Miss Leeds. She wanted to see her son, but not in Tyson's presence. That was a bridge she simply wasn't prepared to cross.

Once they had reported to Alexa all they knew, Lacey pleaded exhaustion and went up to her room, hoping to avoid Tyson altogether until she could come to terms with her feelings. She fell quickly to sleep, but the confusion and turmoil went with her, causing strange dreams. She woke up in the evening, not feeling very well rested, but she was terribly grateful to be home.

❧ ❧ ❧

"Hey, Emma," Jess startled her from the attention she was giving her breakfast, "do you think you can bear sharing Michael's attention with several other people?"

Emma looked up, baffled. Her father seemed almost smug. Michael's face had no expression at all. She wanted to ask what he meant, but her mouth was full.

"Your husband is going to be a very important man at Byrnehouse-Davies," Jess added.

Emma swallowed. "He already is, as far as I'm concerned."

This brought a smile from Michael that deepened when Jess said proudly, "He has consented to be my administrator."

Emma beamed. "That's wonderful!"

"I would have been happy with my old job," Michael admitted. "But considering the circumstances, I think I can make the sacrifice."

Jess caught his subtle humor. "I believe at this point your experience could be put to better use than saddling horses."

"Although he is very good at it," Emma insisted. "And he's good at helping ladies into their saddles," she added with a teasing wrinkle of her nose.

"Pure talent," Michael quipped.

"Does this mean I can leave?" Ben asked eagerly.

"Right now?" Jess tried to act surprised, even though he wasn't.

"Why not? I'm a lot closer to home than I would be tomorrow."

"Pack up." Jess waved a hand toward him. "I think we can manage without you."

Ben was on his feet in a flash. "You've made him a happy man," Jess remarked to Michael, then went to help him.

"When did you discuss all of this?" Emma asked once they were out of earshot.

"Last night, after you fell asleep."

"What else did you talk about?" She was dying of curiosity.

Michael chuckled. "He asked me if I'd slept with you." Emma's mouth fell open in astonishment. Michael put a finger to her chin to close it. "Yes, he really did."

"And what did you tell him?"

"I told him the truth. And I can't tell you how glad I am that I was able to give the right answer, and give it honestly."

Emma squeezed his hand and murmured, "You're a good man, Michael. That's why I love you. Well, it's one of the reasons."

A minute later, Emma jumped when her father spoke too close behind her. "You can kiss her if you want, Hamilton. I won't look."

"All right, I will." Michael put his arm around her like a boasting pirate. "And you can look if you want. I don't care!" Jess laughed, and Michael gave Emma a ridiculously loud smooch. "Let's go home, woman. I want to get married."

"As you wish." Emma sauntered away to saddle her horse, but Michael quickly rushed to her aid.

"Let me do that for you." He took over, and she stood back to watch him. "I'm very good at it. Besides," he looked up at her as he tightened the strap beneath the horse's belly, "such beauty should not work so hard."

🌱 🌱 🌱

The morning after their return, Tyson looked up from the desk to see small blue eyes watching him closely. "Well, hello there, Richard." He stood and came around the desk to squat down in front of the child.

"You were gone a long time," Richard said with a sadness that made Tyson wonder if living without a father had been difficult for this child, despite never knowing who his father was.

"Yes, I was," Tyson said. "But I'm back now, and we're going to make up for it."

"Can we still go on a picnic?" Richard's face lit up as it became apparent that Tyson was still his friend. "You promised before you left that we could go on a picnic."

"Yes, I did. And we'll do that just as soon as—"

"Can we go right now?" he asked with such a tender plea that Tyson could hardly refuse. There was nothing so urgent that a picnic couldn't take priority.

"We'll need something to eat," Tyson said.

"You go tell Mrs. Brady," Richard assigned Tyson carefully, "and I'll go tell my mother."

"Whoa!" Tyson laughed and caught him by the shirt collar before he ran out of the room. "I thought your mother was gone."

"She came back," he announced proudly. Tyson tried to remember what had been said about Richard's mother. She had disappeared, he'd been told. He thought of Richard's imaginary friends and wondered if he had conjured up a mother in the absence of Jess and Tyson, which would have left him with no one to follow around except Alexa. Tyson realized he was choked up as he tried to imagine how it must feel to be abandoned—the way so many of these children were—the way he had abandoned Lacey and his family. Lacey had been right. Tyson had had everything he could want growing up, and he had turned his back on it. And here was a child with nothing, at the mercy of those who would give of themselves to care for him, so lonely that he had created an imaginary mother.

"Then you'd better go get her." Tyson smiled and swallowed his emotion.

Richard pointed a finger at him. "You be sure to tell Mrs. Brady to pack enough for three."

"I'll do that, and I'll meet you on the veranda in twenty minutes."

Richard grinned and ran off. Tyson could only go to the kitchen and order a picnic for three. There was no point telling Mrs. Brady about the imaginary mother and having her pack for two. Richard was sharp for a three-year-old, and Tyson would get a good scolding if there wasn't enough food.

※   ※   ※

Lacey was gratefully interrupted from her reading by a vigorous hug. "Richard!" she laughed. "What are you so excited about?"

"We're going on a picnic."

"We are?"

"Right now. Hurry, we have to meet on the veranda really soon."

"Who is we?" she laughed again, certain her mother had arranged it.

"Tyson and me and you."

Lacey's expression faltered. "What did you tell him?" she asked gently.

"I just told him to have Mrs. Brady pack a picnic for three people, 'cause my mother was coming."

"I see." Lacey sat back while Richard watched her inquisitively. She wasn't certain that she was ready to make the introductions official between father and son, but it was impossible for them to all live in the same house and not have the truth come out. Perhaps now was as good a time as any. At least she'd had a good night's sleep and some time to gather her wits without having Tyson there at every turn.

"Is something wrong, Mama?"

"No," she smiled, "just let me hurry and change into some picnic clothes."

"I'll wait in the sitting room." He grinned and bounced away. Lacey smiled after him, wondering why she had been blessed with such a good child. Perhaps Tyson was to credit for that. Alexa had often said he was always a good boy.

Lacey quickly changed into a dark skirt and cream-colored blouse. She brushed through her hair and left it to hang down her back. Richard was eagerly waiting and they hurried down the stairs, holding hands, the child completely oblivious to his mother's pounding heart and the significance of these circumstances to his life.

"Mama," Richard speculated, "I think Tyson would make a good father."

Lacey stopped walking to look down at him, wondering what power of insight existed in his little mind.

"I'll bet Tyson *would* make a wonderful father," Lacey added, fighting to keep her voice steady. They walked on down the hall in silence, but Lacey knew where Richard's thoughts were, and it made her hammering heart go even faster. Silently she uttered a prayer that this would go well.

Tyson sat on the veranda looking out over the yard. Home. The stress of the kidnapping hadn't given him time to fully absorb it. This place was the most beautiful on earth, and he knew in the deepest part of himself that he could never, never take it for granted again. His thoughts turned to Richard and the formless peace he seemed to find in easing the boy's loneliness. Then he thought of Lacey and felt regret. The combination of emotions was hot in his throat when the door opened and Richard came bounding into his arms. Tyson stood and lifted him up, settling him onto one arm with a hearty laugh. "I believe Mrs. Brady packed up your favorite," he said. "You know, those little cakes with the creamy stuff inside."

Richard grinned. "I'm glad you didn't forget the food."

"I promised, didn't I?"

"And I brought my mother," Richard announced proudly.

Tyson turned to look around, if only to patronize the child. His eyes narrowed in surprise to see Lacey hovering near the doorway. The connection didn't have a chance to sink in before Richard asked, "Will you be my father, Tyson?"

Tyson chuckled, then he turned to Lacey as something indeterminable made his heart begin to pound.

"It's all right, darling," Lacey said, stepping forward. "He already is."

Tyson stood motionless, as if the words had been slow traveling from his ears to his brain. Realizing what she had said, his eyes turned to Richard, who was grinning proudly, as if accepting Tyson as his father was the most natural thing in the world.

Lacey waited tensely for a reaction. A labored gasp was the only sound Tyson made as he sat down weakly, holding Richard against his shoulder, as if he feared dropping him. He continued to look at Richard severely, then finally his eyes moved back to Lacey. She saw tears glistening there.

Tyson was relieved to find the chair beneath him, which compensated for the weakness in his knees. But nothing could stop the thudding in his chest, nor the moisture he felt trickling out of his eyes. The joy, combined with regret and enlightenment, formed a knot that barely let the words creep through. "I have a son?" Lacey's nod was subtle but evident. Tyson turned to Richard, who now looked perplexed. "I have a son!" his quivering voice said with conviction. He pulled Richard closer, holding him tightly, squeezing his eyes shut to absorb the reality. "I have a son!"

Richard pulled back to look at Tyson closely. "Are you sad, Tyson?" he asked.

"Yes," he smiled, "but I'm very happy, too."

"How can you be happy and sad at the same time?"

"I am happy, Richard, because from now on you are going to be my son, and I am going to be your father. Nothing could make me happier than that." Richard grinned, but he was still obviously puzzled over the tears. "And I'm sad because . . ." He hesitated and turned to Lacey, who had tears streaming over her face. "Because I wish I would have been here to be your father right from the start."

"That's all right," Richard said, then he climbed down to get on with this picnic. "Let's go, Mama," he insisted.

"How about if we eat right here," Lacey said gently, "and we'll go out on a better picnic when Aunt Emma comes back."

Richard looked momentarily disappointed, but Lacey added, "Why don't you unload the hamper and sample the food for us." Richard gladly complied, oblivious to the emotion passing between his parents.

Tyson found the strength to come to his feet and take Lacey in his arms. They held each other and cried while their son took a bite out of each of a dozen little cakes.

"Lacey." Tyson took her face into his hands. "Why didn't you tell me?"

The question apparently didn't have an easy answer when Lacey said to Richard, "You stay right here. We'll be back."

Richard hardly noticed them slipping through the door into the library. "Lacey?" Tyson persisted when she continued to hesitate.

"I'd have gladly told you four years ago," she said, unable to hide her bitterness, "but you weren't here to tell."

Tyson felt a whole new compassion for her. But where and how could he even begin to express it? All he could do now was lean against the back of a sofa and listen to her as the truth behind all of her pain finally came out.

"You weren't gone a month, Tyson, when I realized I was pregnant." Her eyes turned severe. "Do you have any idea what it was like, after all your parents have given me, to tell them that I was pregnant?" Tyson bit his lip. "I even tried to keep you out of it. Your father got downright threatening before I told them it was your baby."

"He probably wanted to kill me."

"Actually, he took it rather well, considering. Your mother kept him calm . . . sort of."

Tyson nodded.

"They were wonderful," she continued. "Through all of it they have supported me without question, and they have loved Richard as if he were their own. They say he is so much like you, and they have admitted more than once that they were grateful you left a part of yourself behind."

Tyson pushed both hands into his hair and tugged at it. The repercussions of his thoughtlessness seemed to increase continually.

"You missed so much, Tyson—every day of his life, every little thing he did. All I could ever feel was a longing to share it with you."

"Lacey," he pressed his brow into his hands, "I can understand now why you—"

"No, Tyson," she interrupted, "you don't understand." He looked up to see defiance in her eyes. "You will never begin to understand. I gave myself to you, Tyson, because I believed it would make you stay. I made that mistake. I admit it. But where was *your* self-control all those nights in the attic? And I will never understand why you let it happen, knowing full well that you were intending to leave in spite of it.

"You will never understand, Tyson, the fear and desperation I felt to be left alone with the consequences. You were not here to see the illness that came along with the pregnancy. I was in bed for the last seven weeks. Emma and Mother and Father were there for me constantly, but it never seemed to be enough. And then . . . oh, Tyson," her voice cracked with sorrow, "you will never comprehend what it took to bring your son into this world. Twenty-eight hours of hard labor, Tyson. You can be grateful we have a good doctor available, because Richard was born breech. Without the right care, I might well be dead now. Could you have lived with that?"

"No," he answered firmly. "I'm having a difficult time living with this."

"As you should," she snapped.

When nothing more was said, Lacey went out onto the veranda to join Richard, while her words echoed over and over in Tyson's mind. She was right, and he knew it. The discovery of his son had put a whole new light on the bridges they had yet to cross, but her tone of voice, her cynicism, her bitterness made the true problem all too clear. He looked back over the past week. He'd been so humble and penitent that he'd nearly turned to melting butter, but Lacey had not softened even the slightest. He felt certain she still loved him; that was evident from the way she had responded to his kiss. But her wall of enmity made him fear that what had been done would never be undone. At this moment, he wanted to celebrate with her. They were together. They had a son. He felt peace growing within himself, but he wondered if she would ever relent.

Through the remainder of their picnic, Tyson concentrated on Richard, attempting to comprehend the reality that this was his son—which kept his mind away from Lacey's obvious belligerence. He was relieved when she finally left with some flimsy excuse. He took Richard riding, then they returned to share a nap on the nursery floor.

Tyson woke to find his mother standing above them, smiling serenely. "I was wondering where you'd gone off to. Last I heard, Mrs. Brady had packed up a picnic for three."

Tyson grinned. "Yeah. Have you met my son?"

Alexa's eyes widened while Tyson turned to admire the child sleeping against his shoulder.

"You figured it out?" she asked.

"Not without some help, I'm afraid."

"And how do you feel about that?" Alexa asked, making herself comfortable in the rocker.

"How am I supposed to feel?" He turned to look at her. "I can't possibly regret his existence."

"None of us do, Tyson. Many times good things come out of difficult circumstances. Richard is a wonderful child, and he's given us a great deal of joy—much like his father."

Tyson smiled sadly. "I wish Lacey shared your sentiment."

"All of this has been difficult for her," Alexa justified. "You must be patient with her."

"I have no choice."

"Why is that?"

"I love her, Mother."

"Then you must make your stand."

"I have apologized so many times that I'm beginning to sound like a parrot."

"Then enough of apology. She's heard it; now you must prove yourself."

"I'm working on that."

"So I see." Her eyes smiled down on her son and grandson.

"Thank you, Mother."

"For what?"

"For your wisdom. For raising me with values, then loving me even when I didn't live up to them."

"You are easy to love, Tyson." She rose and moved to the door.

"Would you mention that to Lacey?" he quipped. She smiled and left them alone.

❦   ❦   ❦

Lacey took a careful peek into the nursery and saw Tyson and Richard asleep together on the floor. She watched them for a few minutes then returned solemnly to her room, feeling a dark cloud hanging over her that seemed to grow heavier and darker by the day. None of this was turning out the way she had expected, but she couldn't figure out exactly why. A distinct uneasiness hovered relentlessly inside of her. She didn't understand its source, but she felt too afraid to ponder it deeply. It was as if the events of the past few weeks had triggered something long buried in her mind; something she had no desire to look at. The only thing she knew for certain was that it was somehow linked to the nightmares that often plagued her. Years ago, the dreams had only been a bizarre montage of her abandonment as a child. Then when Tyson had left her, he had somehow filtered into them. And now, Michael Hamilton had become included. All she knew for certain was that something frightening and painful was buried deep inside her—but perhaps not deep enough. All she could do was attempt to ignore her confusion and get on with her life, if such a thing were possible.

❦   ❦   ❦

Tyson had intended to talk to Lacey about getting married and announce it at supper, but she didn't show up. She requested a meal in her room and refused to see even Alexa. By the following afternoon, Tyson had contemplated the circumstances deeply and he sought out

Lacey, deciding he would see her whether she wanted to see him or not. He knocked on her bedroom door but got no response. He tried to open it, but it was locked. She had to be in there, or it wouldn't be.

"Lacey," he called. "Open the door. I want to talk to you."

"Go away. I don't feel well."

"I'm not going away. I am never going away again. Get it straight, woman."

"Leave me alone."

"I said I want to talk to you."

"Later!"

"Now!"

"Later, Tyson."

"Open this door, Lacey, or I will get it open by any means possible."

"Oh, grow up!" she called.

"Why don't *you* grow up?" he shouted angrily, taking hold of the door frame to kick the knob. The lock broke beneath his boot.

Lacey sat up in bed, looking astonished and harrowed. "What do you think you're doing?"

"I am here to talk to the mother of my child," he insisted. "It's dark in here." He strode to the window and pulled back the drapes. Lacey squinted and glared at him. "He asked about you." Tyson leaned against the sill and folded his arms. "How much time do you spend with your son, Lacey?"

"Don't you dare criticize the way I raise my son. I have been a good mother to him. You have a lot of nerve, when you didn't even know he was yours until yesterday."

"And neither of us has seen you since."

"I haven't felt well."

"You've hardly been ill a day in your life."

"You haven't been here the past four years."

"And I suppose you'll blame any illness in that time on me as well."

"I was pregnant."

"Yes, you were pregnant, and if I had been here, you would not have been any more or less ill. And may I remind you that pregnancy lasts about nine months in most cases."

"Did you want to talk or argue? I told you, I don't feel well."

"You said that already. If you want to be depressed, I suppose that's up to you, but you can get out of bed and give your son some attention while you're at it. If you're ill, I'll send for the doctor."

"I don't need a doctor."

"Good. I'll say what I came to say, then you can get up and get dressed."

"Get on with it."

"All right. I have one question for you."

"And what is that?" she asked, staring toward the wall.

"Will you ever forgive me?" She turned in surprise but said nothing. "I am quite serious. I have wronged you as much as any man could. I can see that, and it has filled me with harrowing remorse. I will never cease to regret what I did, Lacey, but I can't turn back time. I can't change the past. And I want to know if it's even possible for you and me to share any happiness together again. If we are going to be Richard's parents, don't you think we ought to have some unity between us?"

"Right now I can't answer that," she said almost coldly.

"Don't you think we should get married?" he asked.

"That would be appropriate under the circumstances," she said, watching him for a reaction. But his expression was unreadable. "I had hoped you would have asked me before now."

Tyson lifted a curious brow. "I might have, if you weren't so belligerent toward me."

She went on as if he'd said nothing. "I would like to spend the rest of my life believing that you and I are together for some reason beyond obligation."

Tyson was so astonished that he could only stare at her blankly. "Obligation?" he finally muttered. "You and I have *never* been together because of obligation. Don't you dare think for a minute that I have ever been anything but completely genuine with you, Lacey. I love you."

"That's what you said before, and then you left me."

"And now I am back, Lacey. There is nothing like pure loneliness to teach a man the true meaning of love. There was not a day out there when I didn't long for you, ache for you, and—"

"But that was different, Tyson. The separation was under your control. You could have come home any time you wanted."

"No, I couldn't."

"What is that supposed to mean?"

"It means, Lacey, that I had to grow up first. It took three years to get the courage to come back here and face it."

"Face what? I don't understand."

"What I am facing right now." He came close to shouting. "I had to come back and face everything that was dear to me and admit that I'd been wrong, that I was a fool, that it was all my fault." His voice rose further. "How many times do I have to say that I'm sorry? How much penitence must I pay?"

Lacey didn't answer, and Tyson lowered his voice. "I have a son, Lacey, and if you think I'm going to spend my life regretting his existence, you are quite mistaken. I am going to marry you, and Richard will have full-blooded siblings. If you choose to be miserable in that situation, that is up to you. I have begged forgiveness until my knees bled. If it takes a lifetime to prove my penitence to you, so be it. That is how long I'll be here, Lacey. I am giving my life to you; my heart and soul. There is nothing more I can give to prove to you how very sorry I am."

"Can four years be forgotten so easily?" she retorted.

"Forgotten, no! But use them to learn from, not to wallow in!"

"You just don't understand, do you."

"I understand how I feel, Lacey, but I'm going to marry you anyway. Not out of obligation, but for me. I'm doing it for me, because I love you and I don't want any man to have you except me. And I love Richard. I will be such a good father to him, he will never remember a time when I wasn't there, even if you will never forget."

He left the room abruptly, while Lacey wondered why he was being so insensitive to all she had faced in his absence.

Lacey didn't see Tyson until supper. He smiled warmly at her as he helped her with her chair. In a gentle voice he whispered, "You look beautiful."

"Thank you," she replied tersely.

"Better than this morning, at least," he added, unable to keep from retorting when she had to be bitter, even toward a genuine compliment.

Tyson talked with his mother about the fine attributes of his son, and Lacey couldn't help but feel his pride and relish it. When dessert was finished, he summed up the conversation and announced without preamble, "Lacey and I are getting married. I was thinking we should do it in a few weeks. I think we'll keep it simple, under the circumstances. We'll make arrangements when Father returns." He stood and tossed his napkin to the table. "It's the least I can do."

The following morning, Lacey was in the nursery playing with Richard when Tyson entered the room quietly. He tousled his son's hair and sat close to Lacey on the floor. Their eyes met, and he took the opportunity to quietly recite his memorized speech. "I love you, Lacey. And I pray that one day you will forgive me. In the meantime, I will not stand for this outward bitterness between us. We have a son to raise, and we will set a proper example of loving parents. If you wish to continue this bitterness, please keep it to yourself."

Lacey was tempted to argue, but he leaned forward to kiss her on the mouth, and she lost all resolve. As his kiss deepened, Lacey couldn't help but feel a subtle relief. She believed they had a long way to go to work all of this out, but she was growing tired of the anger and confrontations. She far preferred this, despite all she felt within.

"Tyson," she whispered as he pulled away, "I love you as well."

"Then there is hope," he smiled.

"I need time."

He nodded and kissed her again, feeling a wary relief.

They both turned at the same time to investigate Richard's silence, and found him staring at them, smiling with mischief.

"What are you looking at?" Tyson asked lightly.

"Grandmama and Grandpapa like to kiss, too."

Tyson chuckled and lay on his belly to help Richard build a castle from wooden blocks, while Lacey looked on, willing herself to forget the pain.

❧ ❧ ❧

Alexa sat anxiously on the veranda for what seemed hours, tensing at every noise she heard, looking around the corner of the house for any sign of someone approaching. Finally defeated by frustration, she went inside and sat at the piano, convincing herself that they would only come when they came. Her impatience would not bring them here any sooner. They were supposed to be three days behind Tyson and Lacey, and that meant today. But they could have run into trouble, or been delayed for any number of reasons. Alexa prayed that all was well and resigned herself to patience. She was so anxious to see them, and to know what had transpired.

Despite all her hopes, Alexa had made up her mind to the fact that Michael was likely lost to them. She had imagined him returning with Jess and Emma and Ben, but after hearing Lacey's report of his behavior, she had achingly forced herself to accept the reality that the hope she had once felt for Michael Hamilton had been lost somewhere in the past few years.

With purpose she became lost in her music, concentrating on the feel of the notes she played, telling herself that seeing Emma safe would be enough. She pulled her hands from the keys with a sigh, expecting to hear silence. Instead she heard distant laughter and men's voices. Then a distinct, familiar shout that sent her heart racing as it had for nearly twenty-five years.

"Alexandra Byrnehouse-Davies!" Jess shouted, and Alexa rushed through the veranda doors, looking out toward the stable yard. She laughed and put a hand to her heart as the team of animals came to a halt. Quickly she counted heads. One, two, three. Her heart sank just a little as she assumed the dark one was Ben. But she had been prepared for the disappointment, and she concentrated instead on her husband. She laughed like a schoolgirl and lifted her skirts high to run down the steps and over the lawn. "I brought your daughter home!" Jess added exuberantly.

"Jess!" she called. He beamed when he caught sight of her, then he laughed when he caught her into his arms, turning circles with her, kissing her as if he'd been gone a year. He'd barely set her down when she turned and squealed, "Emma!" They embraced and laughed. "You're all right?" Emma nodded, grinning.

Michael pretended to be unloading a mule as he observed the reunions taking place. He felt strange sensations as he recalled what Jess had told him about Alexa Davies in relation to him. While they were occupied with each other, he glanced around, distracted by the reality of being here again. Everything looked the same, but there was an unfamiliarity that he couldn't pinpoint. He reminded himself that it was him who had changed, and four years was a long time. It felt so good to be here, and to think of calling it home again filled him with an indescribable peace.

As Emma embraced her mother, Michael longed to blend in with the stable hands who had appeared to unload and care for the animals. He slung the saddlebags containing the money over his shoulder and was beginning to unfasten another when he felt Jess and Emma turn toward him. He increased his attention to the saddlebags as Jess announced, "Emma brought home a friend. I doubt there is a need for introductions."

For all Alexa's hopes, Jess's words didn't quite sink in until the dark-bearded face turned toward her with familiar, skeptical eyes. She'd seen that look hundreds of times in his youth. It clearly said *I dare you to love me.* Alexa had always taken that look very seriously.

For a moment, Alexa just stared at Michael, and he felt tense. She finally smiled, but he wondered if she would even remember his name. Surely there had been so many boys. But without any further delay, she reached out both hands and stepped toward him. "Michael Hamilton," she said as if she was actually glad to see him. "Where on earth did they find you?"

"At the end of a ransom note, I'm afraid," he admitted, taking the proffered hands. "I'm the jackass who kidnapped your daughters."

"Yes, I know," she said as if it were nothing. "Lacey told me."

Michael looked guiltily away. What Lacey had observed and repeated could not be at all good. "I'm sorry about that, Mrs. Davies. I—"

"It's all right, Michael. I'm certain you had your reasons, or you wouldn't be here." He nodded helplessly in agreement. "We can talk about that later. I'm so glad you came back."

"You are?"

She nodded and went on her tiptoes to hug him. "I've been worried about you."

"For four years?"

"Mother," Emma interrupted Alexa's eager nod, "Michael and I are going to be married."

Alexa smiled smugly toward Jess, who was leaning against his horse, arms folded, looking rather smug himself. She squeezed Emma's hand, then looked directly at Michael. "You couldn't have found a better man."

Michael and Emma exchanged a glance that made it clear they were both equally amazed by Alexa's lack of surprise.

Michael said quickly, "You don't need to flatter me, Mrs. Davies. There's no point hiding what kind of life I've lived."

"And now?" she questioned with purpose.

"I'm a different man," he said easily. "But why are you so quick to believe it?"

"A man who can rise above the worst of childhoods to be worthy of my daughter's affection has more to him than most men of this world who rise above nothing to become great."

For the hundredth time this week, Michael was struck dumb, in awe of the love and acceptance he had enjoyed because he was lucky enough to have been found in the gutter. He'd do it again to be here now.

"I hope you don't mind a double wedding," Alexa announced.

"I take it Tyson and Lacey are doing better," Jess said as he stepped forward and took his wife's hand. The slightly harsh look in her eyes caught him off guard.

"I suppose you could say that," she said. "They *are* getting married." The tone in her eyes added silently: *We'll talk later.*

"I don't care what kind of wedding we have," Emma beamed, "as long as it's soon."

"But where is Ben?" Alexa looked around, just realizing his absence.

"He went back," Jess answered, knowing she could figure out the details.

"But what about—"

"I gave Michael the job," he answered proudly.

"How brilliant of you!" Alexa kissed her husband, who winked knowingly at Michael. "Why don't we go inside and get caught up." She put her arm through Michael's and urged him toward the house.

Michael hesitated, concerned with the animals after the journey. "It's all right," Alexa assured him. "The hands will see to it." He turned back, and sure enough, they seemed to have it under control. It was his first perception of being on the other side of the world he'd grown up in.

On Alexa Davies' arm, Michael followed Jess and Emma into the house. He didn't recall ever venturing into this part of their world before. The residence had simply been off limits to the boys for obvious reasons, and he felt like a foreigner in this extension of his homeland. He was at first surprised by the simple elegance of the home. The boys' home had been nice and comfortable, but it wasn't like this. Everywhere he turned, there was the unshowy evidence of wealth. But it had a homey, lived-in feel. He could imagine the Davies women sitting about in feminine elegance, and at the same time he could conceive that the men wouldn't be afraid to put their boots on the coffee table.

"You'll fit right in," Alexa whispered as if she'd read his mind.

Emma felt an indescribable pride in Michael as she watched him stride into the house with her mother. She was filled with intense gratitude for her parents' acceptance and forgiveness of him; it would make the transition much easier. Still, she sensed he feared most having to face Lacey. And despite how deeply Emma cared for her sister, she could understand why Michael was afraid. Lacey was a wonderful, caring person, but the past few years had made her bitter. In truth, Emma had no idea what to expect from her—or from Tyson. At one time she had known Tyson so well that she could nearly predict his every move, but she'd not seen him for four years. She could only hope, for Michael's sake, that they would open their hearts enough to forgive him and try to understand his motives.

"I believe Tyson and Lacey are upstairs with Richard," Alexa said, knowing the next course of events had to be the reuniting of the children. "Emma, why don't you take Michael into the drawing room and offer him a drink. I'll go and find them."

Jess and Alexa moved on down the hall, leaving Michael and Emma alone, but not before Alexa turned back and gave a warm, reassuring smile to Michael, who was obviously tense.

"Are you all right?" Emma took his hand.

"As good as any man would feel stepping onto the gallows," he stated all too soberly.

"It's not as bad as all that." She reached up to kiss his nose, and he took the opportunity to pull her close to him.

A deep severity filled his eyes as he said, "She has every reason in the world to hate me, and this is nobody's fault but mine. I fear it will come between us. I know how dear she is to you."

"Yes, she is," Emma admitted. "And so are you."

"And if you had to choose between us, I'm certain it—"

"Lacey has many people who love her, Michael. If it comes down to such choices, it will only be because she brings it to that. I would choose you."

She said it so easily that Michael wondered if she was sane. "You can't really mean that you would—"

"Do you credit me with less commitment than that?" she asked with an edge to her voice.

"No." He shook his head apologetically.

"It will not come to that, Michael. But I can assure you, I am committed to you, your life, all that you are."

"And all I have been?"

"All you have been has made you the man you are now. And I love you."

"Emma," he murmured and cradled her head against his shoulder, squeezing his eyes shut to perceive the reality. The depth of her love was beyond his own comprehension.

"Besides," she pulled back and smiled up at him, "you need me."

"Yes," he said with strength, "I do." He heaved a sigh. "I think I could use that drink."

Emma led him into the drawing room. "Why don't you sit down."

"I think I'll wait until my clothes won't leave an impression on the furniture." Emma chuckled, but he was serious.

"Is brandy all right?" she asked.

"Fine," he said, biting his thumbnail.

"You really can sit down, Michael. This house is quite accustomed to surviving dirt. Mother always made it clear that houses are to live in, not look at."

"I'm all right," he insisted as Emma handed him the snifter. He emptied it and coughed. He was going to ask for more, but the sound of approaching voices froze him cold.

Twelve
THE REUNION

Tyson was the first to notice Alexa entering the nursery, looking rather smug.

"What?" he asked, rolling onto his back to look up at her.

"Your sister is here," she said mischievously, and Tyson jumped to his feet.

"She's all right?" Lacey gasped.

"She looked perfectly wonderful to me," Alexa beamed. "And she's brought a friend with her. I'll get Miss Leeds to watch Richard, and we'll go down."

"I'm right here," the nanny announced. "I was just eavesdropping a little."

Tyson took Lacey's hand, and she lifted her skirts to keep up with him as they raced down the stairs. Alexa was proud of herself for keeping up. They found Jess in the hall. He grinned and hugged Tyson and then Lacey. "It would seem you made it home all right," he said to Tyson. Then to Lacey, "And that leg must not be too bad off from the way you came down those stairs."

"It hurts some, but it's doing well."

"Did everything go all right?" Tyson asked.

"Couldn't have gone better, I'd say." Jess winked at Alexa.

"Where is Emma?" Tyson couldn't bear the anticipation any longer.

"In the drawing room," Alexa stated, and he hurried to the door with the others following. Alexa added quietly to her husband, "This should be very interesting." Jess nodded dubiously.

"Emma!" Lacey flew through the door that Tyson had opened. "Oh, you're safe!" she squealed, and the girls embraced.

Michael took notice of the easy way Lacey walked before he turned away in a feeble effort to avoid being seen.

"Are you all right?" Lacey added.

"Yes, I'm wonderful." Emma's enthusiasm was genuine.

"Oh, you must be so glad to be home. I know I was. Did that horrible man hurt you?"

Emma tangibly felt Michael's pain at Lacey's words. She was grateful for the distraction of Tyson catching her eye. "Tyson!" Emma couldn't keep from crying as he took her into his arms.

"Emma," he whispered as the flesh of the womb was reunited after four long years.

"You've changed." She touched his face.

"So have you." He laughed, doing the same.

"There's so much I want to talk to you about."

"Me, too." He hugged her again, lifting her off the floor.

Michael turned carefully to observe the reunion, finding a degree of peace in sensing Emma's joy. His eyes shifted carefully over the occupants of the room, all momentarily oblivious to his presence. The proud parents observed the reunion of their children with emotion etched into their faces. Lacey eased into the twins' embrace, and Michael found himself on the outside of a circle that he felt certain he could never be a part of. His heart thudded into his throat as he realized that only seconds from now his intrusion on their happiness would become evident. He wanted to just walk away. He wondered if anything had ever been so difficult in his life. Of course, he'd been through too much that could never compare. But at this moment, the present fear blocked out everything else. He felt some peace, however, in realizing that much of his fear was for Emma. It felt good to know that his heart was feeling for someone else. He found himself uttering a quick, silent prayer, and he wondered when he'd found the ability to pray. He couldn't remember the last time he'd done it.

The circle began to spread apart. Michael drew back his shoulders and lifted his chin. His palms began to sweat coldly when Lacey questioned with expectancy, "Where is this friend Mama said you brought with you?"

Michael waited for Emma to show apprehension, to apologize for falling in love with a criminal. But warmth filled him as her face brightened with pride and her eyes turned lovingly toward him, leaving him momentarily oblivious to the others as their gaze followed.

"You remember Michael," she said, as if he were royalty, giving them the honor of his presence.

Michael's eyes shifted to see that fearing the worst had been optimistic. There was enough hatred, bitterness, and disgust in Lacey's eyes to turn the Nile to blood. He sensed Emma's hand reaching out for his and he moved to take it, but a fist landed against his jaw, not hurting nearly so much as Tyson's accompanying words. "You fiend! How dare you show your face here after what you have done!"

Emma watched in horror as her brother turned on the man she loved. Michael barely took a step backward to receive the blow. His neck snapped forward again so quickly that Emma wondered if he was made of steel. How many times had he been hit like that to learn to take it so straightly?

In the split second it took for him to recover his stance, Emma had her arms about his waist, holding him protectively. Michael's eyes stayed riveted on Tyson while he touched his lip to assure himself that it was bleeding. He wiped the blood on his dusty sleeve and realized that Tyson was itching to hit him again. There was a brief, pounding debate in Michael's head as he wondered whether or not to hit him back.

"No, Tyson," Emma insisted.

Alexa stepped forward to put a hand on her son's arm. "I don't care what he's done," she insisted, "you will treat no man like that."

"It's all right," Michael stated, unavoidably cold. "I think I deserved that."

"You bet you did," Tyson retorted, still full of anger.

"What's he doing here?" Lacey asked with quiet venom. She couldn't begin to fathom what kind of madness was consuming her sister. Just the presence of Michael Hamilton alone made her cringe. A clear image came to mind of him holding a gun to Emma's head.

"Michael and I are going to—"

"Emma," Michael stopped her announcement, certain the direct approach was not the best route at the moment. He wished he could just fight them the way he was used to fighting. It would have been easier. But at the age of twenty-eight, he was finally growing up. It was time to act like an adult, to be civilized. "I think I would do well to speak for myself."

"Why don't you do that!" Tyson challenged, calming slightly, if only for his mother's sake. After the torment Michael Hamilton had just put them through, the present scene seemed like something out of a disjointed nightmare.

"I am here to apologize," Michael stated. "I have wronged this family, and I am willing to admit it. I will do whatever is necessary to make right what I have done."

"Some things cannot be made right," Lacey insisted, folding her arms tightly.

"I am not asking you to forgive me, Miss Davies. Only to tolerate me."

Tyson didn't like the way this seemed to echo his recent conversations with Lacey. The silence following Michael's statement made Tyson begin to realize that Michael would not have gone to such trouble, and come all this way, just to ask for tolerance.

"Tolerate you for what purpose?" Tyson asked. "What exactly do you want from us, Hamilton?" When only silence answered, Tyson's eyes were drawn to his sister and the tight hold she had on this man. He couldn't believe it!

Michael watched Tyson closely and caught the slap of betrayal in his eyes that he knew would not go unnoticed by Emma. But she only tightened her grip, possessively challenging her own flesh and blood to come between them.

"I love Michael," she stated. No apology. No regret. Not even a hint of distaste. It was evident she meant it.

"Emma!" Lacey shouted in a whisper. "Have you gone mad?" She stepped toward Michael as if she'd like to tear him apart. Emma moved between them, holding fiercely to Michael's arms behind her.

Tyson pulled Lacey back, saying tonelessly, "Stop it, now. It won't do any good. She's obviously not going to listen."

There was a severing of bonds in his tone that made Michael ache on Emma's behalf. He felt tempted to turn and run, but a voice inside his head reminded him that he was committed, he loved her, she loved him, and he'd come too far to run now.

"I can't believe it," Lacey gasped in disgust.

"Emma has a right to her own choices," Alexa said gently, finally stepping into the drama as she figured it was time for a parent's wisdom.

"Not when choices are manipulated," Lacey nearly shouted at her mother—something Alexa Davies did not tolerate. It only took a glance for Lacey to regret the tone of voice.

"I have been manipulated into nothing," Emma insisted. "I love Michael of my own free will. He is a good man, and he loves me. He made some mistakes, but if he's humble enough to ask your acceptance, you have no right to treat him like a common criminal."

"He *is* a common criminal," Lacey shot back, as if Michael was not present.

"*Was,*" Emma corrected calmly but with force. "What Michael was before this day is of no relevance. I love him, and I'm going to marry him." From behind, Michael put his arms around Emma in a gesture of support and appreciation.

"I don't believe it." Tyson shook his head in disgust. "After what he has done to you, you would . . ."

"And what has he done to me, Tyson? You're not bothering to ask *me* what happened out there. Michael did not hurt me."

"How can you say that?" Lacey was so appalled she felt lightheaded. "I was there. I saw what was going on." Michael dropped his head forward and sighed. "Do you think I didn't hear how he threatened and—"

"Lacey," Emma pleaded, "you must try to understand his motives. We can talk about this, if you would just—"

"I thought I knew you better than that," Tyson interrupted.

Emma turned on her brother like a she-bear defending her young. "How dare you claim to know what I am, when you haven't even seen my face in four years? You cannot just stride back into my life and expect to pick up where you left off."

"But you were always so insightful, Emma," Tyson said tersely. "I would have thought, of all people, that you would not be blinded by—"

"I would have thought that *you*, of all people, would trust my judgment when—"

"Emma," Alexa interrupted gently, "Tyson." Her voice put all anger on hold. Jess sat down in his outback-dusted clothes and put his boots on the coffee table. "I think something needs to be said here that isn't being said." Alexa stepped between Tyson, who held to Lacey, and Emma, who held to Michael.

"My advocate," Michael quipped, unable to avoid an attempt at comic relief. Emma fought to keep a straight face as she nudged him with her elbow. Alexa gave him a quick smile that was lost on Tyson and Lacey.

"A man is a result of his upbringing." She said it directly to Tyson and Lacey. "You cannot fairly judge his actions without knowing what kind of life he has suffered through, and the motives behind—"

"I object." Michael stepped forward abruptly as he realized Alexa knew more about him than he cared to have spilt here. "With all due respect," he nodded to Alexa, "whatever I might have suffered through in my lifetime is no excuse to inflict suffering on others. I am prepared to take responsibility for my actions. I will not be justified because I had the misfortune of . . ." Michael stopped, realizing what he'd nearly said.

His eyes widened in horror when Alexa finished for him. "Because you were tortured as a child?"

Michael heard gasps and felt eyes widen. His eyes locked onto Alexa's in a silent struggle of wills that brought back vivid memories of the years he had been under her careful tutelage. He knew from experience that power struggles with Alexa Davies were futile. Eventually she always won.

Emma looked on, attempting to comprehend what her mother was trying to achieve. If she didn't have complete faith in her mother's abilities with the human mind and emotions, she would have been angry on behalf of the hurt she knew was close beneath the surface of Michael's suddenly hardened exterior. She saw him now as the man he was comfortable being, bitter and brash. Still, she felt pride in him. His strength, his will, combined with his newfound humility, were all part of the man she loved.

"Was that necessary?" he drawled, barely moving his lips.

"Yes," Alexa answered with confidence, "I believe it was. If you are going to be a part of this family, you've got to learn that suffering does not come alone. When one of us suffers, we all do. When one of us rejoices, we all do. There are no closeted skeletons in this home, Michael. To share in the joy of your rebirth, we must *all* know of the pain."

"My pain is irrelevant," Michael retorted. "It is the pain I have inflicted on others that is the issue here."

"And one is the result of the other."

"That," he lifted a finger, "does not justify it. If I am to be accepted, it will be because I'm worthy of it, not because I have the most scars."

Michael left the room before anyone else had a chance to confront what he was still having difficulty confronting himself. Emma moved to follow him, but Alexa stopped her momentarily. She turned back to look at all of her children, saying carefully, "Emma has made a decision she believes in. It is not for us to disapprove. She is a woman with sound intelligence and a good heart. If Emma accepts Michael, it is for us to accept her decision. If any of you have a problem with that, just keep it to yourself. Enough has been said. Michael has asked for nothing but tolerance. He deserves at least that. Your father has made Michael administrator of the boys' home."

Tyson and Lacey turned to Jess in astonishment. He grinned and shrugged his shoulders.

"Michael is, from this day forward," Alexa continued, "a part of this family. He will eat with us. He will sleep under this roof, and he is entitled to be treated with civility. I did not raise my children to be prejudiced and intolerant. Do I make myself clear?" There was no response. "Well?" she insisted.

"Yes," Tyson answered reluctantly. Lacey said nothing, feeling her bitterness shift to a new scapegoat.

"Now," Alexa continued, "this might be difficult for you to take, but for reasons you may not understand or appreciate at this point in your lives, I believe this is the best thing, and I expect it regardless. The wedding will be in three weeks, which should give us enough time to prepare adequately. And it will be as Tyson and Emma have always planned. Though it may have been in jest, I am quite serious now when I say that my twins will have a double wedding."

Emma could see the fire in Tyson's and Lacey's eyes, but Alexa's will kept them silent. "Enough said," Alexa finished and turned to Emma. "Take Michael to the east guest room, where he can clean up and get settled in before supper. See that he has everything he needs."

"Yes, Mother," Emma said, pausing to embrace her before she ran from the room in search of Michael.

When she was gone, the silence was broken by Jess clapping out a slow, steady applause. "That was quite a performance, my dear." He smiled at his wife. But it was apparent that Tyson and Lacey were not amused as they hurried from the room, each going a different direction down the halls.

"Do you think I was too harsh?" Alexa asked Jess when they were alone.

"On Tyson? No. I think Michael should have hit him back. On Lacey? Hmmm." He contemplated it. "I can see why she's upset, although she was overly brash about it."

"On Michael?"

"Most definitely."

"Oh, Jess, I—"

"But," he added firmly, "I think it was necessary. It's a hard way to face it, but you were right. He'll be better off in the long run if he doesn't feel like he's keeping secrets. He's been doing that all his life. It's time he stopped."

"I just hope he sees it that way." Alexa sighed. "The last thing he needs is to feel like I'm against him, too."

"I doubt it will take long for you to convince him otherwise."

Jess sighed. "I must talk to Sarina. Ben gave me a message for her. She'll certainly be wondering why her son didn't come home."

Alexa sat beside her husband and leaned her head on his shoulder. "That would be fine," she said. "But first you could really use a bath, Jess."

"Why don't you come and help me?" He blew in her ear and she giggled.

"All right. I think I will. And you can tell me everything. I want all the details."

"You want to know about all the times I was silently cursing you for making me promise to keep an open mind?"

"Especially that. Come on, dear." She stood and pulled him to his feet. "Get your dirty carcass off the furniture and—"

The door opened and Tyson stood in its frame, his hand on the knob. "I just figured it out." He pointed an accusing finger at his father. "Those saddlebags he had over his shoulder. You gave it to him, didn't you."

"Yes, I did." Jess didn't apologize.

Alexa looked at her husband in pleasant surprise as she guessed what they were discussing.

"You gave him the money?" Tyson's voice seethed with disgust.

"Let's get one thing clear, Tyson." Jess pointed his finger in return. "I will do whatever I please with my money, and you can do the same with yours."

"But . . . a hundred thousand pounds?" Tyson gasped.

"Kind of puts the two of you on equal terms, doesn't it," Jess said, figuring Tyson could still use a little humility in some respects, like when it came to tolerance.

"I can't believe you just said that."

"And one of these days when you've grown up just a little bit more, I will tell you why I said it, and why I gave it to him. For now, it's my business, and it's Michael's money. But just so you don't have to wonder, I practically had to force it on him."

"Why?" Tyson had to ask. "Why would you pay him, after—"

"For the moment, suffice it to say that we will never have to wonder if he married Emma for the money, now will we."

Tyson gave a noncommittal grunt and left the room. Jess and Alexa sighed in unison.

"You know," Alexa led Jess into the hall and up the stairs, "I always thought when they were grown it would be easier."

"Yes, I know," he said. "And then you thought when Tyson came back everything would be all right."

"And then I was certain that when I had my family back together under the same roof, our problems would be over."

"Perhaps once we get them married, it will—"

"Don't even think it," she said. "It's too pleasant a thought to be possible."

❦   ❦   ❦

Logic told Emma that Michael would have gone someplace he felt comfortable. She found him in the stables. For a moment she wasn't certain if he was packing or unpacking. Panic edged her voice when she asked, "You're not leaving?"

Michael shot his head up in surprise. He closed the saddlebag he'd been looking in and threw it over his shoulder with the other. "And where would I go?" he asked too coldly for the progress they'd made.

"If you had somewhere to go, would you leave?"

Emma didn't like the way he contemplated the question, until he firmly answered, "Not without taking you with me."

Emma smiled.

"What did she say after I left?" The coldness dissipated slightly from his voice.

"She made it clear that she expected tolerance, and if anyone had a problem with it to keep it to themselves. And she announced that we would be having a double wedding ceremony in three weeks."

Michael absorbed this. "Your mother has a way of taking command."

"Yes, she does. She's had to."

"Yes," Michael chuckled, seeming a little more relaxed. "She's had to put up with brats like me. It seems she's learned to handle us brats rather well."

"You're not angry with her?"

"I'm learning that getting angry with the truth doesn't get me very far."

"But it's not easy." She touched his face with compassion.

"No," he admitted, "it's not easy."

"Come on," she took his hand, "I'll take you to your room."

"My room? In the house?"

"Mother just made it clear that this is your home from now on. You'd better get used to it."

"I'd rather share your room," he said in his villain voice.

"Soon enough." She laughed at the thought.

"No." He shot his arm around her waist and pulled her against him, dropping the saddlebags to hold a more precious package. "Not soon enough."

He kissed her, and the drama of the last hour became insignificant. Emma became completely absorbed in it, aching to be his wife. When he held her this way, she felt as if they could take on anything together—even Tyson and Lacey.

Emma sensed her brother's presence and turned away from the kiss to find him there, studying the scene in disgust. Michael stepped back but kept his arm firmly around Emma, holding her steady as she teetered slightly. She held her breath as the two men exchanged a probing gaze. She could feel their strength battling silently as they each firmly believed in their stand.

Tyson broke the silence with a coldness that Michael might have had trouble matching. "I will tolerate your presence, out of respect to my mother."

"And what about your respect for Emma?" Michael asked firmly. Emma watched Tyson closely and saw some of the betrayal come back to him that he'd wordlessly inflicted on her earlier.

"And my respect for Emma," Tyson admitted. "But I cannot forgive the hurt you inflicted on Lacey."

Michael said nothing. He didn't feel he had a right to question that. His actions had hurt Lacey, and he had to take responsibility for it. But there was something he felt compelled to say. "I have a question, Tyson," he said.

"All right. What is it?" Tyson's irritation was evident.

"How does a few weeks in the outback with bad company, and a scar on her leg, compare with four years of being alone with an illegitimate child?"

Emma became tense as she felt Tyson's shock over Michael's brashness. But her eyes echoed Michael's question when Tyson turned toward her. Michael was fighting for her, and she couldn't help but feel pride.

"That has nothing to do with you," Tyson insisted.

"If I'm going to be a part of this family," Michael borrowed Alexa's speech, "I've got to learn that suffering does not come alone. When one of us suffers, we all do."

"What's your point, Hamilton?"

"Has she forgiven you?"

Emma felt the hurt rise in Tyson. Michael had struck a significant chord. Something softened in Tyson's eyes, and at the same time hardened his countenance. But he said nothing before he turned and walked away.

When they were alone, Emma turned her face against Michael's chest and sighed back the tears. Michael buried his face in her hair and matched her sigh. "It would seem we all have pain to deal with in one way or another," he said.

"Let's go inside." Emma bent to pick up the saddlebags and handed them to Michael.

"I think you should keep this one." He indicated the money.

"No," she put it over his shoulder, "you earned it. Besides," she took his hand, "I've already got a hundred thousand pounds."

"You do?" He was genuinely surprised.

"Tucked in the bank, earning interest," she said proudly. "Father gave us each that much on our eighteenth birthday."

Michael's eyes widened. He couldn't help but think there was something significant behind Jess's motives. "If I had known that," Michael smirked, "I could have just married you for your money."

Emma smirked. "How about if *I* marry *you* for your money?"

Michael followed her through the side door of the house, up the back stairs, and down a long hall to the east wing. "Why don't you get settled in," Emma said, "and I'll have Rick prepare you a bath."

"Rick?"

"He just helps around the house. I'm sure he won't mind a—"

"Really, Emma," Michael interrupted, "I don't think that—"

"It's all right." Emma stopped him with a patronizing pat on his chest just before she opened a door and motioned for him to enter. They found the pleasant Rick leaning over a large brass bathtub for a final temperature check.

"It would seem that someone has beat me to it," Emma said.

"It's ready, sir," Rick announced with an easy smile, wiping his hand on his sleeve.

"Thank you," Michael stated, not certain how he was supposed to respond. He'd never had anything done for him by a servant in his entire life.

"I think you'll find everything you need," Rick announced. "Will there be anything else?"

The question was directed to Michael, but Emma responded

when he didn't. "Could you take Mr. Hamilton's clothes to be laundered." She added to Michael, "Do you have any clean ones?"

"I think so," he said, but didn't make any immediate effort to find out.

Emma took the saddlebags and dumped the contents on the bed. Michael took over. "Let me do that!" He quickly separated the dirty from the clean they had washed a few days before. "These will do just fine."

Emma handed the remainder to Rick. "That will be all, thank you."

He nodded graciously and left the room. Emma went to the bureau to be certain everything was readily available. She listed aloud, "Towels, soap, shampoo, combs, boot polish, shaving items, and—"

"I brought most of that with me." He sounded subtly irritated.

"Is something wrong?"

"I'm just not used to being . . . coddled over."

"It's all right, Michael." She smiled. "No one is going to undress you and tuck you into bed. I'm just making certain you have what you need. And if you need anything else," she added, moving toward the door, "my room is down the next hall and—"

"Yes," he grinned, "I know where your room is. You're not going to be trading with Lacey again, are you? I don't think that's a mistake I want to make twice."

"No," she blew him a kiss, "I'll be in my own room, I promise. Supper will be at six. I'll come back to get you."

Michael blew a kiss in return and watched her disappear down the hall, then he closed the door and leaned heavily against it. Never in his life would he have dreamed of living in such a room, in this house—betrothed to Emma Byrnehouse-Davies, no less. And having baths prepared for him in brass tubs! "Oh, well," he said aloud, "life is full of trials."

Deciding he'd do well to get that bath before the water cooled, Michael undressed and slipped into the water with a husky sigh. *Yes,* he thought, *it's such a trial.*

❦   ❦   ❦

Tyson went from the stable to the nursery, knowing it was likely the only place he could presently find any solace. He couldn't believe it. He felt angry with his father, baffled by his mother, and totally torn from Emma. He wanted to beat Michael Hamilton to a pulp, and Lacey . . . well, it made him all the more angry with Michael to hear how plainly he'd confronted him with the truth. Lacey had not forgiven him, and she likely never would. With Lacey, he was reminded continually that his only real chance for happiness had been blown when he'd walked away from here four years ago.

Tyson entered the nursery, but the solace he sought wasn't there. He found his son crying in Miss Leeds' arms.

"What's wrong?" Tyson questioned.

Richard looked up at the sound of his voice and quickly ran to his father's arms while Miss Leeds explained quietly, "It seems his mother is upset over something, and he's taken it rather personally."

Tyson felt angry, but he temporarily swallowed it and gave Richard a bright smile. "Hey there, buddy, what's a brave guy like you doing with such big tears?"

"Mama . . . ," he hiccuped, "yelled at me, and . . ."

"Now, you listen," Tyson explained gently. "What Mama is upset about has nothing to do with you. She loves you very much, and you have been a very good boy."

Richard managed a smile. Tyson wiped his tears and nodded toward Miss Leeds, who shrugged her shoulders. "That's what I tried to tell him," she said, "but he'd far rather believe you than me."

Tyson smiled. "I hope that's a good sign."

Miss Leeds agreed eagerly.

"I think I'll go have a little talk with Mama," Tyson said without any of the terseness he was feeling. "You find something to do now—and smile, will you?"

Richard nodded. Tyson hugged him and moved toward the door.

"Papa?" Richard stopped him, and Tyson had to swallow the emotion as he heard himself called that for the first time.

"What is it, son?"

"I'm glad you came back."

"So am I, Richard. So am I."

The emotion steadied Tyson's anger as he went the short distance to Lacey's room. He knocked, then pushed the door open to find it empty. The sitting room door was ajar, and he peered around it to find her staring blankly out the window.

"Are you all right?" he asked tonelessly, trying not to jump to conclusions.

"Not particularly." She didn't look at him. Tyson sat down and put his feet up. "What are you doing?" she asked without turning.

"I'm sitting." He attempted some humor. "It's a sitting room. Can I sit?" All humor was apparently lost on Lacey, so he added, "I take it you're pretty upset."

"That would be putting it mildly."

"And you left our son in tears," he added, only slightly critical.

"I'll make it up to him. He knows I love him."

"Yes, well," Tyson's voice turned bitter, "I believe you love me, too, but that doesn't mean I enjoy being in your presence."

Lacey turned abruptly toward him. "Haven't we got enough to worry about without arguing about *us?*"

"I was not arguing." He kept a straight voice. "And as I see it, we don't have anything to worry about."

"How can you say that when your twin sister is—"

"It's like Mother said, Lacey, this is Emma's choice. Whether we like it or not, it is none of our business."

Lacey didn't hear him. She was so thoroughly absorbed in Emma's apparent madness that she couldn't think or feel anything else. "After what that man has done," she fumed, "how can she just turn around and forgive and forget as if it were nothing?"

Tyson leaned back to observe the embittered Lacey, and his heart ached. Michael Hamilton's words returned to him like an ominous premonition. How had he been here so short a time and hit the nail on the head so perfectly? In his hesitance to answer Lacey's question, Tyson felt a basic principle of humanity that he'd been taught as a child come back to him now. If he was expecting Lacey—and the rest of the family, for that matter, including Emma—to forgive and forget his leaving here, and the hurt he'd inflicted, how could he not forgive Michael Hamilton? The severity of their deeds was relative, and no man's motives in a deed could be completely understood by anyone but himself. Tyson could look back and understand his motives in leaving, although it made him feel like a fool now. Did Michael feel the same way? He still felt angry with Michael, and he still couldn't understand what Emma saw in him, or his parents' unquestioning acceptance. But he knew he could not support Lacey's bitterness toward Michael and expect her to be free of it toward him. The concept was as old as the Bible, and even though religion had never been a big part of their lives, the basic concepts of Christianity had been. And Tyson recalled his father teaching him the familiar words: *Condemn not and ye shall not be condemned; forgive and ye shall be forgiven.*

"I don't know," Tyson finally said, startling Lacey out of her thoughts. "Perhaps the way she feels about him makes it possible to overlook how he might have hurt her in the past."

Lacey was astonished. "Excuse me, but aren't you the man who just bloodied Michael Hamilton's lip?"

"That's me," he said proudly. "But maybe he should have hit me back. Who am I to cast the first stone?"

"And now you're practically defending him!"

"I was merely trying to point out that there is obviously another side of the coin. Perhaps we should be a little more open-minded. We've only been asked to tolerate him. I think we can live with that."

"Perhaps *you* can. You weren't out there in the middle of nowhere with him, watching the way he treated your sister."

"No, I wasn't."

"Tyson, how can you be so calm?" she shouted. "We're talking about your sister. Our darling Emma is marrying herself to a beast! How can you just sit there and—"

"It's a sitting room," he interrupted, and Lacey became infuriated.

"Get out of here!" she demanded. If he wasn't going to share her concerns to any degree, she didn't even want him here.

"I take it you're implying I can't sit anymore."

"Oooh," she groaned in frustration at his attempting comic relief at such a time.

"Listen, Lacey," he came to his feet and stuffed his hands into the pockets of his jodhpurs, "I understand your concern, and I understand that Hamilton's offense toward you is real and warranted. But I want you to take Mother's advice seriously. Keep it to yourself. If you don't, you're only going to make bad problems worse, and it will surely come back to you."

"You are the most unsympathetic, insensitive excuse for a man I have ever known."

Tyson found it difficult to take that one with any degree of humor. "Then why are you marrying me, Lacey?"

"I have no idea!" she shouted. "When I figure it out, I'll let you know."

"In the meantime," he said in warning, "you keep your temper in check in front of Richard. If you can't, just stay away from him."

"Fine! You raise him, and I'll take four years off."

"All right, I will." He was proud of himself for remaining calm. He walked to the door that led into the hall and opened it. "But when you come back, Lacey, I will forgive you."

Lacey clenched her fists in anger and frustration. His calm defiance of everything she felt made her want to scream and curse. Without the will to hold it back, she did both. "You and Michael Hamilton can both go to the devil!"

❦   ❦   ❦

Emma winced when the door slammed. Tears fell silently over her face as Tyson's brisk footsteps echoed down the hall. There was little of their conversation that she hadn't heard while she'd quietly bathed away the remnants of the outback from her hair and body.

She had no doubt as to where Tyson and Lacey stood in their relationship, and it made her ache. They should have been happy together, and here their forthcoming marriage was nothing more than a farce. No, she stopped herself. It couldn't be as bad as all that. She knew they loved each other. They simply had to overcome these barriers. She only prayed that they could do it soon, before the bitterness became any deeper.

Beyond her compassion for Tyson and Lacey, Emma couldn't help but feel a loss in the wake of their animosity toward Michael. She felt a degree of hope in Tyson's defense of Michael, however slight. But she still sensed his lack of acceptance. And what Lacey felt made Emma cringe on Michael's behalf.

Willing herself not to think about it, knowing there was nothing to be done, Emma sank into the water and pressed wet hands over her face to blend away the tears. Everything she had shared with Michael came back to her with a peaceful glow. There was not even an inkling of doubt that she was doing the right thing. It was right for her, and it was right for Michael. Her parents' wisdom and support added conviction to their cause.

"I love you, Michael," she said aloud, and decided she'd had enough of sitting here in the cooling water when she could be with him.

Wrapped in a towel, Emma stood before her closet, wondering what attire might be suitable. She didn't want to overdress, knowing Michael had little to choose from. But she did want to feel attractive. She couldn't recall ever wanting to impress a man before, and he had certainly seen her at her worst. Thinking they might ride together after supper, she opted for a black split skirt, black riding boots, and a white blouse with lace insets and pearl buttons down the front. Emma brushed through her hair until it gleamed, then she tied it back with a white satin ribbon and put on pearl earrings. A light splash of perfume made her feel well put together—and glad to be home.

The clock on the mantle read five-forty. She hurried to Michael's room and knocked, then opened the door without waiting for a response. She found him leaning close to the bureau mirror, almost finished removing his beard. The mustache remained, but Emma couldn't help feeling a little nostalgic. She had become so accustomed to seeing him bearded.

"Just a minute," he said, his words barely discernible through the contortion of his face to make his left cheek taut to the razor. "I'm shaving."

Emma leaned against the door to watch him, noting the highly polished boots, clean clothes, and damp hair, combed back over his ears and hanging in loose waves that she now realized looked different. He'd cut it, she realized, noticing the evidence of dark hair scattered over a towel on the bureau.

Michael finished and splashed water on his face, blotted it with a towel, then turned to set his eyes on Emma. He looked different, but oh . . . "You're a handsome man, Michael Hamilton." She made no effort to hide the desire in her eyes. He looked more the way he had four years ago—the way she'd imagined him all this time.

Michael was oblivious to the compliment. His eyes were drinking in the woman before him. "You are the most beautiful woman in the world." The words might have sounded trite, but his tone, his eyes, and the expectancy in his countenance made the compliment unequaled.

Michael splashed shaving lotion on his face, wiped his hands on the towel, then turned to lean against the bureau, folding his arms over his chest. Emma sauntered toward him, reaching up to touch his smooth face, relishing the way it felt so different, and the scent that was so familiar. She touched his damp hair. "You look . . . different," she said.

"A new man needs a new look, don't you think?"

"I like it. I think I would like you no matter how you looked." Emma was thinking of his reasons for leaving the mustache when she had intended to imply that scar or no scar, she loved him just the same.

"The mustache stays forever," he said as if he'd read her mind, or perhaps he was making what he considered an important point.

"If that's what makes you comfortable," she touched it with affection, "I'll not argue." She kissed him and smiled. "Just so you don't forget how to kiss me."

"Never," he whispered and tightened his embrace, setting his fingertips against her face in a gesture of respect and admiration. Timidly he fingered the pearl in her earlobe. "Thank you, Emma, for all you are doing for me. I am forever indebted to you." His tone of voice could only attempt to convey the awe he felt in the present reality. He had never once, in all the dirt and disarray he'd seen her in over the past weeks, even considered that she was anything less than beautiful. But the woman before him, complete with fumes of lavender, left him wondering what he had done to deserve this. The question was only deepened by the reality of their surroundings. He was truly a lucky man.

Not knowing what else to say, he urged her toward the door. But she stopped him with an abrupt tug on his hand. He turned back in question. "Oh, I'm sorry. I forgot to clean up and—" He headed back to the bureau, ready to alleviate the mess, but Emma stopped him again.

"The mess can wait," she said. "But let's get something straight." She lifted a finger, much like he would do. "You sound as though I'm making some great sacrifice on your behalf." He lifted that eyebrow. "I am not."

"I know it can't be easy for you, Emma. Don't think I can't see what passes between you and your brother when you look at him."

"No," she admitted, "at times it's not easy, but it's not nearly as difficult as you might think. My motives are selfish, Michael. I want you here with me. I want you in my life, and I will stop at nothing to have you. I cannot expect you to fight for me without giving the same in return. You are a blessing to me, Michael, and nothing less."

Again she left him speechless. He could do nothing but bend to place a warm kiss to her lips. "Let's eat," he said, pressing her hand over his arm. "I'm starved."

They walked to the dining room, pausing momentarily before entering. "Are you all right?" she asked.

"As long as I'm with you, I will forever be fine."

Emma pushed open the door, and Michael sighed with relief. They were the first ones there. "Where do I sit?" he whispered.

"There," she pointed, "next to me."

He contemplated the utensils on the table and couldn't ever recall having more than one fork and one spoon to eat with. Emma read his mind with little trouble. "Don't worry about it. Just watch me. We're actually rather casual."

"It's going to take some getting used to," he admitted. "I'm a student of the streets, Emma. I was never terribly concerned with which fork to use when I was starving." She gave him a compassionate smile. "And meals served in boys' homes and prisons are not generally inclined to etiquette."

"My family is quite accustomed to such things. Stop worrying over silly things like forks. Think about important things, like whether or not we'll be eating beans." He feigned nausea and Emma giggled. "All right, worry about whether or not you're going to take me riding after supper."

Michael smiled, but the family's entrance didn't leave time for comment. The meal went as well as could be expected. Alexa was quick to remark on Michael's changed appearance. She kissed him on the cheek and squeezed his hand, making it easy to forget their encounter in the drawing room. Michael helped Emma with her chair and was seated. It didn't take him long to figure out that this was just a meal, and eating it while pretending he had dined this way before was not so difficult.

He quit thinking about it as his mind turned to concentrate on the food. It all tasted good, especially after what they had lived on in the outback. But he had to stop and marvel at the steak he was given. His first surprise, as he went to cut it, was simply that it hardly needed to be cut. It was so tender the knife nearly slid through it like warm butter. His next surprise was that it had the same effect in his mouth. In all the years he had been eating to sustain himself, he had never imagined anything that mooed when it was alive could taste so succulent.

Though he knew it would draw attention to his ignorance, he couldn't resist the urge to interject into the light conversation, "What exactly does one do to a cow to make it taste this way?"

He first noticed Lacey looking up in astonishment. Tyson and Jess chortled comfortably. Emma answered with perfect ease, "It would all depend on the cut of meat and the way it's prepared. This particular cut was likely simmered half the day to make it so tender."

"Hmmm." Michael made a gratified noise. "Sure beats canned beans, eh?"

"If you think this is good," Alexa said as if they were discussing politics, "wait until you taste dessert. Mrs. Brady made Emma's favorite to celebrate her homecoming."

Emma lifted a mischievous brow toward Michael. "You'll love it."

As the meal progressed, Lacey said very little, and her words were addressed only to her parents. Tyson said nothing. Jess and Alexa kept the conversation light and moving along. Michael avoided meeting the eyes across the table, but once when Lacey caught his glance, she looked at him as if he were the devil himself. Then she turned to Emma with a glare that implied she'd become possessed. Such belligerence seemed out of place in this home, Michael thought. But it was not for him to question it. There was nothing more he could do now but let time prove his dedication to Emma and those she loved.

"I'd like to meet with you, Michael." Jess drew Michael's attention from Lacey's accusing eyes. "When you're finished here, could you come to my office?"

"I'd be happy to," he agreed, "if I knew where it was."

"I'll wait for you so you don't get lost," Jess said. "I need to get you started right away. I'm certain the boys are beginning to test their limits in Ben's absence. We have seventeen at the present time."

"Isn't that a little less than average?" Michael asked, still not accustomed to the idea of being in charge of something he'd once been on the other side of.

"Yes, we generally average between twenty-two and thirty. But the fewer numbers should make it easier for you to get acquainted."

When supper was apparently finished, the chocolate mousse having been thoroughly relished, Michael stated emphatically, "The meal was delicious. Thank you."

"I'll pass your compliment along to Mrs. Brady," Alexa said. "And you girls can come along. Tillie is down with a headache, and I'm certain Mrs. Brady would appreciate some help cleaning the dishes."

Lacey and Emma immediately began gathering dishes, and Michael felt inclined to help. Tyson left without a word. Michael and Emma both noticed Lacey's distress and exchanged a glance of concern.

"We can do that," Emma insisted, taking a stack of plates from Michael. "But thank you anyway."

"Come along, Michael." Jess motioned toward the door.

"I'll meet you in the stables when you're finished," Emma said quietly, and Michael followed Jess out of the room.

"We need to talk," Emma said quietly to Lacey as they followed Alexa to the kitchen. There was so much she needed to explain about the changes in Michael, and she felt certain it would make a difference in Lacey's attitude.

Lacey said nothing. There was a great deal she wanted to say to Emma, but their mother had made it clear that any negative opinions were to be kept quiet. With Alexa present, Lacey couldn't think of anything to say that wouldn't bring on a reprimand from their mother.

When Emma and Lacey were leaning over the deep sinks, sleeves rolled up, cleaning the plates and glasses, Alexa and Mrs. Brady returned to the dining room to finish clearing off the table.

"Don't you have anything to say at all?" Emma asked quietly.

"Like what?" Lacey didn't want to get into it, knowing Alexa would be returning any minute.

"How about congratulations?" Emma intended to prove a point. She was getting married and she was happy, and two of the people she loved most were totally disregarding it.

Lacey couldn't believe it. She stopped to look at her sister with an astonishment that was becoming familiar. "Have you gone mad?" Lacey shouted in a whisper.

"You've already said that once today," Emma stated, turning her attention to the bubbles in the sink. Pushing her hands through them, she was reminded of sitting by the little pool, washing Michael's feet. She smiled to herself. "Perhaps I have gone mad, Lacey." She met her sister's eyes. "But I love him, and I . . ." Alexa returned and Emma added quickly, "We'll talk later."

"I think the roasted lamb would be ideal for tomorrow," Alexa was saying to Mrs. Brady. "And don't forget the mint jelly."

"Couldn't do that." Mrs. Brady set down the table linens and turned toward the girls. "Would you look at that. They've nearly got everything washed except the pots."

"Give us time." Emma smiled, and they continued their chore in silence. When it was finished, Lacey went up to spend some time with Richard. Emma went to the stables, hoping Michael wouldn't be long. She entered to find a small group of the hands gathered, arguing and laughing.

"What are you guys gossiping about?" she teased.

"Hey!" Murphy greeted her jubilantly. "You're still in one piece."

"I'm doing quite well, thank you."

"I heard rumors about you," Jimmy teased.

"I hope they're all true. Only if they're good, of course," she teased back.

"What's this we hear about Michael Hamilton?" Fiddler inquired, getting more specific.

"Did you want the whole story, or just the good parts?" Emma asked.

"All of it!" they said together, and she laughed.

"The man kidnapped me and made me fall in love with him. We're getting married."

"That's it?" Murphy sounded disappointed.

"The rest is a secret." Emma eased her gelding out of its stall, greeting it as a friend she had missed in her absence.

"Sounds like one o' them stupid books you read," Jimmy chortled.

"I suppose it does," Emma replied, as if it had never occurred to her. "So how could I possibly resist?"

"Hey," Fiddler changed the subject, "we could make that bet good right now, boys. Emma's here. I think we have time before dark."

The others agreed heartily.

"What are you betting about this time?" Emma insisted lightly. "And what has it got to do with me?"

Fiddler answered for the group. "We were just betting that Crazy Lad couldn't beat a mule since his leg got healed. Why don't we run that little gelding of yours against him and see?"

Emma leaned close to Fiddler and asked in a loud whisper, "Would Lizzie approve of this?"

Fiddler laughed. "Lizzie would cheer me on."

Emma laughed with him. Fiddler lived in the old house on the estate with his wife, Lizzie. Their three children were grown and on their own now, but Emma had often played with them growing up. And Fiddler and Lizzie were nearly like second parents to her.

Emma turned to see George, their current top jockey, smiling mischievously. He'd obviously been observing the conversation and was in on the bet.

"What do you say, George?" Emma asked.

"I say Crazy Lad's healed up as good as new," George boasted quietly. "I'd wager he could outrun your gelding."

"You're on," Emma said vibrantly. It had been too long since she'd participated in a good race.

Jimmy and Fiddler saddled up the gelding, while Murphy and George did the same for Crazy Lad, a high-spirited descendant of the famous Crazy, the horse that had saved Jess Davies' estate. Of course there was a rule that any betting, except on official races, was to be done purely in fun, with no money involved. The winners of such bets won little more than the privilege of heckling the losers. Emma raced purely for the sport, and she had often helped with training. She simply loved it, as her mother did. It was all just a lot of fun.

The horses were taken to the track to be warmed up and Emma followed, wondering what was taking Michael so long. She had vague memories of his dark form leaning against the rail to watch her race many times in the past. She mounted her gelding and whispered in his ear, "Come on, boy. We'll show them good."

The horses were put into their stalls and made ready. Emma

grinned toward George, who was next to her. "Hold on to those reins, George. My dust is going to choke you."

The boys all laughed, and the horses bolted out. Emma leaned forward and pushed the gelding for all he had, while her heart pumped hot blood to every nerve. Oh, how she had missed this! She would die if she couldn't ride.

Thirteen
OUTSIDE THE CIRCLE

Michael followed Jess down the hall into an elaborate but tasteful office. Jess motioned for him to sit down.

"Now," Jess began, taking a ring of keys from his pocket to select one and open a desk drawer, "I keep the personal files on the boys here. I thought we could quickly go over them to get you acquainted with their situations. Perhaps you would like to study the records more on your own. We keep very accurate records of all we know of their background, and every situation that arises, good or bad."

Jess opened another drawer, pulled out another set of keys, and tossed them to Michael. "That small one is the key to this drawer. Feel free any time." Michael nodded. Jess handed him a sheet of paper. "Here is a list of the boys from youngest to oldest, the youngest being six, the oldest seventeen. It might take some time to place the names with the faces, but you'll get it soon enough."

Jess leaned back in his chair. "I don't think there's much I need to tell you about your responsibilities. The time you put into it depends upon the needs of the boys. They have their study hours, meals, and sports, which are all supervised by others. You are welcome, but not expected, to oversee or participate in any of those things. The boys go out in two different groups daily, except Sundays, to work with the horses. You're in charge there. You know well enough that teaching them to steer their attention to a creature dependent upon them, and in their control, can bring about good things."

Michael nodded. He had always figured that he had been put with a horse because he was expected to earn his keep. And, of course, he was. But it was only long after he'd graduated from the home that he came to see that there had been ulterior motives, and he couldn't deny that it had certainly worked with him. He'd found a genuine affection for horses, and it had been reciprocated from the animals in a way that had given him fulfillment as he'd adjusted to a normal way of life and learned to deal with normal people.

"Sarina will fill you in on the boys' schedules and anything else you might need to know."

"She's still here, then?" Michael smiled, recalling her charming way of being in charge.

"Forever," Jess answered.

"I'm not sure she liked me much. Do you think she'll take kindly to my replacing her son?"

"I think she'll manage," Jess smiled. "Of course, Alexa and I want to be involved as much as possible, where we are needed. We'll often be around in one way or another, but it's you the boys need to look to for authority."

"I'm not well-rehearsed in authority," Michael admitted tensely.

"It's not so difficult. Just remember a few things. The boys need limits. Their behavior might indicate that they don't want them, but limits bring a sense of security. It's more important that they respect you than it is to have them like you. If you keep respect foremost, accompanied by genuine caring, the other will fall into place." Jess lifted a finger. "I don't need to tell you this, but perhaps remind you, that these boys are tough; most of them, anyway. And it will take toughness to match them. You've got it, Michael. And I think you know how to use it in their best interest."

Michael wondered what made him figure that, but he just listened.

"Now, these boys are smart," Jess continued. "They're street-wise, many of them."

"I know the language well."

"Then you know that if you're not sincere, they can see through you, and they'll never trust you. Trust is vital in reaching the truth." Michael thought of Emma and felt the verity in what Jess was saying.

"You're putting a lot of faith in me, Mr. Davies."

"I told you to call me Jess, and I don't put faith where it isn't deserved. Now, let's go quickly over these names, and then we'll go and meet them." He glanced at the clock. "They should be gathering for reading time soon."

Michael tried to concentrate and memorize as Jess went over the papers with him, but his mind was caught in a whirlpool of memories. He recalled the fear he'd felt when Jess Davies had dragged him into a carriage, and he'd had no idea where he was going or what was in store. He had believed that all men were monsters like his father, and being in the custody of one was as bad as another. His adjustment to the boys' home was a mixture of relief at being fed and protected, along with a great deal of fear. Learning to deal with the other boys had always left him defensive and afraid that they would see the scars and find him different. He had been quick to notice that other boys didn't have ghastly scars, and he alone had sat on the sidelines when the boys would swim or strip their shirts to play on a hot day. The tough wall Michael had constructed on the streets become tougher as he'd attempted to keep his secret hidden from the rest of the world. And now Michael felt empathy on behalf of every one of the names before him. He wondered what their pain was, what they were hiding, what they were afraid of. But all he could see was a blur of names that wouldn't stick in his memory.

"Let's go and meet them, shall we?" Jess announced, and Michael took a deep breath.

Tough but kind, he repeated silently in rhythm to his boots on the wood floor of the long hall. *Tough but kind.* Jess took out his keys and turned one in a door that connected the boys' home to the residence. Michael remembered well the other side of that door. He'd spent a great deal of time contemplating what life might be like to pass through it. But he'd never even imagined being here like this now. Jess pointed to the keys in Michael's hand. "It's this one," he indicated. Michael tried to memorize keys while his mind was still on faceless boys.

Michael felt his heart pounding as they came to the door of the library and Jess turned the knob. Eighteen pair of eyes turned toward them. Sarina's were the only kind ones.

"Would you look at that." Sarina came to her feet from where she'd been reading a story to the younger boys. The older ones all held

books on their own. Michael fleetingly remembered being absorbed
with Dickens in this room. He recalled thinking that *Oliver Twist* was
a delightful story. "It appears that Mr. Davies has returned."

"Hello, boys," Jess said warmly. "Miss Sarina, could I speak with
you a moment?"

"Of course. Matthew, would you come and finish reading this
story to the children?" One of the older boys complied, but not without first eyeing Michael skeptically.

"You're a difficult woman to find time with," Jess spoke softly.

"I've been busy, but Alexa told me Ben had stayed. I thought he
might, if he got half a chance."

Michael lost track of the discreet conversation as he concentrated
on surveying the eyes in the room. He didn't know their names, and he
knew almost nothing about them. But he could read their eyes. Some
were cold, some hard. There was only one that was timid, a few were
afraid, one longing, some wary. But all of them were skeptical. Did
they think he was a threat? He couldn't blame them. But he could
prove to them that he wasn't. Michael's apprehension melted into a
warm hope for these boys. They were dependent on him, and he would
not fail them. He blessed Jess Davies for putting such trust in him, and
for giving him the training as a youth to know how to face this.

"You remember Michael." Hearing his name, Michael turned his
attention to Jess and Sarina.

"Of course." Sarina squeezed his outstretched hand. "How are you
these days?"

"Quite well, and you?" he nodded respectfully.

"Fine, thank you. Would you like to meet them now?"

"Now is as good a time as any," he said, taking a deep breath.

"Boys," Sarina said loudly, and all eyes turned toward her. "I have
an announcement. I told you that Ben has stayed in the outback to
spend some time with his family there." Michael sensed the disappointment in the group. He knew Ben was good with these boys, and
it would be a challenge living up to his standards. "But we have a new
friend who will be helping us out from now on." Those skeptical eyes
all deepened in harmony. "This is Mr. Hamilton."

The boys came to their feet, as they knew was expected under such
circumstances. Sarina stepped individually in front of each boy,

announcing his name and age. Michael repeated the name and gave a hearty handshake, in spite of the reluctance he met.

"This is Gene, age nine," Sarina said warmly. "Hans is seven. Michael is six."

That would be easy to remember, Michael thought, smiling down at the small boy who looked like he wanted to kick the newcomer. Michael reminded himself that most of these boys had little reason to trust anyone. Trust had to be earned.

"Alan is eight. Kevin, thirteen, and Kent, twelve. They are inseparable."

Great, Michael thought with sarcasm. The inseparable Kent and Kevin. He'd never get them straight.

"Reynold is thirteen also. Matthew, seventeen, and Joshua is also seventeen. Walter is eleven. Toby just turned ten."

Michael felt something ache when he looked at Toby. He was going to be the difficult one; he could feel it. His eyes reflected something Michael understood, making him wonder what kind of hell this child might have been through.

Sarina continued, "Christian will be fifteen next month. Will is eleven. Kit, ten. Roy, seven. Jack, fourteen. And Bob is also eleven."

"It's a pleasure to meet you." Michael bowed slightly to the group, like a caller in a drawing room.

"Is there anything you'd like to say to the boys?" Sarina asked, and Michael felt put on the spot. He looked over the group with contemplation, and impulsively decided on a method that might at least put them on their toes.

In a split second, Michael transformed into a frozen menace: feet wide apart, body bent forward from the waist, finger pointed in a threatening gesture, teeth bared, narrow eyes moving speculatively over the group of boys, each of whom had jumped a little at his instant metamorphosis.

"Let's get one thing straight," he said cruelly, with a sinister lift of his brow. "If I have any trouble, I will take you one by one, and . . ." He left them in suspense for a long moment while Sarina looked skeptically at Jess, who was obviously amused.

"And . . . ," Michael continued, "I will hang you upside down from the nearest tree, put flowers in your hair, and tickle you within an inch of your lives. Do I make myself clear?"

Michael maintained his sinister expression while a gradual realization seemed to come over the boys that he couldn't be serious. Still, no one dared laugh. Michael turned his back and stepped away a few paces, just long enough to let them relax a little, then he shot back around, instantly retaining his bad-guy pose. They gasped in unison, then became deathly silent.

"Now," he became more serious, though the boys couldn't likely tell the difference, "I bet you guys think you're pretty tough, and because I'm the new kid around here . . . ," he eyed them all one by one through a taut silence, ". . .you might think you can bully me around a little and see who's toughest. Go ahead. I can take it. Because I'm tougher." He smiled like a stuffed cat. "I'll win."

"What makes you so tough?" Toby snapped, and all eyes turned to him as if he were either crazy or stupid.

"You'll only know when you deserve to."

"And when is that?" another boy questioned, apparently realizing that Toby had spoken out and survived.

"When it happens," Michael sneered, "you'll know." No one else posed any questions, so Michael straightened himself and folded his arms. "If you're good to me, I'll be good to you. And if you're not . . ." He drew the last word out with a cruel smile, spreading his lips slowly back over his teeth.

Straightening his expression, Michael looked over the boys, then he casually pointed to Kent. Or was it Kevin? "Nice shirt," he stated as if discussing the weather. "Black is my favorite color. What's yours?"

"I don't have one," came the response.

"That's too bad." Michael remained toneless. "I was hoping it would be black. Black is the absence of color, you know."

"Black is for bad guys," little Michael spoke up, who was wearing a white shirt.

"That's why I like it," Michael replied with a sinister lift of his brow. "Any questions?" he added abruptly, then he only gave them twenty seconds to contemplate before he concluded, "I'll see you tomorrow."

He turned on his heel and left the room without waiting for Jess. Jess had told Michael he was in charge.

Sarina gave Jess a dubious glance as soon as Michael was gone. He just smiled and waved a farewell to the boys before he joined Michael in the hall.

"I didn't realize you were such an actor," Jess said with praise.

"I've been acting all my life," Michael replied, not so proud. "Ask your daughters," he added with an ironic chuckle. "I put on a great act for them."

"I dare say you did." Jess slapped his shoulder lightly, then nodded back toward the library. "I think you're going to do just fine."

"Even if my methods are not conventional?"

"Especially because of that." They moved down the hall. "Now, I would bet that my daughter is waiting for you somewhere. I want you to do your job well, Michael, but don't neglect the woman you love."

"Yes, sir." Michael returned the slap on the shoulder and hurried outside. It didn't take much effort to find Emma. Nostalgia welled inside of him as he leaned over the rail to watch as she settled her mount at the starting line, silhouetted against the setting sun. Michael chuckled as the two horses tore out. The chortling and cheering of the onlookers felt so familiar. He remembered all of these men well, although he had always kept his distance. His eyes shifted to the racing horses, and he felt an uncontrollable tension that had come from spending half his life watching horses race. He couldn't observe it without aching to see which would win, and feeling the drive and suspense of the riders.

"Come on, Emma," he whispered through his teeth, marveling freshly at her grace and talent as she blurred past him and around the track. The horses stayed neck and neck, and he felt the tension rise in proportion to the boisterous cheers of the other men across the track. "Come on," he said again. As they rounded the final corner, Michael saw Emma lean forward just slightly and the gelding responded. She won by a head. "Yes!" Michael gave a subdued cheer.

The hands on the track went wild, some booing, some cheering. By the sound of them, Michael would have thought there were twelve instead of three. Emma slowed her mount and turned back, calling loudly, "You owe me, Murphy." She laughed with all the vibrancy she was capable of, then she turned to George and stuck out her tongue like a child. George laughed and dismounted. "How did the dust taste, George?" she heckled, fully enjoying it.

"Hey, Hamilton!" Murphy called, and Emma immediately looked his direction. Michael ducked beneath the rail to walk across the track. "How did you luck out?" Murphy continued.

"I'm sorry?" Michael put a hand to his ear as if he'd not heard. It was a ridiculous notion to think that anyone couldn't hear Murphy.

"News travels fast around here, boy. You lucky son of a . . . gun," he finished with a chuckle. Their eyes both turned to Emma as she cantered toward them.

"It was my charm and gallantry," Michael said with sarcasm, reaching up to put his hand in Emma's as she came beside him. "Good race," he added to her with pride in his voice.

"Thanks." She winked, then said to Murphy, "He's telling the truth, you know. It *was* his charm and gallantry."

"I didn't stand a chance, is what you're tryin' to tell me." Murphy acted genuinely hurt, but he couldn't keep a straight face for more than a second.

"You were an old man before she was born," Michael chuckled.

"Watch your manners, boy," Murphy chided, still chortling too much to be anything close to serious.

"It's good to have you back, Michael." Fiddler extended a hand and Michael shook it.

"It's good to be back," Michael said firmly.

"You want to race?" Emma lifted her brows toward Michael.

"Not unless the loser takes all."

The men started to cheer, as if they might get another race.

"Aw, shut up!" Michael shouted comically. "I'm not staying around here just to give you guys a good laugh."

"Come along, darling," Emma reached down a hand for him and he mounted behind the saddle, putting an arm around her waist. "So long, guys." She waved back at them as they trotted away. "Thanks for losing!"

"Miserable old chaps," Michael quipped as they could still hear laughter in the distance.

"Most of them have been here longer than my mother. It's a miserable place to be," she finished with light sarcasm.

"So I've seen." Michael put both arms around her to embrace her fully as they galloped toward the hills. "Especially that chocolate mousse. Miserable stuff."

They rode together with peaceable small talk, but they didn't go far since it was so late. They returned after dark, and Michael unsaddled the gelding.

"By the way," he said, "I'm not certain I recall this horse's name. It is the same one you've had for years, isn't it?"

"But of course." Emma stroked the gelding's nose. "Everyone around here claims that his name is so ridiculous, they won't use it." Michael looked up curiously. "I named him exactly what Father said when he was born. You see, he was born with difficulty, and the mare didn't survive. I called him Demented's Daughter's Death."

"That's rather poignant, don't you think?" Michael set the saddle in its resting place.

"Yes, but I didn't want to forget that his mother had sacrificed all for his existence. Father said it was my horse, and I could name him anything I wanted. Everyone else just calls him *the gelding.*"

"As I suppose I did. But," he lifted a finger, "what exactly do you whisper in his ear before you race?" He raised his voice to mimic her. "Come on, Demented's Daughter's Death, take us away!"

"Not exactly." She laughed. "I call him DD."

"How quaint." He tipped his head, then patted the gelding affectionately. "Good night, DD. Don't take the name personally, boy. We love you anyway."

"He knows." Emma laughed softly.

Michael took her hand and walked toward the house. "Yes, I dare say he does."

They walked around the house to enter through the front door, and they were heading up the front stairs when Michael asked with perfect innocence, "Do we come in the front door when we haven't just arrived from the outback looking like heathens?"

"You may enter through the front door any time you like," she insisted with a warm smile. "You are such a silly man, Mr. Hamilton."

"Yes, I believe I am," he agreed, "but you love me anyway."

"Yes, I do. More than I can . . . Tyson!" She let out a startled gasp when she noticed him on the landing.

"Could we talk?" Tyson said to Emma. "Alone?"

"Of course," she said, then turned to Michael.

"I think I can find my way." He gave her a virtuous kiss on the

cheek. "Good night, then," he added and went on up, trying not to
betray his disappointment. He knew this was more important right
now than his desire to spend every possible moment with Emma.

"Outside?" Tyson motioned toward the door, and Emma led the
way. They walked in silence down the porch steps and across the lawn.
Tyson paused, pushed his hands into his pockets, and sighed.

"I didn't imagine our reunion this way," he stated.

"Neither did I."

"I don't know what to say," Tyson admitted.

"You must have something to say," Emma forced her voice to
remain even, "or you wouldn't have brought me out here."

"Isn't there anything I can say to make you change your mind?"

"Change my mind?" She actually laughed. "Tyson!"

"Now, before you get all upset," he put a calming hand on her
arm, "hear me out. If Hamilton has asked forgiveness of us, then I
expect that we should be willing to give it. But Emma, you've got to
look at the facts. Forgive him, yes. But marry him? How can a man
like that be right for you? He's—"

"You don't even know him, Tyson."

"I grew up with him," Tyson retorted, anger rising in his voice.
"He was belligerent and obnoxious. I can't even imagine what he
might do to you if he became angry or drunk. You don't even realize
what kind of life he came from, what kind of blood flows in his veins.
The man is a beast, Emma."

Emma slapped her brother's face without hesitation. Following a
moment of stunned silence, he looked at her in question.

"Now that I have your attention," she glared at him with an expression she had learned from Michael, "I want you to stop and listen to the
hypocrite you've just made of yourself. What was it I heard? Forgive
him, yes, but marry him? What is forgiving, Tyson? Forgiving is forgetting . . . forever. Michael has earned my forgiveness, and I give it to him
freely, because I understand him and his motives. And until you understand the same, you will not stand there and judge him. You have been
asked nothing more than to tolerate the situation. That does not mean
torment; it means *tolerate*. Michael Hamilton has a heart of pure gold,
Tyson. He is the perfect example of rising above one's circumstances to
defy his blood. Perhaps he's right; perhaps his circumstances don't justi-

fy the mistakes he's made, but he's serving his penitence. I have seen his soul turned inside out, Tyson. I have witnessed more pain and humility in that man than you could ever dream of experiencing. There is absolutely nothing in him that I could ever fear. Do you put so little faith in my judgment? I'm the one you always came to for advice, because I had discernment. Have you forgotten me so completely?"

When Tyson said nothing, Emma lowered her voice to a fervent plea. "Tyson, he loves me. Do you realize what he went through for me? His methods were misguided, yes. But his motives were nothing less than pure commitment to me. Can't you see that?"

"Careful that you're not acting on flattery," Tyson said quietly.

"Tyson!" she snarled. She hadn't felt this frustrated since the night she had tried to convince him to stay. "Have you heard anything I've said? Look around you. Would Mother accept him so fully if he was as horrible as you say? Would Father put a man in charge of those boys without having the deepest possible trust in him? No!" she answered her own questions.

"I'm only thinking of your welfare."

"Then accept him as I do," she challenged.

"How can I, when—"

"How can you not?" she interjected, and proceeded with another speech that made Tyson begin to realize he *was* being a hypocrite. Hadn't he begun to figure that out himself earlier today? "You, who grew up with the finest of everything, with love and peace and wealth. And yet you have the audacity to run and leave it, as if you knew everything and no one else could understand. You have inflicted pain on others, Tyson. And I don't see anyone belittling you for it."

"You are," he shot back in his own defense. "And Lacey . . ." His head snapped away quickly, wishing he hadn't let that slip out.

"Is that what this is all about?" Emma asked softly. Only silence answered. "Michael was right, wasn't he. Lacey hasn't forgiven you, so you don't figure anyone else has the right to be forgiven, either."

Tyson chuckled humbly. "You and your psychological analogies." He looked at the ground and pressed the toe of his boot into the grass. "Maybe you're right. I don't suppose I can expect what I'm not willing to give." He straightened his shoulders. "But beyond that, what's between Lacey and me has nothing to do with you."

"Tyson, you and I share the same flesh and bone. It is impossible for anything that happens to either of us not to affect the other."

"That's likely true."

Emma touched his sleeve. "Tyson, I missed you so desperately. Please, don't let this come between us now."

"You're determined to marry him," Tyson tested.

"I love him, Tyson. I believe in him."

"Be careful you don't do it for pity's sake."

"I am doing it for *my* sake, Tyson. I want him in my life."

"Then I can only trust your judgment," he said, looking again at the ground. "I only hope the changes in him are not temporary. I fear he will decide he can't handle it and run."

"I don't." She touched her brother's face. He smiled humbly, and she decided enough had been said. "How was your adventure, Tyson? You haven't told me."

"It was eye-opening," he stated blandly.

"That's it?" She laughed, feeling relieved to change the subject. "You travel the world for four years, and that's all you have to say?"

"I'll tell you about it sometime." He sounded bored at the prospect. "I'm not in the mood right now. Maybe you'd better get some sleep. You've got to be exhausted from your own adventures."

"I'm fine," she replied. He said nothing, and she felt moved to put her arms around him. He responded quickly with a strong embrace, and Emma felt certain everything would be all right. They were too close to have contention between them for long. "I love you, Tyson."

"And I love you," he whispered. "If I'm hard on you, it's only for that reason."

"I understand. I suppose I should be flattered that you care so much."

"Get some sleep, Emma." He touched her chin and turned to walk away, but Emma stopped him.

"Things are not so good between you and Lacey," she said, and the hurt in him was immediately evident.

"I don't know what else to do, Emma. I'm so frustrated I could . . ." He didn't bother to try and finish what he couldn't think of.

"Be patient. She'll come around."

"And in the meantime, walls are being built between us that I fear will never come down."

"She went through much in your absence."

"Yes, so I'm beginning to see."

Emma smiled. "Were you surprised to find what you had left behind?"

Tyson finally showed a glimmer of joy in his expression. "More than a little," he admitted. He looked into Emma's eyes with a once-familiar intensity that only they could share. "Richard is wonderful, Emma. How can I regret his existence?"

"You can't."

"At times I fear that Lacey does."

"Lacey is confused. The hurt is getting in the way of her real feelings. You must be patient."

"Yes, I suppose that's all I can do."

"Come now." She put her arm through his and headed toward the house, but they only ended up sitting on the veranda. "Let's talk. We have four years to catch up on."

Gradually the tightness between them dissipated behind a familiar closeness. Tyson spoke of his journeys. Emma relayed anything significant concerning his absence, which mostly consisted of Richard. She told him all that was good and happy about the child, where Lacey had only repeated the hardships. They held hands, sitting together while the sky filled with stars, and talked of the feelings they had sensed concerning each other during their separation. Emma could feel a bridge being rebuilt between them, and when she mentioned it to Tyson, he echoed her own feelings. They both wondered how they could ever have existed without it.

❦　❦　❦

Michael opted against going to his room. It seemed so early yet. By chance, he found himself in the upstairs hall and looked down through the window to see Emma and Tyson talking in the yard—or, more accurately, arguing. He nearly winced when she slapped her brother. And he ached, knowing they were arguing about him. He didn't have a clue what was being said, but he knew Emma was giving him a good talking to. She could do that, he knew. He'd been on the receiving end more than once. He was relieved to see them embrace.

But not wanting to be caught observing them, he left the window before they parted and wandered to Jess Davies' office, trying five keys before he found the one that opened the desk drawer. He sighed as he realized it was the smallest key, just as Jess had said.

One by one, he opened the files of the boys and tried to place the name with the face. And the eyes. His heart bled as he glanced over harrowing backgrounds. It was Toby's file that caught his keenest interest when he realized that the boy was Rafe Coogan's son.

"Blast!" he muttered under his breath, wondering what complication might have been spurred from his previous stupidity. Realizing there was nothing to be done about it now, he distracted himself by curiously flipping through the older files in the drawer, chuckling to himself as he read names that brought back clear images of boys he'd grown up with. He was actually surprised to come across a file with his own name on it, as if he'd detached himself from literally having been here. He felt an odd sensation as he pulled it from the drawer and opened it, as if he were reading about some distant relative or acquaintance.

Unconsciously Michael bit his thumbnail as he read, hating the way his heart quickened occasionally. And more than once, a sour taste rose in the back of his throat. If he had read all of this concerning anyone else, he would have felt the deepest pity. But all he could feel was sick. The words themselves were not so revealing; they were rather cryptic, in truth. But Michael knew the story between the lines. And it was horrible. But he also read things he hadn't known, things that left him wondering what had been kept from him. Distracting himself to make a quick comparison, he noted that his file was much thicker than most. Had he been so much trouble? Yes, he decided firmly. He had.

Emma pushed open the office door and sighed. She had left Tyson and gone in search of Michael, wanting to tell him that Tyson was softening. But finding his room empty, she had almost been tempted to panic. Perhaps a small part of her did fear his stability. Or rather, she feared the reality of having to live without him, now that she'd discovered what life was like with him. Either way, it was a relief to find him.

Her relief waned, however, when she observed his demeanor. His clasped hands were pressed to his mouth, his knuckles white. His eyes were distant and pained, his shoulders heavy.

"Are you all right?" she asked.

His head shot up, startled. "Yes, fine," he said, but it wasn't sincere.

"What is it, Michael?" She sat on the edge of the desk. He glanced down at the papers in front of him, and Emma's eyes followed.

"What are you looking at that for? It should have been burned years ago."

"On the contrary," Michael stated, "it's a little difficult to swallow, but the reality of these records makes me realize that I wasn't crazy. I didn't imagine it." He turned in the big chair her father usually occupied to stare at the wall. "I didn't realize until now that my father came here, demanding to take me back."

"What happened?" she asked gently, sensing the horror Michael was feeling.

"I don't know. All it says is . . ." He found the correct page. "Right here it reads: 'Jedediah Hamilton was shot and killed in a witnessed struggle of self-defense, following a violent attempt to recover his son, Michael William, for intended purposes I shall leave unwritten. Of all we have ever encountered in our work, this incident leaves me with a strong gratitude that we have the boy in our custody.'"

Emma didn't know what to say when Michael penetrated her eyes with his. He stood and went to the window, stuffing his hands into his pockets and lifting one boot onto the low sill. "Somebody killed my father to keep me from going back to hell."

"It says self-defense. Chances are, whoever killed him might have thought saving his own hide had something to do with it."

"It still kept me out of hell." Michael's voice held a deep sense of gratitude.

"You look tired." She stood beside him, but he didn't respond. Emma returned the file to its proper place in the drawer, then she closed and locked it. Placing the keys in Michael's hand, she urged him to the door, dousing the lamp on her way out. She took the keys back to lock the office door while he wondered how she knew which key went where so easily. She stuffed the keys into his pocket, took his hand, and headed toward the stairs.

"Where are we going?" he asked.

"You've had a long day. I'm putting you to bed."

"Really?" His voice lightened considerably

"Chastely, of course," she said firmly.

"Of course," he agreed with a smile.

Emma hurried up the stairs. Michael took them three at a time to keep up with her. He took her hand and proceeded down the hall on tiptoes. Stopping where the hallways met, Emma looked one direction, then the other. Michael did the same with comical exaggeration before he followed her on down the hall. Quietly he opened the door and pushed Emma into the dark room, pausing to look both ways down the hall before he closed the door.

"I believe we have arrived unnoticed," he whispered, pressing his lips to hers as he backed her against the door.

"Detective Hamilton?" she chuckled.

"Sneaking around like this is rather enjoyable," he said, keeping an arm around her while she fumbled to light the lamp.

"Even if we don't have anything to hide?" she asked.

"Especially because we don't have anything to hide," he repeated, the humor completely absent in his eyes. The day's drama fled as he bent to kiss her again.

Emma pushed her hands into his hair as she became preoccupied with the different feel of his kiss, having all but his mustache shaved away. "I've missed you, Michael," she murmured, wanting only to be close to him, as they had been in the outback.

Michael made a noise of agreement and kissed her again, but it was interrupted by a knock at the door. He sighed and rolled his eyes with disgust.

"Emma, are you there?" Lacey's voice called.

"Yes, just a minute," she called back.

Michael sighed. "It would seem I'll be going now . . . again."

"It's probably safer that way," Emma said, unable to hide her disappointment.

Michael gave her a sideways smile, then his eyes sobered as he said,

"I promised you, Emma, and I meant it." He touched her face and kissed her again quickly. "But I do miss—"

"Emma?" Lacey called again.

Michael sighed more heavily. "I'll never forgive her for this."

"Very funny," Emma retorted. "Tasteless, but funny."

"That's me," he said.

"I'm coming," Emma called. "Just a minute." Then more softly, "I told her we needed to talk. It would seem her timing is poor."

"Quite," he said tersely, then his voice softened with understanding, "but I know it's important."

Emma wondered if Michael would try to hide, or at least feign innocence. She was surprised to see him open the door abruptly, motioning the shocked and disgusted Lacey into the room with an elaborate gesture.

"Never fear," he quipped, "the devil was just leaving."

Emma chuckled, but all humor was lost on Lacey.

"Yes, I know," he added to Emma, "tasteless, but funny."

"I love you." Emma kissed her fingers and waved.

Michael jerked his head slightly as if he'd caught the kiss, then he closed the door with a warm, "Good night, love."

For a long moment, Lacey faced Emma in silence, her expression etched with disbelief, until she finally voiced it. "I still cannot believe it."

Emma wanted to get angry and insist that Lacey be more accepting, but she reminded herself to be positive in return. "Neither can I," Emma said brightly. "It just seems too good to be true."

"Emma, have you—"

"Lacey." Emma took her arm and urged her to the edge of the bed, where they sat close together. "Please, hear me out. We've not had time to talk about this. You need to hear the whole story before you come to such brash conclusions. I know you're upset, and I understand why. But will you please just . . . listen?"

Lacey nodded in response, however reluctantly. She knew she owed Emma at least that much, but she already knew that Emma couldn't possibly be anything but blinded or manipulated—or both.

"After you left, Lacey, I confronted Michael. I insisted that he tell me the truth. I had sensed all along that his motives were not what they appeared to be. Besides, I . . . I must confess, I felt something for him from the start, and—"

"Wait a minute." Lacey held up a hand and squinted her eyes to perceive this. "From *what* start?"

"I suppose I felt something a long time ago, although I wasn't willing to admit to it. I felt terrible when he left here, and I often thought of him. In all honesty, Lacey, my initial reaction when the blindfold was taken off and I saw him was . . . well," she laughed softly, "I was glad to see him."

"I can't believe this!" Lacey stood and began pacing. "Are you trying to tell me that you enjoyed being . . . being . . . kidnapped . . . by that . . . that . . . beast who—"

"Lacey!" Emma interrupted sharply. "Michael is no beast. He is a—"

"I have eyes, Emma, and ears too. Do you think I couldn't—"

"You promised to hear me out," Emma interrupted.

It took great discipline for Lacey to hold up her hands and force herself to silence. She didn't understand how they could have been so close a few weeks ago, and now they were at such odds over something that held Emma's entire future in the balance. "All right," she said quietly, though the anger in her voice was still evident, "I'm listening. But I want to know, if you have liked the man for so long, why didn't you say something? You always told me everything."

"I thought it would sound silly, so I didn't tell anybody. Besides, I knew you didn't like him. You never have."

"That's true. There's something about him that absolutely gives me the creeps."

"What?" Emma asked. She couldn't understand Lacey's complete aversion to Michael, when she found him so attractive, so virile.

"I don't know," Lacey shook her head, "but he certainly proved himself worthy of my opinion through that little jaunt he took us on. Exactly what was he trying to do out there, Emma? I don't understand."

Emma felt hope. At least they were getting to the point. "That's just it, Lacey. What it all boils down to is just that. What was he doing? Why did he do it? That's what I wanted to know. You witnessed a lot of bizarre and apparently cruel things out there, Lacey. But what you didn't bother to notice were the little kindnesses he showed me, the gestures, the glances; things that altogether made me realize he was not what he was pretending to be. Don't you see? He was acting. It was all a big show." Emma lowered her voice. "He loves me, Lacey. The man put everything he had on the line to abduct me and carry me off because he loves me. What woman wouldn't want to be loved to such a degree? I know the changes in him are drastic and difficult to account for. But I saw it happen, Lacey. The changes were drastic because the hurt he was facing inside himself was drastic. I watched that man's soul drop to the depths of hell and come back again." Emma's impassioned speech ended with a soft, "I love him so much, Lacey. You must give him a chance . . . for me."

The clock ticking on the mantle made Emma realize that nothing in Lacey's eyes had changed. She had seen some understanding in Tyson, if only to a degree, and she had hoped for the same with Lacey. But the continuing silence forced Emma to face the truth. She didn't understand why, but Lacey was not going to back down. For some formless reason, she hated Michael Hamilton; always had, always would. And there was nothing Emma or anybody else could say or do to change it. Her assumption was finally validated when Lacey spoke tersely, "I cannot, Emma."

"And it's as simple as that." Emma wanted to cry.

"I suppose it is."

"I'm going to marry him, Lacey."

"Yes, I know," she said bitterly, "at my wedding."

"If you would prefer—"

"Oh, no. What right have I got to defy Mother's wishes? I'm not even a *real* member of this family."

"That's not true, and you know it. There hasn't been a day when you weren't loved as much as the rest of us."

"Yes, I know," she admitted, "but I always felt different."

"I'm sorry about that, but if you weren't a member of the family before, you certainly are now. You're the mother of Tyson's son, and Tyson loves you. We all love you."

"Yes," she gave a bitter chuckle, "Tyson's idea of love is to marry me because, as he so quaintly put it, 'I don't want any other man in your bed besides me.'"

"If he said that, he was implying that he loves you."

"And I believe he does," she admitted with a degree of sincerity, "but he can't just come back and say I'm sorry and expect everything to be perfect."

"From what he's told me, he's done much more than just tell you he's sorry. Perhaps you're being too hard on him."

"We were not supposed to be talking about Tyson and me."

"And why not?" Emma stuck to a point she considered important. "It's apparent everything is not right between the two of you, and I have always been a big part of both your lives. Perhaps talking about it is exactly what you need. Maybe if we talked it through a little, it would help."

Lacey sighed and sat down, emotionally exhausted. "Perhaps you're right. It's as if the world has turned upside down these past weeks. We do need to talk, Emma. But not tonight."

"I think we're all tired. It's been a trying day."

Lacey met Emma's eyes and nodded in agreement. Impulsively Emma opened her arms, and Lacey hesitated only a moment before she rose and embraced her. Their eyes teared up in unison. "I am glad you're home safely," Lacey said gently. "I only hope the rest will work out."

"So do I," Emma agreed, though she didn't agree on what she knew Lacey's idea of *work out* was. Perhaps Michael Hamilton was simply something they would never agree on.

"I'll go and let you get some sleep." Lacey pulled back and wiped at her eyes. "We'll talk tomorrow."

Emma attempted a smile, nodded with an underlying sense of despair, and watched Lacey leave the room. The closeness they had once shared had disappeared forever when Emma had allowed Lacey to sleep in the wrong bedroom on the most fateful night of Emma's life.

Despite the late hour, Emma went quietly to Michael's room. She went in without knocking to find it dark, and moved quietly to the bed where she found him sleeping soundly. Feeling her way, she pressed a kiss to his cheek. He shifted and settled deeper into slumber. Emma lightly brushed the hair off his brow and knew that it would all be worth it.

"I love you, Michael Hamilton," she whispered, then went to her room in search of the same exhausted slumber. She didn't have to search long.

❦ ❦ ❦

Michael had just pulled on his breeches and was about to put a clean shirt over his head when a knock came at the door.

"Come in," he called, certain it would be Emma. With his back to the door, he didn't turn around until he had tucked his shirt in. Seeing Tyson made him freeze.

"I'm sorry," he said without thinking. "I thought you were Emma." He realized once it was out that the implication he'd given wasn't good, but he didn't see any point in stammering some kind of explanation.

Tyson briefly thought that if Michael was allowing Emma into the room while he was dressing, then they had likely been intimate. But his mind was more absorbed with the shock of what he'd just unwittingly witnessed. In the brief second before Michael's shirt had fallen over his back, a mass of raised welts had stood out blatantly. Tyson had read of such things described in books concerning mistreated slaves, prisoners in backward countries, or pirates at sea. But never would he have imagined to find such a thing on Michael Hamilton. He recalled his mother saying that Michael had been tortured as a child, but the reality must have completely evaded him.

"Did you need something?" Michael asked, and Tyson realized he was gaping.

The speech Tyson had prepared suddenly became all muddled in his head. All he could think of now was how right Emma had been. Tyson had been raised with everything a boy could want. He had no right to judge someone who had been through such things in his life.

Michael's impatient stance brought Tyson to a degree of his senses. He'd intended to threaten Michael with a gallant speech about taking good care of Emma or he'd hunt him down, and other such things. He quickly reformed it to a simple, "I just wanted to tell you that I'm putting a great deal of faith in you to take good care of Emma and make her happy. She is very dear to me."

"And to me," Michael said with strength.

"I suppose," Tyson continued, "we all make mistakes of one sort or another."

"Some of us are better at it than others," Michael conceded.

Tyson looked at the floor and chuckled. He felt much better, but he knew there was one point he had to clear, even at the risk of putting tension back where it had just been released. "I understand my father gave you the money anyway."

Michael drew up his chin, contemplating a moment what Tyson might be testing. He couldn't figure for certain, so he made up his mind to simply be honest, which he was coming to realize was the only way to be if he wanted peace with himself, if not with those around him. "I wasn't real happy about taking it. He was quite insistent. I think he gave it to me more for Emma's sake than for mine, and it is Emma who will benefit from it."

Tyson couldn't think of anything to say. There simply was nothing in Michael's attitude, however firm, that encouraged any defensiveness.

Michael was unnerved by the lack of response, and decided his true theory on the money was worth adding. "If you think you need it more than I do, I will give it to you in a minute, Tyson. And I wouldn't bat an eye over it, if it would return peace to this household. I know how to work, and I can support Emma one way or another if I have to." He put his hands behind his back. "It's only money. I've lived without it enough to know that I can still survive."

Tyson couldn't quite pinpoint the basis of the respect Michael had just earned from him, but sure enough, Tyson felt it. Was it that same intangible instinct that had driven his father to give Michael so much? Beginning to feel like a silent fixture of the room, Tyson gave an embarrassed chuckle. He couldn't think of anything else to say that wouldn't sound gushy, so he just held out his hand.

Michael looked pointedly to the outstretched hand and all it represented, then he looked into Tyson's eyes, making certain the representation was sincere. He would far prefer to be blatantly ostracized than to be patronized with hypocritical offerings of kindness. But the sincerity was there. In that moment, his eyes looked just like Emma's. It was easy to reach out and shake his hand firmly.

"I'll do everything in my power to make her happy," Michael said. Tyson nodded and left the room. Michael sat on the edge of the bed to pull on his boots, but he had to stop a moment in an attempt to fully interpret the encounter. Then he smiled. Considering he'd been here less than twenty-four hours, he had to admit that things were looking pretty good. He was getting married in three weeks to the most vivacious, beautiful woman in the world. He had seventeen boys to be responsible for, and he was going to be paid well for doing it. Jess and Alexa Davies had accepted him more fully than he could have ever hoped. And Emma? Emma was simply wonderful. And to boot, he had a hundred thousand pounds. He could still feel a little guilty about that, but Jess had made it repeatedly clear he wouldn't take it back. He looked down at his clothes and wondered if he ought to buy something new. White perhaps, or maybe something in between. He did like black, though. Maybe just something new and black.

Michael finally got his boots on and headed to Emma's room, wondering when breakfast was supposed to happen. He'd eat anything except beans and peaches.

He knocked lightly but followed Emma's example of yesterday and opened the door without waiting for an answer. He grinned like a greedy cat to see her still sleeping. For a moment he just watched her, tiptoeing closer to the bed, marveling at her beauty. Carefully he nudged her shoulder to wake her. He was just thinking about kissing her when a knock came at the door and he muttered under his breath, "Every time I kiss you, someone starts making a racket."

Emma giggled softly and called, "Who is it?"

"It's Tillie, Miss Emma. Your mother was wondering why you weren't to breakfast. Do you need anything, Miss?"

"No, I'll manage, thank you. Tell Mother I slept late. I'll be right down."

"Yes, Miss."

"I think you'd better go to breakfast now, Michael Hamilton, or it could appear rather suspicious."

"I suppose you're right," he agreed reluctantly and slid off the bed.

"I'll see you soon." She looked up at him and stretched.

"Not soon enough." He sighed and went downstairs alone.

Michael paused outside the dining room door and drew a deep breath, recalling the one aspect of this situation that was not so enjoyable. Life was good for him, and he was determined not to let one woman's intolerance of him ruin it.

"Good morning," he said as he entered, smiling nonchalantly. He quickly surmised by the plates and covered serving dishes on the sideboard that this was a help-yourself meal.

"Did you sleep well, Michael?" Alexa asked.

"I don't think I've ever slept in so fine a bed," he commented, wishing he had more room on his plate. Then he reminded himself that he wasn't starving. There would always be plenty. It just looked so good after all those beans.

"I apologize for being late." He slid into his chair and looked around the table as if he'd just noticed that Emma wasn't here.

"It seems she overslept," Alexa said, as if she'd read his mind.

"All that adventure must have worn her out," Jess said with a wry wink toward Michael, who smiled and proceeded to eat. When he finally found the will to look across the table, Lacey was tactfully ignoring him, toying with her food. Tyson exchanged a civil smile that didn't go unnoticed by his parents.

"Are you ready for your first day on the job?" Jess asked, apparently finished with his breakfast, but leaning back in his chair for a little conversation.

"As ready as I can be, I suppose. I looked over the files last night, but it's difficult to keep them all straight."

"Did you find anything interesting?" Alexa asked.

Michael wondered if he should mention his association with Rafe Coogan and the threats he had heard from him, but his eyes turned to Lacey and he decided against it. Perhaps another time. "Tragic would be more appropriate," he replied, recalling the sensation his studying had left him with.

"It truly is." Alexa's voice filled with compassion. "But that's why we're here—to hopefully dispel some of the tragedy."

"Yes," Michael's tone deepened, "I shudder to think where I would be now if . . ." He found he wasn't able to finish the sentence. He'd believed all of the pain had left him the night Emma had forced him to confront it, but he was coming to find moments when it haunted him. He thought of his personal file in that drawer and wanted to ask Jess what had happened. If Tyson and Lacey hadn't been here, he would have. Later, he told himself.

"Perhaps you could tell me, Michael," Jess slid his chair back and folded his arms, "what your perception of the home was when you were brought here."

Michael looked severely at Jess, then cleared his throat tensely. "That would depend on whether or not you want me to be honest."

"The answer would be of little benefit if you were anything but honest."

"Good point." Michael tried to smile. "Well, I hated it." Everyone looked surprised but Alexa. "You said you wanted the truth."

"But why?" Tyson asked. Unable to comprehend the horrible life Michael must have lived before coming here, he couldn't understand such a statement.

"It was different," Alexa answered for him when he hesitated.

"*I* was different," Michael corrected. "Of course, I look back now and I am deeply grateful, but at the time I felt like a foreigner in a strange land. I didn't feel worthy of clean sheets and balanced meals. Education was something I'd never gotten close to, and I was always afraid the others would discover how . . . different I was." He stopped to take a bite of his eggs. "Couldn't we talk about something else?"

"I'm sorry." Jess leaned forward. "I didn't intend to put you on the spot."

"Don't be. It's just that . . ." His voice trailed off.

"I understand," Jess said, and meant it. "Sarina will have the first group ready to go out to the stables at ten. The boys each have a horse they've been assigned to, with their names—"

"On a leather tag by the appropriate stall," Michael finished. "And if they care well for it, they can take it with them when they leave." He took another bite, chewed, and swallowed. "I still have mine."

A lull in the conversation made it possible for Michael to finish his breakfast before it turned cold. He wondered what was taking Emma so long. Tyson got up and left with a polite acknowledgment to his parents and Michael, but not a word spoken to Lacey. Michael felt for him. He could take a lot, but he wouldn't have been able to tolerate such strain between him and Emma. Lacey left moments later, looking her normal melancholy self.

Michael had really hoped to see Emma before he began his work, but with his meal finished, staying could only be awkward. "Thank you for breakfast." Michael came to his feet and walked toward the door.

Alexa reached out a hand from where she sat and took hold of Michael's arm to stop him. Looking up into his eyes, she said in her quiet way, "You're doing beautifully, Michael. I know what you're fighting is tough, and I admire you for it."

"It's not so bad." He chuckled, setting an appreciative hand on her shoulder. "I'm feeling rather spoiled, actually. Emma makes it easy." His voice lowered. "I would fight the world for Emma."

"Yes, I know. That's why I told her she had a good man, and I meant it."

Impulsively Michael bent and pressed a kiss to her cheek. "You're one in a million, Mrs. Davies." He raised his voice to make certain Jess could hear as he added, "The only reason I'm marrying Emma is because she's so much like you, and you're already taken."

"You'd better believe it," Jess said.

Alexa blushed prettily. "You flatter me, Michael. And you must stop calling me Mrs. Davies. I'm not your school counselor any more." She pointed at her husband in mock defiance. "You call him Jess."

"He's just one of the guys." Michael grinned at his father-in-law to be.

"And me?"

"You deserve more respect." He turned to add, "No offense intended . . . Jess."

Jess smiled wryly.

"How about *Mother?*" Alexa squeezed his arm.

Michael bowed slightly from the waist. "It would be an honor." He felt warmed. She was the only mother he'd ever known. In his view, the woman who had given him life had earned no other right to bear such a title.

"We'll see you at lunch," Alexa smiled.

"Actually," he drawled in preamble to an apology, "I must decline. I believe I'll eat with the boys today. You understand."

"Yes, I certainly do."

"We'll see you at supper, then . . . Mother." He turned back to Jess, adding with a comical lift of his brow, "And Father."

"Get out of here," Jess laughed.

Michael went straight into the boys' home to find them all absorbed in lessons. He quietly observed while he contemplated his plans with them. He was mostly ignored until ten o'clock came.

Eight of the boys were put reluctantly into his care, but he found that guiding them through their already trained rituals with the horses was easy and rather enjoyable. They all remained aloof but civil.

The boys began to relax and act more like boys during the noon meal. Michael said little, but he kept his eyes acutely tuned to observing each boy as an individual, trying to figure out what made them tick.

In the afternoon, he took the second group to the stables. From a distance on the way in, he could see Emma riding the track. The sight of her stirred him. He missed being with her every moment, but the fulfillment in what he was doing seemed a fair compensation.

The afternoon was as uneventful as the morning. Once the boys were escorted back into Sarina's care, Michael returned to the track and leaned against the rail to watch Emma work with the trainer, exercising a fine example of racing equine. Memories flooded over him, along with an added sense of peace. Recalling how he'd once felt to watch Emma at her play, Michael realized that even then, he'd never believed deep inside that being in her life would ever be within his reach. Her rejection had only been a confirmation of what he'd always believed, and perhaps abducting her had been just another attempt to prove the same thing. But it was Emma who had done the proving. His devotion to her left him freshly stunned each time he stopped to ponder it. Did all men love so completely? Recalling brash conversations in pubs and other places far worse, Michael felt certain his feelings were unique to a degree. He wondered if pain suffered and dealt with made a man more receptive to a good woman. He thought of Jess and Alexa, and the details of their own story that had recently come to light. The love and devotion was continually evident between them, but their lives had not been easy. And even when wealth and security had come, they had still chosen to complicate their lives by attempting to give happiness to the miserable of the earth. Like him.

"Thank you, God," he murmured aloud before he consciously realized what he was saying.

Emma caught sight of him, kissed her hand, and waved. Michael visibly caught the kiss, returned the gesture, then bent to move beneath the rail. She left the horse in the trainer's hands and walked across the soft earth of the track to meet him.

"How did it go?" she asked.

"Well enough." He took her hand. "But I can't remember half their names."

"It will come." She reached up to kiss his cheek, and he could only think how he longed to be married to her.

"In the meantime," he added, attempting to distract himself, "I just call them *hey you*. And they listen."

"I would bet they do."

They moved off the track when the trainer brought the horse around for another run.

"More importantly," Emma ducked beneath the rail and he followed, "are you enjoying it?"

"It's strange, you know," he put his arm around her shoulders, "I never would have imagined myself in such a position, but already I'm comfortable there. I have a real desire to know each of them, and if possible, help them." He chuckled. "Does that sound like the dreadful man who kidnapped you?"

"Actually, yes."

Emma put her arm around his waist as they walked toward the house, and she realized that Michael was veering more toward the stables. "Where are we going?" she asked, sensing mischief in his attitude.

With no warning, Michael lifted her into his arms, carrying her toward the stable, ignoring the stares they received from the hired hands scattered around the yard doing their various jobs. He chuckled to find the building empty except for the horses. But then, he had figured it likely would be, since this was the family stable, which got little traffic as opposed to the racing stable, the work stable, or the stable that housed the boys' horses. Though Michael had helped where he was needed in the years he'd been employed here, he'd spent most of his time here, and he knew well that it could be a lonely place to work—which had suited him just fine, then and now.

"What are you doing?" Emma demanded with a giggle.

"I am going to find a clean, empty stall, throw you into the straw, and hold you my personal hostage where no one will find us."

He set her down in the straw, then looked both ways to assure himself of their privacy before he knelt beside her, kissing her long and hard. Reminding himself to remember his boundaries, he relaxed, kissing her occasionally, tickling her more frequently. Emma's giggling was interrupted when they heard Tyson call, "Is that you, Emma?"

Michael pressed his face to her shoulder with an exasperated whisper. "I don't believe this!"

Emma giggled again and called, "I'm here." Michael leaned back and put a piece of straw in his mouth, as if he'd been lounging there for hours.

Tyson peered over the top of the stall, but instead of the disgust or disapproval Emma had expected to see, he was amused.

"What are you doing?" Tyson leaned his elbows on the door and grinned.

"Did you want the truth?" Michael asked nonchalantly. "Or should I paint you an illustrious picture of fiction?"

Tyson was obviously intrigued. "If you put it that way, I think I'd like to hear both."

"All right," Michael continued nibbling on the straw. Emma watched him with amused interest, wondering if it was her imagination that there was no tension between the two men. "I followed Emma into the stable, you see, right after she had finished on the track, and we were just standing about chatting, when I heard this horrid, thunderous noise and the ground began to rumble." Emma couldn't hold back a snicker, but Michael glared at her so she forced a straight face for his benefit. Tyson's eyes went wide with wonder as Michael continued. "I turned around just in time to see this tremendous herd of cattle come from nowhere, and they were stampeding right toward my dear, sweet Emma. I knew how awful you would feel if you lost your sister, so I thought quickly and pushed her out of the way just in time. We landed here in the straw, and have just been discussing how fortunate we are to have survived such a dreadful turn of events."

"I see." Tyson gave a patronizing nod. Emma elbowed Michael none too softly in the ribs, which brought out a baffled expression that made her giggle again.

"Now let me hear the illustrious picture of fiction," Tyson said, and Michael grinned. He was beginning to like this guy.

"I was attempting to neck with your sister."

Emma gasped with no amusement. She glared at Michael in astonishment, but he just grinned proudly.

"Michael!" she said, then attempted to give him a good talking to, but Michael put his hand over her mouth.

"It's all right, my sweet. He's your brother, remember? You can't keep secrets from your brother."

"It's not such a big surprise," Tyson said. "Although I did like the story about the cows."

"Thank you," Michael stated, then Emma noticed Tyson's expression falter. She could almost guess his thoughts, but she asked anyway.

"You're thinking of Lacey."

Tyson looked briefly startled. "Always," he said sadly. "But we haven't exchanged a word since yesterday, when . . . oh, never mind."

"When you slammed the sitting room door?" Emma guessed.

A subtle embarrassment filled Tyson's eyes. "Yeah. Since then."

"She loves you, Tyson. She would be indifferent if she didn't. And she's far from that."

"I suppose that's somewhat comforting," Tyson said, then he took a long look at Michael and Emma. An unfamiliar tension filled him as he realized he was on the outside of something he could never share with Emma, and at the moment, there was no compensation to be found elsewhere. He suddenly missed Lacey dreadfully. He missed the laughter, holding hands, stealing kisses, and intimate conversation. Suddenly wanting to be alone, he turned away, saying, "I'll leave the two of you to discuss your narrow escape from stampeding cattle."

"Wait," Emma called. "You were looking for me. Why?"

"It's all right. You're busy, and—"

"Aw, take her," Michael said as he began pulling straw from Emma's hair.

"What did you need, Tyson?" Emma persisted.

"I was just going to see if you wanted to ride, but you're obviously busy, and—"

Emma caught a discreet nod of encouragement from Michael and interrupted Tyson firmly. "I'd love to. Besides, Michael was just going to—"

"Check on the boys," he provided easily, much to Emma's relief. "I was feeling a real need to check on the boys."

"You saddle the horses and I'll be there in a minute," Emma said. Tyson nodded and moved to the other end of the stable.

Emma began pulling straw from Michael's hair. "Did I miss something?" she asked. "It seems that you and Tyson are doing a little better than when he hit you yesterday afternoon."

"He came to my room this morning," Michael said. "We had a little chat. That's all."

"Must have been a good one."

"Yeah," Michael smiled and kissed her, "it was. He's a part of you, Emma. I can't help but like him."

"Good," she smiled.

"You don't want contention between us, of course."

"Not only that, I wouldn't want him to never have the opportunity to really know you."

"Which is something Lacey would rather have never done." He couldn't help sounding terse.

"We can't do anything about that."

"No, but it still makes me wish I had . . ." He stopped himself, knowing such hopes were futile. He couldn't take back the past. "I was hoping the two of you would have made some progress last night after I left."

"I tried, but . . ."

"What did she say?" Michael asked.

"I'd rather not discuss it."

"Discuss it anyway."

"She's convinced that you are a horrible man, and she will not be persuaded otherwise."

"I can't blame her."

"But then," Emma added, coming to her feet, "I think her problems with Tyson are blowing it out of proportion in her mind. I fear for their happiness."

Michael looked down the stable to where Tyson was saddling the gelding. "I think you can make up for a little of it." He patted her back to move her along. "Spend some time with him. He needs it."

"Thank you, Michael." She kissed his cheek in appreciation of his understanding.

"For what? I'm not sharing you with Tyson, Emma. He was here first. It's the other way around. I think he'll feel better about me if he knows I'm not going to hoard you all to myself."

"You know, Michael," she touched his nose, "I think you have a lot more discernment than you realize."

"If I do," he chuckled, "I learned it from you."

"Why don't you come to my room tonight?" she whispered coyly. "About eleven. Everyone will be asleep, and we can talk without any interruptions."

"I just might do that." He smiled gently, longing to just be with her and absorb the sustenance she gave him.

Emma kissed him quickly and walked toward Tyson, who helped her mount the gelding. Michael watched her, recalling his long-time fascination with her.

"Did you want to talk?" Emma asked Tyson as they set out side by side.

"No." He smiled. "I just want to be with you . . . like old times."

"Sounds good to me."

"Emma," he reached out a hand and she took it, "I apologize for my prejudice. Michael may not be conventional husband material, but I can see now what you see in him . . . at least to some degree. I wish you every happiness."

Emma took her hand from his to wipe away the tears. "I wish you the same, Tyson."

Tyson smiled sadly and heeled his mare to a gallop, calling over his shoulder, "I'll race you to the border."

"Eat my dust!" Emma called and galloped past him.

Fourteen
THE RIFT

Michael found himself on the veranda, leaning back in a comfortable chair, his boots crossed and planted on the railing. With his hat down over his eyes and his arms folded across his chest, he contemplated taking a little nap. Then a completely unfamiliar voice startled him, saying firmly, "Howdy."

Michael pushed his hat back to find a small boy only inches away, staring at him with innocent curiosity.

"Who are you?" the boy asked.

"I'm Michael. Who are you?"

"I'm Richard Byrnehouse-Davies." He proudly stated his recently learned surname.

Michael lifted his brows. Of course, he thought. The mention of Lacey's illegitimate child had never quite struck reality. But now he was face to face with it. Michael smiled at the boy, who looked a great deal like Tyson.

"Are you a cowboy?" Richard asked as if he was wondering why the sky was blue.

Michael chortled. "What makes you think I'm a cowboy?"

"The way you were sleepin' under that hat. Grandpapa's told me stories about American cowboys. He's read about 'em in books."

"I hate to disappoint you, boy, but I've never gotten terribly close to a cow. Maybe I'm a horseboy."

"Oh," his eyes brightened, "I'm one of those. Papa takes me riding every day, and we play horses in the nursery."

"The nursery?" Michael tried to imagine horses in a room labeled *the nursery*.

"Do you want to see 'em?" Richard offered as if Michael were another three-and-a-half-year-old boy.

"I think I'd like that."

"Come on, then. We haven't got all day."

"Why is that?" Michael questioned, following Richard into the house and up the stairs.

"It'll be story time soon, and then supper."

"And where do you eat supper?" he asked, wondering why he hadn't seen this child before.

"In the nursery, of course."

"Of course."

"How come you don't know anything?" Richard asked.

"How come you think you're so smart?" Michael retorted.

"Cause Papa says so."

"Then it must be true," Michael agreed.

"Hey, who are you, anyway?"

"I told you. I'm Michael."

"Do you live here?"

"I do now. I am going to marry Emma. Do you know Emma?"

"Of course. She's my aunt. She likes to build castles with me."

"Does she? How quaint."

"What does marry mean?"

"It means we get to share a room instead of having different ones."

"Like Grandmama and Grandpapa?"

"Exactly."

"Why are you going to marry Emma?"

"Because she likes to build castles."

"Do you like to build castles?"

"You ask too many questions, Richard."

"Well, do you?"

"I never have. I like horses. And Emma."

"If you marry Emma, will you be my Aunt Michael?"

Michael laughed. "Not exactly. How about Uncle Michael?"

Richard looked up and wrinkled his nose as if that made no sense at all.

"You'll figure it out one of these days," Michael finished, then followed the boy down the same hall that Emma and Lacey's rooms were in. The nursery was directly across the hall from Lacey's bedroom. Richard opened the door, and Michael had to pause and absorb the fact that such a place existed. He didn't believe he had even known what a toy was when he was Richard's age. But here there was a wooden rocking horse, and blocks of all sizes—for building castles, he assumed. There were toy bows and arrows and guns and shelves of books, balls, and stuffed animals. And spread over the floor were horses—dozens of horses.

"Which horses do you want to play with?" Richard asked, and Michael looked up to see a woman in her fifties enter through a side door.

"That's just Nanny," Richard announced and returned his attention to the horses.

"Miss Leeds," she corrected. "And you are . . . no, wait. Don't tell me. You must be Miss Emma's betrothed."

"I'm the lucky guy," he said proudly. "Richard and I have just recently become acquainted. He invited me to play horses with him."

"What a splendid idea," Miss Leeds said more to Richard, then to Michael, "I will be just in here if you need me."

Michael nodded and was distracted by an emphatic question, "I said, which horses do you want to play with?"

"I like the black ones."

"You can have the black ones, and I'll use the brown ones. You can use Papa's stables since he's not here." Richard plopped belly-down on the floor, and Michael figured he had to do the same. Michael examined these "stables" built from blocks, noting the individual stalls for the horses. He followed Richard's example and put all of the black horses into place "to eat and take a nap," as Richard explained to him. When that was done, Richard announced, "When you have your horses all trained, you can pick the best one and then we can race."

"And how do we know who wins?" Michael asked lightly, realizing at the age of twenty-eight that playing could be fun.

"We take turns."

"I see. And what does the winner get for winning?"

"When me and Papa race, he gets to take me for a ride on a real horse if he wins."

"And if you win?"

"I get to go for a ride on a real horse."

"I see," Michael chuckled. "Well, we'd best get training."

For the better part of an hour, Michael found himself enthralled on the nursery floor. Miss Leeds looked in occasionally and smiled to observe them. They were about to discuss the payment of debts when Michael heard the door open behind him, immediately followed by an angry gasp.

"Hello, Lacey," he said without turning. But he was more concerned for Richard than for himself as he turned and sat up to find her eyes full of fire.

"How dare you!" she said in a whisper, as if Richard couldn't hear her. A quick glance assured Michael that the boy was distraught and confused.

"Richard and I were simply playing horses," he responded with calm innocence, "and having a delightful time, I might add."

Miss Leeds appeared, obviously sensing trouble. "Everything is perfectly fine, Miss Lacey," she stated, apparently baffled. "I've been close by."

"I do not want my child alone with this man," Lacey said angrily to the nanny, and Michael felt his defenses rise on her behalf.

"As I said," Miss Leeds stated calmly, "I was very close."

"Not close enough," Lacey hissed. Miss Leeds, on the verge of tears, ushered Richard from the room and closed the door.

Michael came to his feet with no attempt to disguise what he was feeling. "I don't believe that was necessary. If you must be angry, take it out on me, not innocent children and nannies."

"I said nothing in anger to my son."

"You didn't have to."

"And Miss Leeds should know better than to leave Richard alone with a . . . a . . ."

"Go ahead and say it, Lacey. I can take it. Get it out of your system."

"All right, I will," she spat. "You are nothing less than a monster, Mr. Hamilton. The thought of your even being close to my sister puts my stomach in knots, but I have little to say in that. I will not, however, tolerate your being close to my son."

"I would not harm the child any more than I would hurt Emma."

Michael regretted his choice of analogy when her eyes blazed with added fuel. "Oh? I have seen how you treat Emma. I've seen what you're capable of. How dare you have the gall to even set foot in this house after what you have done? You might have the rest of them fooled, but you will never fool me. I know what kind of man you are. Now get out of here, and don't you ever set foot into a room with my son unless another member of the family is with you. Do I make myself clear?"

"Quite clear, Miss Davies." Michael was proud of his steady tone. He hadn't felt this angry inside since . . . ironically, since he had beat Rafe Coogan to a pulp for hurting Lacey.

Lacey felt so utterly infuriated that she wanted to scream. This entire thing had gone too far. The man was capable of murder, and he had the nerve not only to be living under their roof and eating from their table, but now he was playing in the nursery with her son. Yet here he stood, silently defying her with those cruel eyes that in themselves brought such an intense fear to Lacey that she couldn't begin to comprehend it. It was as if he represented everything in her life that she had ever feared or mistrusted, and nothing could ever bring her to accept, or even tolerate, the way her family had taken him in with open arms. The thought sickened her, and it was all intensified by the silent challenge in his eyes as he stood before her now, taking her lashing words with no response or apparent feeling whatsoever. She wasn't certain he had the capability to feel anything at all.

Through the silent moment that Lacey attempted to stare him down, Michael felt a gut instinct rise in him to fight. If she hadn't been a woman, he might well have hit her. He reminded himself that physical aggression accomplished little, if anything. Plainly seeing the blatant hatred in Lacey's eyes, he decided he would prefer physical injury to her hurtful words. With purpose Michael narrowed his eyes and pushed his face forward. "Go ahead and hit me, Lacey. It'll make you feel better."

She didn't hesitate a moment. It was just the opportunity Lacey had been itching for since the moment he'd had her dragged from her bed in the middle of the night. But she felt even more infuriated when he hardly flinched. She slapped him again. His cheek turned red, but his eyes never left hers, his expression didn't change. He *didn't* know how to feel.

"You fiend," she hissed, not feeling the slightest bit better.

Using great self-restraint, Michael walked past her and calmly went to his own room, where he closed the door and leaned against it. He groaned through clenched teeth and slammed his fists into the hard wood behind him, making them throb. When that did little to help, he kicked over a chair, then willed himself to calm down. He felt certain that destroying furniture would not help his reputation any. His blasted reputation! So painstakingly and unwittingly earned. He had won the woman he loved in spite of it, but he would never be free of the repercussions as long as bitterness and resentment kept slapping him in the face. Literally. He could still feel the sting.

When the calm following the storm finally took hold, Michael had to ask himself what he was doing here. And the answer was easy. Emma. He would do anything, face anything, fight anything, for Emma.

In a desperate need to feel a reminder of the closeness they shared, Michael went to her room. He wasn't surprised, but disappointed, to find it unoccupied. He became distracted by his surroundings when he realized that he'd been in here very little, and he'd always been absorbed with Emma when he had. But now, in her absence, he took the time to study this room that was so much her. Riding boots at the foot of the bed. Novels scattered haphazardly over the bedside tables. A flat-brimmed hat hanging casually over the bedpost. He picked it up and realized it was the one he had bought her; Lacey had worn it during most of their excursion. On the bureau were scattered an odd array of lavender toiletries, a riding crop, the pearl earrings she had worn, and a framed photograph of her and Lacey in jockey silks, obviously taken at the Melbourne track. He guessed they were about fifteen. Their closeness was evident, and it made the sting return to his face.

"Emma," he whispered aloud, not begrudging her time with Tyson, but needing her presence to temper his concerns. In search of a distraction, he sat on the bed and leaned against the headboard, one leg stretched out in front of him, the other foot on the floor. Idly he picked up the closest novel, the one she was obviously reading as evidenced by the folded paper stuck between pages to mark a place. Michael removed the marker and decided to see where she had left off, but the paper in his hand had a vague familiarity. He unfolded it curiously and read: *My dear Mr. Davies, Your daughters are very beautiful. It would be a shame if something happened to them, but beauty has a price . . .*

Michael refolded it tersely and stuffed it into his shirt pocket, forcing himself to read the book for the sake of his sanity.

❧ ❧ ❧

Tyson and Emma returned to the house, full of laughter. Emma felt a deep peace from the closeness they were rebuilding. This moment brought back all the years of kinship between them, and she was compelled to stop him before they parted. "Tyson, it's good to have you back. And I thank you for your acceptance of Michael. You can't know what it means to me."

"It's like you said," he shrugged it off, "I'd be a hypocrite if I didn't."

"Thank you anyway." She reached up to kiss his cheek. Tyson put an arm around her shoulders and guided her to the kitchen.

"I'm starved," he announced to Mrs. Brady. "What have you got hiding to hold us until supper?"

"Supper is in less than an hour," she scolded. "I'll tell you now what I told you all your life. You can wait."

Tyson began searching for food in a way he knew would catch Mrs. Brady's attention. "Come now, you always hide some of those little cakes around here. Where are they? Confess it, Mrs. Brady."

"You're being really obnoxious," Emma laughed.

"Listen to your sister." Mrs. Brady slapped Tyson's hand and gave him a wry wink that made him chuckle.

Alexa settled it as she entered the room to announce, much as she might have fifteen years ago, "You children leave Mrs. Brady in peace. You can wait until supper."

Tyson leaned casually against the counter and popped a little frosted cake into his mouth that he had discovered without the cook's notice. Mrs. Brady acted shocked, but she couldn't keep from laughing as she shooed them out of the kitchen.

"What have the two of you been up to?" Alexa asked, sensing the unity they had once shared.

"Riding. What else?"

"What about you?" Emma asked her mother.

"I just finished a counseling hour with a boy."

"Any progress?"

"None worth speaking of, but I'll keep at it."

"You always do," Tyson complimented.

"I think I'll go and get cleaned up for supper." Emma kissed her brother and mother in turn. "You haven't seen Michael, have you?"

"I caught a glimpse of him heading up the stairs with Richard earlier. I haven't seen him since."

"With Richard?" Tyson laughed. "That boy could coerce Mrs. Brady into playing with him."

"He's already done that," Emma said. "I'll see if Michael's still with him."

Tyson called after her, "Don't let him take all the good horses."

Emma peeked into the nursery and found Richard playing alone. Lacey sat in the rocker, rocking back and forth vigorously. Emma opted to speak to Richard. "What you doing, handsome?" They both turned at the sound of her voice.

Richard glanced at his mother then returned to his play, saying with no enthusiasm, "Nothin'."

Emma noted something unnatural about Lacey and chose to simply say, "I'll see you at supper." She wasn't in the mood to get into anything else. Next she went to Michael's room, but he wasn't there. Certain she would see him at supper, she went to her room. She didn't notice him there until she had closed the door.

"Michael!" Her countenance brightened until she saw him look up from the book in his hands with an expression far too much like the man who had once frightened her. "Is something wrong?" she asked, leaning against the door.

Michael couldn't think what to say. The problem was by no means new or unexpected, so he simply answered, "No, I'm fine. How was your ride?"

"Excellent. It feels good to have Tyson back, and to know we have his blessing."

"Do we?"

"I believe so."

"That's good, then." Michael returned his attention to the book, which Emma felt certain couldn't be as interesting as he was pretending. But the gesture made it clear that he was in no mood to talk.

"I think I'll clean up for supper. Do you mind?" He waved his hand carelessly through the air and continued to read. "It's a hot afternoon. I fear I worked up quite a sweat."

Emma removed her boots and stockings, then went to the closet to find clean clothes. Opting for something a little more feminine, she pulled out a deep gray walking skirt and a pink silk blouse. When it became apparent that Michael wasn't taking the hint, she took the clothes and some fresh water into the sitting room to freshen up and change. She returned to find the book set aside and Michael staring at the wall, his brow furrowed in deep thought.

"Is everything all right?" she asked, brushing the back of her fingers over his face, startling him to the moment.

Michael looked into her eyes, and his lips twitched upward slightly just before he pulled her into his arms. "It is now," he said, and he meant it.

"Anything you want to talk about?"

Michael shook his head with certainty, then Emma noticed a piece of paper sticking out of his pocket. She pulled it out and declared, "You were trying to steal my bookmarker!"

Michael took it back. "It's a little inappropriate, don't you think?"

Emma took it from him again. "I'd say it's perfectly appropriate." She stuffed it down inside her chemise. "A ransom note to mark my place in a story of adventure and romance with a rogue who always looks like you no matter what he's supposed to look like."

"I don't find the memories associated with that . . . worth remembering."

"Well, I find the memories rather intriguing—being kidnapped and held for ransom by the man I end up marrying. The memories will always be there, Michael. You're going to have to learn to enjoy the good ones and accept the bad."

"Apparently there are things you find amusing that I would rather forget. There is a great deal I've done that I'm not proud of."

Emma reached up to kiss his nose. "Well, I am proud of *you*. And everything you have done, good or bad, is a part of you. Enough said."

Michael grunted and leaned back against the headboard again. She was always right, even when he didn't want her to be. He distracted himself by watching Emma put on short boots and lace them up, then she brushed through her hair and tied it back with a pink ribbon.

"Perfect," he said as she briefly surveyed herself in the long mirror. "Now come along," he said, offering his arm as he moved toward the door, "before I forget that we're not married yet."

Emma smiled at him and walked down the stairs by his side.

Michael was glad they had arrived at the dining room early, until the extra time began to make him dread having to sit through another meal with Lacey across the table. He considered requesting a change in seating arrangements, but he didn't want to give Lacey an opportunity to suggest where she would like him to sit.

Emma watched Michael carefully and felt the evidence deepen that something wasn't right. Something had happened while she'd been out with Tyson. She hadn't seen Michael this somber since they'd decided to marry. It was apparent he didn't want to talk about it, or perhaps he did, but the time hadn't been right. With determination, Emma made up her mind to talk to him just as soon as the meal was finished.

The remainder of the family entered together, and Emma saw Michael go visibly tense. As they were seated and the usual greetings were exchanged, Emma paused to study the faces around the table. Tyson appeared as lively as when they'd parted less than an hour earlier. Her mother and father were both normally congenial. Of course, she should have known: it was Lacey. She looked exactly as she had a while ago in the nursery, rocking in that chair in a way that reminded her of . . . Emma gasped. Michael was the only one close enough to hear it, but his eyes turned to her in surprise. She only smiled and returned to her meal, keeping her eyes on Lacey. The way she had rocked in that chair, back and forth with perfect precision, was too much like the way Michael had once clicked his thumbnail against his tooth. There was no similarity in the gestures, but the expression in the eyes was identical. Could it be possible that there was more to this problem with Lacey than met the eye? The thought frightened Emma, but she couldn't begin to know what to do about it. Despite having been through the drama of Michael's facing the truth, she couldn't say for certain that there was anything in particular she had done that had made a difference. She considered discussing it with her mother, but wondered if she was being presumptuous. Apprehension made her decide to wait and see what happened. Perhaps it would take care of itself.

There was an obvious deepening of the bitterness in Lacey's eyes that made Michael feel near despair. But he couldn't understand why. Was it simply the evidence that the tension between them was getting worse instead of better? Was it because he knew how much Emma loved her sister, and he didn't want to be the cause of such animosity? Or was it something else altogether? Whatever the reasons, Michael found it increasingly difficult to concentrate on the pleasant conversation around him. Something in Lacey's eyes seemed to remind him of everything rotten he'd ever done, while the memories became evenly interspersed with his father's sneer, his father's cruel laugh, and the snap of his father's belt. All of it came together in his mind with a booming echo that seemed to scream from the inside: *Are you a product of your father?* Was Lacey the only one in the room who could see the truth?

"What was that?" He shot his head up, realizing he was being addressed.

"I said," Alexa smiled in an effort to cover her concern, "have you been sneaking cakes from the kitchen with Tyson? You don't seem terribly hungry."

"Perhaps I'm not." Michael set down his fork, noting his plate was no less full than when it had been given to him. The food was just rearranged a bit.

"Is anything wrong, Michael?" Alexa asked gently.

Michael caught Lacey's eyes for the first time since the meal had begun, and he suddenly couldn't bear it another second.

"No," Michael said cryptically as he stood and threw his napkin onto the table, "but I think I could use some fresh air."

He was gone before Emma could even think of what to say. She felt stunned and afraid, but her mother's eyes confirmed her instinct to let him go. He likely needed time to himself. But two hours later, when the family was gathered in the drawing room and the coffee had turned cold, Michael still hadn't returned. Emma had gone up to check his room and found no sign of him. Tyson had gone outside and returned to report that Michael's horse was missing.

Lacey, who had sat quietly through the evening, betrayed a rare hint of smugness just before she said, "Things get a little rough around here, and he's gone in a flash. You simply can't depend on a man like that, Emma."

"What things?" Emma insisted. "Rough how?"

Lacey didn't answer, but her expression made Emma angry.

"You know something we don't, Lacey. What happened this afternoon that made him so upset?"

Lacey looked to their mother, hoping for some support in avoiding this, now that she regretted bringing it up. But Alexa gently said, "If you know what's happening here, Lacey, I think you'd better share it with the rest of us."

"Fine!" Lacey snarled. "The man had the nerve to be alone in the nursery with Richard this afternoon when . . ."

Emma was so astonished she couldn't speak, which made her grateful for the way Tyson leaned toward Lacey and took her arm. "Are you trying to tell me that you got upset with him for playing with Richard?"

"And why shouldn't I?" she insisted. "Do you know what he is capable of? I wouldn't trust him to—"

"Lacey!" Jess silenced her, which was something he generally left up to his wife.

"You're all a bunch of fools," Lacey mumbled, moving to sit at the piano in order to take out her frustration on the keys.

Emma felt Tyson's eyes on her before she turned to him. Without a word spoken they both rose at the same instant, knowing they had to go and find Michael. Before they'd taken a step, however, the door in the entry slammed. Emma was in the hall with Tyson close behind her before Michael made it halfway up the stairs.

"Michael!" she called, and he turned reluctantly. Emma moved to the bottom of the steps and held out her hand. Michael hesitated only a moment before he stepped down to take it. "Lacey told us what happened. I'd like to hear your side of the story."

Emma noticed that he was out of breath. His hair was windblown and his face glistened with sweat. Had he ridden so hard? Had he run from the stables to the house? He looked up to acknowledge Tyson before stating, "I told her to hit me, and she did."

"She hit you?" Emma was appalled.

"Slapped me, twice." Michael pointed to his cheek and added in a voice more like himself, "You're welcome to kiss it better."

Emma did so while Tyson chuckled. "Lacey is good at slapping. I can testify to that."

"Emma's not bad at it herself," Michael said to Tyson, who chuckled again and went back to the drawing room to leave them alone.

"You're feeling better?" she asked, pushing her arms around him.

"I suppose I got it out of my system," he replied with a firm embrace.

"Why don't you come in and sit down with us?" she asked.

"Is Lacey there?"

"Yes," Emma squeezed him tightly, "but I won't let her beat you up."

"How kind," he said with sarcasm and reluctantly followed Emma into the drawing room.

Lacey was quietly playing the piano and paid them no mind as they entered and sat down. Jess looked up from his book and Alexa from her needlework, as if nothing was out of the ordinary.

"Would you like some coffee, Michael?" Alexa asked. "I can go and warm it up in no time."

"No, thank you, Mother," he said, and Lacey's eyes flicked toward him briefly, but he glared at her until she looked away. "I think I would prefer some of whatever Tyson has."

"Port or brandy?" Tyson asked.

"Brandy, thank you," Michael said, and Tyson handed him a snifter before returning to his seat.

"I must say I'm rather upset with you, Michael," Tyson said, attempting to sound severe. All eyes turned to him in surprise, much to his gratification. "I understand you were using my stables today, and my horses." Tyson pointed a finger at him. "Next time you play with *my* son, get some blocks off the shelf and make your own stables."

Michael smiled. Emma squeezed his hand, and he decided that he felt better. But he should have known it wouldn't last.

"I have made it clear," Lacey said as the music stopped abruptly, "that I do not want my son left alone with . . . *him.*"

In the silence that followed, Michael wanted to beg these people not to get angry. He was tired of being the source of contention in this house. Alexa handled it perfectly when she answered, "Then we will all have to dedicate a little time to the purpose of allowing Richard to get to know Michael better."

Lacey said with exasperation, "Why do I feel like my entire family is against me?"

"Maybe it's the other way around," Tyson provided.

Lacey turned angry eyes back to the piano. Jess lightened the mood as he asked, "So, Michael, how did the work go today?"

"Good, I believe," he answered with enthusiasm.

"Everything all right, then?" Jess added.

"Fine."

"With the boys or otherwise?" Alexa persisted. Michael knew she was well aware that he was struggling. But he couldn't believe she knew what he was struggling with, when he wasn't certain himself. The worst of it was the memories, centering more and more on his father. For the past several hours they had assaulted him with a demeaning guilt, making him wonder why he was here. He felt so undeserving.

Inwardly longing to find some resolve, Michael figured her question was a good enough opportunity to perhaps get some of the answers he needed. "I would like to ask you something," he said cautiously.

"Yes?" Alexa urged.

"When I was going over the files for the boys, I . . . I came across mine."

This brought Jess's attention away from his book. Michael didn't miss the sharp glance that passed between Jess and Alexa. Tyson and Emma were politely interested. Lacey appeared indifferent.

"There was mention of my father . . ." Michael had to swallow hard to say it, ". . .coming here for me, and . . . it says he was killed."

Emma squeezed his hand and felt him squeeze back until it almost hurt. She knew more than anyone how difficult this was for him, and she held his hand tightly, attempting to convey her support.

"I'd like to know what happened," Michael finished tersely.

Emma was not the only one surprised by her parents' hesitance. Jess glanced uncertainly at Alexa, but she answered him firmly. "You have to be honest with him, Jess. You're not obligated to protect him anymore. He's a man."

Michael didn't know what he'd expected, but this preamble made him nervous. Jess glanced discreetly toward Lacey before he spoke in a tone unnaturally light in contrast to what Alexa had just said. "It was either him or me. Lucky for me, I was quicker."

Michael came to his feet and set the snifter down in one swift movement. With his back to the occupants of the room, he attempted to grasp what he'd just heard. Then he turned back to Jess, ignoring everyone else. "Just a minute. Are you saying that you . . . *you* killed my father?"

The piano stopped. "Does that disturb you, Michael?" Alexa asked.

"Disturb me?" He laughed. "I have lain awake nights, fearing that I would come upon my father on the street and kill him without a second thought. The man was a monster. It took years to realize there was nothing wrong with me; it was him who had the problem. Learning of his death has given me a great deal of peace." He spoke directly to Jess. "I have never killed a man, but I can imagine it wouldn't be easy to live with. I want to thank you for being willing to live with it for my sake."

"Like I said," Jess repeated, "it was either him or me."

"If this is the incident I think we're talking about," Tyson joined in, "isn't there a little more to it than that?"

"Yes," Alexa said carefully, glancing discreetly toward Lacey once again. She sat staring at her hands folded in her lap. "But we're not going to discuss that right now."

Lacey felt the voices around her become distant. The conversation seemed to tease at vague memories. She couldn't recall the incident they were talking about, but the mere mention of it provoked feelings in her that resembled waking up from a nightmare. The sensation became so unnerving that she suddenly needed to be alone. The room felt hot and stuffy. She looked around at her family—and *him*—casually sitting in silence. She felt outnumbered, unwanted, and most especially afraid.

"I think I'll go up to bed." Lacey came to her feet and fled the room before anyone had a chance to say good night.

"Is it possible to discuss it *now?*" Michael asked, his mind still obviously absorbed with the conversation.

Jess nodded firmly toward Alexa. "You said he had a right to know."

Alexa diverted her thoughts from a deepening concern for Lacey and attempted to put together the words to tell Michael what he wanted to know. She tried to determine his reaction and how it might make him feel. And she had to admit, "I think it would be better to discuss this another time." She rose and moved to the door, feeling an instinctive need to be with Lacey. "Right now, I believe I'm needed elsewhere."

"When?" Michael insisted. "If there is something I am ignorant of that concerns me, I want to know about it."

"Tomorrow, Michael," Alexa assured him. "And in the meantime, relax." She smiled warmly. "Everything will be all right."

Jess followed Alexa into the hall, leaving a distinct tension in the room in their absence.

"Alexa," Jess quickened his step to catch up with her, "what's wrong?"

She stopped and took his hand. "I just had the most awful feeling." She put her hand over her stomach, and her expression turned almost queasy.

"What?" he pressed when she didn't continue.

"It's as if I have been overlooking the obvious for fifteen years, Jess, and it just hit me in the face."

"I don't understand."

"What's happening here is not a simple matter of what we see. I fear that what Lacey is feeling now has a lot less to do with Michael than we realize."

"Alexa," Jess bent forward to look her in the eye, "I realize we have been married twenty-three years, and I should understand what you're talking about, but I haven't got a clue."

"Jess," she whispered intently, "I have spent countless hours counseling troubled boys and helping them deal with their fears, while I have totally neglected the fears of my own daughter. Lacey always seemed secure enough, and she was hesitant to talk about what happened before she came here. I never felt a reason to press it. But look what's happening here. Her belligerence toward Michael is unreasonable. Her unwillingness to forgive Tyson is the same. I believe Lacey is not being obnoxious as much as she is simply afraid. I'm not certain of what exactly, but I'm going to find out."

"What you're trying to tell me is . . ."

Alexa finished when he hesitated, "It's going to get a lot worse before it gets any better."

Jess watched her hurry up the stairs and let out a heavy sigh.

Lacey sat with no expression while her mother gently explained how it might be a good idea to discuss things that had happened in the past— things that could possibly be disturbing her now, even if she didn't consciously realize it. Lacey understood the concept; she'd heard it discussed many times before. But she simply felt it had no validity in this situation. It was not her fault that Tyson had abandoned her. Nor was it her fault that the family was condoning this marriage that would permanently bring a savage brute into the household. She calmly expressed her feelings by simply stating, "I appreciate your concern, but there's nothing to talk about. If you want to talk, try talking some sense into your dear Mr. Hamilton. Or perhaps your son could use some talking to."

Lacey got up and went to Emma's room to wait for her to come up to bed. It was Emma she needed to talk to.

Alexa was so stunned that it took several minutes to find the motivation to stand up and go to her room, where she futilely attempted to get some sleep.

"I think I'll leave you lovebirds alone." Tyson came to his feet with a barely stifled yawn. "I'll see you in the morning."

"Good night, Tyson." Emma rose to kiss him. Tyson nodded toward Michael and left the room, hoping he could fall asleep quickly enough to avoid feeling the empty ache that was becoming all too familiar.

"You look tired." Emma took Michael's hand, wishing she could somehow dispel the anxiety etched into his face.

"It's nearly eleven," he stated.

"Already?" She glanced at the clock in disbelief.

Michael took Emma's hand and kissed it, looking into her eyes in search of the strength he knew he could derive from her. "Do you know what I need?" he asked.

"What?" She smiled and kissed him quickly.

"I just need to be with you."

"I think we could arrange that," she said, urging him toward the door.

They hurried up the stairs, holding hands, while Michael could only think of how he needed some time with her. He paused outside Emma's bedroom door to kiss her the way he'd wanted to all day. He was just beginning to forget about the nagging torment of Lacey's hatred when her voice called out, "Is that you, Emma?"

Michael drew away immediately. "Good night, Emma," he said as he turned and walked away.

"Michael, wait," she said in a loud whisper.

His hands came up in resignation. He turned and kept walking backward. "I can only fight so much in one day, Emma. I will see you at breakfast."

Emma felt so torn she wanted to cry. Lacey pulled open the door, and Emma forced a smile.

"It is you." Lacey was genuinely happy. "I need you, Emma. I need to talk. I hope you're not too tired, or—"

"No." Emma went in and closed the door behind her. "I'm fine."

Lacey sat on the edge of the bed, and her expression became severe.

"You're not going to try and talk me out of marrying Michael, are you?" Emma figured that getting to the point could avoid any more drama. "If you are, I don't want to hear it."

Lacey sighed. "Emma, I just don't want to see you get hurt. I fear he will turn his back and run like . . ."

"Like Tyson?"

Lacey ignored it. "Let's say Michael has changed. Do you think a past such as his won't come back to haunt him . . . you . . . us?"

"That is what forgiving is all about, Lacey. Could we talk about something else?"

"If you wish." Lacey sighed. "But be careful, Emma. It would break my heart to see him hurt you."

"So, how is Tyson these days?" Emma asked tersely.

"You've spent more time with him than I have."

"And why is that?" Emma asked as she began to undress for bed.

"I don't know," Lacey admitted. She couldn't explain something she didn't understand. "It's just difficult to be . . . with him . . . after all that's happened."

Lacey then embarked on a long oratory concerning the difficulties she had experienced as a result of Tyson's abandonment. Emma listened politely, then with delicate tact she told Lacey that she had to forgive, to open her heart. And she had to talk to Tyson about it. Emma became so sleepy that she crawled into bed while Lacey rambled on, and she was barely aware of Lacey apologizing for keeping her up so late as she extinguished the lamp and left the room.

Emma awoke to find she had time to spare before breakfast. She dressed quickly in her most comfortable riding apparel and went to Michael's room. When he didn't answer, she peeked inside to find him gone. The bed was slept in, and there was evidence that he had shaved and washed up before going out. A vague sense of desperation rose in Emma as she contemplated the emotional duress Michael had faced the last two days, combined with the memory of Lacey's declaration: "I fear he will turn his back on you and run."

Emma knew with her entire being that Michael wouldn't do it, but she felt relieved nevertheless as she approached the track to see him helping Murphy and Fiddler exercise the racers. Emma leaned over the rail and watched him, intrigued to observe him from a distance—his walk, his mannerisms, the virile aura he bore. And to realize she would be his wife. Her mind turned to how it felt to hold him close, and a fluttery warmth crept through her. The feeling was magnified tenfold when he turned and smiled like the rogue he played so well. She saw the men pausing in their work long enough to tease Michael as their attention turned her way. Emma could hear nothing until something Michael said sent them into peals of laughter and Michael walked toward her, a self-satisfied grin filling his countenance. Emma couldn't deny her relief at seeing that he felt better than he had when they had parted. He seemed more like himself already.

"What was that all about?" she asked when he came close enough to hear.

"They asked how a man like me managed to catch a woman like you." He bent beneath the rail and planted a wanton kiss on her lips. Then he glanced back at Murphy and Fiddler to confirm Emma's suspicion that it was partially for their benefit.

"And what, pray tell, was your answer?"

"I told them to read *Rogue of the Plains*."

Emma laughed. "I seriously doubt that what you learned from that book had much to do with my falling in love with you."

"No," he grinned, "but it didn't hurt."

"Feeling better?" she asked.

He put his arm around her and moved toward the house. "Do you still love me?"

"Emphatically!"

"Then I'm fine. What did Lacey have to say this time?"

"Same old thing, I'm afraid."

"Has she talked you out of it yet?"

"No, and she won't."

"Good," he said and kissed her as they walked. He felt a peace that dimmed only slightly through the course of an unusually quiet breakfast. The tension was undeniable, but it seemed that no one knew what to do about it.

When Alexa was finished eating, she came to her feet and announced, "Emma and Lacey, I would like you to give some time this morning to assisting Mrs. Brady in the kitchen. Tillie is still not up to her usual self, and Mrs. Brady's feeling a bit overwhelmed." She studied their expressions and added, "Is there a problem?"

"No," Lacey stated.

"I suppose I can see Michael later." Emma smiled toward him.

"Eventually, I suspect you'll be spending ample time together," Jess said with an edge of humor. "Husbands and wives tend to do that."

"I've got work to do, anyway," Michael said, pushing back his chair.

"Not today, you don't," Jess insisted, and Michael looked briefly stunned. "It's Sunday, Michael. Your day off."

"Oh?" Michael had forgotten all about that.

"Perhaps while Emma is busy, you could survey your new office. Sarina has it cleaned out now."

"Office?" Michael's voice rose a pitch.

"But of course." Jess came to his feet. "One of those keys you have fits the door."

"Wonderful," Michael said with sarcasm. "It could take me an hour to get in."

"I trust you can all keep yourselves occupied then," Alexa said as she left with her husband. "I've got business to attend to."

Lacey rose and moved toward the kitchen. Tyson was on his feet and after her with half of his breakfast still left on his plate. He knew Michael and Emma were watching him, but he didn't care. Abruptly he took Lacey's arm to stop her.

"What do you want?" she snapped.

"A word with you," he stated firmly. "Which is more than I have gotten the last two days."

Lacey turned to assure herself that they were not alone. "I should get to the kitchen."

"Fine. I'll escort you." They moved through the door while Tyson maintained a grip on her arm. "Am I so distasteful to you that we cannot even speak?"

"You said to keep my bitterness to myself."

"And you have nothing else to give?"

"At the moment, no."

"Lacey, if what I have done is so unforgivable, why are you marrying me?"

"It's the right thing to do. For Richard's sake."

"And what about *my* sake?"

"You made it quite clear that you wanted me in your life, but I don't have to talk."

Tyson regretted even opening this discussion. How could she manage to make her words bite so deeply? How could she misinterpret him so completely? He swallowed his frustration and asked, "Do you find that so distasteful?"

Lacey only looked away, not wanting to betray what just being close to him did to her.

"There was a time when it wasn't so distasteful." He lowered his voice and moved a little closer.

Anger quickly replaced all else, and she turned to him with fire in her eyes. "There was a time when I gave you everything I had. My heart was fully yours, and you broke it, Tyson Davies. You tore it out and broke it. Now, see if you can put it back together and set it back where it belongs." She jerked her arm free and hurried away. Tyson turned and hit his fist against the wall. The ache pounding through his fingers was not nearly as intense as the dagger Lacey kept twisting in his heart.

Fifteen
THE ACCUSATION

Michael squeezed Emma's hand while they helplessly overheard Tyson and Lacey arguing. Neither of them could think of anything to say. When the argument was apparently finished, Emma kissed Michael and came to her feet. "I should go and help in the kitchen. I'll see you later."

Michael nodded and watched her walk away. It seemed he had little choice but to occupy himself. He wandered into the yard and realized he missed the boys, even though he'd hardly had a chance to get used to being with them. He watched them playing ball and felt strongly reminded of his own childhood here. It seemed he was always on the outside looking in.

He decided to follow Jess's suggestion and check out his new office—once he figured out which key to use. With a sense of importance, he sat back in the big chair and put his boots on the desk. Sarina had cleared out all of Ben's things, and the room felt terribly bare, which set Michael to contemplating what he might fill it with. He didn't have any books, beyond a few paperback romances. He had no masculine bric-a-brac, no souvenirs or artifacts of his life. He decided it was a worthy goal to begin collecting such things. He tried to imagine this office in ten years, or twenty. The prospect created a pleasant image in his mind.

A knock on the door made him put his feet abruptly on the floor, as if he'd been caught at mischief. "Come in," he called, attempting an important tone to match the chair he was seated in. The door clicked open, and Alexa Davies peered into the room.

"Hello, Mother." He was genuinely happy to see her. "What can I do for you?"

"Getting the feel of the new office?" she asked, looking around.

"Kind of bare, eh?"

"It will evolve, I'm certain."

Michael sensed that Alexa had a purpose for seeking him out. "Looking for me?" he asked.

"I thought you might be expecting me," she said, and only then did Michael recall that she had promised to talk to him today.

"I must have been trying to forget about that," Michael said quite honestly.

"Let's go for a walk, shall we?" Alexa held out a hand toward him. Michael looked at her closely, then he took it as he came to his feet.

"Now, that's progress," she smiled.

"How is that?"

"I can't count the times I offered you that hand, and you always put your hands in your pockets."

"Did I? I don't remember that."

"Isn't it funny how some memories remain very clear, and others leave us entirely?"

Michael looked around and realized they had crossed through a side door from his office into a room in which he had spent many hours as a youth. He thought it strange that she would be speaking of memories at this moment. Then he realized that she'd probably done that on purpose.

"Does it look different?" she asked.

"Yes." Michael soaked in the room that had been logically dubbed "the counseling room." It was here that Alexa Davies had spent endless hours with the boys who were having difficulties for any number of reasons.

"This room got a lot of business from me," he said.

"Then you know it well."

"I remember it being bigger."

"You were smaller, perhaps."

"I thought the horse in the picture was black."

"It looks brown to me," Alexa said, and they both paused to contemplate the painting of a boy leading a horse toward a home in the distance. Michael had always liked this picture, but it wasn't until now that he grasped the symbolism in it. Still, he could have sworn the horse was black. He turned to Alexa and decided to get to the point. "You didn't just bring me here to discuss memories, did you?"

"Memories might be a good thing to discuss, but I thought we could go someplace a little more appropriate. I just thought you'd like to see this room again."

She led him into the hall and toward the residence. "Appropriate for what?" he asked, noting she still held his hand.

"I'm not your counselor anymore, Michael." They ascended the stairs together and went down another hall that he was not acquainted with. "I'm your mother, or at least as good as. And I think we have some family matters that need to be discussed."

"But why just the two of us?" he asked, following her into a room that he realized was her sitting room. "When one of us suffers, we all do."

"I fear there is a little more suffering going on here than I first realized." Michael drew up his chin defensively. "And I am not referring to you, although I would venture to guess that there is still some pain in there that could stand to be dealt with." Michael said nothing. "Sit down," she added. "Make yourself comfortable."

Michael opted for one end of a sofa, and Alexa took a chair across from him where the sunlight came behind her through an east window. For a moment, he became lost in an intriguing resemblance she bore to Emma that he'd never noticed before.

"You like your job?" she questioned, and he felt familiarity in the tone. This was an opening question, to get him to loosen up and start talking about something he felt comfortable with. He couldn't count the hours he and Alexa Davies had sat facing each other this way. Was that why she knew him so well?

"I've had little time to do otherwise, but I believe I'm going to enjoy it. Why don't we get to the point? Are we here to talk about my father, or was there something else?"

Alexa smiled. "Some things don't change." His brow lifted in question. "You were always sharp and tough. So, all right. We'll get to the point. I'll tell you what I believe you want to know, and then you can do the same for me." Michael nodded. "I assume, and you may correct me if I'm wrong, that you are somewhat distressed over learning that Jess killed your father."

"It took me by surprise."

"And?"

"And what?"

"You must feel something beyond surprise."

Michael thought about it. "Gratitude. Jess has likely prevented me from committing murder."

"Do you really believe you would have killed him, given the chance?"

Again he thought. "I don't know, but I certainly wanted to."

"It *was* your father then?" she asked, and Michael narrowed his eyes. "He was responsible for the scars?"

Michael shifted quickly in his seat and crossed his legs. Alexa noticed the way his fingers tightened over the arm of the sofa. "Yes," he answered tersely.

"It's apparent you resent those scars," she stated, hoping not to betray how difficult this was for her. But she felt it was necessary, however painful.

"I resent being a walking souvenir of somebody's sick mind. I resent not being able to live through a day without being reminded. You still haven't told me what happened."

"I suppose I should start at the beginning."

"That's logical." He nodded.

"You aren't going to like it, Michael."

"Then you'd do well to get it over with."

"Jess told me he mentioned to you that it was when you were thirteen and down with a fever that I discovered those scars. Of course, we weren't certain what—or rather who—had caused them. I suspected, but you blatantly refused to open up about anything, so I continued to pretend I didn't know. It was about the same time that your father finally caught up with you. I don't have a clue how he figured out you were here, but the existence of this place is far from secretive; in truth, it's rather famous. It's not the first time an angry parent has come demanding their rights concerning children they cared nothing for beyond pride or ulterior motives, but . . ." She paused, and Michael felt it coming, whatever it was. "But it was the first time blood was spilt and hostages were held."

Alexa wasn't certain what to expect. In Michael's youth, she had seen him go into angry rages or withdraw into a silent, distant stare when confronted with difficult things. After a long moment, he stated in a quiet tone that defied the intensity of his eyes, "Whose blood? What hostages?"

Alexa drew a deep breath, and Michael felt his rage being fanned by her previous statement. Already he didn't like this at all, but he had a feeling it was going to get worse. "He came into the racing stables and confronted Jess there. He said enough to make it clear what his intentions were for you. Of course Jess told him no, and he . . ." She hesitated in a way that made Michael's heart pump into his throat. "He shot one of the stable hands who died the next day, and he somehow managed to get hold of . . . Emma and—"

"Wait a minute." Michael moved to the edge of his seat and leaned toward her. "My father . . . *my* father . . . had Emma?" The thought left a sick knot smoldering in the pit of his stomach.

"And Lacey," Alexa added. "But it was Emma who . . ."

"What?" he shouted when she hesitated.

"Had the gun pressed to her head."

Michael came to his feet with that youthful rage she remembered well. But he only went to the window and turned his back to her, pushing his hands through his hair and tugging at it. "If he weren't already dead," Michael said through clenched teeth, "I would kill him."

"Then we are grateful he's dead."

Michael attempted to calm down what he felt inside by reminding himself that this had happened a long time ago, and there was no good in raging over it now. "What else happened?" he asked quietly.

"Most of it was over by the time I got there," Alexa said gently. "It was mostly a blur, but when it was all over we couldn't deny that what happened was nothing short of a miracle. Jess rarely carries a gun, but he had been out looking for a dingo that had been in the sheep. He made it clear that he was not giving you back. The gun was cocked at Emma's head. Jess provoked him into pointing the gun at him instead of Emma. Then he pulled his gun and fired."

"Jess said it was either him or my father. It sounds more like it was either my father or Emma."

"We try not to think of it that way. We're only grateful it turned out as it did."

After an unreasonable length of silence, Michael chuckled humorlessly, his back still to Alexa. "And I didn't even know he'd been here."

"What are you feeling, Michael?" She came behind him and touched his arm.

Michael looked down at her. "Gratitude," he said, his chin betraying a barely detectable quiver. "This helpless, humbling gratitude. I don't understand it; I just don't. I must have made your lives miserable back then. Why didn't Jess just hand me over? Why was he willing to let his own daughter's life be jeopardized for me?" His voice lowered as he spoke with an impassioned awe. "Why was *I,*" he hit his chest, "worth so much to you? Why am I *still* worth so much to you? I do not understand!"

"The worth of a soul is great, Michael."

"You're quoting me the Bible?"

"We can all learn something about ourselves there," she said with a tone of wisdom. "Tyson could likely relate to the prodigal son." She smiled. "And you. . ."

"Have a strong resemblance to the devil," he quipped a little too seriously.

"No, Michael," she countered, touching his face. "To me, you are much like Saul."

"I'm sorry? I'm afraid I missed that one."

"As I understand it, Saul was the ultimate persecutor, until one day on the road to Damascus, he experienced such a drastic change of heart that he dedicated the remainder of his life to undoing what he had done. He changed his name to Paul."

"I think I like that story." Michael attempted a smile, but his eyes revealed his true emotion.

"Of course, we don't get all of the details, and I have wondered what put Saul up to such a life. Had someone hurt him? Or was he that way because he chose to be? You say that what you have lived through does not justify what you have done. I admire you for taking responsibility for your actions, Michael. But I want you to remember that it was the pain and the fear that drove you to feel the way you felt, and to be the way you were. Don't use it as an excuse, Michael. Use it as a reason; a means to give you understanding so that you can overcome the past, then let it rest."

Michael could almost literally feel himself becoming rejuvenated from her wisdom. He took a deep breath as if he could absorb it all the more. "I can see where she gets it," he said. Then he clarified, "Your daughter is always saying things like that—things that leave me speechless."

"She loves you very much, Michael."

"Yes, I know. And they say miracles only occurred in Biblical times."

Alexa's smile was a welcome reward for his attempts at humor, but she sobered quickly. "Has Emma seen the scars, Michael?"

"I couldn't have asked her to marry me without knowing she was well aware of what she was getting."

"You've come a long way from the boy who fought so hard to keep them hidden from the world."

"Yes, I believe I have. But not until I came up against something that I couldn't fight."

"And what was that?"

"Emma."

Alexa smiled and they sat again, talking for another hour about the changes and the pain. If Alexa had felt any doubts, they were extinguished in the maturity and courage with which Michael discussed his past. And the more they talked, the more he found her guidance and experience strengthening the remolding within himself that Emma had already helped him to begin. His gratitude deepened with his sense of self-worth, and he admitted to Alexa that he believed he could make Emma happy, he could be a good father, and he believed he had the ability to help the boys in his care. "But still," he had to admit also, "there is a part of me that I fear. Sometimes I could almost believe there is a beast inside of me."

"When do you feel it most?"

He chuckled dryly. "When Lacey glares at me."

"You must be patient with Lacey, and try to understand that much of what she is dealing with has little to do with you. Unfortunately, it appears you are the scapegoat."

"I've been worse things."

"Give it time, Michael. I know all of this seems overwhelming and insurmountable, but in years to come this will seem like a very brief, almost insignificant problem."

"Is that how you feel about losing your first husband?" Michael asked so casually that Alexa was now the one left speechless.

"Jess told you," she finally said. Michael nodded. "I must say I'm surprised. It's something he's never shown a desire to tell his children about. It was a difficult time for both of us. But yes, I suppose in looking back over the years of raising our children and all we have experienced since that time, it doesn't seem so severe. But at the time . . ." Alexa looked down, and Michael nearly regretted bringing it up.

"You know," she said eagerly, standing to pull open a drawer in a small writing desk, "that reminds me of something you might appreciate." She pulled out a stack of papers and carefully rummaged through them until she found what she was looking for. Her eyes glanced over the page with nostalgia, then she handed it to Michael, who read aloud:

> In the mirror I see a man,
>   but the reflection shows a beast
> Does my soul show through my eyes
>   or do my eyes only hide my soul?
> From the distance I watch you there,
>   and I see nothing but beauty.
> Beauty through and through.
>
> I have heard through legend's tongue,
>   from books my mother read,
> The only thing that changes beast to man
>   is true love, pure love, Beauty's love.

Michael finished and looked up at her. "I believe," she said with strength, "that every man who seeks to make something worthwhile of his life has to come to terms with a little bit of an inner beast in one way or another."

"Who wrote this?" Michael asked, feeling a kinship with the piece that he couldn't begin to describe.

"You didn't read the signature?" she laughed.

Michael squinted. "I *can't* read the signature."

"It says Jesse Benjamin Davies."

"Jess?" Michael laughed in surprise, then he looked over it again, trying to perceive this coming from Jess's mind.

"He's quite a poet. You didn't know that, did you." Michael shook his head. "But when I was given that poem, it wasn't signed, and I was under the impression that it had been written by Richard . . . my husband. In a different way, it suited him as well." Alexa sat down and leaned close to Michael. "He could tell you about scars. The first time I came face to face with him, I screamed. Half of his face had been badly burned. But I learned to look beneath the scars, and I found a man worth loving." She smiled. "Like mother, like daughter."

"You are a gem," he took her hand, "Mother."

"Let's get some lunch, shall we?"

Michael put his arm through hers and escorted her to the dining room.

❦   ❦   ❦

Emma stayed busy in the kitchen throughout the morning, while her mind was with Michael. She wondered what he might have found to occupy himself, and she wished they could find more time together. She felt certain it would help him through the difficult adjustment he was going through.

Emma and Lacey remained in an uncomfortable silence as they helped Mrs. Brady set the table for the usual finer-than-normal Sunday meal. Ten minutes shy of noon, she heard familiar laughter and was pleasantly surprised to see Michael come in with her mother. Lacey tersely went back to the kitchen, but Emma greeted them both with a kiss. "What have you been up to?" she asked.

"We were just having a little chat," Michael smiled. "Actually, we were gossiping about you. What's for lunch? I'm starved."

"I'll help Mrs. Brady put it on," Alexa said, and left them alone to share a more meaningful kiss.

"What did you talk about?" Emma prodded.

"I'll tell you later." He kissed her again. "I'm busy now." And again.

Tyson and Jess put a stop to the ardor when they appeared, and the meal proceeded as usual. Emma was pleased to see that Michael was feeling better, but she noticed something different about Lacey. They'd been together all morning, but there was a distant look about her that Emma just noticed as she watched her across the table. Emma was trying to figure it out when Rick came to the dining room to announce, "You have a visitor, Mr. Davies."

"What is this, Rick?" Jess chuckled. "You've taken to answering the door while Tillie's down?"

"Someone's got to do it," he said straightly, but Jess chuckled.

"Who is here?" Jess asked, setting his napkin aside and pushing his chair back.

"It's Mr. Grant, sir."

"On a Sunday?" Jess laughed. Michael was the only one who apparently didn't understand.

Emma leaned over to whisper, "Father's solicitor. They get along famously, and I doubt Father cares much whether he comes on a Sunday or not. They rarely stick to business long."

Michael nodded, and Jess took up his napkin. "Bring him in, and have Mrs. Brady set another place."

"I wonder what would bring him all the way out here today," Alexa said. "Doesn't he usually send word before he makes the effort?"

"Usually," Jess said as he continued to eat, "but not always. I don't recall any warning the day he came to inform us that we were rich."

"Then it must be good news," Emma suggested.

"Ira." Jess stood as the slender, middle-aged man, dressed finely in a business suit, crossed the room to take his extended hand. "I should have known it was you. Smelled Mrs. Brady's cooking, I'd wager."

"Sunday dinner was always my favorite," Ira grinned, then he added more seriously, "No, really, I'm fine. Finish your dinner, and then we can talk."

"Mrs. Brady is already coming with . . . ah, there she is."

"Now, eat up and don't be pretendin' you don't want any," Mrs. Brady said, setting a plate and utensils in front of him.

"You people are difficult to fool." The solicitor grinned up at her as she returned to the kitchen, then he glanced toward one end of the table. "Hello, Alexa. Everything going all right?"

"Fine, and you?"

"Good. I got a new granddaughter since we last talked."

"That's wonderful. Your son's child, is it?"

"Yes." Ira took a mouthful and stopped to savor it. "Mrs. Brady could teach my wife a thing or two."

"Lucy is an excellent cook," Alexa defended.

"I know. I just say that so you'll repeat it to Mrs. Brady, and she'll keep feeding me." Ira glanced down the table, apparently just realizing there was a new face—one he hadn't seen in a long time. His eyes stopped on Tyson. "Well, I'll be. If it isn't the prodigal son!" He laughed. Michael glanced at Alexa, who gave him a little wink. "How are you, Tyson? It's good to see you back."

"I'm glad to be home," Tyson smiled.

"And you girls are looking as lovely as ever," Ira said. They both smiled timidly and he turned to Jess. "Doesn't it seem like these kids were born just last week?"

"Sometimes it does," Jess agreed. "And now they're getting married."

"Married?" Ira laughed and took another bite. "That means you'll be needing me."

"Trust you to find business in every social occasion," Jess laughed.

"So who is marrying whom?" Ira asked.

"Did you come all this way to discuss nuptials?" Jess couldn't stand the suspense any longer. He figured they'd have time for introductions later.

"Actually," he grinned, "I have found out something so exciting, I couldn't wait a minute to get here."

"What? Tell us," Alexa insisted, knowing from his tone that it *was* good news.

"I found a connection to one of your orphans."

Michael's indifference shifted to acute interest.

"Who?" Alexa asked eagerly.

"Michael Hess," he stated. "I believe he's around six years old."

Michael was glad that he could actually put a face with the name as he eagerly waited to hear what Mr. Grant had to say.

"I was doing the standard background search and established what we had already believed. Being an only child of an only child left him with no relatives at all on his father's side. His mother was the youngest in her family, with a space of several years between herself and a brother. Her parents and brother are deceased, as well. But her brother had a daughter who is now living in Adelaide. I wrote to her, explaining the circumstances, and received a speedy response, inviting me to visit them. So I did. Now," he took a bite of his meal and the family hung impatiently on his ability to chew and swallow quickly, "we all know how delicate these things can be. I sometimes hate these visits, because we don't want to put a child into a difficult situation. I was nearly prepared for the worst after some experiences we've had in the past."

Michael watched this man closely as he spoke, and though it was subtle, he could have sworn he glanced toward Lacey as he'd said the last.

"But honestly, Jess, I have never been so impressed with a situation in all my life. The family has seven children, and—"

"Seven?" Alexa laughed. "And they want another?"

"That's just it. When I sat down to talk to them, this woman gets all choked up, you see, and her husband proceeds to tell me how just a few days before my letter arrived, they had both realized there was an empty chair at the dining table. They had discussed how they'd both felt a strange sensation that someone was missing. But they are physically incapable of having more children, due to medical difficulties. They really believe that little Michael Hess is supposed to be in their home. These people are good, hardworking, honest. And the children, well . . . I mean, children are children. But for the most part, all I could see was happy, well-adjusted kids. They aren't wealthy, but they manage well enough. They could provide a good living for him, and a good education. In all my experience, Jess, I have never come across a situation so ideal."

"So, what now?" Alexa asked, beaming.

"Mr. and Mrs. Simpkins are on their way here soon. They should be here by the end of the week, I would guess. I told them they were welcome. I hope that's all right."

"Of course it is," Alexa insisted.

"They want to meet Michael, and they plan to take him with them. I can have the legalities taken care of by then. They did request that nothing be said to the boy until they arrived."

"That's likely best," Jess added. "In my experience, the more time a child has to think about it, the more likely he is to be concerned. If these people are as kind as you say, I'm sure they can win him over."

"Have you had any difficulties with him?" Ira asked, more to Alexa.

"Nothing unusual. He's the youngest here, and came from a relatively calm background. I believe he has some fears related to his parents' deaths, but they're reasonable and understandable. I don't suspect he would have any objection to the offer."

"What do you think?" Jess said to Michael, catching him off guard.

He wiped his mouth with his napkin and said quite honestly, "I'm afraid I haven't been with him enough to say for certain, but I'll keep an eye on him in the meantime."

Ira looked to Jess in question. "Ah, forgive me. We did procrastinate the introductions, didn't we. This is Emma's fiancé, and our new administrator. He grew up here. Maybe you remember him. Michael Hamilton."

If it had taken perception for Michael to notice Ira's subtle glance toward Lacey a few minutes earlier, it took nothing now to plainly see the momentary shock that came over the solicitor's face. He recovered quickly and gave a polite nod, but the glances exchanged over the table made it clear that everyone knew the name meant something to Ira Grant.

"It's a pleasure to meet you, Mr. Hamilton," he said kindly.

"And you, Mr. Grant," Michael replied, wondering what this man knew about him.

"So, you're marrying Emma?" he asked, on the surface seeming to like the idea, while a subtle concern showed in his eyes. "Lucky man."

"Yes, I am," Michael said more to Emma.

"Tyson and Lacey are getting married as well," Alexa provided.

"Really? To who?"

"Each other," Jess said, as if it were obvious.

"Oh," Ira laughed, "of course. I suppose that would make sense after . . ." He stopped himself. "Well, it would make sense."

Tyson looked at Lacey for a reaction, and wished he could see something there beyond terse indifference.

The meal continued with small talk. Jess and Ira discussed mutual acquaintances, and it became evident to Michael that this Ira worked closely with the law in locating children who needed to be here. Michael bet that Ira Grant likely made much of his living from Jess Davies. He wondered if that was how Jess had come to find little Michael Hamilton. His days on the streets had not gone unnoticed by the police. Perhaps that explained Ira Grant's reaction to hearing his name. Was he simply surprised to find a man with a prison record sitting here, a part of the family and the business? It surprised Michael, so why should it not surprise anybody else?

When dessert was finished, Emma leaned over to Michael and suggested in a whisper, "Let's go riding as soon as I help clean the dishes."

Michael's face brightened histrionically. "Can I help too? Can we play in the suds?"

"I doubt Mrs. Brady would deny any help she can get," Emma smiled, squeezing his hand. She stood and began stacking plates. Michael decided to help her.

"You don't need to do that, Michael," Alexa insisted.

"That's all right," he insisted, "Emma and I made a good dishwashing team in the outback. I dare say we can do even better in a kitchen. Besides," he raised his voice to sound like a little boy, eager to have his work done, "if I help Emma with her chores, we can go out to play sooner."

Everyone laughed but Lacey and Mr. Grant, who said to Jess, "Could I talk to you privately?"

"Of course." Jess came to his feet. "It seems the dishes are under control." He kissed Alexa on his way out of the room. "Give our compliments to Mrs. Brady."

"And tell her what I said," Ira added slyly.

"I'll do that," Alexa agreed with a smile.

Jess sat behind his desk and put his boots up. Ira remained standing. Jess knew he didn't need an invitation to sit down, so he figured this must be serious.

"What is it, Grant? Have you lost my bank papers?"

"I never lose anything," he said too seriously for the humor Jess was attempting.

"Then what is it?"

"I must say I was surprised by your dinner guest."

"He's no guest," Jess said lightly, but feeling an uncomfortable twitch at the back of his neck. "As you can see, he's moving in."

"That's what I'm afraid of."

"I realize Michael's background is not exemplary," Jess stated, "but I trust him implicitly. I have no problem with his being here."

"Yet I just heard him say he'd been in the outback—with Emma, was it?"

"Just a little adventure." Jess gave a wry smile.

"That's not what I heard."

Jess leaned forward. "What did you hear?"

"While I was in the constable's office yesterday, I happened to mention that I was on my way here. Knowing that you like to keep track of your boys, he mentioned to me that he'd had a report come in that Michael Hamilton had been charged with murder."

Jess rubbed a thumb over his chin, wondering why this wasn't making him furious. He hoped it was because he instinctively believed it wasn't true.

"What's the story?" he asked with no apparent concern.

"As I understand it, some guy claims to have been in the outback with Hamilton and several other men, for purposes unknown. A fight broke out, and they say Hamilton shot a man and killed him."

"They? You said there was one."

"There were two witnesses backing him up."

Jess turned abruptly in his chair. He cursed under his breath, then hurried to the door and opened it, shouting, "Alexa!"

"What?" she answered with her hand lifted to knock, startling Jess and making Ira laugh.

"Don't do that to me, woman," Jess insisted. "Get in here." He pulled her into the office and closed the door.

"What's the matter?" she asked, noting that the mood was unusually somber once Ira stopped chuckling.

"You tell her," Jess said to Ira.

"I heard from the constable yesterday that Michael Hamilton is wanted for murder."

Alexa sat down. Jess leaned against his desk, watching her closely for a reaction. He was relieved when she smiled. "That's not possible."

"What makes you so certain?" Ira asked cautiously.

"Ira, I can understand your concern, but I spent most of the morning talking privately with Michael. The man has a clear conscience. He said just recently that he had never killed anyone, and I believe him."

Ira hesitated but said with conviction, "I trust your judgment, Alexa, but that doesn't change the fact that there are three men out there who have testified to the contrary. I'm certain it's not a priority case, but it still means there is a warrant for his arrest. Michael Hamilton is a wanted man. You can understand why my learning he is not only your new administrator, but your daughter's fiancé, would surprise me—to say the least."

Alexa sighed. This was not what they needed right now. "Oh, Jess. What are we going to do?"

"I think we'd better start by talking to Michael."

Ira stood. "I really should be going. I promised Lucy I wouldn't stay. She kind of likes to have me around occasionally. I won't say anything to anybody about this, but it wouldn't hurt to keep an eye on him. If he stays here and minds his business, maybe we can work this out."

"Do you know where we can find someone to represent him in court?" Jess asked with a little smirk, since Ira had once fought in the courtroom on Jess's behalf more than twenty years earlier. His education and experience covered a wide range of legal matters.

"As a matter of fact, I do." He lifted a finger. "But I don't defend guilty men, Jess. If you truly believe he's innocent, I'll take him on. But be careful that you're not being misled. The man has a reputation that's difficult to dispel. A previous prison record already makes him half guilty."

"We'll talk to him," Jess said gravely. "Are you coming back with the . . ."

"Simpkins," he provided. "Yes, I am. We'll discuss it then. In the meantime, if you can produce a witness to his innocence, it could make a world of difference."

"Thank you, Ira." Jess shook his hand.

"We'll see you soon." Alexa nodded. "Be careful going home, now."

"Always." Ira turned to leave. "And thanks for the dinner."

Jess smiled and waved him out of the room. Once alone, his eyes met Alexa's. Neither of them could think of anything to say, but they both moved toward the door in the same instant, knowing they had to get to the bottom of this. They were dismayed when Mrs. Brady reported that Michael and Emma had finished the dishes in no time and had gone out to the stables. Going there, they found Murphy, who reported that they had just ridden off together. "Said they might be back for supper," he added.

Jess and Alexa sighed in unison.

"Is somethin' wrong?" Murphy inquired.

Jess trusted Murphy as much as he trusted himself. The man had been in Davies stables for thirty years. But for Michael's sake, he said nothing. The last thing they needed was negative gossip to add to his already tarnished reputation.

"Nothing that can't wait," Jess said, sensing Alexa's relief at his decision to keep quiet.

"Isn't that something about Hamilton?" Murphy said, and they both held their breath. "His comin' back here and bein' such a changed man and all. Who would have dreamed that Michael Hamilton would marry little Emma?"

"Yes," Alexa smiled, "it's really something."

"Have you had much of a chance to talk to him?" Jess asked.

"A little here and there. Of course he doesn't say much; never did. But the biggest difference I can see is that he seems happy. Likes to laugh, that boy. He's sure perked things up around here."

"Yes," Jess put his arm around Alexa's shoulders and embraced her, "he certainly has done that."

❦   ❦   ❦

Emma challenged Michael to race before they were hardly out of the stable, and she left him in the dust before he had a chance to even think about it. When he finally caught up with her she was laughing intolerably, while the gelding danced beneath her, not anxious to stop and wait for anyone.

"Amusing." Michael drew on his practiced cruel sarcasm. "Very amusing."

"Ooh," she eyed him coyly, "aren't we roguish!"

"Yes," he growled in a husky voice, "I believe we are." He dismounted and tethered the horses before he pulled Emma into his arms. She laughed as he carried her a short distance to a thickening of the trees, where he set her down in a grassy spot and leaned over her with a throaty chuckle. "And like any respectable rogue, I intend to take advantage of your vulnerability and your undeniable attraction to me that leaves you breathless each time I take you in my arms."

Emma laughed. "Have you been reading those books again?"

"Reading them? Hah! They were written about me. You said so yourself. Every hero was me."

"I think that was my own personal touch."

"Close enough." He put his mouth over hers, leaving her breathless. She took his face into her hands and returned his kiss with an ardor that left him equally breathless. "Emma," he growled again, then his expression became serious as he gazed into her eyes. "I love you, Emma. I have always loved you."

"I love you, too, Michael," she whispered, and kissed him again.

Emma lost track of the time as they kissed and held hands and talked, gazing up at the sky through the tree tops. She could almost literally feel this time replenishing all the love and strength that had been drained by the difficulties of the past few days.

"Emma?" Michael asked quietly. "Will you marry me?"

"That is the plan, I believe."

"Just checking," he said and embraced her, feeling as if he didn't have a care in the world.

They rode the long way home, circling around the station and farther away from it in the opposite direction to a spot where Emma dismounted and Michael did the same.

"What is it?" he asked, noting the crumbling foundation of what appeared to have once been a large structure of some sort. But it was now mingling with the ground foliage as if it had been this way for a hundred years.

"This is Byrnehouse," Emma stated. "This was the house where my mother grew up. Our family now owns all of this land."

"I'm aware of that, but exactly how did this great Byrnehouse-Davies alliance take place? From what I understand, it's more than a marriage."

"And more than Father has ever wanted to talk about. All I know is that Tyson Byrnehouse left everything to my father, rather than his son Chad, who died when this house and stables burned to the ground. There is a monument over there." She pointed to a stone marker that resembled a flat gravestone when they got closer. Michael went down on one knee to pull away the weeds and brush off the dirt in order to read aloud: "'Here lies vengeance. May it rest in peace on this land forever.'" Michael leaned back on his heel. "I don't get it."

"Neither do I, but don't bother asking them. They won't tell you."

"Really?" he asked in a tone of challenge as he came to his feet and brushed his hands together. "One of these days they might surprise us."

They arrived at the stables, knowing they were late for supper. "Hurry along," Murphy insisted. "I'll take the horses. And you'd best look out," he called jokingly. "Your parents were out here lookin' for you."

This stopped them mid-stride, and they turned back in question. It wasn't like Jess and Alexa to venture this far—together—looking for anyone. Eventually they always crossed paths in the house.

"When?" Emma called back.

"Right after you left. Hurry up now, and eat some dessert for me."

Emma gave Michael a concerned glance. They hurried inside and washed up in the kitchen before they breathlessly entered the dining room and sat down.

"Sorry," Michael appointed himself the spokesman, "we were loitering at Byrnehouse. Fascinating place, what with all those foundation ruins, and the monument there. Intriguing, isn't it?" He lowered his voice dramatically, "'Here lies vengeance. May it rest in—'"

"We know what it says," Jess interrupted.

"But do we know what it means?" Tyson asked, equally curious over the untold story. By the tension that appeared in their father's eyes each time it came up, it was obviously significant.

"Some of us do," Alexa said easily. Jess glared at her. "Oh, come now, Jess, if you told them how Richard died, what is so awful about—"

"He didn't tell *me,*" Tyson protested.

"I'll tell you later," Jess said tersely.

"It was a long time ago, Jess. You told me you didn't want to tell them when they were children because they wouldn't understand. I think they're now old enough to understand."

"Fine, tell them," Jess said with reluctance.

"All right, I will," Alexa announced, and Michael gave Emma a subtly smug glance. "Your father's brother, Chad, was angry because it was becoming evident that Jess was likely going to end up with everything Chad had been trying to keep from him for years. He set fire to the house and stables, declaring vengefully that if he couldn't have it, Jess couldn't either. He died in the fire."

"No," Jess corrected, "he died in my arms after I dragged him out of the fire."

A reverent hush followed the emotion in Jess's voice, until Tyson caught a discrepancy in the story and felt a need to point it out. "Wait. I thought Chad was *your* brother," he said to his mother. This brought on a deep gaze between Jess and Alexa that didn't go unnoticed.

"Half-brother," Alexa corrected carefully.

"But you just said he was Father's brother," Emma said, pointing out the apparent mistake.

"He was your father's half-brother as well."

Another silence made Michael ask, "Am I the only one lost here?"

"No," Tyson said.

"You've got them itching now," Jess said dryly. "You might as well get it over with."

"Don't you think they've ever wondered why their name is Byrnehouse-Davies?"

"I never thought about it," Jess replied.

"I have," Tyson and Emma said at the same time.

"All I ever cared about was the privilege of having the name," Lacey said, much to everyone's astonishment. It was the first words she'd spoken at the dinner table for two days, and the first civil thing she'd said since Michael Hamilton had shown up.

"The privilege is ours," Alexa said gently. Lacey gave her a redeeming smile.

"Get on with it," Jess insisted.

"From the beginning?"

Jess's voice softened. "Tell them the way you told me, the night you figured it out, looking through the gable window."

"All right." Alexa leaned back and set down her fork. "It started when Benjamin Davies came to Australia, a man with nothing. But he was determined to make something of himself. He homesteaded this land and fell in love with a woman. But her father wouldn't hear of a marriage to a man who had no wealth, so Ben went in search of gold. He returned successful, only to find that this woman had been coerced into marriage with a wealthy young man by the name of Tyson Byrnehouse." At this point, Alexa realized the entire family had stopped eating. There was almost an ethereal enchantment in their faces. Jess just looked sad.

"Benjamin had little choice but to live without her, except that, as far as we understand, she couldn't live without him. They had an affair, but Ben's conscience got the better of him and he turned his back on it. Eventually he found another woman and fell in love. Her name was Emma. But just prior to Ben's planned marriage, Tyson Byrnehouse found out about the affair. He was angry and hurt, and he got drunk."

Michael shifted in his chair, recalling (if only he could) what had happened when he'd gotten drunk from being angry and hurt. Whatever happened had landed him in prison.

Jess came to his feet and moved to the window, stuffing his hands deep into his pockets. It was apparent that he didn't like what was coming. But his children would have never believed what they were about to hear.

"Hours after Ben was married, Tyson Byrnehouse took Emma and . . . he . . . forced himself upon her."

Alexa allowed it to be absorbed while she noted that Jess hadn't even flinched. Tyson took the opportunity to say, "And you named me after this man?"

"The story isn't over yet, my dear," she said gently. "Ben's wife, Emma, whom he had never shared a bed with, became despondent, and helpless as a child. She was emotionally ruined from the experience. She was also pregnant. She had a son that Ben raised as his own. Ben loved the child, raised him well, and gave him everything he had worked so hard to have."

"Including his name," Jess added, and a chorus of heavy sighs made it evident that they had perceived the truth. But he added just to make certain, "If you're going to know, you're not going to have any doubts. I am the product of vengeance. My existence ruined my mother, but I had no idea I wasn't Ben's son until I was eighteen, and he was dead. They gave everything to me." Jess pointed a finger at Michael. "I think about that every time you have questioned my acceptance of you. I haven't given you a tenth of what my father gave to me, which was all produced from life's blood and sweat. And I was not even his son." He waved a hand toward Alexa. "Finish the story."

"We can assume that it was Emma's frailty that prevented her from living a normal married life, which drove Ben back to his first love again. Tyson Byrnehouse's vengeance backfired on him, and many years later, he came to realize that. His regrets moved him to make changes in his life. He became a good and humble man. He was everything I could have ever wanted in a father, and what we shared was good. But he was killed before he could sign the will that resulted from his changed ways. I was eighteen when I discovered that I was not Tyson Byrnehouse's daughter. I was disowned and came to Jess for a job. Some time later we discovered the truth. I am Ben Davies' daughter. Jess is Tyson Byrnehouse's son."

Tyson leaned back. "And that made Chad a half-brother to each of you."

"Exactly. And Chad knew it long before either of us did. He worked diligently for years to destroy your father. When Jess finally came up with the means to turn it back on Chad, he attempted to take us both down with him. It was a miracle that we survived."

"A few months later," Jess said, "Ira Grant showed up to inform us the will had been deemed legal. We inherited the Byrnehouse fortune. At the time, we felt the name Byrnehouse-Davies was appropriate."

"That was the day Tyson and I were born," Emma said, recalling that part of the story.

"That it was." Jess sat back down. "And soon after, Ira moved his family closer, and he's been highly involved in our family businesses ever since."

"Now," Alexa said lightly to him, "that wasn't so painful, was it?"

"Some wounds never heal completely," Jess stated, and Lacey fidgeted in her chair. "Some scars just don't go away," he added, and Michael shifted tensely. "I think our supper's getting cold."

Tyson and Emma exchanged an anxious look, attempting to comprehend what they had just learned of their bloodline and their namesakes. The overwhelming nature of the story left the meal to be finished in taut silence.

Lacey was the first to excuse herself and stand up. "Wait," Alexa stopped her, "we're having a family conference as soon as we're finished here. Don't you want to be there?"

"Not particularly," she said. "I promised Richard a story."

Michael couldn't help but be relieved to have her gone when he felt Jess's eyes fall on him and recalled Murphy saying that Jess and Alexa had been looking for them. Whatever a family conference was, he felt relatively certain that this one was about him.

"What did I do now?" he asked like he had when he was sixteen, and he'd been called into the administrator's office for what seemed the thousandth time to be reprimanded.

Jess stood and moved toward the door briskly. "That's what we're going to find out. I want all of you in the drawing room in five minutes."

Michael looked to Alexa for some reassurance that this was not as bad as it was beginning to feel. But all he read there was concern. Emma's expression was the same as they walked together to the drawing room and were seated.

"What exactly is a family conference?" Michael asked Emma quietly, since Alexa hadn't arrived yet and Tyson was looking at a newspaper.

"When decisions have to be made that affect the entire family. I only remember five in my whole life."

"Wonderful," Michael muttered under his breath, "just wonderful." He tried to think what might have happened between his visit with Alexa this morning, and his going riding with Emma when Jess and Alexa had come looking for them. Something sick began smoldering inside him when he pinpointed it. The solicitor. He'd wager his hundred thousand pounds that Ira Grant had told them something they hadn't known, something they didn't like—which wouldn't be difficult. He knew he had a long list of black marks to choose from.

Michael swallowed hard and was grateful to feel Emma squeeze his hand as Alexa entered and closed the doors. She sat demurely next to Jess and nodded to him like a king might nod to give the command for an execution.

Jess hesitated, and Michael decided he'd plunge in with an attempt to get to the point. "What did Mr. Grant have to say about me?"

Emma was surprised, but her parents didn't seem to be.

"Perceptive as always," Alexa said.

"Before we discuss that," Jess began, "I want to ask you a few questions. I want to say first that I feel it is just as well that Lacey isn't present, considering her current state of mind. But I felt it was important for Tyson to hear this. We could likely use his help."

Emma began to feel a seriousness in this meeting that made her heart quicken. If her parents had accepted and forgiven kidnaping, what would bring on such a formal gathering?

"Go on," Michael urged, wanting to get this over with. "I'm not out to hide anything."

"Good. That should make this easier. First off, I've been wondering exactly what became of the men you hired to assist you in your kidnapping ploy."

Emma didn't know what she'd expected, but it wasn't this. A quick glance at Michael made it evident that he was equally surprised.

"They left," he stated easily. "They just . . . ," he chuckled, "packed up and left."

"Why?" Jess asked carefully.

"You really want to ruin my image with the ladies, don't you, Jess." Michael's humor was appreciated, but it was evident that Jess expected a straight answer. So Michael gave him one. "The general consensus seemed to be that they had earned the advance I'd given them, and they didn't figure they were going to get the rest without trouble. It would seem they were right. They also made it clear that they thought I was going soft." He looked at Emma. "I guess they were right about that, too. The fools didn't appreciate my sense of humor. They did not like my temper. And they called me a coward. That about covers it."

"And every man that went with you left without you?"

"Yes." Michael gave a baffled chuckle. "They all rode out together, and Emma and I were alone long enough for her to redeem me before we started home. That's it. I haven't seen or heard from any of them since, thank heaven. And I can only hope I never do."

"Did any shooting occur while you were out there?" Jess persisted, much like the judge who had landed Michael in prison. At least this time he could remember enough to answer the questions.

"That depends on your definition of shooting," Michael said, attempting to keep a straight face. But Emma giggled, and he couldn't hold back a little smile.

"Either there was shooting, or there wasn't," Jess insisted.

"Yes," Michael sobered, "there was shooting, but no one got hurt. The night before we took the girls, I got up in the middle of the night and reloaded all of the guns with blanks. Even mine. There wasn't a real bullet there—at all." Michael didn't miss the glance that passed between Jess and Alexa. "I had no intention of anybody getting hurt. What happened out there was nothing more than a show. I did and said a lot of stupid things, but nobody got hurt."

"Emma?" Jess obviously wanted her opinion.

"Everything he said is true. All the men who started out with us left together. I was with Michael every minute after that. What is this all about?"

"That's what I'm beginning to wonder," Tyson interjected.

Jess looked at Alexa. As if to answer some silent question, she said with confidence, "I'm sticking with my original opinion. I told you he had a clear conscience."

"I wouldn't go so far as to say that," Michael added. "I've told you the truth, but that doesn't necessarily clear my conscience."

"Is there anything you've done since you were released from prison, kidnapping excluded, that would even remotely be considered breaking the law?"

Michael thought about it to make sure. "No," he said firmly, "I'm clean."

"All right then," Jess said just as firmly, "we're just going to have to find a way to clear your name."

"I'm sorry?" Michael leaned forward. "Clear it of what?"

Jess sighed. "Mr. Grant spoke with the constable before coming here. It seems that someone has accused you of murder."

"No!" Emma clutched Michael's arm as if she might lose him that very minute. "He didn't do it!"

"We've already established that, Emma," Alexa assured her.

Michael was so stunned that he barely heard her. The only thing he could think of was what a pity it would be, after all he'd been through to make a new life for himself, to be sent back to prison for something he hadn't done. He wanted to apologize for bringing this kind of trouble to their home, but he couldn't find his voice.

Emma watched Michael's face turn pale and felt his grip tighten painfully over her hand. She spoke earnestly on his behalf. "We must clear his name. I won't stand for anything less. He has enough to live down without having to live with false accusations. I refuse to let somebody's lies come between Michael and me."

Michael put his arm gratefully around Emma and wiped the tears from her eyes before they fell. He turned to Jess. "Who exactly am I supposed to have killed?"

"I don't know."

"And who exactly is accusing me?"

"I don't know that, either. A man who claims to have been in the outback with you and several other men is saying that a fight broke out and you shot a man. There were two others backing up the story."

"Well, now I know who," Michael said with disgust. "Or at least I can be fairly certain it was the same man who hurt Lacey. His name is Rafe Coogan."

Tyson sat up straighter, feeling a more personal purpose coming into this.

"I beat the tar out of him for what he did. I made a fool out of him more than once. He didn't like me at all, but I didn't care because I didn't like him, either."

"So," Jess leaned back, "if we have established the fact that this is nothing more than a fabrication of lies, our goal here is to prove you innocent. Ira told me he would take your case if I was absolutely certain you weren't guilty. I am. In the meantime, I don't want you leaving my land. You stay out of the public's eye until we can get to the bottom of this, and maybe we can keep you out of jail. Tyson, I'm sending you into town tomorrow to see what you can find out. I want names and specifics so we know exactly what we're dealing with."

"It would be a pleasure," Tyson said with vehemence.

"Michael," Alexa spoke softly, "this doesn't change anything. We consider it a temporary setback, nothing more. We will work together as a family to undo this, and in the meantime, life goes on as normal. Those boys need you, and Emma needs you. Just keep on fighting."

"I don't deserve what you give me," he replied with fervency.

Jess pointed an accusing finger at him. "I talked to you about that at the supper table. Mind what you say, boy. You're not the only one here with scars. Now, tell me what I did to deserve becoming one of the wealthiest men in Australia. I'll tell you what I did: I bet everything I owned on horse races, and had the fortunate privilege of being born out of vengeance. I'm a lucky man, Michael, and I am reminded of that every time I look down the dinner table at my family. You're a lucky man as well. Let's leave it at that and attempt to enjoy life."

"Yes, sir," Michael said like an obedient soldier, and Jess smiled.

"Why don't you get some sleep," Jess added. "I hear from Sarina that the boys were rather a trial today. You'd do well to be prepared to snap them into shape tomorrow."

"That's it," Michael stood with Emma next to him, "turn your boys over to a wanted man with a prison record. That's what they need. Example."

"Get out of here," Jess laughed. Then he sobered when Michael held out his hand in a gesture of appreciation. Jess shook it firmly. "We'll make it through this." He put his other arm around Alexa, who stood beside him. "We've made it through worse."

Sixteen

THE GABLED ATTIC

Emma walked Michael to his room without a word spoken. When he opened the door she asked quietly, "May I come in?"

"I doubt Lacey will come looking for you here." He ushered her inside and found the lamp while she closed the door. "She wouldn't dare venture into the devil's lair."

Their eyes met with a desire to exchange a thousand words. Michael chuckled tensely and looked down, putting his hands behind his back. "Have you begun to regret it yet?"

"What?"

"Bringing me home with you like a stray puppy. I don't think either of us counted on something like this when we agreed to be married."

Emma felt angry. "And if we had, would it have made a difference?" He didn't answer. "Tell me, Michael, is it worth it?"

"You tell me."

"You bet your life it is," she said with clenched fists. "At least to me it is."

"I'm sorry, Emma. Sometimes it's just difficult to believe that I could be worth so much to you."

"I will never stop loving you, Michael, and don't you forget it."

"Just keep telling me."

"I love you, Michael."

"Again."

"I love you. And what about you?"

"I have always loved you, Emma. You have made my life worth living."

"And live we will. We'll clear the charges. Father is right. We'll make it through this together."

"But Emma," he drew a deep breath, "what if we can't? If this backfires, I could end up on the gallows or in prison before we even get to a honeymoon."

"It won't happen," she insisted.

He leaned forward and stated emphatically, "But we have to face the possibility that it might. You can't love a man like me without consequences."

"What is happening here has nothing to do with anything you have done or not done. It's a matter of somebody else's lies."

"Whose lies, Emma? I'm the one who chose to get involved with the scum. I'm the one who pushed the game too far and started the trouble. Maybe I'm getting exactly what I deserve." His voice softened. "I only wish it didn't have to hurt you."

"Michael," she took his hand and pressed it to her face, "we can only go on living and pray that we can undo this. There is no good worrying over it. We must be happy in spite of it."

Michael embraced her as if she might disappear before he found the opportunity again. "I love you, Emma."

"Just keep telling me."

"I love you, Emma."

Emma reached up to kiss him. "Do you want me to leave so you can get some sleep?"

"I couldn't sleep right now if my life depended on it."

"Good." She sat down. "Let's have some of those roguish kisses."

Michael chuckled and knelt down to face her. Leaning toward her, he said with a menacing voice, "I would swear that you're daft, woman. Sometimes I think you actually enjoyed being kidnapped by a scoundrel."

"Oh, I did," she said with enthusiasm. "But only because you were the scoundrel." She pressed her nose to his. "Who could resist such a charismatic kidnapper?"

"You're daft!"

"Yes, I am."

"So, hold still and let me kiss you," he said with perfect cruelty, "or I'll. . ."

Emma giggled and put her lips over his. A knock at the door made Michael groan. "If she has come here looking for you, I will personally . . ." The knock was repeated. "Who is it?" Michael called, still sounding like the kidnapper.

"It's Tyson."

"In that case, you can come in," he called more pleasantly.

Tyson opened the door and stuck his head in. "Who else were you not expecting? Oh, hello, Emma."

Michael turned and motioned him in. "I was afraid your fiancée was coming to slap me around a little." Tyson chuckled and closed the door. Michael leaned back against Emma, and she put her arms around his chest. "Before I tell you to sit down, maybe I should ask if *you* came to slap me around a little."

"I'll protect you," Emma said, tightening her grasp.

"In that case, why don't you sit down, Tyson. Make yourself at home. What can we do for you?"

Tyson sat in a chair near the bed and stretched his long legs, crossing them at the ankles. "I was just wondering if there was anything else you could tell me that might help me out tomorrow."

"I honestly can't think of anything," Michael said regretfully. "I thank you for your confidence in me, Tyson. We can only hope it works out."

"Father did say something more after you left. Apparently Ira mentioned that having a good witness on your behalf would help considerably. It would seem that Emma saw enough to do that."

"I don't know," Emma teased. "Do you think my character could stand up against those esteemed gentlemen testifying against you?"

Michael chuckled. "If they don't take a bath sometime this year, the judge won't get close enough to hear their testimony."

"They sound like nice guys," Tyson chuckled.

"Oh, I tend to draw a crowd suitable to my reputation," Michael said too seriously.

"They were nothing like you," Emma insisted. "At least you bathe regularly."

"Yes, at least I'm a clean criminal."

Tyson stood up. "I think I'll leave the two of you to argue on your own."

"Hold on a minute," Michael said. "Emma, my sweet," he said with a phony smile that made her laugh, "would you spare your brother and me a moment alone? I'm in need of a little male gossip."

"Oh, if I must." She exaggerated a mask of dejection as she stood up. "But don't be talking about me."

She kissed Michael quickly while Tyson said, "What else would we talk about? You know our motto . . ."

They said together, "If you're not here, we're going to talk about you." Emma thought how good it felt to be with Tyson again, sharing things that had once been so common.

"Good night, Michael," she said and kissed him again. "Tyson." She kissed him as well and left them alone.

"What can I do for you?" Tyson asked.

"I'm glad you asked that." Michael motioned to the chair, and Tyson sat back down. "I had every intention of going into town sometime this week to take care of something. But it seems I won't be able to do that. I would be forever indebted if . . ."

"What?" Tyson urged when he hesitated.

"I'm not sure, exactly. Maybe you could help me out on that, too." Michael sat on the bed, leaned against the headboard, and folded his arms. "What exactly does a man need to get married?"

Tyson grinned subtly. "I don't know. I suppose I should be thinking about that, too."

"A wedding ring, perhaps?"

"Good place to start."

"How do you go about finding one that will fit?"

"Oh, that's easy. Mother has rings that Lacey and Emma have worn. I'll borrow them."

"I'll leave the choice up to you," Michael continued. "You likely know Emma better than I do," he smiled, "in most respects."

"Yes," Tyson grinned slyly, "I dare say I can choose an appropriate wedding band, at least. Anything else?"

"A gift, perhaps?"

"Good idea. But what?"

"I don't know," he mused. "What do you think would be appropriate? I'm certain she has everything she wants. What does a man buy for the daughter of Jess Davies?"

"The worth of gifts is in their sentiment. Money is not the issue."

"Good point."

While contemplating the idea, Tyson felt a familiar ache settle in a little deeper. He doubted that any gift would soften Lacey's heart toward him. He was beginning to wonder if they should even marry. The regret involved with that thought made him want to die inside.

Michael was quick to notice Tyson's troubled expression. "Something wrong?"

Tyson looked up, startled. "Same old thing."

"Lacey?" Michael guessed.

Tyson nodded.

"Anything you'd like to talk about—man to man?"

Tyson looked away. "What is there to say?"

"Perhaps I could say that I have wondered if my being here is making a bad situation worse."

"I know Lacey is making all of this more difficult for you, but . . ."

"And for you," Michael said.

"How do you figure?"

"Correct me if I'm wrong, Tyson, or hit me if it's none of my business, but somehow I think I'm involved. From what I see, it's you she hates, and me she's taking it out on."

Tyson turned his head as if he'd been struck. His bottom lip betrayed a barely detectable quiver. "Yeah," he chuckled tensely and pushed a hand through his hair, "I guess you and I are a lot more alike than she realizes."

"How do you figure?" Michael borrowed his phrase.

"We're both doing penance for mistakes committed in ignorance and youthful rage, while no amount of remorse will ever make us worthy of her forgiveness."

"Are you saying that you've resigned yourself to living without her forgiveness?"

"It's either that or live without her."

"And you love her."

Tyson looked at Michael with an intensity that reminded him of Emma. He lifted a hand and curled it into a fist. "I would die for her."

"Then you have to fight for her."

"Fight?" Tyson groaned. "All we do is fight. That is, when we speak at all."

"I didn't say fight with her. I said fight *for* her."

"Expound on that, please," Tyson said like his mother might have.

"I'm not so experienced in these things, Tyson, but I can tell you that when I finally admitted to Emma how I felt about her, I had no intention of pursuing it. I mean, look at me." He held up his hands for emphasis. "Imagine—me—even thinking that I could marry Emma Davies. I told her I couldn't do it. I couldn't come back here and face her family. I couldn't be the kind of man she deserved." Michael chuckled. "Mercy, if she didn't put me in my place. She gave me more of a talking to than your mother ever did."

Tyson smiled, and Michael went on. "And what it all came down to was that she *expected* me to fight. I've been fighting all my life, but I've never had a fight like this one. But she's worth it. For Emma I would fight the world. And yes, like you, I would die for her." Michael laughed again. "I got thinking about that later, and I realized from reading one of those silly books Emma likes that fighting is what it's all about. If women like those books, then it stands to reason they want to know a man cares enough to fight for her."

"All right," Tyson leaned forward, "you're a fighter. You tell me, Michael, how do I fight for a woman who apparently wants nothing to do with me? At least Emma gives you something to reward you for your efforts."

"Do you believe Lacey loves you?"

Tyson thought of the brief glimpses he'd had since his return that made him certain she did. He answered firmly, "Yes. But reaching that part of her isn't easy."

"But I'd say as long as it's there, you can find a way to reach it. Think about how you've reached it before, and . . . Well, let me put it this way: when I've had to fight to survive, literally, I just stuck to a few basic rules. The first is to never take my eyes off my opponent. If you let up for a second, it could be fatal. The second is to find their weakness, and then you pound until they fall."

"You have an interesting way of looking at life, Michael," Tyson chuckled. "But I think I see your point."

"Then fight, Tyson," he said deeply. "I believe she loves you."

"A few minutes ago, you said she hated me."

"They say love and hate are very close in the heart, often divided by a very thin line."

"You're beginning to sound like Emma."

Michael smiled proudly, considering that the greatest of compliments. "I have learned a great deal from Emma."

"That's another thing we have in common." Tyson yawned. "Have you decided yet what you want me to get for Emma?"

"I've been busy. Don't rush me." He thought a minute. "I don't know. I wish I could just . . . well, I can't. But I want to get her something special. I don't know. Maybe I should wait."

"I'll tell you what. If I see something I think is appropriate, I'll get it. If you don't like it, I'll take it back. No loss."

"Fine. But don't forget the ring. I can't get married without a ring."

"Neither can I." Tyson stood and stretched, yawning again.

"You need to get to sleep, boy. Wait, I'll get you some money."

"That's all right," Tyson said. "You can pay me back when I know how much it is. I assume you want the best." He gave an accepting smile. "I assume you can *afford* the best."

"I can," Michael grinned.

"Anything else you want?"

"Nothing I can't live without until I can go myself . . . I hope. About that gift: if all else fails, buy her some lavender shampoo." His eyes brightened. "And you might consider buying some for Lacey, too. She likes to wash her feet in it."

"You're joking."

"I saw it with my own eyes." Michael lowered his voice dramatically. "It might be just the right weakness to start with. Tie her up and wash her feet."

Tyson laughed. "Go to sleep, Michael. You're getting delirious."

"That's true."

Tyson opened the door as Michael said one last thing. "Black. Emma likes black. It reminds her of me and my black heart."

"Go to sleep, Michael." Tyson closed the door, and Michael laughed.

❦ ❦ ❦

Michael awoke late and went without breakfast in order to get to work in time to observe the boys and acquaint himself a little better before they set out to the stables. The morning went by without incident until they were finishing with the horses and preparing to go in for lunch.

"Hold it, Joshua." Michael was proud of himself for getting the name right. "I think you've forgotten something."

"I think it's time for lunch," Joshua retorted.

"Not for you; at least not until you feed that horse."

"I'll feed it later."

Michael took hold of his shirt collar and looked him in the eye. "That animal is dependent on you, which means you will not eat, sleep, or breathe until she is fed, watered, groomed, and sheltered. Do I make myself clear? Feed her now, or I will put her in your room tonight, and you can sleep in her stall."

"Yes, sir." Joshua spat cynically and turned back to grudgingly see to the task. Michael watched him to make sure he did it while the other boys hovered around, impatiently waiting to go and eat.

"Kevin didn't water his horse," Bob volunteered.

"Is that true, Kevin?" Michael asked.

"I did so. Will stole my horse's water for his."

"I did not," Will insisted, and in a split second Will and Kevin were attempting to tear each other apart. Michael broke it up with little effort and pointed a silent, threatening finger at each of them. He double checked to make certain the animals were all cared for, then the group headed for the house, Michael taking up the rear to keep an eye on them. They seemed especially restless today, but he figured they were just loosening up with the change in command. They were testing their limits, as Jess had put it.

Michael saw Walter sidle up to Joshua and whisper something with taunting gestures. Michael couldn't hear him, but he guessed it had something to do with the scolding he'd just gotten concerning the horse.

"You wanna fight about it?" Joshua asked loudly enough for Michael to hear. He didn't step in yet, but he kept a close eye on them.

"No," Walter said without any apology, and Michael felt proud of him.

"You chicken?" Joshua pressed, while Michael wondered how many times he'd said that to other boys in his lifetime. More than he could count.

"No, I just don't wanna fight," Walter insisted, obviously wishing he hadn't started this.

With no warning, Joshua turned and planted a fist against Walter's jaw. With Joshua's six years and about thirty pounds advantage, the blow sent Walter reeling backward to the ground. Walter shook his head enough for Michael to know he was all right as the other boys circled around, expecting a good fight. Michael calmly stepped between the two, facing Joshua straightly, hands behind his back.

"You chicken?" Michael asked.

Joshua hesitated, then said firmly, "No."

"Good," Michael drew back and gave him a fist in the jaw. It wasn't half of what Michael was capable of delivering, but it sent Joshua flat on his backside with a bloody lip. Michael leaned over him, grinning proudly. "Then you won't mind if I toughen you up a bit."

"What did you do that for?" Joshua snapped, touching his lip with a martyrish gesture.

"I was going to ask you the same thing." Michael jerked his head quickly toward the recovering Walter.

"He was bad-mouthin' me."

"And you were bad-mouthin' me back there in the stable. I could have hit you then, but I didn't. So what seems to be the problem?"

Joshua and Walter both came to their feet. No one spoke.

"Well?" Michael shouted, holding his arms up and turning slightly, leaving it open for any one of them to speak.

"Joshua thinks he's so tough," Bob volunteered.

"And what do you think?" Michael bent so close to Bob that the child drew his head back to avoid touching noses.

"I think Joshua's just a chicken."

Michael raised his voice to mimic a gossipy old woman. "I think you're a tattler." Someone chuckled, but when Michael turned, all faces were straight. In silence Michael eyed the group, outwardly daring them to defy him, inwardly wondering what to do now. This cycle of toughness had never done anything to benefit his life. What he saw in these boys was no different from what the boys here had been doing years ago. But he wondered how to break the cycle in a group of life-hardened boys who rightfully believed they could only take on the world by being tough.

Realizing he had to think more on that, Michael decided he had to at least deal with what had just happened. He turned to Walter. "Was it worth it?"

"What?" he snarled.

"Whatever you had to say to Joshua must have been pretty important to risk that bruise on your face. I just want to know if it was worth it."

"No," he admitted sheepishly.

"Then perhaps you'll remember from now on that if something good isn't going to come out of your mouth, don't open it."

"Yes, sir."

With that, Michael turned to Joshua and posed the same question. "Was it worth it?"

"He was bad-mouthin' me," Joshua repeated, attempting to justify his actions.

"Let me bad-mouth you a little, and let's see you call me a chicken." Michael slammed his fist into his other palm.

"That's not fair."

"Fair?" Michael laughed, then he nearly touched Joshua's nose with his. "And why is that? You're young and strong. Seventeen years old. Prime of life. Muscles from all that hard work you do on other kids' faces. I'm an old man. Come on, Josh. Take me on. Let's see who's tougher."

"I said it's not fair," Joshua shouted. It seemed he really wondered if this Mr. Hamilton was going to beat him into the ground.

"Why not?" Michael straightened and asked more softly.

"You're a better fighter."

"You'd better believe it, boy," Michael agreed proudly while an idea lit up inside his head. "So, I'll tell you what we're going to do about—"

"Mr. Hamilton!" Sarina called from the distance.

He sighed and rolled his eyes. "What is it?" he called back.

"Lunch is getting cold. Let's get those boys in here."

Michael wanted to argue, certain that what they were doing was more important than food at the moment. But arguing with Sarina in front of them would accomplish nothing.

"Get out of here," he ordered, and they all walked away—very briskly, he noticed.

Michael followed more slowly, stopping for a minute to contemplate the situation. He wondered: if he had found the opportunity to let go of his pain and get rid of his tough exterior at a younger age, would he have been so misguided as an adult? He couldn't question the methods he'd been raised with here, and Alexa had certainly tried to get him to face it. But he was finding a new insight that perhaps only someone with his background could see. He wondered briefly how the other adults might view his methods, but he felt enough confidence in what he was trying to achieve that he didn't concern himself over that.

With a sense of purpose, Michael ambled into the cafeteria and was immediately approached by an angry Sarina. He saw all eyes follow her curiously and managed to stop her with a quick, "If you have something to say to me, you will say it outside."

She walked into the hallway and he followed, closing the door behind him.

"Is it true that you just hit that young man?"

"Yes, ma'am, I did," he said proudly.

"For what purpose?" she demanded, but she didn't give him a chance to respond. "Those boys have had more than enough of such things in their lives. Senseless violence will accomplish nothing when—"

"Miss Sarina," Michael said firmly enough to stop her, "I am as opposed to senseless violence as anyone. But I had good reason to do what I did, therefore it was not senseless. I had a point to make, and I made it in a way that was clearly understood. If you have a problem with my methods, I suggest you speak to Mr. Davies. I will deal with him."

Michael stepped back into the cafeteria and shouted with a grating voice, "There will be no sports time, reading time, or whatever other time you might be having the remainder of the day. I want every

one of you standing at attention in this hall in twenty minutes. Be prepared to be gone a good, long while." He gave Sarina a sinister glow-
er and walked briskly down the hall.

"Please let this work," he prayed aloud, knowing he'd have the
devil to pay if it didn't.

❦   ❦   ❦

Emma was disappointed not to see Michael at breakfast, but she
knew he had work to see to. She went to the stables after she'd eaten,
longing for the day when they could respectfully share a bedroom and
never miss a morning of seeing each other before the day began. She
entered to find Tyson just stepping into the stirrup.

"Going into town now?" she asked, knowing he was by the way he
was dressed. He'd never wear his best hat and a tweed waistcoat to
enjoy a casual ride.

"Yes." He situated himself in the saddle. "And I'm glad you're here.
There's something I want to ask you."

"All right."

"I was thinking of getting a wedding gift for Lacey." He bent over
and leaned an arm on his thigh in order to look at her closely. "What
would you suggest?"

"Something sentimental," she said right off. "Something you can
always look at and be reminded of what binds you together."

Tyson scowled. The suggestion might help in choosing Michael's
gift, but he had to admit, "I'm not sure anything binds us together
right now except Richard."

Emma shrugged her shoulders and Tyson rode away. She helped
on the track for a while, then took one of the racers out for a run. On
her way back to the house, she caught a glimpse of Michael with the
boys, but she chose not to distract him. He looked rather involved.

❦   ❦   ❦

Michael went to the main dining room and quickly wolfed down
some lunch. He announced to Alexa that he might not be in for supper,
and told her to give Emma his regards and not to worry. Then he added

to Jess, "If Sarina comes to you any time today with horror stories about me, tell her I'm the most wicked man alive and I intend to sacrifice each of these children to the great pyramid god of the southern land." He pointed a vicious finger. "But not before I cut off their toes."

Jess widened his eyes and laughed. "I'll do that."

"But we don't have any pyramids in Australia," Alexa said, feigning innocence.

"Exactly!" Michael said. "But how long will it take Sarina to figure that out?"

"Enjoying your job, Michael?" Jess added.

"Quite," Michael grinned.

"I'll give Sarina the message," Jess called as Michael left the room hastily.

He found all seventeen boys lined up in the hall as ordered, Sarina gazing on dubiously. He politely said to her, "Mr. Davies would like to see you."

Sarina huffed away and left him to his business.

Michael quickly took the entire group out to the stables so that the boys who hadn't yet cared for their horses today could take care of them. When that was finished, he escorted them back inside.

"Now." Michael paced slowly back and forth, his hands behind his back, like the miser he was trying to be. "Those of you who weren't present at our little party a while ago should have at least heard about it. Is there anyone who hasn't?" No one moved. "Good. I hate to repeat myself." He stopped and looked them over carefully. He was certain that a few of these boys didn't need this exercise, but he couldn't separate them fairly, so they'd have to suffer through. And hopefully they would all benefit in one way or another.

"With that out of the way," he announced, "let's get down to business." He pointed toward the stairs. "The attic," he ordered, and they all moved in that direction like lambs to the slaughter.

Michael was the last one into the room. He turned back and locked the door with a key. It was hot and stuffy so he ordered, "Open those windows, then everybody get comfortable." He pointed to the pile of blankets in the corner. With expert stalling tactics, they managed to take a ridiculous amount of time to spread them out and sit in a haphazard circle around him.

"No," he decided, "I want you all against that wall." He wanted to see all of their eyes at once. "No," he said again when they were situated. He was thoroughly enjoying beating them at their own game of stalling. "Back in the circle. I'll sit here." He plopped himself onto the floor, folded his arms and stretched out his legs, crossing them casually.

"Ya wanna blanket to sit on?" little Michael asked.

"No, thank you, Michael. I'm fine." He rewarded the boy with a genuine smile, almost wishing he could betray what he knew was going to happen in the child's life very soon.

"All right," Michael stated, "we are here to find out who's the toughest. It seems to be a constant topic of conversation, and I'm getting sick of hearing about it. I know what's going through your minds. You're thinking I've only been here a couple of days. How could I be sick of it? Well, that's none of your business. I'm sick of it, and that's all that matters. Understand? So, we will not leave this room until we know beyond a doubt who is the toughest."

"How we gonna do that?" asked Toby.

"How do you think we should do it, Toby?" Michael retorted.

"I guess we fight it out."

"Hmmm," Michael contemplated, "I suppose we could do that. What do you think, Walter?"

"I don't think it would be fair."

"Why isn't it fair, Joshua?"

Joshua was obviously not pleased to be called on, but he answered dutifully, "Because we're not all the same."

"Brilliant." Michael's face filled with exaggerated enlightenment. "Why are we not all the same?"

"Some of us are older and bigger," Matthew provided.

"Thank you, Matthew. It seems I can depend on your intelligence."

"I could beat you up," Toby said to Matthew, who was his senior by seven years.

Matthew rolled his eyes but said nothing.

"Could you beat me up?" Michael asked Toby.

"I'd sure as heck try," Toby sneered.

"That's 'cause you didn't see him punch out Joshua," Bob offered.

"And watch your language." Michael pointed at Toby.

"So, we gonna fight it out then?" Kent asked. Michael didn't answer right away, and eyes began darting around the circle carefully, as if they wondered if this Mr. Hamilton was going to provoke them into some great fighting match. Some of them were almost itching for it. Others obviously wanted to be somewhere else.

"What do you think, Michael?" he asked the littlest of the group.

"I don't think it would be fair."

"All those who say that fighting wouldn't be fair, raise your hands." It was immediately unanimous. "All right, if it isn't fair here and now, why is it fair in the stable yard?" No one answered. "I'm sorry?" Michael put a hand to his ear. "I can't hear you." Still not a sound. "What? No smart remarks? No jests? No one calling me a chicken?" He folded his arms. "Mercy, didn't I shut you up!"

Michael leaned forward. "If we can't fight it out, then how do we decide who's toughest? Think hard, boys, because I want a good answer."

After a reasonable silence, Michael was surprised for more than one reason when Jack, who'd not said a word in his presence so far, stated blandly, "Whoever has the most scars."

Michael gave a questioning look heavenward, wondering if his feeble prayers were being heard. Not only was he finding the correct keys and remembering the boys' names, but this was actually going exactly the way he had hoped—even sooner than he'd expected. If nothing else, he could certainly prove a good point with this one. Scars were something he knew about.

"That sounds interesting," Michael said. "Any comments?"

"I got a good one," Christian volunteered, and pulled up his pant leg while Michael fought to keep a straight face. "I got this one when a crocodile bit me when I was eleven."

"Christian?" Michael implied doubt by his tone. He considered himself skilled in calling out liars, and little of what he'd heard Christian say in their brief acquaintance had resembled the truth.

"I did," Christian insisted.

The boys moved closer to have a look, and for the next hour, Michael sat back and observed a humorous display of battle wounds. Broken arms, broken noses, broken legs, and broken toes. Burns and cuts and animal bites, all displayed proudly to the other boys. Michael found it was a good release of tension. But his heart fell to the pit of his stomach when his attention turned to the ones not participating. He wasn't concerned about little Michael, who was watching with amused interest, likely too young to have had the opportunity for many boyish accidents. Kit also observed silently, but he was a gentle boy, and likely hadn't had a desire to participate in the foolish things that brought on boyish accidents. But Kit's expression was also amused and interested. And then there was Toby. Michael watched him and wanted to die inside.

When little Michael Hamilton had been brought here at a young age, if such a discussion had come up, and gratefully it hadn't, he would have looked exactly like that. Arms folded tightly, eyes glazed over with cold fear, jaw tight and hard. And Michael knew why. Scars resulting from fighting or accidents or animal attacks were battle scars to be hailed. To a young boy, they were signs of exactly what they believed they were proving now: toughness. But scars inflicted by someone else's cruelty were ugly and scornful, hurting more from the inside out. Michael felt compassion and complete empathy for Toby; for the boy's sake, he wished this wasn't happening. Then he stopped to wonder: if it had happened to him as a child, would he have dealt with it then and avoided hurting so much as an adult?

"Have you decided yet?" Michael asked, keeping half an eye on Toby.

"I think Christian has the most scars," Matthew announced.

"I think Christian is the clumsiest," Michael said lightly, and was pleased to hear them all laugh. All but Toby.

"So why do scars have anything to do with how tough we are?" Michael asked.

"Because they show you've been hurt the most," Kent said. Or was it Kevin?

"Good point." Michael shrugged. "But aren't there ways of being hurt that don't leave scars?"

"You mean like bruises that go away?" Bob asked.

"Yes," Michael agreed, "and also things that hurt in here." He pressed his hand over his chest. The boys didn't seem to completely understand, although he caught a glimmer of comprehension in a few of them. He moved along. "I think there is more to being tough than having scars," Michael said. "Any other ideas?"

"Being tough is not being afraid of anything," Reynold insisted.

"Are you afraid of anything?" Michael came back.

"No."

Michael shot to his feet, grabbed Reynold by the shirt, and drew back a fist as if he might strike him. Reynold made no sound, but his arms went up and he recoiled with a grimace. "Scared you, didn't I," Michael said, relinquishing his hold and returning nonchalantly to his place on the floor.

"What's your point, Mis-ter Hamilton?" Reynold asked, still on his feet.

"My point is this." Michael became as severe as he could manage. "Being tough hasn't got a blasted thing to do with scars, or power, or fighting, or fear. Being tough is having courage."

"Isn't courage what it takes to fight and—"

Michael interrupted Matthew. "I don't know. You tell me."

"Tell you what?"

"Does it take courage to fight?"

"Yes," Joshua insisted.

"And I say you're wrong." Michael pointed that menacing finger.

"And what do you know about courage?" Reynold sneered.

"You really want to know?"

"Yeah," several answered in unison.

"I learned about courage the hard way. I grew up in this room." A hush fell over the group. "You didn't know that, did you. Well, I did. I was sent here nearly every day for seven years, because hardly a day went by when I didn't beat somebody up, and I was good at it. I was tough!"

"You still are," Roy interjected.

"Thank you," Michael smiled.

"But you just told us that courage didn't have anything to do with fighting."

"And it doesn't. One day, not so long ago, I did the hardest thing I ever did in my life. Can you guess what it might be?" No one volunteered. "It wasn't beating somebody up. That's easy. What I had to do took more courage than I had ever mustered up in any fight, even the ones I lost."

Seventeen pair of expectant eyes hung on his words.

"I had to admit I'd been wrong. I had to restrain myself from hitting someone because I knew it wouldn't do any good, and I had to tell someone—someone I want to like me—that I was afraid."

"Sounds like a wimp to me," Toby shot out, still maintaining his hardness from the scars discussion.

Michael gave a quick chuckle. "Yes, it does, doesn't it. But I'll bet nobody here is brave enough to admit they're afraid."

Michael let silence drill in the question, though he doubted it meant much to them at this point. He expected it would take time and some examples to prove all he was telling them.

"I'm afraid of the dark," little Michael said softly. Michael wanted to hug him, but he only smiled in acceptance. Did the child know the ice he had just broken?

"So am I," Michael replied. "Why are you afraid of the dark?"

Little Michael looked around skeptically, and Michael saw him gathering courage. "Because it was dark when my mother died."

"Did the dark take your mother?" Michael asked, fighting the urge to get choked up.

"No, she just died."

"Then is it the dark you're afraid of, or death? Or do you just miss your mother?"

"All of it." Little Michael's eyes filled with tears, but he was quick to wipe them away.

"You're not afraid to cry, are you?" Michael challenged in the same tone he had called Joshua a chicken.

The child let a sob rise, and tears spilled.

"There," Michael motioned toward little Michael with pride, "is our champion. The toughest boy here."

"How do ya figure?" Joshua challenged belligerently.

"Because he's not afraid to admit that he hurts; to admit he has fears, and to cry in front of a bunch of hard-hearted fools who will likely call him a crybaby for the rest of his life because they're too cowardly to admit that they have fears and hurts, too."

Michael looked around the room, wondering where those words had come from. For the first time since he'd come face to face with these boys, all eyes were the same. There was no pain, no fear, no skepticism, no timidity. They were all just open wide, trusting, receptive.

They all looked to him expectantly. He had opened a very big, heavy door. Now it was up to him to lead them through it. At this moment, his biggest fear was that any one of them would reach maturity without having the opportunity to cry over the pain, without learning to trust, without being able to accept love when it was offered, and without learning how to give it in return.

"Well," he finally said, "is there anyone here as tough as little Michael?"

Roy spoke up first, admitting that he feared having to go back to the home where his mother was a prostitute, and he'd had to hide in the cellar most nights while she entertained her guests. Michael gave him ample opportunity to talk it out. They discussed the fears that had no warrant, and they talked about facing the ones that did. Gene was next with an admission that he feared horses, and their time in the stables was difficult for him. Michael helped him formulate a plan to work on it, one step at a time. One by one, each boy admitted his deepest fear, and Michael attempted to make a beginning at working them through. Toby was the only exception, still insisting that he wasn't afraid of anything. Michael passed over him. Matthew was the last to speak.

"I'm afraid of you, Mr. Hamilton."

Michael lifted a brow. "Do you think I would hurt you?"

"No," the seventeen-year-old stated. "What I mean is . . . I'm afraid you know something we don't know . . . about the world; something that we ought to know. I'm afraid you won't tell us before I have to leave."

Michael was touched by his roundabout way at insight. "I've already told you. If you're going to make it out there, you have to have the courage not to fight, except in self-defense. And the courage to admit when you make a mistake, and the courage to feel—not hide from your feelings. It's not me you fear, Matthew. It's the world. And we all know it's not such a great place. There is good out there, boys, and you can learn to find it. But you can only find it if you're willing to give it. People who fight their way through life only end up battered and broken."

"What are you afraid of?" Toby asked Michael. Hard skepticism had returned to his eyes.

"I'm afraid of you, Toby."

The answer apparently threw him off, since he said nothing in reply.

"Why are you afraid of Toby?" Roy asked, genuinely curious.

"Because he's a lot like me."

"Are you afraid of yourself?" little Michael asked, puzzled.

"Not anymore. But I used to be." He looked directly at Toby. "It took me a long time to realize that there was nothing wrong with me. The reason I had so many scars was because somebody else had something wrong with them. Something terribly wrong."

Toby's shoulders slumped forward and his eyes narrowed. Michael knew he was on the right track, and he wasn't willing to let it go just yet. It wasn't going to be easy on Toby, but it was far better that he face it now than wait until he was twenty-eight—or never. Their eyes met in a battle of wills, and Michael knew there was only one way to win his complete trust. Toby's problem was different from the others, and he needed to know that he wasn't alone. With a pretense of changing the subject, Michael turned his eyes away and said lightly to Christian, "You think you've got the most scars, eh?"

"You said I was the clumsiest," Christian replied proudly, and got a laugh out of the others as his reward.

"At least your scars are your own responsibility."

"Or stupidity," Matthew said and the boys laughed again—except Toby, who wore an expression of cold fear. Michael knew he was sensing something significant, but the fear of facing whatever it might be was likely intolerable at the moment.

On that light note, Michael announced with a smile, "You haven't seen my scars yet."

"You got one for every fight you lost?" Joshua asked without malice. His eyes sparkled with friendly humor.

"Actually," Michael started unbuttoning his shirt as he came to his feet, "I got these before I ever started fighting." He drilled his eyes into Toby's as he pulled the shirt from his arms and tossed it aside. He held up his arms and turned. A dumbfounded silence enveloped the room. Mouths fell open. Expressions filled with shock. Toby's eyes filled with tears.

"My father did this to me," Michael said, "before I was Alan's age."

He pointed to the eight-year-old, then picked up his shirt and put it back on. "And the hardest day of my life was when I had to admit that it had hurt, that I wasn't so tough, and it's not so easy to have scars that you aren't proud of. But I know now that it's all right to have them. The people who love me, love me in spite of them—perhaps more because of them." He paused to absorb the profound silence.

"Mercy, it's getting late." Michael noted that the room was becoming dim. "Should we go back? We're probably missing supper." No one answered. "Want to stay a while longer?" They all nodded eagerly.

"Tell us what it was like here when you were a boy," Will requested.

Michael lit a lamp and began telling stories from his boyhood. He soon had them talking and laughing over the good times they had experienced here, and they admitted among themselves something else Michael hadn't been able to see until recently: that the opportunity to be raised here was a blessing. In the gabled attic, Michael watched in awe as this handful of tainted lives became positive and humble. When a brief lull finally came, Michael turned to Toby, who had been observing silently. "You still haven't told us what you're afraid of, Toby."

For a moment, Michael feared he wouldn't answer. He shifted his attention briefly to little Michael, who moved closer and laid his head down in Michael's lap. Michael patted the boy's shoulder and watched him relax, then he looked back at Toby.

"I'm afraid my father will find me here and make me go back," Toby said with a quivering chin. Something inside Michael's head exploded, though he fought to keep his expression steady. Toby's father. Rafe Coogan. Michael's heart pounded into his throat. He had every reason to believe that Rafe was behind this murder charge, but he'd been so caught up in his anger that he'd forgotten all about Rafe's relation to Toby. Michael thought of his own father, and it made him want to kill Rafe Coogan with his bare hands. What kind of man would inflict such horrible hurt on a child? Michael felt the deepest kind of regret as he recalled Rafe telling him about the boy he wanted to get back. Rafe's interest in helping Michael with the kidnapping venture had been mostly due to the Byrnehouse-Davies connection to the boys they were harboring. And now Michael hoped with all his might that his own mistakes would not indirectly bring harm to Toby. He thought of Jess's confessions concerning his own father, and with full sincerity he finally answered Toby, "He would have to kill me first."

Toby only hesitated a moment before he nearly flew to Michael, wrapping his arms possessively around him, sobbing against his chest. Michael held him and found it impossible to keep from crying, for himself as much as for Toby. The child asleep in his lap was oblivious to the drama, but the others slowly moved closer, seeming to want some of the closeness they were witnessing. Michael reached out a hand, and Kit took it and squeezed. Michael took another hand, then another. He touched their faces and wiped their tears. And when they were all huddled together, they laughed. They laughed until they cried some more.

Exhaustion made them all want to sleep, but no one seemed to want to leave, as if doing so might break the spell. Michael lay back on one of the blankets and situated little Michael's head against his belly. Toby laid a head on Michael's shoulder and kept an arm around him. From there, the chain moved out in every direction. The boys used each other for pillows and eventually fell asleep, sprawled over the floor of the gabled attic.

Seventeen
STRATEGY

When supper began without Michael, Emma asked what she had been wondering all afternoon. "Has anyone seen Michael?"

"I believe he's with the boys," Jess answered. "He told us to tell you. Said he might miss supper." Jess smiled apologetically. "Sorry, I forgot to mention it."

"Just so I know he's all right," she said. "I assume Tyson isn't back yet."

"Haven't seen him," Jess said. "I hope he found out something that will help us."

"I believe he was going to do a little shopping, as well," Alexa added.

"For what?" Lacey spoke up for the first time today.

"I can't say." Alexa smiled conspiratorially.

"He could be gone for hours yet," Lacey added. "He never could make up his mind when it came to buying things."

"That's true," Emma said, feeling the first sign of warmth from Lacey since they had returned. Perhaps it was the absence of Tyson and Michael in the presence of their parents.

"Are you feeling all right, Lacey?" Alexa asked gently. "Perhaps we could go for a walk later, and—"

"I'm fine," Lacey insisted.

The remainder of the meal passed in silence. Emma missed Michael, but she tried not to let on as they went to the drawing room for coffee. She knew she wasn't doing a very good job of acting indifferent to his absence when Lacey said with a joking voice and bitter eyes, "Maybe he ran away."

"Amusing," Emma retorted in a sarcastic tone she'd learned from Michael.

The front door opened and closed. With every hope that it was Michael, Emma still wasn't disappointed to see Tyson enter the drawing room.

"You're home safe," Alexa said. "Good."

"How did it go?" Jess asked.

"Not so bad, I suppose." Tyson sat down and fanned his hair by blowing air from his bottom lip. He set some small packages on the floor and put his hat on top of them.

"Tell us what you found out," Jess prodded. "Do I have to squeeze it out of you?"

"A body was brought in by three men. The spokesman was a . . ." Tyson pulled a note out of his pocket. Lacey perked up curiously, just now recalling that she'd missed the family conference. "A Rafe Coogan."

"We figured that," Jess said. "Go on."

"What are you talking about?" Lacey insisted. "That was the man who . . . who . . ."

"We know, Lacey," Alexa said gently. "I'll catch you up later." Alexa motioned for Tyson to go on.

"The man killed was middle-aged, said to have been in and out of jail for the last forty years. When he was out, he made a living as a cook."

"Oh, no," Emma interjected, realizing who they were talking about. She had actually liked the man. "Not Corky?"

"His name was Corky Patterson," Tyson stated, astonished by her reaction.

"Oh," Lacey said matter-of-factly, "that's the man Michael shot in the head."

Stunned silence filled the room. Tyson finally asked, "You saw it?"

"No, but I heard it," she said just smugly enough to make Emma want to hit her.

"Wait a minute," Emma moved to the edge of her seat, "I think that—"

"Hold on, Emma." Jess held up a hand. "One at a time. I want to hear what Lacey has to say. What exactly did you hear, darling?"

"There was arguing outside the tent where Emma and I were . . . well, I don't remember what we were doing exactly. We heard Michael order somebody to his knees, then he said something about removing a hat, then a gun fired twice. After that Michael said, 'Get him out of here.'"

Jess and Alexa looked at each other, stunned and distressed.

"May I speak now?" Emma asked.

"If you'll start by answering a simple question," Jess said severely. "Lacey just said *we*. Did you hear what she heard?"

"Yes," Emma answered straightly, and all eyes but Lacey's went wide. "But that's just it: we didn't see it. I thought what Lacey thought. I was so upset I wanted to die. But you must remember what Michael said last night. The guns were loaded with blanks. It was all a setup; an act."

"I can't believe you're saying this." Lacey became visibly upset. "How can you sit there and defend him, when—"

Emma spoke to her father. "I saw Corky alive after that. The day Lacey was returned to you, I spoke with him. I told him I was surprised to see him alive. He laughed and told me they had just been having a little fun. He said, and I quote," she attempted to mimic the cook, "'Mike Hamilton wouldn't shoot a wallaby.'"

Tyson chuckled, and Lacey glared at him.

"You're certain?" Jess asked.

"Absolutely positive. It's as we said last night: every man we started out with was accounted for and alive. They left together the same day Lacey was returned to you."

Alexa sighed audibly. "I think I feel better now. That was a scare. I would hate to think we had misjudged him to that extent."

"Amen," Jess chuckled.

"I can't believe this." Lacey came to her feet in anger. "I cannot believe how thoroughly he has fooled every single one of you. The man is a cold-hearted fiend."

"Lacey." Alexa rose and attempted to touch her shoulder, but she recoiled and moved toward the door.

"You're all a bunch of blind fools. But one of these days his past is going to catch up with all of us, and his real character will come through. I only hope we all survive that long." She left the room and slammed the door. The family winced in unison.

Realizing there was little to be done about Lacey's opinions, Jess attempted to get back to his original purpose. "Did you find out anything else?"

"Only that they don't have a clue where Michael is. Apparently these thugs said nothing about the kidnapping, or I figure they would have asked me about it. I simply pretended that you had sent me to inquire because you were concerned and wanted to help. From the way they talked, I think the last place they would expect to find him is here."

"Good," Jess said. "Let's hope it stays that way."

"Where's Michael?" Tyson asked, anxious to show him his purchases.

"That's what I'm beginning to wonder," Emma admitted. "Isn't it past time for the boys to be in bed?"

"I believe so."

With impeccable timing, Sarina timidly peered into the drawing room. "Excuse me, Jess," she said, "but I seem to have misplaced seventeen boys."

Jess came to his feet, pretending not to be concerned. "Where have you looked?"

"Nowhere. I just know they didn't come to supper, and they're not in their rooms or the library. I was hoping you'd know where they are."

"At the moment, no. But I know Michael is with them, so I wouldn't be too concerned."

"After that speech you gave me earlier?" Sarina said skeptically.

"Where's your sense of humor, Sarina?" Jess laughed. "Come along. Let's go find them. Where do you think they might be, Alexa?" he added, noting her expression.

"That's easy," she said. "I would start by looking in the gabled attic."

"That's logical," Jess said, and followed Sarina and Alexa into the hall. Emma was close behind.

"You coming?" she asked Tyson.

"I might as well." He took Emma's hand and they walked together, holding back enough to speak privately.

"What did you get for Lacey?" Emma asked.

"I'm not telling," he grinned.

"Why not?" she asked with exaggerated disappointment.

"Because Michael got you the same thing. That's why not."

"Michael got me a present?" she squealed quietly.

"Unless he doesn't like it, then I'll have to take it back."

"Oh, don't do that."

"I shouldn't have even said anything." Tyson nudged her shoulder with his arm to set her off balance. "You'd better keep quiet, or he'll never trust me again."

"All right. I'll act surprised."

They arrived at the attic door and they all waited while Jess tried the knob and found it locked. He located the key and turned it in the lock, then slowly pushed the door open.

"I don't believe it," Jess chuckled quietly. Sarina pushed past him and gasped, as if she feared they were all dead. The others moved into the room, where they all stopped to gaze in amazement.

It was Emma who finally broke the silence. "Isn't he adorable?"

"Which one?" Tyson nudged her again with his elbow.

"The tall one there, in the middle, with the mustache. I wonder if he'd marry me if I asked him."

"Don't count on it," Tyson went along. "I hear he's a rogue."

"Oh, I hope so."

Fortunately, Sarina and their parents appeared oblivious to the conversation. "But they didn't have any supper," Sarina protested quietly once she was assured that they were all sleeping soundly, and all heads were accounted for.

"I'm certain they'll eat a hearty breakfast." Jess patted her patronizingly on the shoulder and ushered her from the room. "Let them sleep."

Michael stirred at the sound of voices and lifted his head. "Hello, Emma," he said, focusing on the face he loved. Then he smiled, as if it was perfectly normal to be found this way. "Did we miss supper?"

"Quite," she smiled.

"We were worried," Sarina insisted.

"I wasn't worried," Jess added.

"Shhh," Emma whispered, "you'll wake them."

"I was teaching them how to be tough," Michael explained through a yawn.

"I can see you were successful." Jess glanced at the two boys firmly attached to Michael, who gently tousled their hair.

"I'll tell you about it in the morning," Michael said, and laid his head back down. Jess reached for the light and Michael added, "Oh, don't do that." He closed his eyes as he finished, "We're afraid of the dark."

"I suppose we can all go to bed now," Jess announced.

Sarina sighed and went one direction down the hall. Jess and Alexa bid them good night and went the other.

Tyson and Emma talked for a while before she went up to her room and was quickly in bed. Her mind went to Michael, and she smiled to recall how they had found him this evening. What a man! She was proud to claim him. "He's so adorable," she said aloud, then she drifted to sleep.

Emma awoke the next morning and went to find Michael's room still empty. She went down to breakfast, hoping he'd be there. But his chair remained empty through the meal.

"Do you suppose Michael's still asleep in the attic?" Tyson asked, coming in only a few minutes later.

"He did appear rather worn out," Alexa commented lightly.

When the meal was finished, Tyson announced, "I'm going to see if I can track Michael down and let him know what I found out yesterday."

"Can I come?" Emma hurried through her last two bites.

"You might as well." He held out his hand. "He's not my fiancé. Lacey?" he added, and she coughed. "Want to come?"

"No," she smiled with her mouth full, "I think I'll pass." She swallowed. "I could likely live without seeing the esteemed Mr. Hamilton this morning."

"It's your loss," Emma quipped.

Tyson tugged on Emma's hand and followed her into the hall.

They went first to the gabled attic and found it empty and in order. They next tried the cafeteria and found the boys all eating ravenously and in good spirits.

"Can I help you?" Sarina called.

"Just looking for Mi—" Tyson began, but Emma nudged him and he finished, "uh . . . Mr. Hamilton."

"You barely missed him. He went to his office, I believe."

"Thanks." Tyson waved and Emma eagerly led the way, feeling the intensity of how much she'd missed him yesterday. How was it possible for two people to be living in such close proximity and never see each other?

Emma knocked on the door and immediately heard him call, "Come in."

Emma pushed it open and peered in. Seated in the chair behind the desk was one of the older boys, and sitting on the edge of the desk, with his back to her, was Michael. He turned to look over his shoulder and gave a pleasurable smile. "Hello, Miss Davies."

"Hello," she replied brightly. "Am I interrupting something?"

"No." He stood. "I think Matthew and I are finished for now." The boy came to his feet, and Michael gave him a friendly slap on the shoulder. "You remember what I said, now. We'll talk more later."

"Thanks, Mr. Hamilton." The boy nodded sheepishly at Emma and brushed past her.

"Oh, Matthew," the boy turned back, "have Miss Sarina save me some breakfast, will you?"

"Sure thing."

When the boy was gone, Emma motioned Tyson back into the hall before Michael saw him, and he knew she wanted to give Michael a proper greeting in private.

"Emma," Michael spoke with a trace of passion, "you shine like the stars on a moonless night."

"A poet now, are we?" She smiled up at him.

"No acting. Just pure feelings." He bent to kiss her, and Emma nearly melted. "I've missed you," he whispered.

"Not as much as I've missed you," she insisted. "Maybe that's why Father gave you this job—to keep us chaste and humble."

Michael chuckled and kissed her again, wanting to never let her go. He was still on an emotional high over his experience with the boys, and Emma's kiss was like icing on the cake.

Tyson cleared his throat loudly, and Michael looked up to see him leaning against the doorframe. "What do you want, Davies?" he snarled wickedly, and Emma laughed.

"My brother is here to protect me."

"Tell him to find his own woman."

"I'm working on that." Tyson came into the room and sat down.

"Do you have any news?" Michael's tone sobered. He sat on the corner of the desk and kept Emma's hand in his.

"Not a great deal. But the man doing the accusing is who you suspected." Michael scowled and Tyson added, "The dead man is Corky Patterson."

"Idiotic fools," Michael muttered under his breath. "They probably killed him because he actually liked me. He was the only one in the bunch who appreciated my sense of humor."

"And he was an excellent cook," Emma said sadly. "Poor man."

"Anything else?" Michael asked.

"They have no idea where you are, and we'll just hope it stays that way. Ira's supposed to be back here later this week; we'll tell him what we know then. In the meantime, I guess we try not to think about it."

"We'll plan a wedding instead," Emma said lightly. "Mother and Lacey and I are going into town tomorrow to make arrangements."

"How quaint." Michael squeezed her hand.

Matthew knocked on the open door and entered with a breakfast tray for Michael. "Thank you, my boy. I may get to eat after all."

"It was Michael's idea," Matthew said as he set the tray on the desk.

"The child's a genius. Tell him thank you from the bottom of my heart."

"You're a strange man, Mr. Hamilton." Matthew gave him a quirky smile and departed.

"Does anyone mind if I eat?" Michael eased away from Emma and sat in the chair behind the desk. "I believe I've had one meal since Sunday evening."

"Michael!" Emma scolded, then she methodically tucked the napkin into his collar. "You've got to keep up your strength."

He tugged the napkin out with a mocking glare and set it on his lap. "Don't you worry about my strength, my sweet. I could spank you good if I had to."

"I dare say you could," she said with a giggle.

"But would you?" Tyson asked, not totally serious.

"If the need arose," Michael stated with an upward twitch of his lips that made it clear he was teasing.

"I realize you can't bear being apart," Tyson said to Emma, "but I need some privacy with Mr. Hamilton." He chuckled. "No, wait. What was it Lacey called him just this morning?"

Tyson and Emma pointed at each other, trying to remember, then they said it together. "The *esteemed* Mr. Hamilton."

The three of them laughed boisterously, and Michael added, "I knew she loved me all along. I just knew it."

Emma kissed Michael ridiculously loud in parting, and Tyson cleared his throat again. "I'm going," she huffed. "I was just giving the *esteemed* Mr. Hamilton a proper remembrance of me to carry him through the day."

Michael growled low in his throat and watched her walk to the door. She blew him a kiss, and he snapped his head back as if he'd caught it.

"The boy was right." Tyson closed the door behind his sister. "You *are* a strange man."

"A rogue," he said proudly and proceeded with his breakfast. After some silence, he looked up in question. "Well?"

"Well what?" Tyson chuckled. "Don't you want to see them?"

Michael's face turned abruptly to wide-eyed excitement. "I almost forgot about that. Did you find something?"

Tyson reached into his waistcoat pocket and felt around for the proper object. He dramatically pulled out the tiny gold band and leaned his elbows on the desk to show Michael, who took it between his thumb and forefinger as if it might break, holding it close to his eyes to examine carefully.

"The stones are black onyx," Tyson said proudly, indicating the three tiny dark sparkles set diagonally into the top of a polished gold band.

"It's perfect." Michael grinned and leaned back in his chair, still enchanted with the ring. "Is her finger really that tiny?" Michael slipped it onto his smallest finger, but it wouldn't go past the second knuckle.

"It really is. Read the inscription."

"Inscription?"

"The jeweler asked if I wanted one. I thought, why not? I did my other business, then went back to get it."

Michael squinted and turned the ring carefully to read aloud from its inner surface: "To Emma, who holds me captive. Michael." He gave a delighted chuckle. "I love it!"

"I thought you might, or rather, I hoped you would."

"You do have a way with words, Tyson. It's perfect. Did you get one, too?"

"Well," Tyson reached into a different pocket, "you know how alike they are, and yet so different. These two rings were side by side. I got them both." He handed it to Michael, who put Emma's into his pocket to take the other one. The rings were identical, except that the stones in this one were red.

"Rubies?" Michael asked.

"That's what I thought, but actually they're garnet. They have a deeper red color than rubies that size."

"It's beautiful," he smiled, "but I like black better."

"And I prefer red."

"I've got an idea," Michael said with enthusiasm. "Why don't you give your ring to Lacey, and I'll give mine to Emma."

"Great idea," Tyson said with amused sarcasm.

"An inscription?" Michael asked, and Tyson nodded. Michael read it aloud: "There is no place like home, no one like you. Tyson."

"I hope she knows I mean it."

"I'd say that about covers it." Michael handed the ring back, and Tyson tucked it safely into his pocket.

"Did you want to see the gift?" Tyson lifted his brows mischievously.

"You found something? Let me see it!" He was like a child at Christmas.

Tyson reached into his pocket and slowly pulled out a gold chain. Michael watched with intense anticipation as it got longer and longer. Tyson chuckled, and Michael realized he was being teased. "Get on with it!"

Tyson dangled it in front of Michael's eyes. He caught it with his hands and Tyson let go. The chain of fine, sparkling gold fell over the back of Michael's hand, while he surveyed the pendant lying in his palm. He liked it, but he wasn't sure why he liked it until Tyson said with a trace of sentiment in his voice, "I thought long and hard about what you said, and all of it just seemed to come together when I saw that. To me, it's full of symbolism."

Michael leaned back, intrigued. "Tell me."

"One half of the heart is ebony, the other ivory. They are attached and surrounded by the highest quality gold filigree. It reminded me of what you said about love and hate being close in the heart, divided only by a fine line."

"I didn't say that, Emma did." Michael didn't take his eyes off the pendant.

"It must have meant something to you, because you repeated it to me when I needed to hear it."

Michael studied the pendant carefully, turning it over in his hand, noting the incomparable quality. "It's like a black heart made white by perfect love."

"Something like that," Tyson agreed. "And knowing Emma, I'd wager that neither of us would have to say a word, and she'd figure it out just by looking at it. She's not one to wear jewelry often, but I think this would always remind her of what the two of you are really all about."

Michael chuckled and looked down abruptly. "Are you trying to make me cry?" he asked with humor, but the true emotion wasn't far from the surface.

"If you don't, I might," Tyson admitted.

"Thank you, Tyson." Michael wrapped his hand possessively around the necklace. "You must know me better than I thought you did."

"Perhaps it's because I can sense Emma's feelings sometimes, and she knows you better than anyone."

"That she does." Michael put the necklace into a little box that Tyson slid across the desk. "I owe you some money. Do you think a hundred thousand pounds will cover it?"

Tyson chuckled and opened the door. "For that much, I'll throw in a little lavender shampoo."

Michael laughed. "Thank you again."

"It was my pleasure. Eat your breakfast. We'll settle up later."

Tyson returned to the house, feeling better than he had in days. Now if he could only think of something appropriate to give Lacey. That might be almost as difficult as winning her back. But he was determined on both counts.

❦ ❦ ❦

Emma was stretched out on her bed reading when her mother came in search of her. "Could you come to my room, darling? I want to show you something. I'll get Lacey."

"I'll be there in just a minute," she said, and hurried to finish the page.

Emma found Lacey sitting on the edge of their parents' bed, watching with interest as Alexa knelt before an old trunk and lifted the lid. Emma turned the chair from the dressing table and sat expectantly.

"I was thinking," Alexa said, carefully folding back layers of fine tissue paper, "that before we go into town tomorrow in search of wedding apparel, we ought to see what we have here first."

The girls gasped in unison as Alexa lifted an elegant white gown up for them to see. "It's beautiful, Mother." Emma stood to hold out the skirt and survey it while Alexa held the shoulders. "Does it still fit you?"

"I don't know." Alexa laughed. "Should I try it?"

"Oh, do!" Lacey pleaded.

Alexa removed her blouse and breeches, and the girls helped her into the fragile gown. It fastened with little effort, and Alexa laughed as she surveyed her reflection in the long mirror. "Jess always tells me I haven't gained a pound since we were married. I suppose he's right."

"I hope I can stay so thin," Lacey mused.

"Just keep riding and chasing Richard," Alexa advised with a smile.

"Where *is* Father?" Emma asked, and the three grinned conspiratorially.

"In the sitting room, I believe." Alexa nodded toward the side door.

Emma opened it and peered in to find Jess reading, his boots on the coffee table. "Father?"

"Hello, Emma." He looked up. "What are you up to?"

"What makes you think I'm up to something?"

He gave a wry smile. "That tone of voice. I heard it the first time when you came to tell me you'd been cutting Tyson's hair."

"And I did a fine job of it, for a four-year-old."

Jess chuckled dubiously.

"Could you come in here a minute?"

"I suppose I could do that."

Jess ambled into the doorway with his hands in his pockets. He stopped and leaned his shoulder against the frame when he saw Alexa. The girls squeezed hands and looked on in wonder as their parents' eyes met, and in their expressions they could almost see more than two decades falling away.

Jess's mind flashed quickly through the bizarre chain of events that had brought him to the day he had married Alexandra Byrnehouse. But he focused on the memory of her standing, much like she was now, in this room, on their wedding night. If the girls hadn't been there, he'd have taken Alexa into his arms and kissed her now as he'd kissed her then. But knowing he had to wrap up his feelings with words, at least until a little later, he simply said, "Will you marry me?"

The girls giggled. Alexa beamed. "I already did."

"Boy," he sighed, looking her over again with blatant desire in his eyes, "that's a relief. I'd hate to think that such a beautiful bride belonged to anybody else."

"You're too kind," Alexa said humbly.

"No," he shook his head, "you're too beautiful."

"Get out of here." She laughed, but he only stepped toward her to whisper in her ear.

"Only if you promise to put that back on tonight."

"For what purpose?" she asked aloud.

"So I can take it off," he whispered, and she turned warm.

"All right, I promise." She smiled. Jess kissed her mouth quickly, then went reluctantly back to his reading.

Alexa stepped out of the dress and into her breeches. Emma held the gown against her and looked in the mirror. "I believe you girls are near my size," Alexa said as she buttoned her blouse and tucked it in.

"I think Emma should wear it," Lacey said quietly. "It wouldn't be right for me to—"

"Nonsense," Emma interrupted. "You have just as much right to—"

Now Alexa interrupted. "I agree with Lacey. I think Emma should wear it, but only because I want Lacey to wear this one." Alexa pulled another gown from the trunk, similar in elegance and quality, but different in style. The girls gasped again, then looked at their mother in question.

"I was married twice. I want Emma to wear this one." She indicated the first gown that Emma was hugging against herself. "I had it custom made by a local dressmaker when I was planning to marry Jess. And this one," she held it up to Lacey, who took it to survey her reflection as Emma moved aside, "I purchased in Brisbane a few days before I married Richard. You have named your son after my first husband. You should wear this gown."

"Thank you, Mother." Lacey embraced her with the gown crinkling between them. "It couldn't be more perfect."

"They're both so beautiful." Emma couldn't conceal her excitement.

"And so alike, yet different," her mother added. "Just like the two of you."

"Does this mean we're not going into town?" Lacey asked.

"We've got to get accessories and shoes," Alexa said, enthusiastically justifying an excursion into town. "We need to arrange for someone to perform the ceremony, and take care of the legalities. And most important, we need to stop in that little tea shop and have some of those divine little cakes they sell."

"How delightful," Emma agreed.

"And I think we should also think about getting each of you some personal items that every bride should have."

"Such as?" Emma asked.

"We'll discuss that later. Let's try on those dresses and show your father."

The girls excitedly got into the gowns with Alexa's assistance. Emma could only think of Michael, and the reality of what all of this meant.

Lacey thought of Tyson coming to her room this morning and felt a degree of peace in the prospect of their marriage, where until today she had only felt an abstract kind of despair. She truly hoped they could get past the hurt. She couldn't understand Emma's excitement and happiness over Michael, but still, she envied it. She longed to have such feelings between her and Tyson again, but she didn't know where to begin. Just thinking about it made her hurt inside. She was simply afraid of hurting anymore.

Alexa stood back to survey the results and got tears in her eyes. "My daughters. How blessed I am." She called more loudly, "Jess, could you come in here?"

"What now?" He pushed the door open, feigning boredom, but his eyes lit up every bit as much as when he'd last entered the room. "I think I know a couple of very fortunate men, who will be marrying two of the three most beautiful brides in Australia."

"Of course the gowns must be pressed and freshened." Alexa surveyed the fit carefully. "But it seems they don't need altering. How about that, Jess? They're both the same size I was when I got married."

This brought to Jess's attention the fact that there were two gowns old enough to be Alexa's. "Where did you get that one?" he asked, and she looked at him dubiously. "Oh, never mind," he added. "I know. I suppose I never saw it."

"You weren't exactly in a festive mood around that time," Alexa said lightly, but Jess wasn't amused.

"By the way," Jess said, "am I supposed to give both brides away at the same time?"

"You have two arms," Alexa said.

"And what are *you* going to do?" he asked.

"Cry."

"Why do I have to do something and you don't? Why can't you give the grooms away or something?"

"That's not the way it's supposed to work."

"Since when have we been conventional? We stopped being conventional the day you walked into my life wearing breeches."

"All right," Alexa accepted the challenge. "Maybe I will give the grooms away. Now, why don't you get back to that book and leave us to our business. You've had a fair look at the brides."

"Yes, ma'am," he said in a tone that reminded Emma of Michael.

When Jess was gone, the girls carefully removed the gowns, then sat with their mother to plan the wedding. Lacey found it difficult to be too enthusiastic, but she had every hope she would feel better by

then. Emma could hardly contain her excitement. And Alexa seemed
to manage keeping them both involved with perfect balance. They all
agreed that it should be kept simple, with a ceremony in the upstairs
hall where Jess and Alexa had been married. They had few friends and
associates beyond those who lived at Byrnehouse-Davies, and a small
list was made of those close enough to invite. They made another list
of all they needed to do in town the following day, not wanting to forget anything when the distance was so great.

When Alexa suggested that they each get some new nightclothes—something a little less prudish—Lacey blushed and Emma
couldn't keep a straight face. The conversation then turned reverent as
Alexa gently reminded them of certain aspects of human intimacy that
had been discussed years before as they had been maturing into
women. But she added some delicate advice concerning some of the
things involved in a marriage relationship.

Their conversation gradually turned back to trivial things, much
to Lacey's relief and Emma's disappointment. While Emma couldn't
help anticipating being married to Michael, Lacey felt more afraid
than anything at the prospect of being Tyson's wife.

They finally left Alexa's bedroom to go down to supper. Emma
was disappointed to find Michael absent. Jess commented that
Michael seemed to be doing well with the boys, and Lacey added that
he was probably more suited to their company.

Emma excused herself early and went in search of Michael, trying
to recall the last time they'd had any real time together. His office was
unoccupied, so she went quietly down the hall, listening for signs of
activity. She peered into the library and found the boys reading;
Michael was sitting near the window, talking quietly to a young man
of about twelve, she guessed. Not wanting to interrupt, she leaned
against the door and waited quietly, hoping he would catch her eye
eventually. All eyes turned curiously toward her over the next ten minutes, except Michael's. Sarina nodded a quiet greeting from where she
was reading a story to the younger boys, but it was several minutes
before she paused to go and tap Michael on the shoulder. She whispered in his ear and pointed toward Emma, who gave a little wave. He
smiled and held her gaze for a long moment. She could feel him
absorbing her as if she were sunlight after a storm. The look alone

radiated more emotion than Emma could comprehend. Already she felt rejuvenated.

Just when their staring nearly became embarrassing, he held up a finger to indicate that he'd be finished in a minute, then he resumed his conversation. Emma watched as he put a gentle hand to the boy's shoulder, while his expression was firm with careful discipline. The boy nodded and gingerly gave Michael a hug that was easily returned. Emma could envision him as a good father—a man who would spend his life proving that he was not what his father had raised him to be.

Emma saw him lean back and sigh while he seemed to contemplate whatever had just been discussed. His eyes became distant, and he bit his lip slightly. With a quick glance around the room, he seemed to be taking a silent inventory. Then his eyes turned to Emma, and he walked toward her with a stride that made her heart quicken. She thought of her wedding gown, and her mother's gentle lecture on intimacy. She couldn't even imagine how wonderful it would be to marry Michael Hamilton. By the time he was close enough to take her hand, it was trembling.

"Are you all right?" he whispered. She nodded and he escorted her into the hall, away from curious eyes. He kissed her hand to stop its trembling, but it only worsened. He smiled, seeming to understand. "Missed me, eh?"

"Quite. And you missed supper."

"Sorry about that," he said sincerely. "I ate with the boys. I . . . well, after what happened last night, I think I need to be close by for a while. They've lightened up some, but there are some pretty vulnerable emotions going on. Does that make any sense?"

"I think so. You can tell me more about it later. Are you finished now? I thought we could . . ."

"I will be," he interrupted apologetically, "just as soon as I have a little talk with Michael about the dark. I promised him, you see, and . . ."

"I understand," Emma smiled. She had to admire him for his dedication, and there was little she could say after all the times she'd spent with Lacey or Tyson, leaving Michael alone.

"Come to my room when you're finished. We have a lot to catch up on."

"Yes," he kissed her hand again, "we do. I think I could talk and kiss all night."

"Sounds wonderful." She squeezed his hand, grateful for his perception. "I'll see you soon, then."

Michael kissed her quickly, then opened the library door. He paused to watch her walk away. What a woman!

Eighteen

ENCOUNTERING MR. COOGAN

Once Lacey had Richard tucked into bed, she went to her room and found the lamp burning. Knowing she hadn't left it on, she looked around carefully for anything unusual, feeling a little unnerved. She figured it out when she found a small package in the center of the bed. Carefully she untied the ribbon and lifted the lid. She folded back the tissue paper to reveal an expensive bottle of lavender shampoo. Pulling the bottle from the box, Lacey removed the lid and inhaled deeply. The fragrance reminded her of the shampoo she and Emma had used in the outback, which was her only good memory of the entire excursion. Noticing a note in the bottom of the box, she picked it up to read: *I love you. Tyson.*

Lacey felt both intrigued and confused, and without delay she went to Emma's room, needing desperately to talk about this. She found the room empty but decided to sit and wait. Surely she wouldn't be long.

A few minutes later Emma appeared, and Lacey realized that she somehow felt better in Emma's company—at least when she was without Michael. Emma had always been the strong and courageous one, and for reasons Lacey didn't understand, she needed Emma now.

"Is everything all right?" Emma asked, beginning to undress for bed.

"I just wanted to show you this." She handed the package to Emma, who smiled. "Did you set him up to this?" Lacey insisted.

"No," Emma answered firmly, "I simply told him how we had played in the shampoo. Why?" she asked.

"Oh, nothing. I was just . . . surprised." Lacey set the package down and said nothing while Emma changed. "Would you like me to brush through your hair?" she offered. "It's been a long time."

"Yes, it has. That would be nice." Emma sat and Lacey brushed. "Have you spoken to Tyson lately? You should, you know."

"I suppose. Oh, Emma. I don't know what to do. I don't know how to be rid of these feelings. I know it's not right, but it's just so . . . I don't know."

Lacey started into an oratory that Emma knew well. She listened politely, hoping Michael would come soon. She knew his presence would frighten Lacey off. It wasn't that she didn't care about Lacey, but she felt certain that Lacey should be telling all of this to Tyson, not to her. And Emma simply needed some time with Michael.

They exchanged places and Emma began to brush Lacey's hair, glancing often at the clock. She politely gave Lacey the same advice she'd given her at least a dozen times, and pretended not to be irritated when Lacey ignored it. She continued brushing and looking at the clock until she began to wonder if Michael wasn't coming. Lacey interrupted her thoughts by saying, "I certainly hope Michael never lets you down the way Tyson did me. When Tyson has so much more going for him, I shudder to think what a man with Michael's background could do to hurt you."

"Michael is perfectly dependable," Emma defended, wishing she didn't feel like a hypocrite.

❦   ❦   ❦

Michael finished with his business and went eagerly to Emma's room. He wanted nothing more than to just hold her and tell her about all that had been happening since they'd last talked. He lifted his hand to knock, but felt a familiar exasperation. He could hear Lacey's voice. He couldn't quite make out what she was saying, but her tone made it evident that she was pouring her heart out to Emma. He contemplated whether or not to interrupt, but as much as he wanted to be with Emma, he couldn't bring himself to take her away from

Lacey any more than he already had. Filled with disappointment, he sighed and walked quietly to his own room and went to bed.

❦ ❦ ❦

Emma was awakened early by Tillie, who informed her they should be off to town soon. While she was getting dressed, she realized that Michael hadn't come last night. Her time was brief, but she wasn't going to spend the day wondering what had happened. When she was ready except for eating, she hurried to his room and opened the door without knocking, only to find him sleeping soundly. Kneeling over the bed, she put her mouth directly over his ear and spoke in a normal voice that made his eyes fly open, "All right, Mr. Hamilton. What's your excuse this time?" He turned to look up at her and she added, "I waited for hours for you to come and rescue me."

He groaned and put a hand over his eyes.

"You forgot," she guessed.

"No," he defended vehemently, "I did not forget! I could hear Lacey in there, and I decided I'd better stay away."

"Oh." Emma sat huffily on the edge of the bed.

"If I had known you wanted me to interrupt . . . well, you know how Lacey feels about me. Every time I come between the two of you, I feel like she's chalking up more black marks against me."

"I understand," she said, taking his hand.

Michael kissed her cheek, then took notice of her attire. "Mercy! Where are you off to looking so exquisite?"

"We're going into town. I told you yesterday."

"So you did. I suppose that means I won't see you today, either."

"We'll be back for supper."

"I promised supper with the boys, but I'd like to see you afterward."

She smiled and kissed him. "I'll be counting on it. I must be going. Go back to sleep. It's early yet."

He glanced at the clock. "Mercy! You women take this shopping business seriously."

"Yes, we do. Especially when it's also wedding business."

"I love you, Emma," he said with a firm squeeze of her hand.

"And I love you. I'll see you later, then." She went to the door, and they shared the usual ritual of blowing and catching a kiss. But this time he blew one back, and Emma stumbled out the door as if it had knocked her nearly off her feet. Michael chuckled and lay back down to contemplate his future.

🌸 🌸 🌸

After a quick breakfast, the women were loaded into the carriage and Fiddler drove the team toward town. Their errands went smoothly, and by early afternoon they were seated in a tea shop, going over their lists. When they had determined that they only needed to order some fresh flowers to be delivered the morning of the wedding, Emma decided they would have time for something she'd been contemplating for days. "Do you think it would be all right if we went to a men's clothing shop?"

"I suppose we can," Alexa said.

"Since Michael isn't able to come into town, I wanted to get some new things for him. I've shopped for Tyson before. I think I can figure out what to get."

"That should be fine. Come to think of it, I believe your father could use something new for the wedding. And Tyson, too, for that matter. Did he happen to think of that yesterday? Do you know, Emma?"

"I don't believe any of his packages were large enough to be clothes."

"Then it would seem we've still got important details to see to. What would men do without us?"

"They wouldn't show up properly dressed," Lacey said.

"And that's the least of it," Emma added, and they giggled.

"Well, if it isn't Mrs. Davies," a raspy voice said, and Alexa turned in surprise.

"Constable Gunn. How good to see you," Alexa said. Emma felt an attack of nerves, but she hid it well. "Do you come here often?"

"Nearly every day." He took her hand in greeting. "But I rarely see such a fine sight." He nodded to the girls, who politely returned the gesture. "How are all those boys doin' these days?" he asked.

"Fine, as far as I know," she answered. She was grateful Ira had informed them of the accusations against Michael, or she might have told the constable about their new administrator.

"Speaking of which, Mrs. Davies, I'm glad I ran into you. Why, just last night after your boy left here . . . he came to see if we had any new cases Jess would want to know about. But then you probably knew that."

"Yes, of course. Go on, please."

"Well, just last night we had a boy brought in who's not talking."

"You mean he won't tell you where he's from?"

"No, he just isn't talking—at all." The constable seemed concerned. "I was going to send a messenger out to Jess. Could you mention it to him and save some trouble?"

"I certainly will. Where is the boy now?"

"We've got him locked in a cell at the moment. We're treatin' him good, mind you. But he seemed to want to run, and he's been in trouble on the streets more than once."

"Sounds like just what we're looking for," Emma said, like she had earlier when they'd found the right shoes for Lacey.

"You're starting to sound like *him*," Lacey whispered in disgust.

"Thank you," Emma said proudly, and Lacey huffed and turned her attention back to the constable.

"Could I see the boy?" Alexa asked.

"I don't know why not."

"We haven't got a great deal of time, but I would like to meet him. I'll send Jess back tomorrow to get him, and we'll proceed as usual from there."

"If you're finished, we can go along right now," the constable offered.

"Girls?" Alexa questioned.

"Oh, we're done here."

They all came to their feet, and the girls followed close behind Alexa and the constable as they continued their usual update of boys that were now grown and on their own.

"The constable's nothing but an old gossip," Lacey whispered.

"Yes, but Mother loves it. She likes to keep track of her boys."

"Speaking of which," the constable said with enthusiasm, as if he'd just remembered a juicy tidbit, "did I tell you what I heard about Michael Hamilton? Of course, I told Tyson yesterday, so you probably knew that already."

"He did mention something about him," Alexa said nonchalantly. "What was it again? Remind me."

"Not a word," Emma whispered a warning to Lacey.

"I'm not about to tell anyone we're harboring a criminal. I can't think of anything more embarrassing."

Emma glared at Lacey, then listened carefully to what was being said. The constable basically repeated everything Emma had already heard. She was proud of her mother when she said with conviction, "I don't know. Michael and I got to know each other pretty well. I can't believe he would be capable of murder." Lacey rolled her eyes and sighed with disgust. Emma ignored her.

"One can never tell what a man is capable of. I've seen the most upright men do some horrifying things, Mrs. Davies."

"But just what kind of men are these who are accusing Michael?" Alexa asked as if she didn't have a clue.

The constable laughed. "Very annoying," he admitted. "You might have a point there. The truth is, this Hamilton case is not our biggest priority at the moment. He's probably not within a thousand miles of here." Alexa glanced discreetly back at the girls as if to check on them, but Emma didn't miss the satisfaction in her eyes. "But these thugs who said he did it seem to think I should be personally combing the country to find him."

"They don't sound very agreeable," Alexa said with compassion.

"They aren't, I can assure you."

The constable opened the door, and the ladies filed in. Lacey and Emma sat dutifully on a bench in the front office. They had been here for such business many times before. Alexa went through a door and down a long hall with the constable. Once alone, Emma said quietly, "I pray they don't find him before we can prove he's innocent."

"I don't think you can prove that he's innocent, Emma."

"Forget that I brought it up. I should know better than to attempt discussing him with you."

"Yes, you should."

They remained silent while Lacey examined a broken fingernail and Emma bit hers, thinking more realistically about Michael's precarious situation in light of where they were. Neither of them paid any notice to the two men who came in from outside. It was the smell that made the girls look at each other, then look up. Emma put a gloved hand to her nose and discreetly looked away. Lacey took hold of the bench and began to breathe so sharply that Emma feared she would pass out.

"Calm down," Emma whispered, putting a firm hand on Lacey's arm. "Don't bring attention to ourselves." But it was too late. Rafe Coogan had seen them.

"Well, look what we got here, Bud." He showed decaying teeth and nudged his companion, who turned a familiar face toward them. "Seems the little ladies got away." He laughed like a mule stuck in a fence. "Here to report a kidnapping?"

"Actually, no," Emma said calmly while Lacey turned as white as her blouse. "But you wouldn't want me to do that. It could get you into a great deal of trouble, Mr. Coogan."

"I suppose it could, at that." His eyes moved over both of the girls with blatant lust. He licked his lips crudely. Emma felt bile rise into her throat. Lacey turned away and put a hand over her mouth to suppress a wave of nausea. "Did yer Mr. Hamilton get away with the ransom?" he asked with obvious intent.

Emma wondered what to say. She didn't want Rafe to be any more angry with Michael than he already was, but she didn't want to give him a clue that anything beyond the expected had happened. She opted for a degree of the truth. "If he hadn't, I wouldn't be alive and speaking to you now."

Rafe laughed and elbowed his companion, who reacted in an equally obnoxious manner. "Do you hear that, Bud? The lady thinks Hamilton woulda killed her. He didn't have the guts to shoot a barn."

Emma smiled. She was amazed at how inane this man really was. "Is that so, Mr. Coogan? And I'd heard he was wanted for murder." Rafe's expression sobered as he apparently realized what he'd said. He looked around to make certain no one had overheard. Bud glared at him for his stupidity. Emma's smile broadened. Lacey was oblivious with fear. "I had also heard it was you making the accusations."

Rafe and Bud were silenced, much to Emma's pleasure. Alexa and the constable came through the door, and the constable immediately sighed with disgust to see the men in his office. He was obviously sick to death of dealing with them.

"Well, no matter." Emma came to her feet and urged Lacey along. "I only hope they catch up with the beast." She added for the constable's benefit, "And when they do, I hope they do the fitting thing and string the two of you up along with him."

Emma's comment brought Alexa's attention to the other occupants of the room as she discreetly put a hand over her nose. The constable seemed puzzled and was quick to ask, "What's this about?"

Rafe looked decidedly nervous. "Oh, nothing," Emma said casually. "This gentleman and I were just discussing a mutual acquaintance. Isn't it a small world?" She spoke to her mother more specifically. "Do you remember Michael Hamilton, Mother? Didn't he work in our stable for a few years?"

"But of course." Alexa smiled. "The constable and I were discussing him earlier."

"Were you? I must have been daydreaming," Emma said. "Well this man . . .what was your name again? Oh yes, Mr. Coogan. Mr. Coogan here is an acquaintance of Mr. Hamilton's. And I'm certain we must be talking about the same man," Emma's voice was a perfect balance of innocence and flawless enunciation, "because he said that Mr. Hamilton didn't have the guts to shoot a barn. It would seem that Mr. Coogan knows Mr. Hamilton well."

Alexa smiled discreetly, took one last glance at the smelly topic of their conversation, then nodded toward the constable, who seemed to be contemplating what he'd just heard.

"I'll send Jess out tomorrow then," Alexa said. "Thank you as always for your cooperation."

"Ladies." The constable nodded, and they filed out.

"Am I correct in assuming that was *the* Mr. Coogan?" Alexa asked quietly.

"That was him," Emma replied.

"Of all the people to come across," Lacey said, her voice trembling.

"Are you all right, love?" Alexa asked.

"No, I am not," she admitted.

Alexa put a comforting arm around her. "Perhaps you would like to go back to the carriage and rest while Emma and I finish."

"That would be fine," she agreed, and they soon had her in

Fiddler's care, who was lounging in the carriage with a good book and a basket of goodies Mrs. Brady had sent.

Emma thoroughly enjoyed choosing a new wardrobe for Michael, and she felt confident she'd found the right sizes simply by visual analysis and comparing him to Tyson's size.

Alexa was going to put everything on the family account, but Emma insisted on buying the things for Michael with her own money, which she produced from her handbag. A boy from the shop helped carry their packages to the carriage, and Alexa rewarded him well. They found Fiddler still reading and Lacey just sitting, staring into space, barely acknowledging them as they informed her they would order the flowers now and start home.

As the journey began, Alexa watched Lacey closely and felt the evidence deepen. There were some very real fears in her that more recent events were bringing close to the surface. She ached to talk with Lacey, but she knew from experience that Lacey had no desire to discuss any of it. Even as a child, talking about anything concerning her life before she'd come to them was something she simply wouldn't do. Alexa could see that her fear of Rafe Coogan was real, but not completely reasonable. If nothing else, she felt discussing the circumstances with Emma might help Lacey face up a little.

"So," Alexa said after a long quiet spell, "tell me more about your adventure in the outback, Emma. We've hardly had a chance to talk about it. And I'm curious as to how exactly this Mr. Coogan fits in." Lacey shifted in her seat but said nothing.

Emma delightfully related to her mother her kidnapping experiences. When she got to the day that Lacey was taken back to Jess, Emma reverently told her mother how she had forced Michael to confront his fears. Omitting certain details, she repeated what a traumatic experience it had been for both of them. She finished by saying that they had spent the remainder of their time together getting to know each other better.

"Someday you can tell that story to your children," Alexa said warmly.

"The way you told us that story at the dinner table the other night?" Emma asked.

"Something like that."

"It's funny," Lacey finally spoke with an edge of cynicism, "but that's not how I remember it at all."

Alexa acted on the opportunity. "Exactly how *do* you remember it, Lacey?"

"Michael Hamilton is a fiend!" she snarled. "He was cruel and malevolent. I think Emma has read too many of those ridiculous novels. Her mind is clouded over with this absurd fantasy, and Michael is just taking advantage of her to further his motives."

"I've known Michael for a long time, Lacey. He was at Byrnehouse-Davies before we found you." Lacey and Emma both looked surprised, but Lacey seemed to take it personally. "He and I have spent a great deal of time together over the years, and I believe I know him very well. You have always trusted my judgment, Lacey. Why not now?"

"I don't know," she admitted tersely. "I only know what I saw; what I heard. He frightens me." Lacey bit her lip, and Alexa heard the closest thing to her true feelings thus far. "And I don't understand how someone so frightening could be as wonderful as you all seem to think."

"Perhaps you're so obsessed with seeing the mistakes he's made that you're not opening your eyes enough to see what we see in him." Emma's words were gentle, but Lacey glared at her.

"I think there is a lot of truth in that, Emma," Alexa said. "But I also think there is much more to it than that. We must respect Lacey's opinions, just as we expect her to respect ours. I can promise you one thing, Lacey: Michael is not going to hurt Emma, and he's not going to hurt you."

"How can you be so sure?" Lacey snapped.

"I can only say that I am. Maybe if we talked more about the—"

"I don't want to talk about it anymore." Lacey turned her attention to the window. Emma looked helplessly at Alexa, who responded with an expression of deep concern.

The carriage stopped in front of the house, and Fiddler jumped down to assist the ladies. With all arms loaded, he followed them into the house, grumbling good-naturedly, "What did I do to deserve the job of taking the ladies shopping?"

"Oh, you love it," Alexa retorted, setting her armload down in the hall, then turning to unload Fiddler's arms. "I remember all those long talks we used to have in the bunkhouse kitchen. Your true enjoyment is helping ladies shop." She kissed his cheek. "Thank you, Fiddler. I know what a sacrifice it is."

"Yes," he grinned, "quite a sacrifice."

He left to take the carriage around, and the ladies opted for supper before seeing to their purchases. They entered the dining room removing gloves and hats. Jess and Tyson came eagerly to their feet.

"Are we glad to see you!" Jess hurried to kiss his wife. "It's pretty difficult to be content with looking at Tyson when I'm used to three beautiful women."

"The feeling is mutual." Tyson helped Lacey with her chair, but she said nothing.

The conversation stayed busy with reports of all they had done, including their encounter with Rafe Coogan. Jess was concerned and interested about that, as well as the prospect of acquiring a new boy.

"You say he didn't speak . . . at all?" Tyson asked.

"Not a sound. But there is a great deal of fear in his eyes, although the general impression he's trying to give is tough to the core."

"Typical case with an untypical reaction," Jess stated. "I'll go and get him first thing tomorrow. It's too bad I can't take Michael. I'd like to have him along."

"They'll get acquainted soon enough."

"Has anyone seen Michael?" Emma asked eagerly.

"I caught sight of him on the tracks with the boys this morning," Tyson said.

Jess rose from the table. "I'm going to talk with him now. Any messages?"

"No," Emma said, "I'll see him later." *I hope,* she added to herself.

"So, are we ready for the big day?" Tyson asked, looking directly at Lacey. But she ignored him as she helplessly toyed with her barely touched meal.

"We will be," Alexa said with confidence. "Emma, if you're finished, why don't we see about putting those things away."

"Of course," Emma agreed, and followed her mother from the room.

Tyson's first instinct was to ask Lacey if something was wrong, but he felt certain it would only get a negative reaction. Instead he leaned toward her and whispered, "Did you get my little present?"

"Yes," she said tersely. "I don't know what you're implying by it, but—"

"I'm not implying anything, Lacey. I am making it quite clear that I love you. It's just a gift. I was also thinking about a little family outing. Richard would enjoy a picnic, don't you think? He could eat those little cakes and play while his parents—"

"A picnic would be fine." She rose abruptly and left the room. Tyson just sighed, then uttered a prayer that they could somehow get beyond all of this.

❦   ❦   ❦

Alexa helped Emma carry her packages into her room and spread them out on the bed.

"Emma," she said carefully, "I want you to keep a close watch on Lacey, as much as possible. I'm not expecting you to tend her by any means, and you've got your own life to live. But between us, we must try to be aware of what she is feeling."

"I'll do my best," Emma said with concern, "but all she'll ever talk about is Tyson and how he's hurt her." She admired a new shirt and tried to imagine Michael wearing it. "I try to encourage her to talk to Tyson about it, but she doesn't listen."

"We must be patient with her. Perhaps once she has unloaded her feelings sufficiently, she'll be able to do that."

"I hope so."

"I'll leave you to your sorting." Alexa kissed her daughter's cheek and left the room. "Good night, love."

When Emma was nearly finished getting her purchases in order, she decided to take them to Michael's room and wait for him, but she barely had an armful gathered when Lacey knocked at the sitting room door. Peering in timidly, she asked, "Can we talk, Emma?"

"Of course." Emma smiled and set the things back on the bed. She could only hope that Michael would seek her out as she settled herself into a conversation beginning with Lacey's horror at encountering Rafe Coogan. Then the discussion turned predictably to the same oration concerning Tyson's imperfections. Emma did her best to be compassionate and understanding, and to say the right things to encourage her, but it didn't seem to make any difference. Emma, like her mother, was deeply worried about Lacey, without having a clue what to do about it.

❦ ❦ ❦

Jess found Michael just walking out of the cafeteria. "Finished already?" Jess quipped, glancing at his watch.

"I thought I might see if I still have a fiancée," Michael retorted with good humor.

"You do," Jess said. "I just saw her, and she's as beautiful as ever. But," he held up a finger, "not as beautiful as when I saw her yesterday."

"I'm sorry?" Michael leaned forward inquisitively.

"I was given the rare opportunity to see her in a wedding gown," Jess bragged.

Michael's eyes sparkled. "I don't have to ask if she looked radiant."

"No, I suppose you don't." Jess slapped his shoulder and urged him in the opposite direction from where he'd been intending to go. "You're a lucky man, Hamilton."

"I can't argue there. Where are we going?"

"We've got business to discuss, I'm afraid. I think Emma will understand."

"If she doesn't, I'm going to blame it on you."

"I think between the two of us, we can handle Emma."

"Perhaps," Michael said, "but don't count on it."

Jess opened the door to Michael's office and motioned him inside. Michael lit the lamp and sat behind the desk. Jess remained standing. "Alexa ran into the constable today." Michael sighed, certain this would be about his standing with the law. He was surprised and relieved as Jess continued. "They have a boy who apparently belongs to no one, or at least he won't admit to it."

"Where is he now?" Michael asked eagerly.

"In the constable's care. He should do all right with him until I can get there. I'm leaving at dawn to go get him. I wish you could go with me, but you can't. I want you to be prepared to spend some time with him when we return. I'll try to arrange it so we arrive after you've finished in the stables tomorrow afternoon." Michael nodded. "The first few days here are always the most difficult."

"You don't have to tell me that."

"I suppose I don't. But this is a special case." Michael lifted a brow. Jess said quietly, "The boy either can't or won't speak."

"At all?"

"Not a sound." Jess sat and crossed his ankle on his knee to tap a finger on the side of his boot. "Alexa met him. She believes he's around twelve. Says he looks hard, but she sensed a lot of fear."

"Which is understandable."

"Yes."

"Do they have any clue at all where he came from, or . . ."

"Nothing. He was caught stealing downtown yesterday afternoon."

"Probably starving."

"Well, he's being fed now. My biggest concern at this time is the other boys. They tend to be hard on a newcomer, and if he's obviously suffering from more than the average trauma, we've got to handle it delicately. Perhaps it's just as well that you're staying here. Maybe you can work on preparing them, if that's possible."

"Oh, it's possible." Michael leaned back. "I would bet, with the progress we've made, they might just do all right. This could be a good opportunity for them to practice what I've been trying to teach them."

Jess stood. "You keep up the good work, Michael."

"I'm trying."

"Oh, and payday is tomorrow. I'll leave your salary in my desk drawer with the files."

"I haven't worked long enough to get paid," he protested.

"All my employees get paid tomorrow," Jess replied. "You'll just have to get paid for what you've worked."

"I hope it pays better than stable hand," Michael teased. "Although rumor has it that your stable hands get paid better than most."

"Really?" Jess seemed genuinely surprised. "Don't worry, Michael. You'll be making more than three times what you made before." Michael's eyes widened. "I think you'll manage."

"As long as you keep feeding me," Michael grinned slyly, "I could almost become as well off as you."

Jess laughed. "I can't afford to let you get that well off. I've got a lot of mouths to feed besides yours."

"Yes," Michael chuckled, "and tomorrow you'll have one more."

"Which means I'd best get some sleep. Alexa claims I'm intolerable when I don't get my sleep, and I have a feeling tomorrow's going to be a challenging day."

"Like the day you found me, eh?"

"No day could be that challenging."

Michael chuckled proudly.

"Oh," Jess remembered something else, "it seems while the ladies were in the constable's office, they came across your friend, Mr. Coogan."

Michael's expression fell. "What happened? What was he doing there?"

Jess repeated the story to him the best he could remember, while Michael quietly took it in, feeling an instinctive desire to hunt the man down and beat him until he barely lived—or maybe worse. He realized that many of his feelings were related to Toby. He was about to mention that situation when Jess opened the door to leave, saying lightly, "I haven't got time to gossip all night. Ask Emma the details; I'm going to get some sleep. I'll see you tomorrow afternoon."

"Good night." Michael turned to look out the window, chewing nervously on his thumbnail. A few months ago, he had walked out of a prison with no attachments and no complications. And now he was more involved with more people's lives than he would ever have imagined possible. The complications could be overwhelming if he attempted to grasp them all at once, but it had payoffs. Life was good for him, and he wasn't going to question it. He'd do it all again just to have Emma.

The thought of her brought him to his feet. As he walked the long halls, he contemplated his progress with the boys. Michael had helped to alleviate a great deal of the tension among them, but as Sarina had declared, "They're still boys."

"Would you want them to be anything less?" he'd replied.

In the time since their drama in the gabled attic, he was finding it necessary to stay close and prove certain points by example and careful coaching. Old habits couldn't die overnight. They needed careful tutelage, and Michael found it nearly impossible to be away from them. They needed him, and he couldn't deny how good it felt to be needed. He was certain it would become easier with time, and his only regret was his lack of opportunity to be with Emma. With another difficult boy soon to arrive, he could be needed even more in the coming days. He only hoped Emma would understand.

He was eager to make up for some of that lost time when he approached her door, and he had to fight to keep from cursing aloud when he heard two women's voices. After what had happened last night, he was prepared to knock anyway, until he quickly realized that Lacey was very upset, and he heard mention of their encounter with Rafe Coogan. No, he told himself, this was not a good time to remind her of his presence in the household. He impulsively went to the nursery and shared story time with Tyson and Richard, then watched as Tyson tucked Richard into bed. When Richard requested a hug from "Uncle Michael" he couldn't deny feeling touched by the little opportunities he'd had to get to know Richard better, and the way the child made him feel a little more like part of the family.

Michael returned to Emma's room to hear Lacey sounding all the more agitated. He loitered in and out of the hallway for over an hour before he finally gave up and went to bed. He realized that Lacey likely had things to work out, but he was beginning to get really irritated.

The following morning he was up early, bathed and dressed and sneaking into Emma's room before she awoke. Carefully he moved a chair close to her bed, leaned back in it, and put his boots up on the edge of the bed. He wanted the proper roguish appearance when she awoke. It was intriguing to watch her sleep, but feeling a desire to be with her, he cleared his throat loudly. It had little effect, so he nudged her with his toe and dropped a nearby book on the floor at the same time. She opened her eyes abruptly.

"Good morning, my sweet," he said.

"Good morning." She stretched prettily and held out her hand. "Come here."

"No, I'm sitting right here."

"Why?" She sounded distressed.

"Because every time I start kissing you, someone comes to that door. If I don't kiss you, I won't be interrupted."

Emma reached for her wrapper and leaned over to kiss him. She drew back and smiled. "Then I'll kiss you."

"All right." He smiled, and she kissed him again. A knock came at the door, and Michael sighed with exasperation.

"Who is it?" Emma lay back in her bed and imitated Michael's sigh.

"I've come to prepare your bath like you asked," Tillie called.

"Come in," Emma called, pulling the covers up to her chin. Michael stayed as he was, enjoying the surprised glance he got from Tillie. She poured water into the tub and left the room for more.

"Stay a while and you can wash my feet," Emma said with a titillating smile.

"I'd certainly enjoy that, my love." He came to his feet. "But I've got work to do. Your father's bringing in a new boy this afternoon."

"So I understand."

"And he tells me you had an unpleasant encounter yesterday in town."

"What else did he tell you?"

Michael quickly repeated what he'd been told, finishing with, "It sounds like you handled Coogan rather well."

"I do have a way with wicked men."

"Do you now?" He bent over to kiss her, only to have Tillie enter the room with more water. "I'll leave you to bathe, my sweet. I can't count on seeing you later when I'm not certain what to expect with the new arrival."

"I understand." She gave him a disappointed smile. "I hope they can manage without you long enough for a honeymoon."

"They will if I have to beat them all up," he said, and Tillie glanced toward him skeptically. He glared at her and she scurried from the room.

"I love you, Michael," she said with strength.

He sat on the edge of the bed and took her hand. "And I love you." He put his other hand to her face and kissed her long and hard. "We'll make up for it, Emma. When we're married, I'm going to take you to a city big enough to get lost in. We're going to get the fanciest room in the fanciest hotel, and no one is going to bother us."

Emma sat forward and put her arms around his shoulders. He embraced her in return, silently reiterating his promise. Then he kissed her again until Tillie returned.

"I'll see you later . . . maybe." He stood and moved toward the door, adding to Tillie, "Your timing is impeccable."

The maid looked up, obviously confused, then she returned to her work with fervor.

After Michael was gone, Emma remembered her gifts for him. But she decided it might be better to wait anyway, until she could spend some time with him and enjoy the experience.

Deciding there was plenty to keep herself occupied, Emma bathed while she planned out her day with wedding preparations, time with the horses, and her usual play time with Richard. Sinking deeper into the water, she thought of Michael's promise. She had a great deal to look forward to.

🐾　🐾　🐾

Lacey said nothing as she watched Tyson throw himself gracefully into the saddle, then he lifted Richard up and situated the child in front of him. Seeing them together still seemed almost dreamlike. And yet they went together so well. She couldn't deny that Tyson had quickly made up for his absence in Richard's life. The boy acted as if he had been close to his father forever. And there were moments when Lacey truly wished she could see the situation with the same innocence and lack of pain that her son did.

Lacey urged her mount forward and followed Tyson and Richard out of the stable. She had told Tyson that she'd agreed to the picnic for Richard's benefit, but in her heart she couldn't deny wanting to be with Tyson. If only she could be free of the confusion that he provoked in her.

Following a lengthy ride into the hills, she wasn't surprised to see that Tyson had brought them to a grassy clearing in the trees, where a clear stream ran over smooth stones. They had come here countless times with Emma in their growing years. It was a perfect picnic site.

Lacey remained silent as Tyson helped Richard down and together they laid out the picnic Mrs. Brady had prepared. But Richard seemed more interested in playing near the stream. Lacey sat on the grass and found herself actually feeling content as she watched Tyson and Richard throwing rocks into the water.

When Richard got a little too close to the bank, Tyson pulled him back, saying, "If you're determined to get wet, little man, then let's take off your shoes first."

Tyson removed Richard's shoes and stockings and rolled up the legs of his breeches. He picked Richard up beneath the arms and dangled him over the stream, slowly lowering him until his toes hit the cold water. Richard gasped, then giggled. Tyson lifted him up quickly, then lowered him again slowly, laughing at the child's anticipation, and his giggling each time his feet touched the water. Lacey couldn't help laughing to observe them. She became so caught up in their game that she was startled to hear Tyson say, "It's so good to hear you laugh."

She turned to find Tyson staring at her with intensity. Lacey couldn't find anything to say, but she couldn't force herself to look away, either. With all her heart she wanted to tell him that she loved him, that she was sorry for being so awful at times. But the habitual confusion and fear settled in to cloud her mind with doubts. She finally forced her eyes elsewhere, wishing he would just play with Richard and stop staring at her that way. When she looked back up, he was doing just that.

A few minutes later, Tyson urged Richard away from the water long enough to eat. The child quickly ate his required portions in order to have some dessert. He ate three of Mrs. Brady's little cakes before he hurried back to the stream, carefully stepping into the water and laughing as he glanced back at his parents to be certain they were watching him.

"Be careful," Lacey called, then she realized Tyson was watching her again. And again she found it difficult to turn away. She panicked when she realized he was intending to kiss her. But before she could think how to avoid it, he whispered, "Richard is watching us. He needs to know that his parents love each other."

Lacey held her breath as she glanced quickly toward her son, only to realize that Tyson was right. Richard's expression was filled with pleasant expectancy. Lacey turned back to face Tyson, trying to convince herself that she was allowing him to kiss her for Richard's sake. But the feel of his lips over hers stirred something deep and wonderful to life inside of her. She was just beginning to enjoy it when she found herself reminded of their romantic encounters prior to his leaving home. The thought startled her with the fear of having him leave her again. She pulled back and gasped as an all-too-familiar fear crept in to squelch any thought of love or tenderness. She sensed Tyson's concern and frustration, but she didn't know what to say. A quick glance at Richard assured her that he'd contentedly returned to his play. She gracefully eased away from Tyson, feeling her confusion deepen as he whispered, "I love you, Lacey. I love you with my whole heart and soul."

Lacey had to bite back the urge to snap at him with the first response that came to mind. If he loved her, why had he taken advantage of her and then left her alone? But Richard's presence kept her quiet. Instead, she just ignored Tyson, praying in her heart that someday, somehow, she could get beyond feeling this way and be able to love Tyson freely again.

Nothing more was said between them through the remainder of the picnic and their return home. Richard fell asleep during the ride back, and Tyson carried him to the nursery. Lacey offered to care for the horses, grateful for an excuse to be away from Tyson's overwhelming presence. She just didn't understand how she could love him so much and be so angry with him at the same time. And again she prayed that eventually she would be able to come up with an answer that made sense.

❦ ❦ ❦

Jess stepped out of the carriage, waited a long moment, then reached in and dragged the boy out by the shirt collar. If he hadn't purposely established the fact that the boy could hear, he might have believed he was deaf, due to the fact that everything Jess had said to him by way of comfort, promises, or even threats had been totally disregarded. He pointed at the boy with one last effort. "Now, listen good. You are going to be fed and cared for, and no one is going to hurt you, but if you don't mind your manners, you're going to wish you had. Got it?" He got no response. "I asked you a question, boy!"

The boy nodded firmly but with defiance.

"Good." Jess rewarded him with a genuine smile and a friendly pat on the shoulder, although he didn't let go of him for a second. He was in no mood to chase him down. He tried to count the times he'd done this and decided he couldn't begin to number them. They came through the front entrance of the boys' home and were met by Sarina. She greeted the child amiably, and was obviously not surprised to be ignored and glared at by the newcomer.

"Will you get Alexa?" Jess asked quietly.

"Right now," she answered firmly.

"And where is Michael?"

"In his office, waiting for you."

"Good, we'll meet Alexa there."

Jess urged the boy firmly down the hall, saying in a friendly tone, "This really isn't such a bad place once you get used to it. It sure beats stealing to eat."

The boy looked up with a subtle hint of guilt shining through the fear. They knocked and entered Michael's office to find him seated on the edge of the desk, arms folded, his face crafted into perfect cruelty. Jess might have been distressed by the way the boy recoiled at the sight of this man, but he'd seen Michael's methods work before.

"Hello." Michael drew the word out carefully, and Jess, who had been fought against all day, was suddenly something comforting for the boy to hold on to. "You may call me Mr. Hamilton. What might I call you?" Michael acted surprised when he got no response. "I'm sorry?" He put a hand to his ear. "I couldn't hear you." Still no response. "Do you have a name?" he asked. Silence still. "All right." Michael leaned forward, and the boy recoiled further. "I'll just call you Marvin."

The boy grimaced but didn't find a voice to object. Jess had to fight to keep a straight face as he caught on to what Michael was attempting.

"So, Marvin, what do you want to do first?" Michael asked, as if they'd been talking for hours. "Are you hungry? No," he answered without giving the boy even a second to think about it. "Want to see the horses? No. You've got to speak up, Marvin. How about playing some ball? Apparently not. All right. We've got a game room. Not excited about games, eh? The library is nice. He must not like books," he said more to Jess. "I understand there's a bed and other necessities with your name on them. That is, they would have your name on them if we knew what it was. We'll just have to put Marvin on them, eh, Mr. Davies?"

"Marvin is nice."

"Would you like to see where you'll be staying, Marvin? I've picked out some good roommates for you. You've got a lot in common with them, I'd bet. You'll all have a lot to talk about. Maybe you would like to see one of the most beautiful women in Australia. Would you like that?"

The boy made no response whatsoever. Michael leaned back to study him in a way that made the boy squirm slightly. He added carefully to Jess, "I don't think he believes there is a beautiful woman waiting on the other side of that door. I would bet he thinks the beautiful woman who came to see him yesterday was simply his imagination. I think that would be a good place to start. What do you think, Marvin?"

Michael moved to the door and opened it. Jess escorted the reluctant boy into the next room. Alexa was sitting prettily in a chair near the window, as if she was an elegant piece of the furniture. She turned warm eyes to the boy, but got no response beyond a brief glimmer of recognition.

"Have a seat, Marvin," Michael said. The boy did nothing. "I said have a seat!" He sat down huffily and Jess finally relinquished his hold, only to stand against the door like a sentry. It was a well-practiced procedure for Alexa to do the talking, and for Jess to guard the door.

"Marvin?" Alexa looked at Michael in question.

"He didn't tell me his name was otherwise," he informed her, then pulled a chair near the other door. He sat down with an exaggerated sigh to indicate that he intended to be here a long time. He motioned toward Alexa, and she leaned forward to look directly at the boy.

"Do you want to tell us what your name really is?" she asked. He only looked away. Alexa proceeded to promise him they weren't going to use any of the information he gave them to allow him to be returned to whoever or whatever he was running from. She told him they would be happy for now just to know his given name, and the rest could wait until he was ready. She gently pleaded, then she kindly coaxed, then she pleaded again. Jess suggested paper and pencil, and Alexa was quick to provide it, asking the boy if he knew how to write his name. Through all of it there was no more response than subtle changes in his eyes. Michael carefully observed those changes and what had been said to cause them. He studied the boy's appearance painstakingly, and analyzed it in relation to his own education on the streets.

When Alexa sighed and leaned back with a concerned glance toward Jess, Michael came to his feet. Without preamble he leaned his face close to the boy's and growled, "If you don't either speak or write your name immediately, I can guarantee that to every one of these boys you'll be living with, you will forever be known as dumb Marvin."

The boy hesitated, but Michael knew by his eyes that he was well aware of the apparent seriousness behind the threat, including exactly what it would mean to a boy who wanted to be tough. Another moment's hesitation sent Michael quickly to the door, pushing the chair out of the way and opening it abruptly to indicate that the threat would be carried out immediately. That very instant, the boy scribbled something on the paper and shoved it toward Alexa, giving Michael a defiant glare. Michael grinned smugly, closed the door, and sat down.

"Trent?" Alexa questioned with pleasure. "Your name is Trent?"

"The lady asked you a question," Michael said firmly, and Trent nodded toward Alexa.

She gave Michael a quick glance of approval before saying, "I think I like that much better than Marvin. Don't you?" He hesitated but nodded. "You know how to write, then?" Trent nodded, and Alexa handed the paper back. "Is there anything else you'd like to tell us?" He shook his head. "It's going to be difficult for a boy who can't speak to get along in the world," she stated. "Perhaps we should discuss the reasons for this, so we can help you." Trent made no response.

"Maybe his tongue doesn't work," Michael taunted.

Trent stuck it out at him in defiance, and Jess chuckled. "Well, I guess that's not the problem."

"Are you afraid?" Alexa asked, and he shook his head firmly while his eyes told the truth.

Alexa proceeded with perfect patience to gently convince Trent that it was all right to speak. She carefully went through every kind of fear he might have, based on her experience with other boys, until she could say nothing more to help Trent understand that it was all right to talk to them. She promised him that he didn't have to say anything he didn't want to; they simply wanted to know that he could talk. Alexa had discussed the situation with Michael earlier. She feared if the boy settled into a routine without using his voice, the present cause of his fear could turn into a longtime infirmity. She believed if she could just get him to say something—anything—before he was put in with the others, the rest would fall into place more easily, even if it took time. Michael continued to study the boy, and when Alexa glanced discreetly toward him to indicate he was welcome to try, he felt confidence in his next plan of action.

Michael came to his feet, making it clear by his stance that he was in charge. "All right," he paced back and forth slowly between Trent and Alexa, "the lady has made a worthy effort. Now you're going to have to deal with me." Trent lifted his chin with defiant courage, but the fear in his eyes deepened. "And I think you can talk." He stopped and put his hands on the arms of the chair Trent was sitting in. "I think you're just scared," he nearly hissed. "You don't trust us, because you've never known anybody worth trusting. You're afraid if you talk you'll have to tell us where you came from, and you don't want to go back. Well, we don't let anybody, ever, go back." He said it as if he was the keeper of a haunted castle, where no one ever came out alive. "You're ours now, and you don't want to know what we do to people who try to take one of our boys once we've got hold of them. But I'm not sure we can tolerate a boy who can't talk. We can't help you fight if we don't know what we're fighting." He moved his face closer to Trent's. "I say you can talk. I say we're not leaving here until you do. I say you're just a cowardly little whelp who hasn't got the guts to open his mouth and fight for the right to have food to eat and live without being afraid. I say a boy who can't talk doesn't measure up to be one of *my* boys." He lowered his voice. "I'd say you're just plain chicken."

"I am not!" Trent snapped, then he looked down guiltily when he realized he'd just lost the game. Jess and Alexa's dubious gazes turned into astonishment.

Michael straightened his back and folded his arms triumphantly. "That's what I thought." Trent looked up, silently questioning the contradiction. Michael tousled Trent's hair and gave him a smile that likely made the boy wonder if this was the same man. "It takes a real man to talk when he's afraid, Trent. Come on," he held out a hand, "let's get you cleaned up and see if we can find you some new clothes before we go eat. Then you can meet my other boys." Trent hesitated only a moment before he stood, and Michael put a hand on his shoulder.

"Trent," Alexa said, "do you think tomorrow you and I could talk some more?"

He nodded, but Michael said, "I don't think she heard you."

"Yeah," he said sheepishly.

"Good," Alexa smiled. "I'll look forward to it."

"Uh . . . Mr. Davies?" Michael said on his way out the door, "you know those . . . ," he enunciated carefully to imply an unspoken message, "little leather tags we put *my* boys' names on? Could you see that one is ready for Trent just after supper?" Jess nodded eagerly. "And that's Trent," Michael added, "not Marvin."

Michael left the room with Trent, and Alexa laughed. "I don't believe it."

"I do." Jess sat in the chair Trent had occupied. "You're good with the boys, Alexa. I've seen you do phenomenal things. But Michael's got something you'll never have."

"And what might that be?" she asked, although he was certain she already knew.

"He knows how they think, what they feel. He's *been* there."

"Yes," she smiled, "and I think he's one of the best things that ever happened to this place. He's working miracles out there, Jess."

"Yes, I believe he is."

❦   ❦   ❦

Trent said almost nothing as he was introduced to the other boys and sat through a meal in their company. Michael kept a close eye on him from a distance, gratified to see more relief in his eyes than fear. He didn't think Trent was going to be nearly so difficult as he'd imagined. He had been pleased and receptive when shown his new living quarters and given the usual allotment of personal belongings. He seemed to appreciate the meal. And the boys, having been carefully instructed and threatened earlier, were quiet but polite to Trent.

When supper was finished and the other boys went to the library, Michael escorted Trent to the stables, talking casually about the horse business that the Byrnehouse-Davies family was into as much as the boy business. He told Trent, just as he had been told when he'd come here, that he would be given the opportunity to help in the stables and earn his keep. Trent said nothing, but he listened attentively. They entered the stable, and Trent's eyes widened at the rows of stalls running down both sides, most of them occupied by beautiful horses in a variety of colors and breeds.

"You like horses?" Michael asked. Trent nodded. Michael walked with him to the appropriate stall and stopped. "You like this one?" he asked.

Trent looked at the animal with speculation, then up at Michael, who looked completely innocent. The boy seemed to wonder why they were standing here so long, then his eye caught his name engraved in leather and tacked to the stall.

"That is your name, isn't it?" Michael asked.

"Yeah, but . . ." He couldn't seem to find the words, so Michael helped him out.

"This animal is yours to care for as long as you do it properly. If the two of you get along well, you can take him with you when you leave here."

Trent appeared both stunned and pleased. "You mean he's like a present?"

"In a way. But you have to earn the right to keep him."

"Nobody ever gave me a present before."

"Then it's about time somebody did," Michael said, wishing he could tell the boy that he knew exactly how he felt. The only "presents" he had gotten as a child had left scars. Trent smiled up at Michael, and none of that mattered now.

Through the following days, Trent settled into this life as if it were heaven sent. He wouldn't say a word to anyone concerning his background, or even his surname. But he was cared for nonetheless, and Jess and Alexa were pleased with his progress.

Michael felt confident that the boys were adjusting to his new expectations of toughness, and he was glad that he'd had the insight to follow through as he had. He felt certain it was making a difference. Little Michael was sleeping without a lamp, and Matthew was beginning to talk eagerly about turning eighteen and his plans for the future, which included a college education.

While Michael cultivated blossoming boys, Emma kept busy with wedding plans, building block castles with Richard, working with the horses, reading romance novels, and playing Cupid for Tyson and Lacey. Things seemed to be looking up when Tyson went away for a few days with some of the hands to take two of their horses to participate in a derby. And Lacey actually seemed to miss him. Emma could relate, even though Michael never left the station. She was amazed to realize that their time together could be tallied up in minutes, where trivialities were exchanged along with a few stolen kisses. Knowing the circumstances, she wasn't concerned. But on the other hand, as Lacey seemed to be warming to Tyson, her attitude was freezing even more deeply toward Michael. She rarely passed up an opportunity to remind Emma of his lack of presence. Lacey was convinced that Michael was not here for Emma's love, but to get gain; that a day would come when he would decide he didn't want commitment and he'd leave; that his past would catch up with him and leave Emma hurting. Always before, Michael's presence and the evidence of his love had dispelled such fears in Emma; but as Michael remained most-ly absent, and Lacey became more free in her opinions, Emma began to feel the stress.

Her mind was preoccupied with the problem one morning as she dressed for breakfast and hurriedly pulled open the door to leave her room. She gasped to see Michael leaning against the door frame as if he'd been there for hours. "How long have you been out here?" she asked.

"Long enough to make certain I'd be here when you opened that door."

"Who are you, anyway?" she asked lightly, but Michael caught the severity in her eyes.

"Your fiancé." He tapped the toe of his boot on the floor in disgust.

"I don't recall whether or not I've even met you." She thought about it. "Oh, I know," she pointed at him in mock enlightenment, "you're the one who kidnapped me and took me to that cave and—"

Michael clamped a hand over her mouth and looked warily down the hall in both directions. "Yes, that's me," he said quickly, and Emma laughed. In her opinion, Michael Hamilton was the funniest man in the world.

He retained his stance against the door frame and put his hands into his pockets. "I've tried to see you every evening, but you're always with Lacey."

"How am I supposed to keep track of you?" she retorted. "You've not shared a meal with the family for five days. Or is it six? I bought you a present, and you haven't even been around long enough for me to give it to you."

He grinned like a child. "A present, really? What is it?"

"I'm not telling you. You don't deserve to know."

"Oh, Emma," he said, his voice becoming sincere, "the boys need me. I know I've been with them a lot, but it's getting easier now."

"I need you, too, Michael. Do you think perhaps we could expect you for supper this evening?"

"I promise." He took hold of her hands and squeezed them, then he pressed his nose menacingly to hers. "Now, where's my present?"

"Keep your eyes open, and you'll find it if you're where you're supposed to be." Michael scowled, but she ignored him and added, "You coming to breakfast?"

"I need to be with the boys," he apologized. "Your father said he got word that Mr. Grant would be here later this morning with the Simpkins. It could likely be little Michael's last morning here. But tomorrow I'll—"

"Yes, I know," Emma interrupted and walked away, dreading another meal with Lacey's *I told you so* attitude.

"Emma," he called, and she turned back expectantly. "I love you."

"I love you, too," she said and hurried down the stairs.

Nineteen
BALANCE

Michael sighed and promised himself he'd make it up to Emma later. He hurried to the cafeteria, and as his eyes fell on little Michael, he decided he didn't want the boys here when the Simpkins arrived. He wanted the prospective parents to wait and wonder a little.

He told Sarina he would be taking all of the boys together this morning, and he herded them out to the stable to saddle their mounts. They rode together to a spot in the hills where he had often gone on his own. Then they all lay in the grass, and he initiated a discussion about what they felt was good about their lives.

In due time they returned from their excursion and tended to their horses, getting back to the home barely in time for lunch. Michael opened the door to the cafeteria and held it while eighteen heads filed past, but his eyes were on the finely dressed couple sitting across the room with Ira Grant. They came to their feet expectantly as the boys took their places and began to eat. Michael felt a mixture of emotion. Part of him felt the joy of a lost boy finding a home, while another part of him didn't want to lose little Michael. His youth and vulnerability had naturally made him become more dependent on the new administrator, and parting would not be easy.

Drawing a deep breath, Michael approached them, holding out a hand to Mr. Grant. The farthest thing from his mind was the accusation of murder against him.

"Mr. Grant, it's good to see you again."

"And you," he replied. He gestured toward the couple. "This is Holt and AnnaBelle Simpkins."

"A pleasure to meet you," Michael smiled, already feeling good about this. Their kindness left an unmistakable aura about them. He knew little Michael would be in good hands.

"This is Michael Hamilton," Ira continued. "He is the administrator here."

"Why don't we have some lunch, and then we'll go to my office and discuss the situation," Michael offered.

Sarina motioned them to an empty table where lunch was set out for the four of them, and they sat to eat. "Which one is Michael?" Mrs. Simpkins whispered discreetly.

"He's the youngest, there between the tall ones." He nodded unobtrusively, noting that Michael was the boy least interested in what these people might be doing here. "Adorable, isn't he?" Michael added like a proud parent.

Mrs. Simpkins smiled, and Michael was aware of her squeezing her husband's hand across the table. Jess and Alexa came in before they were finished, and they all went together to Michael's office. The women were seated and the men leaned against the wall, except for Mr. Grant, who set a leather case on the desk and proceeded to pull out papers and organize them. Michael felt an unnerving sense of importance as these people looked to him expectantly.

"Please tell us about him, Mr. Hamilton. Mrs. Davies tells me you've spent a great deal of time with him."

"I haven't been here terribly long, Mrs. Simpkins, but I can tell you he's an agreeable child. I've never had a minute's trouble from him. His latest accomplishment is a great personal triumph for him." All eyes widened in question. "He can sleep in the dark now without being afraid." Michael leaned against the desk and folded his arms. "It seems, according to him, that it was dark when his mother died, and he's had difficulty with that. You should be aware of his feelings, I believe." The Simpkins nodded eagerly. "Beyond that, I would say he's a typical six-year-old boy. He likes to be rowdy. He wants to be loved. He likes adventure stories. He's learning to read. He hates green vegetables and he loves meatloaf. He thinks the moon is prettier when it's full, and he wants to be an aborigine when he grows up."

They all chuckled, and Michael went on. "I told him he can't do that, and he's coming to accept that he'll just have to live with them. But that's only when he's not thinking about being a crocodile hunter. He loves cookies with raisins, as opposed to cookies without. He believes that new shoes can make him run faster than old ones. His favorite color is yellow because he likes the sun, and he carries sugar cubes in his pocket at all times, which are supposed to be for his horse, but less than half of them make it to the horse's mouth. His horse's name is Smiley. He tells me that he and Smiley are one day going to discover the outback and be home in time for supper."

Alexa was left in awe when Michael had finished. It was evident that he wasn't just spending time with these boys. He *knew* them. Jess simply said, more to the Simpkins, "Smiley comes with the deal."

"Any questions?" Michael asked.

"I can't think of anything," Holt Simpkins said. "How about you?" he asked his wife.

"No, I think we know how to take care of a boy. We're quite accustomed to the rowdy kind. Mr. Grant has filled us in on the circumstances that led to his being here. I just want to meet him." She added with a slight quiver of her lip, "Do you think he'll . . . I mean, what if he doesn't want to come with us?"

"I think he will," Michael said easily. "Why don't you all wait here for a few minutes, and I'll go and get him."

Michael had to fight the urge to get choked up as he walked briskly to the schoolroom and opened the door. "Michael," he called, "could you come out here, please?"

The boy came eagerly and took his hand. The door closed, and Michael squatted down in the hallway to meet him eye to eye. "Hey there, tough guy, I've got a surprise for you. A very nice man has come to tell me that he has found something for you that I always wanted when I was a boy here."

"A kitten?" little Michael asked.

"No," Michael chuckled. "It's even better. How would you like to have a family?" The child said nothing, but his eyes were more curious than afraid. "There are some very kind people in my office right now; they are related to your mother. They have some children who want another brother to play with, and they have a special chair for you at their dinner table. They also have a special place for you to sleep and to keep your things. And they said you can even take Smiley with you." Michael took his hands. "Do you think you would like that?"

"Can you come, too?" he asked, and Michael had to swallow hard.

"No, Michael. I can't come. But the dark will be no different there than it is here, and I want you to always think of me when the light goes out, and I will always think of you."

"Do you think they'll let me have a kitten?"

"I don't know. Should we go and ask them?"

"All right," he said, as if this was no different than going to the library or the game room.

Michael pushed open the door to the office and leaned his head in while he held the child's hand, who remained in the hall. "He doesn't want to come unless . . ." He hesitated purposely and was gratified at the tension he had created in the room. "Unless he might get a kitten one day."

The Simpkins chuckled, and little Michael was ushered in. He held Michael's hand as he was introduced, and the child speculatively observed these people.

"Do you know what, Michael?" AnnaBelle Simpkins said in a tone that caught his attention. "At our house there is a big gray cat with a white nose and three white paws. She lives under the porch, and in another week or two, we believe she's going to have some kittens. She likes to come in the house and lounge on the sofa, and we always have to clean her fur off when company comes to visit. But she likes to play with the children. And if you would like to come and live with us and our big gray cat, I would bet she'll let you have first pick of her kittens when they're old enough to be on their own."

Little Michael smiled. "Do you think she'll get along with Smiley?"

"She's never seemed to mind the other horses in the barn, and she really likes the cow because she sometimes sneaks a taste of milk when we get it in the mornings for breakfast."

The child turned to Michael. "Can I take my things with me from my room?"

"Of course you can," Michael smiled. "Why don't you take your new friends there now, and you can pack them up. I think Mrs. Davies has a bag you can use. Then you can come back down and say good-bye to the boys. I'll go and get Smiley for you."

An hour later, Smiley was being tied to the rear of the carriage, and little Michael's bag was set inside. Michael hovered in the background as final formalities were exchanged. Little Michael looked accepting and pleased. The situation was ideal, but Michael felt a degree of the ache that many of the other boys had betrayed subtly in their eyes as the child's leaving was announced. But envy was expected. Every lost boy wanted a real home and a real family.

Mrs. Simpkins stepped into the carriage, and Mr. Simpkins bent to lift little Michael up. But he turned suddenly and ran to Michael, who squatted down to embrace him.

"I'm going to miss you, Mr. Hamilton."

"I'm going to miss you, too." He looked right at him and said, "But you remember what I told you about the dark." The child nodded firmly.

"I love you, Mr. Hamilton."

Michael felt the long-fought emotion trickle into his eyes. "I love you, too, Michael."

"How come you're cryin'?"

"Because I'm not afraid to let you know that I mean it."

Michael received a fervent kiss on the cheek, and then he watched as the child ran to his new father and was lifted eagerly into the carriage. As it drove away, Alexa put an arm around Michael.

"Sad?" she asked quietly.

"A little. But more happy, I suppose."

"Tell me."

Michael looked down at her, nestled beneath his arm. "I know how it feels to finally become part of a real family. To finally come home." He smiled. "It just took me twenty-two years longer."

Alexa opened her mouth to compliment him on his work with the boys, but Ira Grant, who had stayed behind for other business, turned to Michael and said firmly, "I think we need to talk, Mr. Hamilton."

Michael had been so absorbed that it took a moment to remember why. "I suppose we do," he answered dryly. "But only if you'll believe me when I tell you I didn't do it."

"I wouldn't be standing here if I believed otherwise."

"Then let's talk."

"Your office?"

"Fine."

Alexa gave him a quick embrace and moved to Jess's side. Michael led Ira inside and back to the office, wanting to do anything else but this.

❧ ❧ ❧

Emma sat down to supper and gazed at Michael's empty chair. She avoided Lacey's eyes as the meal progressed, feeling more sad than angry. This was beginning to be unbearable.

When the door opened, she looked up brightly. But her expression faltered when Ira Grant entered alone.

"I was wondering when you'd show up," Jess said, motioning him to the place set for him. Ira sat and eased his chair to the table. "You've been with Michael all this time?"

"Until about ten minutes ago," Ira reported. "On our way out of the office he was summoned to deal with some fighting boys. He's quite a man."

Emma toyed idly with her food. She didn't miss Lacey's sigh of disgust.

"I must say," Ira continued, "I am as convinced as you are of his innocence, but it's touchy with his record and . . . ," he looked at Emma, "his kidnapping ventures."

Emma relaxed when she realized he was mostly teasing.

"Actually," Ira took a bite and waited until he'd swallowed, "I think we've got a pretty solid case if Emma will testify on his behalf of the things she's witnessed, including what Mr. Coogan said yesterday. I've debated whether or not to inform the constable of his whereabouts."

Emma felt herself turn pale. Ira apparently noticed as he looked her direction while adding, "Considering that he's needed here has made the decision difficult, but there is only one possibility. Forgive me, Emma, but I have to tell them."

"No!" She came to her feet with vehemence. Tyson did the same, as if he shared her response. "You can't. Please. I know that—"

"Emma," Ira said carefully, then he looked around the table to include the others. "Please hear me out." Tyson sat down and gave a comforting nod to Emma, who reluctantly did the same. "I understand the dilemma, I really do. But I cannot waltz into the courtroom to represent a man and let them find out that I knew where he was and didn't inform the law. Dishonest solicitors don't get very far in representing questionable clients. However, I believe the constable trusts me as much as I trust him. I'm going to tell him the situation, promise him that Michael will not leave the premises until the case is cleared, and hope he will agree that an arrest is not necessary at this time."

"It's me they'll arrest," Jess said, "for harboring a fugitive."

"I wouldn't be too concerned about that," Ira said. "The best thing we have going for us here is character. This family has a spotless reputation when it comes to dealing with the law. I think the constable will understand."

"And what if he doesn't?" Emma had to ask. "Michael and I are supposed to be married next week."

"I'll do my best," Ira said apologetically. "That's all I can do."

"I don't know why they don't just hang him and get it over with," Lacey shot into the conversation.

"Lacey!" Emma retorted.

"I fear she's not very fond of Michael," Tyson stated to Ira.

"Yes, I know," Ira replied, then he added to Lacey, "Jess has told me what you heard that could sound incriminating. But with Emma having heard the same, and then having witnessed enough to counteract it, I'm afraid your testimony won't make much difference."

"That's nothing new," Lacey grumbled. She wanted to say more, but Tyson put a firm hand on her leg beneath the table, accompanied by a strong stare that kept her quiet.

When dessert was brought in, Emma ate hers and Michael's too, but she was still in a bad mood. "I think I'll go find Michael," she said, rising to leave.

"He probably ran away when he realized we weren't going to keep him hidden any longer."

"Lacey," Emma said with the kindest tone she could muster, "you are welcome to your opinions, but I'd prefer that you keep them to yourself."

Emma couldn't hold back a rush of tears as she searched for Michael. After looking everywhere she could possibly think of and crying herself out, she decided there was only one other place he could be, and she headed up to the gabled attic, almost afraid that Lacey was right.

❦   ❦   ❦

"Getting hungry?" Michael asked in genuine anger, thinking of his broken promise to Emma. "I am. I think supper is over. But we're not leaving here until your stories match. One of you is lying, and I want to know who."

Silence met him, just as it had for the last hour.

"Fess up, before I start to get *really* upset."

Still, both boys just stared at him, then at each other, then at the floor. Michael knew the liar was Christian, and he hated to make Will suffer through this for telling the truth, but he'd make it up to him later. This was the only way he could figure to get Christian to admit to it. Of course, when he'd threatened that they were going to sit here until the truth was told, he was expecting five or ten minutes. But he'd threatened it, and he had to carry his threats out.

A knock came at the door, and Michael fully expected Sarina to be looking for the boys. "Come in," he called, and Emma peered carefully into the room. Michael attempted to portray apology with his expression, but the disappointment in her eyes was evident.

"What are you doing?" she asked timidly, more grateful than she could admit to see that at least Lacey hadn't been right.

"Trying to get the truth." Michael glared at the boys.

"I told the truth, Mr. Hamilton," Will insisted, and Michael believed him.

He looked at Christian severely. This was beginning to get on his nerves. Trusting his instincts, Michael finally got to a point he'd been avoiding. "You're lying to me, boy, and I want the truth now. You've already gotten me into trouble." He glanced at Emma, and the boys' eyes followed. "Now speak up!"

Christian looked at Michael, then at Emma, as if he'd just comprehended a connection. He then looked straight ahead, folded his arms, and scowled. "All right. I did it."

"Thank you!" Michael drawled, slapping him on the shoulder. He came to his feet, leaned over Christian, and pointed a finger at his nose. "It'll never work, boy. You'll never get away with it. You lie, and someone will always find out. I don't want it to happen again."

"Yes, sir," Christian said humbly.

"I think you owe William an apology."

"Sorry, William."

"That's all right." Will stood, offered Christian a hand to help him up, and they left together.

Michael met Emma's eyes, wondering where to begin to remedy the situation.

"You scared him," he stated. "I've been sitting here for over an hour, trying to get the truth out of him. You give him the evil eye, and he's out with it in a second." Still Emma said nothing. "Ah, so it's me getting the evil eye, as I well deserve it." Still nothing. Michael threw up his hands. "I'm sorry, Emma. What can I say?"

"When I told Mother you would be there for supper, she had Mrs. Brady prepare chocolate mousse. I ate yours."

"You'll get fat," he said, but she didn't even smile. "I'll still love you."

"How gracious of you. Good night, Michael." Emma turned and left, unable to face him and her emotion at the same time.

Michael wanted to follow her, but he wondered if she wanted him to. It was one of those times when he wished he could just fight. He could handle a good fist fight a lot easier than this. But was it any different? Blast what Emma might want! He gave himself some of his own advice and ran after her. She was worth fighting for. He called her name, but she ignored him.

"Emma!" He caught her arm and turned her to face him. "I'm sorry. What could I do?"

"Michael, I understand your dedication to the boys, and I do not resent it."

"Then what's wrong?"

"Other than knowing the law will know your whereabouts sometime tomorrow?"

Michael looked down. "Other than that."

"Your dedication to your family has got to be equally important."

"It is," he insisted, liking the way she'd called them *his* family.

"Not from what I see."

"Emma, you know that I love you. I . . ."

"Yes, Michael," she took hold of his arms, "I know. And I understand that there are times when the boys need you and they can't wait. It's not exactly that. It's just . . ." She looked at the floor, and Michael realized there was something she wasn't saying.

"The truth?" He lifted her chin with his finger.

Emma's eyes filled with tears. "I don't want to talk about it right now." She ran down the hall, and Michael felt he had to let her go—for now. He sensed that perhaps she needed time alone. He shuffled slowly back to his room, wondering if this was the way Tyson felt most of the time. He often seemed to be dragging around, exchanging tense glances with Lacey. Michael felt pure pity for him. Now he knew how it felt.

He had to admit that Emma was right. The boys were important, but it had been well established that he cared for them. The family— most especially Emma—was equally important. No, more so. Emma was his life. Of course, he couldn't abandon the boys; but then, she wasn't expecting him to. Balance—that's what he needed. Balance between the two. He couldn't spend his life waiting around for Emma. She had her pastimes, her family relationships. Nor could he hover continually around the boys. They might come to depend on his always being there, and that wasn't good. They had to learn to make it on their own.

By the time Michael got to his room, he had his mind made up to achieve balance. Six days a week he was expected to be with the boys from ten until three, including lunch. That still left ample time to drift in and out of their other activities, give some time to the special problems, and still eat breakfast and supper with the family. And he could spend most of his evenings with Emma, if he could only get Lacey to spend hers with Tyson. There. That was easy enough to figure out. The hard part would be convincing Emma that he'd learned his lesson.

Michael pushed open the door of his room and fumbled to find the lamp. He barely had it lit when a knock came at the door and he eagerly opened it, hoping to find Emma. Instead he found Tillie, carrying a dinner tray, complete with chocolate mousse.

"Mrs. Davies asked me to bring this up when Sarina said you'd not eaten with the boys."

"Thank you, Tillie." He took it gratefully while his stomach growled in response. "Give Mrs. Davies my thanks, and tell her that I'll see her at breakfast."

Tillie curtsied and scurried away. Noticing little of his surroundings, Michael sat to eat his meal, appreciating its fineness but wishing he'd shared it with Emma. Here he sat, a few doors away from the woman he loved, and there might as well have been a thousand miles between them.

When he'd had his fill, Michael decided to get cleaned up as much as possible without having someone bring up buckets of water. He contemplated whether or not he should try to talk to Emma tonight. He doubted he could sleep if he didn't, but he wondered if she might be more receptive tomorrow. Or would she be insulted if he waited until morning? She had once waited until morning to talk to him, and he'd been gone.

It was only then that he noticed the things left on the bed. He stopped to inspect them. New clothes. The last time he'd been given new clothes, it was by Miss Sarina at the same time all the other boys got new clothes. But they had always been practical clothes. Michael fingered the fabric of the breeches, the waistcoats, the handkerchiefs. The feel was fine and expensive. He was contemplating the quality of the handkerchiefs when he noticed the shirts. They had almost blended into the light-colored spread because they were white.

"White." Michael had to say it aloud to see if he could. If anyone had tried to make him wear a white shirt at any other time in his life, he'd have thrown it in their face. But Michael picked one of them up, fingered it, touched it to his face as if it might renew him. Emma was trying to tell him something. He wasn't a bad guy anymore.

With a sense of pride he pulled it over his head, noting there were also some that buttoned. She knew he liked both. He gazed in the mirror as he fastened the cuffs and adjusted it. She knew his taste. It was full and old-fashioned. Michael tucked it into his new breeches and put a new waistcoat over it, but he left it unbuttoned. He didn't want to cover up too much of the white.

Pulling on his boots with determination, Michael combed through his damp hair, checked the mirror once more, and left his room dark before he peered into the hallway and moved stealthily to Emma's room, muttering a quick prayer in his heart.

He tapped lightly on the door, and a moment later it flew open with a terse, "Really, Lacey, I'm tired, and I . . ." She gasped. "Michael." He noticed she was dressed for bed, with a wrapper hanging loosely over her usual prudishly modest nightgown.

Emma lost her breath and couldn't find it until she had plenty of time to absorb his appearance. He'd always looked good in black, always been suited to the rugged clothing he wore. But the man before her was striking in contrast. The face was etched with experience, street-hardened and world-wise. The eyes were deeply faceted and capable of more depth than most humans could even imagine. The damp hair looked black as a moonless night, hanging in striking contrast over the white collar that flowed into clothes that enhanced the studied appearance and belied the clean, calloused hands.

"You look nice," she said, thinking it sounded trite.

"Thank you," he stated, fully sincere. "Only you could understand."

"What?" she asked.

"That a new man needs to feel like one. Look like one."

"Something like that." She smiled, but silence followed, bringing them back to the tension. Michael glanced warily down the hall, fearing he might be caught here when he knew there was nothing to hide.

"Come in." Emma motioned him into the room. She closed the door and leaned against it. Michael turned to look at her, hands behind his back. There was so much that needed to be said, but words seemed lost. Michael wondered how he could begin to express the humility he felt for his mistakes; his gratitude for her acceptance and love; and the dedication they shared that filled his heart to overflowing.

Emma waited expectantly, wondering where the apologies should begin. It was true that he'd been negligent, but for good reason. And her being so upset was for reasons he didn't understand. She was about to say so when he fell to his knees before her, taking both her hands into his and kissing them tenderly, reverently. The gesture sent her heart pounding as no words could have. The drama of his gallantry made her wonder briefly if he was acting, but his eyes moved up to meet hers, and her throbbing heart nearly exploded with the realization that Michael Hamilton was the most honest and sincere of men. His dedication to her was boundless, his love for her incomparable. Lacey's words, however well meaning, evaporated like steam beneath the melting heat in Michael's eyes, glowing with the kind of love that could only be understood by a man who had known the ultimate hatred.

Emma put her hands to his face, and he closed his eyes to relish her touch. Emma's hand moved into his hair, then she slid to her knees and pressed her mouth over his. With their kiss, everything else became nonexistent.

A knock at the door shattered their oblivion. Michael sighed and pressed his face to her shoulder. "Every time I start kissing you . . . ," he whispered, finding no need to finish what was obvious. "I just don't believe this."

"Who is it?" Emma called.

"It's me," Lacey called back.

"As if we didn't know," Michael said with quiet sarcasm, then his eyes filled with apology. "I'm sorry, Emma. Sometimes that old me just slips out. If she needs you, I understand."

"Emma?" Lacey called. "Are you there?"

"Yes, just a minute."

"But," he pointed a finger as he came to his feet, helping her along, "I'm taking you on a very long honeymoon—and not a double honeymoon, either."

Emma gazed at Michael while Lacey knocked again. A quick assessment of the circumstances made her realize she had some important points to prove, to Michael *and* Lacey.

Emma moved to answer the door, but Michael stopped her. "Did you want me to hide or leave?"

"Neither," she insisted, pulling the door open just enough to see her sister.

"What's going on?" Lacey insisted.

"I'm sorry, Lacey. I know you're having a difficult time, but I'm just not up to it tonight. There is something else I need to see to. Perhaps we can talk tomorrow."

"But Emma, I—"

"Lacey," she interrupted in a voice that was gentle but firm, "you know how I care for you." She took her hand. "But we've had the same conversation several times now. You need to talk to Tyson, not me. I can't solve it, but you can—the two of you, together."

"But, Emma," Lacey insisted, "it's not that easy. Surely you know that I—"

"I know that I need this time to work out some things of my own, and I just gave you the best advice I can give. If you're not willing to heed my advice, why do you ask for it?"

"Are you angry at me for what I said at the supper table?" Lacey asked.

"No, it's not that. I—"

"Emma," Lacey pleaded, obviously not listening. Emma opened the door further. Lacey interpreted it as an invitation and stepped forward, only to realize the gesture had been to indicate that Emma wasn't alone.

"Hello, Lacey," Michael stated, coming behind Emma to place his hands on her shoulders.

"Oh, I see," Lacey's voice turned bitter. "It's plain now where your priorities are."

"That's not fair, Lacey. Michael and I have hardly had an evening together since we returned because I've been with you. But if you must have it straight out, Michael is the most important thing in my life. That doesn't mean you and I can't remain close, but it does mean that Michael and I need time together. Perhaps if you spent more time with Tyson, you would be able to mend some of those bridges." Emma pleaded, "Confide in Tyson. He needs you."

"He loves you, Lacey," Michael said gently.

"And what would you know of love?" she retorted.

Michael borrowed Emma's wisdom. "I know that no amount of pain can stand with truth in the face of genuine love and forgiveness." He drew Emma close to him. Lacey was quick to notice, and her disgust was evident. "Love healed me, Lacey. Perhaps it can heal you, as well."

Lacey's eyes filled with fury as she perceived that Michael was putting her into his category. She turned on her heel and hurried to her room, slamming the door with fervor.

"Did I say something I shouldn't have?" Michael asked.

Emma closed the door and turned to him. "No, I think you said exactly what she needed to hear."

"You said some interesting things, too, Emma. I caught your point, and I want to apologize to you. You didn't need to tell Lacey it was her fault we've not had time together. It's mine, and I know it."

"No, what I told her was true. I can't accept your apology without making one of my own. I wouldn't have been so angry with you if I hadn't spent the week listening to Lacey's criticisms every time you didn't show up. She's been working very hard to convince me that you're not committed, not dependable. I believe in her heart she's only concerned for me. She fears you will leave me the way Tyson left her, and she doesn't want me to get hurt. I don't think she trusts any man, and she's looking for every reason in the world not to trust you. It's all blown out of proportion in her mind because of the pain, but she's not seeing that she's the only one who can let it go." Emma touched Michael's face. "She could learn a thing or two about that from you."

"You can't reach someone who doesn't want to be reached."

"And did you want to be reached, Michael?"

"When you forced me to face myself with honesty, I realized that every part of me wanted nothing but to love you and to be free of the pain." He kissed her lips timidly, watching her eyes, brushing his thumb over her flushed cheek. "Forgive me, Emma. I can see that I need balance in my life, and I will do my best to achieve it. I'm still learning. I need you to guide me."

"I'll always be here, Michael. I have never loved or trusted anyone as much as I do you."

Michael brought her hand to his lips. Emma watched him kiss it, noting the coarse feel of his mustache as it brushed her skin. Without taking his eyes from hers, Michael lifted her hand to brush his face with it, then he threaded his fingers through hers, pressing their palms together.

"Why?" he whispered. "How is it possible for you to trust me so much? Trust must be earned, proven by time. I don't understand, Emma."

"I have seen you fight for me, Michael. That alone proves you worthy of my deepest trust."

"I would die for you, Emma," he breathed against her face. Emma felt tears sting her eyes, but she turned them willingly to Michael, unashamed of the evidence of how deeply the meaning of his words affected her. If only every woman could be so blessed, she thought, to know with all her being that a man loved her so completely.

"I would prefer that you live for me," she breathed into his ear, knowing her life would be nothing without him. If Lacey loved Tyson this much, Emma could understand the pain of his abandonment. In her heart, she prayed they would find together all that she and Michael shared. Mutual trust and perfect devotion.

Her words and thoughts combined to bring the reality flooding back to her. "Michael," she cried, "if they take you away from me, I couldn't live. I absolutely could not—"

"Hush." He put his fingers over her lips. "You're forgetting something very important, Emma." He whispered with vehemence, "I'm a fighter, and I have something worth fighting for. I also have Ira Grant, who is convinced of my innocence. I have witnesses of the highest character, and my accusers are of the lowest. We will take it as it comes and do the best we can. Now, we will speak of it no more."

He pushed a stray lock of hair behind her ear as he said, "Let's talk, Emma. I've missed you. I need you."

"And I need you," she said, missing the closeness they had shared briefly before their journey home from the outback had begun.

"I want to tell you everything that's been happening with the boys," he said, sitting on the bed. Recalling Michael's promise to keep their relationship chaste until they were married, Emma sat close to him, holding his hand as they talked into the night. He told her all he was feeling and learning, and she shared their wedding plans and the arrangements they had made. When a lull came in the conversation, Michael yawned loudly and Emma noticed that a button on his shirt was about to fall off.

"Here," she said, knowing too well that putting off such a thing would result in a lost button. "Slip your shirt off and let me fix this before you go to bed."

Emma thought how far Michael had come when he took his shirt off with no apparent hesitation or embarrassment. She found needle and thread and sat close to the lamp to quickly tighten the button. When she turned to hand the shirt to Michael, she found him dozing. She smiled, thinking that those boys certainly wore him out, then she pulled an extra blanket over him. She contemplated going to his room to spend the rest of the night so she wouldn't have to disturb him. But knowing she was too wound up to sleep for a while yet, she curled up in a chair and decided to read until she got sleepy.

Emma was startled by a light knock at the sitting room door, which made her realize she'd dozed off with the book in her hand. Glancing toward Michael to assure herself that he was still sleeping, she tightened her wrapper around her to ward off a subtle chill and opened the door just enough to see that it was Lacey.

"I know it's late," she said quietly, "but I couldn't sleep. I've been thinking, and I realize I've been dreadful to you." She paused. "Is he gone? May I come in?"

Emma glanced back toward the bed and opted to allow her into the dimly lit room. "He's here, but he's asleep."

Lacey looked surprised but stepped quietly inside, and Emma closed the door. "As I was saying," Lacey continued, "I know I've been hard on you, and I want to apologize. You must know it's only because I'm concerned for you that I . . ."

Lacey stopped when Michael shifted in his sleep, and her attention was drawn to the bed. He lifted an arm out of the blanket and rolled onto his side. For a moment, Emma tried to think quickly of a way to distract her sister, but it was too late. Lacey gave a brief, breathy gasp, then she turned to silently question Emma concerning the scars visible on Michael's back.

"His father did that to him," Emma said quietly, "when he was a child."

Emma turned her sister away, inwardly hoping that the incident might soften her toward him. "You were saying?" Emma prodded, wanting a chance to further discuss Lacey's apology.

Lacey glanced once more toward the bed, then spoke tersely. "I certainly hope Michael isn't like his father. I shudder to think what he might do to—"

"I can assure you," Emma interrupted, "that Michael is nothing like his father."

"How can you be certain, Emma, when—"

"If I'm not mistaken, a moment ago you were apologizing. Now you're at it again."

"Emma, you know I'm only concerned for your future, and—"

"Then let me live my life in peace."

Michael rolled over and asked softly, "Emma? Did you say something?"

"It's all right," she said. "Lacey was just leaving."

Michael's eyes flew open in surprise, then they softened to non-chalance as he leaned up on one elbow. "Oh, it's you."

Emma expected him to show apprehension at having his chest bare, but he didn't seem to notice.

"Yes," Lacey said tersely, "I was just leaving."

"Please don't tell Mother," Michael said like a frightened child. Lacey looked at him in disbelief, but he only grinned.

"I've no desire to repeat it," she snarled. "It's too late, anyway. It's apparent that Emma is already in far too deep."

Emma realized by her comment that Lacey was assuming she and Michael had been intimate. Of course the situation certainly appeared that way, but she felt certain trying to convince Lacey that nothing had happened would be as futile as convincing her that Michael was a decent person.

"Emma is the most wonderful woman in the world," Michael stated soberly.

"Even Emma has her faults," Lacey said, glaring at Michael to indicate that he was one of them. Then she hurried from the room.

"She really likes me, you know," Michael quipped. "In truth, I think she's simply jealous."

"If she's not, she ought to be," Emma said distantly.

"What are you thinking, Emma?" he asked tenderly.

Emma sighed and sat in a chair near the bed. "Well, Lacey just came in here full of apology, then a minute later she was doing exactly what she had apologized for. It reminded me of something."

"What?"

"You." She looked at him, and his eyes widened. "There was a time when I was nearly convinced you were mad." He grinned proudly. "I'm serious!" she insisted. "You would look at me and say something fully serious, and minutes later you would outwardly contradict it."

"I think I was confused."

"That's just my point. I believe you were very confused. The pain inside made it impossible for you to know where you stood. You didn't know what to think, how to feel."

"That's likely true," he said, more sad than anything. "I think I understand what you're saying."

"I'm worried about her, Michael. She's always been timid, and easily frightened. But it wasn't until after Tyson left that she ever showed signs of real unhappiness. And now, so much has happened these past weeks that seems to have affected her adversely."

"And a lot of that is my fault," he admitted with a concerned scowl.

"You might have added a little fuel, but I don't believe you're as much the cause as she seems to think."

"I hope not."

"And as for you," she smiled, "you have made remarkable progress."

"How is that?"

"You, sitting there, scars and all, while my sister is in the room. I recall that until recently, you had fought very hard to make certain no one saw them."

"What scars?" he asked so seriously that Emma had to laugh.

Michael finally smiled and came to his feet as he picked up his shirt to put it on. He kissed Emma at the door and returned to his room. Emma crawled into bed, liking the way the pillow held a subtle, lingering aroma of Michael. She drifted quickly to sleep, and her next awareness was Michael kissing her awake.

"When did you sneak back in?" she asked dreamily.

"Just now," he said and kissed her again. "I don't mean to intrude upon your blissful rest, my sweet. But I promised I would share breakfast with the family, and it's nearly time now."

Emma sighed and looked at the clock. "Yes, of course. Breakfast."

"How long until we're married?" he asked.

"Six days."

"Good. When we're married, we'll miss breakfast and let them wonder."

Within just a few minutes, Emma opened the door and peered carefully into the hall, checking both directions. Michael stuck his head above hers and did the same, whispering in mock fear, "Do you think we're safe?"

Emma took his hand and nearly ran down the stairs, dragging him behind her. She paused before the dining room door and straightened herself into the proper demeanor. Michael did the same, tugging fitfully at his new waistcoat. Emma fought to keep from laughing as she pushed open the door and Michael followed her in, grateful to find that the family was just being seated.

"Good morning," Jess boomed.

"Good morning, sir." Michael bowed slightly and followed Emma through the buffet set out on the sideboard.

"You look nice, Michael," Alexa added warmly.

He turned and nodded in appreciation. "Emma bought them for me." He set down his plate to briefly turn and model in a way that made everyone but Lacey chuckle. "She's always doing things like that, you know." He proceeded to load his plate, adding a little more to Emma's as well. "She's always trying to—"

"I don't want that much," Emma protested, loading the extra helpings back onto his plate.

"You could afford to gain some weight, my love." He moved it back to her plate. "I'll not have a skinny wife."

"You will," she said and gave it back to him, hurrying to the table before he had a chance to continue his antics.

"You were saying," Alexa prodded as Michael followed Emma to the table.

"Ah, yes," Michael said, pausing to help Emma with her chair. "She's always trying to butter me up or something, saying all kinds of nice things, buying me presents. Personally, I don't know what she sees in me."

Michael and Emma exchanged a knowing smile. Jess, Alexa, and Tyson seemed to appreciate his satire, but Lacey shattered the warmth of the moment with a cool, "Neither do I."

Michael gave her a quick, terse smile that was gone from his lips as soon as it appeared, indicating clearly that he didn't appreciate her humor. He suspected, just as Emma did, that there was more to her lack of forgiveness than met the eye. And Michael could certainly feel empathy for her. But still, it really got on his nerves at times. He glanced down the table both directions and decided there was enough acceptance in this room to make up for anything. But his eyes went back to Lacey, and he still felt a distinct emptiness. She was Emma's sister, even if they shared no blood, and her acceptance was important to him—worth fighting for. If only he knew what he was fighting, and exactly how to confront it.

Emma's hand came discreetly to his leg beneath the table, squeezing with gentle reassurance. He momentarily forgot about Lacey.

"I was beginning to think you were doing your job too well, Michael," Jess said.

"I suppose that's better than telling me I'm fired."

"I understand the boys are doing well," Alexa commented.

"As well as boys can do, I would assume," Michael replied.

"Actually," Alexa continued, "beyond what I have seen with my own eyes, Sarina tells me she is quite pleased with the changes."

"Really?" Michael looked up in surprise. "I didn't realize the changes were so obvious."

"I don't know how you do it, Michael," Jess's voice held respect, "but I am impressed. After so little time, those boys really love you."

Michael swallowed and looked down at his plate. Emma turned to investigate his silence. There was nothing physically evident in his face to indicate he was choked up, but Emma knew that he was.

"I'm pleased to hear that," he finally said with an even voice, "because I'm rather fond of them, too. They're good kids, every one of them."

"It would seem that you know how to pick your administrators," Tyson said to Jess while his eyes were fixed on Michael. He turned to smile at Emma, and Michael saw evidence of renewal in their relationship. But again the mood was shattered by a cold glare from Lacey.

"It's all right, Lacey," Michael said as if he were complimenting the color of her blouse, "he's just humoring me."

Following a long moment of silence, Lacey rose and threw her napkin to the table, leaving the room without another word.

"Perhaps I should talk to her." Tyson rose reluctantly, as if facing a daily chore that he dreaded. "She's a little more testy than usual today." Tyson lumbered out of the room, giving Michael enough time to realize that he couldn't let Tyson wonder over what was going on.

"Excuse me a moment." Michael stood and followed Tyson into the hall, leaving Emma to pick helplessly at her food while her parents displayed obvious concern over the dramas going on beneath their roof.

"Tyson," Michael called, and he turned back at the foot of the stairs. "I'm sorry. I fear I'm not helping the situation any. It's likely my fault that she's more . . . testy today."

"How do you figure?"

"Just a suspicion. I don't want to make things more difficult for you by—"

"I don't think you have any reason to be apologizing. But thank you anyway."

"Is everything all right?" Emma appeared from the dining room.

"Yes," Tyson assured her, "everything is fine." He nodded toward Michael, emphasizing his words. "Perhaps we could have another of those talks."

"Man to man?" Michael offered, and Tyson nodded. "You know where to find me."

"Thanks." Tyson smiled briefly. "I'd best find Lacey."

Michael turned to Emma. "It would seem I have a way of bringing a great deal of tension into this home."

"That's not true," a feminine voice replied, but it wasn't Emma's. Alexa stepped out from behind her. "There are problems in this house that have nothing to do with you, Michael."

"And there are problems that do," he retorted. "The last thing I want is to brush it under the rug. I will live here in straightforward honesty, or not at all. If I'm making a bad situation worse, I want to know about it."

"Tyson and Lacey need to work out their own problems." Jess, too, appeared in the hall.

Michael appreciated their encouragement, but he hated this feeling of taking on the entire Byrnehouse-Davies household as they stood opposite him, telling him, of all things, that he was doing all right, that this wasn't his fault. But he knew within that he wasn't helping it any.

"I'm certain that curbing my tongue wouldn't hurt," Michael admitted. He thought of how it seemed they were only scratching the surface of some deep, festering wounds that he wanted to aid in healing, but he was helpless to even get near them.

"You do have a way with words," Jess chuckled. "But if you didn't, mealtime would be rather dull."

"It has been dull without Michael, now that you mention it." Alexa took her husband's hand.

"Come on," Jess motioned toward the door, "let's eat before it gets cold." He pointed a finger at Michael. "And if you feel the need to say something, you'd best say it. Because if you're not going to live here in straightforward honesty, you're not going to live here at all."

"Yes, sir." Michael saluted elaborately.

"Honesty is my number one requirement of all my employees," Jess added as they were reseated.

"Don't I know it," Alexa laughed. "That's the first thing he said to me when I came along begging for a job."

"I'm sorry?" Michael leaned forward. He obviously hadn't heard this part of their story.

"I was eighteen, homeless, and I marched into his office demanding a job," Alexa said.

"Under false pretenses." Jess shook his fork at her.

"You wouldn't even have given me the time of day if you had thought I was a woman."

"You're probably right."

"So I had to lie on the application in order to get an appointment with you."

"A lot of good it did you. Did you think when you walked in I wouldn't be able to tell the difference?"

While the bantering continued, Michael leaned over to Emma and whispered, "When we tell our children that I kidnapped you for ransom, it couldn't be any more colorful than this."

"What was that?" Jess demanded when he realized they weren't listening.

"I was just asking Emma if it worked out," he said, as if he sincerely didn't know. Jess gazed at him, looking so dubious that Michael couldn't hold back a little chuckle.

"I got the job, if that's what you mean," Alexa volunteered.

"She saved me, is what she's trying to tell you," Jess added.

"Someone had to," she retorted.

"She still saves me." Jess lifted a brow toward Michael, and Emma wondered if her attraction to Michael had anything to do with the way he could lift that brow so much like her father.

"This is all very enlightening," Michael pushed back his chair, "but the boys are expecting me. Emma can finish my breakfast."

"Michael," Emma stopped him, smiling sweetly, "it's Sunday."

"Oh?" He smiled back, liking the idea of catching up on some time with Emma. "Well, in that case, I'll just go check up on Trent, and I'll see you shortly."

"I'll be in the drawing room." Emma kissed him quickly and watched him walk out. He paused to thank Alexa for breakfast and squeeze her hand.

"What about me?" Jess called. "I paid for it."

"Yes, I know," Michael retorted, "but saying nice things to you isn't going to get me kisses and hugs. And even if it did, well . . . Alexa is much prettier than you. No offense."

"Get out of here," Jess said, and Michael did.

Twenty
THE FIGHT

Emma and her parents went to the drawing room to relax in a way not uncommon for Sunday mornings. They weren't surprised when Tyson showed up a few minutes later with Richard.

"Where is Lacey?" Alexa asked.

Tyson was about to answer, but Richard volunteered, "Mama has a headache. She won't talk to Papa." He sat down by Emma on the floor. "Can we play chess, Emma?"

"Chess?" Tyson chuckled. "Aren't you a little young for chess?"

"That depends on the rules you play by." Emma winked at her brother. "Why don't I play a game with you," she said to Richard, "and then I'll play a game with your father."

Richard liked this idea and quickly retrieved the chess board and figures from a shelf. Tyson watched in amusement at the childish rendition of the game, and Richard's triumphant announcement, "I won again. Aunt Emma just can't beat me."

"Move over." Tyson tickled him until he moved. "Let's see what Aunt Emma can do with an opponent her own size."

Richard watched until he became bored and perplexed by the way they played the game, then he resigned himself to a stack of picture books. Michael came in and sat next to Emma on the floor opposite Tyson, who was sprawled over the rug on his chest with an outwitted pawn in his teeth. After he got a hug from Richard, Michael watched the game with interest, but soon realized he didn't have a clue what was going on.

"So how is Trent?" Alexa asked, interrupting his futile concentration on the game.

"Fine," Michael smiled. "Actually, I'd say he's thriving."

"That's really good news," Alexa said while she continued with her needlework.

"And you might be interested to know," Michael said proudly, "that his name is Trenton Joseph Lasset." Alexa's eyes widened, and Jess turned his attention from his newspaper. "He was born January second, nineteen hundred. His mother died mysteriously a little over a year ago. His father is an opium dealer, using his millinery business as a front. Trent was being threatened into giving out free opium to his peers until they became addicted and were forced to pay a high price. Trent ran away when his closest friend died of an overdose. Trent tells me he never touched the stuff. Fortunately, his father wouldn't let him—said he couldn't afford to support bad habits, only to make money from others." Michael absorbed the expressions meeting his and added, "We had a little chat yesterday."

"What a dreadful thing," Emma remarked.

"Yes," Michael folded his arms, "another tragic story for the Byrnehouse-Davies desk drawer."

"But Trent is doing well, you say?" Alexa asked to reassure herself.

"He's fitting in beautifully, and seems quite grateful to be away from all of that. He told me he's not necessarily afraid his father will come after him. He doesn't believe his father cares whether he's gone or not."

"I'm certainly glad he's here," Alexa said, and Jess turned his nose back to the newspaper with a grunt of agreement.

"Don't mind him," Alexa said, "he's absolutely boring when he's reading. As soon as he's finished with the paper, he'll be back into his current book. He started doing it soon after he became rich."

Jess glared at her over the top of the paper. "I beg your pardon. You make it sound as if I've never lifted a finger since. I'm simply less . . . preoccupied with money, that's all."

"Yes, dear," Alexa said, and he went back to his reading with another grunt. Michael chuckled and turned his attention to the chess game, thinking more about how he admired Jess and Alexa. He had personally seen countless times when Jess Davies had worked up a healthy sweat, working side by side with his hired hands. The man hadn't stayed trim and strong enough to take on defiant boys by sitting around reading.

Neither was Alexa one to be lazy. He had noticed that she enjoyed her time with her needlework, and he believed that she wore skirts more now than she had in years past. But it wasn't uncommon to see her in riding breeches, helping with the horses on the track, giving her opinions to the trainers, helping the house servants with any number of tasks, and she was always on hand if a troubled boy needed some help or understanding. Michael felt a fresh burst of gratitude. He couldn't have been part of a better family if he had hand-picked them. Their example was worth studying as he contemplated starting a family of his own. That thought made him put an arm around Emma and play idly with her hair while she continued to play chess. He still couldn't understand the game, but he had a suspicion that Emma was winning, mostly from Tyson's deepening scowl.

The calm was interrupted by a light knock on the drawing room door, and Tillie peeked her head in. "Mr. Davies, a gentleman is here to see you."

"Who is it, Tillie?" Jess asked, coming to his feet.

"It's me." The constable stepped past Tillie and set his eyes directly on Michael. Concern fell mutually over all their faces, except for Richard, who totally disregarded the intrusion. Emma instinctively put her arms around Michael, feeling his heart pounding in time with her own, although his expression betrayed nothing. The fear she felt was indescribable as Michael came to his feet to face the situation head-on. Emma stood near him, holding to his arm. Tyson sat up and leaned against the sofa. Alexa set her work aside and held her breath.

"I wish I could say that we're glad to see you," Jess stated coolly.

"I wish I could say I'm glad to be here." The constable's eyes moved to Jess. "I think we need to have a little talk, Jess. And then I'd like to do the same with Mr. Hamilton."

"Please," Emma said, "you mustn't take him. We—"

"And you, young lady." He pointed a stern finger at her and Michael put a protective arm around her. "That was quite a little show you put on for me the other day. If I didn't know this family well enough to know there must be good reasons for this, I'd be pretty upset."

"It seems you're rather upset anyway," Tyson said.

"As I should be. I realize now that you were in on this as well, young man." His eyes went to Jess again. "But it's your father I want to talk to—privately."

Jess sat down. "This is private enough. We're all involved here. Let's have it."

Michael didn't like the way that sounded, knowing that Jess really meant the whole family was in trouble. And it was his fault.

"All right." The constable sat down and looked up at Michael. "Make yourself comfortable, Mr. Hamilton. We could be here a while."

Michael sat reluctantly on the sofa, and Emma sat as close to him as possible.

"Now," the constable began, "I had a real long talk with Mr. Grant last night. He seems to think Hamilton is innocent. I've never known Grant to be wrong, but I've also got three other men who swear he's guilty, and they are hounding me blue until I get my hands on him. But I don't much like these guys. So, considering Mr. Grant's plea on your behalf, I'm going to let it rest for now."

The tension in the room fell several degrees with a unified sigh. Michael whispered a quick "Thank you, God," toward the ceiling.

The constable continued, "The only way I can justify the family's involvement in keeping a fugitive is by stretching the purpose of your intent, and by knowing for all these years that you're decent people. We'll let that drop. Seeing that I'm the only one aware of it, we'll just pretend it didn't happen."

He turned to Michael. "The only way I can justify not arresting you now is by officially putting you under what I'm going to call a premises arrest." He pointed a finger for emphasis. "You will not leave Byrnehouse-Davies property until these charges are cleared, not for any reason—not one little step. I want to know that I can send a man out here any hour of any day, and you can be found in a real big hurry."

Michael nodded in agreement, saying humbly, "Thank you."

"Now, I believe I got the story pretty straight from Mr. Grant, but I want to hear it again from you."

Michael sighed. Considering that he was trying to forget certain aspects of his past, he was certainly getting the opportunity to talk about them a lot. With a firm voice he told his story, trying not to be embarrassed by the ridiculousness of some of his actions. He ended with, "I'm a strange man, Constable, but I'm not a killer."

"I'd say I have to agree with that," he replied, and Michael managed a tense smile.

"How does the case look, in your opinion?" Jess asked.

"You want the truth?" he returned, and Jess nodded. "I'll admit that these lowlifes who are making the accusations don't have much character to stand on, but their story is pretty firm, even though it appears to be a lie. Grant is good, but one of our big drawbacks is that Hamilton's only sound witness is emotionally involved with him." Emma looked anxiously at Michael. "It's not uncommon for such involvement to affect a witness's testimony. What it comes down to is our word against theirs, unless we can finagle the truth out of these thugs." The constable came to his feet. "I guess that's about all." He pointed at Michael again. "You keep yourself clean, Hamilton. I don't want any trouble, or I can almost guarantee that you won't come out of this alive."

Again Michael nodded, and the constable moved toward the door. Jess stood and followed him into the hall. "Let's get you something to eat before you go," they heard him say before the sound of his voice grew faint as they moved down the hallway.

"Everything will be all right," Alexa said, but it was followed by a tense silence that persisted through the day. Hardly a word was exchanged at lunch, which Lacey ate in her room due to the headache she was suffering. Emma urged Michael to go riding with her in the afternoon, but words were few between them, and their eyes couldn't meet without a sense of poignancy.

They returned to share supper much the same as lunch, except for the change in menu. Michael barely touched his food, and he was relieved when Emma said, "I think Michael and I will go for a walk. It's a lovely evening."

Once they were outside, however, the tension only deepened. They idly wandered the yard with little to say, holding hands with a grip that only seemed to emphasize the fear. It was long after dark when they came up the back stairs, pausing at Emma's door.

"No, wait," she said quietly, and led him by the hand to his room, where she pushed open the door and lit the lamp. "We're less likely to be disturbed here."

"Why didn't you figure that out a week ago?" Michael asked, leaning against the door.

Emma knew the question was meant to be humorous, but what she saw in his eyes left no room for a light retort. The full spectrum of the situation came back to her, and she couldn't fight back the sob that rushed into her throat. "Michael!" she cried, touching his face, his hair. "I couldn't bear to lose you."

He took her by the shoulders, watching her form blur from the mist that rose into his own eyes. "I won't let them defeat me in this, Emma. I won't! I'm going to fight this with everything I have inside of me."

Emma found relief in his conviction—a relief that deepened when he kissed her with all the passion he was capable of. Then he held her in his arms in peaceable silence. Just before she left for the night, she said gently, "I'm not going to think about it, Michael. If you do as the constable asked, there is nothing more to be done. We must go on living."

"Yes," he agreed. "And somehow, I believe that everything will be all right."

Emma embraced him tightly, then returned to her room and managed to sleep in spite of having strange dreams.

Michael woke up with a determination to act happy, if only for Emma's sake. Acting was something he could do well, and he was pleased to see that the results were positive as Emma returned to his room as soon as she was dressed the following morning. She watched him shave and they went down to breakfast together, teasing and laughing as if nothing were wrong.

The meal passed by less tensely than the last two, although Tyson looked downright glum, and Lacey remained absent. It was evident that what little progress they had been making had come to a halt. Tyson's discouragement made that plain enough. Michael had a suspicion that Lacey was absent mostly to avoid him, but he said nothing.

"I should be getting to work," Michael said as he came to his feet.

"May I come along?" Emma asked, not wanting to be away from him for a minute.

"You would have to ask the boss." Michael glanced to Jess. "I was under the impression he didn't want my love life interfering with responsibilities."

"I'd say you've established yourself enough not to be concerned about that," Jess acknowledged. "And I'd say Emma's well rehearsed at handling rowdy boys."

"Yes, I know." Michael took her hand, grinning proudly. He paused next to Alexa's chair and bent to kiss her cheek. "Thanks for breakfast." He called down the table as if it were a mile long. "You too, Jess. Even if all you did was pay for it."

Alexa laughed as they disappeared into the hallway. "You know, I always liked Michael, but I never dreamed . . ."

"Good things do come in strange packages," Jess stated as if it were scripture.

"That's what you said when the twins were crawling, destroying everything in sight, always dirty from head to toe."

"Did I?" Jess laughed. "Then I must have meant it."

❦ ❦ ❦

Michael walked into the classroom with Emma close behind. She was quick to notice the way the boys lit up at his appearance. Whatever he had done to win them over, he had done it well.

"You boys ready to go?" he called, glancing over some papers on the tutor's desk at the head of the room to check their progress with mathematics.

The morning group lined up eagerly at the door, while they speculated among themselves in whispers over Emma's presence.

"What about you?" Michael pointed to Kevin.

"Mr. Johnson says I can't go until I finish my problems."

"Then you'd best finish them, and hurry up about it. That horse of yours will be waiting." This seemed to motivate Kevin, and he quickly got to work while Michael exchanged a quiet word with Mr. Johnson, the tutor, who nodded agreeably to whatever Michael had said.

As they followed Michael out the door, Will appointed himself spokesman. "How come she's going?" he asked, looking skeptically at Emma.

"If I were you," Michael retorted, "I wouldn't question the presence of a pretty lady. I'd just shut up and enjoy it."

The boys sniggered, and Emma realized they could see through the brusque exterior Michael used to keep them in line. No wonder they liked him, but it was readily evident that they respected him as well.

"I know why she's here," Bob volunteered as if he knew some great, dark secret.

"And why is that?" Michael asked casually as Bob moved into step next to him.

"Cause you're gonna marry her."

"Brilliant!" Michael slapped him on the back just hard enough to add an extra step to his gait. Bob looked up at Michael and grinned sheepishly.

"Are you really gettin' married?" Matthew asked as they stepped outside, Michael pausing to count heads passing by him to make certain they were all there.

"Wait!" he said and they all stopped immediately. "There's supposed to be eight. There's only seven. Where's the—"

"Doing his math," Emma provided.

"Yes, of course," Michael said with an embarrassed scowl, and the group moved on.

"Well?" Matthew pressed.

"I really am," Michael said proudly, with a sideways wink toward Emma.

"To Miss Emma?" Gene asked, and Michael smiled at him. The boy rarely said a word.

"Yes, Gene," he put a gentle hand on the boy's shoulder as they walked, "to the charming Miss Emma."

"When?" Walter asked.

"Later this week," Michael provided, lifting a mischievous eyebrow toward Emma.

"Do we get to come?" Will asked.

"I don't know," Michael said. "I'm not in charge. I'm just planning on being there."

"Is that why you got a new shirt?" Bob prodded.

Michael sighed from the drilling questions, stopped abruptly, and instantly assumed a pose he was becoming famous for. "Yes, that's why I got a new shirt. Black shirts are for bad guys. Emma wants to marry a good guy, so she bought me a new shirt. Yes, I'm going to marry her—and, so you don't have to ask me any more ridiculous questions, the only reason she is marrying me is so I can keep my job. She got me this job, so if you want me to stick around, you'd do well to treat her with some respect. Got it?"

"Yes, sir," they all said in haphazard unison, moving on to the stable with total disregard of his threats.

Emma stayed with Michael through the morning, assisting as they went to the track to take their horses through some basic racing exercises. She felt a deepening peace to see Michael so content and capable in his work, and she enjoyed the prospect of being able to take part on occasion without feeling out of place.

Michael held her hand as they returned to the home to share lunch with the boys in the cafeteria, then they escorted the second group to the stables, plus Kevin, who had finally finished his math.

"Any potential jockeys?" Michael asked Emma, leaning against the rail to observe the boys riding the track.

"Possibly." She watched them all carefully, one by one. "The biggest problem, as Tyson and my father will tell you, is that once a boy passes a certain age, he generally becomes too tall and heavy."

"That's why you make such a fine jockey," Michael smiled.

"It doesn't hurt."

"No," Michael watched Emma walk back toward the stable, "it doesn't hurt." There was nothing like Emma in breeches.

❦   ❦   ❦

With Lacey present at supper that evening, Michael was careful to hold his tongue and mind his business. He feared he was getting a reputation for disrupting meals. Afterwards, the family went to the drawing room for coffee as they often did. Lacey was tersely cool, but she kept quiet while Jess and Alexa entertained them with stories about their younger days. As details were added to the story Alexa had recently told them concerning the origin of their names, Tyson, Lacey, and Emma were surprised to hear things they'd never known—things that Jess claimed he wouldn't have admitted to until his children were adult enough to accept the fact that their father had made some serious mistakes in his life.

Emma was enjoying herself, but as she kept an eye on Michael, she couldn't help but anticipate being his wife. She was glad when they were finally able to slip away and be alone together. They took a lengthy stroll in the moonlight, then they went together to Emma's room. Michael had every intention of kissing her good night at the door, but Emma urged him inside, declaring soundly that she didn't want to be alone. They held hands and talked as the desire to be together outdid their desire for sleep.

They were both startled by a loud pounding at the door. Emma glanced at the clock as she called, "What?"

"Emma!" her mother called in a frenzy. "Do you know where Michael is?"

"Oh, great," Michael whispered while Emma turned the lamp up brighter.

"We have nothing to hide," Emma reminded him quietly, even though it was nearly two o'clock in the morning.

"Emma," Alexa called urgently, "it's all right. I understand. If he's in there, we've got to know. It's important."

Michael pulled the door open, and Emma swallowed hard to imagine the scene before her mother's eyes and how it must appear.

"What?" he insisted, panic in his voice.

"It's Toby. He's gone."

"Gone?" His panic rose. "Where?" he demanded. "What happened?" He turned to look around him. "Where are my boots? Blast!"

"Here." Emma provided them, and Michael frantically sat on the edge of the bed to pull them on.

"What happened?" Michael repeated.

"Sarina said the boys were talking rather seriously about something at supper, and Toby seemed upset after that. She checked beds at ten and they were all there, but Matthew just woke her up, saying that he saw Toby sneaking out. They've searched the home and he's not there. Jess went to the stables and found Toby's horse missing."

"Blast!" Michael repeated.

"Do you know where he might have gone?"

"I might." Michael came to his feet and gave Emma a quick kiss before he headed for the door.

Alexa called after him. "Jess is saddling your horse."

"Thank you," he called back, running down the stairs.

When Michael was gone, Alexa turned to Emma, obviously leaving her concern for Toby in his hands.

"It's really not what it appears to be," Emma said.

"All right," Alexa said.

"Do you believe me?"

"I've never had reason to believe you'd tell me anything but the truth."

"And now?"

"Of course I believe you, Emma." She sat on the edge of the bed and patted the spot next to her to indicate that Emma join her. Alexa took her daughter's hand. "You'll be married very soon, and I know it can be difficult to keep things under control, especially when you spend a lot of time together. Believe it or not, I remember what it was like to be young, single, and in love. But you know how strongly your father and I feel about waiting for such things until after marriage, even if it is less than a week away."

"I know, Mother. I swear to you that nothing has happened between us that shouldn't. Michael has been a perfect gentleman. He told me it was important to wait so he could prove to me, and to himself, that he could be a good person, and that he could be disciplined. And he has proven it. We've spent a great deal of time alone together, but he's never been even the least bit inappropriate with me."

Alexa smiled and squeezed Emma's hand. "Thank you for sharing that with me. I must admit that it gives me some relief."

"Were you concerned?"

"Well, I know you were taught that such things were to be kept within marriage. But then, Tyson and Lacey were taught the same thing. I know how passion can be a difficult thing to keep under control, and I know that the situation with you and Michael is unique. But I had really hoped you would wait. And I'm proud of you."

Emma smiled timidly and Alexa added, "I love you dearly, Emma. You are such a joy to me."

"And Michael?" Emma asked. "You truly like him, don't you?"

"I always have." This surprised Emma, but she listened attentively. "I always sensed that something in him was hurting. It was when I attended him through a fever that I discovered the scars. I don't think I ever cried so hard in my life. It was as if the evidence of Michael's pain represented all that every boy we've ever had has suffered, but I don't think any of them ever suffered as much as he did. It was difficult to touch him, to reach his heart, but I worked hard at planting seeds that I felt confident would grow eventually. You see, I believed that deep inside of Michael was fertile soil, you might say. Some hardened hearts could never accept the truth or face the pain, but I felt very strongly that Michael had it in him to do so. He wasn't very old when I realized that he was keeping a close eye on you."

"He what?" Emma gasped.

"You heard me," Alexa laughed.

"You knew?"

"I suspected. He was quite adamant that Jess let him stay on and work, and I encouraged it. He'd had it rough, and I felt he needed the constancy of life here. But I suspected that Michael's biggest reason for staying had to do with you. Of course, I had no idea how his life would turn out. Seeds can turn bad, weeds can out-root them, and I think I cried the night I heard he was in prison. But when I figured out that Michael Hamilton was likely the man who had kidnapped you, I couldn't help hoping that he'd finally come around."

"You figured it out? How?"

"It was a combination of clues, I guess. Of course, when Lacey returned and told me what had happened, I had some concerns. But a part of me wondered if it was all just a big show. I figured that I knew Michael well, and . . . I would have been surprised if something good hadn't come out of it sooner or later. You are the best thing that ever happened to him, and perhaps the other way around, too."

"I have no doubt of that," Emma agreed. "I would find life too bothersome and dull with a man any less roguish than Michael."

"Well put," Alexa smiled. "Now, you should get some sleep."

"I don't think I can. I believe I'll go down to the stables and wait."

"If that's what you want." Alexa rose and moved to the door. "I believe you'll find your father there. He won't rest until Toby is found.

I won't either, but I'd rather wait in bed. I got used to the fact long ago that if there was nothing I could do, it did no good to pace myself into a frenzy. Good night, dear."

When Emma was alone, she quickly put on her boots, muttering a silent prayer for Michael and Toby to return safely.

❦ ❦ ❦

Michael rode hard and fast, depending on the horse to make it safely through the darkness. With any luck, Toby would flee to the only place they had ridden that was any distance from the main grounds. He recalled how Toby had liked the meadow Michael had taken the boys to, and he prayed now that he would find Toby there.

When he finally came through the trees into the clearing, he sighed audibly to see the silhouette of a horse grazing near the stream. Quietly he plodded toward it and looked down to see Toby curled up on the grass, sound asleep. Michael dismounted and stood over him, gently nudging him in the ribs with the toe of his boot.

"If you didn't want to eat your vegetables," Michael shouted, "why didn't you just say so?"

"What are you doin' here?" Toby growled after a brief moment of panic.

"I came looking for you. What are you doing here?"

"I was bein' alone till you came."

"There are places where you are welcome to be alone that are not quite so far away. The attic, for one."

"I didn't wanna stay there. I don't wanna go back."

"Want to talk about it?" Michael sat on the grass beside him. Toby said nothing. "You can't tell me that I wouldn't understand, because I bet I would."

"I guess you would," Toby admitted reluctantly, as if he'd have preferred not to talk about it.

"Well?" Michael prodded.

"The boys wanna go swimming next week. They asked me if I wanted to go."

Michael was only subtly sarcastic. "I can see why that would upset you." Toby looked up skeptically. "They're just being kind, aren't they?

Don't you want to go swimming? I bet it would be fun."

"I don't wanna. I never went before. Why should I now?"

"Why not?"

"I just don't wanna. And just because I don't, they were talkin' about me."

"Were they being rude?" Michael asked.

Toby thought about it. "No, they were just talkin'."

"So, what's the problem?" Toby didn't answer. "The problem isn't really swimming or being talked about, now is it," he stated rather than asked. "The problem is that secret you have that you're afraid somebody will find out about."

Toby looked shocked. "How do you know so much?" he insisted.

"You think about that, Toby, and you tell me." He didn't answer, so Michael went on. "When I was growing up here, I didn't ever go swimming. Do you know why?"

"Yeah, I guess I do."

"Is it the same reason for you?"

Toby bent forward, and Michael heard a sniffle.

"It's all right to talk about it, Toby. If I had learned to talk about it ten or fifteen years ago, I would have saved myself a lot of trouble." Toby sniffled again. "And it's all right to cry about it, too."

"I don't wanna talk about it," Toby growled.

"Why not?"

"Cause I don't even like to think about it."

"Yes, I know. But I'll make you a deal. You tell me about it, and I'll throw the memories away. Then you don't ever have to think about it again if you don't want to. And when you do think about it, you can remember that you gave all the hurt to Michael Hamilton, and he threw it away, so the memories will just be memories. That's all."

Michael put his arm around Toby and waited patiently. After a lengthy silence, Toby began to speak quietly about the things that had been said and done in his young life to cause such pain and fear. Michael cried silent tears and held him. When he seemed to be finished, Michael asked gently if there was anything else he wanted to have thrown away.

"No," Toby said straightly.

"Do you feel any better?"

"I think so," he admitted.

"Good. So do I."

"Did your father do things like that to you?" Toby asked, looking up through the darkness.

"Yes, Toby. He did. Even worse."

"Why?"

"Because my father was a very sick man. His mind was sick. Do you understand that, Toby? It had nothing to do with me, just like it has nothing to do with you. You're a good boy, Toby. It's your father who has the problem." Michael tousled Toby's hair affectionately. "So how do you feel about going swimming?" Michael asked.

"I don't want anybody to see the scars," he admitted.

"Yes, I can relate to that," Michael assured him. "But do you think they won't like you because of them?"

"I don't know, but . . ."

"But what?"

"What if somebody asked where I got 'em? I don't wanna tell 'em."

"Well then, you can either swim with your shirt on, or you can tell them they're battle wounds and you won, so they'd better mind their own business. Or. . . you can tell them the truth. Whatever feels good to you."

After a contemplative moment, Toby stated firmly, "I love you, Mr. Hamilton."

Michael swallowed the knot in his throat. "I love you, too, Toby."

They sat in the darkness until Toby began to relax against him. "I think we should get back. Miss Sarina and Mr. Davies will be worried about us."

"And Miss Emma," Toby added.

"Yes, and Miss Emma." He smiled as they came to their feet.

"Can I come to the wedding?" Toby asked as Michael helped him onto his own horse and mounted behind him, holding the other reins to lead Toby's horse.

"Sure. You can be the flower boy."

Toby chuckled, and they rode home at a brisk pace.

❦   ❦   ❦

"Where can they be?" Emma paced frantically while Jess sat in the straw with a lamp burning low in the stable.

"They'll be back. If Michael hadn't found him yet, he would have come for help. I suspect they're talking."

"How do you know Michael so well?" she asked.

"Just do," Jess stated as he folded his arms over his chest and closed his eyes. A few minutes later, Michael and Toby rode into the stable as if they'd just been on a Sunday jaunt.

"Everything all right?" Jess asked through a yawn as he came to his feet.

"We're fine," Michael announced.

"I told Mr. Hamilton you'd be worried," Toby said to Emma as he was helped to the ground.

"You're a smart boy, Toby," she replied.

"Come along, Toby." Jess held out a hand. "I need to talk to Miss Sarina anyway. I'll see that you get to bed."

"Good night, Mr. Hamilton," Toby waved. "Don't forget to throw those things away."

"I promise." Michael held up his hand in a pledge. Toby grinned and walked away with Jess's hand on his shoulder.

"What was that all about?" Emma asked while Michael removed the saddle from Toby's horse.

"It's a secret—between me and Toby," he said, and Emma couldn't help but admire him for keeping a confidence.

Emma secured Toby's horse in the stall, then followed Michael into the other stable, where he removed the saddle from his own horse and put it away while Emma escorted the animal to its appointed place.

"He's to bed," she announced. "All tucked in."

"Now it's my turn." He put an arm around her and they walked together into the house. He asked what Alexa's reaction had been after he'd left, and they discussed it briefly before he kissed her good night at the door to her room.

Michael awoke with barely enough time to meet his usual appointment with the boys. He was pleased to meet Emma in the hall, and she opted to go along again, finding enjoyment in spending this time with him. Again they shared lunch in the cafeteria, then returned to the stables with the afternoon group. The boys began vying for Emma's attention to help them with their mounts, and Michael watched with amused interest.

While the boys were currying their horses and providing them with feed and water, Michael stood at the end of the row of stalls, keeping a careful eye on their work while he chatted with Emma about the endearing traits he noted in their behavior with the horses.

A muffled noise that Emma hardly noticed caught Michael's attention, and he moved stealthily to find its source. He quickly made a head count and realized that one was missing. Checking himself to know how many were supposed to be here, he quickly put names to the numbers.

"Where's Toby?" he demanded. A muffled moan reached his ears. The horse in Toby's stall moved testily back and forth. Michael's body became tense and agile, setting Emma and the boys on edge as they watched him move cautiously like a stalking animal toward the stall, not trusting Toby's absence, strange noises, or the animal's behavior to coincidence.

The facts on Toby's records flashed before Michael's eyes, and a sick dread settled into his gut long before he realized what was happening. Instinct alone made him stop a few yards from the stall.

"Toby?" he called carefully. "Where are you, boy?" The normalcy in his voice belied both his manner and the taut expectancy of those observing.

That muffled moan came again, immediately followed by a loud thud against the side of the stall, which sent the horse into an agitated fit. A streak of cursing sounded amid a struggle, and suddenly Toby came flying over the side of the stall, screaming with terror as he scurried behind Michael for protection. "Don't let him take me!" he cried. "Please don't let him!"

In answer to Michael's unvoiced question, Rafe Coogan came to his feet and sauntered out of the stall to face Michael's cold, expressionless stare and wide stance. Emma gasped and took a step backward to instinctively clutch the post behind her.

"Imagine how surprised I was to show up here and find you," Rafe sneered.

"I was just thinking the same," Michael said coolly.

"So," Rafe's lips spread back to show his decaying teeth, "you did go soft."

"Mr. Hamilton's not soft!" Toby defended, clutching Michael's arm in a fearful grip.

"And what would you know about that, boy?" Rafe's tone of voice degraded the child in a way that no attempt at tough discipline on Michael's part had ever come close to. Toby winced, and Michael fought to keep his mind on the present. His own father had used that tone of voice regularly.

"I came for my boy," Rafe demanded.

"He's our boy now," Michael stated, perfectly calm and confident.

"Not as far as I'm concerned," Rafe retorted. "Now, give me my boy. He's mine, and I need him."

"I won't ask what for, because I don't want to know."

"And it's none of your business."

"Toby is my business, Mr. Coogan, and he's going nowhere unless it's with me."

Rafe produced a knife out of nowhere. Emma gasped and the boys all moved back, except for Toby, who clung to Michael even more desperately. Michael couldn't help recalling his promise to Toby, and somehow knew it was being tested.

"I'm takin' my boy, Hamilton," Rafe snarled.

"Not without killing me first." Michael actually smiled. He wasn't worried. He'd bested Rafe before, and he could do it again. The knife was a concern, but nothing he couldn't handle.

Emma felt her nerves go completely taut with fear. Intently watching Michael's every flicker of movement, she realized that his fingers were twitching. He was going to fight this man. All she could think of was the harm Rafe had done to Lacey, and the knife Rafe held that put the odds in his favor. She recalled the constable's words, warning against any trouble on Michael's part, and her panic soared. There had to be a better way, she told herself. She was not going to stand here and watch Michael get himself killed—or into enough trouble to send him to the gallows.

Without taking his eyes off Rafe, Michael let his mind wander into the past. He thought of Jess Davies killing his father, and wondered if the feelings had been much the same. In his mind, the man standing before him became Jedediah Hamilton. He was going to enjoy this. Carefully he eased Toby away without taking his eyes off Rafe. "You stay by Miss Emma," he said softly.

Toby did as he was told, while Rafe gave a demented laugh. "Yeah, hide behind the woman's skirts, boy. Just like yer precious Mr. Hamilton." He then spoke to Michael. "She really did you in, didn't she." Rafe began to pace, hunched forward, ready to lunge. "Now let's see if I can do you in. The winner gets the boy."

Michael curled his hand into a fist and was ready to make the first move when Emma's voice called, "No, Michael. Don't do it!"

He wanted to ask exactly what she would have him do, but he wasn't about to argue with her in front of this lowlife. He chose to ignore her and took a step forward.

"Michael, no!" she called firmly.

Rafe laughed, and Michael was itching to do him in. He should have killed him when he'd had the chance.

"You're a coward, Hamilton," Rafe sneered. Michael kept his cool. He'd taught the boys that it took courage not to fight in the face of insults. But insults weren't motiving this fight. It was Toby's life. "You're a stinkin', money-grubbin' coward," Rafe added.

"Coward, perhaps," Michael stated as if they were having tea in the drawing room. "Money-grubbing, true. But I do not stink. Unlike some people, I bathe more than twice a year, whether I need it or not."

"Well, you've taken your last bath, Hamilton. Now stop talkin', and let's get down to business."

"Fine." Michael motioned him forward with a taunting challenge.

"Please, Michael, no!" Emma's voice turned desperate. She couldn't believe he was going to do this.

"Listen to her," Rafe laughed. "She's probably got more guts and brains than you do."

"How true," Michael quipped.

"And I bet she's feisty too. I'd like to show her a thing or two."

That did it! Michael could take being called just about anything, but insulting Emma was something he wouldn't stand for. In a movement so quick the spectators hardly saw it, Michael kicked the knife out of Rafe's hand, landed a studied fist into his belly, another to his face, and a knee in the groin.

Emma sighed with premature relief as Rafe came back with an unexpected blow that sent blood spewing from Michael's nose. But it hardly seemed to faze him as he came back with blow after blow of controlled force. In Michael's mind he fought away his own childish fears on behalf of Toby, pummeling this man who was not fit to walk the earth. In his opinion, any man who would maliciously harm a child deserved nothing better than to die and rot in hell. Even hell wasn't bad enough for such a crime, he decided, just as Emma's voice brought him back to reality.

"Stop it! You'll kill him!" Michael looked down at the bloodied face cowering beneath him on the ground, then he looked up at Emma. She was disappointed in him, and at the moment he couldn't figure why. He turned to take in the boys' stunned faces as he came to his feet, wiping Rafe Coogan's blood on his breeches.

Rafe groaned and attempted to sit up. Toby clung tightly to Emma. Michael put a boot on Rafe's chest. "The lady just saved your pathetic life. Now get your stinking carcass out of here before I get serious."

Rafe spat blood and made an effort to wipe off his face. He groaned his way to his knees and looked up at Michael, his eyes full of rage. This wasn't the first time Michael Hamilton had made him look like an utter fool, and he obviously wasn't pleased.

"You just wait, Hamilton." He spat blood again and lumbered to his feet. "One of these days yer gonna turn around and I'll be there, if they don't hang you first." He managed a smug laugh that made Emma cringe.

"Get out of here," Michael hissed through clenched teeth, fighting the urge to start on him all over again.

Emma turned to see her father and Murphy slowing from a run as they entered the stable. It was apparent that Murphy had overheard the commotion and gone for him.

"What's going on?" Jess demanded.

Michael didn't take his eyes off Rafe. "Mr. Coogan was just leaving." All was silent until the thug left the stable.

Jess said quietly to Murphy, "Get someone to follow him. Make certain he leaves, and see that he didn't bring anybody with him."

Michael finally lifted a hand to examine his injury. He was pleased to find that his nose wasn't broken, but he groaned in disgust at the blood on his fingers. He pulled out a handkerchief and wiped it over his mouth and nose as he turned to face Emma. Not liking what he saw in her eyes, he turned to Jess.

"What happened, Michael?" he asked.

Toby ran from Emma to Michael, clutching him with an embrace that fully expressed his appreciation. "It's all right, Toby," Michael assured him, putting a comforting hand on his shoulder as he turned again to Jess. He didn't know where to begin in admitting that all of this was probably his fault, and he sincerely wished he had taken the time to explain the connection long before now. According to Emma's eyes, he hadn't handled it correctly, although he couldn't imagine how else he could have handled it. All he could manage to say was, "Mr. Coogan felt entitled to take back his son. I was simply making it clear that we wouldn't allow that."

"You mean . . ." Jess pointed to where the fight had taken place. "This is the same Mr. Coogan who . . ."

Michael nodded. Jess sighed, showing an acceptance in his eyes that was absent in Emma's. Facing Jess again, a silent exchange of feelings filled the air between them. Michael knew that Jess was thinking of the day he'd killed Jedediah Hamilton. Michael hadn't been there, but he was thinking about it, too.

"Are you all right?" Jess questioned.

"Me? I'm fine," he chuckled in an effort to ease the tension as he glanced around at the boys, all watching the drama in hushed silence. "I'm pretty tough."

The boys chuckled with obvious relief while Michael looked again at Emma. He decided he wasn't fine. She looked like she wanted to walk away. He decided he couldn't stand here and give her the chance. He wanted to talk to her, to know what she was feeling. But he couldn't. Not now, not here. In that moment, he found so many pains and dramas and fears overpowering his mind that he felt as if he'd explode. And he had to get out of here before he did.

Taking first things first, Michael squatted down in front of Toby, motioning for Jess to come closer. "Are you going to be all right?" The boy nodded firmly. "I've got to take care of something right now, but Mr. Davies will take you and the others back inside. I don't want you to ever be alone, Toby. Don't go anywhere without an adult or one of the bigger boys. Don't leave the home unless you're in a group. Do you understand? We don't want to lose you, Toby, and we won't. I would hunt the ends of the earth to find you, but we'd rather not lose you in the first place." He said the last with a grin that brought a smile from the boy. Jess nodded firmly to Michael and took Toby's hand.

"Now, get to your lessons." Michael motioned toward the door, and the boys all followed Jess out. Michael looked at Emma, then turned quickly and walked out the other direction.

Emma panicked. True, she was upset over what had just happened. But somehow she knew there was more to it than met the eye. She felt angry with Michael for resorting to brute force, but as he turned away, she had to wonder if her anger stemmed more from the fear of losing him. With so much left unspoken, she couldn't let him walk away.

"Michael," she called, running after him. He paused at the pump for only a moment to splash water on his face, then he disappeared into the other stable without acknowledging her. Emma entered to find him bridling his horse, but he didn't bother with a saddle. With a glance toward her, he jumped onto the horse's back and galloped out. Emma ran out the door and quickly grabbed the nearest mount that was coming in from the tracks.

"Thanks, George," she spouted quickly, and was glad for the racing saddle beneath her as she lifted her feet high in the stirrups and followed the cloud of dust heading toward the hills.

Emma was surprised at how long it took her to catch up to him. Even with her significant weight difference and racing experience, Michael's speed was phenomenal. She finally came to his side, riding in perfect time with him. But as they moved into the trees, it was impossible to stop him.

"Michael!" she shouted, but he ignored her. "Don't you dare turn and run after what I have been through for you!"

Michael pulled back the reins and halted so quickly that Emma was a good distance ahead before she could stop and turn back. Their eyes met with a hundred emotions passing through the trees, while both horses danced impatiently at being halted in their free run.

"Are you going to talk or run?" she challenged. Michael thought of what he'd been trying to teach the boys. He drew courage and knew he couldn't run. He had hoped the intense speed of the ride would have alleviated his doubts, but it had only driven them deeper. Now he looked into Emma's eyes and realized the question he read there was difficult to face, only because it was forcing him to admit to his own guilt. What had happened back there was his fault. But still, how could she have stood there and told him not to fight, when it was so plainly evident that he'd had no choice? She had always given him such unquestioning trust, and now her seeming lack of it left him on unsteady ground. He didn't know whether he was hurt or afraid, but at the moment the only thing that came through with any strength was anger.

"All right, talk," he said, a once-familiar cruelty seeping into his voice.

"What exactly happened back there?" she asked, attempting to open up the topic, but she regretted the question when she heard her own accusing tone. She wanted to take it back, but it was too late.

"Do I need to explain it?" He leaned forward, tightening his legs around the horse. "The boy was in danger. What was I supposed to do, just stand there and let the creep have his way?" He raised his voice in sarcasm. "Oh, hello, Mr. Coogan. Here's your son, Mr. Coogan. Don't beat him too badly or—"

"Enough!" Emma cried.

"That's what I say! Enough! Enough of children being abused and battered by sick people who call themselves parents. I won't stand for it!"

"I didn't ask you to."

"No?" He slid abruptly to his feet and tossed away the reins. "But you asked me not to fight him." He walked toward Emma like a stalking beast.

"Fighting is not always the best method," she stated, attempting to keep a steady voice, realizing she was afraid.

"That," he pointed back the direction they'd come, "was not one of those times. If I hadn't taken him on, he'd have killed me, or taken Toby, or both. Don't stand there and tell me that what I did back there wasn't right!"

"Was it?"

"You'd better believe it!" he hissed.

"You might have killed him."

"Better him than me," he stated, recalling what Jess had once said.

Emma's voice softened. "You knew, didn't you." Michael looked down, knowing what was coming. "You knew Rafe Coogan had a son here. It's difficult to keep track of all the boys' surnames, and I doubt anybody else figured out the connection. But I think you knew."

Michael turned away and pushed his hands into his hair, tugging at it almost brutally. "Yes," he said through clenched teeth, "I knew. It all goes down to the same thing. Every problem in my life, everything the people I care for are suffering through, all goes down to my idiotic indiscretions." He looked up and sighed, but he kept his back turned to her. "If I had not been fooling around with a bunch of brainless thugs for the sake of a stupid kidnapping venture, a lot fewer people would be suffering right now."

"And where would I be now?" Emma asked gently.

"If you had any brains, you'd be flirting with some respectable banker's son, or somebody equally stodgy."

"And the boys?"

Michael turned hesitantly toward her, grasping the implication.

"Yes, Michael. They, like I, need you. And all I could think back there was what I would do if . . . What if he had . . ." Emma's voice quivered as her true fear came to light. "What if he had killed you?" she finally managed. "Where would that have left Toby? And me? And the other boys? You go about being the gallant hero, totally oblivious to the fact that there are people depending on you now, Michael. Your absence wouldn't go unnoticed. If you had died today, Toby would be gone, and I would be left alone."

Michael quickly stepped toward Emma and hauled her down from the horse. He gripped her shoulders with his hands, pulling her close to his face. "You should never have done it, Emma. You should have known better than to get involved with a man like me. You must be crazy!" He almost shook her, speaking through clenched teeth. "My past is my past, Emma. We will never be free of it. The scars will always be there. You were right, Emma. The truth of the matter is that Rafe Coogan would not have been in that stable today if I hadn't led him there by my actions last month. Now, tell me how I'm supposed to live with that!" He shook her gently. "Tell me!" he demanded.

"Just live!" she shouted back. "You have to live, Michael, because I cannot live without you. Don't you understand? If you had killed him, it might well have sent you to the gallows for certain. I can't live with *that!*"

Michael searched the glistening moisture in her eyes. In an instant his hands left her shoulders, and she might have fallen had they not gone around her back to catch her. He crushed her against him and kissed her in a way that expressed more than words ever could. Emma felt all the guilt and anguish and fear come through his kiss, and she absorbed them without hesitation. She could perhaps fear Michael's anger, but never his passion. She returned his kiss feverishly until she felt herself sob in the midst of it.

When Michael realized she was crying, he just held her, attempting to offer comfort in spite of being certain that he was the perpetrator of the pain. He wondered what could make a woman shout in anger, kiss in passion, and cry in anguish, all in five minutes. The answer became clear as he repeated, "You must be crazy. Do you see what loving a man like me has done to you? You should listen to your sister, Emma. I'm no good. I'm not predictable or dependable. And I have a nasty temper."

Emma pulled back to search his motives. He managed a stilted smile. "And if you left me I would die," he added. "Where would I be without you?"

"Oh, Michael!" She clutched him tightly and pressed her face to this throat. "Please be careful. Don't let the past destroy you."

"I have to face it and deal with it, Emma. And yes, I have to fight it." He pulled away and stepped back to face her. "But don't you see, Emma? It's all for you. If I fight, it will be for you, for the life you would want me to live, for the man you would want me to be. And if I die, it would only be for the same reasons." Emma's eyes brimmed again with frightened tears, moving him to add, "But I will be careful. Of course I will. I have something to live for."

Twenty-one
LACEY'S RAGE

Michael sighed and looked to the trees above him. "And it's time I got everything out in the open, once and for all."

"What do you mean?" She sounded panicked.

"There is a great deal you have accepted without question, Emma. And I realized, when I met your eyes back in the stable, that without your acceptance I could not face any of this. You're the rock upon which I stand. I feel like a child when it comes to living with honesty and goodness. And I need you. I'm not afraid to admit that now—not even to people like Rafe Coogan. What I am afraid to admit is that I do have a past that will likely bring more consequences into our lives—and to your family, as well. Your mother told me there were no closeted skeletons in her home. I think it's time I let all of mine out."

"Like what?" she asked carefully.

Michael sat on the ground and set his forearms on his knees. "Emma, if you had come across me on the street two months ago, you'd have had nothing to do with me." He gave a humorless laugh as she sat beside him. "You'd not have been on the same street with me. I was wallowing with the lowlifes of this world, just like I was before I was brought here at the age of eleven."

"Yes," she said, "I know."

"And what do you think you know?" he retorted unkindly.

"I know you were in prison for three years. I know you're well studied in lying and stealing, and I've seen the lowlife you were associating with. I'm still here."

"Yes, lucky you," he said with a hint of sarcasm.

"So tell me, if you're so determined to have it out. I can take it. Why did you go to prison, Michael?"

"I don't have a clue."

"I'm sorry?" Emma said, imitating him.

"I was drunk. I was so drunk that when I woke up in a cell, the last thing I remembered was sitting down at a bar on the other side of the city. The charge was disturbing the peace and disorderly conduct; the last resulting in a significant repair bill to a particular bar. But they said that what I started that night resulted in a life being taken. Apparently I had nothing to do with the death directly, but they figured if I hadn't been there, it wouldn't have happened, so they gave it to me good and hard."

"And why were you drinking?" Emma persisted.

"You want the truth?" He turned to glare at her.

"No," she mimicked his sarcasm, "I want you to lie to me, coat it over with sugar and pretend it didn't happen." Her tone sobered. "Of course I want the truth."

"I was thinking of you." Her eyes widened. "That's right. I had thought I could erase you from my mind, and I had tried. But no matter what I did, no matter how hard I tried to lose myself in a different life, you were always there, always haunting me." He turned to stare blankly ahead. "I had gotten a job after I left here, and I was doing pretty good. I was saving money, staying off the streets, and pretty much living an honest life. And there was a woman who . . ." Michael stopped so abruptly that Emma had to look to see if he was all right. He watched her cautiously, contemplating just how much Emma should know.

"Well?" she insisted. "What about this woman?" He didn't seem apt to speak, so she provoked him. "How many women were there, Michael?"

"One!" he snapped. "I've had my problems, Emma, but I was never prone to catching some disease by sleeping in brothels." Emma looked away in disgust. "Yes," he proceeded, "I'm a brash man, Emma. You asked for the truth. Not that such a life hadn't crossed my mind. I felt worthy of it at times; felt certain that the only way to get love was to pay for it. But I couldn't bring myself to do it. I would hope you find that redeeming. I do. But I met a woman, a widow with two children. I was fond of her, and she was lonely. I saw her regularly for nearly six months. I became rather attached to the children, but when I finally allowed myself to actually be passionate with her . . ." He put a finger to Emma's chin, wanting her to look at him when he said this. "She was the only other woman I ever got the least bit passionate with, but I didn't sleep with her." With his point made, he continued, "But do you know what I did?"

Emma said nothing. This conversation was putting knots in her throat.

"Do you know what I did?" he repeated angrily. "I called her Emma. In the middle of a tender moment, I had the audacity to call that kind, good woman somebody else's name. Your name."

Emma jerked her chin from his touch, but he went on. "I apologized. She assured me that she understood, but I didn't know how she could when I didn't. I told her she deserved better than someone who was cursed to a life obsessed with a woman he couldn't have. And that's when I got drunk. Blindly, hopelessly drunk. I cursed you from the depths of my soul for ruining my life—what little was left of it after my father had gotten through with me. And when I woke up sentenced to three years, I realized that you were still there in my head, and you continued to be there every hour of every day and night for three years. All I thought of was you, how I hated you for doing what you did to me. I wanted vengeance. I wanted to see you hurt the way I had hurt." He drew a ragged breath. "But if the truth be known, all I really wanted was to love you, and to have you love me. I wanted to be close to you. But you figured that out before I did, didn't you."

"Anything else?" Emma said without showing him the tears streaking her face.

"Nothing you won't hear at the supper table tonight."

"Is that necessary?" she asked.

"Yes, I think it is."

Michael studied the silence and heard sniffles. He couldn't blame her. After that speech, he couldn't blame her for getting up and walking away. But if she was going to do it, he wanted to know now.

"Emma?" He put a hand to her shoulder, but she turned further away. "Emma!" He forced her to face him while she wiped helplessly at her tears. "That's what I am, Emma. I'm the one your sister is afraid will only bring you pain."

Emma was slow to respond, searching for the proper words, while Michael hung vulnerably on her silence.

"No, Michael," she finally muttered hoarsely. "That is the man you were, and I would hope that you haven't changed enough to for-get that I was the one who drove you through your actions. You told me that yourself."

"What are you trying to say?" He needed it straight out.

"I'm saying that a woman would have to be a fool not to feel flat-tered by such undying devotion, however misguided it might have been."

Michael touched her face. "And you don't think any less of me?"

"As my mother once said, you have risen above the worst of things to become more than most men of this world who rise above nothing."

"Emma," he breathed fervently, pulling her to him in an effort to express all she meant to him. She returned his embrace with ardor.

"Come along." He rose reluctantly to his feet and pulled her up beside him.

Their ride home was mostly silent. But he felt better.

❦   ❦   ❦

Michael was the last to enter the dining room, freshly bathed and sporting new clothes. He sat at his usual place next to Emma, who reached beneath the table to squeeze his hand just as the first course was brought in from the kitchen. He smiled at her and she whispered, "You look handsome."

Emma thought it sounded trite in describing the desire his very appearance aroused in her. She was proud of him, past and all.

"I trust everything is all right?" Alexa said to him in greeting.

"Yes, fine," he replied politely. "I checked on Toby before I came down. I think he'll be fine."

"Father told me what happened," Tyson added with concern in his voice.

"What happened?" Lacey turned to Tyson, irritated at being left ignorant.

Tyson looked at her innocently, wanting to tell her that if she would stay around him for more than five minutes at a time, she might know what was going on. "Oh," he reported lightly, as if it were an everyday occurrence, "Michael just beat up some guy who was trying to get his son back this afternoon."

Lacey looked as if she'd bite Tyson, then she turned to Michael. "Something you're quite good at, Mr. Hamilton."

"Quite," Michael said and took a spoonful of soup.

"I'm just grateful you weren't hurt," Alexa said.

"I did get a bloody nose," he said as proudly as one of the boys would have displayed a battle scar.

"I trust it's doing fine," Alexa smiled.

Michael touched his mustache and looked at his fingers. "No more blood."

Emma smiled timidly, but she heard Michael draw a serious breath and knew he was intending to make severe confessions. She put a hand to his thigh with enough pressure to make him look at her. "Not now," she mouthed carefully. She narrowed her eyes, and he perceived her implication that his conversations often put a stop to the meal. It would be better to wait until they at least got to dessert.

The meal passed with small talk, while Emma wondered if anything would change after their wedding day. Would Tyson and Lacey reconcile their differences? Would Lacey let up on her lack of forgiveness once she knew that Michael was committed by marriage? Realizing that Lacey seemed detached and distant, Emma felt a growing concern for her. She tried not to let the tension affect her, but it was difficult at times, and she longed for her and Lacey to be as close as they used to be. But she had told Michael that if she had to choose, it would be him. She had made her choice, and she didn't regret it.

When dessert was brought in, Emma held her breath as Michael turned to her for silent approval.

She did or said nothing, which he interpreted as consent. He cleared his throat and said carefully, "Jess, there is something I need to tell you." All eyes turned toward him curiously.

"Yes, Michael. What is it?"

"What happened out there today was very much my fault."

"Well, I don't see how you—" Tyson began in a way that Michael appreciated, but he put up a hand to stop him.

"I think I need to go back a little and explain myself. I hope you won't be . . . offended, but I think it is necessary."

Lacey's eyes reflected a daring challenge. She obviously hoped he would say something to make the others see him as she did.

"You've figured out now that Toby's father is the same man making these accusations against me. The connection is no coincidence. It's no secret that I served a prison sentence." Alexa looked up, surprised at the turn this was taking. "And when I was released, I was full of an anger I won't bother trying to explain or justify. I had made a decision to bank everything I had on a certain . . . venture."

"He wanted to kidnap me," Emma declared proudly.

Michael attempted a glare of disgust, but it was so much like something he might have said himself that he could only smile at her. "Yes, well, that about covers it. Now, I didn't figure I could do it alone, so I started hanging around the pubs and bars, and . . . I was recruiting help, you might say." He paused to look around while everyone waited for him to continue. "The night I was to set my plan into action, one of these . . . bums came to me with the announcement that he had his own plans. The only reason he wanted to help me was because he saw a chance to check out this place so he could get his boy back."

At this point, Jess put down his fork and leaned back. Michael was glad they had finished the majority of their meal. "I told him I wanted nothing to do with it, and I expected him to do what I had paid him to do. Beyond that, he and I had . . . other run-ins, none of which I am proud of, but . . ." Michael sighed. "What it amounts to, in essence, is that I led Rafe Coogan here, and I gave him good reason to be sour about my being here, defending his son."

Lacey gasped as she finally caught the connection at the mention of the name. "He was here?!" she shrieked. "How could you possibly . . ." She couldn't finish beyond a frightful gasp.

Michael voiced it for her. "How could I possibly allow the man who tried to have his way with you to become involved in our lives again? That is a very good question, my dear Lacey; one that has caused me a great deal of anguish, I can assure you." He turned to Jess. "I hope what happened today will have resolved it, but I can't live with keeping anything from you. I should have told you about the connection a long time ago. The problem is my responsibility, but it's come to affect many more than just me. For that I am truly sorry, and I will do everything in my power to rectify it. The problem is, I'm not sure what to do. I've already done what I do best, but I'm not certain if that helped or made the matter worse."

"I'd say he deserved it," Tyson cheered.

"It's not a good situation, Michael," Jess stated, "but there is much in life that isn't. There's no good in punishing yourself for what's in the past."

"We all make mistakes, Michael," Alexa added.

"Hear, hear," Tyson cheered again, this time with an edge of self-recrimination.

Emma looked to Michael, expecting to see peace at their acceptance. Instead she saw his head bowed, his fists clenched against the table. He came to his feet so quickly that his chair nearly tipped. "Sometimes," he said, barely remaining calm, "I wish you would all just yell at me and call me names and even hit me. Yeah, hit me, like Tyson did when I first showed up in the drawing room. I can take it. I can take it a whole lot better than I can take all of your perfect forgiveness of things that I'm having a hard time living with. How can it be so easy for you to forgive and forget, when I can't look at myself in the mirror without being torn apart inside? I don't understand!" he nearly shouted.

"I tend to agree with Michael," Lacey stated smugly.

"Lacey!" Alexa scolded. "I don't believe your present frame of mind warrants your judgment of this conversation."

"What exactly would warrant my judgment?" she insisted. "I can't believe how blind you all are. He stands there and boldly admits to his heinous life, and you accept him off the streets like some starving hound, totally oblivious to what he's done and what he's capable of."

There was so much Michael wanted to say, but he'd just asked to be yelled at, so what could he do but take it?

Emma moved to stand, ready to tell Lacey exactly what she thought, but she felt Michael's hand come down with pressure over her shoulder, urging her to be still.

It was Tyson who voiced the retaliation, at the risk of losing everything he was fighting to gain with Lacey. "And just where do you think we found you?"

"Tyson!" Alexa scolded him as well. "That is uncalled for."

"Is it?" Tyson came to his feet and pressed his palms onto the table. "You know, Lacey, you have been given nothing but complete love and acceptance in this home. I will be the first to admit that you have suffered from my mistakes, but that doesn't warrant your judgments of Michael, or anyone else under this roof. I'll not have my wife taking the justice of another man's life into her own self-righteous hands."

"I'm not your wife yet," she spat.

"Nor will you be if something doesn't change." Tyson strode from the room, leaving Lacey to glare at Michael with a clear implication that this was all his fault.

"Lacey," Alexa said gently, but with no room to doubt that she was serious, "I think you owe Michael an apology." Alexa was concerned for Lacey, and knew there was a great deal that needed to be worked out, but she figured their allowance of her bitterness had gone far enough.

"I owe Michael nothing," she hissed, "and it's clear that no one here owes me anything either. Perhaps I don't belong here any more than Michael does."

"Lacey!" Jess shouted. "You're as much a part of this family as anyone else. Your mother and I have *never* treated you any differently from the twins since the day you were brought here. We have *all* made mistakes and faced difficulties. Your mistakes don't make you any less one of us. You are our daughter, the same as if we had given birth to you. Do you understand?"

"No," she insisted, "I do not. If I am your daughter, then why do you totally disregard any opinion I might have?"

"Opinions are fine, Lacey," Jess retorted. "Judgments are not, especially when you're too lost in your own pain to realize how much hurt you're inflicting on others concerning things that you're barely aware of."

Lacey looked at her father with a pained expression, then her mother, then she fled from the room.

Michael sighed and hung his head in frustration. "I do have a way of bringing out the best at the dinner table."

"It's all right, Michael," Emma consoled.

"No, Emma, it's not all right. It seems at the moment that everything is quite wrong." He turned to leave the room.

"Wait," Emma stopped him, "where are you going?"

"I thought Tyson and I could wallow in our misery together."

"I love you, Michael," she said with passion.

He managed a smile and said to Alexa, "I guess that makes something right."

"I would say so," Alexa assured him.

"Michael?" Jess added.

"Yes, sir."

"Chances are that Rafe Coogan would have found us anyway. We're not so difficult to locate. I'm grateful that Toby has you to protect him, and that you were there when it happened. We'll watch out for him, and if Rafe comes back, we'll deal with it." He narrowed his eyes to indicate a hidden meaning as he added, "I've dealt with worse."

"Yes," Michael chuckled dryly, "those Hamiltons keep you going."

"My daughter is about to become a Hamilton," Jess smiled, "so watch your mouth. Not to mention that I intend to have Hamilton grandchildren. How does that suit you?"

"I think you're all crazy," Michael chuckled, "and I'm grateful to be with so many crazy people." His eyes went warmly to Emma. "It makes me feel right at home."

Michael left the dining room, trying to figure where Tyson might have gone, then he opted for the side veranda. "That was easy," he said when he came out the door to find him there.

"What's that?" Tyson asked absently, leaning back in a chair, his boots up on the porch rail.

"Finding you." Michael pulled up a chair opposite the table where Tyson sat, and lifted his boots in the same manner.

Tyson gazed blankly at the moon beginning to appear in a dusky sky.

"What you thinking?" Michael asked.

"There's no place like Australia. I only wish I had realized that five years ago. Lacey and I would be married, and . . ." His voice trailed off, and he took a swallow of brandy from the snifter in his hand.

"Australia is quite a country," Michael mused. "Of course, I've never been anywhere else, but I used to read a lot. I always found our history rather fascinating, and I have come to realize that I'm much like this great southern land."

"Do tell." Tyson turned toward him with interest.

"Raw and unrefined, but perhaps longing to make more of myself. You know, Tyson, I wonder which of us is more truly Australian: you, the descendant of adventurous men searching for fortune and a new way of life, or me, the descendant of lowlife outcasts, sent here when the island was first established as a prison land."

"Perhaps a combination of both," Tyson said, giving the matter great contemplation.

"Then that would make mine and Emma's children the true Australians," Michael concluded. "And with Lacey's background unknown, I guess it might make yours the same."

Tyson grunted, preferring not to talk about Lacey. He took another swallow of brandy and put the empty snifter back on the table next to the decanter. "Want a drink?" he asked.

"You've only got one glass," Michael replied.

"That's all right. I'll use the bottle."

"Thanks." Michael stood up, poured himself a small amount into the snifter, drank it, then casually took the bottle and dumped its contents over the side of the porch while Tyson watched in astonished dismay. Michael set the empty bottle down, returned to his chair, and put his feet up. "Getting drunk won't help. The last time I got drunk over a woman, I . . . well, I guess that was the last time I got drunk. And I ended up in prison for three years."

Tyson laughed. "You went to prison because of a woman?"

Michael laughed in response. "Yeah, your sister."

"That's incredible," Tyson quipped. "But you didn't have to dump out my brandy."

"I'd rather not wallow with a drunk man."

"Wallow?"

"In our misery."

"Ah, so we are. I suppose you and I are much alike, as we come to find out more all the time."

"How is that?" Michael asked, leaning back to gaze at the moon becoming more apparent as the sky darkened.

"We're both doing penance for mistakes made in ignorance—mistakes that inflicted suffering on others, however unintentional."

"Well put," Michael agreed. "But how does a man know when he's paid enough?"

"Perhaps some things are not possible to ever pay off."

"If you said that to your mother, she would quote the Bible to you."

"So she would. Perhaps Lacey hasn't read it recently."

"I fear my presence here is not helping matters with you and Lacey."

"So you've mentioned before. But I believe your presence here is the only thing that will force us to face the reality of what's happening. Better to face it now than wait until it's too late."

"Too late?"

Tyson waved a hand through the air. "Oh, never mind. Maybe it's already too late."

Michael couldn't think of a response, so they sat in contemplative silence, except for when Tyson said with dismay, "I really wish you hadn't dumped out my brandy."

❦ ❦ ❦

When Michael was gone, Emma said to her parents, "I'm worried about Lacey. I see things in her that remind me of Michael before he dealt with all that buried hurt and fear. What if she doesn't deal with it?"

Jess and Alexa exchanged a concerned glance, making it evident to Emma that this had been a frequent discussion between them. "We can only hope she does," Alexa said quietly. "I've tried to get her to talk, but she just won't." Alexa chuckled and added to Jess, "It's too bad we can't get Michael to make her talk the way he did Trent."

"I don't think that will work in this case," Jess said, appreciating the humor but remaining serious.

"She's spent a lot of time talking to me," Emma said, "but it's the same things over and over. If she's not telling me how awful Tyson is, she's telling me how awful Michael is."

"Perhaps I should try again." Alexa rose from her chair. "It can't hurt."

Emma stood also. "I think I'll check up on Tyson and Michael."

They turned back briefly to notice Jess sitting alone at the end of the long table. "Go on," he waved them out, "leave me here by myself. Just don't be picking at me for reading all the time. You force me to it."

They only gave him a patronizing smile and went their different ways.

Emma quickly found the men on the side veranda. She stood in the open doorway for several moments, expecting to hear some conversation, but neither of them said anything.

"Aren't the two of you a pitiful sight." She stepped out and leaned her hands on the table to look down at both of them. She picked up the empty bottle and glared at them. "All right, which one of you finished this off?"

"I just had one little drink." Michael held up his hand in a pledge.

"I'm afraid I did, too." Tyson sent a glare of disgust toward Michael, but it had an edge of humor. "Your betrothed dumped the rest out."

"Good." Emma put her hands on Michael's shoulders and kissed his cheek. "I'm proud of him."

"So am I," Tyson said, "but he didn't have to dump out my brandy."

"You'll thank me tomorrow morning when you don't have a headache," Michael stated.

After another length of silence, Emma spoke up. "If the two of you have so much to talk about, I'm going to kidnap my betrothed and do some talking of my own."

"Take him!" Tyson said in mock anger. "I can't tolerate a man who dumps out my brandy."

"I dare say you could find more if you wanted it," Michael retorted.

"But you won't, will you," Emma said firmly.

"No," Tyson stood, "I think I'll just go to bed. Maybe Richard is still awake. I think I could use a bedtime story."

"Good night," Emma said, and Tyson paused to kiss her. He gave Michael a healthy slap on the shoulder and went back into the house.

"You said you were going to kidnap me," Michael said. "I'm waiting."

Emma pressed the point of her thumb to the back of his neck. "All right, just keep quiet and move real slow, or I'll have to shoot you, and I don't want to clean up the mess."

Michael looked up at her in disgust. "That was pathetic. You couldn't sound cruel if you tried, and that thumb of yours isn't very threatening."

"All right," she said. "How about this? Either you go for a walk with me, or I'll . . . I'll . . ."

"You'll what?"

"I don't know. Let's go for a walk, and I'll think of something."

They walked arm in arm over the grounds and through the stables. Then they walked through the carriage house, where Michael nostalgically talked about the years he had lived in a room above it while he'd worked in the stables. Michael was surprised to learn that it was the same room Alexa had lived in when she'd initially worked for Jess. He found the idea ironic. They sat in one of the carriages and talked until it was quite late, then Michael roguishly hauled her out of the carriage and urged her toward the house.

❦   ❦   ❦

Alexa found Lacey in her bedroom, staring blankly out the window.

"Are you all right, love?" she asked.

"I suppose I will be," she answered tonelessly.

"Perhaps you and I should have a little talk, and—"

"Really, Mother." Lacey stood and moved away, straightening things on the bureau that didn't need straightening. "There is nothing to talk about."

"I think there is, and I think if you would open up a little bit about the things that are bothering you, we could work them out much easier."

"There is nothing I have any desire to talk about," Lacey insisted, feeling so confused that she wouldn't know where to begin.

"Perhaps you should whether you want to or not." Lacey said nothing, so Alexa persisted. "For a long time after you came to us, I tried to get you to talk about the experiences that led you here, but you never did. Maybe you should now."

"I'm not certain I remember." Lacey laughed tensely. "Besides, what has that got to do with the way this family is turning against me now?"

"We're not against you, Lacey."

"That's not how I see it."

"Then perhaps you should attempt to change your perspective."

"How can I, when . . ." She stopped cold. "I don't want to talk about this. There is no point in it." She walked out of the room, even though it was her own. She didn't know how else to get away from the fear and discomfort she felt at the prospect of a conversation she preferred to avoid.

She went into the sitting room from the hallway and knocked at Emma's door. When no answer came, she peered in and found no one there. She decided to wait and made herself comfortable in the late evening light. After some time, as Lacey began to wonder where Emma could possibly be, a recent lack of sleep became too much and she drifted off, curled in the chair with her head against one of its arms and her legs draped over the other.

❦   ❦   ❦

Michael and Emma returned to the house to find it dark. They groped their way up the stairs, trying to keep their laughter quiet to avoid waking anyone. Michael tripped halfway up and laughed as he whispered, "I've walked better when I'm drunk."

"Who needs to drink?" She tried to help him up, but he pulled her down instead to sit on the step beside him.

"How true!" He kissed her and wrapped her in his arms. "I get everything I need to feel from you."

"Michael," she gasped for breath, "only a rogue would kiss a woman like that . . . on the stairs."

"Exactly!"

"Michael," she giggled quietly, "considering that we're not quite married, I think you should stop behaving quite so roguishly and—"

Michael laughed and stood abruptly, throwing her over his shoulder. Taking hold of the bannister with his free hand, the stairs suddenly became a trivial obstacle and he ascended with agility.

"I think we're here." Michael set her down, and she opened the door quietly.

"I can't find the lamp, Michael. You've sent all the blood rushing to my head."

"Who needs light? Rogues work better in the dark." He pulled her into his arms, lowering his voice to that practiced mock cruelty. "Now that I've got you, my sweet, you'll never escape what I have planned for you." He laughed like a villain and threw her to the bed. Kneeling over her, he growled and added, "I shall kiss you and tickle you until you beg for mercy. And if you don't cooperate, I will have to shoot a hole through your pretty little head."

Emma giggled softly and whispered in his ear, "Shut up and get on with the kissing, Mr. Hamilton."

Lacey awoke to muffled voices in the darkness, but as her ears tuned in to discern their source, an indescribable panic tightened her chest and set her groping frantically for the lamp. As Michael uttered his last threatening remark, the room became diffused with light, accompanied by a shrill, piercing scream.

Michael and Emma both turned in terrified shock, their hearts pounding, as Lacey flew toward them hysterically, screaming Emma's name in fear and lunging for Michael, who came quickly to his feet on the opposite side of the bed.

"Lacey!" Emma shouted. "Calm down! I'm all right. Calm down."

"The fiend!" she hissed, scrambling to get close to him while Emma barely managed to keep herself between them. "How dare he do that to you! I'll kill him! I swear I'll kill him!"

Emma's suspicions concerning Lacey were confirmed as she realized that this was not normal dislike, and the fear of what was happening in Lacey's mind far outweighed any fear of the hurt she was struggling to inflict on Michael.

"Let me go!" she insisted as Emma grabbed her from behind in an attempt to keep her at bay. "I'm going to kill him! I will not tolerate him in this house any longer, I swear it!"

"Lacey," Emma soothed, "you must try to—"

Lacey mustered all of her strength and pushed Emma aside. She scrambled over the top of the bed and lunged at Michael, who tried to get hold of her instead of running. Her fingernails raked his face and drew blood. Emma cried out while Michael cursed under his breath and spun Lacey around, holding her wrists to her sides with his arms locked firmly around her.

"I know who you are now," she spat, attempting to kick him and occasionally succeeding. Emma looked on helplessly. "I should have known it the first time I heard your voice. You fiend! You're nothing better than scum! You . . . Ooh! Let me go!"

She kicked him harder and Michael hollered at Emma, "If you don't want me to hit her, I think you'd better get some help."

Emma flew out the door and opted to get Tyson. His room was closer. She was grateful to approach the door and see him coming out, barely in breeches and an unbuttoned shirt.

"What's going on down there?" he questioned, running past her.

Emma fell into step behind him, realizing she was crying. "I don't know. Lacey just went mad. I . . ." She couldn't say any more before Tyson bounded into the room to find Michael barely managing to control Lacey, who squirmed and clawed and kicked. The blood on Michael's face made it evident that she was quite serious.

"Lacey!" Tyson took her shoulders while Michael kept a good hold on her wrists. Michael had heard that madness could give people incredible strength, but he'd never believed it until now. He was exhausted.

"Let go of me!" she snarled. "I'm going to kill him!"

"Calm down," Tyson shook her. "You're not going to kill anybody."

It wasn't a surprise to see Jess and Alexa fly into the room, wearing wrappers that were barely tied over their nightclothes. For a moment they paused to observe the scene and try to figure out what was happening.

"I am!" Lacey kicked Tyson and he groaned. "I'm going to kill him! His father tried to kill *us,* and I'm going to kill *him.* He's a fiend, just like his father. It's in his blood. He'll hurt Emma. He'll hurt us all." She clenched her teeth. "I'm going to kill him!"

Tyson moved closer, sandwiching Lacey between himself and Michael so she couldn't move her legs enough to hurt either of them.

Alexa stepped in and put a comforting hand to her daughter's face while the men continued to hold her. "Lacey, calm down and we'll talk about this. You have got to calm down. Do you understand? Your raging will do no good. You can't kill Michael, because we're not going to let you."

"That's a relief," Michael said too seriously.

"Looks like she nearly succeeded," Tyson observed, nodding toward his scratched face.

"I am!" Lacey insisted. "Now let me go!"

"We're not going to let you go until you calm down, Lacey," Alexa said gently. "Now breathe deeply, and try to think clearly."

"I'm going to kill him!" she continued to insist.

"No." Alexa kept a soothing hand on her face, stroking her hair back from it, touching her with assurance. "We're going to calmly go into the other room, and we're going to talk about why you want to kill Michael." Alexa looked up at Michael with a quick warning in her eyes, then added, "If your reasons are valid, we'll help you."

Michael had a good idea what Alexa's motives were, but he couldn't resist a terse, unappreciative smile.

The display of trust was immediately noticed when they felt her relax, if only a little. Alexa sensed this and persisted, "You are very dear to us, Lacey. We want to talk about this, and then we'll decide what to do."

Lacey gave one last fervent struggle, then she slowly relaxed and hung her head in defeat.

"All right, Michael," Alexa mouthed more than whispered, "you let go, very slowly, and be on guard. Tyson, keep a tight hold." They both nodded, and with careful slowness, Michael released his grip. Lacey nearly collapsed against Tyson, who caught her and held her against him. "Lacey," Alexa said gently, "will you come with your father and me into the other room?"

She barely nodded with her face buried against Tyson's shoulder. Tyson felt irony overwhelm him, along with an indescribable fear.

"Tyson," Alexa said gently, motioning Jess closer, "let your father take her. I think it best that we handle this."

Tyson felt an aching helplessness as he carefully shifted her, like a lifeless rag doll, into Jess's embrace. He thought of the story of Jess's mother, who had lived out her life with the mind of a child after a traumatic experience had broken her spirit. Would his Lacey ever be whole again? He felt tears burn into his eyes as he watched Jess move carefully toward the door with his arms encircling her.

Alexa followed, turning back to lift a finger and say quietly, "I want all of you to stay right here or in the sitting room. I may need you."

They all nodded in helpless unison. Emma moved into Michael's arms and cried. Tyson sat numbly on the edge of the bed and choked back the emotion as best he could. When Emma gained control of her emotion, she poured water into the basin and wet a cloth to clean the blood from Michael's face. Michael took over and nodded toward Tyson. Emma sat beside her brother, taking his hand. "Are you all right?" she whispered, knowing it was a stupid question.

"No," he replied and put an arm around her, pulling her head to his chest and setting his chin on it. "What . . . happened?" he muttered. "What brought it on?"

Emma tried to put it together in her mind. "Michael and I . . . came in here in the dark, and we were talking . . . and laughing. Michael was teasing me."

"And we were kissing," Michael felt it important to mention.

"The lamp came on," Emma said, "and she started screaming, and . . ." Emma didn't finish, but she added breathily, "I just don't believe it."

Michael sat down and swallowed hard. "I think it had something to do with that roguish voice of mine." Tyson and Emma both looked to him inquisitively. "She was ranting about my father, how he tried to kill you." Michael put a hand to his face that betrayed the emotion he was trying to hide. "It's not so unreasonable to think that I sound like my father."

"Wait a minute," Emma said as something occurred to her. "How would Lacey know how your father . . ." Suddenly the memory came together for Emma as she made a connection that should have been obvious. "It was your father," she said, "that my father shot in the stable when . . ." Her voice broke, and she couldn't finish.

"That's right," Michael said, wondering why it hadn't come up before now. Perhaps it was because he'd had no desire to remind her of such a horrible connection.

"Good heavens," she said, her eyes becoming distant. "That could explain a great deal."

"If I remember correctly," Tyson said, "the incident was rather traumatic for both you and Lacey."

"Yes," Emma said, "but once it was over and done, I got beyond it. Apparently Lacey didn't."

"Apparently not," Tyson said.

"So," Emma added thoughtfully, turning toward Michael, "perhaps it's your father that Lacey is really afraid of. Maybe she . . ." Emma couldn't quite put the remainder of her thoughts into words.

"It's possible," Michael shrugged. "And aren't I a product of my father?"

"Not in the way she's implying," Emma insisted.

"Perhaps not," Michael said, "but it certainly helps me understand why . . ." He paused and his voice cracked. "Why she's afraid. My father could be a . . . frightening man."

Nothing more was said as they all slipped into deep thought. They took turns pacing and moving from chair to chair. They exchanged concerned glances and attempted to offer each other comfort.

The hours dragged by in silence, broken by an occasional raging outburst that filtered through from Lacey's room. It was nearly dawn before Alexa opened the door to meet their anxious faces. For a moment she hesitated, and they expected her to make some request for assistance. But she moved inside, closed the door with a deep sigh and sat down, looking thoroughly exhausted.

"Is she all right?" Tyson pressed, unable to bear the tension.

"I think she's closer to being all right than she was before this happened. But I also think she has a long way to go." Alexa drew a deep breath and began what she knew was a necessary report. "We did accomplish a great deal as far as finally getting her to open up all the hurt she had bottled away."

Michael shifted in his seat, feeling a deep empathy for what Lacey had just gone through.

Alexa went on. "But the problem is that she showed very little emotion as she spoke. With everything she just told us, she should have cried and screamed and let all of the emotion out with the facts. But the only emotion I saw at all was rage, and that only came when she was discussing you." She nodded toward Michael. He sighed with exasperation.

As long as she was talking to Michael, she persisted with an important point. Her tone was mildly scolding. "That must have been quite a show you put on out there on your little venture into the outback. She has such a suppressed fear of you that discussing her experiences out there was like squeezing blood from a rock." Michael's eyes filled with apology and concern, but there was nothing he could say. "However," Alexa sighed and continued, "that is only a small part of it. As far as I can figure, her encounter with your father when she was a child frightened her so badly that she simply locked the memory away. Your attempts to sound cruel subconsciously tugged at those memories. Perhaps that's why she's always felt uncomfortable with you. From what she managed to tell us, hearing your voice in the dark earlier set it off. But your father's part in this is only a link in the chain that started with her experiences on the streets before she was found and brought here."

"Did she tell you what happened?" Tyson asked. The mystery of her past had always tugged at him.

"As much as she can remember, and what memories she has are very clear. It's as if they've been locked away and preserved. Apparently her parents were killed in an accident; she doesn't know for certain. She just remembers being told they were dead. From what she tells me of her life before then, I am assuming she came from a comfortable, moderate home where there were good feelings. She was taken to the home of a distant relative, who simply didn't want her."

Tyson sighed, feeling his heart pound with angry frustration as his mother continued. "She overheard a conversation concerning orphanages and boarding schools. It frightened her and she ran away, borrowing clothes from another child in the house to dress like a boy."

Alexa paused to put her emotion under control. "In my experience, I have come to learn that in some cases running away is more a cry for help. With most of these children, the appeal of a roof over their head and food to eat soon sends them home, grateful to be there. But Lacey . . ." Alexa put a hand over her mouth, and tears flowed down her face. It was the first time Michael had seen her cry. "She couldn't find her way back, and they . . . apparently made no effort to find her."

Emma clamped a hand over her mouth, and Tyson pushed a hand into his hair. Alexa swallowed carefully and went on. "She was found

huddled in the garbage in an alley, and that's when the constable con-
tacted us, thinking she was a boy." Alexa wiped at her tears. "I am so
grateful she was dressed that way. How lost I would be without her!"

"As we all would," Tyson agreed.

Alexa smiled toward her son. "Her name is really Mary." The
twins glanced at each other, attempting to absorb an entirely new
insight on the sister they had grown up with. "But she told me," Alexa
nearly laughed, "that she much preferred the name Lacey; it wasn't so
dull. She has Tyson to thank for that."

Alexa sighed again and continued with the difficult task of unfold-
ing the story. "Her insecurities about her experience on the streets,
however brief it might have been, were apparently insignificant when
she was brought here and given love and stability. She didn't want to
talk about it, and we didn't press it. She always seemed to be doing
well enough." Alexa looked pointedly at Tyson. "It was your leaving
that began to pull all of those feelings to the surface again."

Tyson hung his head in humble frustration and regret. "The more
time you were gone," Alexa went on, "the more she began to feel that
she had been abandoned, just as she'd been by her parents when they
died, and her guardians when they allowed her to be lost."

Inwardly Tyson cursed the immaturity and lack of insight that had
led him to his careless act. "I should have listened more," he muttered.
"She told me over and over that she didn't want to leave here. Why
didn't I see the fear? Why didn't I—"

"There are things we all could have done differently, Tyson," Alexa
soothed. "Think how your father and I feel for not trying harder to
confront this when it was not so painful. But there is no good in harboring regret."

If Michael could find a bright point in this, it was the reminder
that he, for all his horrendous mistakes, was not alone in regret.

"The rest of the problem, I believe, is a matter of poor timing,"
Alexa concluded. "The combination of being kidnapped and Tyson's
return had a very severe emotional impact. Either experience alone
might have been easier to face, but the two together left her overwhelmed with confusion and fear. And lashing out at Michael and
Tyson was the only way she could justify what she was feeling.
Michael received the worst of it, because I believe his situation is more

black and white, and she has a lot of tangible evidence against him. Her anger toward Tyson is very real, but she had a difficult time expressing it when he approached her so humbly. Deep inside she really loves you, Tyson, and she wants it to be as it once was between the two of you."

"Is that possible?" Tyson asked his mother severely.

"It simply has to be," she insisted. "And you can start right now by just being with her." Tyson was on his feet before she had a chance to explain. "Your father is with her now. She was sleeping when I left. I don't want her to be alone for a minute. I once had a boy with similar symptoms, and he became suicidal. Tyson, you go in there and stay with her. Let her wake up in your arms. Let her know you love her. And stay with her every minute until Emma or I take over."

Tyson nodded and Alexa added, "Go to your room now and get whatever you might need to get you through until this afternoon." She turned to Emma. "I want you to stay in this room with the sitting room doors open, so you can hear Tyson call if he needs anything. We'll change positions later in the day. Michael, you go get some sleep before you have to get to work. I'll have Tillie bring up some breakfast and wake you so you can meet the boys on time." He nodded.

Alexa turned to take them all in. "We'll work together to pull her through this. The important thing now is to be completely loving and accepting, and to watch her closely. I suspect that the emotion she didn't let go of will likely explode at some point." Michael and Emma exchanged a knowing glance. Emma thought it curious how much Michael and Lacey had in common when it came down to dealing with their struggles.

"What do I do if that happens?" Tyson asked his mother.

But it was Emma who answered. "You just hold her, and listen, and absorb it and give nothing but love in return." All eyes turned to her—Alexa's with pride, Michael's with nostalgia, and Tyson's with surprised gratitude. As he noticed the expression on Michael's face, it was easy to guess where her wisdom had come from, and it touched him. If he could help Lacey through this and come to share with her what he had witnessed between Michael and Emma, he could ask for no more.

"Go along, Tyson," Alexa prodded. "Your father is likely exhausted, and he becomes so intolerable when he doesn't get his sleep." Alexa moved to the door. "We'll make it through this. Get some sleep while you can."

Emma met Michael's eyes and could find no words to express all she was feeling. Michael rose and extinguished the lamp that was no longer needed as the hues of dawn filled the room with a dim glow. Emma put her arms around him, and they shared an embrace that expressed a thousand words of love and gratitude, concern and regret.

"Good night, Emma," he said, touching her chin.

"Good morning is more appropriate, I think."

Michael kissed her quickly on the lips and quietly left the room. Emma put on a nightgown and crawled into bed. Despite her worry, exhaustion soon put her into a heavy sleep.

❦   ❦   ❦

Tyson went into Lacey's room without knocking and deposited some belongings into a chair. "How is she?" he asked his father, who sat up straight and stretched.

"Still sleeping."

"I'll stay with her now," Tyson said without taking his eyes off her. She looked so beautiful, sleeping peacefully, without the usual bitterness etched into her face. Tyson thought of the sources of her hostility, and his heart ached for her.

Jess came to his feet. "We just escorted her to the depths of hell, Tyson." He put a hand to his son's shoulder. "Now it's up to you to bring her back."

"I'll do my best," Tyson uttered.

"You'd better." Jess pointed a finger. "That's my daughter there."

"And I love her," Tyson said with strength.

"I know you do." Jess softened. "Get some sleep, but stay close."

Tyson nodded and was left alone with Lacey. Holding a prayer in his heart, he lay down beside her and eased her close, recalling his mother's advice. But he wished he had any idea in the world what to expect.

Tyson's next awareness was of Lacey stirring. He opened his eyes and leaned onto one elbow to watch her come awake. He was reminded of their reunion in the outback, and he hoped her reaction would be a little less painful.

"Hello, Lacey," he said when her eyes focused on him.

"What are you doing here?" she asked tersely, glancing around the room to orient herself. She pressed her head back against the pillow as the memories of the night before fell into place. Just to think of the words that had spilled out of her mouth made something inside her twist into heated knots. And now, Tyson had the nerve to be right here next to her, acting as if everything was ordinary and fine.

"Are you all right?" he asked gently.

"I don't feel particularly well, if you must know," she said. "You didn't answer my question."

"I'm here because I think you need me."

"I think I've learned to do without you," she snapped.

"Lacey," he stopped her from moving away, "you can argue with me and avoid facing it as long as you want, but it will never change what happened last night."

"I should have killed him," she insisted.

"I'm not talking about that," he said, and she looked at him carefully.

"Just what are you talking about?" For a moment she wondered if she had been delirious and missed something.

"Mother told me," he said gently.

"Oh," she said, angrily coming to her feet, "so now it's another of those family matters, is it? Lacey has gone crazy. Let's talk about it."

"We are nothing less than concerned for you." He leaned against the headboard and folded his arms. "Why is it so difficult for you to accept that you are loved and wanted here?"

"Perhaps because I am the outsider. I've always been the outsider. And now . . . now? I am the only one around here who doesn't think Michael Hamilton is the best thing that ever happened to this family."

"Personally, I think *you* are," Tyson said with sincerity.

"Then why do you constantly oppose me, Tyson?"

"I would define it more as sticking up for myself."

Lacey groaned in frustration and began haphazardly looking through drawers and slamming them shut when she apparently couldn't find what she was looking for. Tyson watched her and realized she hadn't faced it yet. She hadn't even come close. All that pain was still neatly fenced in by a wall of bitterness. He felt certain there was nothing he could say that wouldn't be opposed. But he had to try.

Standing behind her, he set his hands on her shoulders. "I love you, Lacey. You are my life. Please, let's talk."

She turned to him with skeptical eyes. "I'm sick to death of talking. Why don't you just go away and leave me in peace?"

Tyson couldn't answer her. He only looked at her in disbelief and wondered how to possibly mend their breaking hearts.

❦   ❦   ❦

Emma awoke to hear shouting filter through the sitting room. She dressed hurriedly and went through the open doors to find Tyson and Lacey standing face to face in a silent battle of wills. The despair in his expression made it evident that little had changed.

"Good morning," Emma said cheerily. "Do you realize it's past noon? I wonder if we can get something to eat around here."

"I'm not hungry," Lacey insisted, "but Tyson was just leaving."

Tyson wanted to protest, but Emma gave him a discreet nod to indicate she would take over. He gathered his things and left the room.

"Why don't you have something sent up for us," Emma added before he closed the door.

"Did you sleep well?" Emma asked, straightening the bed.

"Once I got to sleep." She began to rummage through drawers again in frustration.

"Looking for something?" Emma asked, sitting casually to toy with a lace doily on a nearby table.

"I don't know." She slammed the drawer shut, and Emma could clearly see that her nerves were so tightly strung she was ready to snap. Perhaps snapping was what she needed, but Emma remembered her mother's advice. Love and acceptance.

"So?" Emma said. "Did you read that book I loaned you? It was a good one."

"I don't remember," Lacey said. But it was enough for Emma to begin rambling in a way that Lacey was comfortable with, and she began to relax. Tillie brought up some food and together they ate and got cleaned up, washing and brushing each other's hair in a way that was familiar. The afternoon wore on with little of significance happening, but Emma could feel the tension close beneath the surface and had to fight to keep a cool, nonchalant exterior. What she felt on behalf of her sister was little less than pure fear. It was when Lacey's expression changed abruptly that Emma realized she was packing, and that fear came to the forefront with a surge of panic.

Twenty-two
CHARGED FOR MURDER

Michael finished with his work and found Tyson on the front veranda. "What? No brandy?"

"No," Tyson stared straight ahead, "but I should thank you for dumping it out last night. I was grateful to be sober when everything broke loose."

"We never know when things like that will happen. I suppose that's why we should stay sober." Michael made himself comfortable.

"Wouldn't hurt."

"Is Emma with her now?" Michael asked in a softer tone.

"Yeah."

"Any progress?"

"No."

"Do I have to beat it out of you, boy? What else happened?"

"She woke up, looked at me, and started in with the old routine." Tyson shifted in his seat. "I don't know, Michael. I wonder if I can handle this."

"Oh, you're pretty tough."

"Tough? Me?"

Michael's tone turned severe. "You know what I told my boys about being tough, don't you? Being tough is not being afraid to admit that you're afraid, or hurt, or that you're not so tough."

"Well, I'm not so tough, Michael. And I'm scared to death. I keep thinking about that story about my grandmother."

"Jess's mother, you mean?"

"Yeah. She never recovered. Father told me later that he was nineteen when she died, and she had never recovered from the trauma. He said he believed that her mind was sound, but her spirit had been so completely broken that she couldn't function."

"Don't you think what she experienced was a lot more severe?"

"I believe that trauma is relative. One person's strength is another's weakness. Emma could survive almost anything, I think."

"Even me."

"But Lacey," he said her name with reverence. "She's always been timid, more sensitive, and . . ." He came to his feet and kicked over the chair. "Blast it! I feel so helpless. So blasted helpless!"

Michael couldn't think of anything to say that might console Tyson. His fear on Lacey's behalf was evident. Michael sighed and put his boots up, then immediately put them down as feminine voices, arguing, moved closer from inside the house. Michael met Tyson's eyes, and together they headed for the door. It flew open just as Tyson was about to open it, and Lacey strode past them, oblivious to their presence.

"Lacey, wait!" Emma followed quickly, oblivious as well. "You can't just walk out of here without a word. Don't be a fool. Where would you go? What would you . . ."

Tyson caught sight of the bags Lacey was carrying, and his heart leapt into his throat. He hesitated only a moment to gather his wits, and Michael's voice whispered behind his ear, "Fight, Tyson! You've got to fight!"

"Lacey!" He ran down the steps, but she didn't even slow down. Michael saw the visible relief in Emma as Tyson took over. "Lacey!" he shouted and caught up with her, grabbing her arm and forcing her to face him. "How dare you even think of leaving here!"

"You did!" she retorted.

"Spite? Is that it? There is no point in your leaving to teach me a lesson, Lacey, because I've already learned it."

"I'm just leaving. That's it."

"I don't believe this. What about Richard?"

"He's better off without me."

"That's not true!"

"Let me go, Tyson. I'm leaving. I never belonged here. It's time I faced that."

She jerked her arm free, and Tyson glanced to the steps where Michael and Emma stood. Michael nodded firmly, and Tyson felt a fighting spirit rush through him. With a combination of anger and fear, he caught up to Lacey again and grabbed her around the waist. Her bags fell to the ground, and he calmly threw her over his shoulder.

"What are you doing?" she demanded as he carried her back toward the house.

"I'm saving you from yourself," he answered. "It's about time we had this out, once and for all." He walked with his cargo up the steps, past Michael and Emma. Emma held the door for him while he said to Michael, "Would you take Lacey's bags to her room, please. I'm taking Lacey to mine."

"I'd be happy to," Michael said, waving casually to Lacey as she looked up from where she hung over Tyson's shoulder. She snarled at him, and he was glad Tyson had a good hold on her. His scratched face and bruised shins from the night before were sore reminders of Lacey's wrath.

"It would seem that Tyson has everything under control." Michael actually smiled.

"I hope so." Emma watched them disappear up the stairs, biting her lip in concern.

"And how are you?" Michael asked.

"I'll be all right," she said softly.

"Would you like to go riding, Miss Davies?" he asked.

Emma smiled up at him and took his offered arm. A distraction was exactly what she needed.

❧   ❧   ❧

Tyson hauled Lacey into his room and kicked the door shut. He managed to lock it before he threw her onto the bed and stood back to place his hands on his hips.

"How dare you!" she hissed.

"I'll tell you how I dare." He calmly pointed a finger at her. "You are as good as my wife, as much as my sister, and you are the mother of my son. I love you and I believe you love me, and I am *not* going to stand by and watch you walk away from here, when I don't believe that's what you really want."

"How do you know what I want?" She glared at him through narrowed eyes.

"I believe you want me as much as I want you, Lacey. And I believe if you would just face up to what's hurting, the possibility of what you and I could share is immeasurable."

"Oooh," she snarled, "you're nothing more than an arrogant . . ."

Tyson leaned forward and grinned in a way that stopped her flat. "Go ahead, Lacey. Tell me what I am. Just get it out and get it over with. Tell me how much you hate me."

"I hate you!" she shouted.

"Say it again!" he shouted back.

"I hate you!"

"Again!"

"I hate you, Tyson. I *hate* you." She jumped off the bed and lunged at him. He managed to keep her hands from his face, but she hit his chest with incredible strength and said it over and over. "I hate you! I hate you!"

Tyson allowed her to rage, while his mind played over things Emma had told him of her experiences with Michael and the theory of love and hate being close in the heart. When Tyson figured she'd said it enough, he shook her just enough to get her attention, then said close to her face, "Now, look me in the eye and tell me that you want to leave here, to leave Richard, and Emma, and the only home you've ever known. Look at me and tell me you could last one day out there without falling apart. Look at me and tell me you don't need me, Lacey."

"I hate you," she said softly, but with fire in her eyes.

"Go ahead and hate me, Lacey, but don't leave me."

"I will do as I wish, Tyson Byrnehouse-Davies, and don't you—"

He shook her again. "I *will* stop you! I will not let you leave here unless you can look me in the eye and tell me, reasonably, that it's really what you want."

Lacey looked up at him, confused and distraught and angry. She didn't know what to feel or what to say, but in that moment she felt a desperation to be away from here, as if leaving might keep her from facing this pain. She tried to will herself to say what he was demanding, but it wouldn't come. Instead, she went back to her only present defense. "I hate you," she muttered from deep in her throat.

"You already said that. Now tell me you want to leave."

"I want to . . ." She faltered. "Let me go!" She squirmed, but his grip on her shoulders remained firm.

Tyson felt hope from the evidence of doubt in her eyes. He could see her emotions surfacing, and decided that he could lose nothing by provoking them further. She had talked it all out, but she needed to *feel* it. He remembered Emma's advice about ushering someone through facing their pain, and he held to her tighter, determined to lead her back from the depths of hell, even if it meant being burned on the way out.

"You can't say it," he said with a husky voice. "You couldn't leave me, or anything else you have here."

"Oooh, you arrogant bully. I hate you." She began a fresh struggle. "Now, let me go."

"Not until . . ." Tyson faltered for words. He was afraid to let go of her, sensing that her true emotions were close to the surface, but his mind was so caught up in those emotions that he couldn't find a proper response. Following nothing but instinct, he pressed his mouth over hers with a kiss that surprised even himself.

Lacey struggled and pushed against his shoulders, fighting this without knowing what exactly she was fighting. The confusion engulfed her freshly, landing in the pit of her stomach, and a wave of pain diffused through her. She tried to hold it back, but the force was like the tide crashing against a weakening dike.

Tyson felt a flicker of response in her kiss, then her body went briefly limp with a lengthy whimper. He crushed her against him and felt something almost tangible move through her, stiffening until her fists curled against his shoulders and she shot her head back with a cry that pierced his soul. She groaned from deep within and wilted like a dying flower. Tyson fell to his knees with her and held her as if letting go would leave her to drown. Tears filled his eyes as he watched her rage and wail with anguish and grief. He lost all track of time as her pain went on and on. He held her and whispered assurances, kissed her brow and cheeks and salty eyelids, telling her over and over how he loved her, he would always love her, he would never leave her again. When she finally fell into an exhausted heap, he pulled her into his arms and carried her to the bed, where he pulled off her boots and eased her between the sheets. He sat on the edge of the bed to kiss her brow again, then turned to pull off his own boots.

"No!" she cried and grabbed his arm. "Stay with me. I need you."

"I'm not going anywhere," he assured her. He tossed his boots aside and lay close beside her.

Lacey put her head against his shoulder and clung to him as if she might die if she let go. She didn't know what had just happened to her, only that in this moment all she could feel was grateful that he had stopped her from leaving, that he cared enough to fight for her regardless of all she had put him through, to carry her into this peace of knowing that somehow they were finally reunited.

Tyson eased her closer, and emotion burned through him as he felt her soften in his arms, holding to him the way she used to before he'd left her to follow his foolish disillusionments.

Following a lengthy silence, Lacey leaned on one elbow to look down at him. "Tyson," she said with affection, "forgive me." Her chin quivered. "I'm so sorry for the way I've behaved. I think I understand now why it was so . . . hard, but I . . ." She sobbed. "Oh, Tyson. I'm so sorry."

"Lacey," he cried, touching her face, smoothing her hair, "tell me you'll marry me. Tell me it can be like it used to be, and we'll put the past away and forget about it. None of it matters now, none of it."

Lacey pressed her face to his throat and cried. "I love you, Tyson. I love you. I would die without you. I feel so lost sometimes. You were right; you must save me from myself. You must."

"It's all right," he whispered. "Everything is all right now."

Lacey cried again until she couldn't cry any more, and Tyson relished it. He would never have believed that the love he'd felt for her could have been any more intense than when he'd returned home, wanting only to have her back. But what he felt now was worlds beyond that.

When Lacey quieted again, Tyson wondered if she was asleep, but he looked down to find her watching him with big, tear-swollen eyes.

As the pain diffused from around her, Lacey felt her senses awaken with a newness of life. And in the midst of those senses was the warmth of the man she loved. He had been her brother through childhood; she had borne his son; and now he had saved her soul. For the first time since his return, she felt the reality of what was happening in their lives—things she'd been too buried in pain to think about, let alone feel. She was to be his wife. It was what she'd always wanted, always hoped for, all she had longed for in his absence. And now he was here, holding her, making it clear that he loved her.

"Tyson." She touched his face, and his eyes filled with what she read as a desire that matched the sensation sifting through her, achingly familiar from a time that seemed forever away.

Lacey eased herself up to put her lips to his. Her kiss was timid, but Tyson felt the meaning in it and responded with a kiss that left her breathless. And then he laughed. With pure, perfect joy, he laughed. And she laughed with him. He'd never been so happy in his life. He felt as if he'd finally come home.

❦   ❦   ❦

Michael and Emma returned to the stables after an exhilarating ride through the hills. He took Emma's waist to help her down and immediately drew her against him. He was about to kiss her when she put a hand to her heart, as if she'd felt some kind of shock.

"Are you all right?" he asked, moving his hands to her shoulders to study her face.

"Yes." She smiled slightly, then her eyes narrowed in concentration. With careful effort, she attempted to discern what she was feeling. Her thoughts had gone to Tyson for no apparent reason, and what she felt on his behalf was . . . She checked herself. Yes, it certainly was.

"Michael," she smiled slyly, "I think everything is going to be fine. With Tyson and . . ." She felt it again and laughed. Michael caught on by the distant look in her eyes.

"You feel something?" he asked, and she nodded. "What?"

Emma laughed. "He's happy. That's it. He's just . . . perfectly happy."

Michael laughed, too, and hugged her tightly. When the feeling had subsided a little, Emma said, "I think it's about time for supper."

They saw to the horses' needs and walked to the house, holding hands. Michael looked up first, and stopped abruptly halfway up the steps. Emma nearly ran into him, then lifted her eyes to investigate. Her heart fell to the pit of her stomach. She clutched onto Michael while a raging fear burned through her. Before them stood two law officers, and hovering behind them were her parents. Their expressions alone made it clear what was happening.

"Mr. Hamilton?" one of the officers said. "We've been waiting for you."

"So I see," Michael said tersely. Emma held to him tighter, and he tried to convey some comfort with a squeeze of his hand.

"We're here to arrest you for the murder of Corky Patterson."

"And then what?" Michael demanded. Emma put a hand over her mouth to keep from making a scene. She wanted to scream and drag him away from here.

"You'll be given a fair trial," the officer stated dryly.

It didn't take much for Michael to realize that this was unavoidable. He tried to remind himself that he had a good attorney, and he had the family behind him. But it was still difficult to step forward and hold up his hands in a resigning gesture, which he knew would be far better than making them force him to go.

Emma whimpered behind her hand and had to use great restraint not to cling to him. An officer produced a pair of handcuffs, and Michael sighed with disgust. "Is that necessary? I can assure you I'll go of my own free will."

"With the stories we've heard about you," the officer said blandly, motioning for Michael to hold out his wrists, "I think we'll all feel a lot better with these on."

Michael met Emma's eyes as the cuffs clicked into place. He gave her a wry smile that defied the fear in his eyes. He wanted to tell her that he was thinking about the time he had put handcuffs on her. Instead, he said in a tone far too light for the circumstances, "When you visit, bring me something lavender. And for the funeral, flowers aren't necessary, but a good eulogy would be nice."

"That isn't even funny." Emma's voice trembled with anguish.

Michael's voice nearly cracked. "I suppose it's not." He turned his eyes to Jess. "Tell the boys I'm sorry."

"We'll look out for them until you come back," Jess said with good faith.

Michael smiled at Alexa. With tears in her eyes she said, "It will be all right."

He turned to Emma and wanted to fall down on his knees and beg for mercy from these men who were forcing them apart. "I love you, Emma," he said.

She stepped forward and touched the officer's sleeve, saying quietly to him, "One moment, please." He stepped aside but kept a hand on Michael's arm. Emma put her arms around him and Michael felt frustrated that he couldn't return her embrace.

"I love you, Michael," she whispered and kissed him. "Don't you forget it." Her voice lowered even further. "Fight, Michael. Don't give up on yourself. Don't give up on me."

"Never!" he whispered in reply. She kissed him again, and he nearly felt his life's strength slipping away as she drew her lips from his and stepped back.

Without another word spoken, Michael was led away. Emma couldn't bear to watch, and she ran into the house. Without the strength to go farther, she put her head against the wall and sobbed. She felt her father's hand on her shoulder and turned to gratefully accept his loving embrace. She cried and he held her, stroking her hair and whispering soothing words, just as he had for more than twenty years.

When she had quieted somewhat, he said intently, lifting her chin, "We'll go into town first thing in the morning, and we'll do everything we possibly can." Emma nodded and squeezed her mother's outstretched hand.

"Come along," Alexa said. "We must eat. There's nothing more we can do for now."

They were seated only a moment before Jess said, "I'm assuming that Lacey is with Tyson."

"She's not in her room, and Tyson's door is locked," Alexa provided. "I'm assuming the same. I didn't disturb them."

"How did your time with her go this afternoon, Emma?" Jess asked, startling her.

"Well enough . . . until she started packing and—"

"She what?" Alexa interrupted.

"She was trying to leave. I'm sorry. With all the commotion, I assumed you had already figured it out. Tyson stopped her. The last I saw of them he was hauling her up the stairs, much to her dismay."

"I see." Alexa nearly smiled. "Well, we can hope Tyson has made some progress."

Another deathly silence took hold. Emma found she could hardly eat a bite. All she could see in her mind was Michael sitting in a cold cell, alone in fear and despair.

"I'm sorry." She rose from the table. "I just can't eat. Perhaps I'll take a tray up to Tyson's room and see if everything is all right."

"Excellent idea," Alexa said.

Emma went to the kitchen, and with Mrs. Brady's help she prepared a supper tray sufficient for two. She carried it upstairs, feeling the numbness deepen. She couldn't believe it. She just couldn't believe what was happening.

Quietly she knocked, wondering if they might be asleep. Before she wondered long, Tyson pulled open the door just slightly. "Good. It's you," he whispered. Glancing to the supper tray, he opened the door further and motioned her in. Emma set it down, then her eyes went to Lacey, who was sleeping peacefully.

"Is everything all right?" she asked quietly.

"I think so." He glanced with affection toward the bed. "She seems to be herself again. And from what I saw, I think she must have felt it all. I can't say it was a pretty sight."

Emma closed her eyes and sighed with a quick, silent prayer of appreciation. "Oh, I'm so grateful," she said.

"So am I," Tyson added.

As the relief on Lacey's behalf settled in, Emma felt the reality of her own situation surface. Tyson was quick to notice the change in her countenance. "What's wrong, Emma?"

She looked up at him and couldn't hold back the tears.

"What's happened?" he asked in panic. Emma put a hand to her mouth and pressed her face to Tyson's shoulder. "Emma? What is it? Is it Michael?"

Emma drew back and nodded. "They took him in," she muttered.

"He was arrested?" Tyson whispered in astonishment. Emma nodded a second time and Tyson pulled her close again, letting her cry. "I'm so sorry, Emma. So sorry." He took her shoulders and looked at her. "It's not over yet. He'll get a fair trial. We'll get him back. I swear it."

There was appreciation mixed with doubt in her eyes, and he knew how she felt. Only hours ago, he had wondered if Lacey would ever be whole again. And now, no one could deny the possibility that Michael might not survive this.

"I think I'll get some sleep." Emma wiped helplessly at her face. She could tell the tears weren't going to stop, and she wanted to be alone. "Father and I are going into town in the morning." Tyson nodded, and she quietly went back to her room. She locked the doors and cried far into the night, finally falling into a fitful sleep, sprawled over the bedspread, fully clothed.

Her next awareness was a knock at her door. She oriented herself to the morning light with a sigh of dismay and lumbered to answer it.

"Hello," she said through a yawn to her brother.

"I'd like you to meet my fiancée." He smiled broadly and pulled Lacey from behind him. Lacey laughed and threw her arms around Emma. They held each other and laughed and cried.

Lacey pulled back and took both of Emma's hands into hers. "I'm so sorry, Emma. I know I've been just dreadful, and I hope you will forgive me."

"It's all in the past," Emma smiled.

"That's what Tyson said." Lacey smiled up at him with affection.

"You look awful," Tyson commented to Emma, and reality descended. She turned away in helpless search of a hairbrush as Tyson and Lacey moved into the room. Emma sat in front of the dressing table and pulled the ribbon from her disheveled hair, then she sighed and did nothing more.

Tyson nodded toward Lacey, and she calmly took the brush from Emma's hand to begin brushing. "Tyson told me what happened," Lacey said carefully.

Emma met Lacey's eyes in the mirror, wondering if the changes would also bring an acceptance of Michael.

Tyson observed, wondering the same. He had informed Lacey of the circumstances, but he'd gotten little response.

"You may not appreciate my saying this," Lacey spoke gently, "but I wonder if it isn't for the best."

Tyson sighed. Emma turned abruptly to face her sister, saying just as gently, "I know it's difficult for you to understand, but I love Michael. I don't want anybody else."

"I do understand that you love him," Lacey replied. "But I . . . still fear that he . . . won't make you happy. What if he turns and runs when it gets down to the heat of it?"

Emma drew a patient sigh. She felt better seeing that Lacey's opinions were spoken with concern more than spite, but Emma too had a point to make. "Lacey," she took her sister's hand, "I appreciate your concern. I do. But Michael is not gone today because of any lack of commitment. He loves me. He has already faced the heat of it." Emma took a deep breath and said carefully, "He's had to face you, and he didn't turn and run."

Tyson and Emma held their breath. They could both well imagine Lacey flying into a rage that would set all of their progress back. But Tyson understood Emma's point: Lacey's coming to terms with herself included coming to terms with these attitudes that so greatly affected her relationship with Emma.

Lacey sighed. "You're right, Emma. I'm sorry. You have the right to live your own life. You've made your decision. I should keep my opinions to myself."

Emma squeezed Lacey's hand in appreciation, then she impulsively stood and embraced her. Tears were shed as the bridges between them were rebuilt. Tyson allowed them a moment alone, then he put his arms around them both. For the first time in more than four years, the three of them felt truly united.

❧   ❧   ❧

Jess and Alexa sat at the dining table and looked at each other long enough to realize that they were alone. The emptiness resembled feelings they'd shared when the girls had been kidnapped, and Tyson was still gone.

They both rose in the same instant with a silent decision to investigate, knowing there had been some high-strung emotions here in the last day or so. They had barely moved from the table when Tyson opened the door and followed Lacey into the room.

"Good morning," he said brightly. Jess and Alexa hesitated expectantly.

"Is everything all right?" Alexa asked.

Tyson put an arm around Lacey, and she looked up at him with warmth. "Everything is fine," Tyson smiled.

Lacey embraced each of her parents. She offered them gratitude and apologies that were easily accepted, and they proceeded with breakfast.

"Emma will be down in a few minutes," Lacey said. "She just wanted to be ready to leave right after breakfast."

"How is she?" Alexa asked.

"Not very good," Tyson answered just as Emma entered the room, proving with her quiet reticence that Tyson was right.

She hurried to eat a good breakfast, determined, if nothing else, to have the strength to get through what she knew would be a difficult day. "Can we go now?" she said to Jess.

"Murphy is saddling the horses. I'll meet you in the stable in five minutes."

"Fine." She rose and moved to the door.

"Emma," Tyson called and she paused, "our hearts are with you."

"Yes," Alexa echoed.

"Thank you," Emma said and walked out.

Emma attempted to fill her mind with everything positive concerning Michael and this situation as she rode side by side with her father at a brisk pace. They slowed when a rider approached in the distance. There was nothing behind them but Byrnehouse-Davies, so there was no question that the rider had to be heading there. He stopped when they did, and Jess recognized him as one of the constable's men.

"I was just on my way to see you, Mr. Davies," he said. "Got a message for you."

Jess took it, tore open the envelope, and read to himself. "Thank you," he said. "We're on our way, as you can see." The messenger nodded and rode back toward town.

"What?" Emma insisted, and Jess handed it to her. Hurriedly she read: *Jess, I need to see you here immediately. Bring Emma. This is serious. Ira.*

Emma handed it back and heeled her gelding into a gallop. Jess could only follow and try to keep up, wishing at times like this that the women in his family weren't trained jockeys.

They arrived in good time, and Ira looked up in surprise to see them enter his office. "You're early. That's good. We'll have a chance to go over this before the hearing."

"Hearing?" Jess questioned. Emma chewed her lip anxiously.

"I pulled every legal string I could to get this going quickly. The judge will hear the case in a little over an hour. Right now, we've just got to make certain he hears a good case."

Ira carefully went through all of the points he was going to emphasize, and he coached Emma on the best way to word her testimony. Without being the slightest bit dishonest, they could paint a better picture with the right words.

"He's good," Jess commented to Emma. "He's saved me before."

"One of my best cases," Ira said proudly.

When everything was rehearsed as much as it possibly could be, and the three of them had freshened up, they rode in Ira's carriage across town, where they were escorted into a courtroom and seated. They had only been there a few minutes when Michael was escorted in, the constable close behind. Michael looked so refined, so dignified. Emma caught her breath and squeezed her father's hand as she watched him move to his seat with an officer on either side of him. His eyes quickly scanned the room, filling with a glimmer of warmth when he saw her there. Jess gave him an encouraging nod. Emma kissed her fingers and waved. Michael jerked his head subtly to catch the kiss as he was seated. Emma had to lean forward to see him, but when she did, he leaned forward, too. He winked just before their attention was drawn to the judge as he entered. They all rose until he was seated, then the drama began while Emma contemplated the fact that this man held Michael's future—her future—in his hands.

Only then did Rafe Coogan and his friends bound noisily into the courtroom. The judge looked irritated at their tardiness as he announced that they were here to decide whether the defendant, Michael Hamilton, was innocent or guilty, based on the testimonies heard, or whether the case warranted going on further to a jury trial. Emma decided that despite having it delay their wedding plans, she would far prefer the trial over an immediate declaration of guilt.

Emma was impressed with the way Ira handled the case, representing Michael with the utmost respect. She could see now why Ira wouldn't want to represent someone unless he was confident of their innocence. He would have to be blatantly dishonest otherwise. The three witnesses against Michael each testified with a story that was apparently tight and consistent. Emma fidgeted nervously, and when she managed to catch a brief glimpse of Michael, he was chewing his thumbnail.

Emma felt nervous as she was called to testify, but she felt Michael's eyes on her and concentrated on them, filling her with the support she needed. And his gratitude was evident. When she returned to her seat, Ira whispered in passing, "That was perfect."

Jess was called forward as a character witness, and he gave a perfect, concise account of what he had witnessed in Michael's work with the boys. He testified of his integrity and his firm belief that Michael was a changed man, certainly not capable of murder.

Finally, Michael was called to testify on his own behalf. Emma was proud of him, and touched by his firm humility. He spoke to the judge with perfect respect, and finished his testimony with a statement concerning a man's right to change his ways and begin a new life. His words brought tears to Emma's eyes.

The judge left the room to make a decision, and Emma wondered if Michael's heart was hammering the way hers was. She could only see one of his booted legs stretched out in front of him, but she noticed it twitch occasionally and felt certain his nerves were raw.

A breathless hush accompanied the judge back into the room. He sat down and took a deep breath while Emma squeezed her eyes shut in fervent prayer. "In light of the testimonies that have been given," he began, "I would like to see all of the witnesses individually. Therefore, a decision will be made tomorrow. That's all for now." His words dismissed the session, and Emma didn't know whether to feel better or worse at having to wait another day.

Ira hurried to speak privately with the judge, then returned to Emma and Jess. "I asked if he could see the two of you first so you can return home. He's agreed. He'll see you," he nodded to Emma, "right now."

Emma accepted the squeeze of her father's hand and moved with Ira toward the door where the judge had just disappeared. She caught

Michael's eye and saw a subtle fear there before she entered the room and the door was closed. She repeated everything she had said before, answering the judge's questions carefully and concisely. He listened and thanked her, then she went back to the courtroom to find that Michael had been escorted away. Her heart fell, but she could only sit quietly next to Ira while her father went in to be questioned.

"How did it go?" Ira asked, looking over some papers.

"Fine, I believe." She chewed at her little finger. "Where did they take him?"

"Back to his cell. The judge will see him later." He turned to Emma directly and answered a question that he had obviously guessed she wanted to ask. "No, you can't see him. They want to make certain you're not given the chance to make your stories match. It's a common procedure with this particular judge."

Emma tried to hide her disappointment, but she felt a sense of despair. When her father was finished, Ira advised them to go home; he would send word the minute he knew something.

Jess said nothing as he took Emma to get something to eat, then they headed home. She was grateful when her father took over explaining to the family what had happened. Tyson and her mother showed compassion. Lacey said nothing, but Emma did catch an expression of sympathy, if nothing else. She couldn't deny that it showed some progress.

Through the evening, the family tried to distract Emma. She played a game of chess with Tyson and lost badly. Alexa spoke of wedding plans that Lacey now took great enthusiasm in, while Emma could only hope that Michael would be here. Tyson and Lacey were obviously happy by the way they looked at each other, often talking and laughing. But to watch them, Emma could only think of the irony. These past several days, she and Michael had been exchanging loving glances and laughter, while Tyson and Lacey had been separated by an emotional wall. And now it had turned around. But the wall between Michael and Emma was of brick and bars, and her future lay in someone else's hands.

When Emma couldn't bear it any longer, she resigned herself to going to bed, and once again she cried herself to sleep without bothering to undress. She awoke with a conscious resolve to have a positive attitude. She was determined that Michael would be declared innocent and be back for their wedding the day after tomorrow. But deep inside there was a nagging doubt, tempting her to entertain the idea that she wouldn't see Michael any more than to kiss him good-bye before he went to the gallows.

Emma arrived at breakfast on time, but found she couldn't eat. Halfway through the meal, she looked up at her father and asked, "May I go into town? I can't bear this waiting."

"I'll take you," Tyson volunteered.

"That's fine," Jess agreed. "But mind yourselves. Don't be making the situation worse."

"We'll be good," Tyson promised, then he turned to Emma. "You want to go now?"

"Could we?"

Tyson nodded and came to his feet, saying to Lacey, "I'll see you later." He bent to kiss her while Emma moved toward the door. She paused to take her mother's outstretched hand and the comfort it offered. Then she moved on, only to have the door come open before she reached it.

Emma had to blink several times to make certain she wasn't hallucinating. But there was no denying the reality of his voice as he said, "Hello, Emma."

"Michael!" she gasped and flew into his arms. There was nothing so wondrous as feeling him hold her as if his life depended on her, as much as hers depended on him. She touched his face and found tears there to match her own. They laughed and he kissed her.

"Oh, Michael!" she repeated. They laughed and embraced again until Alexa came beside them, silently demanding a hug of her own. Michael gladly complied.

"You were going somewhere?" he asked Emma while she dabbed away his tears with her fingers.

"To find you," she smiled.

"I assume you're here legally," Jess boomed from the other end of the table.

Emma turned with her arm around Michael as he announced proudly, "I am a free man."

"What happened?" Emma asked, urging him to his usual chair. She was going to sit beside him, but he pulled her onto his lap.

Tyson sat back down, literally feeling Emma's happiness and relief. Alexa was also reseated, and they all waited anxiously to hear his report.

"I was called in late yesterday afternoon to give the judge my testimony again. We talked for quite some time, but I honestly had no idea where I stood. They woke me up this morning to tell me the judge wanted to see me again. Mr. Grant and the constable were there. The judge said that he was throwing the case out. He said that during the hearing he had found the stories of accusation almost too sound. As he questioned the three individuals, he found that straying from the memorized story at all led every one of them to give a different picture. He concluded that it was unknown how the death took place, but he felt certain I was not responsible for it."

Emma threw back her head in laughter and hugged him so tightly that he groaned in mock suffering.

"Did I miss breakfast?" he asked, looking around. "That stuff they were trying to feed me was despicable."

"Help yourself," Alexa said.

Before he managed to move Emma enough to stand, Tyson said with sincerity, "Welcome back, Michael. It's nice to have the family back together again."

Michael absorbed what he'd said and fought back his emotions, which were already too close to the surface. "Thank you, Tyson. It's good to be back. With any luck, my past won't haunt us anymore."

Michael's eyes settled on Lacey. He sensed something different about her, and wondered what had transpired in his absence. "Hello, Lacey," he smiled in a teasing way. "Did you miss me?"

"No," she answered tonelessly. Tyson put his arm around her and lifted a warning finger that wasn't totally serious. She laughed and kissed Tyson quickly. Michael felt warmed to observe them. If everything was all right between Lacey and Tyson, he could live with the animosity between Lacey and himself. "But," she added to Michael, "I'm certainly glad you're back." Everyone in the room betrayed their surprise as she added quite seriously, "I don't think any of us could bear another day with Emma brooding around like that. For Emma's sake, I'm glad you're here."

"Thank you," Michael said, knowing from experience that it could be much worse. They were definitely making progress.

"Get some breakfast, Michael," Alexa urged, "before it gets any colder."

Michael filled a plate from the sideboard, then sat to eat. Emma just leaned on her elbow and watched him. Michael said to Tyson while he pointed his fork at Emma, "I think she missed me."

"You'd better believe it," she smiled. "I was scared to death."

"So was I," he admitted soberly. He shook his head in disbelief. "I'm glad it's over." He added to Jess, "How are my boys? Were they impressed by my example when you told them I was in jail?"

Jess chuckled. "I sat them down and told them the truth, as much as they needed to know. They were concerned. Fiddler and Mr. Johnson managed to get them through the day, just as they did while Ben was gone with me. Fiddler tells me they were pretty somber and quiet. I suspect they missed you almost as much as Emma did."

"I missed them, too," Michael said, and continued to eat as if he'd been starved. "This is wonderful," he said to Alexa. "You must give Mrs. Brady my deepest regards."

"I'll do that," Alexa smiled.

Michael finished his breakfast before Tyson and Lacey, who had started much earlier but were preoccupied with looking at each other. Michael glanced at the clock and came to his feet. "I've got just enough time to interrupt their studies," he said slyly, taking Emma's hand to indicate that she was coming with him. He paused, his eyes scanning the length of the table, to add with sincerity, "Thank you all for helping me through this. A man couldn't ask for a better family."

"That works both ways, Michael," Alexa said.

"And you're quite welcome," Jess added. "I'm in agreement with Lacey. I'd have done just about anything to keep Emma from brooding."

Michael caught the humor in his eyes and moved to the door, pausing for the usual exchange with Alexa. He bent to kiss her cheek. "Thanks for breakfast, Mother. You look radiant."

"It's good to have you back," she replied. He winked and pulled Emma into the hall. Once the door was closed, he laughed and pulled her up into his arms, turning around with her until they both fell back against the wall from dizziness.

"Oh, Emma," he whispered while her face spun before him. "I cannot begin to tell you how grateful I am to be here now, to have you back."

"You don't need to," she said, and put her mouth within reach of the kiss she knew was coming.

"Come on." He took her hand and headed toward the stairs. "I think I could stand to put on a clean shirt before I go to work."

Emma lay over his bed, leaning against the footboard to watch while he peeled off his shirt and splashed water over his chest, sponging himself there and beneath his arms. He found a clean shirt and waistcoat and put them on before he threw a towel around his throat and quickly shaved.

"Michael?" she said dreamily while he was splashing that delicious shaving lotion on his face.

"Yes, my love," he said, wiping his hand on the towel and tossing it aside.

"Will you marry me?"

"If I couldn't," he bent to touch her nose with his and she inhaled the scent of him, "my life would be worth nothing."

Emma went to her knees to touch the fresh smoothness of his face. "Are you certain you have to go to work?"

"Yes," he grinned, "but later . . ." He gave a roguish chuckle and dragged her toward the door.

Michael held up his finger to indicate that Emma remain still as they came to the door of the boys' study room. She hovered behind as he slipped inside, but she couldn't resist watching.

He stood just inside the door, putting his weight casually onto one leg, his arms folded over his chest. With a booming voice he said, "What's this I hear?" All eyes turned to him in astonishment. "I'm gone one day, and you all start brooding around like a bunch of wilting pansies!"

The boys all cheered and applauded as if he'd given them a great performance. They remained seated as they were expected to, but Michael moved among them, greeting each boy with a squeeze of the hand or a tousle of the hair. He turned last to shake Mr. Johnson's hand.

"It's good to have you back, Mr. Hamilton. You put a lot of spirit into this place."

"Too much, perhaps," Michael quipped.

"So they're not gonna hang ya?" Toby called.

Michael turned to lean against Mr. Johnson's desk. "No, Toby, they're not. The judge decided I was telling the truth and I didn't do what they had accused me of. I'm afraid you are stuck with me for good." They all cheered again. Michael pointed a severe finger. "But don't get too comfortable. I've still got a nasty temper. Now get to work so we can move along."

The boys reluctantly turned back to their studies for the few minutes left before the first group departed with Michael, and Emma tagged along.

The day went smoothly, while Emma could only enjoy being with him, her heart full with the realization that the threat of a murder charge was no longer hovering over them.

They rarely saw Tyson and Lacey, but when they did it was apparent they were happy. It only added to an overall sense of fulfillment and anticipation.

The following morning at breakfast, Alexa announced that other than the time Michael would be working, she expected all of them to be helping prepare for the wedding tomorrow. Michael was about to ask what could possibly take all of them all day, but she spouted off a list without any encouragement.

"And everything must be in order before the minister arrives this evening. He will be sharing supper with us, so come looking your best, and then we'll have a brief rehearsal."

Michael looked at Emma, feigning an expression of nervous fear. But what he really felt was more like unquenchable excitement. Next to the day Emma had declared that she loved him, tomorrow was going to be the best day of his life.

"Don't forget to show up, Michael," Lacey said a little too seriously.

Michael gave her one of those brief, terse smiles that she often earned, and said tonelessly, "Where's your sense of humor, Lacey?"

"I think it was kidnapped." She imitated the smile he had just given her.

Michael just nodded to compliment her wit.

He was soon off to see to his work, while Alexa ordered Tyson and Jess to get started on tasks that took a masculine hand, and she carted the girls to the kitchen to assist Mrs. Brady in preparing the food for tomorrow's guests.

ANITA STANSFIELD

The girls chattered excitedly, filling Alexa with a sense of peace. At last, she thought, it was how it always should have been.

She left them with instructions, then went to the boys' home to find Michael eating lunch with them in the cafeteria.

"May I?" she asked quietly, and Michael moved over to make room for her on the bench. She glanced over the boys with appreciation. Trent caught her eye and waved timidly. Alexa smiled and waved back.

"I think he likes you," Michael whispered. "I can't blame him. I like you, too."

"But I'm not certain you did when you were his age."

"One of many regrets in my life." Michael turned to her directly. "I don't think you came here to discuss my childhood."

"Actually, I came to make certain the guest list is complete."

"I'm sorry?" He leaned forward.

Alexa smiled. "I have a hunch that these boys would feel rather badly if they weren't invited to your wedding. How do you feel about that?"

"I think that would be fine." He gave a crooked smile. "But I didn't feel it was my place to suggest it."

"It is your place to suggest anything you like, Michael. Whether or not I'll do it," she added with a teasing chuckle, "is another matter."

"I appreciate your insight." He glanced around the room. "I think they would enjoy being there. I know I will. I'll threaten them to be on their best behavior."

"Tell them there will be a lot of goodies for them afterward if they mind their manners."

"That ought to work."

"I thought after the ceremony they could come back here to eat, but we'll give them the same as the other guests."

"That ought to work," he repeated.

"Why are you so agreeable?"

"I'm getting married tomorrow."

"Which reminds me, Jess has already made arrangements for the boys so that you can take some time off."

"Ah, yes." He grinned. "I suppose I'm entitled to a honeymoon."

"Is two weeks sufficient?"

"I think I can manage with that."

"Good." Alexa stood and squeezed his shoulders, adding as if he were a child, "Now don't go running off this afternoon. I've got work for you to do."

Alexa went back to find the girls finishing a lunch of sampling the food for tomorrow. With the kitchen preparations under control, she took them upstairs, where they tried on the pressed and freshened gowns with all of their accessories. The only things missing were the flowers ordered for their hair, due to arrive in the morning. The girls ooh'd and ah'd and giggled. Alexa couldn't help but join in.

Everything was placed carefully in Alexa's sitting room, where she would help them dress tomorrow. Then they went to their own rooms, packed for their honeymoons, and put everything in order.

A nervous excitement took hold when they both realized it was time to get dressed for supper. They helped each other choose appropriate gowns and chattered excitedly while Alexa went downstairs to check over the last-minute details and see that the minister was treated properly when he arrived to stay the night.

"I'm so happy, Emma," Lacey admitted, her eyes betraying that she meant it.

"So am I," Emma agreed.

Lacey's expression turned serious. "I'll only ask it one more time, Emma, but are you certain you're doing the right thing?"

Emma felt dismayed to see Lacey's continuing lack of acceptance, but she only smiled and said with confidence, "Yes, quite certain." With that the subject was dropped, and they hurried to be ready in time for supper.

Twenty-three
INTO THE CIRCLE

Michael finished with his appointed chores and went to his room to clean up. When he was ready, he was dismayed to realize that he had a great deal of time to kill. He first went to Emma's room. Not only did he hear Lacey with her, but he wondered if it would be inappropriate for him to be with her right now. He went to Tyson's room and knocked.

"Come in," Tyson called, and Michael entered to find him polishing his boots. "All ready?" Tyson looked up briefly and continued his task.

"Yeah." Michael sat down casually.

"Nervous?" Tyson asked after observing him for a minute.

"I think I am," Michael chuckled. "How about you?"

"Most definitely."

"It's not being married that makes me nervous," Michael explained. "I think it's more . . . well, all the formality stuff, I guess. I'm not accustomed to such things."

"I dare say we'll survive it." Tyson set aside the brush and pulled on his boots.

"Did you ever figure out what to give Lacey?" Michael asked for the sake of distraction.

"I sure did. Want to see it?"

Michael nodded, and Tyson took a wooden box off the bureau. It looked old, and Michael was puzzled. "Open it," Tyson said. When he did, he found only a used match.

"How quaint." Michael examined it closely. "I can see the value in such a—"

"Oh, shut up," Tyson chuckled. "It's symbolic."

"I'm sorry?"

"I used to keep that box filled with travel brochures and clippings about exotic places. I used the match to burn them."

"Ah," Michael's face filled with enlightenment. "Then the real gift is a promise to stay home."

"I'm not going anywhere unless Lacey willingly goes along."

"That's nice." Michael put the match back and closed the box.

"Still nervous?" Tyson asked, almost to taunt him.

"I think I'll go for a walk," Michael said lightly. "I'll see you at supper."

"Don't forget to show up." Tyson pointed at him, mimicking Lacey with an endearing grin.

"Don't *you* forget to show up." Michael returned the gesture, and decided on his way down the stairs that perhaps a visit with the horses would soothe his nerves. It was either that or the boys, and the horses were less likely to make his nerves more taut. The boys would probably tease him mercilessly.

The stables were a place Michael felt comfortable, and he casually sauntered down the row of stalls, pausing to stroke or talk occasionally with a horse. He hovered longer over Emma's gelding, feeling a closeness to her that made his heart quicken. He had felt in the recent weeks of his life that he was starting over, but tomorrow would be the ultimate beginning for both of them.

He moved on to his own horse, the only breathing being that had really accepted him during a time when he had believed his life was worth nothing. He'd been given the animal to care for as a youth, and he had taken it with him when he left here. It had been left with an acquaintance during his years in prison. And now this horse had taken him through his adventures with Emma. He talked to the animal and stroked it gently, finding that nostalgia was a good way to soothe his nerves.

He had nearly resigned himself to returning to the house when the animal twitched beneath his hand. Michael turned alertly to look around him. He couldn't see or hear anything, but instinctively he made a decision to hurry to the house. He only wanted to see Emma and feel the reality of what was to come.

Michael walked briskly toward the stable entrance, and was nearly there when the silhouettes of two men appeared against the evening sun. Michael first thought it was some stable hands, but he stopped cold as they took a stance to indicate they intended to keep him from leaving. Then familiarity took hold, and Michael's palms began to sweat.

"What are you doing here?" Michael demanded of Rafe Coogan and the man he called Bud.

"That's what we intend t' tell ya." Rafe gave a demented laugh and stepped toward him. Michael kept his stance, calculating moves in his mind. He wished the sun wasn't behind them; it kept him from seeing their eyes. Being outnumbered was a concern, but he'd fought two to one before and survived.

"Ya see," Rafe said, stopping close enough that Michael could smell him, "we was kinda upset about you gettin' that judge to set ya free. But thinkin' on it a little further, we decided we could get it all anyway."

"All of what?" Michael was afraid to ask.

"Well, first we're gonna have a little fun with you, softie. Then we're gonna find my boy and—"

"Over my dead body," Michael interrupted, but Rafe only laughed.

"That's kinda what we had in mind. But actually, we don't want ya dead. We want ya t' live with what else we're gonna do. After we're finished with you, I'd just like t' see ya stop us from havin' our way with those pretty little women you've gotten so cozy with."

Bile rose in Michael's throat, and he unwillingly clenched a fist. He decided then that whether he survived this or not, he wouldn't leave either one of them capable of hurting Emma or Lacey, not to mention Toby. He hoped Emma would understand his missing supper as he stepped forward to have the first blow. But he'd barely moved to lift his arm when a strong grip came out of nowhere from behind, holding his arms against his sides. *Oh, great,* he thought. *Three to one.* This was not going to be a good evening. A fist landed on his jaw, but Michael leaned back blindly against the man holding him and lifted both feet to push them into Rafe's belly and knock him onto his back. He then lunged back against his captor and broke his grip long enough to turn and land a heavy fist right between his eyes. He added a boot in the groin for good measure. Michael didn't wait for that one to fall before he turned to send his fist into Bud's nose, feeling it break. Then he immediately threw his left into Rafe's belly as he was coming back to his feet. He was considering running while the three were stunned, but the man behind him came around enough to grab Michael's ankle and sent him reeling to the ground. Michael kicked him and scrambled to his feet, and the next thing he knew, both his arms were being held behind him, while Rafe hit him over and over. The only satisfaction Michael could find was in knowing that it took three men to do him in. But losing a fight now was not a matter of losing his pride or his reputation, or keeping his hands on whatever he'd just stolen. Something priceless was at stake here, and Michael decided there was only one way to have any chance at saving it.

❦   ❦   ❦

Emma felt an all-too-familiar emptiness as supper began and Michael's seat was empty. Even Lacey looked concerned.

"Where is the other groom?" the minister asked from where he sat near Alexa.

"I saw him just a while ago," Tyson reported. "He was all dressed for dinner; said he was going for a walk to calm his nerves."

"I hope he didn't . . . ," Lacey began, but Emma stopped her with a cold look.

"Don't even think it! He'll be here soon."

Five minutes later, Tyson came to his feet. "I wonder if Michael's run into a problem. I think I'll go see if I can find him."

Emma looked up at him gratefully, and Tyson hurried out. He wondered if Michael might have gone to the boys' home, but he had a feeling he should try the stables first. He was a short distance away from the main stable when he heard the signs of fighting and ran to investigate, his heart pumping dread into his veins.

Tyson stopped in his tracks at the scene he'd come upon. Michael's body hung limp from his arms that were being held by two dirty-looking thugs, while the third threw a heavy punch into Michael's middle, as if for good measure.

"I think he's dead," one of them proclaimed. The one doing the hitting took hold of Michael's hair to lift his face into view, and Tyson gasped aloud. There was so much blood that he was barely recognizable.

The sound made the three turn toward Tyson, who could only stare in disbelief as Michael was dropped face down into the dirt, then kicked to roll him over. Tyson couldn't begin to think what to do. He was no fighter, and it was apparent that even Michael's skill had been no match for these three. He barely had time to think about what to do before a fist came toward his face and everything went black.

❦   ❦   ❦

"Now," the minister said as if it were humorous, "I wonder where the *other* groom has gone to."

"I'm certain they'll be back soon enough," Alexa said. "Perhaps Michael had some difficulty with one of the boys. They'll work it out."

Dessert came, but Tyson and Michael didn't. "I think I'll go look for them," Emma volunteered.

"And I'm coming with you," Lacey insisted.

"No." Jess came to his feet, unable to fight the uneasiness he was feeling any longer. "You girls go find something to keep busy. I'll look for them."

Jess left the room in a hurry, heading for the boys' home. Emma and Lacey excused themselves and decided to wait upstairs, since Lacey wanted to recheck her packing. Alexa took the minister to the drawing room for coffee.

While Emma was watching Lacey rummage through her bags, trying to determine if she had everything she needed, neither of them said much. It was Emma who noticed the drapes moving. Instinct made her heart pound and she moved quietly toward Lacey, unable to ignore the prickly fear spreading down her back. She touched Lacey's sleeve and pointed toward the movement. She was ready to urge her sister quietly from the room when the drapes were thrown aside.

Lacey wanted to scream, but her mouth fell open in silent fear. Emma scrambled toward the door with Lacey in tow, but two other men appeared from nowhere, one barring each door, while Rafe Coogan moved his smelly carcass closer, backing the girls into a corner.

"We figured you'd show up here sooner or later," he said.

"What do you want?" Emma attempted to sound in control.

"I think you'll see soon enough." He licked his lips, and his eyes turned lusty. Lacey covered her mouth to suppress the nausea that always rose in his presence.

Emma urged Lacey behind her and wished she had a clue how to get out of this. Just the thought of what she knew they were intending to do made her want to vomit. She tried to ignore her fear and disgust and think rationally. There were other people in this house. She decided to scream, but he saw it coming and moved close enough to slap a dirty hand over her mouth. Lacey screamed instead, but it came out more like a squeaky whimper.

"You won't get away with this," Lacey managed to say, cowering behind Emma.

"If you're talkin' about those boyfriends o' yours," Rafe sneered, "we're not too concerned." The three men laughed intolerably. "Last we saw Michael Hamilton, he looked pretty dead to me."

Emma began to struggle as the aching, pounding horror of what he'd said drove her nearly to madness. But she was thwarted as the others stepped forward to help keep her under control. "And the other one," Rafe continued, so close to Emma's face that she could hardly breathe from the odor, "ain't lookin' very pretty, either. We knocked him out cold."

Lacey whimpered again as Emma was dragged away from her. Emma wished in that moment that she could take it all. If Michael was dead, then life was over for her; and she knew Lacey would never recover from such an ordeal. But Lacey was dragged out of the corner, and Emma knew that what had been worth living for was lost to them. Beyond Michael's death, there could be nothing worse than this.

🌿 🌿 🌿

Michael waited until the footsteps faded and all became silent, then he spat the blood and dirt out of his mouth and sat up with a groan. It had been a long time since he'd been bested, and he'd been a lot younger. He came to his knees and groaned again. Blood dripped into his eyes and he searched for his handkerchief to wipe it away, making a noise of disgust to see the blood on the white fabric. Looking down at his white shirt, now covered with blood and dirt, his disgust deepened. But that was of little importance now. He managed to lumber to his feet, grateful he'd found the insight to play dead before they got him so badly that he likely would have been, which would have left the dirty bums to have their way.

Michael put his hands on his knees and steadied himself into some reasonable equilibrium. He slowly brought his head up and took a sidestep to balance himself. Then he saw Tyson.

"Oh, that's just great!" he said aloud for no one to hear. He cursed the supper hour, knowing all of the hands were in the bunkhouse eating. Otherwise, there was always somebody around who could have appreciated a good fight. But here he was, barely able to walk, and Tyson out cold. Logically he realized that if he could rouse Tyson, he could have some help. He found water and threw a bucket of it over him. Tyson sputtered and spat and leaned on his elbows to look up at Michael.

"I thought you were dead!" he shouted.

"I thought so, too." Michael held out a hand to help Tyson to his feet, taking another dizzy sidestep from the effort. "But we're all going to wish we were if we don't get moving. Do you think you can?"

"I think I'm better off than you are."

"I'm all right." Michael wiped blood on his sleeve from a cut below his left eye. "But those blasted idiots were not just here to have their way with me."

"Toby?" Tyson questioned.

Michael nodded, then wished he hadn't. "And . . . the girls."

"They wouldn't!" Tyson snarled.

"You'd better believe they would," Michael retorted. "Now, you go find Toby and make sure he's protected, then I'll meet you upstairs. I suspect they'll go to the girls' rooms."

"Why?" Tyson asked as they moved quickly out of the stable, sheer determination overcoming the effects of their injuries.

"Because they got in that way before, you twit!"

"How did they know where their rooms were?" Tyson shouted.

"Because I told them," Michael shouted back. "Just move!"

Tyson ran toward the boys' home, and Michael headed toward the back of the house. He lumbered up the stairs with much help from the bannister, and went first to his room in search of his pistol. From the hallway he could hear evidence of what he'd suspected, and he was grateful to have found them, hopefully in time. Drawing strength and courage, Michael prepared himself to do something he'd never done before. He kicked the door open, and in one swift movement he was filling the doorframe, the pistol held firmly with both hands, pointed straight ahead.

"Michael!" Emma gasped with relief as Rafe's hand fell away from her mouth in surprise. For the second time in two days, Michael had shown up when she had thought he was dead or as good as. She didn't know how much more of this she could take.

Lacey was so relieved to see him that she could have cried, but she was still being held firmly by one of these bums, and she wasn't about to relax prematurely.

All remained still until Michael said with a genuine cruelty that Emma realized she had honestly never heard before, "Let her go, or I'll kill you." The gun was pointed at Bud, who had Lacey in a firm grip, a dagger in his free hand.

"You haven't got the guts to shoot me," Bud snarled. Michael drew his courage again. His eyes flicked to Lacey's for only an instant, then he pulled the trigger. Lacey screamed as her abductor fell to the floor in a lifeless heap. A moment of stunned silence was broken by Michael's announcement. "Real bullets."

Rafe let go of Emma as he and his remaining friend seemed to perceive that Michael was serious. The girls held to each other and scrambled quickly out of firing range. Michael was trying to ignore the realization that he'd just killed a man and decide which one he should point the gun at next. He'd nearly made up his mind when Tyson came bounding into the room behind him. The distraction was just enough for Rafe to knock the gun out of Michael's hand, and it slid across the floor. Emma saw it slide under the bed, but she doubted that anyone else had. Tyson was quick to take on Rafe's cohort, and was managing to get the better of him. Michael immediately turned to take on Rafe with his fists, and was doing a good job of it until the other thug hit Tyson and sent him reeling backward, where he lay unmoving. Lacey screamed, but Emma held onto her to keep her where she was. The man Tyson had weakened somewhat crawled over the floor to grab Michael's leg. Michael started to fall, and in the same instant, Rafe hit him. Emma screamed as she watched Michael go crashing through the window, and before she could even grasp what it meant, Rafe was dragging her away from Lacey, obviously determined to have his way with Michael Hamilton's woman. He snarled crude vulgarities and threw her on the floor.

Lacey panicked. Tyson was unconscious. Michael was dead somewhere on the ground. And she couldn't find the gun. She frantically looked around her, searching for something, anything that might help, while she prayed that someone would have heard the commotion by now and come to the rescue.

Fresh energy pumped through her veins when she noticed the fire poker. She picked it up, and with little thought sent it crashing down on the head of the man attempting to recover enough to assist Rafe. His body slammed again to the floor and Lacey dropped the weapon, backing away as she realized what she'd done. Deciding she could do it again, and that Rafe Coogan was a worthy target, she bent to pick up the poker. Just then she heard a muffled groan rising above all the noise Emma was making as she made it extremely difficult for Rafe to make any progress. Turning to look around, she realized there were hands gripping the window sill.

"Michael!" She leaned her head out the window.

"Hello, Lacey," he said as if they were at the breakfast table. "Would you mind?"

Instinctively Lacey grabbed the side of the window frame with one hand and reached down to wrap the other around Michael's forearm.

"Bless you," Michael whispered, sighing with a degree of relief as he attempted once again to press his boots up over the side of the house. Lacey groaned and tugged with everything she had, finally feeling the momentum take hold. Michael came crawling breathlessly through the window, and they fell together to their knees. With no thought of anything but the joy of her success, Lacey threw her arms around him. Michael took her face into his hands and kissed her, saying with fervor, "Bless you, Lacey. I love you!"

Their attention turned to Emma, and Michael was quick to pull Rafe off her by the back of his shirt collar, sending him sprawling with a healthy punch to his chin. But Rafe recovered quickly while Michael broke his first rule and momentarily turned his eyes toward Emma to make certain she was all right. She had all of her clothes on; that was a good sign. But in the next instant, a blow came to Michael's belly and he doubled over. Normally he could have taken it, but it had already been hit too much for one day. Emma screamed as Rafe pulled her to her feet. "The gun, Lacey," she shouted. "It's under the bed!"

Rafe put a knife to Emma's throat to quiet her. Michael slowly straightened up and absorbed the situation. Lacey shoved the gun into his hand, but he wasn't certain he could use it without Emma getting hurt. He wasn't in control as he had been when he'd first entered the room. He tested it by just attempting to lift the weapon, and Rafe pressed the point of the knife more firmly against Emma's throat.

"All right," Michael said, "you win." He held up his hands, but kept the gun dangling from his finger. The women gasped. But Michael was relatively certain that in the brief time it had taken for the drama to transpire, someone in the house would have had time to hear his first shot and come to investigate. A distraction was all he needed, and distractions were something he'd learned to count on and take advantage of as a boy on the streets.

Rafe barely had time to give a smug, demented laugh before Jess Davies appeared in the doorway, Alexa right behind him. Rafe turned toward them, and it was just enough for Michael to take careful aim and fire twice. The women gasped as Rafe fell to the floor in a heap beside his friends. Michael fell to his knees. The combination of being beaten, thrown out the window, and killing two men had finally gotten the better of him.

Jess muttered a breathy, "What the . . ." Tyson groaned. Lacey moved to his side as Emma moved to Michael's.

"Michael," Emma cried, gingerly touching his face where he'd been hurt. "What have they done to you? Are you all right? Oh, Michael."

"I've never killed a man before, Emma," he said numbly.

"It's all right. You had to."

"I know," he muttered with disgust. "Did he hurt you? Are you all right?"

"I'm fine," she assured him. "I gave him a good fight."

"I'll bet you did." Michael gave her a proud smile and pulled her close, ignoring the pain it caused. They were alive and together. Nothing else mattered.

"Tyson!" Lacey shook him. He groaned and managed to sit up. "Tyson? Are you hurt?"

Tyson rubbed his head, and Michael laughed. "You've got to learn to take your punches, boy."

"I'll just keep you around to take them for me," Tyson grumbled.

"You did him in pretty good, though," Michael complimented, glancing toward the man in question. Then, taking a second glance, he added, "I don't know who finished him off."

"I did that," Lacey said proudly, holding Tyson's pounding head against her shoulder.

"Good girl," Michael complimented.

"And I'd do it again in a minute," Lacey added with a clear indication that some genuine courage and determination had replaced her fears. "I had to save my sister."

"And you saved me, too," Michael added. "Thank you."

"I have no desire to spend the rest of my life with Emma brooding around here because she lost you." Michael caught the teasing in her eyes and grinned.

"What are you talking about?" Alexa finally spoke up. "What exactly happened here?"

"Michael fell out the window," Emma provided.

"But Lacey pulled me back in."

"These guys came and beat Michael into a pulp out in the stable," Tyson added.

"But I pretended to be dead."

"They knocked me out."

"And I woke him up."

"I went to make sure Toby was being watched."

"And I came here, because I knew they were coming here."

"And Emma and I were just about to be in some real trouble," Lacey joined in.

"But our heroes came to save us," Emma said proudly.

"Yeah," Tyson groaned. "I got knocked out again."

"Not before you did some damage," Michael provided.

"And then I hit him with the fire poker," Lacey stated.

"And Michael fell out the window."

"And Lacey saved me," Michael repeated.

"I think we heard that part already." Jess put up his hands to stop the prattle. "Let's just say you're all alive, and things are obviously under control."

"And we are grateful." Alexa took a deep breath, glad it was over.

"I'll send for the constable," Jess said. "And we'll get somebody to come out here to get the bodies out of my house," he added with disgust.

"Don't tell them I did it," Michael said, not completely serious.

"I'm going to tell them everything," Jess replied. "And you might just end up a real hero."

"He always has been." Emma beamed toward Michael.

"Why don't all of you see if you can get yourselves cleaned up," Alexa suggested. "We've got a wedding tomorrow, remember. I'll send some dinner up for Tyson and Michael. Lacey, you get what you need and go to one of the guest rooms. We'll get this cleaned up later. I'll see if the minister has recovered yet."

"Recovered?" Emma asked, coming to her feet and pulling Michael along. He groaned and leaned against her.

"He passed out when he heard the gunshot."

"What about the rehearsal?" Lacey asked, helping Tyson to his feet as he unwittingly imitated Michael's groan.

"I suppose you'll have to do it impromptu," Alexa smiled. "But I think we can figure it out."

"Just so we get the vows said and the rings on the proper fingers, I don't care what happens," Jess said in exasperation. "The day after tomorrow, all of you brats will be off honeymooning somewhere, and I am going to take a long nap and read a good book."

"We'll be looking after Richard," Alexa announced, "and helping Fiddler with the boys."

Jess sighed. "Well, I'm still going to take a nap. A long, peaceful nap."

He left the room, and Alexa said quietly before following him, "He's so unbearable when he doesn't get his sleep."

"We'll see you in the morning," Tyson and Emma said at nearly the same time, then they glared at each other in mock disgust. Michael and Lacey chuckled, Michael turning it to a groan when he realized it hurt.

Emma and Lacey each escorted their wounded heroes to their rooms, coddling over them just enough to leave them longing for tomorrow to come.

❦ ❦ ❦

Alexa sent breakfast trays to the girls' rooms early, knowing well how much time a bride needed to feel perfect. She met them a while later in her sitting room, where they slipped their freshly bathed bodies into fine silk chemises and petticoats. Their nervous excitement was a pleasure to observe, but there were other things that needed attending to. She left them to work on each other's hair and personally took a breakfast tray to Michael and Tyson to wake them and give careful instructions concerning the rehearsal they had missed. She added emphatically that it was totally improper for them to even attempt to see the brides before the wedding.

With all the members of the wedding party seen to for the moment, Alexa went down to share breakfast with Jess and the minister. Then she checked on the food preparations in the kitchen, and the setting up of chairs and flowers in the upstairs hall. When she felt confident that everything was under control, she took the fresh flowers upstairs. She helped arrange a cascade of a variety of white flowers into each bride's hair. Then she took a budding rose to her bedroom, where she found Jess looking through the closet in search of the proper attire.

"Wear this one." She pulled out the new jacket she'd bought for him and helped him into it. Then she proceeded to pin the rose to his lapel. "For the father of the brides . . . and the grooms."

"And what about the mother?" he asked.

"Don't worry. I'll look beautiful."

"Oh, I've never worried about that."

Alexa studied his appearance with appreciation, then she turned back to his closet and rummaged until she pulled out another jacket, looked it over, and headed out the door.

"Where are you taking that?" he asked.

"You never wear it anymore. You hardly ever did. I've got better uses for it."

Jess grunted and Alexa took it, along with another rose, to Michael's room, where she knocked softly. "Come in unless you're the bride," he called.

Alexa opened the door and smiled to see him looking perfect, from his highly polished boots all the way up to his carefully combed hair. He was struggling to tie a cravat, and Alexa set her things down to help him. "There," she said triumphantly. "You look almost perfect."

"Almost?" Michael questioned, and Alexa looked closely to survey yesterday's damages. "What do you expect, after my face was used for a punching bag?"

"Actually," Alexa concluded, "it doesn't look so bad. Other than this cut," she referred to the healing slit below his eye, "there are just some light bruises. How do you feel?"

"A little sore," he assured her, "but it's not as bad as I thought it would be."

"Good." Alexa held up the fine dinner jacket and said, "I don't believe you have one of these. It seems that Emma overlooked it when she went shopping. A groom should wear one, I think."

Michael admired the coat as she helped him into it and adjusted the shoulders to assure herself the fit was close to perfect. "It's fine," Michael commented, looking in the mirror. "Where did you get it?"

"Jess never wears it." She admired his appearance again. "You can keep it."

"Only if I can tease him about it," he grinned.

"You can do whatever you like."

"Am I perfect now?" he asked like a little boy going to church.

"Not quite." She pinned the rose to his lapel, and Michael watched her closely as she did so. The reality suddenly settled in.

"White?" he asked, questioning the color of the flower.

"It was Emma's idea." Alexa touched his chin and kissed his cheek. "To match your heart." She stood back and looked him up and down once more. "There. Perfect. Now all you have to do is kill time while I get the others ready."

"Great!" he said with severe sarcasm.

"It's a fact of life, Michael. Grooms should feel nervous while brides are primping."

"I see."

"But do me a favor," she said on her way out the door. "Don't leave the house. We don't want to have to come looking for you."

"I'm staying right here."

Alexa went to Tyson's room and found him shaving. His jacket was spread over the bed, and she pinned the flower to it. "Nervous?" she asked.

"A little." He smiled the best he could with his face contorted to meet the razor.

"You'll be wonderful."

"You're just saying that because you're my mother."

"Don't hurry too quickly," she cautioned. "You'll just have to wait for the brides."

"I know." He paused to rinse his razor in the basin. "But I think I'll keep track of Michael."

"Good idea," Alexa said, then went back to check on the progress of the girls. She helped them into their gowns and left them on their own while she quickly changed, put a few flowers into her own hair, then went down to find Jess greeting the first of their guests, most of whom had come all the way from the bunkhouse.

Leaving that in Jess's capable hands, Alexa went back up to help Emma and Lacey with the final touches.

"The two of you look positively radiant." Alexa leaned against the door to take in the sight, and tears came to her eyes. The girls beamed, but their nerves had reached a point where their throats were tight and words were difficult to find.

Alexa finally pronounced them ready, then went out to make certain Tyson and Michael had already left so they wouldn't cross paths. She returned to usher the brides to one of the side corridors leading into the upstairs hall. She kissed them both and left them as the music began to play, turning back just long enough to caution, "You stay out of sight until your father gets here and I give him the signal."

They nodded firmly and squeezed each others' hands. When Alexa was gone, they looked at each other, wanting to say so much. But they only laughed and shared a careful embrace. Jess joined them a moment later, giving the appropriate appraisal for a father with two beautiful daughters about to be wed. He then moved into the narrow archway that opened into the hall.

Tyson and Michael waited in the opposite corridor, drumming their fingers and tapping their toes. They said little and listened attentively to the noises emanating from the hall, rising above the music of a hired string quartet. Michael smiled to himself as his ears told him the boys had arrived and he heard familiar voices attempting to remain quiet. Unable to avoid peeking, he peered around the corner to see the chairs mostly filled by people they worked with, and a few faces he didn't know. He saw Ira Grant with a woman, who was apparently his wife. And he had to chuckle to see seventeen boys under Sarina's watchful eye, all with hair slicked back and their best clothes on, making them all look dreadfully uncomfortable. He motioned to Tyson, who peered around the corner and chuckled as well.

"What are you doing?" Alexa demanded, startling them from behind. "I told you to stay out of sight."

"No one saw us," Michael said like a guilty child.

"Are you ready?" she asked.

"Ready to get on with the honeymoon," Michael said with a nervous edge to his voice.

Tyson gave him a scolding slap on the shoulder, and Alexa held out her arms for them to each take one. They took a deep breath in unison and moved into the elaborate hall. Alexa couldn't help but think how this was the very place where she had married Jess, with many of the same guests in the audience.

Alexa escorted the grooms to the center of the hall, leaving each with a kiss. They stood on either side of the minister, who surveyed them skeptically. He'd obviously been told what had happened last night, and the evidence showed in their bruised faces.

Lacey and Emma each took a deep breath and met their father's proud eyes before they moved into the hall on his arms. Jess felt the significance and emotion of what this day meant to his children, but his eyes were on Alexa, and his mind was consumed with memories.

Michael could hardly breathe when his eyes fell on Emma, slowly approaching with her father. He had to wonder what he'd ever done to deserve this. It was simply too wonderful to be happening to a man like him. She was simply too beautiful to be his. In all the fantasies he'd indulged in through his years of wanting her, he could never have conjured up anything that even came close to this. But any doubt of its reality fled as he watched Jess kiss Emma's hand and place it carefully into his. He caught Jess's eye for the brief second he could manage to keep them away from Emma. There was no denying the complete trust Jess was displaying in this ritual.

Emma could hardly contain her joy as she finally came to face Michael in this most precious moment. Her mind wandered briefly to that first moment she had found herself held captive as they'd ridden into the night. She smiled at the thought. He smiled in return, a barely roguish sparkle in his eyes, as if he'd read her mind.

Tyson felt an overwhelming rise of emotion burn through him with a sense of irony, peace, and gratitude when Lacey's hand was placed into his, as it should have been long ago. The childhood they had shared, the evolution of their passion, then their separation—all seemed to combine into a carefully pieced love he felt for her. It was simply a love that could not be described. Looking into her eyes, he could see the evidence of change in her—a change that had made her more like the Lacey he had grown to love. But she was finer, stronger, and more beautiful than ever.

Lacey wanted to laugh and cry, dance and shout. This day had been too long awaited, too much ached for not to absorb every minute, every second of every feeling, every glance, every touch, and keep it to treasure always. Tyson was the epitome of all that was worth living for. He loved her, and that made all else good.

Jess was impressed with the careful way the minister kept all of the vows straight as each segment of the ceremony was spoken in turn by each couple. There was sincerity in each word.

Richard was sent forward at the appropriate moment, carrying both rings with careful instructions on which one to hand to which groom. Alexa covered her mouth to keep from chuckling when Tyson and Michael looked at the rings they were holding and quickly exchanged them.

The minister finished with a carefully memorized statement. "I now pronounce you, Tyson Benjamin Byrnehouse-Davies, and you, Lacey Mary Byrnehouse-Davies, husband and wife, for as long as you both shall live. And I pronounce you, Michael William Hamilton, and you, Emma Alexandra Byrnehouse-Davies, husband and wife, for as long as you both shall live." He smiled with obvious pride at his success, then he added more lightly, "Gentlemen, you may kiss your brides."

"Thank you," Tyson and Michael said at the same time and gladly proceeded, neither of them the least bit nervous. This part was easy. They all four laughed as the kisses parted. The couples embraced, then the brides clasped hands. Tyson hugged Emma. And, surprising everyone—especially Michael—Lacey put her arms around Michael with a warm embrace and a not-so-quick kiss on the cheek while her hand came against his face. "Welcome to the family, Michael," she said and he hugged her again, laughing as he did.

Lacey kept her arm around Michael as she turned to put the other around Tyson, who was still holding to Emma, who was holding to Michael. The four of them moved closer into a tight circle, laughing and kissing until their parents intruded and Richard scrambled between their legs into the middle, where he jumped into his father's arms.

"Grandmama?" he said.

"What, dear?"

"Everything is all right now, isn't it?" he said triumphantly.

"Yes, precious." Alexa's moist eyes spilled over. "Everything is perfect."

❦ ❦ ❦

A photograph was taken of the newly wedded couples, and another with Jess, Alexa, and Richard added. The celebrating officially began and became more jubilant as the day progressed. There was so much food spread out that Michael was left in awe. The champagne seemed endless, but spirits were high even without it. The real fun began when Fiddler did what he'd been nicknamed for, and to his skilled fiddle there was dancing in the yard until well past dark, when

Michael finally decided he'd had enough of this. With a boisterous "Good night, all!" he deftly swept his giggling wife up into his arms and roguishly carted her into the house and up the stairs. Tyson was quick to follow his example, and with Lacey in his arms he was right behind Michael and Emma on the stairs.

They paused a moment in the hall, only long enough for Michael to say, "Tyson, I really like you, but after we leave this house tomorrow morning, I don't want to see either one of you for weeks."

"The feeling is mutual, I can assure you," Tyson replied. They all laughed and went their separate ways, leaving only the echo of two doors being kicked shut.

"You know, Tyson," Lacey said as he put her down carefully and pressed his hands down her arms and back up again, "Michael really is a funny man."

"Yes," Tyson agreed, "he is at that." He put his lips to her throat with a husky growl.

"And I must say, I think I'm beginning to like his influence on you."

Tyson laughed and picked her up again, tossing her gently onto the bed. He sidled up next to her, kissing her wildly while her gown and petticoats crinkled with his every move.

"I love you, Lacey," he whispered. "Thank you for waiting for me."

"Now that we're here, I can say that it's all been worth it."

"Which reminds me," he said, "I have a gift for you."

"Really?" She smiled. "What is it?"

"You want it now?"

"I certainly do."

"It's on the bureau," he said, leaning back against the headboard and removing the rose from his lapel to smell it.

Lacey lifted her skirts to climb off the bed. She looked over the objects on the bureau and couldn't see anything that resembled a gift.

"The wooden box there," he said. "Open it."

Lacey took it into her hands and turned to face him as she lifted the lid and pulled out the match. He wondered for a moment if she would grasp the meaning without explanation. It had been a long time—even long before their love had been declared—since she'd seen that box and what it had contained. But she looked up at him with moisture glistening in her eyes.

"Welcome home, Tyson," she said. She set the box aside and came into his arms, feeling her whole life fall into perfect perspective. Tyson kissed her fervently, recalling Richard's profound declaration. Their son had put it perfectly. Everything was all right.

❧   ❧   ❧

Michael set Emma down and looked her over with greedy eyes. "My sweet," he murmured.

"You may call me Mrs. Hamilton," she said snobbishly.

Michael grinned. "I think I like that."

"Do you realize," she said, turning her back to him so he could unfasten the buttons, "that it hasn't been so long since you kidnapped me? What would you have thought if you had hauled me into the saddle with you, and I'd said, 'By the way, Mr. Hamilton, in little more than a month I am going to be your wife'?"

"I'd have laughed in your face," he said almost spitefully, then his voice softened. "And I would have thoroughly enjoyed every minute of having you prove that you were right."

Michael pushed the dress down over her arms, and it rustled to the floor. Emma turned to face him, saying dreamily, "I think I'd just like to look at you for a while longer. You look so ravishingly handsome." She smelled the rose on his lapel.

"Well, while you're standing there mesmerized," he said, "take a look at this." He pulled a fisted hand out of his pocket and held it near her face. Watching the anticipation in her eyes, he opened his hand to reveal the chained pendant lying in his palm. "Tyson picked it out," he said as she lifted it up reverently to admire. "One half of the heart is ebony, the other ivory." He was going to tell her what it reminded him of, but she looked up with tears glistening in her eyes, and he knew there was no need.

Michael motioned for her to turn around, and he clasped it about her throat. Emma touched the pendant where it lay against her skin. Michael moved around to face her, pressing his hand over hers. "Don't ever forget, Emma," he said with quiet strength, "how you purged my heart."

"And don't you forget," she touched his face, "how you have filled mine."

Michael bent to kiss her and blessed the day he had fallen in love with Emma Davies, whenever that may have been. He couldn't recall for certain.

"I love you, Michael," she whispered. "I'll love you forever." He picked her up and carried her to the bed. "Will you love me forever?" she asked, barely distracting him from his passion.

"Every chance I get, Emma Hamilton."

She laughed. "You're a rogue, Michael."

"Yes, I am," he said proudly. Emma giggled. Michael kissed her again and added, "Yes, Emma, yes. I will love you forever."

EPILOGUE

Michael and Emma Hamilton were blessed with a son, who was christened Jesse Michael. But not until after they had been blessed with five daughters, including a set of twins. Jess made a point of taunting Michael about it, declaring regularly that he deserved five daughters, and he hoped that every one of them grew up to fall in love with rogues who brought a great deal of trouble into his life. Michael thoroughly enjoyed the prospect.

With Emma by his side, Michael continued his work in the boys' home, gradually taking over Jess's role and handling all the business as well. After twenty years, Michael's greatest fulfillment was a stack of letters to verify that all but one of his boys had earned college degrees. Emma played a big part in this as she gradually took over her mother's role in counseling the boys, and found she was rather good at it.

Tyson and Lacey Byrnehouse-Davies stayed at their home except for an occasional lengthy vacation. Together they toured Europe and the Americas, jaunts that Lacey enjoyed so thoroughly that Tyson declared he had to handcuff her to get her home. In addition to Richard they were blessed with three daughters, the last one coming with complications that left Lacey unable to have more. But she found a great deal of contentment in assisting with Emma's children while Emma aided Michael's work. Tyson eventually took over full management of Byrnehouse-Davies, broadening the breeding and racing and working away from the running of sheep entirely. He hated sheep.

On the twins' twenty-fifth wedding anniversary, the family celebrated with dancing in the yard and food galore. Jess and Alexa sat back to watch their posterity, now including three great-grandchildren. And Jess had to declare, "I swear, we must be crazy."

Alexa only smiled and squeezed his hand.

PHOTO BY "PICTURE THIS . . . BY SARA STAKER"

ABOUT THE AUTHOR

Anita Stansfield has been writing for more than twenty years, and her best-selling novels have captivated and moved hundreds of thousands of readers with their deeply romantic stories and focus on important contemporary issues. Her interest in creating romantic fiction began in high school, and her work has appeared in national publications. *Gables Against the Sky* is her fourteenth novel and second historical work to be published by Covenant.

Anita lives with her husband, Vince, and their five children and two cats in Alpine, Utah.

Tyler awoke feeling groggy. He must have fallen asleep at the desk in his office. He shook his head. That was odd. He never slept at work. As he stretched, he smelled the pungent aroma of a kerosene lamp. The light coming from outside appeared to be fading, and the lamp offered little help.

Something was very wrong. He was on the floor. With a sudden swiftness, he remembered being attacked by the two men from the mailroom. He raised a shaky hand to his head and felt the unmistakable lump from the shotgun butt. His eyes slowly surveyed the room. Instead of his desk, computer, and small couch, he saw two beds and two desks. He looked at the floor, which should have been adorned by plush, cream-colored carpet; instead he found hardwood planks.

He slowly stood and walked over to one of the beds in confusion, examining the faded patchwork quilt that lay neatly folded upon it. Apparently, the two idiots hadn't been content with assault and battery. They'd abducted him, as well.

Trying to make sense of his surroundings, Tyler looked up at the dim light entering the room from the small window. There was a knock at the door. "Come in!" he barked, wincing at the noise he'd generated. The door slowly opened, and a young boy of fifteen or so ventured uncertainly inside.

"Hello, sir," he stammered. "I wasn't sure if you were here. No one saw you arrive." The boy looked Tyler up and down, taking in the white shirt, tie, dress slacks, and immaculate shoes. "Do you not have a uniform?" he asked. "If you'd like, I can go now and get whatever you need from supplies."

Tyler was on the boy in a flash. He grabbed him by the neck and slammed him into the wall. "I don't find any of this funny in the least," he said, his voice dangerously low. "Why don't you just relay this message for me. You tell those two racist bigots that not only will they face jail time for this, I'll personally see to it that they suffer. Now, you go tell them that I am not amused."

The boy was clearly frightened. "I . . . I . . . don't know what you mean, sir. I was told that the old accountant finally died of typhoid and that a new one was coming to take his place. Your regiment will be in the area soon, and you'll meet up with them when they get here."

Tyler released the boy and stared at him. "What are you talking about?"

The boy squirmed uncomfortably. "Perhaps you'd rather speak to the colonel." He turned and ran from the room. Tyler slowly followed him out the door and turned to his left. He stared in disbelief at the sight before him.

I've died and I'm not in heaven, he thought as he looked at a long, narrow room with beds down either side and an old-fashioned wood-burning stove in the middle. The floor was wooden, as was the ceiling, which came to a peak at the top. There were large kerosene lamps approximately twelve feet above the floor, suspended from studs that crossed from one wall to the opposite side.

Tyler turned around and looked to his right, only to see the scene repeated before him. When the stench of the place fully assailed his nostrils, he recognized the odor as a mixture of alcohol and bodily filth. He heard soft moaning coming from the beds. His eyes widened a bit as he stepped closer and saw rows and rows of what appeared to be wounded people. Some had bandages around their heads and faces, others were missing an arm or leg. Some slept, while others who were conscious looked miserable.

"Young man?" Tyler jumped at the voice. He turned around to see a man dressed in a full Civil War Union Army uniform.

"I'm Colonel Duncan. I'm the commanding officer here," the man stated, his gaze slowly traveling the length of Tyler's body as though viewing an oddity. "How long have you been in the Army, son?"

Tyler's head was pounding. Surely this was a prank. The two mailroom idiots had somehow managed to ship him to some sort of play-acting camp. He'd heard of Revolutionary War reenactment scenarios; apparently a Civil War arena had been created as well.

"I said, how long have you been in the Army?" the man before Tyler repeated his question.

"Actually, I was in the Navy, sir," Tyler replied truthfully. "I served overseas, mostly, off the coast of Japan." *Two can play at this,* he mused to himself with a measure of spite. When he caught up with those responsible for his abduction, they'd never know what hit them.

Tyler shifted under the "colonel's" skeptical gaze and avoided the man's eyes; something he normally never did. He couldn't place a finger on the source of his discomfort.

"I understand you met Boyd, and I'd thank you to treat him kindly in the future. That boy just lost his father and two brothers to this wretched war. He'll be back shortly with a uniform for you." The colonel turned to leave and suddenly turned back.

"Oh," he said. "I don't believe I know your name, son."

"Stuart Tyler Montgomery VI, U.S. Navy, sir," Tyler replied dutifully.

The colonel came to stand mere inches away from Tyler's face, and he sensed the urgency and seriousness in the older man's voice.

"I don't know exactly what it is you're up to, Montgomery, but let me tell you something," said the colonel. "This country is tearing itself apart. There are sixteen Union Army hospitals here in the Washington D.C. area alone, and every single one is full to capacity. Why, we even have wounded being cared for in the House and Senate chambers, the Georgetown Jail, and the Patent Office.

"I have seen more boys die in here than I can count, and I don't have time to play games with you. I was given to understand we'd have an Army man here to serve as a new accountant. If you're not certain which branch of the military you've been serving in, then perhaps we should have you committed to an institution for the mentally insane. Now then, Mr. Montgomery, what is your *Army* rank, or do you even have one?"

The first stirrings of desperate unease began to manifest themselves as Tyler stared in response to the man's outburst. Something was horribly, frighteningly wrong. He found himself beseeching a God he didn't believe in to make the whole odd situation disappear.

"I'm sorry, sir. I'm a captain," he lied, stammering. What was going on? He gazed, transfixed at the man standing opposite him and regarded the kind yet tired face, the graying hair, and the short stature. The man was an effective actor. Tyler sensed his exhaustion as though it were a tangible thing.

He spied a door that he hoped would lead to the world outside. If he could just make it to the door, he'd see and hear the hustle and chaos of the city. Keeping the colonel in his sight, he made his way to the door, and upon reaching it, flung it open with a vengeance. The sight before him wrung a groan of frustration from his lips.

Venturing outside, Tyler realized that he was either on a set of a Washington D.C. Civil War reenactment camp, or that the impossible had occurred. The second possibility didn't warrant contemplation from a man who'd lived his entire life grounded in harsh reality. Perhaps, if he just played along, he'd be allowed to return home.

He turned at the sound of approaching footsteps.

"Are you ill, Captain?" asked the colonel.

Tyler sucked in several gulps of fresh air and willed himself to remain standing. "I think I'll go back in the bedroom and wait for Boyd," Tyler murmured, his apprehension mounting with each passing moment.

The colonel saluted. "Very well. I'll expect to see you at 1800 hours for dinner. It's just in the next building over," he said, pointing. He paused for a moment in reflection. "Did you say your name was Stuart Tyler Montgomery?"

"Yeah," Tyler muttered. "The sixth."

"Are you familiar with Stuart Tyler Montgomery, the Army general?" asked the colonel. "In fact, I'm sure you must be aware that it's his regiment you'll be joining up with in about a week."

Tyler stared for a long moment before answering, his anger mounting. "No, *sir*. I wasn't aware of that."

"Well, Captain, do you at least have your transfer orders with you? Any proof of identification at all?"

Tyler was furious. "Well, you know," he spat with sarcastic energy born of fatigue and rage, "I was in an accident not too long ago, one involving a fall from my horse. I was out surveying the area, searching for old Johnny Reb, and the next thing I knew I was on the ground and my horse had taken off! Must have hit my head pretty hard, because I haven't remembered much since then!"

The colonel gave Tyler a long, hard look and said, "I'll see what I can do for you, Captain." He gave one more backward glance at Tyler's clothes and was gone.